RAISING THE STONES

APPLAUSE FOR SHERI S. TEPPER'S PREVIOUS NOVELS

GRASS

"A rigorously constructed parable about necessary (and unnecessary) trade-offs between independence and interdependence. Richly imagined action scenes . . . alternate with lively dialogue that wrestles with fundamental questions of good and evil. Ms. Tepper is as successful in bringing to life intelligent aliens as she is in creating believable human characters. . . . Marjorie Yrarier is one of the most interesting and likable heroines in modern science fiction."

The New York Times Book Review

"*Grass,* a new novel by the remarkable Sheri S. Tepper, is so good you may want to lend it to friends who don't like science fiction. The title suggests a kinder, gentler *Dune,* and there is a structural parallel between the two books. . . . We meet brave men and women, traitors, tradesmen, hypocrites, healers and monsters—plausible and terrifying monsters—and all are deftly drawn. . . . Among Tepper's achievements is a moral dialectic that, for once, is truly informed and entertaining. . . . A writer who can box with God need not genuflect before microbiology."

The Washington Post Book World

"Tepper delves into the nature of truth and religion, creating some strong characters in her compelling story."

Publishers Weekly

THE GATE TO WOMEN'S COUNTRY

"It's grand . . . one of the most involving, serious, and deeply felt studies of the relations between the sexes that I have ever read—and then some."

Marion Zimmer Bradley

"Manages to explore seriously the relationship of the sexes in the context of a well-rounded story, without the use of stereotypes, falling into none of the traps that swallow most such books, forsaking bitter feminism for a successful humanistic approach."

Dean R. Koontz

"Lively, thought-provoking . . . [Tepper] takes the mental risks that are the lifeblood of science fiction and all imaginative narrative."

Ursula K. Le Guin, *Los Angeles Times*

AFTER LONG SILENCE

"Magnificent . . . I give [Sheri S. Tepper] full marks for a tremendously exciting and inventive novel, with excellent characterization and a taut plot. Particularly clever is the communications gap between species . . . Absolutely fascinating."

Anne McCaffrey

"Impressive. . . . [Tepper's] protagonists are appealing, rounded characters who inhabit an intriguing, romantic world readers should enjoy visiting."

Publishers Weekly

"[Tepper] has the gift of detail, so that she imbues with grand immediacy her world. . . . Kept me reading well past my normal bedtime."

Analog

Raising the Stones

the

Stones

—

Sheri S. Tepper

BANTAM BOOKS
NEW YORK · TORONTO · LONDON · SYDNEY · AUCKLAND

This edition contains the complete text
of the original hardcover edition.
NOT ONE WORD HAS BEEN OMITTED.

RAISING THE STONES

A Bantam Spectra Book / published by arrangement with Doubleday

PRINTING HISTORY
Doubleday edition published September 1990
Bantam edition / September 1991

Sinks whoever raises the great stones;
I've raised these stones as long as I was able
I've loved these stones as long as I was able
these stones, my fate
Wounded by my own soil
tortured by my own shirt
condemned by my own gods,
these stones.

—George Seferis, "Mycenae"
Collected Poems
Princeton University Press

Raising
the
Stones

—

Hobbs Land

ONE

· *The God's name* was Bondru Dharm, which, according to the linguists who had worked with the Owlbrit before the last of them died, meant something to do with noonday. Noonday Uncovered was the most frequent guess, though Noonday Found and Noonday Announced were also in the running. Only a handful of the Owlbrit had been still alive on Hobbs Land when it was settled by Hobbs Transystem Foods. All but one of them had died soon thereafter, so there hadn't been a lot of opportunity to clarify the meanings of the sounds they made.

The settlers on Hobbs Land, who rather enjoyed using what little had been preserved of Owlbrit language, called the God by his name, Bondru Dharm, or sometimes, though only among the smart asses, Old Bondy. It was housed in the temple the Owlbrit had built for the purpose, a small round building kept in reasonable repair by the people of Settlement One under the regulations of the Ancient Monuments Panel of the Native Matters Advisory of Authority.

No one remembered exactly when the settlers had begun offering sacrifices. Some people claimed the rite had been continued from the time the last Owlbrit died, though no mention of the ritual appeared in Settlement One logs of years one or two. The first mention of it was in the logs of year three. What was certain was that sacrifice had been recommended by the Owlbrit themselves.

Every word the Owlbrit had spoken from the moment the first settlers met them had been preserved in digifax on the information stages, and among the few intelligible exchanges with the last Owlbrit was the reference to sacrifice.

"Necessary?" the linguist had asked, relying heavily upon his Alsense translation stage to convey the meaning of the word. The question had been directed to the last surviving Owlbrit in its tiny round house near the temple.

"Not necessary," the Old One had scraped with his horn-tipped tentacles in a husky whisper. "What is necessary? Is life necessary? Necessary to what? No, sacrifice is not necessary, it is only recommended. It is a way, a convenience, a kindness."

It took the Owlbrit about thirty seconds to scrape, in a sound like wood being gently sawn, but it had taken the last thirty years for the xenolinguists to argue over. They were still disputing over *way, convenience,* and *kindness,* with the reconstruction school arguing strongly that the delicate rasp of the Old One's tentacles actually conveyed the meanings of *system, lifestyle,* and *solace.* No matter what it meant, sacrifice of a few mouselike ferfs every month or so had been instituted no later than the third year of the settlement and had been carried on regularly since, with the ritual gradually gaining complexity as the Ones Who added flourishes. One Who, these days, since Vonce Djbouty had died the previous year. The only One Who who was left was Birribat Shum. · ·

A Birribat who had lately been rather more evident and importunate than usual.

"I tell you Bondru Dharm is dying," he said to Samasnier Girat, the Topman, meantime wringing his hands and sticking his knees and elbows out at odd angles, making himself look like some ungainly bird. "Sam, he's dying!"

Young Birribat (no longer at all young, but called so out of habit) had been saying the God was dying for some time, though not heretofore with such urgency.

Samasnier Girat looked up from the crop report which was already several days late, from the set of planter-and-furrower repair-part requisitions which needed to go to Central Management on the following morning, furrowed his handsome brow in executive irritation, and said, "Give it a few serfs."

Birribat made a gesture. The movement had no meaning so far as Sam was concerned, being a kind of swoop with the left hand, and a grab with the right, as though Birribat caught hold of a loose line someone had left flapping in the wind. The gesture obviously had meaning for Birribat, however, for it ended with the hands gathered together in prayer position and with Birribat gulping uncomfortably as he said, "Please, Sam, don't. Don't say disrespectful things like that. Please. It makes it very hard for me."

Sam gritted strong white teeth and held onto his patience. "Birribat, you go find Sal. Tell Sal whatever it is that's got you in an uproar. I'll talk to Sal about it tonight." Or next week, or next year. The God had been squatting in its temple since Settlement, thirty some odd years now, without showing any evidence of "doing anything" whatsoever. Sam Girat had the evidence of his own observation for that; he spent time in the temple himself, mostly at night and for his own private reasons. However, he didn't believe the God was truly "alive," and the thought of its dying did not greatly perturb him. Still, as Topman, he had to keep in mind that anything Birribat said was likely to create unexpected reverberations among the credulous, of whom there were more than enough in the settlement—in all eleven of the settlements.

Birribat took himself off, and a moment later Sam saw his angular form lurching along the street toward the recreation center. When Sam looked up from his information stage again, it was to see Birribat and Sal striding in the opposite direction, toward the temple.

Salunicl Girat, Sam's sister, who was serving a more or less permanent term as recreation officer, was both gentler and more patient than her brother. Besides, she rather liked Birribat. At least, she found the bony pietist odd and interesting, and when he told her the God was dying, she was sufficiently concerned to go see for herself. As Birribat did, she stopped at the temple gate to pour water over her hands, stooped on the stone porch to take off her shoes, and knelt at the narrow grilled door in the ringwall to take a veil from the rack and drape it over her head and body. Sal wasn't a regular temple-goer, but she had observed the sacrifices often enough to know what was appropriate for someone entering the central chamber. The room inside the grill was like a chimney, about twelve feet across and over thirty feet tall. On a stone plinth in the middle stood the God, a roughly man-sized and onion-shaped chunk of something or other, vaguely blue in color, with spiders of light gradually appearing on its surface to glimmer a moment before flickering and vanishing.

"What does it say?" Sal whispered.

"That it's dying," cried Birribat in an anguished half whisper.

Sal sat on one of the stone seats along the grill and peered at the God, watching the lights appear and disappear on its surface. The last time she had been here, the sparkles had been rhythmic, like the beating of a heart, flushes of light that started near the rounded bottom, gradually moved toward the top, then went out, only to be replaced a moment later by another galaxy lower down. Now there were only random spiders, bright centers with filaments which seemed to reach almost yearningly into darkness.

"Dying?" she asked, "Is there anything about that in the records?"

Birribat nodded, not taking his eyes from the God. "The Owlbrit told the linguists that Bondru Dharm was the last of the Gods, that there had been others. I think."

Sal resolved to look up the matter in the Archives. After watching for a bit longer, she left Birribat in attendance on the deity, went out the grilled door, hung up the veil, resumed her shoes on the porch, and went down the empty street to her brother's office, which she found as empty as the street. At this time of day—except for the kids in school, the babies in the creche, and a few specialists like Sal—the whole village would be out in the fields. Sam had probably gone out there as well and was busy supervising, leaving the Supply and Admin building vacant, which was fine. Saluniel could get more done without interruptions.

The storage files of the Hobbs Land Archives were located deep in the well-protected bowels of Central Management, a considerable distance from any of the settlements, but the files were completely accessible to settlers through their personal information stages, including the high resolution model on Sam's desk. Sal insinuated herself between chair and desk and told the stage to search Archives for anything to do with the Gods. She was promptly shown an endless catalogue of choices, words, and images, beginning with ancient deities named Baal and Thor and Zeus who had been worshipped on Manhome, and continuing through all the ages of exploration in a listing of every human and non-human deity encountered or invented since.

"Gods of the Owlbrit," she said impatiently, which made the stage splutter at her in a tiny explosion of red and purple fireworks before the new listing floated by. Most of it was devoted to boring scholarly disputations filed in the Archives since settlement, and she didn't want any of that. "Original accounts of," she muttered, wondering why it always took her three or four tries to get anything. "*By* the Owlbrit," she instructed, grunting with satisfaction at the appearance of the original interview with the Old One. He or she or it squatted in a corner in turniplike immobility, delicate legs spread like a lace frill at its rump, confronted by one pallid linguist and an Alsense machine with an irritating squeal in one search drive. All in all, the interview wasn't notable for either clarity or dramatic impact, but when she'd viewed it through to the end, she knew Birribat had been correct. Old One had said this God, Dondru Dharm, was the last. "Only the Owlbrit last," said the Old One, giving the linguists something else to argue about.

From the interview alone, it wasn't clear when the former Gods had been around. However, there were

enough remnants of other temples in Settlement One—
two of them squatting on high ground beyond the north
edge of the settlement and two others clustered near the
temple of Bondru Dharm—to answer that question. Since
one of the temples north of the settlement was almost
complete except for its roof, it was logical to infer at least
one other of the Gods had lived in recent historic time.

Sal didn't need the archives to tell her about the ruins.
They had been a topic of settler discussion for years.
Should they be razed? Could they be used for something
else? Except for the most recent ruin, the rest were only
tumbled circles of outer and inner walls, stubby remnants
of radiating arches, a few fragments of metal grills, and a
few square feet of mosaic. Even the most recent one had
no roof, door, or windows, no seats in what must have
been the assembly space, though the trough-shaped area
wouldn't have been at all suitable for any human gathering. It was a wonder, considering all the disputation about
them, that the ruins had never been disturbed. The two at
the center of the settlement certainly occupied sites that
could have been put to better use. If Bondru Dharm actually died, the whole question would undoubtedly come up
again.

Sal looked up from the frozen images in the stage to
find her brother standing beside her, his face not saying
much, which was rare for Sam. He usually either grinned
or scowled at the world, furrowing his handsome brow
and making a gargoyle of himself, managing to evoke
some response from even the reluctant or taciturn. Still
unspeaking, he sat down next to her, looking preoccupied
and rather ill. She could hear many people moving out in
the street. The shuffling of feet sounded faintly where
there should have been no people before dusk.

"Sam?" she asked. "Was there an accident or something?"

He didn't answer. She went to the window to see a
silent throng gathered down the street, not precisely in
front of the temple, more or less to one side of it: several
hundred men and women and their children as well—
virtually the entire population of the settlement. As she
watched, they fell to their knees in one uncontrolled wave

of motion. A cry rose in her throat and stayed there as she fell to her own knees, possessed by a feeling of loss so great that she could not speak, could not moan, could only kneel, then bend forward to put her head on the floor, then push out her legs until she was pressed to the floor, utterly flat, arms and hands pressed down, legs apart and pressed down, cheek pressed down, as though to imprint herself deep into the surface below her, knowing in some far-off part of herself that Sam was beside her and that out in the street the whole settlement was lying face down in the dust, possibly never to rise again, because Bondru Dharm had just died.

· *A day later,* when they came, more or less, to their senses, there was nothing left of the God. The altar, if it had been an altar, was empty and dust-covered by the time the first settler was able to get up off the ground to go look. Birribat was where Sal had left him, in the central chamber, except now he was curled on the floor, covered with fine black dust, dead.

Sam and two or three other people wrapped Birribat's body loosely in a blanket and carried it out to the north side of town, near the ruined temples, even though the burying ground was nowhere near there. The burying ground was on a hill east of the settlement, but it seemed more fitting to those who took Birribat's body that a One Who should be buried near a temple, even a ruined temple. They laid him in a shallow grave, and it wasn't long before people were saying that when a God died, he took his interpreter with him.

But that was after everyone in the settlement lay idly about for eight or nine days, unable to do anything. People started for the fields and then found themselves back in their clanhomes, looking at the walls. People started to cook meals and then found themselves lying on the floor. Mothers went to look at their kids and never got there, and the kids slumped in logy groups, not moving a lot of the time. Even the babies didn't cry, didn't seem to be hungry, scarcely wet themselves.

About the tenth day, however, whatever-it-was began

to wear off, and someone had enough energy to call Central Management. Within hours there were med-techs and investigators swarming over the place, hungry babies were yelling, and hungry, grumpy people were snapping at each other.

"Has it happened anywhere else," Sam wanted to know, rubbing his itchy beard and scraping gunk out of the corners of his eyes, feeling as though he'd slept quite badly for about a week. Sam had been in the habit of meeting with a private and personal friend every two or three evenings, rather late, and he had just realized he hadn't seen his friend since this event began. This made him even more snappish and apprehensive. "Has anything like this happened elsewhere?" he repeated, snarling.

"This is the only settlement built on the site of an Owlbrit village," the harried med-tech in charge told him as she took a blood sample. "All the other Owlbrit ruins are up on the escarpment. So, no, it hasn't happened anywhere else."

"Any ideas about what caused this . . . this depression?" He could remember feeling depressed and inexpressibly sad, though right now he just felt edgy and annoyed and his legs jumped as though he wanted to run away somewhere.

"One theory is that the thing had some kind of field around it that you'd all gotten used to. Chemical, maybe. Pheromones, possibly. Electromagnetic, less likely. Whatever it was, when it was shut down, you had to readjust."

"That's all?" It hardly seemed an adequate explanation to Sam. He was of a mood to be belligerent about it, and only common sense and long experience as a Topman, who had learned more by listening than talking, kept him quiet.

"Isn't that enough? It'll keep some of us busy for some little time."

Sam couldn't let it alone. "Did the initial Clearance Teams find any kind of field? I mean, nobody objected to the settlement being put here in the first place, did they?" The idea that some carelessness might have taken place only increased his feelings of annoyance. He took a deep breath and controlled himself.

The med-tech was getting a little annoyed herself, and her snappish tone reflected that fact. "Topman, nobody had any reason to. We've called up everything available from the Archives and found nothing. Nobody found anything strange at this site except for the thing itself."

Sam growled wordlessly.

She went on, waving her finger at him. "Since it was sacred to the Owlbrit, the decision was made high-up not to bother the thing except to test for radioactivity or harmful emanations, and there weren't any. By the time the last of the Owlbrit died, your village seemed to have adopted the God as a mascot, and Central had more important things to deal with than investigating some animal, vegetable, or mineral which wasn't bothering anyone, which might resent being investigated, and which was, so far as we knew, a unique phenomenon. Until ten days ago, nobody found anything weird about anything."

Sam shrugged, his best approach to an apology.

The tech sighed. "Speaking of weird, I understand you buried a body elsewhere than in the approved burying ground. That's a public health matter, and it ought to be reinterred."

Sam vaguely remembered Birribat had been buried, but he couldn't remember who had done it, or exactly where, and after a brief and aimless search for the grave, the health people gave up on that.

"You think we're over the worst?" Sam asked the woman in charge finally, having run out of everything else to ask.

"You've been mourning," the med-tech said. "The psy-techs say the whole settlement had all the symptoms of grief. Even though you didn't know what you were mourning about, that's what you were doing. It's pretty much over, I'd say. The biologists are pissing themselves for not having investigated earlier, but except for that everything is on its way to normal."

The medical person could be forgiven. She spoke as medical people have often done, out of a habit of authority and reassurance, in a tone that admitted of no doubt or exceptions or awareness of human frailty. She was, as many medical people have always been, dead wrong.

· · ·

· *First time visitors* to Hobbs Land, at least
those who came on official business, were usually sub-
jected to an orientation session conducted by someone at
Central Management. Production Chief Horgy Endure
often got stuck with the duty since he did it very well,
even though he called his presentation, with stunning
unoriginality, "All About Hobbs Land." On a particular
morning not long after the death of Bondru Dharm
(which Horgy had had no responsibility toward and had,
therefore, ignored), he had a group of five to instruct: two
engineers from Phansure (Phansuri engineers being as
ubiquitous in System as fleas on a cat, and as itchy,
though rather more benign) as well as the latest trio in
Horgy's endless succession of female assistants, three
lovelies from Ahabar, not one of whom was actually
brainless. The engineers, specialists in robotic design, were
going out to Settlement One to meet with Sam Girat, and
the lovelies were staying at Central Management to learn
what Horgy could teach them. Two of them had already
had a sample and longed for more.

Horgy had gathered the five of them in the Executive
Staff Room around an information stage, which he had
programmed to display eye-riveting visuals concurrent
with his well-practiced oral presentation. Horgy enjoyed
orientations. He liked the sound of his own voice, which
was rich and warm and did not belie the sensual curve of
his lips.

When they gathered, the stage was already showing a
neat model of the System, the three tiny inner planets
twirling in their orbits, then Thyker, Ahabar, the Belt,
and finally Phansure. The truncated model included all of
the occupied worlds and most of the occupied moons but
not the outer planets, which didn't fit the scale and
weren't important for orientation anyhow. When Horgy
cleared his throat, the model gave way to actual holography of the Belt as taken from a survey ship, skim-
ming past Bounce and Pedaria and a few of the other
fifteen-thousand Belt worlds, the stage pointing out, unnecessarily, that though some of the Belt worlds were set-

ed, some were merely named, while others were only
umbered and not even surveyed yet. Belt worlds were
ny to smallish, by and large, a few with native life, some
vith atmosphere of their own, some with atmosphere fac-
ories, many of them with great light-focusing sun-sails
ehind them, gathering warmth to make the crops grow,
arm worlds for the System.

"This world we now call Hobbs Land," said Horgy,
vatching it swim up on cue, a tannish-green blob with an
ngular darker green belt, blue at its poles, fishbone
triped by wispy clouds slanting in from the polar oceans
o the equator, "was mapped and sampled by the un-
nanned survey ship, *Theosphes K. Phaspe,* some sixty
feyears ago. About twenty years later, when the relative
rbits of Phansure and the newly mapped planet made the
ttempt economically feasible, Hobbs Land was optioned
or settlement by Hobbs Transystem Foods, under the di-
ection of Mysore Hobbs I."

"Mysore One died last year," said the older of the two
*hansuris to one of the lovelies. "Marvelous old man,
Mysore. Mysore Two's running things now."

Horgy smiled acknowledgement without missing a
eat. "Transystem headquarters on Phansure sent a settle-
nent ship with parts for a continuous feed Door and the
equisite technicians."

The stage showed the technicians putting the Door
ogether, leaping about like fleas. The newly assembled
Door glittered with blue fire as construction materials,
nen, and machines began coming through on a con-
inuous belt. Time-jump holography showed men and
nachines creating the Central Management structures—
dministration tower, equipment and repair, warehouses,
taff and visitor housing blocks, and recreation complex—
ll of them sprouting from the ground like mushrooms.
At the top of the Admin building, a sign flashed red and
ellow: *HOBBS LAND, a Farm Settlement World of
TRANSYSTEM FOODS.*

Horgy went on, "Construction of the Central Manage-
nent complex was already well underway when on-planet
urveyors discovered that the world, which had been
hought to be uninhabited, was actually the home of the

Owlbrit people, a presumably ancient race, only twelve of whom were still living at the time of first contact."

Visuals of tiny villages, tiny round houses, fat, turnip-shaped creatures dragging laboriously about on their fragile legs.

"Only twelve of them?" asked Theor Close, the older of the two Phansuri engineers, "Were there really only twelve?"

"Only twelve," said Horgy, firmly. "That is, only twelve anybody could find. Plus three or four of their Gods, and all but one of them died immediately."

"That's sad," said one of the female assistants, a willowy blonde with impossible eyelashes. "Even though they're not very pretty."

Horgy smiled at her, his meltingly adoring smile, the smile that had convinced whole legions of female assistants—Horgy never had anything else—that each of them was the most wonderful woman in the universe. "It was sad," he admitted, his voice throbbing. "Though, you're right, they weren't pretty."

"So," said the other engineer, Betrun Jun. "What happened to the twelve survivors?"

"Ah . . ." Horgy reviewed what he had said and found his place again. "Through the immediate efforts of topflight philologists and xenolinguists, it was learned that, far from resenting the presence of humans upon their world, the Owlbrit people welcomed settlement. Such had been foreseen, they said. Such had been promised by their Gods, in order that the will of the Gods could be accomplished."

"Nice for us humans," said Betrun Jun, with a wink at his companion.

Horgy acknowledged this with a nod and went on. "The last of the Owlbrit people died about five years after settlement, though the last of their Gods remained in the condition which has been called 'alive' until just recently."

"Why didn't I ever hear about the Owlbrits?" asked the brunette member of Horgy's trio, a young person of astonishing endowments. "I never heard a word about them."

"It seems they didn't build anything," said Theor Close, thoughtfully. "No roads, no monuments, no cities."

"They didn't create anything," added the other Phanuri. "No art, no literature, no inventions. What did they leave, Endure? A few ruined villages?"

Horgy, badly off his track but grateful for their interest, regrouped with his charming smile once more. "That's about all. From space, the clusters of little structures look much like multiple meteor strikes, which is probably why they were missed on first look-see. The onsite surveyors found ten live Owlbrit, in ones and twos, among the ruins on the escarpment. They found one mostly ruined village down on the plain containing two Owlbrit who said they'd been waiting for us. 'Waiting for somebody to show up,' is the way the linguists translated it. That's where Settlement One was put. A couple of xeologists were housed there until the last Owlbrit died. I recall reading that the last Owlbrit told one of the linguists that watching the humans had interested him so much that he stayed alive longer than he would have otherwise."

"So there's really nothing left of them," Theor Close said, his voice conveying both wonder and regret.

"The ruins and a few words and phrases of their language we've adopted as localisms," admitted Horgy. "Names for places and things. *Creely,* that's a kind of local fish. *Bondru,* that means noon. We can make only an approximation of their sounds I'm afraid. We can't really duplicate their language vocally."

"That's why I never heard of them, then," said the brunette with satisfaction. "They were all gone before I was even born." Her tone conveyed the unimportance of anything that might have happened, anywhere, before she came upon the scene. Horgy's assistants tended to be self-approving.

However self-absorbed, she was right. The Owlbrit, an enigmatic people, less than legendary, were indeed gone, as the people of Hobbs Land knew. Xenologists in various places read books about them, or wrote books about them, but in the last analysis there seemed very little to say

about the Owlbrit except they had lived once but were n
more.

Turning to the engineers, Horgy said, "Before you g
out to talk to Sam Girat at Settlement One, a few bri
words about the geography of Hobbs Land. . . ." And l
summoned up pictures of undulating and remarkably du
plains to get himself on track once more.

·   *When Samasnier Girat,* his sister, Salunie
and their mother, Maire, had arrived on Hobbs Lan
when they had first set foot upon the glassy sand beyon
the Door, with the wind of a strange world riffling the
hair, Sam's mam had knelt down to touch the soil.

"Thanks be to God!" Maire had cried. "There are n
legends here."

She had uttered the words with a certain fatalistic sa
isfaction, in the manner of a woman who is packing u
house and has resolved to abandon some troublesome po
session even though she knows she may miss it later. He
words, uttered coincident with their arrival, had carrie
the weight of prophecy, and the whole event had seeme
so pregnant with intent that Sam never forgot it. Eve
when he was grown he could recall the feel of the wind
the smell of the air—an empty smell, he had thought the
and often since—his mother's haggard but beautiful fac
under the dark kerchief she wore, her heavy shoes besid
his small ones on the soil, the very sack she had set down
the one that held their clothes and Sal's doll and his ow
carved warriors, Ire and Iron and Voorstod, though Mar
had not let him bring his whip. The sack had been threac
bare and stained, with a leather drawstring, and Mam ha
carried it all the way from the town of Scaery, in Voorsto
upon Ahabar.

After that, during his childhood, Sam thought of leg
ends as things Mam had left behind; not valueless thing
like worn out shoes, but things difficult and awkward t
transport, things that were quite heavy perhaps, with od
knobs on them, or even wheels, difficult but fascinatin
things. Without ever saying so in words to himself, an
certainly without ever asking Maire, he assumed that on

of the difficult things Mam had left behind had been Sam's dad, Phaed Girat. Sam was never sure from day to day whether he could forgive Mam for that or whether maybe he had forgiven her for it already, without knowing.

Maire had offered Sam his choice, back in Voorstod upon Ahabar, in the kitchen at Scaery, where the fire made shadows in the corners and the smell of the smoke was in everything. Sam could not remember that time without smelling smoke and the earthy scent of the pallid things that grew along damp walls. "Sal and I are going away," Mam had said. "You can stay with your dad or go with us. I know you're too young to make that decision, but it's the only choice I can give you, Sam. Sal and I can't stay here. Voorstod is no place for womenfolk and children."

He had wanted to stay with Dad. Those were the words crowding at his throat when she gave him the choice, but they had stuck there. Sam had been born with a quality which some might have thought mere shyness but was in fact an unchildlike prudence. He often did not say what came to mind. What he thought at the time was that he wanted to stay with Dad but it might be difficult to survive if he did so. Dad was unlikely to help him with his reading, or cook his dinner, or wash his clothes. Dad didn't do things like that. Dad threw him high in the air and caught him, almost always. Dad gave him a whip and taught him to make it crack and to knock bottles over with it. Dad called him "My strong little Voorstoder" and taught him to shout, "Ire, Iron, and Voorstod" when the prophets went by and all the women had to hide in their rooms. But there were other times Dad scarcely seemed to notice him, times when Dad growled and snarled like one of the sniffers, chained out behind the house, times when Sam thought this big man was really someone else, someone wearing a mask of Dad's face.

Besides, with Sam's brother Maechy dead—Mam said he was dead and would never come back—wouldn't Mam need a son to take care of her? Dad needed nobody, so he said. Men of the Cause needed nobody but themselves and Almighty God, whether they had been men of Ire or of Iron or of Voorstod to start with.

So Sam, prudently and dutifully, had said he would go
with Mam and Sal. Even when Maire had told him he
would have to leave his whip behind, Sam had figured out
it was his duty to go, but he wasn't sure then or later he
had made the right choice. As he got older, he still wasn't
sure. Sometimes he dreamed of Dad. At least, when he
wakened, that's who he thought he'd been dreaming of.
He also dreamed of hands over his eyes and a voice whispering to him, "You don't see them, Sammy. They aren't
there. You don't see them." He woke angry from those
dreams, angry that he'd been kept from seeing something
important, or that he'd chosen to come to Hobbs Land, or
that Dad hadn't come along.

Remembering what he could of Dad, however, he
could imagine why Maire had left him behind with the
rest of the legends. Dad had been much too heavy to
move. When Sam remembered Phaed Girat, he remembered him that way: a ponderous and brooding shape with
no handles a person could catch hold of. The thought was
comforting, in a way. If Dad was too unwieldy to be
moved, then he was still there, in Voorstod, where Sam
could find him later if he needed him. Voorstod upon
Ahabar would always be there, half-hidden in mists,
smelling of smoke and of the pale fungi growing along the
walls.

On Hobbs Land—as in most places elsewhere in the
System—children had uncles, not fathers, and Sam had to
grow up without an older man of his own. Though Maire
had had brothers in Voorstod, they would not have considered betraying the Cause by leaving it. Sam pretended
his carved warriors were his father and his uncles. He put
them on the table by his bed, where he could see them as
he fell asleep. Clean-shaven Ire, with his sandals and jer-
kin, his shield and sword; bearded Iron, wearing flowing
robes and headdress, carrying a curved blade; and mus-
tached, heavy-booted Voorstod, with his whip at his belt.
Voorstod's name meant "Whip-death," and he was the
fiercest of the three. Sam believed he looked like Dad, the
way Dad had sometimes been.

Sam grew up to be both dutiful and willful, a boy who
would say yes to avoid trouble but then do as he pleased.

He was biddable, but not docile, innovative in his thinking and tenacious in his memories. He had an occasional and peculiarly trying expression, one which seemed to doubt the sensations going on inside himself. Sugar was not sweet, nor vinegar sour, his face sometimes seemed to say, but to hide some other flavor concealed therein. "It's all right, but . . ." his face sometimes said, to the irritation of those around him. Beneath each sensation, within each explanation, Sam felt there must be others, more significant and more profound.

When Sam was about twenty, he sometimes lay on his bed looking out at unnamed constellations, thinking deep thoughts about who he was and what Hobbs Land was and whether he belonged there. The settlers talked about all kinds of worlds, real ones and ones they had only imagined. Hobbs Land had to be real, for who would bother to dream up a world like this? No one. Hobbs Land was dull and bland, and not worth the effort. Except for a few blotches (scarcely more than pimples, really), a few thousand square miles of field and farm and vineyard and orchard where the people were, there was no human history or adventure in this place. No human-built walls staggered across the shallow hills; no menhirs squatted broodingly upon the escarpment; no painted animals pranced at the edge of the torchlight in chambered caves, full of wonder and mystery and danger, evoking visions of terrible, primitive times.

Of course, men had never been primitives on Hobbs Land. They had come through the Door already stuffed with histories and memories and technologies from other places. They had come from troubled Ahabar and sea-girt Phansure and brazen Thyker and this moon or that moon. They had arrived as civilized peoples—though not as *a* civilized people, which might have given them the sense of common identity Sam thought he wanted.

And so far as monuments were concerned, it made no difference what kind of people had come there. Hobbs Land had no monuments of any kind, civilized or not. No battles had been fought here, no enemies defeated. The landscape was bland as pudding, unstained by human struggle, empty of triumph.

So he told himself, lying on his bed, longing for something more. Something nameless.

A few years later, Sam kissed China Wilm out by the poultry-bird coops on a starlit evening and thought he might have found what he wanted. He sought among unfamiliar emotions to tell her how he felt. He couldn't find the words, and he blamed Hobbs Land for that. He told himself he wanted similes for the feel of her lips, which were silken and possessed of an unsuspected power; he wanted wonderful words for the turmoil in his belly and groin and mind as well, but nothing on Hobbs Land was at all tumultuous or marvelous.

"Sam, she's a child!" Mam had exclaimed, not so much horrified as embarrassed for him. China Wilm was only twelve and Sam was twenty-two.

Sam knew that! But Sam was willing to wait for her! Sam had watched her grow from a glance-eyed toddler; he had picked her out! He had no intention of despoiling a child, but she was his, he had decided, no matter whether she knew it yet or not. Even at twenty-two, he was an ardent and articulate lover who loved as much in his head as in his body. So he kissed her chastely, said only enough, he hoped, to be intriguing, and let her go—for a time—while telling himself it must be those missing *legends* that frustrated him. Among them, he was sure, he could have found all the similarities and examples he needed. Surely if he'd had a chance to talk with his dad, Dad could have made it clear how it all fit together.

Unthinkingly, Sam said as much to Maire Girat. The words left his mouth and he knew in that instant they should never have been spoken. She turned away from him, and after a time he realized she was crying. Her tears made him uncomfortable, and he tried to remedy matters.

"But there were good things on Voorstod! You were important there, weren't you, Mam. People used to ask me if I wasn't proud of you, you were so famous."

"To some I was famous," she said, wiping her eyes. "To a few."

"Because of your singing," he went on, keeping the conversation going with an effort and wondering—oddly, it was the first time he had wondered that—why she no longer sang.

"Yes. That," she said in a dismissive tone, her mouth knotted uncomfortably.

"Did you sing of love, Mam?"

Surprised, she laughed harshly. "Love, Sammy? Oh, yes, I sang of love. Out of love. For love."

"Were there legends of love then, there in Voorstod?"

Her lips twisted at one corner. "It was said by the prophets in Voorstod that what men call love is merely lust, to be controlled at all costs. We women were said to provoke this unholy lust unless we covered our faces and bodies and stayed well hidden. Men were too valuable to be exposed to such feelings. What we felt was of no matter. They could walk with their faces showing, but we were instructed to hide ours. Such teaching leaves little room for songs of love."

His expression told her this wasn't what he had meant. "What is it, Sammy?" she had asked him.

"I need to know about it," he cried, though he had not planned to do any such thing. "I need to know about . . . where we came from." He had almost said "Who I am," and had caught himself just in time. He was twenty-two then, and a man of twenty-two should certainly know who he was. The truth was, he did not. He had tried on this mask and that, but none of them had suited him, quite. Maire did not understand him well enough to tell him. "Where we come from," he repeated, thinking this was what he had really meant.

So, Maire had told him of her own life in Voorstod and of the little dark Gharmish people who were slaves in Voorstod and of her marriage to his Dad and why she had left. Before she was well started, that peculiar expression had settled on his face and he had stopped listening. What she had said was not what he had wanted to hear. Her words had slipped from his preconceptions like rain from a leaf. She had spoken of Fess, and Bitty, the Gharm friends of her childhood, but these had not been the memories he had wanted. He had never seen the Gharm, had he? He had shaken away the fleeting memory of hands across his eyes and had told himself her words did not describe the Voorstod of his heart.

Still, at some level, the words had stuck. Later, in a far place, he would remember Fess and Bitty as he might have remembered a story he had once read or a drama he had seen. At the time Maire told him, however, he simply did not hear.

· *About four years* after Sam first kissed China Wilm, she became old enough for real lovemaking. She was sixteen, an acceptable age for love affairs or mothering among the matrilineal Hobbs Landians. Sam was twenty-six, by that time fairly experienced in the joys of love, which a good many settlement women had been eager to teach him. He gave China Wilm no chance to take up with anyone else. He adored her with every part of him, and in good time China bore a son. The boy was named Jeopardy Wilm. In his heart, Sam called himself Jeopardy Wilm's father, though no one else did. If people had mentioned the relationship at all, they would have said that Sam was Jep's progy, short for progenitor, and even that word wasn't bandied about in casual conversation. Unless a woman did something blatantly stupid, genetically speaking, *who* progied a child was considered to be nobody's business but the woman's own, and that was true on Hobbs Land as it was on Phansure and Thyker and even most of Ahabar.

Whatever Sam's role was called, he went on coveting, adoring, and desiring China Wilm—and arguing with her and fussing at her until Mam took him aside one day and told him he'd inherited Old Phaed's meanness with women that he couldn't leave the girl alone.

"I found her crying," said Maire. "It isn't the first time I've seen her crying. I asked her what the matter was, and she said you were, Sam. She said she didn't know what you wanted! I told her to join the group, for I've had that problem with you myself, but at least you've given up badgering me long since! Now take her as she is or let her alone, laddy. We're not on Voorstod where you could hound her to death and then beat her because she cries.

You're here on Hobbs Land, and you owe her some courtesy!"

He ignored what she said about Voorstod as he had come to ignore everything she said about Voorstod. As to the rest of it, though, he paid attention. He had not realized he was being tiresome. It was only that he felt so close to China Wilm, it was as though she were part of him and could help him figure out things he didn't understand himself. He wanted her to help him know what it was he needed to know—things about belonging to a place, about longing for a place, about the way Hobbs Land sometimes felt to him, prickly and raw, like new wine, rough on the palate, or vacant and empty, like trying to swallow wind. He'd thought if he progied a child, he might feel more a part of China and of Hobbs Land, but it hadn't happened. What happened instead was that China Wilm's son was so completely a Wilm clanmember, it made Sam Girat feel even more at a loss, more an outsider.

All of which connected somehow to the legends Mam had left behind, and his father back there on Voorstod. Mam may have left them, he screamed to himself silently in the privacy of the brotherhouse, thundering on the wall with his fists in a tantrum that would have satisfied any three-year-old; Maire may have left them behind, but Sam hadn't! And even if he tried to be gentler with China Wilm, he wasn't going to let Jep alone, no matter that custom demanded it. He'd find something he could do to ingratiate himself with the boy!

Sam went to the Archives, all innocence and sneaky good intentions, and asked for stories for children. He thought he would become a storyteller, an unobjectionable hobby that would entertain the young ones without offending anyone. The Archives, however, didn't categorize stories for children. What one culture considered appropriate for children, another culture might taboo. All the Archives heard was "stories," and it called up everything, a flood of epics and sagas, rulers and vagabonds, monsters, wars, crusades and quests, myths, tales, dramas, jests and frolics, which frothed upon the stage until Sam was dazzled and dizzied by it all. He would never have thought of coming to the Archives for the legends he'd wanted, but here they were. All of them. Everything.

For a while he buried himself in the Archives, living and dreaming what he saw there, soaking it in, swimming in it like a creely. There were homelands and fathers aplenty in the Archives, gods and heroes and kings, most of them. Which is what a father should be, thought Sam: a god, a hero, a king!

One particular legend leapt out of the stage at him, almost as though he had made it up himself. A king had gone on a journey, and he'd progied a child on a woman. A noblewoman, actually, for heroes wouldn't consort with anyone ordinary. The king had to continue his journey. His mission couldn't be interrupted for her or for a baby, so he'd buried a sword and a pair of his own shoes under a heavy stone, and he'd told the mother that, when the boy was strong enough to lift the stone, he could get the sword and the shoes with which to make the journey to find him, the father. In time the son had grown strong and found the shoes and the sword and found his father, too, and met his destiny.

Destiny! Fate! That purpose larger than mere existence that shone like a distant beacon upon a dark height! His heartbeat said, "Scale it." His very breath urged him, "Find it." It was *destiny* that called Sam Girat. He knew it as though an oracle had whispered it in his ear. This story was about *him*. In a stroke of revelation, sudden and sharp as lightning, he understood that Phaed Girat had never really intended to let him go. Somewhere there was a stone with the secret thing under it, the thing that would take him back home, where his dad was.

Never mind there were no chains on Sam and he could have gone to Voorstod any time he liked. Settlers weren't serfs, they were free to come and go. To Sam, "going home," meant something more than that. To him, the meaning of the tale was clear, evident, absolutely without question. The illogicality of it only made it more sure, more intriguing. Of course it was illogical. Of course it was strange. Legends *were* strange, and destiny might be illogical. Sam had never heard *credo quia absurdum est,* which a few Notable Scholars still quoted on occasion, but he would have understood the phrase in a minute.

Even though that particular story was the best one, Sam soon came to believe that all the stories were really one story. Every legend was one legend. At the root of every tale was someone with a need or a question, setting out to find an answer to that need, meeting danger and joy upon the way. All the heroes were looking for the one marvelous thing: for their fathers or for immortality or goodness or knowledge or some combination of those things, and it was their *destiny* to find what they sought. It was almost always the men who went, not the women, and that told Sam something too, confirming him in a former opinion about Maire and China, that it did no good to ask women some kinds of questions because they weren't interested in the answers. Women just didn't understand these things!

Thereafter, he often took long walks north, in rocky country, shifting boulders along the way, believing that any one of them might be the one beneath which his father had hidden the sword or the shoes or some other thing, whatever it might be. He did this even after he realized that both "stone" and "sword" might be symbolic rather than real. He did it even knowing that Phaed Girat had never set foot upon Hobbs Land. In a marvelous world, Phaed could have sent someone, some miraculous messenger who flew around between worlds. And who was to say it wasn't so. The power of the father, the hero, the king, resided in that ability: to make the impossible real.

· *Jeopardy Wilm had* a cousin, Saturday, the daughter of his mother's sister, Africa Wilm, who had chosen her daughter's name out of old Manhome sources from the Archives. It was a language no one spoke anymore. Sometimes settlers chose old Manhome names for their meaning, sometimes for their sound. Africa Wilm had chosen *Saturday* for its sound, and because it was part of a series of words that could be used for the five or six other children she intended to have. So far Africa had added Tuesday through Friday, three boys plus another girl, and had decided a total of five might be enough.

From the time she was tiny, Saturday sang. Even when she was a toddler, she twittered like a bird. There were few birdlike things on Hobbs Land, and none of them sang very well, so Saturday had no competition in becoming the settlement songstress. She was much petted over this, and it was due to Africa's good sense she didn't become spoiled. It was a gift, Africa told her child in a stern voice. A gift which Saturday hadn't earned or even earned the use of. She must work hard at other things as well and use the gift for the happiness of all.

Saturday worked hard at everything, and she sang, and when she was about ten, she got to know Maire Girat, who, though she didn't sing now, had once been a singer of great reputation. At least, so said many of the settlers, even those from Phansure or Thyker. Many of them knew of the songs of Maire Manone, which is what she had been called back in Voorstod. It was Maire who taught Saturday how to breathe, and how to bring the air up in a glowing column from her lungs, without break or pause, stroking the notes into life. It was Maire Girat who taught her to embellish her songs with trills and scales and leaps, so the voice trilled and purled like water running.

They became friends, the tall, haggard, broad-shouldered, often-silent woman and the slight, talkative, flyaway girl. They spent much time together, Saturday questioning and Maire answering in her slow, deliberate voice with the furry roughness at its edges.

"Why do you sing no more, Maire?" Saturday asked her one day. It was a question she had wanted to ask for a very long time, but something had kept her from it, some sensitivity or scrupulosity which told her the answer would be painful.

"I cannot," the woman said sadly. She did not want to talk to this happy child about Fess and Bitty, or about the dreams she once had of great anthems sounding among the stars. Once music had dwelt in her mind, every watch of every day. She had left Voorstod when the music died, but she did not want to talk about that.

Instead, she said, "None of the things I sang of exist

here, child. I sang of lashing seas and looming mountains. Here, the land is like a child's sandbox, all patted smooth. What can I sing of?"

To Saturday, there seemed a good deal to sing of. Though Hobbs Land was dull, so everyone said, Saturday had always found it beautiful. Very simple and plain, but beautiful for that.

"In Voorstod," Maire said, "the mists gather around to make a little room wherever you stand. If a girl had a lover they could walk all alone, closed in, as though there were no other people in the world. Women could take their veils off, in the mist, and kiss their sweethearts, daring greatly for love, for the winds might come down off the heights to blow all the mists away, and suddenly everything would be there, the monstrous stones, black and towering, with the sea reflecting the sun in a great mirror, everything green and blue and gold, meadow and mountain and sea, and the lovers would have to flee lest they be discovered. That is what I sang of, there."

"That's all you sang about? Sweethearts in the mist?" Saturday's voice held a great deal of doubt.

Maire considered this. The sweethearts were entirely a fiction. Women did not dare do such things, and men would not have risked their lives so, but it had been pleasant for a moment to pretend it was true. The lie turned to bitterness in her throat, and she spat it out as truth. "I'm lying to myself and to you, child. I did not sing of lovers. I sang of death. When my boy Maechy died, I wrote a song. It was called 'The Last Winged Thing,' and it spoke of the angel of Hope coming to Scaery to ask if I'd called it there as I'd called the other angels. Hope was the last one, the last winged thing."

Saturday gazed into the woman's hooded eyes, wonderingly. "What happened? In the song?"

"What always happens in Voorstod. The angel died, just as all the other angels had died. Love, Joy, Peace, all dead. Voorstod is into the habit of death, so we women always said. With hope dead, I could not sing anymore, so I came away."

"How did it go, Maire? The song?"

"I cannot sing it. The last words were, '. . . kiss me

my child, farewell my child, follow me, child, and we'll go.' "

Saturday shook her head in puzzlement. "I don't understand."

"We women of Voorstod understand it. We've been leaving Voorstod for hundreds of years now. When we're ready to leave, when we've told our husbands we're going, and they've laughed at us, not believing us, when we've packed what we can carry and cried until we're blind, we say *kiss me* to the sons and husbands who will not come with us; *farewell* to them and to all the friends and children who've died; and then *follow me* to the little ones and the daughters who come along. When I came away, there was no one for me to kiss goodbye. I said farewell to my son Maechy who had died at Voorstod's hands. I said follow me to Sam and Sal. That was my last song. I will never sing again."

• *Comes a certain* night on Hobbs Land, which is, though no one even suspects such a thing, different from all other nights. It breathes of brooding pregnancies awaiting birth, monstrous winged truths lying coiled and glimmering in wombs of shadow, ready to erupt at any moment. Such nights need no moon, being lit by their own quiescence.

Sam, some twenty-eight lifeyears old now, finds himself unable to sleep. Darkness gathers in palpable shapes that are peopled with possibilities. A word may be spoken on such a night. A truth may be told. A thing may happen. Sam is not moved to push over boulders on this night, or to peer beneath them with the aid of a tiny torch to see what mysteries lie there. Sam is tired of that. So, he walks east, out beyond the settled lands and back again, searching for the unknown, striding along fields where the little ditches gleam silver in the starshine and the growing crops stretch upward, murmuring, almost as though they were sentient. This thing, that thing, everything is glossed with glamor on this night, as though a cloud of miracles has descended. His feet are guided as by invisible hands; they fall softly on paths Sam feels he would not even see by daylight. The stars turn above, making great wheels of light, which he can feel turning, like an engine. So Sam Girat, moving through the night in great, ground-eating strides, returns to Settlement One with dawn not far off and no sleep at all behind him.

Close by is the temple of Bondru Dharm, small and dark, making a sound like breathing, a suspiration, gentle as the breath of a child sweetly sleeping. Air rises in the temple, bringing in the cool. The God squats in a column of rising air, flushed with light. So Sam remembers him, quite suddenly—though he has not been in the temple for years—suddenly remembers with affectionate regard or perhaps only a vagrant curiosity which has distilled itself into something like fondness.

The temple door opens easily, almost of itself. The scoopy floor presents no hazard. Sam finds the grilled door into the enclosure and squats before it, peering into the darkness to see the lights, pale galaxies of fire which appear low on the body of the God and ascend gradually, disappearing into darkness once more, over and over, rising lights, drifting as though in unlimited space, up, and out, and away.

Sam's eyes grow heavy. His legs feel the long miles of walking. He will rest, he says to himself, a few minutes, he will rest before he goes home to the brotherhouse. And he is all at once curled like a worm in a nut upon the mosaic floor, head pillowed on one muscled arm, legs drawn up, sleeping like a kitten, all limp, while the lights of the God pulse and dim, pulse and dim, pulse and dim.

The air rises. The night gathers itself like a net drawn in before it is flung, darkness folding upon darkness, leaving light at the edges where dawn pushes against the horizon. When Sam wakes and rises, the tiny tendrils between the stones tickle his flesh and he is amazed at himself, amazed at the presence he senses even before he sees or hears it, something molten and golden warming the air in the temple like a brazier bright with burning coals.

"Restful here," the presence says.

Sam sees the hero then, sees him and knows him at once. The hero glows, as though lit from within, a bronzy fire that shines through his short tunic, flames around his

sandals and sword. On the floor beside him, as though
casually dropped, is a high crested golden helmet which
burns like a little sun.

"Theseus," Sam breathes, making it a prayer. "Here!"

"Why not here?" asks the hero with a brotherly smile,
head cocked benignly, beaming, his eyes alight. "I came to
extend a fraternal hand. You wanted me, didn't you?"

For the moment Sam cannot remember. Wanting Theseus has not occurred to him, even in the same instant
admitting that perhaps he has wanted . . . someone.
Why not Theseus? "Did I?" he murmurs, wondering if he
is dreaming. It would be churlish, he decides, to deny the
hero whether it is a dream or not. "Of course, I did."

"As I said," the hero goes on, striding to and fro upon
the mosaics beneath the arches, "it's restful here, but dull.
The possibilities for adventure are limited. The immediate
landscape creates no feelings of awe or majesty. It creates
no feelings at all except apathy. There are no canyons, no
precipices, no caverns. You seem to have no bandits, no
despots, no Procrustes, cutting you to fit . . ."

"We're all cut to fit," Sam objects, coming to himself,
aware that he is merely listening, mouth open, taking no
part in this happening. "Oh, yes, we're all cut to fit!
There's only room for certain habits and attitudes here.
Constructiveness. Dependability. Honesty and reliability.
There's no room for epics, for sagas, for legends." He
babbles, surprised at his own lack of surprise. He sees the
hero. The hero is not an imaginary image, not a delusion,
not a hologram. When Sam puts out his hand, it meets
flesh and leather and metal. When he sniffs, he smells
sweat. Of course, he could be dreaming that he touches,
feels. . . . "We're all cut to fit, psychologically," he cries.
"All our legends have been lopped off. Like limbs, from
trees."

"Which leaves life boring," the hero challenges, smiling at him, mocking him only a little. "Bored, Samasnier
Girat. Aren't you? You feel the need for a quest, don't
you? Yours is probably the same as mine was. We're fellows, aren't we? Comrades? I've come to help you."

"Help me?"

"Raise the stone. Find the sandals, swing the sword. Find your father."

"But I know where he is . . ."

"I knew where mine was, too. That doesn't mean it was easy, getting there. There were many, many barriers in the way. Many villains to dispose of. Many heroic deeds to accomplish. And then while I was doing all that, there were the women, following, clinging. You have to be careful of them . . ."

"Careful of them?"

"Women. They're tricky."

"Yes," says Sam, realizing the hero has just told him a great truth, "Yes, they are."

"They don't understand men. They pretend, sometimes, but they really don't understand men," says Theseus, his voice growing faint. "They don't see the world as we see it. . . ."

Sam nods, believing the words though he is not sure what the hero means.

"You need a sword belt, Sam Girat," the hero whispers. "You have no sword belt for your sword, when we find it."

"Don't go!" cries Sam, aware that the hero is becoming tenuous, misty. Sam puts out his hand and feels something spongy and unreal.

"I'll be back," the hero whispers. "Later. Watch for me."

And he is gone. Night is gone. Through the slit windows, the pale tentacles of morning are insinuating themselves, sucking their way across the temple floor. Sam goes out where dawn marks the eastern sky with a long, violet line which spreads upward in shades of purple and plum, exploding instantly into pink daylight.

"I saw him," Sam erupts with joyous laughter. "I really did see him. Theseus! I saw him!"

He capers like a goat. He dances. He frolics his way to the brotherhouse, occasioning interest, wonder, perhaps a little fear in those who are up very early and see him leaping along the path like a young milk-vlish. At home, he crawls into bed and falls at once into deep sleep while the day-to-day world wakes and surges around him.

• • •

· *In later years* Sam remembered wakening after the episode in the temple with the absolute certainty the hero was real. That same day, Sam had started making a sword belt from a pattern found in the Archives. He made it of worked leather with semiprecious gemstones set into it. One could pick up the stones along the little streams anywhere in Hobbs Land. Sam had made a special trip to borrow a polisher at the craftsmen's market at Central Management. He hadn't been accustomed to doing that kind of work, and it had taken him some little time, doing it right, doing it over until it was right.

When he had finished with it, Sam kept the sword belt hanging in the back of his closet, behind his off-time robes. Later on, again at the hero's suggestion, he had made a helmet decorated with gold medallions, so he could be properly dressed when he found the thing under the stone. He never doubted he would find it or them, or something else like them. Theseus was clear on that point. Sam would not only find the sword, he would find adventure and challenge and heroism of his own. He would find a destiny fitting who he actually was, which was not a farmer upon dull Hobbs Land, dedicated to grains and legumes and increasing the production of hairy-legged milk-vlishes.

"Patience," said the hero, again and again.

Even though years were going by, Theseus was surprisingly little dismayed. "Patience. The time comes," he told Sam. "Inevitably, it comes. When it is meant to be, it happens, that's all."

Sam had been patient. He had become thirty lifeyears, and thirty-one and thirty-two, and then he had become Topman. Becoming Topman, in a way, helped solve his problem with patience. Being Topman was kingly and heroic and even godlike enough for him to go on with, for a time.

And in Voorstod, upon Ahabar, his father lived still, as he had always lived. Among the legends.

• • • •

· *In Voorstod, in* the town of Cloudport (often called simply, Cloud), on the cobbled street that went from the square on up the hill to the citadel of the prophets, stood a tavern sign called the Hanged King. The tavern sign showed the king hanged by his feet and pierced through with daggers, his crown still jammed tight on his head. It was a measure of Voorstod's hatred for the royal family of Ahabar that the face on the king was that of the first ruler, King Jimmy. Scarcely a season went by that some drinker did not suggest repainting the sign with the face and figure of the current monarch, Queen Wilhulmia. Since that would mean changing the name of the tavern, however, the owner had held out against the suggestion. "Kings and Queens come and go," he had chuckled. "The Hanged King goes on forever."

At a corner table covered with the circled stains of tankards and charred places where men had knocked out their pipes, Phaed Girat, with his usual bull-necked imperturability, sat talking with a little man he had only just met, one who had been sent down to meet Phaed, so he said, from Sarby. He had a few amusing words to say about Sarby, up there in the far north, where the mists gathered thick as wool. Things washed in Cloud would stay wet for a week, he commented, but things washed in Sarby never dried. People went wet like frogs in Sarby, where they saw the sun only once every ten years or so. So said the little man in a jokey voice belied by the pinched look of his nostrils and the suspicion in his eyes.

"So what are you folk doin' up there, in Sarby?" Phaed rumbled at him, stroking the whip at his side with one thick thumb. "You have wise prophets, I suppose, and many of the Faithful. Awaiting apocalypse and strong for the Cause, are you?" He pushed his big cap back on his head, letting the front of his hair show a little, wiping his forehead with his sleeve. It was warm in the tavern, for the provisioner had built a fire to drive off the damp.

"Strong as any, I imagine," said the other. His name was Mugal Pye, and he was known as a quick man, with a word or with a knife. He was also known for his handiness in the assembly of various deadly explosives and sneaky weapons. People, speaking of him, said he was clever as a

Phansuri in that particular way. "We in Sarby do our part," he said.

"Well, that's what it takes. Men strong for the Cause, wise prophets, and a little luck."

"Almighty God directs, Almighty God assures," said the other sententiously. The prophets taught that the Cause was inevitable because Almighty God ordered it so, and never mind that the Queen of Ahabar seemed to have temporarily countermanded the order. Luck had nothing to do with it.

"So they sent you down here to quote aphorisms at me, did they?" Phaed wanted to know.

Mugal laughed, silently, his tongue showing at the corner of his mouth. He had a twisty face with protruding cheek bones triangulating a pointed chin. From squinchy wells of wrinkled lids, his eyes peered like two dagger points, bright and sharp. It would have taken two or three of him to make one Phaed Girat, but he did not seem dismayed by that.

"Not likely they sent me only to quote at you, Phaed Girat. Perhaps they sent me to get your opinion about things in general. About drink, perhaps. Or women."

"About drink? Well I approve of it, unless there's a prophet nearby. As for women, would you be needin' some or have some you want to dispose of? Or perhaps you'd like instruction in what to do with one who's botherin' you? Or, if it's mere fuckin' you've on your mind, I can sell you a juicy little Gharmlet, only ten, and you can whip her up to suit you."

Mugal laughed again, this time biting his tongue between narrow white teeth. "I'm less interested in Gharm than I am in real women. Voorstoder women."

"What trouble are they causin' now?"

"Why would you say that?"

"Why would I say trouble? What else? If there's any that get in the way of the Cause, it's the women. They bleat and weep and carry on, cryin' woe, cryin' peace. The prophets promise joy, indeed, Mugal Pye, when they say we'll have no need of wives after apocalypse." Phaed drank deeply from the tankard and sighed in the manner of a man sorely tried. "Women! With their priests and their churchin' and their nonsense. Oh, they grieve so over their children that they're unbearable to live with, or they contract to go settle on some farm world, or they spend their time frettin' over the Gharm pups. You wouldn't argue with me would you, Mugal Pye? That women are a burden to the Cause."

The little man had been watching Phaed narrowly, and now he nodded, though not with any great show of agreement. "I suppose they are. And seein' how you feel about 'em, it's a good thing then I wasn't sent to talk to you of that."

"I'm relieved to hear it."

They drank a while, not saying much, until Phaed demanded, "Well, did they send you to talk of anythin' then?"

The little man made circles on the table top with his tankard. "They sent me to talk of one certain thing, the matter of a certain Gharm harp player out in Ahabar who's come to our attention."

Phaed growled a little between gritted teeth. "I know which one you mean! Have you in Sarby heard what the Queen of Ahabar intends? Have you heard she's holdin' out some mysterious great honor for this Gharm? What are they thinkin' of out there! It's a slap in the face of every man of Voorstod."

"Of all of us," agreed Mugal Pye, the dagger-points in his eyes glinting. "All of us, man. Too long the Gharm's been out there in Ahabar, attractin' attention, mockin' us, while those of Ahabar make much of her. It's time the matter was put an end to."

"So," growled Phaed. "What do they call her? Stenta Thilion, is it not? Two names they've given her, as though she was a human. Was there spawn of hers?"

"She had a mate, but he's long dead," said Mugal. "As for her spawn, they're not in the Three Counties. They're out in Ahabar somewhere."

"And where did they settle?"

"In the eastern provinces, so I've heard. Near Fenice."

"We've managed before, in the eastern provinces."

"That's true, that's true. But we've made it look like

accidents, Phaed. That's what we've always thought best. Not to do anything openly in Ahabar."

"It's time we did! It's time we started takin' out the Gharm in Ahabar, in bunches, if we can manage it."

Mugal Pye squinted and turned his glass, musing. "There's those who say we'd bring the army in."

"You know that's foolishness. Wilhulmia won't order the army in without Authority sayin' so," Phaed declared with a fine brave thump on the table.

System government resided on Authority, one of Phansure's many moons, while the army was stored on another, called Enforcement. On Authority and Enforcement the governance of System depended, or so it was assumed, though some felt Authority had outlived its ability to govern anything larger than a fairly small committee.

Phaed went on. "It's time, I tell you, Mugal Pye. What will Ahabar do? I'll tell you what they'll do. The Queen will weep and rage, and then she'll call for Authority to discipline us. And Authority will hem and haw and say maybe yes and maybe no, and they'll refer the matter to the Religion Advisory to tell them whether our ownin' slaves is religious or not. And the Religion Advisory will refer the matter to the Theology Panel. And what have we paid all that metal and gems to this one and that one on the Theology Panel for, except to guarantee they say maybe yes and maybe no for a thousand years if need be. And what will happen in the end is nothin'. The Panel will say nothin' to the Advisory. The Advisory will say nothin' to the Authority. Authority will do nothin'. And Ahabar will do nothin'. Meantime we'll have rid ourselves of a traitorous Gharm and put the fear of Almighty God into ten thousand more!"

"Phaed Girat, though I may live to regret it, I tell you the truth. There are those among the prophets who agree with you."

"So then, let's do it."

"Well, we would do it, save no one knows quite where Stenta Thilion is, there in Ahabar. The Queen has kept her and her family guarded and hid. Which is why I've come to you, Phaed Girat."

"You need my nose, is it? Need my nose to sniff her out. Well, we'll find her!" Phaed puckered his brow in concentration. "Any musician worth her keep has to come out of hidin' to play a bit, once in a while. I'll find out, myself, when that is and where that is."

They drank in silence, not seeing the Gharm who swept the floor or the Gharm who polished the tables or the Gharm who carried bottles up from the cellar. The Gharm were small and ruddy-dark and as human in intellect as any Voorstoder, but they were invisible in Voorstod except when they ran away. Phaed did not think of them as he stroked his whip and frowned deeply, plotting how he would find Stenta Thilion, the harpist, whose family had been three generations in Ahabar and who was reknowned throughout all its provinces; the harpist, whose great grandparents had fled from Voorstod over a hundred years before, but who was still accounted an escaped slave by those of the northern counties.

· *When he had* drunk slightly more than he could hold, Mugal Pye left the tavern, staggered up the hill and around a corner to find himself at the door of a dark narrow house with blind windows, where he knocked three times, then three again, then one, holding onto the door to keep himself from slipping.

The door creaked open to disclose an old man with white hair to his knees, one Preu Flandry, who looked carefully up and down the street before standing aside to let Pye enter.

"So you've met him," Preu said, as Mugal took off his cap and shook loose his own wealth of hair, like a tangled dark rain falling almost to his thighs. So the men of the Faithful wore their hair, for their power was in their hair.

"I've met him," the other agreed, shortly, thrusting his tangled locks behind his ears and bowing with perfunctory reverence toward the niche with its resident skull. So the Faithful, among themselves, made ritual obeisance to death.

"And what d'you think?" his host asked, leading the way into a dusty room to the right of the hallway.

"About what?"

"About Phaed, man! Will he help us or won't he?"

"He's a zealot for the Cause. He'll help find the Gharm woman." Mugal Pye hiccuped and shook his head.

"We already knew he'd do that! That was somethin' for you to talk of, is all. It's his wife we're wonderin' about. He was besotted about her, that we know, too."

"That was years ago. She was young and pretty then. Likely she's neither anymore."

"Did you talk to him of women?"

"I did." Mugal nodded slowly, for a long time, as though he had forgotten his head was moving up and down. "He did not seem overly interested in 'em. Rather the reverse, I'd say."

"Ah, but we've been taught that," the older man said softly. "Oh, yes, that's what we're taught. The prophets have said, often enough. 'Let women go,' they've said. 'Our faith is a faith for men.' Throughout all Voorstod, that's what's been said."

Mugal kept on nodding, accepting this as the simple truth it was. "So Phaed had a wife he was besotted about. And so she left, as women do." He sat down and collected his thoughts with difficulty. "The thing I don't understand is why you lot want her back."

The older man shook his head, pursing his lips. "The prophets want her back, Pye. After tellin' us for generations to let the women go, now somethin's happened to make them think we may not have women left enough to bear us sons." The old man said it almost apologetically, but not enough so to stop the flare of anger in the other's eyes.

"I thought eschatos was imminent, Preu Flandry!" Mugal Pye cried in a strident voice. "The end of things was to be sudden and soon. We've been promised the apocalypse. In our lifetimes, we were told!"

"And so it may be," whispered the other.

"The eschatos, the end of things, when we will stride across worlds with the sword in our hands." The little man's voice rose in impassioned complaint, like the wail of a hungry child.

"And so it may be," the other repeated, patting the air with his hands as though to calm the other down.

Mugal Pye thumped the table in time with his words, "The eschatos, when we stride among the worlds, with the sword in one hand and the whip in the other. When we bring the worlds to their knees. When the unbelievers cry woe and the heathen gnash their teeth, for lo, Almighty God comes as a pillar of storm." His eyes were wide and staring. In the dark narrow room the light seemed to flicker and pale, as though some fatal and hideous presence had reached into it, shadowing the light even as it stroked their hearts into flame. Mugal's voice became a chant, "Eschatos: when rivers run with blood, when the bodies of apostates are piled into mountains, when the space between worlds stinks of death!"

"And so it may yet be," agreed the old man, caught up in Mugal's drunken reverie. He nodded in time, as he joined the chant, the two voices rising in unison: "They do not know their death awaits them all. They do not know it comes from us. Yet it comes."

Flandry gulped in air, making a tiny orgasmic sound, a grunt of pure pleasure, as though something had touched him intimately. When he had been a boy, the telling of apocalypse had been accompanied by such touching so that he might always associate the words with pleasure. His chin was wet, and he dabbed at it impatiently.

In the hallway, just outside their vision, the Gharm slave who had been cleaning the stairs heard the crooning and huddled against the wall. At times like these it was not wise to draw attention to oneself. He put his head down and thought, silently, of a snake.

The Gharm often thought of Voorstod so. Like the snake, Voorstod could lie in full sight and look like something else. Like the snake, it could secrete a poison for which there was no antidote. Like the snake, it did not care what it bit, and it could kill before the victim quite realized it had been touched.

The room where the men sat throbbed like a heart clenched tight in a fist. Gradually, the chant faded. The men's eyes lost their ecstatic opacity and saw the world once more.

"So, if apocalypse dawns tomorrow as we've been told it will, what need have we of sons?" Mugal Pye demanded harshly.

"There's been a delay," gasped the older man, gulping air through his engorged throat.

"What delay?"

"Somethin' happened on Enforcement. Somethin' that wasn't planned for. Our agents there failed in their duty, so it's said. The Prophet was white with fury, but when he got control of himself a little, he said he felt we must plan for another generation, just in case. If the end comes soon, there's plenty of us to do the job, but if we must go on longer than that. . . ." Preu Flandry's voice trailed away to angry silence.

Mugal whined, "But the end was to come soon! Practically tomorrow, that's the word I had. We stood upon the doorstep of the end! I've been savoring it, Flandry. Since I was a mere boy."

"Well, and so have I, but there's this postponement for some reason or other. What's certain is, if we must go on longer, we'll need another generation to do it."

"Well, then, what's this nonsense about Sam Girat's wife? We've Armageddon to bring upon the System, and here we are, talking of one silly woman!"

The old man sighed windily, wiping his chin again. "I've only told you half. Because there's so few women left in Voorstod, the hot-bloods have been followin' their lechery out into Ahabar, out among the Abolitionists in Jeramish, where they've been takin' women by force. And if that goes on, it won't be long before Ahabar mobilizes the army."

Mugal Pye shrugged and sneered. "So? That means less than nothing. Authority won't let 'em act."

"Oh, we've paid the Theology Panel enough to assure they never give an answer on the slavery question, but rapin' and abductin' is another question entirely!"

"They won't consider that a religious matter, eh?"

Preu scowled at this levity. "Not likely, no. And the army of Ahabar is nothin' to make light of. Though the

Queen hasn't struck at us over the Gharm, the prophets think it likely she *will* strike at us over a few hundred rapes in Jeramish, and the one thing the prophets do not want, not so close to the end, is an army of occupation!"

Mugal went to the cupboard and found himself a bottle and brought it back to the table, together with two glasses. He poured and drank deeply, considering this.

"You've told me nothing yet to say why we'd want Maire Manone brought back! She's an old woman by now! Past childbearing. And it's not likely you want her to preach abstinence to the hot-bloods."

The white-haired man snorted. "Mugal Pye, I gave you credit for more imagination than that! We need her for propaganda! We must do somethin' to keep the women here and bring others back, some voice to rally them. And what woman was listened to in all Voorstod more than Maire Manone?"

"Propaganda, you say? No more than that?"

"A symbol, so say the prophets. What I say ten times is true, as we well know, but the thing has to be *believable*! The prophets have told us a symbol is needed. Someone whose voice will be heard, a woman to make the business seem real. Who better than she who was called the Voice of Voorstod? The Sweet Singer of Scaery?"

"Only propaganda!"

"Ostensible, at least, though it's likely there'll be recruitin' done as well. If we're accused, we can say, 'A girl kidnapped? Nonsense. The maiden saw Maire Manone singing and she came of her own free will.' "

Mugal Pye shook his head, considering how far from apocalypse it seemed, this fiddling about with abduction. How small a thing. How insignificant and unworthy. He pursed his mouth, as though to spit, then thought better of it. The true Faithful did unquestioningly as the prophets commanded, and if this had been commanded. . . .

"That's why we wanted to see how Phaed might stand on the matter," said Preu. "He's her husband still, after all."

"But you're not telling him about this."

"Not yet. Not until we're closer."

"And how do you intend to bring her back?"

"We'll give her good reason to come."

"You're not thinkin' Phaed will go get her, are you?"

"We've not quite settled on that yet, Mugal Pye. She must seem to come of her own free will, and we must think up a way to be sure she'll do that."

"I'd be careful how you talk to Phaed about this business. She's his wife, after all. He may still have feelings there."

"Well surely," murmured Preu Flandry. "Which is why we had you soundin' him out, Pye, to see where he'd stand. When it comes to sacrifices, all of us have to make them, all of us."

"Oh, yes, all of us," agreed Mugal Pye. "For we will have our reward. For there is nothing to stand against us. Nothing in all the worlds to oppose us." And he smiled again, his tongue-bitten angry smile, while the skull smiled from its niche in the wall and the Gharm slave crept away from the hallway, wondering if there was anyplace the Gharm might go to escape the holocaust which Voorstod would certainly bring very soon upon all the worlds, wondering if there was anyone, anywhere, who could stop the horror that was surely coming.

· *Beside the ruined* temple north of Settlement One, shallow in the soil lay Birribat Shum. Shallow he lay, with fragments of roots and crumbs of leaves on his eyes, with particles of sand between his toes, with the small creatures of the soil at work upon his hands where skin gave up its chemistry cell by cell. In the soil lay Birribat Shum, shallow in the soil, with the sunwarm earth over him and the shaded depths below, moisture rising beside him and in him, gasses bubbling up into the porous dirt, a daily percolation as sun rose and hung above at noon and set. In the soil lay Birribat Shum when night came and the earth cooled and all things sank down, as though snuggling more deeply into the bed of earth, only to rise and percolate once more with the dawn. In the soil lay Birribat Shum, and the soil ate him.

In his clothes the small invaders made a home, legged

and legless, the ones too small to see, the ones too small to
hear, the invisible ones, the unheard ones, creeping along
the seams, settling in the wrinkle of a rotting shirt to multiply their legions, to nibble on the soaked fiber, to carry
bits and pieces out into the surrounding earth, the troops
of dissolution, the army of decay, gathering in ever greater
numbers.

The soil above—unmounded over the grave, as though
no one had cared to make it visible—sank gradually as
Birribat Shum was disassembled, leaving a basin, a shallow declivity where water accumulated and filtered slowly
downward when the sun returned and the earth warmed,
a declivity where Samasnier Girat sometimes lay, late at
night, talking to his friend, unaware of who or what lay
beneath him.

On the skin of Birribat Shum, in the tatters of his
clothes, on the edges of his shoes, in the sodden felt of his
hair, in the cavities of his eyes lay dust from the temple of
Bondru Dharm, dust which came suddenly at the moment
the God disappeared, dark and fine as pigment ground in
a mortar, feathery light. A breath could have dissipated it,
but there was no breath here below the soil, where Birribat lay.

The dust brooded wetly in the manifold womb of the
earth, brooded and soaked and changed. Individual particles swelled and replicated themselves, and again, and yet
again. From a single grain, a filament came, thinner than
hair, white as the light of stars; palely gleaming, it snouted
its way between infinitesimal grains of sand, among mi-
croscopic remnants of flesh, stretching outward through
the rags of clothing into the earth beyond. First one, then
two, then fifty, then five thousand, then an uncountable
number, until the body that was Birribat Shum was
thickly furred with fragile fibers, wrapped with them, pen-
etrated by them, eaten and used up until nothing remained but the hard bones around which the threads
gathered more thickly still, weaving themselves into a
solid, cottony mass, a tough cylindrical mattress of com-
pacted fiber, its edges thinning and fading undetectably
into the surrounding soil. There the fibers continued to
grow outward in a gauzy circle, now diving under the

nearest ruined temple, now encircling it, now moving on
toward the settlement, toward its houses and shops, its
equipment stores, its fields and meadows, where people
were.

Where the felted mattress of fiber lay, something was
slowly created. A cell grew there, a seed, a scion, a nucleus, something quite tiny, something that grew a little
with each warming, day by day.

Beneath the soil lay Birribat Shum: what was left of
him; what he had become.

TWO

· *After receiving their* orientation from Horgy
Endure, Theor Close and Betrun Jun took themselves to
the vehicle park, checked out a flier, and—during the brief
but boring flight to Settlement One—told one another
their original impression of Hobbs Land had been wholly
substantiated. The world was uniformly dull. The two engineers came from volcano-lit Phansure, ocean-girt Phansure, cosmopolitan Phansure, with its ten thousand cities
and clustered billions of mostly very clever persons. All
Phansuris knew their world was the most beautiful and
only civilized world in System, perhaps in Galaxy, and
Betrun and Theor were unreservedly Phansuri.

They were not chauvinists, however. They told themselves that Hobbs Land was probably quite nice, just un-
derendowed to start with and pitifully underdeveloped.
Each assured the other they should be kind to Sam Girat,
poor fellow, having to live in such a place.

Sam, meantime, gave himself similar assurances. Since
Mysore Hobbs II was always sending batches of Phansuri
engineers and designers to the Belt worlds to improve this

or that, playing host was something Sam did fairly frequently. Before welcoming such visitors, Sam always reminded himself of what his upper-school teacher had said about Phansure, sneering just a little. Too many people, she had said. Like a swarm, she had said. Hardly any forests, almost no animals, and everyone living in each others' armpits. When the various Phansuri visitors introduced themselves to Sam with their flourishes and politenesses, as Phansuri were wont to do, Sam was always very kind.

With both sides trying so hard, their mutual greetings were protracted and exceedingly warm, and only when the rituals were over did Theor Close and Betrun Jun refer to the problems Sam had listed in anticipation of their visit. After a brief discussion, the three of them went down to the heavy equipment barn, where they looked first at a blackened launcher.

"We didn't design this," said Theor Close with distaste.

"I know," said Sam patiently. "If you'd designed it, we wouldn't have the problem." Phansuris were all geniuses. Everyone knew that. They didn't need to rub it in.

Theor preened. "What's the problem?"

"A settler got burned, on the face and neck. He was too close to the thing, and the back blast off that fire shield got him."

"What do you use if for?" asked Betrun Jun.

"Certain trace elements in the soil get used up and we need to restore them. The quantities are so minuscule, it's not economical to try to mix them evenly into the bulk fertilizers, so we wait for the wind to be right, then we go way, way upwind of the settlement, and use this launcher to kick an explosive cannister up about two miles. The mix is very fine, the dust gets wind-spread over hundreds of square miles and it drifts down for days. It's primitive and untidy, but it's effective and efficient."

"The launcher needs a blast control chamber," said Betrun Jun. "A torus-shaped ring at the base." He sketched rapidly, holding out the result. "With baffles."

Sam snorted. "It's funny-looking. Like a doughnut with a pipe through it."

"Well, whatever it looks like, the blast will buffet around in the ring shaped chamber without getting loose to burn anybody. This one is easy, and we'll see to it at once. How many do you need?"

"Eleven, one for each settlement, plus a few spares."

Jun added the eleven settlements to his list of Hobbs Land facilities, which already included the mines, the fertilizer plant, and Central Management.

"What's next."

Sam ticked off the second item. "There's something faulty in the fuel feed on that 1701 cultivator over there. We had a driver sick from gozon fumes."

"Anybody hurt?"

"Just the driver. He was kind of woozy and angry, that's all."

"You're lucky," said Theor Close. "We had an operator on Pedaria get a good whiff of gozon and kill three people before they finally stopped him."

"Funny the chemists can't come up with something safer," said Sam.

"They have. It just isn't as efficient. With the proper safeguards, gozon is all right." Theor Close took a protective mask from his tool kit, put it on, then opened the pod hatch on the 1701 and drew out the pod. "Where shall I put this?"

Sam looked around and indicated a bare work bench standing to one side.

Theor laid the pod upon it, then returned to the pod hatch. "If you've got fumes, likely the problem is in the seal-valve unit. That was the problem on Pedaria. We're redesigning the whole assembly, and you'll have these replaced very soon."

"And until then?"

"Until then, we'll fix this one." Theor inserted himself into the hatch and mumbled to himself. Then he came out, with an audible pop, and said to Betrun Jun, "Will you look at it? There's got to be a flaw in the sphincter-gasket, but I can't find it."

A settler drove into the barn on a small multipurpose tractor towing a spray unit behind it.

Betrun inserted himself into the hatch. After a time,

he said, "You can't find one because there isn't one." Hi
voice reverberated in the closed space, before he poppe
out, like a ferf out of a hole. "Are you sure this is the unit
Sam?"

"This is the one," said Sam, firmly, checking the num
ber painted on the hatch against the one on his list.

The man at the door began to back the tractor.

Jun took another look and popped out again. "Th
flaw has to be in the fuel pod itself. Where did you put it?"

Sam turned, seeing the pod and the bench and th
tractor all in one terrible vision, the sprayer hitting th
table, the table falling, the faulty pod going over with it
and the cloud of violet mist that erupted from it, catchin
the tractor driver in its midst.

"God," whispered Theor Close, jerking open his too
kit and finding another mask. He shoved it at Sam, wh
took it almost without thinking. Sam's eyes were fixed o
the driver, who had gone completely blank-faced, like
manikin. Then, slowly, the blankness was replaced, firs
with craftiness, then with rage. The driver looked aroun
and saw the three of them. He began, slowly, to get dow
from the tractor.

"He'll kill us if he gets a chance," said Betrun Jun
almost calmly. "Us or anything else he can find."

The man picked up a steel brace bar from the floo
and came toward them. He was a very large man, Theo
thought. A very large man, moving with the inexorabilit
of a robot.

"Hever," said Sam. "Give me the bar."

"He won't hear you," whispered Close. "He can't
He's all shut in on himself."

"Hever," said Sam again. "Give me the bar. Give it t
me." He moved away from the others, drawing the driv
er's eyes after him, his feet dancing slowly to one side, s
the driver would not lose sight of him.

"Is there an antidote," asked Sam, almost conversa
tionally.

"No," said Close. "Not here."

"Do you have something that will put him out?"
asked Sam.

"No," said Close. "Not with me."

"What the hell good are you?" asked Sam, still dancing. "There's an emergency medical kit on the wall over there. That red thing. You'll find a full kit of painkillers, in slap ampules. You think you could get your hands on those?"

"You have a weapon on your belt," Jun pointed out. "You've got a plate cutter."

"You have some particular reason for wanting Hever dead?" Sam asked, his voice conveying slight astonishment. "Or maimed? He will come out of this, won't he?"

"Eventually," said Close, from a dry throat as he watched Jun backing toward the medical kit. "I'm just not sure painkillers will put him out. Those fumes he breathed make the victims three or four times as strong and quick as usual."

"We can try, can't we?" Sam asked, still dancing. He had led the ominous, silent driver almost to the door and was now turning to bring him back again. "Can't risk leading him outside. He might see somebody else moving."

"I've got the ampules," whispered Jun.

"You think you could . . . ah, put them down somewhere in the direction I'm moving in. Like on the breaker guard of that small harvester?"

Jun moved quietly toward the harvester and sneaked the kit onto the guard.

"Open!" pleaded Sam. "For God's sake, man, I'm not going to have time to open it."

Jun took the kit down again and opened it, shaking half a dozen of the ampules into his hand and laying them in a pile on the flat guard.

"Now," said Sam, still conversationally, still dancing, still keeping the man moving, the bar moving, the expressionless, silent man moving. "Now, there's an emergency med alert over by the kit. Would you please go press that button and say, very clearly, that we need restraints and immobilizers."

"Sam, you could at least take that cutter into your hand," pleaded Close.

"I need my hands," said Sam. "Why don't you get

over behind that harvester, Theor. So Hever won't see you when we come around."

Theor went.

The silent man attacked, rushing Sam, swinging the bar in a lethal arc. Sam moved to one side, put out a foot, tripped his attacker and danced away, toward the harvester. The ampules were within reach and he grabbed them, dropping all but two into his pocket. He stripped off the needle guards and palmed the two ampules. As Hever came up off the floor, Sam sped by, slapping him on the back with both hands.

He dropped the empty ampules and palmed two more.

"Come on, Hever," he whispered. "Give old Sam the bar, like a nice guy, will you."

Hever did not hear, did not care, did not change expression. The two ampules might as well have been water. If anything, he moved slightly faster. The bar swung again, missing Sam's head by inches. Sam ducked under the swing and slapped Hever on the chest with both hands. Hever clutched at him. Sam dropped and rolled, coming to his feet with his hands already at his pocket, reaching for the last two ampules.

"Restraints and immobilizers," Jun was saying, over and over again. "There's been a fuel pod leak. We need restraints and immobilizers. Hurry, please."

"Sam, for God's sake," pleaded Theor Close. "You could at least take off one of his legs. He can be sent to Phansure and grow a new one!"

"Not soon he can't," panted Sam. "He'd be out of commission for a long time, and I need him. Production's already down." He darted forward, then back, then forward. "Besides, it's painful losing a limb. It's painful growing new ones!"

The bar swung again. This time it caught Sam a glancing blow, a mere brush down one arm, and the arm fell at his side, the hand clenching, the ampule dropping.

"Damn," said Sam. "Oh, damn." He dropped to one knee and picked the ampule up again, trying to bend the arm. It moved reluctantly.

Hever moved in, the bar swinging. . . .

And then he fell. All at once. Forward, almost where

Sam was kneeling. He fell, and squirmed briefly, and was still.

Three settlers appeared at the barn door with restraints and immobilizer guns.

"Is he dead?" asked one.

"He's got four ampules of painkiller in him," said Sam. "And he could still come out of that raging. Don't take any chances with him."

"What about you, Sam?"

Sam shrugged with a decidedly pained expression. "I think my arm is broken."

Theor and Betrun went with Sam to the infirmary, and stayed with him while his arm was examined and put into an immobilizer, while he was given a shot of quick-heal, while he was given a painkiller of his own and told to go home and rest for the remainder of the day.

"Sorry," said Sam to the Phansuris. "It's not broken, but I don't feel much like going back to work."

"That's all right," murmured Theor Close. "Really, Sam, that's all right."

"You can go back and finish what we'd started," Sam suggested. He stumbled a little, and they both caught him, one at either side and turned him in the direction of his brotherhouse.

"We could do that," said Betrun Jun. "Tell me, Sam, was that man—Hever, was he a friend of yours?"

Sam looked at him blankly. "Not particularly. No."

"Ah," said Jun. "Well. I guess we could go do a little work. Then maybe we could . . . oh, go sightseeing until you're feeling better."

"I don't know what you'd sightsee. It's all pretty much like this," Sam gestured at the fields around them with his good arm. "North of us is the escarpment," he pointed again, toward the single upland that twisted like an angular snake around the girdle of the world, edged on both sides by precipitous and columned cliffs. "That's where all the ruins of the Owlbrit villages are, if you're interested in ruins. There are some lakes up there, some wildlife, a thing called the upland omnivore. It eats most everything, including rocks for its gizzard. You might see one of those."

"The escarpment doesn't sound very interesting," said Jun, gloomily. He was annoyed with himself. With Theor. With everything. In future, every Phansuri engineer should have an immobilizer gun in his tool kit. The need for it was self-evident, but he had never thought of it until now. "This planet is really pretty dull, geographically speaking."

Theor Close kicked him, without effect.

Jun switched to his pedantic tone. "That has an advantage, of course. It makes things easier from a design point of view, removes the extremes, so to speak."

"Dull, maybe, but good for agriculture," Sam insisted, wondering why he felt personally offended.

"I think we'd better get back to that cultivator," said Theor Close with a glare at Jun's suddenly embarrassed face. "That faulty fuel pod is still lying there after all." He patted Sam on the shoulder and tugged Jun away with him, leaving Sam to go into his brotherhouse alone.

"What in hell did you get off on that subject for?" snarled Close. "It isn't his fault the place is dull."

Betrun Jun thought about it, as Phansuris thought about most things, carefully and analytically.

"What I think it is," he said at last. "Usually, anywhere we go, I sort of feel . . . superior. It doesn't matter where. On Thyker. On Ahabar. Anywhere we go. We're the smartest. The best. You know."

"I know," said Theor, flushing.

"But. But he made me feel . . . I don't know."

"Because he wouldn't hurt his man."

"Yes. Yes, because of that."

"I know," said Theor. "I found it rather . . . unsettling, as well."

"I mean, he didn't even consider it."

"I know."

"We could all have been killed! He could have at least considered it!"

Theor Close nodded, then said, "Of course, he was fairly busy at the time. And if you were the man involved, you'd probably rather Sam didn't cut your leg off."

Betrun Jun scowled. "I suppose."

"If there were ever anything going on . . . anything

dangerous, I mean, I'd rather like someone like that to be in charge."

"I'd already decided that."

Theor patted his colleague on the shoulder. "Let's go get that fuel pod put away before someone else gets hurt."

· *Sam went into* his brotherhouse in no very pleasant mood. He was hurting, and now that the whole incident was over, he felt a little foolish getting injured that way. It wasn't . . . well, it wasn't heroic. He should have moved faster. Old Hever wasn't that quick, not usually. The painkiller was making him feel drugged and remote, and on top of all that he was annoyed at the two Phansuris. He knew Hobbs Land wasn't much, from the point of view of adventure—Theseus himself said that— but it wasn't up to two damned smart ass Phansuris to tell him so.

Sam dug a bottle of wine from the place he had hidden it and sat down in his own room to drink it and play with his books until he got sleepy or felt better, one. Playing with his books generally improved his mood.

He had taken up the craft of bookbinding a few years before he became Topman, and he kept it up, despite the many claims on his attention and the assumptions of others that he would not be able to continue with the hobby.

"You won't have time for your books anymore," his mother had sympathized after he had been selected Topman. "What a pity. Oh, I do like them, Sammy. They smell so good." Which, indeed, they did, being rare leathers and woods, whatever he could lay hands on at the artisans' market at CM. The pages were generated by Archives, of course, though Sam had taken some pains in determining the size of them, and the type style and the spacing and arrangement of paragraphs. He had selected the pictures also, deciding for each book whether it was to be illustrated in the style of woodcuts or of engravings or of paintings, or even with something that looked like photographic images, any of which Archives could produce as easily as it could spew plain print. Each book had one or more of the stories he had found in the Archives—he had done Theseus's story first—each one modified and augmented by Sam, written and rewritten until it suited him, until it was properly heroic. When they were printed, he enclosed them in hard, well-made covers with fancy endpapers handmade by a woman in one of the other settlements, and with titles embossed in gold. When Sam finished a volume, it looked very much like the ones the Archives showed him, the ones the museums kept in vacuum containers, their millenia-old names going back even to Manhome.

"They smell so good," Maire had said, never thinking of reading what was inside. She had never read an old-style book. Outside the universities or the great libraries, few people had. If you wanted to know what was in some old volume, it was so much easier to ask the stage to summarize for you, or do a commentary, or even dramatize it, if you were in the mood for that.

"Why do you take all this time?" Sal had asked, holding the children back from the shelves, lest they pull one of the things out onto the floor and ruin it. Sam, however, had reached for his favorite volume and had sat down with one child in the lap and one over each shoulder as he showed them the pictures, fascinated them with the story of the hero of ancient Manhome time whose father had left him a sword and a pair of shoes buried under a heavy stone. And then, when he found his father at last, he was sent away to fight the wicked Minotaur.

"Why would the King do that?" breathed Sam's oldest nephew. "The boy just got there."

"What's a father?" asked the next oldest.

"Like a progy," Sam had replied, slightly annoyed. "And the King knew his son wanted to be a hero, so he sent him to do something heroic." The Archives hadn't really said that, but Sam thought that's the way it should have been, and Theseus had not contradicted him.

"I could have been safe in Athens," Theseus had told him. "But mere safety wouldn't have been worthy of me. So I volunteered to go to Minos. I went to face the Minotaur with a song in my heart. At least, so my face said." He turned up his lips and became a mask, beaming with confidence and courage.

"I know," Sam had breathed. "You had to face danger and death without flinching to be worthy of the King."

Sal's comment was, "The hero and his father did get together at the end of the story, I suppose?" She said it with a certain wry emphasis, which Sam ignored. "That's the point of the story, isn't it?"

"I suppose," said Sam, remembering that the story hadn't ended all that happily. The hero's father had died, at the end, because of something the hero did, or didn't do. But then, that was destiny, working itself out. He had been destined to die all along.

Sam also read the children the story of Heopthy Jorn, who promised his father he would care for the kingdom, whose older brother imprisoned him as a sacrifice for the horrible Chagrun, which was eating the people, and how he escaped and came back to win the kingdom as his own and father many sons.

"There's a lot of fathering in those legends," Sal commented, disapprovingly. "A lot of fathering, a lot of kinging, a lot of death and violence, and very little uncleing and ordinary kindly living. We are a matrilineal society, Sam, and there's good reason for that." Sal wholly approved of the society the way it was, but then she'd been too young to remember anything else.

"Some of the legends do say uncles," Sam had admitted, a little wearily, wondering momentarily why he bothered to show Sal anything at all. She was so unrelentingly . . . *female*! Tricky, as Theseus said. Not at all understanding.

"The children could punch up Archives and get the same thing," Sal had persisted, still curious as to why Sam did these things. She had always wondered why Sam did the things he did.

Sam had not bothered to set her straight. They couldn't punch up Archives and get any such thing. They could get an account of the hero, sure enough, comparing him with a hundred other similar tales and telling what he symbolized, and what the monsters meant, and what the psychological significance was of the tensions between the hero and the King, but one couldn't get the tale itself. It was Sam who had restored the tale to itself, by pulling it out of the commentary which was strangling it and giving it back its power and blood. If anyone wanted to know the true stories, they would have to take one of Sam's books and read.

Now, sipping his wine and stroking the soft bindings, Sam reflected that he had never answered Sal's "why." Why was simply that he needed to hold the past in this way, to preserve the tales, to make sure he didn't lose them as he would if they were left in the Archives, lose them as he had lost his dad, lost his whip when he came to Hobbs Land. People vanished, and their stories died with them or were left behind to be buried under a thousand other things. It wasn't enough that they were in the Archives. Things could stay buried in the Archives forever, like geological strata, layer on layer, never to be raised up again. Here on his shelves, the ancient stories were like bones dug up and made live again, fleshed out, peopled, creatured, whole. He couldn't make them for his own son (which rankled), but he could for Sal's sons. When they were old enough to come live with him here in the brotherhouse, then they would read the books together. He had never mentioned that to Sal.

He had mentioned it to Theseus, when he met with him out at the old temple during the night watches. After Bondru Dharm had died, Sam hadn't seen the hero for quite a long time, but then he showed up again, out north of the settlement, even stronger and more sure than he had been before. Theseus had understood about the books, about tales, about epics and how important they were. He had told Sam to look in his books for tales of monsters, for undoubtedly there were some Sam could fight here on Hobbs Land, to get in shape for his eventual quest.

Sam doubted there were monsters, but he could not doubt the large number of very heavy boulders Theseus found for him to turn over. Sometimes Sam woke at dawn, far from the town, sore and exhausted from the night's effort.

"Patience," Theseus always told him, laughing. "The time will come."

Sam, drinking his wine and stroking the covers of his

books with his uninjured hand, leafing through them in search of pictures of monsters and heroes, forgot the minor annoyance of the Phansuri engineers and hoped the time of his own destiny would come while he still had the strength to meet it.

· *In Settlement One,* the favorite game of the children of the middle school (lifeyears ten through fourteen) had for some time been "Exploring Ninfadel." Ninfadel was the larger of the Ahabarian moons, home of the Porsa, one of System's three indigenous intelligent races. What the Porsa were, and how they were, was sufficient explanation for the fact that, except for a guard post, Ninfadel was left strictly alone. It was also sufficient reason for all adults to consider playing at Porsa utterly disgusting, which was probably the reason the children enjoyed it so.

Recently, however, there had been a new game. The children didn't call it anything except "Going out to Play," which children had been using for millenia as an excuse for being elsewhere. This particular play was the discovery of the cousins, Saturday and Jeopardy Wilm, who were friends, possible sweethearts (though at around fourteen lifeyears they weren't ready to admit that to themselves), but constant companions in any case. After afternoon classes, when Saturday wasn't scheduled for a voice lesson and Jeopardy wasn't at sports practice, they often went exploring beyond the northern edge of the settlement. In every other direction, cultivated fields stretched for mile after endless mile, but north was the creek with its groves of ribbon willows, north were the ruined temples on their gentle prominence, north was a wide stretch of rising, rocky, undisturbed semi-wilderness reaching all the way to the escarpment.

Though Saturday was slim and dark and Jeopardy was light and sturdy, there was a certain likeness in the expression of the eyes and the curve of the mouths and the tenderness with which their hands found one another's sometimes, quite by accident. They had discovered the new amusement on a certain afternoon shortly before Saturday's lifeyear celebration.

"I want to find some glaffis," Saturday had announced. "I want it to flavor my birthday cakes." She had tossed her head back, making her dark hair ripple.

"You want *glaffis*-flavored birthday cakes!" Jep had exclaimed. "Yech."

"It's almost like new-cinnamon," she had argued. "And we're out of new-cinnamon."

"It's *nothing* like new-cinnamon. It's more like . . . like famug."

"Honestly, Jep, your taste buds are all on your ears. When did you ever taste famug? Huh? Your mom and my mom *talk* about famug, but CM hasn't brought in any famug since our moms were little girls because the blight on Thyker wiped out all the famug plantations, and they ran out of what was left in storage, so when did you ever taste it, huh?"

"Mom told me what it tastes like," he said, trying to remember if she had.

"That's what I meant. Your taste buds are in your ears."

"Well, I know what glaffis tastes like, and I still say, yech. Don't expect me to eat any."

"Wait until you're invited."

"I'll be glad to."

They had left the edge of the settlement behind them and were crossing a brookside line of ribbon-willows, beyond which the ruins of two old temples sprawled in the amber sun of afternoon.

"If you really want the stuff, I saw some growing inside one of these temples," Jeopardy offered.

Saturday made a face. She'd been into the old temples now and then, along with others, when they were exploring or playing last man, but she didn't really like being there. Something about the arches or the way the floors scooped made her slightly uncomfortable, like certain styles of music, kind of creepy. However, she didn't dislike them enough to complain about going there. Provided they didn't stay too long.

They splashed through the narrow stream, circled two

squatty ribbon-willow trunks, parted the straplike leathery foliage, which hung in curtains around the tree, and walked slowly up the slope toward the temples. From this angle the temples looked like building blocks, each a round fat lower layer with a narrower chunk on top.

"They're funny looking," opined Saturday. "Like a muffin with a candle stuck in the middle."

"In the middle is where the God lived," Jeopardy instructed her. "Like Bondru Dharm. And they wouldn't look so funny if they had roofs on them." They clambered over fallen stones and piles of trash to reach the opening and went through it onto the narrow flat place inside. Before them the floor swooped down in a gentle arc, then up at the far side to the base of the stone ringwall perforated by grilled arches. Over this declivity stretched a radiating series of arches, each outer leg buried in the outer wall, each inner leg resting on the ringwall. Saturday decided that, from the inside, the thing was shaped like the doughnuts Africa made sometimes, when she felt like it.

"Let's go in where the God lived," Jeopardy suggested, sliding on his bottom down the sloping floor and then scrambling up the other side on all fours. Tiny stones rattled behind him as fragments of the original mosaic floor gave way. At the ringwall, he peered through one of the grills, waiting for Saturday to join him, before they both walked clockwise around the wall to the single door. Inside the central space, they found drifted soil and dried leaves around the waist-high stone pedestal at the center. The tops of the walls ended against the sky. Nothing was left of the roof.

The perfume reached them before they saw the glaffis bush against the stones, waving its sprays of bright oily leaves in the rising air.

"See there," Jep crowed. "I told you. Mom says it grows in natural stone chimneys along the escarpment, too. It likes to grow where the air goes up, to spread the smell, so the pollinators can find it."

Saturday took a filmbag from her pocket, nipped off a few leaflets with strong fingernails, and stowed them away in a pocket. "Okay, now what do you want to do?" she asked, sniffing at her fingers. Glaffis was aromatic, not sweet, but very pleasant. Saturday's mother, Africa Wilm, sometimes hung twigs of glaffis leaves over the heatsource, letting the warm air spread the smell throughout the sisterhouse. Now that Saturday had smelled the herb, the ruined temple seemed suddenly familiar, and she felt almost reluctant to leave. It was cool and shady under the arches, and it smelled nice; why should she want to go?

They went out of the central space to slide into the trough again. This time, however, they stayed there, making the circuit of the temple, kicking at the small stones which had made up the mosaic floors. When they came to a patch of intact mosaic, Saturday knelt and stared at it.

"This is pretty," she said. "See, it's a leaf pattern. Leaves and vines and fruits. See this, this is a willow, and this one is wolf-cedar."

"Where's fruits?" he knelt beside her. "Oh, I see. You mean nuts."

"And you a botanist's son. Nuts are fruits." She began extending the intact pattern into the surrounding area, laying out the small, flat stones that were scattered around her. "Jep, can you get any stickum."

"What kind of stickum? Construction? Machinery parts?"

"To stick these down." She had completed a leaf and the long section of stem which bordered it. "I'd really like to fix this. It would be fun."

Jep, who was working on a section of his own, merely grunted. They stayed in the temple for an hour or more, leaving behind them several completed leaves and a long stretch of twining vine. The next afternoon, when they returned, Jep brought with him several varieties of stickum, one of which proved to be suitable for gluing the scattered tesserae to the larger paving stones beneath. By the following week, they had acquired a dozen helpers from among the settlement kids around their age.

The ten-year-old twin Miffle girls who were not and would never be interested in crawling about on their hands and knees, joined the eleven- and twelve-year-old Tillan brothers, whom they admired greatly, in cleaning out all the mess: the stubby rooted sulla daisies and the pinch-bush coming up through the stones; the dust that had settled in knee-high mounds along the walls; the bits of scattered human trash, containers and paper and plastic bits and pieces. When that was done, the girls decided to continue their help by sorting stones into small boxes, so that the workers did not have to search for the correct size or color. The smoothly washed stones, though all shaped very much alike, came in a wide assortment of colors and shades: grays ranging from very light to very dark; several distinct greens; cream and white; various shades and tints of rose. Sorting them could be done anywhere, which meant the Miffle girls could work near the Tillan boys, wherever they happened to be.

By the end of the third week, the reconstruction was in full swing, with the entire floor being worked on as though it were a giant jigsaw puzzle. Boxes of accurately sorted stones stood ready. Tubes of stolen stickum were ranked at the bottoms of the arches. Crews ranging in size from three to a dozen youngsters showed up at odd times and, without direction, continued to rebuild a pattern which none of them had ever seen.

When the floors were four-fifths done, Saturday began to complain about the dust. "I wish we had some big beams," she said, wielding a makeshift broom made from bundled stipweed. "The wind keeps blowing dirt all over the pattern, and we have to keep sweeping it off to see what we're doing. If we had some big beams, we could put a roof on."

"It doesn't take big beams," Jep commented. "Haven't you ever been in the Bondru Dharm temple? Didn't you ever notice the ceiling?"

Saturday had been there and had not noticed the ceiling. With an extended finger, Jeopardy drew in the dust two concentric circles, one about a fourth the diameter of the other. He pointed at the center circle and invited consideration.

"That's the middle, where the grills are, where the God goes, right?"

The other children, who gathered at any excuse for a break, agreed that the God went in the middle.

Jeopardy drew a series of radiating lines from the small circle to the larger one encompassing it. "Those are the stone arches," he said. "There's twenty-seven of them in this temple. So, all we need is stuff long enough to go crosswise from one arch to the next. That's about six feet at the outside, and it's hardly anything in the middle where they get skinny. In the Bondru Dharm temple, the roof's made of wolf-cedar trunks laid up tight to each other."

"How come you noticed that?" Saturday was moved to ask.

Jeopardy started to answer, then stopped, aware of some vacancy inside himself where the answer should have been. He should have had a reason, more than mere curiosity, for what he had actually done several days before, which had included climbing a set of footholes along an arch at the Bondru temple and cutting a sample of the ceiling, which he had then taken to his mother for identification. He really couldn't say why he had done that. "I just did," he replied lamely. "I just did."

"I guess we could cut wolf-cedar with a lase-knife," one of the Tillans remarked in his usual imperturbable manner. All the Tillans looked and sounded alike. "I've got one."

Several others of the children also had access to tools suitable for the cutting of wolf-cedar, including the other Tillan boy and the two Quillow boys, Deal and Willum R., as well as their girl cousins, Sabby and Gotoit. While the main body of their colleagues continued repairing the mosaics, these larger and stronger young people began exploring the wolf-cedar forest and marking slender trees from which to build a roof. They returned from the forest at dusk, singing, Saturday's voice darting and hovering above the youthful chorus like a prophet bird.

• *Maire Girat was* drawn to the porch of her sisterhouse by the sound of Saturday's singing. The child's voice was unmistakable, unselfconscious as rain. Maire's earliest memories were of similar music. Not herself singing, but voices singing, marvelous voices in her head, solo and chorus, making wondrous melodies inside herself.

Saturday's voice was like one of those she had heard within her when she had been a child.

When Maire was only four or five, she had wakened early one morning, before the rest of the family were up, and had seen the curtain moving in a light breeze with a sunbeam shining through it, had felt a song welling up in her throat, and had let it spin out, into the room, into the moving light.

Mam had come running, and Dad, and the four older brothers and sisters, all to stand with puzzled faces around the cot where she'd lain, still a little drowsy, letting her mouth make music. After that, there had been songs for everything. Gradually, the inner music had moved into the background, returning in its full glory only at that borderland between sleep and wakening or when she dreamed at night of great choruses crying ecstatically in the spaces between worlds.

They had lived just outside Scaery in the county of Bight, where the eastern shore and the northern shore of the peninsula of Voorstod came together to make a knobby heel thrust against the gray seas of Ahabar. Here the fields were pillowy and green, and the fogs gathered thick, like the wings of angels, soft and protective. Her brothers and sisters were all much older, so her playmates were the Gharm children. They were smaller than she, and darker, and they had quick, clever hands. They had a private language from some former time, too, which they spoke among themselves, but only when they forgot, for they were forbidden to speak that language. When they were caught speaking that language, the Voorstod pastors came with their whips and punished them, so Maire was told.

Morning times, Maire went out into the mists, around the corner of the house to the quarters out back where the Gharm lived. Fess and Bel were there, the daughters of the Manone house-Gharm, and also Bitty, a son of a Manone field-Gharm.

"What'll we play?" asked Maire.

"Adventures," suggested Bitty. "We'll adventure to a far place and slay a monster."

"I get to be the monster," said Fess. Fess was the biggest of the Gharm children, almost as big as Maire. Fess liked to be the monster, or the great ally-gaggle in the swamp, or the giant who had caught them all in her tea-pot.

So Fess was the monster, and the monster caught Maire and held her fast until Bitty came, just in time, and rescued her.

Fess's mam, Lilla, had been Maire's nurse-Gharm. When Maire was a baby, in nappies, Fess's mam had taken care of her. Sometimes when Maire was unhappy, she still went to Lilla to hold on to her until things were right again.

Sometimes the children went out in the fields to play hide-and-seek. The Gharm were very clever at hiding, because they were so small. It was hard to find them, and when they were found, they collapsed in giggles, scarcely able to walk.

"I love you, Fess," said Maire Manone. "I love you, Bel."

Fess hugged her, and then Bel, but neither of them said anything.

"I love Fess and Bel," Maire told her mam.

Mam became suddenly very quiet.

"What's their last names, Mam?" Maire asked, only to be slapped quickly across the mouth with Mam's two fingers, not to hurt, only to say shush, we don't say that.

"Gharm have no family names," said Mam, whispering. "Call names only, Maire. No family names. If you want a Gharm, you use the call name. That's all you need."

So Fess was only Fess and Bel was only Bel, but Maire was Maire Manone with a family name.

"I have two names, and you don't," she crowed at them. "I have two names."

Fess turned to Bel, eyes wide. Bel frowned. Both of them looked shocked and puzzled and then, all at once, cool, as though some little fire inside them went out. Lilla was standing by the back door of the house, listening to what was said. She always listened to them, very carefully. "Fess, Bel," she said, "Come in now. There's work to do."

They turned away, without a word, and went to Lilla before vanishing in the mists.

"They won't play with me!" Maire said to Mam.

"They have work to do," said Mam in a quiet voice. "Let them alone, child."

"But, I want them to play with me," Maire cried.

Dad heard her, and Dad said, "You call those whelps by their call name, Maire Manone, and you tell them what you want them to do, and they'll do it."

So she called "Fess," and Fess came. "Play with me," she said, and Fess stayed and did everything Maire told her to do. Everything. Sit here. Say this. Say that. Get up and go there. Fetch. Only Fess didn't do anything herself, not anything. Everything Maire said, she did, but nothing of her own.

"You're not playing!" Maire cried.

"I'm doing everything you tell me," said Fess in her quiet voice without any giggles in it. "As I must."

"But you used to play with me!"

"That was before you told us you had two names. When you say that, then you're master and we're slaves, and that's that."

Maire went in the house to cry. Dad came in. He was tired and mad from something that had happened. He asked her what the trouble was, and she told him Fess wouldn't play with her. So Dad took his whip and went out, and Maire heard Fess scream.

Mam was looking at her, tears running down her face. "I thought you loved Fess."

"I do," Maire said, frightened at the screaming, which went on and on, the animal sounds, as though the throat uttering those sounds had forgotten whose it was and went on uttering without a mind behind it.

"She'll play with you now," said Dad, coming back into the room, coiling the whip up. It was wet, and it dripped on the floor, little spots of darkness that nobody saw but Maire.

Maire saw Fess's back, next day, when Mam went to the Gharm quarters with medicine and food. "Look at it," Mam hissed at her. "Remember it. That's what you did when you let Dad hear you complain of the Gharm,

Maire. There's some might send for the pastors to do their whipping, but not your dad. Remember that!"

Fess's back was bloody, striped, raw, like meat in the kitchen, the startling white of bones showing through. Fess lay with her face to the wall and didn't speak. Her breath came into her throat like a little scratching thing, trying to get out. Fess died, lying that way, with her face buried in the corner between the bed and the wall. She burned with fever and she died, and after that none of the Gharm ever played with Maire again, and she never asked them to.

That's when the music inside herself began to fade. There had been a dream in which white curtains blew softly from tall, arched windows, while voices sang upon a green hill. Sometimes she dreamed of it still and wakened, weeping at what had been lost.

"Why are you crying, child?" Mam would demand, impatient of her tears.

"I miss the voices in my head," she'd wept. "All the voices in my head." It was Fess she missed, and Bel, and Bitty. It was innocence she missed. The little dark spots were still there on the floor. No one washed them away. The broom in Lilla's hands slid over them, leaving them there. How could she say she missed Fess? She talked of the music in her head, instead.

Mam shushed her and told her not to talk foolish or somebody might tell the prophets, and they'd come take her away. "Bad enough that you sing out loud, where people can see you, where men can see you," she said. "If you weren't so young, it wouldn't be tolerated. If you start talking crazy, they won't tolerate it, no matter how little you are."

So she learned not to complain of the Gharm. Unless one wanted them killed, or crippled, or maimed, one did not complain of them. If one complained, a man took up his whip—even some women did that—or they sent for the pastors, and the Gharm ceased. It was easier not to see them. The mists made that possible. If one didn't go out back, one never saw the Gharm houses. If one didn't pay attention, one never saw the house-Gharm or the field-Gharm. One learned to look by them, over their shoulders, as though they were invisible. One learned not to speak of them, for someone might act on that speech.

Maire went to the girls' Ire-school, to be taught by the celibate teachers there, and in school she sang. She went to County concerts, and once to an all-Voorstod one, held in Cloud, on a platform built over the whipping posts in the public square. She was twelve lifeyears old, and it was the last time she went anywhere without a veil. She became a woman then, and could not sing to anyone except women, or her family, or on sound recordings, which did not show her image. She put on the robes the prophets commanded all women wear in public until they were old women, past stirring lust in anyone, for men were too important and precious to be exposed to the evil temptations women exuded like sap. Why should men risk paradise over some woman's face or the line of a woman's breast? Only when Maire was old would she be allowed to take off the robes once more and be herself, her face exposed to the sun and wind as it would not have been since childhood.

Before she was veiled, she began writing songs of Voorstod, songs of meadows and copses and stony shores, songs of love for uncomplicated things, songs of eagles over the crags and crows among the corn. The flying things in Voorstod were not precisely eagles or precisely crows, the crop was not precisely corn, but the ancient names did well enough, and the prophets commanded that no new words be coined if old ones could be found to fit.

She was fourteen when she first sang for money, a musical background for an information stage diversion, with other female musicians. It was Maire's voice in such diversions which gave her the name the Voice of Voorstod. The recording was arranged for, and the money was given to her father, not to Maire herself, though he passed on a bit of it to her, "to encourage her," he said. He liked the money and wanted more. It came in handy for treating his cronies at the tavern or buying more Gharm or having new jeweled coup markers made for his hair. The best coup markers were very expensive, made by craftsmen on Phansure.

It was the first money Maire had ever held in her own hands. She remembered looking at it on her palm, sitting there looking at it as though it might hatch into something else. So peculiar a thing, money. A few coins, three strips. And yet it would buy a dress or a pair of shoes or a ticket to the crowded women's balcony of the concert hall.

Maire didn't buy anything, however. Instead, she took the money to Lilla, an older Lilla now, but with her face still unlined and fur still dark on her head and neck.

Maire whispered, "I want to pay for your escape. Yours, and Bel's, and Bitty's."

Lilla stared at her from unfathomable eyes. "Escape?"

"Into Ahabar. Don't look at me like that, Lilla. I know that Gharm escape into Ahabar. Women go away into Ahabar, too. I hear them talk of it when they don't know I'm listening."

"We could be killed trying that."

Maire wept. "You could be killed staying here. Fess was."

"My daughter," said Lilla with great dignity. "My daughter, Fess Salion, of the Green-snake Tchenka."

Maire didn't understand the word *Tchenka,* but she gathered what it signified. "You do have names."

"Of course we have names. Did you think we had no history, Voorstoder."

"The men say . . ."

"The men say lies," Lilla hissed, going back to her sweeping. "They suck lies into their lungs and breathe them out like smoke!"

They did not speak of it again, but Maire went on saving all the money her father let her have. When she had what she thought was enough and more than enough, she put it into a crock and set the crock on the front stoop of the Gharm quarters. Lilla said nothing, but the crock was gone in the morning. That year, in the spring, all the Gharm at the Manone place vanished.

Dad raged. Mam wept. Maire kept silent, shaking her head as though in dismay.

"Disloyal scum," Dad screamed. "Traitorous animals."

"Wise," whispered Maire to herself, needing desperately to reassure herself. "Courageous."

Later that summer, her father bought other Gharm, two men and a woman with children. Maire never spoke to one of them, or uttered a single order or instruction. The Gharm could not fail or disobey orders they never got. It was the only way Maire had of rebelling.

Thereafter, she spoke to other women, carefully, taking her time about it. There were those who used the whip, those one didn't dare speak to. There were those who sympathized and helped. There were Gharm, arriving in the middle of the night, tapping with ghost fingers on the windows. There were Gharm, hidden in cellars and under haystacks, sent on their way again, fed and clothed and provided with money.

"Have you any idea how all these Gharm are getting away?" Dad demanded of her.

"I try not to think of such things," she told him. "My music takes all my time."

"They're our servants, you know," he'd instructed her. "We have a contract, signed by them, agreeing to serve us for a thousand years, and there's five hundred yet to go."

"I've heard of it," she said, for she had heard of it until she was weary of hearing.

"They're bound to us," he'd gone on, trying to get something out of her, meeting only a level unseeing gaze and no emotion whatsoever. He wondered aloud to Mam when the last time was she had kissed him and called him Dad, and was reminded of the whip and the little Gharm child, Fess. Well, he said to Mam, she couldn't still be grudging him that. That had been years ago.

"I don't know," Maire's mother said. "I don't know anything about it. Her songs take all her time, and she doesn't talk to me."

Even with Lilla and her family gone, memories were bitter in Scaery. When Phaed Girat came courting, all the way from Cloud, she thought things might be better in Cloud, or at least different. She was not the first, even among women much older and wiser than she, to marry for such a reason. Seventeen lifeyears old was not too young to marry, and Phaed was a handsome man with glittering eyes and a manner to him like a cock strutting. He loved to hear her singing, so he said, praising her to the skies. She sat in the parlor while he said pretty things to her, she veiled to the eyes and with Mam just outside the door, he on the chair across from her. Sometimes he told her instructive stories.

"Long ago, Almighty God took us to a new land where we found the Gharm," Phaed said. "Our God was stronger than the little gods of the Gharmish people, for they had Gods as small as themselves. We took the land and renamed it Voorstod, for this was the name of our prophet. We drove the Gharm into the deserts and into the frozen wastes, and we used the world according to God's word. Almighty God had told us to be fruitful, to fill up the worlds, to multiply, and so we did until that world was used up, as we had used up other worlds, before."

When Maire spoke with the Gharm who were escaping, softly, secretly, they told the tale differently. They told of land misused and overpopulated until it was a slag heap where the rain burned when it fell and nothing would grow but thorn. The Gharm starved in the wilderness, and the Voorstoders had short rations in the towns, and the land lay dead beneath their feet, for the Voorstod God was a rapacious destroyer who created nothing and ate everything, planets as well as people, and who cared only about beings in the shape of men.

"In time we had taken what the place had to offer," said Phaed, in the manner of one instructing a child, "But Almighty God had prepared for that by providing us with a Door which would take us to another place. And when we got ready to go, who should come crawling after us but the Gharm, begging to go along."

The Gharm knew about that Door. The Door had been bought with lives, a hundred thousand Gharm lives given to slavers. One learned of roundups, of forced marches, of cages, like those used for livestock, full of the Gharm.

"We would rather have died there," said the Gharm, whispering to Maire in the night. "But they captured us, and sold us, and those they did not sell, they brought with them to this place."

That wasn't the way Phaed told the story. He could tell it over and over, or, if he'd had several glasses of spirits, he could sing it. No matter how he told it, or sang it, or rhymed it, it was lies, so said the Gharm. The Gharm would rather have died on their ruined planet, but they had not been given the choice. As for the contract, it was the greatest lie of all. No Gharm had ever agreed to such a thing.

All of this was what Maire had tried to tell Sam, that time he had asked about her songs. "There were all the things of the land in my songs," Maire had said to her son when she had told him the story of Fess and Bitty and Bel. "There were forests and seas and the sun on the water. But there were no Gharm, Sammy."

Sam didn't know Gharm. When he'd been tiny, Maire had held her hands before his eyes and told him he didn't see the Gharm. What he didn't see, he couldn't hurt. He didn't know Gharm.

He didn't know Gharm, and he hadn't understood. She had told him things she had never told anyone, and he hadn't understood. Not about Fess, not about Lilla, not about the day she'd gone away from Scaery to marry Phaed Girat and had seen the hem of her robe moving across the little dark spatter on the floor. Not how those small dark spots had become the symbol of their marriage, of everything between the two of them.

"No Gharm in my songs," she said to herself now on the porch of her sisterhouse in Settlement One, where she stood listening to Saturday Wilm's voice floating on the evening air. No Gharm, no voices crying between the stars, no magic, no more music. Her throat was too full of baby Maechy, lying still in the street. Her heart was too full of the spatter of Fess's blood that no one had ever washed away.

· *China Wilm heard* Jeopardy come in and clatter off to his room. She filed the last of a corrected pile of hybrid-yield reports and turned off the information stage after sneaking a quick look at its time pulse. Daywatch seventeen point two. Workdays, which began at this time of the year around daywatch five or six, were considered to end at daywatch sixteen or seventeen. Daywatch seventeen was time to knock off, pushing dusk, but still early enough to walk down through the settlement and take a look at the old temple.

She hadn't been particularly interested in the temple until Jep brought her the wood sample and asked what it was. His question made her remember something she'd read about dendrochronology, an ancient system for determining the age of buildings by dating the wood in them by seasonal growth rings. Why not, just for fun, find out when the temple had been built? Nobody knew, which made it a rather exciting idea. She could build up a tree ring sequence from local samples. It would make an interesting activity to fill in her spare time for a while, maybe she'd get an item for the Archives out of it, get her name recorded for posterity.

Besides, it would help her not think about Samasnier Girat. Some days it took a good deal of energy not to think about Sam, but she was determined to keep him out of her head, and out of her bed. As it was, without him, things were peaceful. With him, things were impossible. She had been through it before, more than once, and was determined not to go through it again, even though she was eaten up with curiosity over this new game Sam had, if it was a game. Walking around half the night, shouting at nothing out on the hills. Challenging dragons, Africa said. One of the herdsmen had encountered him early one morning on the western ridge and reported that Sam hadn't known him, hadn't even seemed to see him, but had gone by him with a heavy club, a broken-off branch raised to strike, veering away only at the last minute as though deflected by something, or someone. The herdsman had come back to the settlement at top speed, not bothering to inquire after reasons. He'd told Africa, of course—Africa was his Team Leader—and Africa had told China, wondering what it meant. Not that she expected China to know what it meant. China had never known what Sam meant.

China gave herself a quick looking-over before she left her sisterhouse. Her hair lay properly, in a fluffy black cap over her unlined brow. Her face was clean, and her clothing was neat if not stylish. Not that anyone in the settlement was stylish. Stylish was a word grandmothers used about clothing in some other place, some Phansuri city, in some former life. Even at Central Management they weren't stylish, though China had heard they were sometimes sexy. Which meant naked, China assumed. Skin showing. Maybe tits, or upper legs. China sometimes tried that in front of the big mirror, a gauzy scarf here, another there, lots of self showing. Sam would go crazy. Do it in public, though, and earn the disapproval of the entire settlement council! Time for baby making, yes. Time for sexiness, no. Though some people were. Sam, for instance. Very, very sexy.

Samasnier, Samasnier Vorcel Girat, she chanted to herself. Samasnier was hyper, that was his trouble. Over the top. Maybe Topmen needed to be hyper, but Sam overdid it. China could have been lastingly in love with Sam if he just hadn't been so picky and strange. What did he want! He wanted to know what life was about? He wanted to know why? Why everything? He didn't know the answers; he wanted her to know the answers, but she didn't. Now he was going out in the night, dressed up in a funny hat and a belt he'd made for himself, being weird. He thought nobody knew, but everyone in the settlement knew. Strange, wild Sam. And if the herdsman had been right, perhaps it was more than merely strange. Maybe it was crazy.

The trouble was, nobody wanted Sam to be crazy. He was too good at his job. That business with Hever, for example. Anybody else would have had Hever's legs off in a minute, but not Sam! If anyone from Settlement One told anyone from Central Management that Sam was crazy, they'd take Sam away, and nobody wanted that to happen. Even if they fixed him and sent him back, nobody wanted that, because fixing him might change him somehow. Fixing people did change them. Sometimes they were just dull, after. Easier to stay out of his way, when he was out there on the hills, yelling at nothing.

She put thoughts of Sam aside and stalked down the pathway toward the temple, pausing to wave at the Theckles, sitting on the porch of their singlehouse. Mard Theckles had been the oldest of the original settlers, fifty at least when Settlement One started, including among the younger people for his years of experience on another Hobbs farm project. His brother, Emun, had joined Mard here on Hobbs Land when Emun had retired from Enforcement a few years ago. Emun had worked on Enforcement for fifty years, maintaining the pseudoflesh soldiers there. The thought of that buried army, like something ready to hatch enormously from its moon-egg, was enough to give China the cold grozzles. So now she waved at the sibs (who were North Province Phansuri, bigger and slower than most Phansuri), and tried not to think about where Emun had spent most of his life.

Past the Theckles's place were only two more clanhomes, Tillans and Quillows, then the small equipment yard, one slab-walled mushroom house and two fragile-vegetable houses, their transparent sides reflecting the sunlight into her eyes, before she came to the temple. She was surprised to see that the building had already come to look dilapidated. Ancient Monuments Panel had had other things on its mind, perhaps.

She went through the narrow door to stand on the lip of the inner declivity, a dipping arc with the arches rising above to make up the other three quarters of the circle. Above her, straight trunks of wolf-cedar stretched side by side from arch to arch to make up the corrugated ceiling. How Jep had managed to get his roof sample, and how she was going to get one, was a riddle, however. All the logs were well out of reach.

She strolled down into the mosaic-lined trough, bending over to get a closer look at the designs. She had never before noticed the fibers protruding through the clay into which the stones were set, like a fine fabric nap around every tessera. She put her hand upon the nap and drew it away covered with dry segments. The same fine dry fur protruded from the rocky walls. Whatever this fine fur had been, it was now dead.

Back on the circular walkway, she examined both

sides of each arch for possible footholds. It was only when she came to the easternmost pair that she found the way up, a set of foot-holes running up one side of the arch, as though certain stones had fallen from the arch leaving treads no wider than a single human foot, the climb made possible only by the pierced decorative border carved into the stone of the arch. One could hold on to that.

Dust filtered onto her face. A flash of light caught her eyes. She looked up to see daylight where no daylight should have been. One hand wiped her face and came away red with dust, wood dust, sifting down from the wooden ceiling. The parallel beams were crumbling at the edges. More dust fell, white this time, telling her that the clay above the wood was breaking up as well. If she climbed the narrow stairs to take a core from one of the beams, she could bring the whole thing down on herself! It was ridiculous! The Monuments Panel wouldn't let the building fall to pieces!

More dust fell, accompanied by a subtle shifting in the mass above. Prudently, she moved under the arch, only to feel it shivering behind her. It might hold fast under the shifting weight of the roof, and then again, it might not. The door she had entered by, the only door, was across the full width of the building.

China had never been accused of indecision. She ran. Behind her, logs creaked, dust spilled. There was a tortured rending of beams when she was still six arches from the door, and she did not pause to look back. The door had swung shut behind her when she came in, and it took a moment for her to force it open, but the instant it came free, she threw herself out and away from the building, pausing only at the road to turn back and see what was happening.

What was happening was the roof falling in, all at once, very deliberately, with no very loud noises in the process. The roof of the central space was at least ten feet higher than the lower roof and was not connected to it. Nonetheless, it fell when the lower roof fell, simultaneously, almost soundlessly.

The stone arches stood bare, like the ribs of a stripped carcass, looming over the clutter of dust and thatch. The temple of Bondru Dharm now resembled the other temples, the ruined ones, those nearby and those beyond the north edge of the settlement.

"Looks like it was hit by a de-bonder," remarked a quavery voice at China's side.

China turned to find a considerable crowd gathered. The Theckles stood close behind her—Mard looking dismayed, but Emun displaying a proprietary interest.

"Some of the soldiers packed away on Enforcement do stuff like that," Emun announced. "They have this kind of gun, call it a de-bonder. Stuff just falls apart into dust."

"People, too?" China could not keep herself from asking.

"Oh, people, animals, houses, everything. Of course, if a de-bonder had hit this, the stone arches would be gone as well."

The two old men stayed beside her for a time, shaking their heads and mumbling to one another. The other bystanders, who had been on their way home from the fields, muttered, pointed, and departed, nodding or waving to China as they went.

When the dust had settled, China went back to the doorway and searched inside for a wolf-cedar trunk she could take a core from. There were none. There was only dust and a few punky chunks that fell to powder as she handled them. No one was going to learn from these remains when the temple of Bondru Dharm had been built. "De-bonded," she said to herself with a shiver. It had an unpleasant sound.

· *The courtyard of* the citadel of the prophets in Cloud had various uses. Rallies took place there, when the prophet felt inclined to address the Faithful. Apostates and recalcitrants were skewered, live, upon its walls to serve as a rebuke to backsliders. Sometimes fliers came in from other parts of Ahabar, slipping across the high walls to bring official visitors of one sort or another.

The two cloaked, masked figures who were landed in the courtyard one late evening and escorted inside the ramified bulk of the great stone pile had to be official visitors. They would have gotten no farther than the main gate, otherwise.

The men went silently through the corridors of the public part of the citadel, those parts the Faithful of the Cause were allowed to frequent. When they came to the iron door marking the private quarters of the prophet, the door was unlocked with much ceremony, and the two were escorted into warmth, light, the smell of roasting meat, and the piled softness of carpets and cushions. It was one of the younger prophets who had let them in and who nodded to them both.

"Altabon Faros," he murmured. "Halibar Ornil. Faithful Ornil, if you will wait in the chamber . . ."

Halibar Ornil smiled and bowed and went into the chamber to wait while Altabon Faros was escorted past the chamber and into the quarters of the prophet Awateh himself. In the foyer, he removed his heavy cloak and was disclosed as a tall, aristocratic-looking person in nondescript clothing, distinguishable from other men in the citadel by the short, military cut of his hair.

The prophet sat in the next room on a comfortable divan, sipping fruit juice and reading a commentary upon the Scriptures. Faros knelt before him, placing his forehead on the floor.

"Altabon Faros," breathed the prophet, briefly looking up from the page.

"Holy One," said the other, adding nothing, merely waiting. He and Ornil had been summoned, and they had come. Perhaps, later, he would have the opportunity to ask . . . beg. . . . Not now. It was not a good idea to ask for anything during an audience, certainly not early in an audience.

"How fare you upon the moon Enforcement?" asked the Awateh.

How fare I? wondered Altabon Faros. I fare alone and lonely, except for that fanatic Ornil. I fare frightened most of the time. I fare in desperation when I think of Silene and of my children.

"We move toward our goal, Awateh."

"I was distressed to hear there is a delay," the voice was kindly. Only long experience with that voice would

have led the hearer to shiver at the tone. Such kindliness
Such iron. "I have been put to some trouble over this
delay."

"There is a delay, Awateh."

"There were to be no more delays."

Faros swallowed desperately, trying to wet a dry
throat. "Alas, Holy One. We do not control everything
the men of Authority do or say."

"Explain," the prophet demanded. Faros looked up
wondering if the aged man would be able to understand
Evidently so. His eyes were as sharp and perspicacious as
Faros had ever seen them. Perhaps the vagueness came
and went. Last time Altabon Faros had seen the Awateh,
he had seemed barely able to hold up his head. "Explain
from the beginning," demanded the prophet. "As though
I knew nothing."

This was a favorite device of the prophets. Make a
man tell the whole story, checking the details each time to
see if he left anything out or told it differently or remembered things he shouldn't.

Faros gathered his thoughts. The true beginning had
been two generations before, when a dozen zealous members of the Faithful had cut off their hair and gone secretly
out into Ahabar where they had established themselves as
well-to-do planters. Planters were anonymous and, for the
most part, socially acceptable, whether they had gone to
the proper schools or not. Wealthy planters were particularly well-accepted.

The false-planters had raised children who learned to
speak and behave as Ahabarians, though when they
reached the age of reason they had been sent "away to
school." The school was in Voorstod, in the citadel of the
prophets, from which the satisfactory sons returned to
raise families of their own and the unsatisfactory sons and
the daughters did not return at all. Women fully trained in
the total self-effacement required among the Faithful
could not be expected to show themselves in the outside
world. Second generation wives and mothers were recruited from among Ahabarians.

As Silene Faros had been.

Faros and Ornil were the end result of all this endeavor, two apparent Ahabarians who had obtained positions on Enforcement. Faros and Ornil, both with impeccable records and a generation's worth of references.

The prophet didn't want to hear all that, no matter what he said, so Faros began with his own history.

"Ten years ago, I obtained a post on Enforcement after serving in the Ahabarian army for five years following my graduation from the Academy at Fenice." He kept his voice expressionless. One never knew what might set the Awateh off into one of his rages. "The Faithful of the Cause had already smoothed my way by bribing certain officials in the personnel office of Enforcement, thus assuring I would be accepted and given a suitable command. At first I was too low in rank to have access to the information needed by the Cause. I was promoted as rapidly as it is possible to be promoted, each step upward aided and assured by my brethren. Two years ago, I reached the rank of Overmajor, which is the minimum rank necessary to be admitted to the secret levels of Enforcement." He ran his tongue over his lips, longing for water. He dared not ask for it.

"It was then your family were brought here, for safekeeping," purred the prophet.

"Indeed, Holy One." They hadn't told him they intended to pick up his wife and his children. Silene and the children had always lived in Ahabar. He had gone there for his holidays. He had never told Silene anything about Voorstod. He wouldn't have told her anything. She had been safe and happy in Ahabar, on the plantation. She and the children could have been left there, perfectly safely. And instead this old . . . the Holy One had had them kidnapped and brought here!

"To assure there would be no unnecessary delays," said the prophet in the same kindly tone, sipping at the goblet in his hand.

Faros, who knew that tone, held his breath. When he could go on, he said, "As soon as I could, I learned the procedure by which the army of Enforcement is mobilized."

It had taken the better part of a year to learn the exact sequence of events necessary to get the soldiers moving.

"First, at least fourteen of the twenty-one Actual Members of the Advisory create an ineradicable record of their intention to mobilize the army. A copy of that record is then carried by the Commander-in-Chief, in his own hands, to Enforcement, where it is verified by the two Subcommanders. The Commander-in-Chief then uses his key . . ."

"Key?" asked the prophet, as though he didn't know what Faros meant. He knew exactly. He had been told.

"A device keyed to his living person. The Commander uses this key to open a certain panel on the moon Enforcement. Behind that panel is a control to which the Commander and the two Subcommanders simultaneously speak a command. This command releases the locks upon the army and allows them to be programmed as desired.

"It was clear, Holy One, that many of the details were mere ritual, that if we had the key and the living body of the Commander-in-Chief—regardless of its condition—and a record of the three voices uttering the proper command, nothing more was actually necessary. The command was 'Open Sesame.' It had some connotation I do not understand. It was not a phrase any of the three highest ranking officers would use in their daily lives.

"Still, the words were not difficult. The word *open* was easy to collect from the three officers. I recorded two men and Ornil recorded one. The other word, we had to build up from phonemes, which took longer, but soon we were ready to make the recording." Faros licked his lips. They had been so close, so very close.

"We had understood your success was imminent."

"It was, Holy One."

"But then you sent word of delay. Delay necessitates explanation." The words were icy, like cold iron.

"The message was ready, telling you of our success, when Subcommander Thees suddenly was removed from his command."

"Could you not have used the key before he was actually sent away?"

"He was not 'sent away,' Holy One. He was at a banquet on Authority when it happened, and he never returned. The Commander was at the same banquet, and so we had no access to him. The password had already been changed from Authority by the time the Commander returned, which was the first we learned of the incident."

"Incident?"

"It had nothing to do with Thees's work at Enforcement. He went to a banquet on Authority and said something improper to a young woman. The young woman was the daughter of a Baidee family of some exalted position, and, as even an officer recruited from Ahabar should have known, Baidee do not *mix*. The young woman's family demanded his removal."

"You should have foreseen this difficulty."

"I abase myself, Holy One." How in all Satan's realm was he supposed to have foreseen that a damned Ahabarian would drink too much and make a pass at a Baidee woman!

The prophet snarled. "How long, then?"

"We have already learned the new password. We have already put together those words in the voices of the two men available to us. Mobilization requires three voices, however, and Subcommander Thees's replacement has not yet been selected. Nothing moves very fast on Authority, and Enforcement is dependent upon Authority for this particular decision."

As soon as it had happened, Faros had sent word to Voorstod, to this old man, giving every detail. Patience, he had said. A small delay. Patience. This old man already knew what had happened. He had been told!

But Voorstod had long ago learned what passed for patience among the prophets: a rage they barely bothered to suppress. According to the prophets, if a man failed in his mission, he failed because Almighty God was unhappy with him and willed it so. If God were happy with him, he could not fail. If he failed, God was unhappy with him, and so were the prophets. It was all very logical.

"I understand," said the prophet in a lofty and unforgiving tone. "A pity I did not understand earlier that the delay may not have been entirely due to your own dalliance and negligence. I am afraid your family may have suffered somewhat because of your lack of foresight."

Faros held his breath again.

"No doubt Almighty God has forgiven you," said the prophet. "No doubt His victory over the false Gods of the unbelievers is imminent. No doubt your destiny is in His hands."

Faros abased himself. Vagrantly, for no reason, he had a vision of some other man, somewhere, kneeling before some other prophet or some other God, hearing these same words. Somewhere, was there another poor vassal being assured of his destiny? Some servitor of a false God, perhaps? Faros caught his breath and fought down an almost uncontrollable urge to laugh hysterically. Perhaps it was not Almighty God who had allowed him to fail. Perhaps Almighty God had an unknown enemy. Perhaps, somewhere, some other God was unwilling to lie down and die before the feet of the Faithful.

Altabon Faros choked and said nothing. His thoughts were enough to condemn him. "I would like to visit my family," he murmured at last, when it was clear the prophet had nothing more to say.

The prophet smiled peculiarly and signaled his permission. As Faros took up his robe in the foyer, Halibar Ornil entered. There was to be another inquisition, just checking, to be sure they both told the same story.

"Holy One," he heard Halibar Ornil say in the adjacent chamber.

The prophet's voice came fatefully, as Faros went through the door. "Explain this delay. Explain from the beginning, as though I knew nothing . . ."

The women's quarters were at the back of the citadel, where it touched the forests of the mountains above Cloud. There were a number of houses set in forest glades, surrounded by high walls and guarded by the Faithful. Faros was taken to one of these, and the tall, solid gate was unlocked for him.

The Gharm woman he had seen last time he had been here was inside, sweeping the walks of the garden. She looked up at him from under her eyelids, pityingly.

"My wife?" he asked.

She pointed down a path toward the pool. When he had gone a little way, he saw Silene and the children, beside the pool where flowers bloomed, very ancient flowers, brought from the gardens of Ire and Iron on Manhome, thousands of years ago. The boy was seven now. He had grown. The little girl was still a baby. Only three. Faros went swiftly toward them. The children saw him and ran away from him, scattering like birds. His wife turned a startled face on him and did not move.

"Silene!" he cried, reaching out his hands.

She looked down, her own hands writhing in her lap.

"Silene!" he cried again, gathering her into his arms. She was stiff, like a carving, all bones, no softness, nothing yielding. Her black hair cascaded halfway down her back, untidily, as though she had not combed it recently. The skin of her face looked rough, untended. The nails of her hands were torn.

"What?" he said. "Why?" He shook her, making her look at him.

She opened her mouth and showed him that she had no tongue.

"The prophet had it cut out," said the Gharm voice from behind him. "He came here, raging at her, telling her you were not doing your duty. She should have knelt down and kept quiet, but she wasn't wise enough to do that. She defended you. She told him he should not be angry at you, you were doing your best. At first he threatened to kill the children because she spoke so, but in the end he only had the guards cut out her tongue."

Silene made a gargling sound, as though she were trying to speak. Tears ran down her face in runnels.

"Next time, if there is more delay, it will be worse for her," said the Gharm. "Next time it will be her hands, her breasts, her eyes. Or maybe it will be the children's hands and eyes. The prophet told her that."

Silene looked at him with terrified eyes and he pulled her close to him. She was not Voorstod. She was Ahabar. The children were not Voorstod, they were Ahabar. In his heart, was he Voorstod? Or Ahabar? Or something else, which had no name?

The Gharm servant gazed into his face and said wonderingly, "They do it to us Gharm all the time. I was surprised when I saw them doing it to you, too."

THREE

· *Queen Wilhulmia of* Ahabar was no longer young. Her hair was an aged silver and her eyes a mature gold. The robes of state and the heavy Collar of Ahabar did not dwarf her formidable figure. With her great prow-like jaw under a firm mouth, her sizeable nose, and a wide low brow that sloped back to a wealth of flowing hair, she was, so her people said, every inch a Queen—though it was true she was no longer young.

Wilhulmia said sometimes in fits of depression that her youth and beauty had been spent upon the Voorstod Question. "Wasted," she said, for there had been no profit or return from all her years of effort, and everyone knew it. She was only the latest in a long line of rulers of Ahabar who had spent more time on the Voorstod problem than on all other issues of government combined. Five hundred years before, when the conflicts and confusions of the colonial period had ended and the people had sat down to create a lasting government under which they could live in peace, all had consented to and welcomed King Jimmy and his parliaments-several—except Voorstod. That people had never changed since they had come plunging through their illicit Door into the wastes of the peninsula, dragging the Gharm behind and claiming the land for the prophet. "Ire, Iron, and Voorstod. Death to Ahabar," had been the cry then and ever since.

Luckily for the Voorstoders, they had arrived on Ahabar during a time when that world had been disunited and unprepared for hostilities. Later, after many Gharm had escaped from the peninsula into Jeramish and points south, spreading their stories of what Voorstod really was, Ahabar had wanted to act but was prevented from doing so by Authority. Ahabar would have solved the problem by invasion and war, but Authority forbade it. Authority regarded the conflict between Voorstod and Ahabar as a "possibly religious matter" and referred the matter to the Religion Advisory, who referred the matter to the Theology Panel, who said, well, maybe slavery and cruelty weren't religious, but possibly they were.

Let us consider, said Theology Panel: "Is Voorstod a slave state, or is it merely pious?" Everyone knew someone(s) on the Panel had been bribed, though thus far it had been impossible to prove.

Each time Ahabar brought itself to the brink of intervention, Authority insisted upon considering the matter afresh. Voorstod demanded the return of its escaped slaves. Ahabar said no, and threatened to invade. Authority forbade invasion while it considered the matter. Should the escaped Gharm be returned as breakers of contract and apostates, as Voorstod demanded? Or should the Gharm be given sanctuary as common sense and good nature dictated? Where did humanity stop and interference with religion begin? Authority couldn't decide. From time to time, Authority suggested negotiation.

Elsewhere negotiation might have worked. With other religions, it could have worked. Voorstod's God, however, was a jealous and vindictive deity who ruled by murder, terrorism, and malediction. How did one negotiate with that? Where other Gods might have allowed representatives to talk to the parliaments-several of Ahabar, the God of Voorstod demanded that past insults be revenged by blowing up the parliaments. Where other Gods might have advocated making life a garden, the Voorstod God promised the garden only after death, preferably violent death. Then might the Faithful lie about on the greensward sucking grapes and fucking virgins, so the prophets promised.

As with other peoples who had focused their lives upon wrongs in the past and heaven in the future, Voorstod made an everlasting hell of the present.

All of which led Queen Wilhulmia to cry from time to time, as she did when told by her counselor that Voorstod had some new demand, "What do they want now?"

Old Lord Multron cleared his throat and prepared to say, for the thousandth time, what Voorstod wanted from Ahabar.

"Independence, Your Pacific Sublimity." He ticked this off on his first finger, holding it up for her to see.

"Forget the *Sublimity,* Ornice. If we speak of Voorstod, we can forget the *Pacific,* as well. I am Uriul, whom you have known since childhood. Speak to me."

"Uri, they want independence." He waved the admonitory finger, ready for the second point.

"They have independence. We've told them ten thousand times we'll make no effort to rule in Voorstod. We told them that when they squirmed through that damned Door of theirs onto land they had no right to, and we've told them ten thousand times since."

"They want their Gharm returned, as well, Uri. As you well know." The middle finger marked this demand.

"There, Ornice. You see, you're doing it, too. *Their* Gharm, you say, as though you accept ownership."

He flushed. "One gets in the habit, Sublimity."

"*I* don't. I won't. I will not say, *their* Gharm. Is Vlishil Teermot, he who won the Sabarty Prize for poetry, is he one of *their* Gharm? Is the harpist Stenta Thilion one of *their* Gharm? Are those horticulturists who have made the valley of the Vhone bloom for the past three generations *their* Gharm? Shall we round them up and return them to Voorstod to be tortured and executed when their parents and grandparents have been free in Ahabar for five generations or more?"

Ornice merely shook his head at her, as though he

were her grandfather. She sighed and fiddled with the Collar of State, thinking it heavier than she liked. "Has your daughter learned anything of interest?"

Ornice looked hastily around himself, laying his finger across his lips. "Her relationship to me is not known, Uri. Lurilile feels I would lose dignity if it were known my daughter is a spy."

The Queen nodded. The things one had to do as a spy were often undignified. So she had been told. Ornice had not liked the idea of his daughter becoming a spy, but Lurilile had been determined on the matter.

"But you're a woman!" Ornice had cried, unforgivably.

"So is the Queen!" his daughter had replied, with more relevance. Not only that, Lurilile had come to the Queen, begging her intercession in the matter. Lurilile was strong-willed. Her family, an ancient one, was known for its strength of character. "Someone must do something about this Voorstod mess," she had said. "Why should I hang back, feeling forgiven any effort because I am a woman?"

"It may be unpleasant," the Queen had told her. "Spies have to do unpleasant and undignified things."

"I am sure they are no more unpleasant or undignified than dying with one's guts blown out by some terrorist bomb in Green Hurrah," Lurilile had answered, and the Queen had had to agree.

Sweet, strong Lurilile. The Queen thought of her often, wishing her well.

"Has she found out anything about the bribes."

"She has attached herself to one of the Thykerite members of Authority, and through his contacts has found everything but evidence we can submit to Authority."

The Queen snorted. "However those bastards are being paid, someone is being exceedingly clever about it." She sighed. "What else isn't new about Voorstod."

"Uri, why ask if you already know?"

She nodded, curtly. "Sometimes I have to hear you say it, Ornice. Sometimes I have to hear myself say it, just to realize it is not a pervasive nightmare I have come to believe in."

"It is not dream," he bowed. "Further, as I mentioned to you, this morning I have been advised of Voorstod's newest demand." He ticked off first and middle fingers once more, holding the remaining ones in reserve.

"What more?" she asked. "What more could there be?"

"The three southern counties, those in which people of Voorstod have intermarried with people of Ahabar, those in which the people have watered down or changed their religion, and become, so say the northerners, a bastard race—those counties, says Voorstod, are to be ravaged and sewn with salt." Third finger. "After every man, woman, and child within them has been slaughtered." Little finger. "They give notice that Ahabar is to withdraw the army and is not to interfere while Voorstod takes care of this internal matter for itself." Thumb, and all five points were made. The hand could rest.

The Queen paled. "You can't have understood them. The difference in dialects . . ."

He bowed, one nostril distended to tell her he had understood them all too well. "They speak System as well as we do. They may be intransigent, but they are not stupid. Either they see a threat in the southern counties and want it stopped or this is a feint, to draw our attention while they do something wicked somewhere else. The Gharm escape through the southern counties, Uri. The people of Wander and Skelp and Green Hurrah have become reasonable and peaceful. They have lost the fanaticism of their forefathers. They are, therefore, apostates and heretics, anathema to the prophets of Voorstod. Killing a man of the southern counties is now counted a meritorious act in Voorstod. Killing a child is more meritorious yet, for it chops that many more years of heresy away. Killing a child in the womb, or a woman of childbearing age, or a virgin girl . . ."

"Don't say any more," she cried. "Oh, who would be Queen in a world like this!"

"They don't get away with it," he soothed. "Commander Karth keeps the peace."

"You believe the peace is what he keeps!" she cried. "My harried soldiery have prevented the slaughter of some innocents in Green Hurrah. That is true. I went there and presented the medals myself. Karth's battalions lately stopped a murderous battle in Skelp. Our intelligence network intervened in the planned assassination of the Squire of Wander. All true, and yet we are powerless to prevent the killing which goes on, hour by hour, day by day. You know it. I know it. Commander Karth knows it and says so. Why do we lie to ourselves!"

She turned away from him to look out the window into her gardens, tears threatening to fall. "The killing goes on, old friend. The Voorstod Question is the curse of Ahabar and the woe of her Queen. Voorstod has crawled into a tomb of darkness and pulled the heavy stones down upon it. Oh, yes, Voorstod is far into the habit of death!"

· *Since Emun Theckles* had seen the temple of Bondru Dharm falling apart, the old man had become distracted and depressed, uncommunicative, and obsessed by old times. He stared at walls and did not answer his brother Mard's attempts at conversation. After a few days of putting up with grunts and silences, Mard decided Emun needed to be jostled. Mard did the jostling by inviting Sam Girat to breakfast, a meal which the aged brothers often took on their porch so they could watch what went on in Settlement One. As an elder settler, Mard could get away with insisting Sam wander by at an appropriate time and sort of drop in. Sam was also instructed to ask Emun about his former life.

"Maybe he'd rather not talk about it," Sam had suggested to Mard.

"Talking about it's the only way he's going to get himself back on track," said Mard. "You be there, Sam."

So Sam dropped in for breakfast, and after a few general words about the weather asked, "What was it like, up there?"

Mard set a sharp elbow into Emun's ribs to wake him up.

"Up where?" asked Emun, coming to himself with an effort.

Mard jabbed him again. "You know what he's asking about, Emun. Up there." Mard pointed generally upward, though Phansure was in quite another direction, with all its moons. "Answer the Topman."

"On Enforcement?"

"Of course on Enforcement, where else have you been!"

"It was . . . it was gloomy."

Mard shook his head in exasperation. "How d'ya mean, gloomy? Sam wants to know!" He raised his eyebrows at Sam, who said, yes, indeed, he did want to know.

Emun, who was accustomed to obeying those in authority, turned his full attention to the question and thought about it. When he had thought for a time about what he had meant, in fact, when he said it was gloomy, he told them.

The maintenance quarters were above ground, he said, liberally fenestrated so the workers could see the stars and the wheeling, clouded orb of Phansure above them. The gravity was light. The quarters were luxurious. "Real nice," said Emun. The food was delicious, just as it was on Authority. The chefs were trained on Authority, after all; none of them had to stay very long; and they received hardship pay plus bonuses if they kept the staff happy. Emun could recall nothing really unsatisfactory on Enforcement. There had even been a properly maintained brothel, for both sexes.

Sam nodded. "But you said 'gloomy,' Emun."

Emun allowed it was more a matter of perception than reality. One rose in that place to the quiet whisper of air, the stroking of banal music—"Without any umph to it," Emun said—the flurry of water as one cleaned oneself of one's own dirt. There was no other dirt, no extraneous filth, no foreign organic or inorganic impurity from which the morning body needed deliverance. It was only sleep dirt, sleep sweat, the flake of no-longer-living skin, the fall of no-longer-living hair, to be cleansed away before submitting oneself to the dustless rooms, the sterile walls, the endless, empty ducts down which men moved in their white garb like ghosts on felt-padded feet. Ghost-servitors. Ghost-prowlers, along the edges and down the aisles of static madness. Perhaps that was what had been gloomy.

Or maybe it had been the cars, like coffins, with their padded, almost reclining seats, their airtight lids, their number pads greenly glowing in the shadows of the tube. One found the proper tube, one got in, one shut the lid, one entered the destination number. BB5601. An almost silent whoosh and a feeling of heaviness. A screaming above the level at which one could hear and the heaviness again. Then the lid opened of its own accord to let one out in green-lit Vestibule BB5601 with the closed door and the green light washing all the walls. Green meant as usual. Green meant no worse than yesterday. Green meant boring, uninteresting, but vastly preferable to yellow, or red. Certainly it was preferable to purple which meant it was already too late.

"Ah," murmured Sam, sensing interesting danger.

But Emun didn't talk about that. He went on to something else that had always disturbed him: the sound the doors made. The doors clanged. No matter what one did to them, or how carefully they were shut, they clanged—a deep, clamorous sound like an ill-tuned bell, a tocsin pealing danger. Clang, and then the whisper of feet as one went through. Clang, again. Inside, the cobweb aisles stretched ahead and back to infinity, vanishing in gloom, in distance. Gray light, there in the aisles. Coming from nowhere. Throwing no shadows. A long walk down the main aisle from Vestibule BB5601 before one saw Aisle BB5617 to the left. Past it would be Aisle BB5618 and Aisle BB5619 to the left again. "Those three were mine," he said, almost with pride. "Those three were all mine." Emun's province, his kingdom, where the unlit eyes looked only to him, where the unspeaking throats quivered, almost ready to utter, only to him. Between him and Vestibule BB5601 were five other men, each with three aisles. Beyond him were five more, each with three aisles, and then Vestibule BB5635.

Sam imagined it and shivered.

On the first day of shift, one got the cart out of its

garage, stocked it, led it down the main aisle, then turned left into BB5617 and began the slow trip down the side aisle, looking at telltales, tapping at dials, peering at signal lights, reading tapes, refilling tape registers, replacing telltale lights, running test patterns, the soft-tired little cart buzzing along behind like an obedient pet. There was a toilet on the cart, and a little kitchen, which would open at quarter-shift to give him drinks and snacks. By midshift one would have got a tenth of the way down the first aisle, and the cart would offer a comfortable seat and a built-in little table, where it would serve him a hot meal.

"That sounds well-managed," Sam said, approving.

Oh, yes, that was well-managed enough. One would eat while listening to music or watching a recreation on the little information stage on the cart, and then the afternoon would go by, doing the same things. Replace. Repair. Check. Monitor. Sometimes something would actually be wrong! Then one could take out the tools, do a dismantle and repair, something different, something unusual. At quitting time one rode the cart back to its garage on the main aisle to be there, waiting, when the services scooter came ding-ding-dinging down behind him, with five other men already aboard, being taken back to Vestibule BB5601. They knew you were tired by then. They didn't make you walk.

Every fifteen or twenty days, the route would be completed. Then there was time off to do what one pleased: to drink or dance or play games of chance, or simply to sleep or read or go to the brothel or to religious services. And then Aisle BB5617 once more, Aisle BB5618, Aisle BB5619.

"A little boring, perhaps," suggested Sam, feeling goosebumps.

Oh well, yes, but not always. Once in a great while, a true malfunction. The monitors quivered in excitement, something wrong. Pseudoflesh is rotting, pseudobrain is not functioning, something awry, dangerous.

"And then all of a sudden you knew how dangerous it was," said Emun. "Then you didn't need no telltale to tell you anything. You didn't need no monitors. You'd feel it, all the way down the aisle you'd feel it, like something reaching at you, like some great animal creature, evil and hating you every minute and not wanting you to get away."

A brute malevolence, he went on saying, though not in those words. Sam supplied the words. A killing horror, barely withheld.

"You pick up that communicator so scared you can't hardly breathe," said Emun. "And at the same time your old heart's poundin' away like you was runnin' a race from the excitement. And you say, 'Technician Theckles, reporting possible malfunction.'

"And he says, 'What is it Technician Theckles?' "

"Who was he?" asked Sam.

"Oh, that there was Faros, we called him Chilly Faros. Never no more emotion to him than to a circuit scanner. Except when he talked of his wife, then he got all soft. Old Chilly Faros, he was only a subaltern then."

"So what did you say?" asked Sam.

"Oh, I'd say, 'Brain malfunction, Subaltern Faros. I recommend power shutdown at once.'

"And he'd say, 'Do so, Technician.'

"An' you'd go to pull the plug. Disconnect the power source for the whole section. An' you'd pray the whole time the things would let you do it."

There had been cases of soldiers that didn't want to be unplugged, he said. Cases where men had been found, what was left of them, like a splash of mush on the floor, red jelly.

Then young Lieutenant Halibar Ornil would come zipping up on a scooter, full of rumbling amusement. "Got a rogue, have we?" he would ask, as though it didn't matter. "Got a rogue?"

A rogue, said Emun. A devil. A killer designed to be unstoppable, unappeaseable. A thing the height of three tall men, on clawed treads that could climb a fifty-percent grade, with disruptor circuits and de-bonder guns and no feelings. A thing that would blow up a schoolyard full of children without blinking. A thing, so thought Emun occasionally, like a Voorstoder, only bigger.

Sam blinked, setting that aside.

And the eyes, staring over his head blindly, but pick-

ing up reflections of the red telltales, as though the eyes
themselves were glittering.

"Gloomy," repeated old retired Emun Theckles to
Sam Girat at the end of his tale, wishing he could forget it
entirely since he had come to this better place. "Oh,
Topman, it was gloomy there."

·   *That night, in* Settlement One, Topman Samasnier Girat tapped his gavel impatiently and, when this had
not the desired effect, bellowed at the small clot of people
arguing in the doorway of the settlement hall. "Can we
get this meeting started, people!"

Quiet came reluctantly. Outside in the dusk, children
shouted at one another. On one window sill an orange cat
groomed herself in the pink light of sunset, while her gray
colleague sniffed along the base of the walls followed by a
staggering line of half-weaned kittens. All three hundred
seats were filled, with room at the back for any young
person who decided to take an interest in community government.

"All right," Sam said. "Short meeting tonight. We all
know of the recent crop shortfalls. I've made a complete
report to Central Management, and they've asked me to
come in for a meeting in a few days. They're also sending
some people to run tests, so they say, though what tests
they can run we haven't already run I don't know. You all
know that even after the shortfalls our production is still
within the parameters set by the project, so the settlement
is in no danger. Our production balance is going to suffer
quite a bit, but that's all." Production over and above
ninety percent of the reasonable quotas set by CM was
converted into land credits for the settlers. Settlement One
had long had an enviable production balance.

"Now, the reason for this meeting tonight is to discuss
the conflicts we've been having among the production
teams. . . ."

There were groans of resentment and voices raised at
once, each blaming some other team or individual for
whatever had happened. Sam demanded order, and got it,
only to have the discussion degenerate again. It was like a

grass fire, he thought. You stamped it out in one place, and then the wind took it running off somewhere else. The arguments generated heat but not light; the meeting threatened to degenerate into a brawl; finally Sam shut them up, talked them into relative peace, and adjourned the meeting before they got started again.

Africa Wilm, who had been standing by the door, keeping herself quiet with some difficulty, slipped out into the night. China went after her. Quick as she was, Sam managed to intercept her at the door.

"G'night, Sam," she said hurriedly, increasing her pace, even as he reached out a hand to detain her.

By the time Sam got outside, the children seemed to have gone elsewhere. There were no shouts in the dusk, no squeals or cries of outrage. Sam stood in the quiet, snarling to himself. Everyone was behaving . . . behaving like something or other. Not like themselves. Now China. Well. Always China.

Rebuffed, Sam stalked north of the settlement, toward the temples, stopping only briefly at his brotherhouse to pick up his sword belt and helmet. Theseus didn't like it when he showed up without them.

"It means you're not serious," Theseus had explained. "You haven't the proper attitude."

"I do have the proper attitude," Sam had growled. "I'm tired of waiting, that's all." He said the same thing again tonight as he settled on the hillside near the old temple.

"You're agitated," accused Theseus.

"We're all agitated. There's lots of anger floating around. We're not used to that."

"What are you angry about?"

"Me?" Sam thought about it. What was he angry about? "I don't know. Nothing specific."

"Something in your past, maybe?"

"I guess I've always been angry that my father let me leave that way. He didn't try to stop Mam from taking me. He just let me go."

"That's a very old anger."

"Old ones are the worst. New ones you can yell about and get over. When you grow up, you learn that. Yell about it, then forget it. But when you're a kid, you're afraid to yell. Somebody might punish you for it, for the way you feel, so you put the anger away, deep, store it, and it festers. I imagine old angers are like abcesses, deep ones, full of nasty pus and sickness. You can feel them boiling inside you."

"So you hate him because he didn't keep you?"

"I hate him because he didn't even try."

"I hated mine, too. He could have sent someone to Troezan to learn how I was, whether I was growing up strong and healthy. He never did. He didn't even know he'd had a son until I showed up in Athens."

"So if you hated him, why did you go?"

"Why will you?"

"I'm not, yet."

"But you will. Just the way I did."

Sam thought about this. "I guess I'm curious. I want to ask him why. I want to ask him lots of things."

"Let me tell you, fathers don't always give you good answers. In my experience, they sometimes tell you things, but it doesn't satisfy. They tell you why, but it isn't a why that matters, you know what I mean?"

"I'm not sure I do."

"Well, say you ask your father why he wasn't there when you were born. And he says, he was off fighting a war with the Atticans or something. That's the reason, but you still feel he should have been there."

"You're saying there aren't any reasons good enough for some things."

"Isn't that the way you feel?"

Sam stared at the sky, wondering if it was the way he felt. He thought it was. There were no reasons good enough for some things. Certain things simply had to be. Fathers had to put their sons first. No war or cause was that important. Sons came first. If fathers didn't do that, they failed, no matter what the reasons. He turned to explain this to the hero and found him gone.

It was all right. He'd explain it next time. He curled into the slight declivity he had been sitting in. The night was warm and windless; it was very quiet there; gradually he drowsed into sleep.

Two persons had followed Sam from the settlement, had hidden among the ribbon-willows, had listened to his conversation with whomever he had been talking to. They had seen him put on his belt and his helmet. They had seen him sit on a hillside. They had heard him talking to someone, maybe to himself. There had been nothing wild or crazy or violent going on. Just a man dressed up and talking to himself.

"How often does he do this?" asked Dern Blass, who had come to Settlement One that afternoon, disguised as a peddler, in response to certain rumors he had heard. "How often does he sit out here talking to himself?"

"He rambles every other night or so," said Africa. "Sometimes he walks a long way. Sometimes he sits and talks like this."

"But he's all right in the daytime?"

"So far," she said. So far he had been. "So far he's done his job as well as anyone could do it." Africa thought this was true. She could not think of any improvements she herself could make over Sam's performance.

"Any idea what he meant by '. . . there aren't any reasons good enough for some things . . .'?"

Africa shook her head. She didn't know what Sam had meant. She knew what she would have meant. The words were true. There weren't any reasons good enough for some things.

· *Jeopardy Wilm saw* himself as a future Team Leader, like Saturday's mom. Jep felt his Aunt Africa was the best, better than any of the uncles, though they were all right. Africa's Team Five was recognized, even among the children, as being extremely well led.

Thus, when it came time to cut the wolf-cedar for the roof of the temple the children were restoring, Jeopardy went to the sisterhouse next door to China's to consult his aunt about the proper system for doing things.

"Let's say," he told her over her work table, while Saturday and her sibs did homework at the other end of it, "let's say I've got fifteen men." Actually he had eight, but fifteen sounded better. Friday Wilm, who was eleven and knew very well how many workers Saturday had, looked up and winked at him, but Jep pretended not to notice. "I've got fifteen men, and the job I have to get done is to cut wolf-cedar logs and transport them and lift them up about twelve feet."

His aunt stared at him, trying to show interest without curiosity, ashamed of herself for feeling impatient. She had been up half the night, watching Sam with Dern Blass, and she was tired and unusually fractious. If she could have, she would have postponed this little conference. What the hell were these kids up to now?

"What's the total weight of the logs and what's the distance you need to move them?" she asked, keeping her voice calm with an effort.

Jep had been prepared for these questions and came up with reasonable estimates as to total weight and distance. After a computation session, in which Saturday joined, Africa suggested the use of a dilapidated utility vehicle which, while it was no longer sufficiently reliable to be used regularly in the fields, could certainly carry larger loads than twelve- to fourteen-year-olds would find possible without mechanical help.

When Jep had gone, Saturday said into her book, "Mom, do you feel all right?" The other children looked up expectantly, wanting to hear the answer to this question.

"Not really," Africa remarked with an apologetic look at all of them. "I think I must be coming down with something."

"I thought maybe you didn't feel good," Saturday said, giving her mother a troubled look. "You almost sounded as though you didn't like Jep, and I know you do."

Africa started to say she didn't like anybody much right now, but decided that would be misinterpreted. Instead she merely smiled apologetically and hoped whatever was wrong with her and everyone else would soon go away.

Jep got his eight-man crew into the wolf-cedar forest the following day. For several days they cut, trimmed, and stacked the slender trunks, trying to pick ones that were straight and uniform in size, being careful not to clear-cut any area of the forest, a deed which Jep's mom would have regarded as only slightly less dishonorable than genocide. When enough wood had been assembled in widely dispersed piles to do the entire job, Jep borrowed the utility vehicle Africa had offered, drove it slowly and solemnly to the forest, and then made a dozen trips back and forth to the temple. When he returned the vehicle to the equipment sheds, he was dirty, weary, and unmistakably triumphant.

The children started the roof the following afternoon. Jeopardy had promised everyone a potluck picnic when they got to the center. Someone—probably Gotoit Quillow, it was her kind of thing—swiped ale from the settlement brewery for the occasion, enough for the children to enjoy becoming a little high and happy. Though, when Jep came to think of it, it seemed they had felt that way most of the time since they had started work on the temple, which is why they kept coming back.

"Jep," Gotoit asked from her sprawled position in the bottom of the completed trough, "what are we going to do with this place when we finish it?" Over their heads the neatly laid logs glimmered with the light that sparkled between them. "And how are we going to finish the roof? This'll rain right through."

Ignoring Gotoit's first question, Saturday said, "First, we put a layer of straw over the cedar to keep the clay from coming through. I've already begged the straw from the meat foreman. He says it's last year's and he doesn't need it for the animal pens. Then over that we put a layer of wet clay and straw, mixed. And when that dries, we thatch it with ribbon-willow."

Willum R. Quillow, who, between sports practice sessions, spent as much time recumbent as possible, adjusted the pad of grasses he had accumulated for a cushion and asked, "What about the middle part. Over where the God goes. We haven't done anything about a roof for that yet. It's going to take bigger wood. The cedar sags if you cut pieces that long."

"Trusses," said Saturday and Jep at the same moment.

The picture had appeared in their minds at once—triangular structures made of small logs, not too heavy to move, which could be assembled into a multisided peak. The settlement was built entirely of sponge panels. Neither Saturday nor Jeopardy could remember seeing a truss, but the pattern was there in their heads.

No one noticed that Gotoit's original question had gone unanswered.

Over the next several days, the children cut, hauled, trimmed, and joined with stickum and lashings of rope the wolf-cedar logs that made up a conical roof for the center of the temple. Over the next several months they worked at thatching the roof. When they needed some extra muscle to haul their carefully constructed roof-cone over the central well, several adults stopped by to see what was happening. The grownups seemed unsurprised to find themselves helping and were sufficiently unimpressed by that fact not to make anything much of it. Africa mentioned to China something about the children's project, but China, along with everyone else, paid very little attention.

When the roof was complete, the children finished up the last few bits of mosaic, washed the stone walls inside and out with borrowed brushes and buckets, and then went back to the settlement to resume their more usual recreations. The rebuilt temple stood as they had left it, sound and tight, thatch and walls gleaming, needing only a coat of mud plaster and a door to look almost exactly as the temple of Bondru Dharm had done, before the death of the God.

• *Specialists arrived from* Central Management to duplicate, first, the tests China Wilm had already done, and then the results of those tests. No one could find any reason whatsoever for production to have dropped, and no one could think of any possible way to get it up again. Settlement One, despite thirty-odd years of above normal crop production and below average internal conflict, seemed destined to be one with Settlements Two through Eleven: simply average.

• • •

· *Once each ten* days or so Dern Blass held a staff meeting in his office, complete with lunch laid on and assorted interesting drinkables. In Dern Blass's opinion, food and drink went some way to ameliorate the boredom he almost always experienced during meetings. He knew that no matter what the purpose of the gathering, Jamice Bend would take offense at Horgy Endure's handling of some situation with personnel implications; Horgy would suggest yet again that he should have the last word on any personnel decisions involving production; Spiggy Fettle would point out—in either his who-cares or his God-this-is-portentous voice, depending upon where he was in his joy-pain cycle—that the organizational structure of CM was mandated by Hobbs Transystem, and there wasn't much they could do about it; and Zilia Makepeace would raise some angry though specious concern about incursions against the natives, all of whom were dead, Departed, and thus beyond incursion.

Today Sam Girat had been summoned to Central Management to take part in the meeting, so maybe the others would behave themselves, though Dern didn't count on it. Dern was trying to think of some way in which their behavior might be permanently altered when his ruminations were interrupted by the arrival of Tandle Webster who gave him a knowing look, to which he returned one of bashful innocence. This was their usual relationship. The perfect secretary, Tandle. Self-effacing. Modest. Mean as sin.

"What's on the agenda this week," he asked.

"Spiggy's dramatizing about the shortfall at Settlement One," she said, as she stacked papers at each place around the conference table. Dern was a primitive. He liked paper. He liked something he could fiddle with, doodle on, write scurrilous comments in the margins of.

"What about Zilia? What's she up to?" Dern asked.

"She has convinced herself yet again that the earliest settlers committed genocide against the Departed."

"The shortfall is something we'll have to deal with," growled Dern. "Since I've asked Sam to come in, put that item first and Zilia dead last. We can hope Sam will have left before she starts accusing him of anything."

Tandle had time to enter the revised agenda before the first of the staff members arrived: Horgy Endure, trailing his trio of girlies. If Dern had no objection, he murmured to Tandle, they could sit along the wall and observe. Dern had, as usual, no objection, said Tandle.

"Another of your usual beauty pageants?" commented a chill voice as Jamice Bend stalked from the door to the table, flicking a dismissive finger at the pile of papers before her chair. She moved like some creature from a jungle, all sinew and grace and predatory intention. Her red hair was wound tight on top of her head, the knot pierced by two Phansuri spirit rods, which gleamed green with cabochon gems. Whenever Tandle saw them, she gritted her teeth at the arrogance which could stick millennia-old artifacts in its hair. Nonetheless, the effect was striking—as emerald-eyed, ochre-skinned Jamice well knew.

"Morning," tolled the third member of the meeting, slouching across the room and into his chair, not looking at anyone, his ugly face made plainer yet by its pained expression, lank beige hair dangling across his rippled forehead, his lithe, long-muscled form twisted into a tortured skein. Spiggy's eyebrows, which could be clownish, were this morning raised at the center like a mask of tragedy. "Morning," Spiggy tolled again, his voice a dolorous bell rung across watery meadows.

Tandle sighed. When Spiggy was up, he was delightful, though wearing. When Spiggy was down, he drained energy from a room as though someone had pulled the plug. Abruptly, the day seemed dim. Tandle sighed again and turned up the light and heat. By the time this meeting was over, Dern would be fit for nothing but escape. He said having Spiggy around during a depressive cycle was like giving a continuous blood transfusion.

Of course, Spiggy could have been treated. Any of them in the room, Tandle often thought, *should* have been treated, including Dern himself. The technician in charge of the CM medical center was totally competent to straighten Spiggy out, but Spiggy's parents had been Thyker Baidees, High Baidees, a sect which rejected all psychotropic intervention because (supposedly, though Tandle had her doubts) the prophetess had commanded so. Spiggy wasn't a Baidee observant. He held to no other tenets of the faith—most certainly not the elaborate dress or the complex and difficult food taboos—but this one canon he was adamant about.

"Am I late?" Zilia Makepeace asked from just inside the door. "I was afraid I was late." She knew she wasn't. Dern wasn't present yet, so she couldn't be late. It was her way to start each conversation with an apology, so she could be offended when the apology was accepted. The response she expected now was, "Yes, you're late, Zilia. Only a little." At which she would be annoyed, pointing out that Dern was not yet present.

"No, not in the least," said Tandle offhandedly. "In fact, you're a little early, but then, so is everyone else."

"Come on in, Zilia. Don't hover," sneered Jamice, totally wiping out any good Tandle's stratagem might have accomplished.

"I wasn't aware," Zilia responded in a defensive voice verging upon anger, "that I was hovering."

So much for peace and tranquility.

Sam had been waiting outside until the staff assembled. Now he strode to the table, his tall, vital presence making the rest of them seem juiceless and pale, even Jamice, even Horgy—poor Horgy, who surprised a couple of calculating glances thrown Sam's way by Horgy's very own new brunette.

Tandle subvocalized into her com-link that everyone was present, and Dern came through the door smiling, nodding to each of them, asking about this and that, giving Sam a firm hand on the shoulder, skipping over Spiggy the moment he looked at his face, kissing Zilia's hand, admiring Jamice's hair, slapping Horgy on the shoulder, smiling at the wide-eyed row of trainees along the wall, being the good fellow all round, finally seating himself at the head of the table to reach for the piled papers topped by the revised agenda.

"Spiggy," he said in an interested tone, after they had all settled down, "we've asked Sam to come in today to talk to us about the shortfall at Settlement One. What's your final count?"

Spiggy pulled himself together, barely, took a small, battered memo-rizer from one pocket, leaned across the table until he was half-lying on it, and said in a half-moan, "Settlement One had a thirty percent shortfall on projections."

Sam felt blood rising in his neck.

Dern said, "That much?"

Spiggy sighed. "Oh, all in all, it doesn't make that big a difference." He tapped the memo-rizer, frowning at the figures which floated to its surface. "It only makes a two or three percent difference overall, somewhere in there. Two point four, I think . . ." His voice trailed off, then began again, as he began a recital of production statistics and what it meant to the transport crews on the recipient planets.

Dern fought down a yawn. Sam looked at his hands, annoyed, wondering why he'd been asked to come here when Spiggy was doing all the talking.

"Quit going on about the transport crews," demanded Jamice in a nasty voice. "They're not the problem. The problem is the actual shortfall. That and a breakdown in morale."

"What do you mean, breakdown in morale?" Horgy had been leaning back, alternately smiling with enormous forbearance at his colleagues and throwing knowing little glances toward the girls along the wall, but now he came suddenly alert, glaring at Jamice. "What breakdown in morale?"

"Personnel matters," Jamice said crisply. "I've had reports of interteam hostilities at Settlement One."

Sam felt his neck get even hotter. He did not like meetings. He particularly didn't like meetings where his settlement was being discussed in this way.

Horgy leaned back, relaxed, smiling, the brows raised once again as though to say, well, is that all. "Jamice, sweetheart, for a minute there, I thought there was a problem. Now, don't tell me there's a week goes by you don't have reports of interteam hostilities, or rivalries, or whatever. Of course you do, dear. Rivalry is one way to keep production up." He shrugged at his sycophants along the wall, as though to say, "You see what foolishness I have to put up with."

"That isn't how you've kept it up in Settlement One," she snapped. "There were no such reports from Settlement One until recently. Settlement One has virtually no deaths, and those they do have result from unmanageable illnesses. As a matter of fact, when I took this job, I noted the variation from norm and made a trip out to Settlement One to see if perhaps the Topman or the Team Leaders weren't fudging their reports. They were not. The mortality and morbidity rates have always been vanishing low at Settlement One. People simply didn't get belligerent out there."

Dern looked at Sam, raising his eyebrows.

"She's right," said Sam, trying not to give further evidence of Settlement One hostilities. "We never used to have people getting angry with one another."

Dern cleared his throat. Three heads swiveled in his direction. "I don't recall your ever mentioning that, Jamice, or you, Sam," said Dern. There was iron under the velvet of his voice.

Sam frowned and snapped, "What was there to mention? We don't report negatives."

Jamice leapt in. "There was nothing to report, Dern. It was simply an anomaly. I've always assumed the higher production was due to the lower conflict rate. Which seems to be the case. At least, the two seem to fluctuate together."

"Are you attributing a causal factor to one or the other?" he asked gently, looking first at Jamice, then at Sam, then back to Jamice.

Horgy didn't give Jamice time to answer. "The production levels were high because they have the best leadership of any of the settlements, that's all. All five of the leaders out there are absolute gems. Africa Wilm should be used as a paradigm."

"She is that," said Sam with relief, glad to be off the hostility topic but wondering why he was attending this meeting. They all seemed to be getting along fine without him. They all knew everything he knew.

Dern gave Horgy a polite you're-out-of-order look and returned to Jamice. "A causal factor?" he demanded.

Jamice flushed once more. "I can't go that far. It's a bird-and-egg question, Dern. When you only have one incident, you'd be a fool to predict on the basis of it. The fact is they fluctuated together. Production down, hostilities up. Or in reverse order. But it's only happened once."

"Has anything else happened? Anything noteworthy?"

"For heaven's sake," cried Zilia angrily, going off all at once in a clatter of wings, like a ground bird startled from its nest. "Of course something happened. Their God died." She glared at Sam as though he'd personally committed deicide and then stared, red-faced, into her lap once more.

"Bondru Dharm," murmured Tandle, fishing the proper references up on the stages. "Perhaps we should not go so far as to call it 'their God.'"

"The Departed God that was there when you people settled," amended Horgy with a nod to Sam. "You settlers probably have your own religion or religions, don't you? Most of the Settlement One people are from Phansure, aren't they, Sam? Phansure has lots of religions."

"They probably do," Spiggy interjected in a gloomy voice. "Last thing they'd want would be a God who was actually present. Last thing anybody'd want would be a God who actually worked."

"Worked?" asked Jamice, sneering. "A God who worked? What do you mean, Spig?"

Sam, seeing Spiggy drifting away again, said hastily, "Our people come from a number of backgrounds, but all of us had this thing, this so-called grief reaction, which lasted about ten days. We just blanked out. I hadn't seriously considered it as the main factor in the production drop, but I suppose it could be the cause."

"If production dropped, and if your people out there had always taken pride in being number one," Dern said, "could their chagrin and disappointment lead to annoyance? To hostility?"

Sam shrugged, not pleased with the thrust of the conversation, but not able to refute it.

Spiggy murmured, "You know it could."

"So?" Dern asked. "It could be causative?"

"I suppose," Sam admitted. "I suppose it could."

"It wasn't," Zilia murmured. "I know it wasn't. It's because they killed their God. Guilt, that's what it was."

Silence. Against the wall, the blonde whispered to the brunette, and the two of them covered their mouths, either in laughter or in shock. The third girl stared at Zilia, as though she could not believe what she had heard.

Dern said, "Zilia, that would be upsetting, if indeed, any such thing occurred. What makes you think it did?"

"Because of the way they acted afterward. I don't believe they grieved over the God. I've been out there. Ninetenths of the people didn't pay any attention to it at all. No, it's something else. I think they killed it."

"How did we do that?" Sam asked in a dangerous voice.

"Starved it, poisoned it, I don't know."

"And who do you think did it? My sister? Maybe my mother?" Sam felt fury flooding upward from some central reservoir, felt himself becoming flushed, every muscle tightening. "Me?"

"I don't know who. You all had reasons."

"What reasons," Sam thundered, infuriated by the holier-than-thou expression on Zilia's face.

"The God got in the way, it took up personnel, it . . ."

"Shit," said Jamice. "Do we have to put up with this utter, damnable nonsense from this silly woman!"

Damn all paranoids, Tandle thought. Oh, somebody treat this damned Native Matters person or get her off our necks.

The lights in the room seemed to pulse. Dern took a deep breath, rather more interested than otherwise. At least the current discussion was something new. "We've had no evidence of any such hostility, Zilia. Indeed, from everything we've ever heard, Settlement One took good care of its God. Right, Sam? I scarcely think that after thirty, almost thirty-five, years they would do any such thing."

He shook his head at Sam, apologetically, sighed in fatherly fashion, and went on, "Suppose you and Horgy and Jamice put your heads together, my boy, and see whether we need to take any action at Settlement One. Horgy and Jamice can fly out there and take a look." Which would get them out of his hair for a few days, at any rate. Horgy had a good head and was reliably discreet. Dern could ask him to check around, see what people were saying about Sam. Though he had to admit, Sam looked fine. That's really why Dern had had him come in, to look him over, see how he behaved around people. Nothing abnormal, so far as Dern could see. A little hostility, but then Zilia could do that to anyone.

"I'll go with them," said Zilia. "I must."

"If you wish," said Dern, annoyed. "All of you go, if you like. Make it a holiday."

"If that's all you wanted me for . . ." murmured Sam, rising to his feet, longing for escape.

Dern nodded, irritated at them all, without exception. "Sorry to have interrupted your work schedule, Sam. Give my best to your family," and then when Sam had gone, "Zilia, that was really quite outrageous, even for you. Horgy, tell your girlies to go study the previous ten years' production schedules. I don't want them at another staff meeting until they know what's going on. Jamice, stop fiddling with those things in your hair. It's annoying. Now, Spiggy, if we've aggravated ourselves sufficiently over the crop shortfall, may we get on to the budget reports? What is this ridiculous set of figures listed under 'Miscellaneous'?"

At lunch, Tandle sat next to Spiggy and tried to keep him from vanishing under his own weight of woe. "What did you mean when you said the last thing anyone would want was a God who worked?" she asked, just to get him talking.

He focused on her with difficulty. "Well, it is," he said. "Early on, of course, it was assumed there were lots of gods who caused various things, and one needed access to them to propitiate them or ask them to undo what some other god had done or, in rarer cases, to say thank you. Since there were lots of them, one always had a god to go to if some other one was acting up. Not a bad state of affairs, really, very much the system Phansure has today.

Of course, it carried the seeds of its own destruction, because some of the priests that rose up around the man-gods got carried away with their own greed or need for power.

"So, some of them became prophets, each of them claiming his particular god—or some new one he'd thought up—was the biggest or the best or the only. Sometimes they said God was all-good or all-powerful or all-something-or-other or even, God knows, all-everything, which inevitably created dualism, because if God was all-everything, why did these contrary things keep happening? This required that man postulate some other force responsible for contrariness, either a sub-god or a bad angel or man himself, just being sinful, and that placed man squarely in the middle of this cosmic battlefield, always being told it was his fault when things went wrong.

"And as long as man was in the middle, nothing could happen but a kind of tug-of-war. Man constantly prayed to God for peace, but peace never happened, so he decided his god must really want war because the other side was sinful. Man invented and extolled virtues which could only be exemplified under conditions of war, like heroism and gallantry and honor, and he gave himself laurel wreaths or booty or medals for such things, thus rewarding himself for behaving well while sinning. He did it when he was a primitive, and he went on with it after he thought he was civilized, and later on just before the Dispersion he was still doing it, making war like crazy, while praying for peace the whole time, of course.

"Most of the monotheisms were tribal, pastoral, retributive religions that committed holocausts and built pyramids of skulls and conducted organized murder for a few thousand years, so there were lots of opportunities for one guy's god to fight some other guy's god. Each tribal religion claimed that its god was the One True God. Every prophet had his own idea about what that meant, of course, and as a result man was always being jerked around between different people's ideas of god, depending on who'd won the most recent war, or palace coup, or political battle.

"This meant mankind was always being asked to accept deities foreign to his own nature. I mean, if your prophet was sexually insecure, or if his later interpreters were, that religion demanded celibacy or repression or even hatred of women; if the prophet was a homophobe, he preached persecution of homosexuals; and if he was both lecherous and greedy, he preached polygyny. If he was luxurious, he preached give-me-money-and-God-will-make-you-rich; if he felt put upon he preached God-of-Vengeance, let's kill the other guy; and no matter how much well-meaning ecumenicists pretended all the gods were onc god under different aspects, they weren't any such thing, because every prophet created God in his own image, to confront his own nightmares."

Tandle was deeply regretting she had ever asked the question, but by this time Spiggy was in full spate and couldn't be stopped.

"For example, during the middle years of the Dispersion, the three largest of the surviving tribal-retribution religions left Manhome, to unite and eventually become Voorstod. Nobody ever accused them of having a god that worked. And so far as I know, nobody has accused any human society of having a god that works!" Spiggy took a mouthful of stewed poultry-bird and dumplings and chewed, sadly, grieving over the state of mankind. "The ones on Phansure are among the best. They don't do anything, but there's always one of them around to blame."

Tandle, who had until now always believed herself to be quite respectful of religion in general, could think of no response to this and moved quickly to another topic of conversation.

· *While Preu Flandry* and his fellow conspirators had agreed to fulfill the desire of the prophets by luring Maire Manone back to Voorstod and possibly back to her husband and house, they had not yet agreed on the best way to accomplish this end. They believed it best not to mention the matter to Phaed Girat, not yet. Phaed might be dedicated to the Cause, but he had a streak of contrariness in him likewise. Better wait until Maire was back before telling old Phaed.

Openly forcing the woman to return would be counterproductive. A forced return would be worse than no return at all. She must seem to return of her own free will, without any Voorstoders along, coming out of longing for her homeland and its people. "Have you heard?" they would ask in the taverns. "Maire Manone has returned to Scaery. She sang there just the other night."

To guarantee her cooperation, they could come up with no better plan than the abduction of one of Maire's children or grandchildren as a hostage against her return and good behavior. They had not, however, decided yet which hostage would work best.

"By now her son Sam's a grown man," said Mugal Pye in a judicious tone. "He'd be forty lifeyears if he's a day. If he takes after Phaed, he could be hard to handle." He sipped his ale and waited for comment. "Also, maybe he and his mam don't get on all that well."

"Maire's daughter Sal's younger by some," said Epheron Floom. "She's what? Five years younger?" Epheron had lately become active in the Cause after some years spent out in the fatlands among the Ahabarians as a reporter for the Voorstod news, which was to say, as a spy for the prophets. He was youngish yet, smooth-faced, plump, and quiet looking, with dead-calm eyes and a naturally cruel nature.

"Maire's kept in touch with her mother's sister here," said Mugal Pye. "She's sent messages from time to time. She's mentioned that Sal has young kiddies. Two or three."

"Young ones and their mams are a problem," Epheron opined. "Separate them, and you have trouble with them. Babies need a woman to keep them in good condition. That means we'd need to bring Sal as well, or come up with some woman here to keep the kids, and every extra mouth is a mouth that might talk. Besides, if anything happened to one of 'em, the word might get around. Dead babies aren't what'll bring the women back."

"We know Sam has a son," said Preu Flandry. Preu was the oldest of them, his white hair and slightly lame right leg speaking of long years at risk. "A boy called Jep. Maire mentioned him thirteen or fourteen years ago, in messages to her aunt. There's been no mention since, but likely she would have said something if he'd died. Likely if you brought him, Maire would behave herself."

"The boy'd be old enough to get along without his mam, but still young enough to be manageable," agreed Mugal Pye.

They went on arguing, with this one opting for Sam, and that one for Sal, and then changing their minds and settling on one or more of the children.

"Whoever we take, we can keep them at Elsperh's farm above Sarby," said Mugal. "It's well hidden in the hills; even if Ahabar sent troopers in from the sea, they wouldn't look for a hostage there. And Maire never knew Elsperh, so she'll have no thought where her offspring might be."

They thought about this for a time, exchanging specifics. How old was each of the children? Their plan might involve some mutilations before they were done, were the children strong enough to survive such treatment for however long it took?

"Whoever we take, he or she or they'll have to be carried or forced off Hobbs Land, either by subterfuge or by threat of harm," said Mugal Pye. "Which means we'll need a party of at least three or four to handle the matter. Why don't we wait until we get there to decide who we take? There's nothing like seeing the ground before we decide on tactics."

"Who will it be going from here, then? Who goes?"

"There's you two, and me," said Epheron, "and I think some relative of Maire's, just to make our inquiries seem natural."

"We'll find someone, no fear," said Preu. "Someone Maire knew, or at least knew of."

"Not Phaed?"

"No, I think not."

They drank to the project, and laughed about it, and so set in motion the chain of events that would end with the taking, and possible killing, of someone's child far from love and home and hope.

Or perhaps they started the sequence that would only begin there.

· *Shallow under the* soil, near the temple at Settlement One, straight fibers ramified into feathers and the feathers into lace, which reached beneath the houses and the storage yards, beneath the settlement buildings, beneath the old temples, out toward open country in a tenuous, cottony web which enclosed in its fibrous reticulation all the land from the temples north of the community to the fields in the south. Under roads and paths, where people walked and machines rolled, the web grew thick, almost feltlike, able to absorb the repeated pressure of men and their tools. Under the fields, it spread itself in random polygons, leaving and finding itself, again and again.

As it spread, it encountered the gullies and channels of former, similar networks. Tiny canals led through clayey soil. Grooves had been cut along subterranean strata. The rock-hard roots of stone-oaks had been bored through long ago by a million thread-thin fingers. The evidence was everywhere that other webs had gone this way before, but the new net did not care. It took the easy way, the path of least resistance, the way of former times. The net that had run in these channels before had been old and weak, barely able to hold itself and its environment together. Finally, it had died. The smell of that death still clung, the fragments of that dissolution were still present. Some places, recent places where the ancient and moribund net of Bondru Dharm had run, stank of it. The Birribat net was new and strong and full of questing. It did not pause to consider the past.

Upon the hill, where the burying ground had been established by the earliest settlers, the web sent out curious wormlike extrusions to snout along old bones, to twist through dried skulls, to find a few rags and tatters, a few shreds of organic material. Nothing recent. Nothing of interest. Nothing usable.

Under the temple where the children had labored, beneath the flat-topped pillar where a God had sat one time long past, the net sent fibers upward through hair-thin channels in the stone. Near the top they stopped, the end of each fiber sealing itself off into an oval button, hard as tooth and tiny as a grass seed.

And in the thick, mattressy felt where Birribat had once lain, the hard, strange nucleus continued to grow, laid down molecule by molecule, aggregated as stalactites are aggregated, patient as time itself. At the center of the mass something was taking shape, growing faster the larger it got.

· *Maire Girat and* Saturday Wilm went out into the countryside so that Saturday could practice vocalizing. Usually Saturday sang in the recreation hall, but Maire had told her that nothing contributed more to humility in a vocalist than to sing in the empty out-of-doors, where one's voice went away into nothing at all, like a little wind blowing at elsewhere.

When they had spent their usual time at it, she and Maire sat on the bank of the nameless little stream that flowed across the high ground west of Settlement One.

"You're looking happy," said Saturday. Maire Girat usually had an air of grief about her, not an ostentatious thing, just an aura, like that of a woman who had suffered a loss she could not forget. Lately, though, she had seemed more content.

"Do I now?" she asked. "Well, I guess so, Saturday. Recently the days have seemed more comfortable, as though something had changed, though there's nothing changed I can see."

"I think it's everybody," said Saturday. "I heard my own mam singing this morning, and she hasn't done that in a while."

"I believe you're right. Sam was chipper as a sparrow when I saw him earlier today. And three people said good morning who haven't done anything but growl recently. Even the babies in the crèche have been better tempered. As for me, yesterday I made a small song about a ferf. I didn't sing it, mind you, but I thought it up."

"Teach it me," demanded Saturday.

Maire taught it to her, all three verses, croaking out

the melody, and they two laughed over the troubles the ferf had getting his grain home to his children.

"It must be *her* children," instructed Saturday. "A mother ferf. Either that or an uncle ferf."

Maire nodded, shamefaced. "I forget, sometimes, that we are not in Voorstod where it is fathers, not uncles, who are expected to bring bread. Not that they often do. Anyhow, I made it up for the children in the crèche. Sam's assigned me to work there. He says I'm too old for fieldwork."

"Perhaps he just knew you'd be good for the babies," said Saturday, thinking, meantime, that it was the babies who were good for Maire. "To give them some of the love you could not give your own little one who died."

"That's true," said Maire, looking at Saturday with clear eyes.

"How did he die, Maire?"

The older woman knotted her hands and twisted them together, a gesture she often made when she was thinking or remembering. "There was a representative of the Queen come to talk to the Phyel, which is a kind of parliament we have in Voorstod. And he was given safe conduct by the Phyel, but not by the Faithful of the Cause, which I found out later was an agreement between the two, so the Phyel could lay the blame on the Cause later and the Cause could take credit for the kill. So, the men of the Cause laid an ambush. They didn't tell me, nor any of the women, and our children were playing in the street, where it was dry, for we didn't know anything special was to happen. But when the attack started, the vehicle the man was in came our way, down our little street, and Maechy was there in the street with Sal, playing, and then there was noise and flame and my baby lying quiet, bloody, with tiny red holes in the side of his head, only the dear child lying there and me weeping."

She took a deep breath and stared at the sky where one small linear cloud chased another toward the escarpment away in the north. "And when Phaed came in, full of sour words—for the Queen's man had got away—I showed him his son lying on the bed, white and still, and he said it was bad aim had done it, for if the man had shot straight it wouldn't have happened. But that it was really the man from Ahabar's fault, for being in Voorstod at all."

"What did you do?"

"I wrote my last song that night, the one I told you of. And I sang it, here and there. And I talked to Phaed and asked him to leave Voorstod with me. I'd sworn an oath, and that was the least I could do. He laughed at me and told me I'd never leave him. He pinched me on my bottom and told me to behave, to go sing my songs and get paid in good coin, for he needed everything I could earn. I tried to sing, but a day came my throat closed up. I could hardly breathe. I had to go then, or die from lack of air. I packed up our things, Sam's and Sal's and mine, and we started walking down the back roads from Scaery, where we'd moved to from Cloud, since my Dad had died and left the house to Phaed. We walked nights and hid days, going south through the rocky fields of Wander and Skelp into Green Hurrah, where the gentle forests are, and then across the border into Jeramish, with all the little farms spread like toys on the meadows. And then, after that, we came to the city of Fenice and the Door and here, girl."

Saturday, looking into Maire's eyes, felt Maire's grief as though it had happened to Saturday herself. She thought of Jep, and how she would feel if Jep were killed. Or Friday, her own brother. Or any of the people of Settlement One. She laid her hands upon Maire's callused ones where they were knotted together in Maire's lap, wet with the tears that dripped from her eyes unheeded.

"No more, Maire," she said. "It will not happen anymore." It was only a comforting phrase, not a promise. She had no way of making it a promise, and yet it was as a promise that Maire heard it, or perhaps felt it, not for this land alone but for all those she had left behind in Voorstod as well.

FOUR

· *In Settlement Three,* hostilities between production teams had kept Topman Harribon Kruss occupied for a good part of the afternoon. Someone on Team Two had said something derogatory to someone on Team Four. No, not someone. Jamel Soames had said it. Jamel Soames, backed up by the five other Soames brothers. Then Team Four had retaliated with fists and a few hand tools. Team Two had been working with an irrigation pump, so they had escalated the battle with a quickly devised water cannon. One field had been completely soaked and trampled and would have to be dried out and replanted. Another one had been almost ready for a leaf-crop harvest which was now futile. One settler had a broken jaw; there were other broken bones, as well as assorted abrasions, strains, and cuts.

Topman Harribon Kruss heard carping (which the carpers called testimony), assigned fault, and assessed fines. Jamel's allegation that had started the ruckus had concerned Team Four's alleged snobbishness in "thinking it was Settlement One, better than anybody else," or words to that effect. Settlement One had definitely been mentioned, and it wasn't the first time this week that Harribon had heard those words under stressful circumstances. "Settlement One and its crazy Topman." Jamel Soames was fond of that phrase.

By the time Harribon was finished with the last of the combatants, Jamel himself, with whom he had had some angry words—final ones as it turned out—he was late for his visit with his mother at the skilled care center. When he entered her room, Elitia Kruss turned worried eyes from her bed.

"You're late, Harri." In her wasted face her eyes were huge but completely alert. She was having one of her increasingly rare good days. "What kept you?"

"Big fight, Momma. People throwing punches, throwing rocks, firing high-pressure water at one another. Lucky nobody got killed." He sat down beside her and fanned himself with one flapping hand, indicating how hot things had been. "I finally told Jamel Soames to get out, leave. Leave the settlement, go somewhere else. He'll probably take all five of the brothers with him, and maybe Dracun, too, but good riddance." He shook his head, thinking of the relative inconvenience of keeping the Soameses versus recruiting replacements. Recruiting was no fun either.

"Dracun Soames will be furious," she said, referring to Harribon's assistant, sister to the belligerent brothers.

"She'll have to be furious. It's in my authority, Momma, and I've had enough."

She shook her head sadly. "Such children," she said. "Grown-up people acting like such children. And now you're so late. You'll miss your dinner at the brotherhouse. Slagney said he was cooking this week. You should run on while it's still hot."

"Nonsense!" he growled. "I'm going to have my visit with you. I can always heat my dinner up if it's cold when I get there, but Slagney will probably keep it warm for me."

He sat down comfortably, making himself obviously ready for a protracted stay. Elitia Kruss was dying. She knew it and the family knew it. If her condition had been curable, the techs would have kept her in the medical facility at CM. She wasn't curable, so they'd sent her home to die in the skilled care center of her own settlement, a center staffed only as needed by people who worked in the fields when there were no sick or dying to care for, but who had been trained to provide expert supportive care. Harribon reflected that no matter how much humankind learned about disease and hurt bodies, there was always something new coming along they didn't know how to cure. They could grow hands and feet and even whole arms or legs. They could take out organs and put in new, cloned ones. They could inject rectified DNA into a person and change all his cells. But this thing, a strange, rare kind of half-cancer half-fungus, nothing worked on at all. Less than a hundred cases, Systemwide, and one of them had to be Momma. They didn't even know how it was transmitted, or if it was transmitted, or whether it might be some genetic thing they hadn't figured out yet. They called it the ghost disease, because they couldn't find it. The gene manipulations that had cured a thousand other diseases did no good in this case. Fifty generations of science, and people still died before their allotted five score lifeyears.

They talked for quite a while, she continuing alert, and he being unwilling to waste a moment of it. When she fell asleep suddenly, in the middle of a sentence, he left her and went home to the brotherhouse, where his younger brother Slagney hadn't waited the meal for him, though he had left a plate of food to stay warm in the cooker. Harribon sat late over this no longer very succulent supper and, in order not to think about Momma, considered the problem of envy.

Settlement One, long a thorn in the side of all other settlements on Hobb's Land, had begun to fester. Now even the children were talking. The defeated teams returning from the last game with Settlement One had been rife with rivalry, rumor, and rebellion. Settlement One didn't play fair, so ran the tale. Settlement One ought to be excluded from the games. Dracun Soames had brought this version straight from the lips of her son, Vernor. More worryingly, it had been accompanied by threats from Jamel and Vernor's other uncles. They would, by damn, see fair play, they said, seeing no irony in this claim despite the fact that they themselves were well-known to strike the unwary and the unprepared without warning and from behind when they thought they could get away with it. Fair play was not what they had in mind. Settlement Three had had two homicides since the Soameses had been settlers, people bashed from behind, people Jamel had had words with. Harribon had always been sure it was Jamel, though he had been unable to prove it.

Early in the day, before the fight had started, Harribon had directed his home stage to print compilations of inter-settlement sports standings from the Archives, though he hadn't had a chance to look at them until now. He ran a horny thumb down the standings, adding mentally. Settlement One had won about half their games. Seldom by much. They had lost about half. Seldom by much. They had stayed consistently in the middle most years. Twice in thirty-two years they had won the series. Three times in thirty-two years they had come in second. As they might have done by chance, all else being equal. Of course, all else was never equal, so the one-in-eleven win was, in it-self, interesting.

More interesting was the fact they had never been at the bottom of the list. Never. Neither had Four. Not in the thirty-two years the games had been played. So, to that extent, people were right. Though Settlement One didn't win top place any oftener than they should, they did not lose as often as some.

Harribon stared at the wall, wondering what that meant. If it meant anything. Someone settling onto a chair across from him broke his concentration.

"Dracun," he murmured to the woman who was perched there like some great flying lizard, ready to dart off at any moment. She had come in without knocking. Her narrow face was drawn into harsh lines.

"What's this about Jamel?"

"I told him to leave, Dracun."

"I'll go with him. We'll all go." It was a threat.

He sighed. "I knew you might when I told him to go, Dracun. I guess that should tell you something."

She flushed. "He's that bad, huh?"

"He's that bad. It's gone past what we can tolerate. Now you and your other brothers are welcome to stay, if you like. Without Jamel stirring things up, the other Soameses are only a little more belligerent than ordinary people." He was trying to make a joke of it.

She chose to change the subject. "You said you were going to check about what Vernor said today. About Settlement One cheating. I suppose you're going to tell me the fight put it out of your mind."

"I did check," he snapped, annoyed by her tone. "I had the listings printed here, so I'd have time to look at them. And if anything could have put it out of my mind, Dracun, it was the fact my momma is dying, which is happening only once. Thanks to your brothers, fights we have every day. Almost."

She had the grace to look ashamed, but it didn't prevent her asking, "Well?"

He tossed the compilation to her, pointed out the figures that were pertinent, waited while she read them for herself.

Her glare turned into a frown. "Are these accurate?"

He furrowed his low brow into three distinct horizontal convexities, pulled his stocky form out of the chair, and stalked to the window to stand staring out at his settlement. "That's the way Archives gave it to me."

"What about the production figures."

"Well, yes. They've been consistently on top in production and at the bottom in disruptions. Considering how much time you and I spent today, sorting out who said what and who did what and who broke who's arm, I think the two are intimately related."

"That's possible," she admitted.

"Dracun, your son was wrong, but that doesn't mean there isn't something to . . . well, to the impression he had. Why would Settlement One have no conflict?" He rubbed his face, feeling the scratch of his beard on his fingertips. "It isn't natural, is it? I don't know quite how to put that question to the Archives."

She thought, rising to stalk about the room, settling again to say, "Religion, maybe? I mean, it can't be genetics, can it? There's been movement of population. Kids have grown up and moved from one settlement to another. People have moved up to management. People have given up their land credits and moved away. Other people have applied for vacant places, some Belt worlders, some System people. Haven't they?"

Harribon paused for some time before he answered. "That's all true, here, in Settlement Three."

"And there? In Settlement One? Have they had people coming and going, too?"

"I don't know. I didn't think to ask."

"Will you find out soon?"

"Yes. I'll find out soon. And, Dracun? Let me know if the whole Soames family is going to go with Jamel."

She shook her head. "No. We won't. You're right. He's too much, even for us. Better he go somewhere else. Celphius, maybe. Become a prospector."

He smiled, relieved. So. He offered her a sop. "Maybe I should plan to take a trip over to Settlement One sometime soon, just to find out what's really going on. I'll message the Topman and tell him I'm coming."

• *"They're coming here,"* said Sam, annoyance in his voice and his stance. "Here. To question me."

"Why?" asked Theseus. "What have you done?"

"Nothing!" Sam cried. "Everything! Production is down. Not much, not overall, but it's down. Or, we're a curiosity. So they're coming here!"

"Who? Can we fight them? Challenge them? Set an ambush?"

Sam shook his head, half-laughing. "No, no. It's not an invasion. They're harmless. Just people. Like the courtiers in your father's court."

"Who plotted," said Theseus loftily. "Always!"

"Well, these plot too, but they don't go about killing people." Sam shook his head, amused once more.

"Who are they?"

"Horgy, Jamice, Spiggy. A crazy woman named Zilia Makepeace. Harribon Kruss, the Topman from Settlement Three, but he's coming later on. It's no problem,

really, just an annoyance. We'll show them around, they'll
ask a few questions, they'll go back home."

"They don't need to come," said Theseus. "Whatever
happened was only temporary. Everything will be as it
was. Better than it was."

"Settlement One will be first again?" asked Sam,
doubtfully.

"How can you doubt it? With you in command?"

Comforting words, which Sam wasn't sure he understood. How would Theseus know about farm quotas?
Hardly his kind of thing.

As though aware of this scepticism, the hero whispered, "Have I told you about the monster? Of course I
haven't. I've been saving it!"

"What monster, where?"

"Just a little west of here. In a cave. It hasn't been
there long. I found it. You don't have your sword yet, so
you'll have to kill it with your bare hands, but you can,
Sam. I know you can." The hero moved toward the west,
beckoning.

"Tomorrow," Sam suggested, feeling a bit weary.

"Now," whispered the hero. "Tonight!"

At the western edge of the fields, Theseus left him, just
beyond the dorge crop, tall rustling stalks bearing globu-
lar clusters of almost ripe grain heads, the rows alive with
hunting cats. Sam carried a glow-bug lantern, and everywhere he turned he saw twin disks of cold fire, cat eyes,
reflecting his own light back at him.

"Out there," Theseus said, pointing westward.
"There." Then he turned on his heel and vanished among
the dorge, glowing through the leaves, though none of the
cats turned their heads to follow him with their eyes.

Sam looked westward, in the direction Theseus had
pointed. Nothing was out there except undulating plains
covered with sparse growth, dotted with short curlicue
trees, runneled with streams so insignificant they did not
even gurgle as they ran. Here and there water sneaked
along the ground, over clean pebbles, silent as a snake.
Nothing was out there but dullness and more dullness.
Sam thought of refusing to go, then reconsidered. The
walk wouldn't hurt him.

His feet found water, first, and then a flattened trail beside the water, one easy for the feet to keep to. Something walked here, something cropped the scanty grasses, keeping the trail low and flat. Pocket squirrels, maybe, coming to drink. Legions of ferfs, marching by companies and battalions. Maybe an upland omnivore or two, fallen off the heights to be bored to death by the plains. There wasn't anything larger native to the place.

The sound stopped him, one foot just lifting, so that he stood heronlike, poised, unable to move. A howl. A strangled paean of fury or hunger or . . . A guttural sound, a coughing roar. What?

Westward, whatever it was. Where silence was now, not even echoes to tell him he had really heard it.

Sam ran his hands over himself, taking inventory. Sword belt, helmet, work clothes, lantern. Tools on his belt: spy-light, knife, memo-rizer, trouble-link. His hands lingered on the link. If he triggered it, Africa and Jebedo Quillow would be alerted to his location. Both of them would arrive within minutes.

Not yet. He took off the sword belt and helmet, placing them carefully beside the trail. The memo-rizer went in the helmet, along with the spy-light. It wasn't good for anything except disclosing the innards of machinery. Knife he would keep. Trouble-link he would keep. Lantern he would keep, though, just now, he would turn it off.

When his eyes had adjusted to the starlit surfaces around him, the faint glimmer of water, the barely discernable trail, he went westward once more. Up a tiny slope and down a tiny slope, the streamlet cutting through, between dwarf banks, edged with white flowers. The scent rose from them, dizzying. He had never seen them before.

At the foot of the slope, the stream dropped, suddenly and shockingly, over a bank. The sound of falling water alerted him before he stepped off into air, and he lit the lantern to find the source of the sound. It lay beneath him, the height of two tall men, a pool at the head of a . . . a canyon?

Hobbs Land had no canyons, Sam told himself, quite

seriously. Therefore, he was dreaming, sleep walking, or in some other place.

The sound came again, closer. A coughing roar. A growl of fury. He turned off the light and scrambled over the edge of the bank, dropping onto a soggy patch beside the pool. More of the white flowers bloomed beside the pool, filling the canyon with their sweet smell, spicy, faintly resinous. A trail led along the stream, a larger stream than the one above, augmented from some source, some spring or underground brook which had joined it at the pool. The canyon grew deeper and wider as he walked. The little stream became a small river. There were holes, large and small, in the canyon walls, the smaller ones full of the flutter of wings. Trees rustled along the banks. Large stones stood blackly in the water, making it purl and chuckle as it roiled around them, starshine gleaming on the curved ripples.

The thing attacked him from behind. Sam fell forward, dropping the lantern, feeling teeth at the back of his neck, rolling frantically to get out from under it. It stank. It held on with clawed feet, clawed hands. Sam rolled into the water, and the thing broke from him, choking, then roaring, ready to attack again.

Sam had the knife in his hand. He didn't remember getting it there, but it was there, open, sharp, something better than teeth, though not much. It was only a tool, something to cut vegetables with, in the fields, something to cut fruit from a tree or bush. Not a weapon, not intended as a weapon.

He felt claws rake his arms, smelled the breath of the thing, hot and stinking. He struck out with the knife and was rewarded with a howl, not so much of pain as of surprise. He leapt forward, knife out, slashing it, trying to wound. The knife encountered something hard, bone perhaps, and the howls increased in fury.

The thing came at him again, brushing his knife hand aside. Sam ducked, getting under the clutching arms, feeling the heavy body go by him. He whirled, grabbed, touched the head, lunged forward to get his arm around the creature's thick, muscle wrapped neck.

He was whipped from side to side, knocked against the

stones. His knife flew away, somewhere; he thought he heard a splash. He had his hands locked, arm around the throat of the thing, pressed tight as he hung on. Warm, metal-smelling blood ran over his chest. His own? The thing's? He couldn't tell.

Time crawled. He was dizzy and weak. He held on as long as he could and then let go. The thing went away from him, or fell, perhaps. He couldn't tell. After a time, he struggled to his feet and staggered back the way he had come. When he came to the pool, the high bank defeated him. He couldn't climb it. A star shining through a notch showed him the way to get out, a rocky defile, like a flight of monster stairs. He was barely able to climb them.

· *Sal just happened* to be up around dawn—little Sahke had had a stomach ache, which had kept her restless through the night—when Sam came home. She saw him in the street, covered with blood, as though he had been run through a harvester. She screamed and ran to him.

"All right, all right," he said, pushing her hands away.

"But Sam, you're cut, you're bleeding, you're . . . come inside, let me wash . . . call the medical techs . . ." And all the time he was pushing her hands away.

She got him into the kitchen of the brotherhouse and went at him with a wet towel, finding to her astonishment that it wasn't all his blood he was covered in. Oh, there were one or two cuts and tears, nothing too serious, as though something had sliced at him with a knife, or fangs. One tear on his arm might need closing up, but most of the thick, horrid blood wasn't Sam's. It didn't even smell like human blood.

She took his helmet and sword belt and put them away. No need for the med-tech to see those.

"What . . . how?" she cried into his peaceful face. "What did you . . ."

"Something out there in the dark," he said at last. "I was walking, and it attacked me."

"But what was it, Sam?"

He sighed, blinking at her sleepily. "It had teeth and claws and bad-smelling breath. It came at me from behind. It was dark. I'm pretty sure I killed it. At least I hurt it, I know that."

"Why didn't you use the link, Sam?" She slapped it with her hand, angry at him. "Why didn't you use the link?"

He only blinked at her, not answering as she used it, summoning Africa and Jebedo Quillow, who went to get the Tharby men up. The settlement had no sniffers or dogs or anything like them, but Jebedo Quillow was a good tracker. Meantime the med-tech had arrived and was busy sealing up the long tears on Sam's arm with ooag and body glue.

Jebedo and his group returned midmorning, saying they'd found where the attack took place right enough, blood all over everything and the bones of something biggish, the size of a big man. But the birds and ferfs and pocket squirrels had been at it, and nothing was left but the bones, and they didn't look mannish, somehow. Not quite.

"Where?" she asked.

"Out in that strange canyon with the little river and the caves," they told her.

"What little river? *What* strange canyon with the caves?" she demanded, never having heard of any such thing.

"That one," said Jebedo Quillow, "that funny little old one that's out there."

Sam slept peacefully, a slight, wondering smile on his lips.

· *Saturday Wilm wanted* her cousin Jep to go fishing with her. Jep was as determined to spend the off-day playing scissor hockey with the first level team as a possible substitute player.

"They won't take you until you're fifteen, Jep," she told him. "No matter how good you are."

"They haven't seen how good I am, yet," her cousin

announced. "I'm really very good. I'm better than Willum R."

"You could be the best they've ever seen, but they still won't let you on the team until you're fifteen."

"Who told you that?"

"Mam. It's a Settlement Rule."

"A big rule, or a little one?" Big rules had to be changed by CM; little rules could be changed by the Topman or by settlement vote.

"It's a big rule. It's part of the child labor prohibitions."

"Playing scissor hockey isn't labor!" he objected hotly, his voice squeaking in disbelief.

"It is if you play a lot of games against bigger people and your bones aren't grown yet. That's what Mam said."

"Crap," said Jep. "Why didn't they tell me that when they said I could come around and play?"

"Because you've been pestering them for ages, and they figure if they let you play with them once and get knocked around a little, maybe you'll get some sense and quit bothering them."

"Why didn't they just tell me about the rule, for shish sake. I'm not about to waste time with them if there's no chance they'll let me play."

"Well, there's no chance until you're fifteen, I'm telling you. And if you don't believe me, you can go ask Africa."

"I believe you," he mumbled furiously, angry mostly at himself for not checking. His own mam would have told him if he'd asked. And he wouldn't soon forgive the coach who hadn't told him, either. Just wait until next year when they asked him to be on the team and he told them no. He'd switch to Settlement Four, that's what he'd do. "What do you want to fish for."

"Creelies. Mam said she's been hungry for creely legs for ages."

"That means climbing all the way up to the Gobbles."

"Doesn't take any more energy to climb the Gobbles than it does to play scissor hockey all afternoon," she told him sarcastically.

"Maybe that monster that got Sam is up there. Have you thought about that?"

"Sam killed it, Jep. And everybody's looked everywhere for more of them, and there aren't any. If anybody thought there were more of them, we'd be confined to settlement, and nobody's said one word about that."

Jep scowled at her, conceding the point. "Have you got bait?"

"I've got half a poultry-bird, cut up in pieces, then left out for a couple of days."

Jep made another face and went to get his jacket, thinking about creelies. In the Archives, creelies were listed somewhere between octopuslike and lobsterlike animals, in that they had both tentacles and a jointed exoskeleton—which they sometimes left to wander around in the nude—but they were fishlike, too, for they had fins and scales and almost an endoskeleton as well. The finned, scaled, tentacled critter moved around under the banks of mountain streams, sometimes in its hinged, legged shell, and sometimes, sans shell and sans legs, it just swam off naked while the legs and shell stayed under the bank. A neuropad at the top of each leg matched up to a neuropad on the body, and when the animal entered its exoskeleton, it simply reestablished neural contact. The legs had a separate heart-lung system as well, to protect them during long separations. There was some controversy among the biologists as to whether the creelie was actually one animal or two, acting in symbiosis.

Whether one or two, the object in creely fishing was to attract the creature, naked or housed, to a blob of half rotted meat. If the creely was in its shell, one pulled it out of the shell and dropped the tentacled creature back into the stream while retaining the shell and legs. If one caught it nude, one tied a thread to it and let it flee back to its legs, then pulled it out and stole the legs. A nude creely was inedible, but the detached legs were delicious. Those arguing that there were two animals involved used this fact to telling effect. Those arguing for one animal pointed out that the nude creely soon grew new legs and a new shell. Those not bothering to argue ate the steamed legs with butter and a touch of sour juice from the thick leaves of the cit tree, amid much gourmandish delight.

Bringing the spice of danger to the sport of creely fishing was the possibility of fishing up a creelylike creature that, when separated from its legs, sprayed an unpleasant and foul-smelling irritant in all directions. This creature, differing from the creely only in insignificant details of tentacle arrangement, was called a bomber. Both Jep and Saturday had been sprayed, more than once, but not for several years.

"What you'll do today is catch a bomber," Jep announced as they went toward the mushroom house to fetch the half-rotted poultry-bird. "Only, you won't get it all over you. You'll get it all over me."

"I haven't done that since we were ten," Saturday protested. "And I didn't do it purposely." She opened the door to the mushroom house and took a lantern from the rack by the door.

"You got it all over Willum R., too."

"He forgot about it. He doesn't keep reminding me all the time the way you do. Willum R. is a true friend," she said loftily.

"I only remind you to focus your mind, Saturday Wilm. That's what you need, focus." He followed her down the aisle, stepping in the puddle of light she allowed him from her lantern.

"I don't need any more focus than you do," she said, throwing a fresh-picked mushroom at him, which bounced harmlessly off his head and rolled away down the stone-floored aisle between the beds. "Your mom tells my mom all the time that you're a scatterhead."

"Who's a scatterhead?" He leapt at her in a low tackle, knocking her down and sitting on her. "Now, who?"

"You."

"Not me."

"Let me up, you loader-bottom. You weigh a ton."

"One kiss, that's the price."

"Oh shit, Jep."

"One."

"I'm not old enough for kissing."

"That depends who wants one."

"Just one."

He took his toll chastely, not trying for any ardent effects. He liked kissing Saturday and didn't want her offended at him. He liked hugging her even better, because she was soft and sort of supple in ways he wasn't. He tried a hug when he'd finished with the kiss, then let her up.

"If my mom knew you were all the time kissing me, Jep Wilm, she'd baby-proof me so fast . . ."

"Kissing!" he cried, red-faced. "That's all."

"Well, just don't get any ideas."

He glared at her. "Saturday Wilm, I've had that idea about you ever since I was about nine, but I'm not going to do anything about it yet." He helped her up. "And when I do, we'll both know about it in advance, believe me."

She flushed, not willing to tell him she'd had the same idea. She had gone so far as to consult the Archives from the information stage at the school, to determine whether there was any genetic problem with the Wilm family, and to consult her own birth records to determine whether, by any chance, she and Jep had the same progenitor. They didn't. Jep was Sam Girat's get, which everyone more or less knew, but she was the get of the man from CM named Spiggy Fettle.

Spiggy was very, very smart, Africa had said, despite being a rather ugly man. "Which is no handicap as I have enough beauty for both of us," she had announced, wrinkling her nose at her daughter. "I know that for a fact because you turned out fine." Spiggy was also a manic-depressive, but Africa had checked to be sure Saturday was okay before she continued the pregnancy. Fixing MD was no harder than fixing other developmental errors. The doctor just fiddled with the DNA and injected it into the growing fetus. What Saturday couldn't understand is why Spiggy got born without that being done, though Africa said it was something religious.

She turned left at the next corner, tripping over something and almost sending herself sprawling, catching herself on the side of a planting bed. In the lantern light she could see one of the heavy floor slabs heaved up a hand's breadth.

"What in hell did that?" murmured Jep.

They peered beneath the stone, seeing a pallid fungus piled beneath the stone, shoving up. "I didn't know they could do that! A little thing like that!" Saturday exclaimed. "When it dies, will the stone fall back down?"

"Maybe it'll just keep growing," suggested Jep. "Maybe it'll push the stone through the roof." He stepped over the raised stone and asked, "Why'd you leave the creely bait in here?"

"Because nobody would smell it in here," she replied. "The whole house smells sort of decayed." She found the sack, picked it up, and led the way back to the door.

Both of them sighed with relief when they reached the open air. The mushroom house was entirely too wet and cavelike. They galloped out of the settlement, keeping up the pace until they were well on the trail to the Gobbles.

Saturday had returned to her thoughts about Spiggy Fettle. She didn't mind being smart as he was, but she didn't want to look like him.

"Do you think I'm pretty?" she asked Jep.

Jep turned to examine her brown face, the curly black hair that surrounded it, her dark glowing eyes, the imperious beak of her straight, delicate nose, her olive-rose mouth, which was usually open, usually full of words. "Sats, I think you're beautiful. How about me? Am I pretty?" He grinned at her.

Jep always reminded her of one of the little settlement tractors, square and tough and unstoppable. His eyes were pebble-colored, like rocks seen in shallow water, but his eyelashes were long and thick and brown, and there was nothing stony about the neat, full curve of his lower lip. He looked quite a lot like Sam, and Sam was a very handsome man.

Satisfied both with his response and with the way he looked, she gave him a kiss. Jep was surprised, but not displeased, and he returned the kiss. The result astonished them both. They drew apart, unable to catch their breaths, and took up their climb again.

The way to the Gobbles was not interesting. It was a

steady ascent among uniformly blobby bushes, which had neither a particular scent nor any discernable blossom or fruit. The path was littered with round, ankle-breaker rocks, too, and the smart climber kept his eyes on his feet. It was the dullness of the trip which made the climb laborious, rather than the physical effort required. Therefore, when Jep looked up from the path to find himself confronted with an enormous tree in a place where no such tree had ever been, he was startled into absolute immobility.

Saturday ran into his back with a whoof.

"Clummox," she growled, before looking up, and then, "Ohowee, oh my. Where did that come from?"

"Them," said Jep. "There's about a hundred of them, plus little ones."

She looked beyond the first huge trunk to see others standing at either side of the path and down the slopes, with smaller feathery growths beneath them, unmistakably young ones of the same type.

"They've never been here before," she said unnecessarily. "Unless we're lost."

He nodded. There hadn't been trees before. And they weren't lost. The trail led to the foot of the tree and resumed at the other side of the trunk.

"Do you suppose it's like the mushroom house, where everything sort of grows overnight?" she asked. "Like that thing that was pushing up the floor stone?"

Jep had his head back and was trying to estimate the height of the tree he had almost run into. He thought it looked about the same as the width of a scissor hockey court, which would make it about a hundred feet. It was almost as wide as it was tall, great branches spreading to every side, each one supported from below with stout growths which curved down and back into the main trunk. Some of the larger branches had several supports, some only partway grown, half-curved down toward the trunk.

"Overnight?" he asked, incredulously. "It had to take longer than that. When was the last time we came up here?"

Saturday thought about that. "It's been a long time,

but Willum R. went creely fishing about ten days ago, and this is the only way to come. If he'd seen these trees, he'd have said something. We can tell your mom. She'll come look at them, and she can tell us what they are."

Jep, swallowing deeply, went around the tree and proceeded on his way. If Willum R. hadn't seen these when he came up ten days ago . . . Well then, it was very strange, that's all.

As the day went on, they came back to the subject of trees, more disturbed than either of them let on, but worrying away at it as they tried to reach a solution. Though they picked at the subject of the trees, they avoided the matter of the kiss and were careful not to get too close to one another, not knowing what would happen. Anything that happened might be more than they could handle. The world they knew was tenuously balanced on nothing much, teetering upon oddities. Until they returned at evening, tiptoeing through the new forest, which loomed even more strangely in the shadowy light, they kept everything very ordinary.

Then, at Saturday's door, Jep tried the kiss again, just to see if whatever had happened would happen again. Whatever it had been was still there and kept being there, each time they did it, and they did it quite a lot, hugging one another in pleased wonder and undisguised anticipation.

When Saturday came into the sisterhouse, Africa saw the slightly swollen lips and glowing eyes and turned away to hide a mixture of peevishness and chagrin, self-awareness and parental anxiety. She herself had been kissed—really kissed—first when she was what? Thirteen? About Saturday's age. It had happened in one corner of the equipment yard, behind a big loader. Africa could still remember the smell of the lubricating grease, the hard bite of the steel edge as she had been pressed against it. Who had it been? Not anyone currently in the settlement. His name trembled in her mind, ready to announce itself. Someone who had gone away.

"How'd the creely fishing go?" she demanded. "Let's see what you've got."

Saturday dumped the sack on the kitchen table, laughing at the pile of wriggling legs, joyous about life in general.

Africa watched her daughter as she might watch a sprouting field, half apprehensive, half gloating. Things lay in wait for the ripening grain, danger was in store, but there was also the hope of harvest. A name swam into memory. Osmer. Gard Osmer. He had tasted of salt and apple-eating boy and smelled like the grass. He had kissed her and said sweet, fumbling things, his eyes alight. They had gone for walks together, holding hands. His family hadn't really been happy on Hobbs Land. No, she dug into memory. It had been Gard's father that hadn't been happy. He had insisted upon their giving up their accumulated land credits and moving to Pedaria. Africa had been fourteen. She had cried on and off for months. It was Spiggy who had rousted her out of her pain, Spiggy who was at the holiday camp the same time Africa was. He told her to have a baby and study leadership. He started her on her career. He was only a few years older than she, but he knew things she didn't. "Apple-sweet," Spiggy had called her childhood romance. "Apple days," he said. Apple days with Gard. And apple days with Spiggy, too. Five children since, three boys, two girls, but this, her eldest, summoned up so many memories.

"You had a good day," she said gently to her own child, in memory of Gard, in memory of Spiggy, in memory of apple days.

"Oh, yes," Saturday cried. "Oh, yes, it was a good, weird, wonderful day, and listen to my surprise! I have to tell you what we found!"

• *China was amazed* when Jep told her about the grove of giant trees. A complete catalog of native flora had been made during the decade after Settlement. She requested a copy, and the inventory swam upon the stage, from mold to tree, with nothing in it at all resembling giant trees with upcurving support branches. She would go up there the next day, she resolved.

When Jep asked her later that evening—apropos of nothing much so far as China could tell—how old she had been when she had had her first love affair, one part of her mind was grateful that he had waited until his little sister was in bed and had couched his question in terms of love rather than sex, but another part wished fervently he had been satisfied with what they learned at school—which was quite complete enough—and hadn't asked her a personal question. She did not speak of Sam, of what had happened between them when she was twelve. That had been only confusing and wild, like being at the center of a storm. She had never thought of herself as a participant in that, or as a victim, but rather as a kind of observer.

Instead, she said, "I had what I'd call my first love affair when I was fourteen," she said. "I was terribly fond of this wonderful boy. It went on almost two years, and then his mother was offered a position at CM, and they moved. We never became sexual lovers, though I think we would have in time, but being together was very sweet, nonetheless."

China was pleased with her reasonable tone, until she saw the pallor on her son's face, the darkness of the skin around his eyes, like a member of the chorus in an ancient tragedy, ready to cry woe. "Jep, what's wrong?"

"You never saw him again? He just went away, and you never saw him again?" he cried dolefully.

"Of course I saw him again," she said, wondering what was going on. "Of course I did. I rode in to CM on off-days, and he came here. And we sent one another messages. But, after a while he found someone else and sort of . . . stopped keeping in touch."

"That's rotten!" he proclaimed. "You must have just hated that."

It would have been easiest to agree with him. "No," she said honestly. "By that time, I had found someone else, too." She had found Samasnier, or found him again, or he had found her. Samasnier, through whose enjoyments Jep had been conceived. Sam, who at that time hadn't yet achieved Topman status, but who was on his way. Sam, whom she loved then, and probably now, still, despite everything.

"This isn't like that," he cried in protest, as he carried

the bowl of creely shells into the kitchen. "This isn't like that at all."

China, wondering what *this* was, decided not to badger him. Since Jep had spent the day with Saturday, she could extrapolate the probable cause of his anxiety. It would probably be a good idea to talk with Africa early tomorrow. With their children growing up so quickly, perhaps it was time the two sisters got together with their brothers, Asia, Australia, and Madagascar Wilm, and discussed clan strategy. Africa said she had enough children, but China had thought of having another. If she was going to do that, better do it before Saturday made her a grandaunt.

Having another child was rather an attractive idea. The problem was, of course, that there hadn't been anyone she had felt particularly drawn to. Not except Sam. No other than Sam. As though she had chosen Sam once and for all, as in some marriage culture. There were others who would become her lover in a moment, of course. Jebedo Quillow had been hinting around for at least two years, priming his sister Fearsome with self-touting little messages designed to be dropped into China's ears. Jebedo did not move her. Nor did any other person in Settlement One, or in CM, or any of the other settlements. She didn't want just anyone. She really didn't. Sam was the only one she wanted. Even crazy the way he was getting to be. Even if he was out of his mind, wild, the way people said.

Even if that thing he had killed out there in the strange canyon was the missing person from Settlement Three everyone had been told to watch for. Jamel something. Who had run off rather than emigrate as he'd been ordered to do, and everybody thought he'd attacked Sam, because he was known to do things like that. Even though the skull and bones hadn't looked human at all. The teeth were too long. It had claws. It was more like some monster.

Jep, who was observing her troubled expression from his hideaway in the kitchen, wondered at her concentration and thought she might be worrying about him and Saturday. Smugly, he thought she didn't need to worry. Saturday had a very good head on her, and so did he.

• • •

·   *There was always* routine business to take care
of at CM, and—since the situation at Settlement One was
not an emergency—it was over thirty days before the department heads and Zilia Makepeace made the trip Dern
Blass had requested. None of the four had been content to
leave matters in the hands, or to the interpretation, of the
others, and scheduling a date when all four were free of
conflicting appointments or responsibilities took time.
During the journey, they went over the reports of hostilities in the settlement and agreed that was the priority item
to be examined, immediately upon arrival.

When they reminded Samasnier they wanted to discuss the recent outbreak of incivility, however, Sam stared
at them blankly and responded, "But that was all over
long ago! Right after I got back from CM."

They were initially doubtful, and Zilia was sneeringly
incredulous. Sal made her logs available. Sam pulled out
stacks of filed reports. The five Team Leaders, interviewed
individually, said they'd had no trouble for twenty or
thirty days now. Since there was no evidence of current
difficulty, the visitors could only agree that whatever-it-
had-been seemed to be over.

Horgy wide-beamed a gratified smile, even as he admitted to himself that he'd been more than a little worried. Though he dealt with hostilities in the settlements on
a daily basis, dealing with hostility here in Settlement One
was not something he had done before. He wasn't sure
which emotions to push, whose egos to stroke. He didn't
like situations that lay outside his experience, because
then he had to rely upon improvisation. While he impro-
vised quite well, supremely well when he was in a panic,
originality was strenuous and anxious and never as comfortable as the experience-tested solutions to familiar
problems. Familiar problems were like old friends. They
were like a girl you'd made love to enough that she knew
what you liked. They made one feel adept and serene and
avuncular. Women liked men who were experienced and
serene and . . . well, perhaps not avuncular.

"Do you have any idea what caused the hostility before?" Horgy asked Sal, turning up his radiance slightly. He had always fancied Sal, though until now there had been no opportunity to do anything about it. Besides, if anyone knew about Sam and his strange new hobby—if that's what it was, and Dern was sceptical about that— wouldn't it be Sal? "Even though the whole business is over, there *were* some problems, weren't there?" Horgy liked gossiping about problems that either he or someone else had already solved: showing an interest, smiling sympathetically, nodding to show he understood. Women liked that, too.

Sal melted, as women almost always melted for Horgy, and described the trouble, which came out sounding like nothing much, really. "My personal opinion is that we were simply very upset because of that thing that happened when the God died."

Zilia pressed her lips together, and there was an uncomfortable silence.

"Of course, now there's this new thing," said Sal, wanting to break the silence. "There's the beast that attacked Sam!"

This not only broke the silence but also the complacence of everyone present who had been assured repeatedly there were no dangerous beasts on Hobbs Land. Sam's story was solicited, and he gave it, briefly. Seeing the doubt in their faces, he asserted that Jebedo Quillow had found its bones.

The Central Management people looked at one another in wonder. Sam had said he'd had his knife out of his belt.

"Knife out of your belt?" asked Spiggy, who had heard about the sword belt.

"I always carry one," said Sam, pointing to his replacement knife. He had gone back to the canyon to see if he could find his own knife—and because he wanted to see the bones—but without success. The replacement was an ordinary tool in a vlish-leather sheath.

"Jebedo did find the bones," said Sal, firmly. "The skull and everything. Rather primatelike, we all thought, though it had monstrous teeth, and claws. And Sam had to have the bite in his arm sealed shut. The thing bit him."

Incredulity changed to apprehension. "We certainly want to see where that happened," Horgy said. "Meantime, you don't mind if we wander around and talk to people? Just to see if anyone's seen any strange . . . beasts. Later, we'll want to go see that canyon you mentioned."

"Just don't bother any of the work crews until quitting time," said Sam in a firm but friendly voice. "After that, do as you like. Be our guests." He had previously assigned a settler as escort to each of the four visitors so the people from CM wouldn't wander off alone and kill themselves by stumbling in front of a harvester.

Zilia, accompanied by China Wilm, made straight for the temple of Bondru Dharm. When she got there, she turned, glared, and asked, as China had almost known she would, "Someone destroyed it, didn't they? Who was it, really?"

China shook her head. "I'm sure you've seen the report I sent to CM, Zilia. Sam assigned me as your escort just so I could tell you about it personally. I was right here when it happened, and nobody did it. The thing just fell in. The Theckles were here, too. You can ask them."

"I find that very hard to believe," Zilia sniffed, watching China from the corner of her eye, "considering the way you all felt about the God."

"I think most of us rather liked Bondru Dharm," China commented, not at all put off by Zilia's manner, which everyone in Hobbs Land had encountered at one time or another. "Actually, Zilia, I don't think you have any idea how we felt about Bondru Dharm. He was ours. He was Settlement One's own thing. It was kind of prestigious to have something none of the other settlements had. We rather liked it."

"You didn't pay any attention to it!" Zilia charged, as though this neglect had been China's personal fault, and ignoring the fact that in the two years Zilia had been on Hobbs she herself had visited Bondru Dharm only once. "None of you paid attention to the God."

"Most of us didn't," China admitted, "but your inference from that fact is all wrong. Most of us went to a sacrifice maybe once a year, out of curiosity more than anything. But we all put in our share to support Vonce and Birribat, and they spent all their time maintaining the temple and serving the God, which means they spent no time helping with production. Settlements aren't required to support nonproductive personnel, except for children and the disabled and their own retirees. In this case, we all voted to do it, and, as I recall, it was a unanimous vote."

Zilia shook her head in her customary expression of skeptical disbelief and turned back along the road toward the recreation building where Sal was flirting with Horgy. Zilia ignored them, taking plenty of time to peer into each of the other ruined temples as they went by. When she and China came up to Sal and Horgy, Zilia interrupted their fun to say she was going on out the north road to inspect the other ruins. Horgy let go of Sal's hand, which he had been stroking in a suggestive way, and said he'd go along.

China gave Sal an exasperated glance, which Sal ignored, and they walked on toward the northern edge of the settlement. On the way they picked up the other two visitors with their escorts—Jebedo and Fearsome Quillow, uncle and mother, respectively, of Gotoit and Sabby Quillow—outside the Supply and Administration building. All eight of them continued northward along the dusty road, all the settlement people except Sal, who had enjoyed flirting with Horgy, feeling that this visitation was a total waste of valuable time.

As they crossed the stream north of the settlement, they were joined by children: the two Tillan boys and all four of the Quillow kids, as well as Jeopardy and Saturday Wilm—the entire wolf-cedar logging crew. Horgy and Zilia led the group, closely followed by Spiggy and Jamice, as they strode up the slope to the temple.

Though the CM people had noticed the restored roof while they were still a good distance away, no one said anything until they were close enough to be sure it was no illusion. It was Zilia who put what they were all wondering into the most accusatory words possible.

"On whose authority was this temple rebuilt?"

Jebedo and Fearsome stared at the roof with their mouths open and shook their heads to say they didn't

know what it was or who had done it. Sal was equally
ignorant. China had a kind of idea, based on something
Africa had told her. "The children did it as a recreational
learning experience," she said mildly.

"On whose authority," Zilia quivered. "Who gave
fhem permission?"

"I don't think they needed authorization or asked for
permission," China found herself saying in a dead-calm
voice, without emotion or apprehension. "You didn't ask
anyone, did you, Jep?"

"No, Ma'am. We didn't think anyone would care,"
said Jep in an equally casual tone. "It's outside the settlement proper but within the utilization zone, so we didn't
need to ask CM. We did it outside schooling time, a whole
bunch of us, so we didn't need our teachers' permission.
Since we were rebuilding, not tearing down, we didn't
need Ancient Monuments approval. The AM Panel directives say reconstruction doesn't need approval. I did ask
Aunt Africa about proper crew management when we put
the roof on, and some of the grown-ups helped with that."

"I don't think anyone knew they were doing it until
the job was nine-tenths completed," remarked Sal in the
same disinterested voice China had just used.

Zilia started a complaint with, "You can't just let your
children . . . ," and Spiggy laid his hands on her shoulders, calming her down.

"Come on, Zil. No damage done. For heaven's sake,
girl! Make up your mind. The kid is right! This is exactly
what the Native Matters Advisory would like to see done,
isn't it? Exactly what *you'd* like to have had the Ancient
Monuments Panel doing. Quit screaming about it and
take a look."

"Come see the beautiful job they've made of it," called
Jamice from the temple doorway. "Look at these mosaics,
Zilia. If you'd had artists sent in from Phansure, they
couldn't have done better. And see how neatly the children have laid the roof logs." She went in, still talking,
leaving the others to follow.

The children sat down where they were, watchful but
quiet. After a time the visitors came out of the temple,

trailed by their settlement escorts, the latter looking slightly puzzled though not at all concerned.

The children rose politely, as they had been taught to do in the presence of elders.

"Are you going to reconstruct another of the temples?" Jamice asked them, using her sweetest tone of voice. She was moved to make much of the children, partly by her scorn for Zilia Makepeace, and partly by her well-developed esthetic sense. The graceful complexity of the designs in the newly laid floors had impressed her greatly.

"No, Ma'am," said Saturday in her most courteous voice. "We don't plan to. It was very hard work, and we learned just about everything there was to learn about it."

One of the men was watching her very closely, a rather ugly man. He smiled at her, and she blushed, suddenly realizing who he was. He wasn't nearly as ugly as Africa had said.

"What are you going to do with it, now that it's done?" the ugly man wanted to know. It was the same question Gotoit Quillow had asked, months before. Now, as then, no one answered it. Saturday looked at the questioner from beneath her lashes, shrugging. Jeopardy glanced at Willum R.

"Would you like to come to our Settlement Series tonight?" Willum R. asked Spiggy, with an ingenuous smile and a gesture indicating that all the visitors were included in the invitation. "We're playing Settlement Three, and winner gets to play Settlement Four in the semifinals."

• *Guest quarters in* Settlement One, as in all the settlements, were on the upper floor of the Supply and Administration building: half a dozen bedrooms with bath and sanitary facilities, a kitchen, and a comfortable room furnished with information stages, which could be used for relaxation or meetings or work. As was customary during visitations by CM staffers, a kitchen crew had been detailed to cook for the visitors.

The people from CM were served a plentiful and well-prepared supper, after which they separated: Horgy and

Jamice going off to attend the game they'd been invited to by Willum R; Spiggy and Zilia announcing their intention of taking a walk out to see the place Sam had been attacked. Once Horgy and Jamice had left, however, the other two found reasons to put off their exercise, lingering over the cheese, sweet filled cakes, and dried fruits which had been served as "finishers."

"What are these?" wondered Spiggy.

"Plum willow," she said. "They grow here and over around Settlement Five."

"Amazing," Spiggy murmured. "I've been here for over fifteen lifeyears, the last six in management, and I'm still learning things every day. You know a remarkable amount to have been here such a brief time."

"My father always said I was a fast learner. And it's been almost two years, now."

"You came from Ahabar, didn't you?"

"How did you know that?"

"You used the word *father*. Hardly anyone does, unless they're from Ahabar."

"I was born on Ahabar, in the southern counties of Voorstod. A county called Green Hurrah. I grew up mostly in the Celphian Rings."

"I've never been to the Rings."

"Nobody with any sense would ever go there."

"You must have had some reason for being there."

"My *father* was sure he could find moon-gems where other people had failed. Father always had this conviction that he was destined to succeed where others couldn't. He took other people's failures as favorable omens. If they couldn't do it, he'd try it. If other people were successful at a given endeavor, father wasn't interested. He needed to succeed at something other people had failed at. It made his life, and ours, a succession of disasters and disappointments. In the Rings, we lived in a environment container unit with a faulty recycler. Father was out prospecting for fire opals most of the time, and he got food at the outpost, but Mother finally died, mostly from malnutrition. I was very sick, too."

"Your family had a marriage tradition?"

"All the Voorstoders do, yes. Mother was from there."

"How do you feel about that tradition?" he asked curiously.

"After watching Mother wither away among the Rings? I feel the same way I feel about slavery and genocide," she snarled at him. "Which are also Voorstod traditions. Why do you ask? Were you going to propose a contract."

He laughed shakily, set back by her sudden ferocity. "No, I was just curious. Cultures with marriage traditions are so much in the minority, I find them exotic, that's all. I'm from Thyker, and Thykerites regard marriage as a kind of slavery. I know Voorstod has one of the old tribal religions that allows slavery."

"That insists upon slavery," she spat. "They have an interesting doctrine. According to the prophets, the only men who are free are those who do only what they want to. Doing what someone else wants you to is the sign of a slave. However, since there are always things that must be done, but that no one wants to do, a free man must have slaves to do those things. According to the Voorstoders, slavery is God's signs of approval to his people. It isn't allowed, it's required." She made an angry sound and rubbed her forehead, "Luckily, my father's family wasn't pure Voorstoder. In Green Hurrah there's been intermarriage for generations."

"So, how did you get away from the Rings?"

"After Mother died, Authority wouldn't let my father leave me in the Environmental Containment Unit alone. Child endangerment, it's called. At the time I thought that was pretty funny. Wife endangerment isn't a crime under the Authority—or among the Voorstoders. Perhaps they see women as consumables—and if the child is with the wife, you can endanger them both and nobody cares. Once the mama dies leaving minor girl children, though, then the Authority gets very exercised. Some kind of incest taboo, probably, for the Authority certainly has no religion to move it in that direction. My father sent me back to Grandmother Makepeace, and I left as soon as I could. Fifteen years ago now."

"That long."

She fished in the neck of her blouse for the life-timer

which hung between her breasts, flicked open the cover and read the numbers glowing at her. "This read almost sixteen when I got off the moons. It reads thirty now. Almost fifteen lifeyears." She subsided, simmering.

He said nothing more but merely stood at the window, watching the darkness come down. Gradually she calmed as the quiet remained unbroken. In the kitchen, the settler crew finished cleaning up and left, one man poking his head through the door to ask what time they wanted breakfast.

"We said we were going walking," Spiggy suggested, when the kitchener had gone.

She shook her head. "It occurs to me that going out in the dark to a place a settler was attacked by a large unknown predator may not be very intelligent."

He nodded. "You have a point. Would you like a game of some kind? Chess, maybe. Or four-way?"

She shook her head, rose, and went to the window where she stood, looking out at the settlement. "What did you think of that temple. The one the kids rebuilt. Or say they rebuilt."

"Do you really doubt they did it?"

She thought about it, trying to set her usual skepticism aside. "Not really, I guess. But I don't believe they thought it up all by themselves."

"Why is that?"

"Because of the amount of work involved. I looked at the ruined temples in the settlement. I estimate there's somewhere between two thousand and twenty-five hundred square feet of mosaic in the floors with four or five hundred stones to the square foot. There's over two thousand square feet of roof, with clay laid several inches thick over all of it. The labor involved . . ."

Spiggy shook his head at her, grinning.

"Why are you grinning at me?"

"When I was about eleven, back in Serena on Thyker, where I grew up, six of my friends and I built a clubhouse. We dug a tunnel over twenty feet long, shored it up and cased it with sponge panels we stole from a construction site. Then we dug a twenty-by-twenty cave, eight feet high. It took us one whole year, every spare minute we had. Nobody urged us to do it. Nobody even knew we were doing it. When we were finished with it, we used it half a dozen times, then we had some heavy rains and the thing collapsed, luckily not when we were in it. Kids do things like that. Of course, they'd think it was slavery if their parents wanted them to do it. Part of the attraction is that nobody knows, that it's a secret."

She shook her head at him. "I suppose that's true, Spiggy, but the difference is that this temple isn't going to collapse. Children can exert enormous amounts of energy, but when they build things, they usually do it as you and your friends did, not quite competently. They haven't gained the experience and knowledge they would need to build competently. The temple we saw today couldn't have been done better if the settlers had done it themselves under expert direction. I believe it's exactly as it was originally. Where did the kids learn how?"

"Archives?" he suggested.

"Archives! When I knew we were coming to Settlement One, I looked up everything there is in the Archives about the God and the Departed and the ruins. There was never an architectural study done of the Bondru Dharm temple. It was occupied when the first settlers arrived, so Native Matters instructed that it not be disturbed. All Archives had were a few pictures of the outside, a sketchy floor plan and the verbal description given by the xenologists. Nothing else. Either there's an unsung genius among the children, or . . ."

"Or the settlers are lying," he suggested.

"Or the settlers are lying," she agreed. "Someone helped the kids. Someone used the kids."

"Are you sharpening your claws?" he asked gently. "Who are you out to get, Zilia?"

She turned to him, hands out and open, mouth making a lopsided grin. "I know what you all think of me, Spiggy. Everyone at CM thinks I'm crazy. Hell, everyone back at Native Matters thinks I'm crazy. Well, everybody thinks you're crazy, too, with your ups and downs. And most people think Jamice has the terminal nasties. About the only sane one among us is Horgy, and he has this little satyriasis problem he keeps asking his friends and acquaintances to help him with."

"And Dern," grinned Spiggy. "Don't forget Dern."

"And Dern. Who is usually out in the settlements, running around in disguise, thinking no one knows who he is. Tandle actually runs CM, and anybody who doesn't know that is blind, deaf, and has no sensation left in his extremities. So, we're all mad in one way or another."

"My question was, who are you out to get?"

"I learned growing up that people always exploit others if they can get away with it! My father exploited my mother and me. My grandmother exploited her sons and daughters and grandchildren; the Voorstoders exploit the Gharm. I was born a child and a girl and therefore a victim, and I didn't like it. I want to stop there being other victims. So I go around accusing people of genocide and corporate torture and child-eating, watching to see if anybody turns pale. And no, I don't believe what people tell me! Grandma always had a ready answer. My father always had a ready answer. In Voorstod, they've got a whole catechism of answers. I'm not ready to accept what people say. Almost always there could be some other answer, you know."

"No, I don't know. What other answer?"

"Maybe not all the Departed died. Hobbs Land has been surveyed, but nobody claims it's been thoroughly explored. Maybe some of them have shown up here at Settlement One, and the first thing they did was restore a temple for one of their Gods."

"Farfetched, but possible."

"Maybe the Departed didn't show up here. Maybe they're back in the hills, and some of the settlers have restored the temple to bait them in."

"Bait them in?"

"To use as forced labor."

"Equally farfetched. Have you seen the Owlbrit? You might as well try to get labor out of a cabbage."

"That may be true. But it seems to me that restoring a Departed temple for no special reason is also farfetched, especially when I'm told children did it! There's something else going on here, Spiggy. Count on it!"

"So what are you going to do about it."

She shrugged again, widely, both arms out as wide as she could reach, as though some solution lay just beyond her fingertips. "What can I do? Make recordings. Ask the Native Matters Advisory for an engineer to do a structural study, or maybe even ask for an Ancient Monuments survey. There's never been a survey done here." She became thoughtful. "Actually, that's a pretty good idea. It would at least tell us what we're dealing with. They can't survey the monuments without getting around most of the planet. There are ruins of villages scattered all over the escarpment."

He sighed, shaking his head. She was being fairly reasonable, for Zilia. "So, do it then, and consider you've done your duty! Come on, Zilia. Let's not waste a pleasant evening. If you're afraid to go out among the beasts, let's take a walk around the settlement."

· *The game was* a doubleheader, the Settlement One first- and second-level teams against the first- and second-level teams of Settlement Three. Settlement One, with several very young players—including Willum R., who had just turned fifteen—on its first-level team, did not expect to do very well and was pleasantly surprised at ending with a tie score.

"You wouldn't have if you hadn't cheated," sneered a frustrated Settlement Three player to Willum R. in the changing room. Settlements didn't lean toward frills, and there was only one changing room for each sex, share and share alike, visitors and the home team.

"We didn't cheat!" cried Willum R., stung by the accusation. "That's a rotten thing to say."

"Vernor Soames," snapped the Settlement Three coach, "that's not sportsmanlike. You owe the player an apology."

"Well they do something," whined Vernor. "Settlement One always wins more than they ought to. They've always had that God-thing around, kind of a good luck charm. The rest of us don't have one." So his Uncle Jamel had always said, though nobody had seen Uncle Jamel for a good while now.

"The God died!" retorted Willum R. "It died a long time ago."

"So you say," sneered Vernor, almost silently.

"Vernor," growled his coach.

"I apologize," said Vernor, covertly displaying a bent index finger to turn around what he said, showing he didn't mean the apology.

From the nearby toilets, Horgy heard the conversation and made mental note of it. So the other settlements thought Settlement One had an unfair advantage. Interesting. Perhaps Sam knew that. Undoubtedly, he knew that. Perhaps the pressure of being on top, and staying there, had cracked him. Thus far during the trip, Horgy had heard nothing but praise for Sam, but that could be loyalty talking. Now that Settlement One was doing no better than some of the other settlements, that loyalty might change.

And then, too, there was this odd business about this thing that had attacked Sam? Had anything really attacked him? Had he killed something, or seriously wounded something. Or someone. Horgy sat, ruminating. There was that man who had disappeared from Settlement Three. What had his name been?

Well, tomorrow they'd go look at the place the attack had taken place. They'd collect the bones. Then they'd go back to CM. Dern would be most interested. He'd keep it quiet, of course. Dern wouldn't want biologists and zoologists from System flocking onto Hobbs Land to investigate this possible new life-form. It would upset production. No, Dern would keep it quiet. But Horgy himself intended to find out as much as he could.

• *Technically speaking, Authority* consisted of twenty-one members, appointed for life, who had final and irrevocable power over all the worlds and moons in System. Unofficially, however, the word *Authority* was used to mean the moon upon which these members were housed, as well as all the rest of its inhabitants, whether or not they were members of any official committee or Panel or Advisory. The official bodies included the Advisories of Defense, Intelligence, Science, Religion, and so forth, as well as the Native Matters Advisory with its four subordinate panels: Ancient Monuments, Linguistics, Interspecies Relations, and Advanced Studies. The latter was a catchall panel to which all matters were referred which pertained to indigenes and seemed to fit nowhere else.

The staff of the Native Matters Advisory was relatively small, inbred, almost incestuous. Great-great-grandchildren of early members now occupied offices their forebears had built and sat at desks their great-grandparents had ordered made by Phansuri craftsmen. Inbred though they were, Native Matters persons were sincere. When Phansure, Thyker, and Ahabar, worlds without native peoples, had filled up and spilled colonists into the Belt, where there were native peoples, the citizens of the sister worlds had reviewed their history, ancient and recent, and determined with rare unanimity that genocide and slavery, which had stained the skirts of humanity for millennia, would not take place in System. They had resolved that the prior inhabitants of the system were to be compensated for, or protected against, all human damages or harms which might already have taken place, which might be anticipated, or which might eventually and inadvertently occur.

The purity of mankind's vision could be determined by the fact that included in the protectorate with the gentle Osmers and placid Glothees were the Ninfadelian Porsa, a race of raucous mucusoids so foul and unloveable that even graduate students in xenology, hardened by years of study among primitive and even disgusting societies, could seldom be found to live near the Porsa and study their ways.

Because Native Matters Advisory had real creatures to concern itself with, it met regularly, unlike certain other advisories, to discuss real issues and problems. Often these included personnel problems, a nuisance that knowledgable persons accepted as inseparable from any human institution.

"We have received a new complaint about Zilia Makepeace," the current Chair of the Advisory told his members. The Chair was Rasiel Plum, a stout and elderly Phansuri gentleman of generally unruffled disposition, who happened, also, to be one of the twenty-one official Members of Authority.

"Zilia Makepeace?" murmured a new Advisory member to his neighbor.

"On Hobbs Land," came the response.

"She's still accusing the Hobbs Land people of killing off the Departed," said Rasiel Plum.

"Who's the complaint from, Rasiel?" asked one of the younger members, a Thykerite. "Someone reliable?"

"The CEO. Dern Blass. He says she makes accusations at most Central Management meetings, but he's recently picked up on the fact that she makes accusations out in the settlements, as well.

"So?"

"So he was in a settlement, in disguise, pretending to be a drifter while selling spice graters or System world cheeses or something, and someone told him Zilia Makepeace is still accusing the settlers of killing off the Departed."

"What has the Makepeace woman said recently?"

Rasiel fumbled with the keys of the information stage, refreshing his memory. "She says the children of Settlement One have reconstructed a ruined temple, and she finds that highly suspicious."

General sighs and one, quickly stifled, giggle. At the far end of the table, someone began to whistle recognizably though almost tunelessly, a bawdy song, "The Beheading of Sarafin Crowr." Sarafin had been a notable witch on Phansure, disposed of in remote though historic times by her fellow villagers, and the tune was often used, particularly at sporting events, to suggest imminent eradication of the opposing side.

"Back on Ahabar, my kids and some others in the neighborhood built a first-century fortification out of insublocks once," said a member who had not, like many others, spent his whole life at Authority. "It cost me half a year's pay to get the thing disassembled and the blocks taken back to the site they'd swiped them from. Kids do things like that."

"We could send the Makepeace woman to Ninfadel. The Porsa don't build anything." A Moon and Belt representative made this tentative suggestion, which was greeted with ribald cheers.

"We could simply fire her," said someone else in a grumpy tone. High Baidee, probably.

"Retrain her," suggested a third, more mildly.

"Knock her off," growled a fourth, the whistler.

"We could deal with the problem by recommending to Ancient Monuments Panel that they send a monuments survey team to Hobb's Land," Rasiel Plum replied, "which is what the Makepeace woman asks for. The easy way out is to recommend just that. We haven't sent a survey team to Hobb's Land in . . ." He punched up *Advisory involvement* and *Hobb's Land* on the desktop stage, asking for coincident files and referring to the sequence number attached to the account of the most recent team. Another quick punch gave him the elapsed time in lifeyears. "Not in thirty-three lifeyears, and even then it was only an aerial mapping of sites," he concluded.

"We've always kept a staff member there," complained an elderly Ahabarian woman. "Since Settlement. Since the last Departed died. Even though there was nothing to look after. None of the staff has ever done anything at all on Hobbs Land. Why does this one have to *do* anything?"

"Maybe that's Zilia's problem," Rasiel Plum smiled. "That she has nothing to do or look after. But before we remove her, reprove her, or replace her, shouldn't we be absolutely sure she's wrong?"

The members looked around for guidance, for expression, for some indication by smile or frown or nod that their colleagues felt one way or another about the question. No one seemed to feel strongly; no one seemed to be even slightly doubtful that there was nothing-at-all on Hobb's Land to be concerned about.

"Since she's asked for a survey of the villages and temples," Rasiel added, helpfully, "referring the matter to Ancient Monuments Panel with our recommendation will be responsive."

The members shifted and muttered. Being responsive was a Good Thing. Sending a team was not that Big a Deal. If a survey of the monuments hadn't been done yet, now was as good a time as any. The AM Panel's budget for the year was not yet spent. By all means, they muttered. Recommend a survey team.

"May I have a formal utterance to that effect?" Rasiel Plum suggested, promptly receiving several.

The Ancient Monuments Panel received the recommendation with general disinterest. After arguing about it in desultory fashion, the Panel decided to implement the recommendation with a three-man Baidee team from Thyker, mostly because there was a three-man team on Thyker which was immediately available. They also decided not to tell Zilia Makepeace the team was coming until it was on the way.

"The last thing we need," the Panel leader agreed, "is manufactured evidence."

•　*When blight had* struck Thyker a lifetime ago, there had been enormous loss of both human and animal life, as well as the loss of many native species. Even after the disease had been controlled, no one had been sure the Blight would not strike again, and there had been wave after wave of emigration to the other habitable words. In the Belt, Bounce and Pedaria particularly had received numerous non-Baidee immigrants from Thyker, and there had been considerable thought given by some groups to looking far out, outside the orbit of Phansure, for homes, though there wasn't much out there of interest.

Next beyond Phansure was Celphius, a frozen planet whose gem-rich rings were inhabited mostly by prospectors. Beyond Celphius was giant Tandorees, with more rings and dozens of possibly habitable moons of its own: gassy Tandorees, hot with its own belly rumblings. And after Tandorees came blue Siphir and far, cold Omnibus, and that was all, save the comets and the trash and the occasional strange visitor that came plunging in from outer darkness to fling itself into a sun or around them and out into forever-black once more.

Nothing ever came of the far-out colonization schemes. When all was said and done and the Blight was truly gone, it turned out that the habitable planets and moons had been hospitable enough to make room for the frightened and the desperate. Once they had departed, Thyker had found itself greatly depleted but much more homogenous. By coincidence (though there were those who alleged otherwise), the largest number of surviving and remaining inhabitants on Thyker had been High Baidee, devotees of the Overmind, followers of the prophetess, Morgori Oestrydingh, who had appeared on Thyker a thousand years before through a Door which no one had known was there.

The Door had been and still was—if anyone wanted to go look at it—near an oasis park a little beyond the western suburbs of Serena. It most resembled a twisted loop of timeworn metal set on a spacious dais of native stone, which, because of its undoubted antiquity and its convenient location, had acquired a certain mythic reputation and had come to be used as a site for all kinds of concerts and celebrations.

On that dais, during the solemn celebration of the bicentennial of the colonization of Thyker, while the patriarch of a local sect was delivering his annual blessing of the herds (drought-tolerant vorgashirs resulting from a cross between the ancient Manhome camel and a horny lizardlike creature found originally in the Vlees System), the twisted monument suddenly lit up with a curtain of fire and a dragon came through. The patriarch's blessing was being recorded for posterity, and thus, perforce, the arrival of the dragon was recorded also: a great horned and callused beast with fangs and a fiery mane. Said some. Actually, the dragon did not show up terribly well on playback. Everyone saw something, but few people could describe or agree upon what they saw. Archives was no help. It could not recall what it had never actually seen, and there was not enough there to extrapolate from.

Everyone agreed, however, that the prophetess was riding upon a partially visible and quite formidable creature, that she dismounted and came forward to take the patriarch by the hand and pat him familiarly upon his shoulder. The patriarch, whose back had been turned to the monument, had not seen her arrive and believed for a moment she was part of the celebration, a notion of which he was disabused when he turned and caught a glimpse of the dragon before fainting dead away. A brave subdeacon had carried him to safety, and after a moment's hesitation the prophetess had turned to address the crowd in archaic and imperfectly understandable language, which was later transcribed and annotated by the Circle of Scrutators and thereby made perfectly clear.

"My name is Morgori Oestrydingh," she had said. "My companion has no name."

A student of ancient languages in the crowd appointed himself translator and asked her why she had come. She told them the dragon had come to explore, and she herself had come to preach the opening of the mind. It was all there, on the recordings, the old woman with her feathery white hair floating like mist around her head, her intensely bright eyes seeming to stare into the hearts of those she spoke to, and, hanging like mist upon the air behind her, confused elements of tooth and claw and scale, which added up to an impression of dragonhood without ever condescending to be representational.

Prophetess Morgori Oestrydingh stayed on Thyker long enough to teach them that the twisted structure was an ancient Door to non-human worlds, that it had been built by—and those worlds had once been occupied by— the Arbai people, and that the Arbai people had been of surpassing abilities and goodness. She stayed long enough to preach at them for the better part of a season, naming them the Baidee, or "New Bai" people. They must become a new Bai people she had said. The first Bai people had been the Arbai, inventors of the Doors, and there were other Bai people on worlds Morgori had visited since. The prophetess's life had been spent in a search for the Arbai, throughout a thousand worlds and over some thousands of years, so she said, and she told stories of those worlds and times that astonished the people.

She also said other things:

"God does not know our names any more than we

know the individual cells in our brains," she had said. "God is the Overmind of which all minds are part."

And, "It is our minds and not any other attribute which gives us personhood and value. We share intelligence with other living things, and they are no less important than we. Even creatures without detectable intelligence have adapted themselves to play necessary roles. To make God in our image or we in God's is blasphemy."

And, "When our minds are gone, our purpose is gone, and we are only meat, whether living or dead. Personhood resides only in the mind, not in the body, though once the mind has gone, there are always those who will try to maintain the body, because the body and what the body did are all they knew or cared about."

And, "Freedom comes only with uncertainty. Because man does not like to feel impotent, he would rather believe himself guilty of causing evil than to know he is helpless before uncertainty. If there is uncertainty, there must be evil, just as there must be good. You must accept that evil and pain may be among the inevitable consequences of every action, just as goodness and joy may be. Do not attempt to find explanation either in good intentions or in guilt. Man neither merits joy nor earns pain, nor will he learn from either alone, though, if his race lives long enough, he may be informed by both concerning the nature of what is."

And, "There is no sin inherent in any mind save the sin of pride in believing one has seen or been taught the absolute truth. The second greatest sin is refusing to search for the truth one must acknowledge one will never absolutely find."

Her last and greatest commandment was said to be the words she had whispered to her favorite disciple just before she left. "Even when people are well-meaning, do not let them fool with your heads."

So she taught, this old, old woman, before she got onto her dragon and went away through the Door once more. The first Baidee, the Low Baidee, were those who followed her teachings. That is how the Baidee began, and that is how they thought they had continued, century af-

ter century, cleaving always to the teaching of the prophetess. They still began their services with the first words
the prophetess had spoken to them as a teaching. "This I
say unto you, be not sexist pigs."

The Primitive, or "Low," Baidee still clung to the na-
ive prophesy, claiming that Morgori had never meant to
prohibit brain surgery and the techniques to cure mental
illness, but only psychological manipulation, particularly
religious cultism. The High Baidee, however, had carried
the word forward, through generations of theological disputation and political manipulation. Over the centuries
they had defined meaning and eliminated heresies and had
set up a canon against which future innovations might be
judged. Where the Low Baidee found a prohibition
against sexual discrimination in the words of the prophetess ("be not sexist"), the male Scrutators of the High
Baidee found a warning against bestial behavior ("be not
pigs"). It was not long until bestial behavior was defined
as consorting with the *other kind,* that is, the Low Baidee.
Though the Low Baidee were at first the only people
shunned, as a practical matter, the prohibition was soon
extended to everyone else as well.

In order to make recognition of the real, or High,
Baidee immediate and unfailing, certain distinctive dress
and food habits were ordained by the Scrutators assembled, who claimed to find justification for these singulari-
ties in the words of the prophetess herself. "Be not pigs"
obviously meant "take not into yourself the substance of
pigs," and that obviously meant "eat nothing resembling
pigs," such as anything having four legs or hairy skin or a
snout and so on. Since on Bounce there were creatures
which resembled pigs but laid eggs, eggs were likewise
prohibited. Other such interpretations were used to order
the dress of the High Baidee, which included such items
as the zettle, a small scarf of precious material hung from
the belt, on one side of which were embroidered the words
"Stuff happens," and on the other "Not guilty."

The Low Baidee had mostly died out or emigrated,
though there were sizeable colonies of them left near
Chadnarath and Bajasthan, where they maintained Temples of the Original Revelation and held ceremonies nota-

ble for the cheerful frenzy of their dancing. As for the High Baidee, they revered the prophetess (who would have been astonished at their interpretation of her teachings), clung to her last and greatest commandment, and considered their own beginning to have been a large and fortunate one. It was from among these folk that the Native Matters Advisory chose the team to do the Ancient Monuments survey.

The three were residents of the capital city, Chowdari, and members of one family, the Damzels. They were two brothers, and a sister: Shanrandinore (Shan) and Bombindinore (Bombi) Damzel, fraternal twins sharing the same progenitor; and Volsalobinag (Volsa) Damzel, their younger sister whose progenitor had been, their mother said, the randomizer on the Baidee sperm bank at the Temple of the Overmind. All three Damzel children had spent the requisite three years of late adolescence in religious and military service. All had attended a prestigious university on Phansure; all had specialized in xenology; all were committed conservationists. Shan's commitment (or arrogance) was so great that he had gone to Ninfadel to do postgraduate study of the Porsa, and though he spoke of that time frequently and feelingly, he actually remembered the realities as little as possible. He had undergone a ten-day cleansing at the Temple of High Baidee when he returned, and he had learned self-hypnosis to allow him to forget, but he still woke up yelling in the middle of the night.

All three, when advised of the appointment, went immediately to the Temple of the Overmind, to give thanks that they were considered capable of service. In the Sanctuary of the Scrutators they were admitted to a solemn reading of the sayings of the prophetess (two chanters and a dozen intoners), given instruction for those faithful to the Overmind, and supplied with the names of coreligionists on Hobb's Land. A notable thing about High Baidee was the way it kept young people of breeding age in touch with one another. First among the names they were given was that of Spiggy Fettle.

.   .   .   .

· *In Settlement One,* Jeopardy awoke one off-day morning with a feeling of intense anticipation. That feeling had recently had only one cause: his cousin Saturday. Therefore, when he had dressed himself and eaten and found a small spade in the tool room, he wandered over to the next-door sisterhouse, his aunt's place, knowing he would find Saturday waiting for him. She was, in fact, leaning on the front stoop with her own spade lying beside her.

"Did you bring film bags?" she asked him.

He shook his head, realizing for the first time that they would need film bags. Of course they would. He just hadn't thought of it.

"It's okay," she said. "I've got fifteen. That's enough."

"We'll need the Quillow kids," he said. "Suppose they'll meet us there?"

She shrugged. They would need the Quillow kids. Maybe Willum R. and Deal and Sabby and Gotoit would meet them there, and maybe they wouldn't. Maybe Thash and Thurby Tillan would be there, too. No telling until they got there. No matter, either way.

They went north out of the settlement, down the slope to the creek, through the curtain of ribbon-willow and up the opposite slope toward the rebuilt temple. Near the temple they found a slight declivity in the soil, and they sat down near it to share a drink from Saturday's canteen before beginning to dig. The digging was a gentle process during which they slowly laid small neat spadefuls of earth in a sculptured pile at each side of the armspan-wide trench they were making.

Saturday sang as she dug. "Owee, owee, owee, janga, janga." The words made no sense, but her voice was tuneful and happy sounding. Jeopardy contented himself with grunting occasionally. When Willum R., Deal, and Gotoit came up the slope to join them, each with spade, Deal and Gotoit joined Saturday's psalmody, and Willum R. grunted along with Jeopardy. Neither of them had enough sense of music to notice that the grunts were rhythmic, that they punctuated the song the others sang, that the whole was greater than its parts.

Six cats appeared out of the surrounding grasses and

sat in a circle beyond the piled earth, waiting curiously. The trench slowly deepened. The deeper it became, the slower the children dug, until they were moving in a gesture ballet full of long pauses. First Willum R., then Deal, then Gotoit got out of the trench and watched while Jep and Saturday went on uncovering, quarter inch by quarter inch.

"Here," said Gotoit, bending forward to offer Saturday a paint brush. "You'll need this."

Saturday did need it. Of course, Gotoit had brought it, because Gotoit's mother was a hobby artist and the brush was right there where Gotoit could lay hands on it. Saturday leaned down and began to brush the soil away. She had come to a thick, felty mass, like a mattress. "Knife," she said

Willum R. handed Jep his knife, a very sharp one. Willum R. had spent most of the previous evening sharpening it. Jep slipped the knife into the felty mass and began to cut it, a long cut, from the head of the trench to the bottom. Then he made cross cuts, from side to side, a dozen of them. Finally, he cut fifteen palm-sized pieces of the mat loose and handed them one by-one to Saturday, who put each into a film bag, sealed the bag, and put it into her knapsack.

"Now," said Gotoit.

Saturday and Jeopardy laid the fibrous mat back at either side. Beneath it was . . . something. Dark. Hard. Faintly sparkling. As big as a grown man, or bigger.

"We can't raise it," said Gotoit.

"Wait," said Jep. "It's all right."

"Anybody got anything to eat?" asked Saturday.

"We do," someone hollered. The diggers hadn't noticed Sabby Quillow and the Tillan kids coming through the trees. Thash and Thurby had brought fried poultrybird, salad, and fresh bread, and Sabby had brought fruit.

"What are we waiting for?" asked Thurby from his seat on the dirt pile, his mouth full of crisp bird.

"We can't raise it," said Saturday. "We got it uncovered all right, but we can't raise it."

"How much do you think it weighs?"

"A lot," said Jep. "As much as four men, maybe more."

They had almost finished eating when the men came through the willows: Sam Girat and Jebedo Quillow and the two other Quillow uncles, Quashel and Quambone, as well as Thash and Thurby's uncle, Tharsh Tillan. A little later, the three Wilm uncles showed up: Asia, Australia, and Madagascar. Eight of the strongest men in Settlement One, all nodding to the kids and looking into the hole to see what was lying there.

"Where does it go?" asked Sam, totally unsurprised. Last night Theseus had told him about this. He couldn't quite remember the conversation, but he recalled Theseus had mentioned he'd be needed to help.

Saturday pointed. To the rebuilt temple, of course.

The men had brought ropes and long bars. They levered the mass up, got ropes beneath it, then hauled it out. No one suggested using a machine. Instead, the men made loops of the rope and put the loops over their shoulders, then carried the heavy thing the short distance to the temple door, through that door, making a rhythmic grunt with each step as they went around the temple and through the door into the central room, where they stood their burden erect upon a network of crossed ropes before heaving it in one muscle-straining effort onto the plinth at the center of the room.

"Raised," they said, as they lifted, all at once, eight voices speaking together in the same pitch, like a growl, like distant thunder, deep. Then again, "Raised."

They tilted the mass to one side, then the other, as they removed the ropes, then rolled up the ropes and left, chatting to one another of inconsequentialities, Sam already offering suggestions to Team Leader Jebedo Quillow about one of the delicate vegetable houses. Outside, all the children except for Saturday and Jeopardy were filling in the hole, bringing spadefuls of soil from other areas to make it level and invisible. In the central room, the cousins were cleaning off the thing with the paintbrush Gotoit had brought, brushing away the remaining webs, which had clung to the mass but which were now shriveling into ash. When they had finished, they stood back and looked at it. It stood the height of a tall man upon the plinth: dark, rugged, and angular, like a surrealistic sculpture of an almost human form. It had nothing that could be identified as a head or limbs, and yet it gave the impression of personhood. A sound came from the pedestal, the slightest whisper, as though something were moving slowly inside the stone. After a time, dim lights gathered at the foot of the new thing, ascended very gradually to the top and disappeared.

A black-and-white tabby cat came into the room with a live ferf in her jaws. She jumped onto the plinth and laid the animal against the base of the mass, then jumped down and left the room, purring loudly. Two other cats came in with similar burdens.

"That was Gotoit's cat," Jep remarked after a time. "That stripey one. She calls it Lucky."

Saturday nodded and brushed the surface of the plinth with her bare palm, cleaning away the few scraps of scruffy ferf hair that remained on the stone. The bodies of the ferfs had disappeared silently into the mass before them.

"The God was hungry," said Jep. "We're the Ones Who have to take care of that."

"I think the cats will take care of that," returned Saturday.

"How come the cats didn't take care of it before? With Bondru Dharm?"

"Bondru Dharm didn't know about cats," Saturday answered. "There weren't any cats here when Bondru Dharm was raised. But we know about cats, and Birribat was one of us, so the cats will take care of that. We're the Ones Who have to take care of all the rest of it."

FIVE

· *Scattered among the* relentlessly cheerful and dedicated hosts of the High Baidee, who were so conscientious and hard-working they had little time to be introspective about their religion, there were a few whose natures demanded that they do more for the faith than merely dress and eat correctly, keep the four hundred positive ordinances, and engage in the conventional daily recitations of the words of the prophetess. They were the enthusiasts, the sectarian devotees, zealots of the Overmind, whose heads, unfooled-with by any outside force, urged them to stricter vigilance and more extreme effort.

One such fanatic, though his family and friends did not know it, was Shan Damzel. Another such was his friend and mentor, Howdabeen Churry. Though there was almost no difference in their ages, Shan considered himself Churry's disciple. He went so far as to call Churry teacher, though only when they were alone. He did it to be daring, to share a secret between them, like a small boy sharing a newly learned dirty word. The word *teacher* was, like the words *evangelist, missionary, apologist,* or *advocate,* a word to which implications of head-fooling stuck like glue. High Baidee preferred words like *lecturer, expositor,* or *commentator,* words without any imputation of coercion. When one said *teacher,* the hearer might infer that someone was being *taught,* a thing no right-minded Baidee would consent to. Explaining something was all right. Teaching it was not. With the exception of religious matters, of course. Or military ones.

Howdabeen always demurred when Shan said *teacher.* "Perhaps I may clarify your own thoughts," he was apt to say. "Perhaps my ideation throws your own conceptions into brighter light, but I make no effort to convince you of the correctness of my own mental processes or the position I take because of them." Indeed, he had no reason to do so. Though Howdabeen was very young, only in his early twenties, he had enormous charisma. This attribute alone made him believable in the way that actors and demagogues are believable: he was so overwhelmingly convincing he was never required to demonstrate relevance. Though he was not particularly handsome, Howdabeen Churry was unsullied. He had that clarity of eye and clean sweetness of skin which spoke of a calm conscience housed in an uncorrupted body. Others might chant, "Stuff happens, not guilty," responsively in the temple. Howdabeen intoned it, believing it utterly. He could not be guilty because his heart was pure. He was as assured of his purity as he was of his correctness, and he maintained his correctness by constant attention to himself and what he was doing and what he thought about things.

He carried this tendency toward self-autopsy into his professional life. When young Baidee joined Churry's brigade, even those with appropriate backgrounds and acceptable habits were examined microscopically, as Churry, so he said, would have wished to be examined himself. Churry wanted no mere time-servers. He believed that danger had come and would come, that the Overmind intended recurrent tests of the readiness and dedication of its parts. Churry was convinced of it. His own senses, of which the Overmind obviously approved, confirmed it. Danger lurked. It was out there, somewhere, getting ready.

Thus, when Shan Damzel showed up in some excitement, announcing that he had been picked as part of a family team to go to Hobbs Land, ostensibly to do a survey, but really because of some unspecified danger that a probably paranoid woman had almost certainly invented, Churry eliminated all the qualifiers as he heard them and rubbed his mental hands together over the opportunity that remained. Of all the words Shan Damzel uttered, Howdabeen Churry heard fully only *Hobbs Land* and *danger* as the operative syllables.

Churry had a personal interest in possible dangers. Over the past two years he had been organizing a secret strike force, an association of several hundred like-minded Baidee brigadeers too young for the regular army and too zealous to sit on their hands. Older, perhaps wiser Baidee, if they had known of this covert corps, might have called it a bunch of foolhardy young hotheads. Churry called it The Arm of the Prophetess. The Arm had been formed to protect everything the Baidee stood for. It was designed to move so swiftly that it would have struck and withdrawn before anyone knew it was there.

"Be careful," said Churry to Shan in the voice of one devoted, though superior, friend to another. "When you get there, be exceptionally careful. Don't take anything on faith. Don't accept anyone's word for anything."

"Actually, we're only supposed to keep our eyes open while we're doing an Ancient Monuments Survey," Shan demurred, a bit taken aback at Churry's unqualified enthusiasm. "There won't even be people where we'll spend most of our time."

"When there are people, note exactly what they say and what they do, Shan. Look for signs of mental control. Oh, well, you know. We've discussed it at brigade conference time and again. The last time, when the invaders came, the threat was overt and easy to see. Next time, I feel it will be more subtle. The Overmind is testing us, Shan."

"Yes, teacher," said Shan, greatly daring.

Churry smiled and preened inwardly. He relished this

and other attentions from the handsome Damzel scion, though in his most private heart Churry thought Shan a bit of a fool. All that quivering frailty about his studies on Ninfadel!

"How have the dreams been?" he asked, rather daring in his turn. One did not lightly mention dreams to Shan Damzel.

"Controllable," said Shan, offhandedly. "The doctors are really very good. They've taught me some excellent techniques." He ignored the drops of cold sweat which had sprung from his hairline immediately on hearing the word *dreams.*

"I've never asked you," said the other, curiously. "While you were on Ninfadel, did you ever have any feeling at all that the Porsa might be a threat to us?"

Words stuck in Shan's throat. His eyes bulged slightly. He shut them and nodded, as though reciting something to himself, some kind of rhythmic chant. At length he opened his eyes again and managed to say, "No. Not in the way you mean. No."

The barely controlled terror in Shan's eyes shamed Churry. He hadn't meant to set the boy off that way. He turned away, pretending he had not seen Shan's reaction. "Well, be careful," he said lamely. "Come see me the moment you get back."

By the time a day or two had passed, he forgot Shan's discomfiture while keeping clearly in mind that there might be something dangerous on Hobbs Land. The Arm of the Prophetess had been doing push-ups for a very long time. Now he dared hope, more than a little, that on Hobbs Land there might be something dangerous for that well-muscled Arm to strike at.

· *On Hobbs Land,* unconcerned with possible dangers, Sam Girat slept and dreamed. He was deep in the canyon of caves, exploring each cave as he came to it, finding strange and remarkable creatures living there.

China Wilm dreamed of a sapphire lake where bubbles rose from vents in the depths to float like balloons above the gentle water, where beaches of diamond sand gleamed in every direction, coruscant and marvelous. She had seen that lake, or invented it, in a fantasy when she was a child. She came back to it now and then, for comfort and peace.

Maire Girat dreamed of the Voorstod of her childhood, of precipices from which bridges of stone reached into low hanging clouds, of small creatures singing among the leaves, of fruit-laden vines, dangling over sunwarmed walls. It was an idealized Voorstod, without shadows. The land she had thought was there, when she was young.

Others dreamed: children, old people, men and women. Even the cats dreamed, curled in their dens, and the kittens, warm at their mothers' teats. Saturday dreamed. And Jep. And, shallow beneath the soil, Birribat Shum dreamed with them.

· *Topman Harribon Kruss* took two days leave from Settlement Three in order to make his visit to Settlement One. Topmen were encouraged to share experiences: he could have made the trip on Hobbs time, but he wanted no picky-picking at his schedule or second-guessing as to his motives by Spiggy's minions in the finance department. Before he left, he sat by his mother's bed for an hour or two, but she woke only briefly to smile her haggard smile and murmur something indistinguishable. He made the trip alone, leaving Dracun in Settlement Three to bite her fingernails in frustration. Though she had been content to have Jamel gone, ever since he had disappeared, Dracun had acted like a smudged copy of Zilia Makepeace, all too ready to make incoherent accusations. Harribon didn't want to get off on the wrong foot with the Settlement One Topman, about whom he had heard interesting, or perhaps disturbing, things.

Topman Samasnier, however, was all charm and pleasantries as he welcomed Harribon, gave him the pick of the guest rooms, bought him a drink at the canteen, and invited him to dine with him and Saluniel that evening.

Harribon demurred appropriately. "Ah, Sam, that's too much work for Sal. She's got, what? Two little ones?"

"Three. Sandemon, Sahkehla, and Sahdereh." He laughed. "Nine, seven, and five. They're a handful all right, but it's no problem. Some of the older folks are fixing dinner at the brotherhouse for us. We've got a handful of retireds now, Harri. Doesn't seem it could be that long, does it? I remember first day we stepped through the Door. I was six, and the oldest settler here at the settlement was what? Fifty lifeyears? And we've got great-great-grandmas now! Of course, they were grandmas or mommas when they came, but it won't be long before people have enough land credits to get their land rights."

Harribon, who was somewhat younger, merely nodded and smiled, wondering a little at how relaxed Sam seemed, Samasnier Girat who was known for being tight as a guy wire. Sam Girat who was supposed to be so hyper he wandered around half the night, fighting monsters. It couldn't be the drink; they'd only had this one. Unless Sam was on something, which was possible. Maybe the med-techs had come out and settled him down.

"What brings you over, Harri?"

The question took Harribon almost by surprise; he choked on his drink. He'd thought Sam knew why he'd come. "I came over, Sam, to find out how in hell Settlement One manages to keep its people so peaceable."

"Ah well," Sam made a deprecatory gesture, as though it was nothing much.

"Don't *ah well* me, Sam. I've heard all the rumors; I've scotched a few of them. I don't think you've hexed the rest of us, which some few of the younger workers seem to believe. I don't think you're getting favored treatment from CM. But get rid of all that nonsense and the fact remains, Sam, Settlement One does it somehow. It was true even before your time as Topman, according to the Archives, so I'm not blaming you personally." He laughed, cocking his head to show he'd intended no offense.

Sam stared at him, almost incomprehendingly. "I've always thought that was . . . just stories," he said at last. "We had a while during peak season, you know, when everything went to hell. It was after our God died, old Bondru Dharm." He laughed, shrugging. "We had a hell of a ten days there. I figured all the meanness that happened afterward was because of that. That's what I told them at CM. But once we quit fretting over it, we got back to normal pretty soon."

"Normal for you," said Harribon, squeezing the words out between his teeth. "Sam, what's normal for you isn't normal for the rest of us, that's what I'm trying to tell you. By my grandma's left tit, you know what I'm saying. We need to know why. Thirty-some odd years, that's long enough to say it isn't chance! Not an accident! Something's at work here, Sam, for shish sake."

Sam shrugged again, still uncomprehending or giving every appearance of it. "Well, if you think so, maybe so. I don't know what it is, Harri. Maybe it's just because the way we are is the way we are. I've lived here all my life, almost. I don't know how we're different from anyone else. People come from CM now and then, look us over, sort of stamp around, make a fuss, and then go away again. You'd think if there were anything, they'd see it, wouldn't you? They've been looking at us for all that time. Wouldn't they have seen it?"

"Will you let me look?" Harribon asked, holding his breath and his temper.

"Sure! Look! Anywhere. Ask questions. Get a flier from the garage. Go on out to Bubble Lake, if you want to see something pretty. Or Cloudbridge."

"Bubble Lake? Cloudbridge?"

"Sure. They're close by. Anyone down at maintenance can tell you how to get there. Supper's at nightwatch two. That'll give you time to clean up after you go digging around." He bowed and swept one arm in a long arc toward the door, giving his guest the freedom of the settlement.

Harribon had never heard of Bubble Lake or Cloudbridge. Besides, he hadn't come to look at scenery. So far as he knew, no one ever went anywhere on Hobbs Land to look at scenery. What he wanted to know would be in the settlement, anyhow, so he went first to the barns and equipment yards, looking for nothing in particular. He found nothing in particular. People seemed to be fully occupied, not hurrying, but not wasting time either. They greeted him, introduced themselves, seemed pleased to see him, but didn't stand around looking for an excuse not to work. He stood for a while in the door of the main tractor shed, watching a man and woman working on a fertilizer pump. She was doing the repair. He was fetching and carrying. Harribon saw her put out her hand for a tool and the tool being slapped into it, then the hand again and another tool. He watched for some little time, then left, realizing only after he'd left that the two hadn't exchanged a word. That's the kind of teamwork he envied. He saw it sometimes at Three, but it was a rare and wonderful commodity.

In the fields the weeders and fertilizer spreaders moved slowly down rows of rootcrops, across the tops of grain fields. Water ran in glittering rivulets here and there. Harribon stood on a bridge over a main ditch, watching the threads of silver sparkle away into the distance. Beneath him, the bank of a ditchlet had recently given way, letting the water spill onto the surrounding soil to make a tiny swamp. Harribon looked up to see if anyone was near enough to call. No need. From across a field, a quarter of a mile away, a man was moving toward him with a shovel, grinning as he came. Three strokes of the shovel fixed the ditch wall.

"Nice day," said the worker, looking out over the field. "You visiting?"

"From Settlement Three," Harribon told him. "How'd you know this ditch was broken?"

"Thought it was likely," the man grinned, giving him a knowing look.

The place must have broken before, Harribon told himself. The settler evidently knew it was likely to break again.

A power truck moved out from the central garage, stopping at field side at the same moment that the robot weeder drew up to the road. The operators exchanged chitchat while the weeder was fueled, then they went their separate ways.

"How'd you know he was out?" Harribon asked the truck operator.

"Usually runs out about now," was the casual answer.

He walked back through the settlement, stopping to peer into the ruined temples, to walk around on the shattered mosaic floors and stare at the grillwork and the central stone. He'd made a trip here, years ago, to see the God. He didn't remember it as having been anything very impressive. A chunk of stone with sparkles in it. Now it was gone. He went out to the north, stopping briefly at the crèche and again at the school, to find they appeared to be much like the Settlement Three crèche and school. Here, however, the children weren't yelling at each other. Yelling, yes, but not at each other. The sonic effect was the same, but the psychic effect was quite different, noisy but purposeful. Like an orchestra tuning up.

North of the town the path dropped into a streambed, up the other side, and out onto fairly level ground where the other ruined temples stood, just as he'd seen them the last time he'd been here.

Except that one of them had been rebuilt. Where had he heard that? Someone from CM had told him. Jamice. Last time he'd consulted her about a new chief mechanic, she'd told him how surprised they'd been at the reconstruction. So this was it?

He circled the structure, startling several cats and surprising four children who were busy plastering the exterior walls with what appeared to be a mixture of clay and straw.

"Hi," he said. "Sorry to have startled you."

"That's all right, sir," the largest of the boys said. "You must be the visitor from Settlement Three."

"Harribon Kruss," he said, holding out a hand.

Each took it in turn, announcing his or her own name. Saturday Wilm. Jep Wilm. Gotoit Quillow. Willum R. Quillow.

"That's quite a big job," Harribon commented. "You going to do the whole outside?"

"It's traditional," remarked Gotoit. "To do it every year."

"After it's smooth and dry, we can paint it," said Saturday. "We're thinking up the designs now."

"What do you plan to put on it?"

"This year we think some kind of aquatic motif," said Gotoit. "Creelies and water weed and all kind of little creepers. Like out at Bubble Lake . . ."

"This Bubble Lake," interrupted Harribon. "I don't think I've heard of that before."

"Well we only found it recently," said Jep. "It lies out west of the settlement, in a little fold, sort of, where you wouldn't happen on it ordinarily."

"Anywhere near Cloudbridge?"

"No, Cloudbridge is more up toward the Gobbles. Past the New Forest."

Harribon nodded. He hadn't heard of a New Forest, either, trees being in short supply anywhere except up on the escarpment.

"Okay if I go inside?" he asked.

There was a moment's hesitation, only a moment, as though they were thinking this over.

Then, "Sure," said Saturday. "No reason why not. Don't scuff up the floors, though. They were a lot of work."

He took off his boots when he went inside, slipping along the curved floors in his socks, floors curved to fit the rumps of the Departed, so he'd been told. The place had a strange beauty. He didn't remember the temple he'd visited before as being beautiful, but this one was. Very dim, of course, with only the light reflected through the grills from the central space and the tiny amount that came in through the ventilation slits and open door. Would the Departed have used the temples at night? How would they have lighted them? There were no candle sticks, no lanterns. He roamed around the scooped floor, stopping at the grilled door to peer into the central space.

It stood there, regarding him. He remained poised, almost off-balance for a long, frozen moment as he stared at it, then he stumbled back the way he had come. The children were outside the door, mixing more mud plaster.

"You have . . . you have another God," he said, wondering if they knew.

"Oh, yes," said Jep offhandedly. "Did it startle you, sir? I'm sorry."

"It's name is Birribat Shum," said Saturday. "Jep and I are the Ones Who take care of it.

"We help," protested Gotoit and Willum R. simultaneously.

"Oh, yes," Saturday agreed. "Lots of people help. And cats."

"How long have you had it?" Harribon asked, pulling on his boots, his blood pressure slowly returning to normal, now feeling slightly ashamed of his first reaction.

"He was raised fifteen days ago," said Saturday. "Between the tenth and the eleventh hour of the daywatch. Like his predecessor, he was Noon Discovered." She laughed, the others laughing with her. "It's a pun," she told Harribon. "Or maybe a riddle. Bondru Dharm means 'Noon Discovered,' so Birribat is also Bondru Dharm."

The children went back to their plastering. Harribon sat where he was, just outside the door of the temple, listening to them bickering back there. They sounded like any children anywhere. Willum R. was teasing Jep about being Saturday's sweetheart, threatening to paint a big heart with an arrow through it on the temple when they got it plastered. Gotoit was telling him to quit teasing and get more straw. After a time other children came through the willows, greeted him, and went to help the plastering crew.

Harribon sat and listened. There was a mud fight. There was much squealing and laughter, but no one was hurt, though Gotoit spoke vehemently to Willum R. about his getting mud in her ear. Several faces were washed down at the stream. Still Harribon sat. When it began to grow dark, Saturday and Jep Wilm came from behind the temple and offered to walk with him back to the settlement. They stopped at the stream to wash.

"The only problem with this job is it's really filthy," Saturday complained. "It's like monstrous mud pies."

"Should you say that?" Harribon asked in slight wonderment. "Since it's for the God?"

"Why shouldn't you?" she asked him. "The God doesn't care about stuff like that."

"I thought Gods were very strict about stuff like that," he persisted. "Strict about, ah . . . blasphemy. Joking about . . . sacred things."

"There's nothing sacred about plastering the temple, is there, Jep?"

Jep was drying his face on his shirttail and only grunted in reply.

"Isn't the God sacred?" Harribon went on, wondering why he was asking these children questions like these. "I mean, you do call it *God.*"

"Oh, we could call him anything," Saturday announced. "We could call him Bafflebreeze. Or Chinless. Or Australia. It doesn't matter what you call him, for shish sake. He's Birribat Shum, just like I'm Saturday, and Jep's Jep. Just like you're Harribon Kruss, Topman of Settlement Three. It's just a name, that's all. Kind of a label, you know."

"It's just a way," said Jep. "A convenience. A kindness." He stopped abruptly. "Here's where we have to cut off for our clanhome, sir. A pleasant nightwatch."

Harribon stood and watched them darting away through the dusk, down a sideway toward a cluster of houses, which were no doubt fully occupied by the Wilm clan. They were no different from the clanhouses found in Settlement Three, and yet he found himself examining them, trying to find something strange or exotic about them. Everything was built of foam panels. There wasn't much a builder could do to make a sponge-panel structure look distinctively different from any other sponge-panel structure. The brotherhouse had a wide porch and welcoming door. The several sisterhouses spread from it, each with its private entrance leading to private spaces inside, space for women to entertain their lovers and friends, private space for older women, too, grandmas and such, along with plenty of room for growing children. Jep would probably be moving out of his mother's place and into the brotherhouse within the next year or so. Willum R. probably already had. Most boys moved when they started having love affairs—or thinking about having love affairs. Just thinking could go on for a considerable time without anything really happening, not like those marriage cultures, where all the women were trying to cling to their virginity and all the males were trying to take it away from them, everybody panting and rushing, trying to grab off acceptable partners under acceptable conditions before they got too old.

Thinking of getting old: if there were retireds in Settlement One, people who were no longer contractually obliged to work in production, it wouldn't be long before brotherhouses would hire them as housekeepers and cooks for the clans. And then it wouldn't be long before some of the settlers would have land rights of their own. And after that Hobbs Transystem Foods would turn Settlement One over to the people in accordance with the contract and begin recruiting for a Settlement Twelve, off in the nowheres. Harribon had once asked Spiggy how many settlements there would be, altogether, when Hobbs Foods was finished planting and harvesting. Hundreds, Spiggy had said. Hundreds, spread across the arable plains of Hobbs Land, with wide stretches of the original Hobbs Land left untouched between.

"Land left between, so there will be no extinctions," Spiggy had said. "Not of plants. Not of animals." Authority frowned on extinctions. At least, the Science Advisory did, which was pretty much the same thing.

It was all so familiar, and yet it felt foreign, exotic. It was too peaceful. Perhaps that was it. At home, in Settlement Three, there were always problems. Always the subliminal whine of discord, somewhere, like the snarling of a trapped cat. Here, Harribon was aware of no problems. If there were problems, Sam would handle them.

Or, he told himself, perhaps Birribat Shum would handle them. Before they ever happened.

• *"You look tired,"* Sal told Harribon over the liqueurs as they sat by a window of the Girat brotherhouse, looking out over the fields. Behind them in the kitchen they could hear the bustle and clatter of two of the retireds who were cleaning up after dinner, mixed with the treble chatter of Sal's young ones.

Harribon smiled, shaking his head. "Not really. Just thoughtful. Your brotherhouse is very quiet, Sam. You were an only son?"

"I had one brother, Maechy. He died as a child, before we came to Hobbs Land. In fact, it was his death that prompted my mother to become a settler. My parents were married, in Voorstod upon Ahabar, but mother was the only one who came to Hobbs Land."

"Sam's brotherhouse will fill up when Sande and Sake get to be big men," Sal laughed. "Then Sam can play uncle, right enough." About fourteen, that's when boys needed to live with men, so said the conventional wisdom. Up until then, mothers did well enough.

"What about your mother?" Harribon asked them, trying to remember what it was he had heard about Sam's mother.

"Maire? She has a small sisterhouse to herself," Sam said. "She works at the crèche, which she enjoys. We invited her to join us tonight, but she said she was too tired of people to eat with people. Some of the older settlers are talking about building a retireds home when we get land rights, maybe up north of the settlement, where it's quiet."

"Up by the temples," Harribon offered.

"West of there. But fairly close."

"I was up there today."

"Were you?" asked Sal. "How were the kids coming with the plastering job?"

Somehow, Harribon had not expected her to know about the plastering job. "They seemed to be enjoying it."

"Yeah, they get a kick out of doing stuff for the God," said Sam. "The way Birribat Shum and Vonce Djbouty used to. Did they tell you they were the Ones Who?"

Harribon nodded. "They said everyone helped."

"Oh, well, yes. If something needs doing. But mostly the kids. It's good for them. Teaches them a lot about planning a job and sticking with it until it's done. And with the child labor provisions in the settlement contract, they can't be involved in production, so it gives them something they can feel good about having accomplished."

A peaceful silence. Harribon swallowed again, almost painfully. "I didn't know you had another God, Sam."

Sam furrowed his brow, scowled into his drink. "I guess we haven't made any announcement about it."

"Stirs things up too much," agreed Sal, making a face. "Can you imagine Zilia Makepeace if we tell her we have

a new God. 'Who authorized you to have a new God.'
'Why wasn't Native Matters consulted about this new
God?' " She laughed. "Or what about Jamice Bend?
'What are the personnel implications of your having another God.' We just didn't want to bother. We figure eventually they'll find out, and then we can say, 'Zilia, Jamice,
it's been here for years. Why make a fuss now?' "

"Where . . . where did you get it?"

"The children found it," said Sam. "And since they'd
already prepared the temple, of course we raised it."

"Found it? Raised it?"

"It was buried. In the soil." Sam regarded him
thoughtfully. "Does that bother you, Harri?"

"Don't let it bother you, Harri," said Sal, regarding
him with lovely, luminous eyes.

"It isn't fair," he said, his voice rising uncontrollably,
angrily. "It isn't fair!"

There was a slight noise at the door, and they turned
to see Saturday and Jeopardy Wilm standing there.

"Excuse me," said Saturday. "I'm terribly sorry to
interrupt, but we had to bring something for Topman
Harribon."

"For me?" The anger which had flooded him flowed
away in an instant, leaving him feeling empty and
ashamed. He looked at the package the child was offering
him without understanding anything. He didn't understand why he felt as he did. He didn't understand who he
was mad at. He didn't understand why he was standing
here holding a film bag with something white inside it. It
meant nothing to him.

"Isn't there someone at Settlement Three who's dying?" Saturday wanted to know.

The words caught in Harribon's throat. "My . . . my
mother," he said at last. "How did you know?"

Saturday drew him away and talked to him in a low
voice, giving him the package, touching his face with her
hands. Jep was talking too, patting him, stroking him.

"It'll be all right," the children said. "All right. We're
the Ones Who know about these things. You'll see." Then
they were gone.

"What did she give you?" Sal asked curiously, taking the packet from Harribon's hand and peering at it.

Harribon stared through them, not seeing them, not sure what he saw. "A God for Settlement Three," he said at last. "They knew I thought it wasn't fair. So they gave me a God for Settlement Three."

· *Elitia Kruss died* at the sixteenth hour of the nightwatch three days after Harribon returned from Settlement One. Her passing was peaceful. She went from alive to not alive on a passing breath. Harribon, who had spent the past two nightwatches on a couch in her room, did not even realize she had gone until the breathless silence woke him from a drowse.

Harribon had one brother, Slagney, and two sisters, Paragon (Parry) and Perfection (Perfy). The four of them wrapped their mother's body loosely in a blanket and carried it at the first daywatch hour to a place just west of the settlement where there was a considerable tract of high, wooded ground and a shallow grave they had all helped dig the day before. They laid her in the grave. Parry recited a poem her mother had been fond of. Harribon knelt above the body for a moment, tucking something inside the blanket, then they picked up the shovels they had left the day before, covered their mother's body, and went back to the brotherhouse, where they prepared breakfast for the children.

"I don't understand why she didn't tell *me* she wanted to be buried out there," wept Parry, who was the eldest daughter. "Momma always told me everything."

"I think it just came to her within the last few days," Harribon said in the calmest voice he could achieve, one somewhat liquefied by swallowed tears. "She told me during the night. I was the only one there. I should have mentioned it to you before she died, but I just didn't think of it until yesterday." He remembered the conversation, almost. Perhaps he had mentioned how lovely the view was from out there. Something.

"What was it you put in the grave with her?" Slagney

wanted to know. Slagney was the youngest, the baby, and he had a habit of petulance.

"Her locket," said Harribon honestly. There had been a locket in the packet, along with the thing Saturday Wilm had given him. "The one you gave her when you moved into the brotherhouse. She treasured it. She asked for it when she told me where to bury her."

"Oh," said Slagney, his petulance detoured for the moment by sentiment. The locket had been his "leaving home" gift to his mother. Sons often gave their mothers gifts when they moved into the brotherhouse, gifts to say I'm still with you, I still love you, I'm no farther away than next door. "Isn't CM going to be upset at us, burying her outside the authorized cemetery?"

"If anyone tells them, probably so," said Perfy, the second daughter. "Since she wanted to be buried out there and not in the burial ground, I'm not going to tell CM. Are you, Slagney?"

"Don't be a fool," he snapped. "Of course not. But people here will know there was no grave dug in the burial ground."

"I had one dug there," said Harribon. "Yesterday. We'll go fill it in after breakfast." He chewed his bread and nodded and made quiet conversation and wiped the faces of young children in between repeatedly wiping the palm of his hand against his trouser legs. He could still feel the warm stickiness of the white stuff when he had taken it from the filmbag and pressed it against his mother's body. She had been cold and dead, but the fiber had been warm and alive. When she had died, he couldn't remember what it was the Wilm children had told him that made him so sure, so very sure. He still couldn't remember, not exactly. Something. Something very important. And even if he couldn't remember what they'd said, he had remembered what to do.

And now, now, now what was going to happen?

• *Shan, Bombi, and* Volsa Damzel arrived on Hobbs Land middaywatch, immediately following the arrival of four men from Ahabar, and since both contingents were gathered simultaneously in the small reception area, the welcoming committee consisting of Zilia Makepeace, Dern Blass, and Tandle Wobster encountered them all. Dern, without displaying any of the interest and suspicion he felt at the advent of men who were unmistakably Voorstoders, asked for their names—Mugal Pye, Epheron Floom, Preu Flandry, and a young man called Ilion Girat —without giving his in return. The name Girat rang a bell, of course, and Dern had to remind himself to show no sign of recognition.

"And what brings you to Hobbs Land?" he asked.

Preu Flandry claimed they would be doing a comprehensive survey of Hobbs Land for the Archives, and certainly they were laden with enough recording equipment to make this explanation seem reasonable. Even in Ahabar there were few barriers against travel by Voorstoders. Dern had no reason to act upon what he told himself was merely prejudicial dislike.

Since Dern was being his usual casual self and Tandel was being her usual efficient one, the Voorstoders were speedily sent off to travelers' housing without having any idea who it was they had met—or who had met them. Then the three Thykerites were escorted to VIP quarters, where they were introduced to their assigned servants (cook/chauffeur/valet/guide/interpreter/factotum) and generally welcomed with remarkably little fuss. Dern and Tandle soon bowed themselves away, leaving the three visitors with Zilia, as she had been mentally urging them to do for some little time.

Zilia had been keeping herself very much under control. She hadn't known the Thykerites were coming until this morning. She certainly didn't want them reporting back to the Native Matters Advisory that she'd gone off her head or was being wilfully capricious. She might be capricious while no one was watching, but not when Rasiel Plum and the whole Native Matters Advisory membership could pin it on her. Zilia had met Rasiel Plum and had the highest regard for his perspicacity and his determination.

"Well," she said in a shaky voice when they were left alone. The three of them were looking at her as though she were something doubtful and possibly dangerous. She looked back, thinking they were the dangerous ones, the whole ensemble of them: three stocky white-tuniced figures, each tunic diagonally slashed by a wide purple belt with a zettle tucked into it; three dark, round faces turned toward her under three immaculate and identically folded white turbans; three triangles of ochre hair showing over three unwrinkled brows; three pairs of pale yellow, very glittery eyes, which seemed to be examining her soul. Under those turbans, the hair would be long enough to sit on, but done up in tight braids. In obedience to the prophetess's command, High Baidee did not cut their hair. The prophetess had said, "Do not let people fool with your heads," and heads included hair. The Scrutators had ruled, however, that faces were distinct from heads, and the male Baidee were not bearded.

"Well," assented Shan, curving his straight lips into a narrow arc, like a slice of melon. "That was all very nice. I feel properly welcomed. Now, what can we offer you, Lady Makepeace."

"Zilia," she said, still in the shaky voice. "Zilia, please. Nothing, nothing at all. I had luncheon shortly before you arrived. If you and your clanmembers are hungry, please feel free . . ." Shan was, she decided, the slenderest one of the three. And the handsomest. Not that she, Zilia, should care about that. Baidee did not mix.

"I think something light," declared Volsa in a surprising hungry-beast voice. "Something green or orange, with leaves in it. What's good on Hobbs Land."

"If you'll permit me?" Zilia went to the door and spoke softly to the CM steward waiting there. A salad dressed with cit juice and grain oil. Fruit. A bottle of the mild, sparkling wine made at Settlement Eight. Cheese from Six. A few small creely leg sandwiches. The High Baidee ate no mammalian meat, no eggs, and nothing contaminated by either, but they did eat fowl and fish. Zilia hoped creelies would count as fish.

Evidently they were close enough to fish, though Bombi did ask if the creature had fins and scales. Bombi was the plumpest one, the one with the slightly exaggerated manner.

"Both," Zilia assured him. "Both fins and scales, yes."

"And what's it called?"

"Creely," she said, leaving off the *legs*. Most things with fins did not have legs. So far as Zilia knew, the High Baidee had never ruled on the acceptability of creelies, which meant that eating them was, at least, not forbidden. "A creature unique to Hobbs Land. So far as we know."

"Now," said Shan, chewing away at a piece of fruit, "What's all this we hear about the Departed."

"What we have here is not about the Departed, at least not on the surface," Zilia murmured. "What's on the surface is human children rebuilding a temple of the God. The Departed God, one presumes."

When she had finished telling her tale, clarifying whenever they liked, she waited for judgement. Inasmuch as she was alleging—or at least suggesting—some form of coercion, anathema to any Baidee, the situation demanded a pronouncement of some kind.

"Do you have any reason to believe, any real reason," Volsa asked at last, "that the children were coerced into rebuilding that temple?"

Zilia shook her head miserably. She didn't. Not really.

"Do you have any reason to believe *anything* got them to rebuild that temple against their will?"

She shook her head again. "I just have this feeling," she admitted. "A feeling that something isn't . . . isn't the way it's being represented."

"Hmph," said Dombi. "Well, I, for one, am going to get *proper* charts from the Central Management office and lay out a schedule for an Ancient Monuments survey. That's what we're here to *do*, after all. We'll do a little back-country, then a little civilization. There's only the *one* village with temples in it, right? Settlement One? When we get to that point, we'll see what we can find out, right? See if we find anything to *confirm* your 'feelings.' "

"Do you want me to come along?" Zilia asked, not sure whether she wanted them to say yes or no.

"Perhaps. Let us do a bit of surveying first," Shan asserted. "We may not ask you to join us when we get to Settlement One either. Just to avoid any appearance of undue influence, you understand."

She smiled, indicating she did understand. Then she left them to go back to her apartment at CM staff housing, where she spent the night chewing her nails to the quick and wondering if she were really going mad. What did she think was happening here? She honestly didn't know.

Meantime, the Damzel team got hold of Spiggy Fettle and invited him to dinner. They caught him with a companion, and he spoke to them with the screen blanked out, which his companion much preferred.

"I'm not observant," he told on-the-screen Shan. "I don't own a kamrac or a zettle. I wouldn't know how to wind a turban if my life depended on it, and I eat eggs."

"Not at our table, you don't," laughed Shan. "As for the rest, wear a loin cloth if you like, but we need to talk."

Spiggy, who was having one of his all-time top highs, thought having dinner with a troupe of Thykerites would be great fun or ridiculous, one or the other, but in any case good for a laugh. Besides, his companion had to be elsewhere that evening.

As it turned out, the Damzels were nobody's fools and gave him a good deal to think about. No, he told them seriously over the finishers of dried fruit and confections, he didn't really think Zilia was mad.

"I rather like her, you know," he admitted. "Despite her paranoia. She told me about her traumatic upbringing, and I've decided it's really some kind of supersensitivity she has. She seems very alert to nuance. I don't think she honestly *believes* anyone on Hobbs Land ever did anything naughty to a Departed, but she feels *something* covert is happening, and her quivering nerves translate that into something personal. By that, I mean something that affects Zilia or Zilia's purpose in life. There are no remote and irrelevant sins with our Zilia. If there's anything going on, she's sure it pertains to her. She's the only person I know who could overhear some harmless sexual hanky-panky between two settlers and translate it into a threat against the Departed."

"So you think something could be going on?" Volsa asked.

"I know *something* is going on. Have you read

Chaniger's work on settlement applications of the classic
Gaean hypothesis?"

Bombi shrugged at Shan who shrugged at Volsa, who
said, "He was one of our instructors on Phansure."

"He claims," said Spiggy, ignoring the sceptical tone
Volsa had used, "that the introduction of any strange species or, indeed, the loss of species causes great changes in
the planetary psyche. Man has been on Hobbs Land some
thirty-odd lifeyears, so, if Chaniger is right—and I've always felt there is a great deal to be said for his theories—
we may expect the *persona* of Hobbs Land to be changing.
It won't be anything too obvious, I shouldn't think. We
occupy only a tiny land area and have been careful not to
threaten local species in any way. Nonetheless, some
change is probably occurring, and I think Zilia senses that
change. It may be the most minor of adjustments. Some
barely discernible shifting, but I think she feels it, as animals are said to feel the precursorial tension of climatic or
tectonic events."

"An interesting theory," said Bombi, without expression.

"Of course, during this recent period, the Departed
did die out," murmured Volsa. "Assuming they were a
predominate species, their demise might create considerable change in the planetary ecology. However, I think it
only fair to tell you that the High Baidee do not accept the
idea that planets or planetoids have *psyches.* To do so
would imply that worlds have minds, and the proscrip-
tions of the Baidee . . ."

"Oh, I'm well aware of all that," Spiggy laughed. "I
was born and bred on Thyker, after all. I lived there long
enough to learn all about the Overmind and the Baidee
prophetess. My stance upon such matters—which I will
not allow you to call backsliding—is not due to ignorance
of the words of Morgori Oestrydingh. No, my beliefs are,
I like to think, my own device, not merely a reaction
against revealed truth. However, you asked me a question,
and I gave you an answer. You are free to reject the idea,
or put it in terms you can accept if you like. Isn't that
what Baidee is all about, after all? Not allowing our minds

to be controlled by others, so that we can be responsive to various ideas?"

He was laughing at them, and all three of them knew it. The prophetess had declared it a sin to believe in absolute truths, but the Scrutators claimed that didn't apply to religious truths, of which they had manufactured a good supply over the centuries.

"If you can't accept a planetary persona," Spiggy went on, "then think in terms of shifting ecologies. No doubt they would also cause a bit of a premonitory tension. My real point is, I don't want you to discard Zilia's concerns as *mere* paranoia. She's paranoid, yes, as many of those who share Voorstod heritage seem to be, but that doesn't mean there isn't something going on."

"Would you be interested in joining our survey? If we could get you time off?" Bombi put the question as a hypothetical one, but Spiggy took it seriously.

"No," he said, after some thought. "If I went with you, it would be for pure curiosity's sake; I might do some damage, and I can't imagine being of any help at all. My refusal isn't due to lack of interest, however. I feel bound to suggest that, if you could record your travels, there'd be a ready market among the settlements for your records. Settlers are intensely curious about the unsettled parts of Hobbs Land."

He accepted their lifted brows as sufficient consideration of his idea, and then fell back on hospitality. He invited them to walk about CM, to visit the Admin club as his guest, to use the sports complex, to take advantage of the Archives. He made appropriate small talk, then left them to settle into familiar patterns of half talk, half musing, which was their family trait.

"Personas . . ."

". . . not likely, but . . ."

"Something they haven't even thought of . . ."

". . . seems to be alert and responsive . . ."

A very long silence.

Then, "Tomorrow," said Shan.

And with that and their evening obeisance to the Overmind, they ended their day.

· · ·

· *In the upper-level* personnel office of CM,
Mugal Pye was attempting to impress Jamice Bend rather
more than he had impressed a number of lesser function-
aries on the floors below.

"You see, Ma'am," he was saying in his insinuating
voice, "this boy here, Ilion Girat, is a nephew of Maire
Girat, who came here to Hobbs Land snorbel's years ago.
All the boy wants is to convey the greetings of members of
the family and get to meet his aunty, and we've had all
these persons below and outside telling us it was impossible."

"Mr. Pye," said Jamice. "You would be amazed to
learn how many uncles and nephews and sisters and sons
come to Hobbs Land in order to escape from their kin and
their families and all entanglements of the past. Even
when so much is clear, we have all manner of relatives
coming here saying they only want to talk to dear old
aunty or advise dear sister that mother has died or that
they only want to say hello and carry greetings back to the
family. It may well be that this young man's aunt will be
glad to see her nephew, but it is equally likely such a
meeting is the last thing she desires. We've learned this to
our sadness. It's why there is no roster of personnel available to visitors. You won't even find it in the Archives.
Casual visitors are not told where our people are."

"But what if she wanted to see him," pressed Mugal.
"Would you forbid her doing so?"

"Of course we wouldn't. I have a form here which
you, or in this case, the young man should fill out. He
should give us the name of his aunt, or the name she was
known by before she came here, for she may have changed
it since. He can tell us what the relationship is, and what
the purpose of his visit is. Then we'll transmit the message
to the person involved, and if he or she wants to meet you,
he or she will take time off from the work of the settlement and come here to CM to do so."

"We can't go there?"

"No, you can't go there for that purpose unless you

have a written invitation to be a guest in her clanhome. The settlements are not set up to receive casual visitors."

Mugal, since he was already committed, had Ilion Girat fill out the form and then watched while Jamice herself fed the information into her desktop stage. He had little hope Maire Girat would want to see her nephew, but anything was worth a try.

They left the office to join the others outside, and Ilion asked, for the dozenth time, "How long am I going to have to stay here? This place is so empty."

It was true that Hobbs Land had no mists to create walls and ceilings among which men could move, half-hidden from others of their kind. Here the horizon was far and clear, and vision disclosed more than Voorstoders were accustomed to see.

"You'll stay until they send you home," said Mugal. "And they'll ask you how come you got left, and you'll say you don't know. You don't know, do you?"

Ilion shook his head. He didn't really. He only knew that someone else would go home in his place, someone who had some connection to a woman named Maire. The whole thing, so far as Ilion was concerned, was pointless.

· *In · Settlement Three,* Vernor Soames was learning how to lay stone. He and six or seven of his friends had fallen prey to an urge to build something. Vernor wasn't sure what. A clubhouse, maybe, he thought.

"I told them it would be all right with you," Dracun had told Harribon. "I told them you wouldn't mind their being fully occupied doing something sensible."

"Where do they want to build it?" Harribon had asked, in a flat and unsurprised voice which seemed natural to the occasion.

"Out west of the settlement. There's some open ground out there and a lot of broken stone at the bottom of a ledge."

Harribon not only agreed to the project, he also used some personal credits to hire an ancient-arts hobbyist, two-jobbing from CM, to come give the boys lessons in stonemasonry. At least, it had started with boys, but there were as many girls involved by the time the lessons had progressed through foundation digging and stonecutting and mortar-mixing to actual stone-laying. So far as anyone could tell, the young people had no plan, but as the central ringwall and radiating arches took shape, Harribon relaxed into a mood of fatalistic acceptance. He seemed to be the only one who noticed the resemblance of the stonework to an architectural form already found upon Hobbs Land. But then, he was probably the only one who had traveled to any part of Settlement One except the sports complex. The ruined Owlbrit villages up on the escarpment were out of bounds for settlers.

While the older children cut and laid stone, whole teams of younger ones combed the stream beds for flat colored stones, which they sorted into boxes by color and size. Many such boxes sat near the construction site, waiting. Sometimes adults wandered out to the site and helped with the digging. The area inside the arches had to be scooped, just so, and then lined with large, flat stones, with the interstices filled in with clay, to make a surface on which mosaics could be pieced together with construction stickum.

"What would you do if you didn't have stickum?" Harribon asked Vernor one day as the boy took a brief respite from lifting stone.

Vernor thought about it. The whininess which had always distinguished his manner was almost totally absent, Harribon had noted. "Clay," he said finally. "We'd set the stones in a bed of clay. But stickum's better."

Harribon agreed that stickum was probably better. So long as Central Supply didn't cavil at supplying such large quantities of it.

After the arches had been completed and the central ringwall had risen to the height of three tall men, Vernor came into Harribon's office and announced, "We need some grills. Each three of the radiating arches comes down over one arch in the ringwall. There's twenty-four radiating arches, so that means there's eight arches in the ringwall. Each of those needs a grill, and one of them has to open, like a door. There's nothing in the settlement that will do. None of the machine grills will fit. They need to be metal, and we can't make them here." Vernor was not in the least apologetic as he explained his needs.

Harribon told the boy he would take care of it. He made another trip to Settlement One, this time with an engineering recorder capable of sampling materials. He made a record of the grills in all six temples, the rebuilt one, the recently ruined one, and the four others, where only fragmentary bits could be found. The grills differed mostly in details. Some were wrought with leaves, others with blades of grass. Some had curlicues, others were plain. Harribon's mother had been fond of certain aromatic native plants, which she had grown in pots. Harribon made pictures of the plants and took the recorder notes and the pictures to an artist hobbyist at Settlement Nine who sent the resultant plans on to the artisans' shop at CM for bid by any metal-working hobbyist. When the grills were delivered, subtly decorated with entwined metal leaves and stems, the children working on the structure did not seem at all surprised.

Harribon helped with the central roof truss, as did seven other men of the Settlement, including a couple of the Soames brothers. By that time, the thatching on the lower roof was complete and the mosaics were nine-tenth's laid on the scooped out floors. This building had a slightly shallower scoop to the floor than in the Settlement One temple, Harribon noted. As though something had realized humans weren't built at all like the turnip shaped Departed.

When the building was complete, except for plastering, everyone went back to doing what they had done before. Except, of course, that they got more done these days because people had almost totally stopped getting angry with one another. At the end of the quarter, Harribon looked at the stats on production and permitted himself a wry and slightly fearful smile. If this kept up, Settlement Three would be neck-and-neck with Settlement One.

• • •

• *"Mom,"* *asked Jep* one evening when Jep's little sister was soundly asleep and the two of them were alone, a time that was increasingly rare. "Do you know anything about mycelium?"

"A little," China replied. "Fungus isn't my specialty, but I know what any competent botanist knows."

"What does it do?"

"Well, I suppose mostly it's like roots. It isn't structured like roots, but it acts mostly like them. Mycelium is the mass made up of the interwoven, often underground threads that make up the body of a fungus."

"I thought the thing on top was the fungus. The mushroom part." He was thinking of the things that grew in the mushroom house.

"No, the thing on top is only what we call the fruiting body. Fruiting bodies don't even need to be on top, sometimes they're buried. Let's see, there was a classic delicacy, way back, what was it? One still sees references to it. The truffle! That was an underground one. The actual fungus is the rest of it, the filaments, the interwoven threads, the part you don't see."

"What does it grow on?"

"Different things for different kinds. Tree roots. Straw. Manure. Rotted leaves. Often on something that's decaying, like a dead tree or dead animal. What are you doing, homework?"

Jep nodded. Yes. He was doing homework.

"Where'd you find the word mycelium?" his mother asked.

"I was asking the Archives. About things that grow underground."

• *"Are you worried* about the children?" Africa inquired of her sister. "I get a little worried sometimes."

"About their getting involved with one another? No. The genetics look all right, and they make each other happy."

"It isn't that so much. More this business of their identifying themselves as the Ones Who. I keep remembering poor little Birribat Shum. And Vonce Djbouty. Now, there was a misfit."

"You think there's some similarity? Between Jep and Birribat Shum?" China was properly horrified. "They're nothing alike. Nothing at all. Poor little Birribat took care of the old temple very nicely, but honestly, Africa, it's all he was good for. Once the elder Shums died, I was always grateful he'd found something to do."

"Did he, do you think?"

"Did he what?"

"Did he find something to do? Or did something find him?"

"You think the God came looking for Jep and Saturday?" China laughed, not at all bothered. "Well, what if it did? They aren't creeping around like little Birribat, dusting and sweeping and catching ferfs in little traps. For heaven's sake, Africa! Saturday and Jep are completely normal kids with a particular hobby, that's all."

Africa shook her head ruefully, agreeing. Certainly Saturday was a completely normal kid.

· "*People have to* be dying somewhere," Saturday murmured to Jep and the others. "I just don't know how we find out where."

"We could start a kind of club," offered Gotoit. "To visit people who were sick. To take them flowers and fruit. Things like that. Then when they died, we'd know."

"An intersettlement club? Who would we ask?"

"Horgy Endure," suggested Jep. "If we could convince him it has something to do with production."

"Well, it would have," said Gotoit. "If people's sick relatives were made happier, then people wouldn't worry about them so much, and production would be up."

"We could make the same argument to personnel," said Willum R. "If Horgy doesn't bite on it."

"He'll bite on it," said Saturday, as though she had been assured of it. "He'll bite."

Trips to CM, particularly to the surplus and specialty food exchange or to the hobby and artisan center, were not infrequent. Each settlement sent a vehicle at least once every ten days or so. Saturday Wilm called ahead for an appointment with Horgy and arrived at his office just before noon. She had come alone. Horgy's reputation was such that she felt she would get a better hearing if she went by herself, and Horgy was probably, so she and Gotoit had agreed, not at all dangerous to someone her age. In furtherance of the mission, however, she had paid particular attention to her dress and appearance.

Horgy invited her to lunch in the officer's dining room, telling himself he would be offering this child a treat she would talk of for weeks. Saturday, who thought dressing up and being served was a bore, smiled and dimpled in gratitude. During the meal she told him about the idea of a visitation committee, being carefully inarticulate at times to show him how overcome she was at the honor of dining with him. Saturday could sound like Africa when she chose to, but she and Jep had agreed it wouldn't be a good idea today.

"You know, finding things for kids to do is one of the problems we've got in settlements," she said confidentially, when she figured she had been with him long enough to have regained some degree of poise. "Everybody knows that. Mothers and uncles are always telling us to go out and play, but you can only play so long. We're not allowed to be involved in the work; we can only spend so many hours on studies or athletics. That's why we did the temple rebuilding, really, just for something to do. Now we think this committee to visit sick people might be very interesting."

Horgy was impressed, though he thought it best not to show it. "There aren't many people who are very ill," he said. "We're a healthy lot, and mostly young enough that the diseases of aging haven't caught up with us."

"I know," she admitted. "Even if there are only a few, it would be kind of fun to meet the kids from the other settlements, get to know them better. Really, the only times we see other kids are at the games, and there's not a lot of time during a game to get to know anybody."

"I don't see why your committee wouldn't be useful," he said. "You'll need a vehicle, I suppose."

"We figure we'd need to use a settlement vehicle once

in a while," she said, smiling encouragingly at him. "The
older ones of us will operate the vehicles."

"On a trial basis then," he agreed, giving her his
charming look. "And you'll report to me at intervals. I'll
also inform the Topmen. If they have a problem with it
we'll discuss it later."

None of the Topmen had a problem with it. The visitation committee was well-accepted, not only by the few
sick and injured, but also by the people of the settlements.
Many of them were particularly touched by the little ritual the children worked up of keeping all-night vigil at the
gravesides of those who died. Though there were only a
few who were sick, there were always accidents, always
fatalities. As time went on, the committee conducted vigils in every one of the settlements except One and Three.

Horgy was so moved when he heard of this that he
wrote the whole thing up as one of the "innovations" reports Dern Blass demanded from all of them. Sometimes
Horgy thought the damned innovations reports were the
only ones Dern read.

· *The four men* from Voorstod had spent some
time at CM, recording everything, bothering everyone.
The policy of Hobbs Foods was to have everything open
and aboveboard and available to anyone who wanted to
look, but by the time the Voorstoders left CM, there were
those who felt the policy went too far. The Voorstoders
had burrowed, and they had snooped, to no purpose.
None of the people who worked in the personnel office
were at all susceptible to Mugal's sly charms, and what
Jamice Bend had told them had proved perfectly true.
There was no available roster of settlement personnel.

If they were to find Maire Girat (always assuming she
did not meet with them voluntarily), then they could look
forward to recording all eleven settlements in addition to
the fertilizer plant, the vacation camps, and even, so said
Ilion in a depressed voice, the mines.

"It's all for the Archives," Mugal told the fertilizer
plant supervisor, with a wave of one hand that seemed all-
inclusive. "The settlements, the mines, everything."

"Make pretty dull viewing," said the supervisor. "One settlement is pretty much like another. And Hobbs Land is no great shakes for scenery."

"Ah, well, it's for students," said Pye. "The duller, the better for them, eh? Make them dig. No point making it easy, no point letting the inadequate rise in the world. Patience, fortitude, that's what does it every time, Lord knows. Dogged determination."

"Still dull," repeated the supervisor. "It's all dull, when you come right down to it. Planting. Growing. Harvesting. Shipping out. Planting again. Everything flat, so the ditches will work right. Everything flat."

"You sound bored, friend."

"I'm not your friend, and I'm not bored," the supervisor said, offended. "I chose a quiet life. I'm not a slave. But then, you Voorstoders would know more about that than I." He said it with a certain cocky arrogance, a touch of hostility, his eyes watching Mugal's hands, as though getting ready to counter a blow.

Mugal was quiet for the moment, his eyes drifting away from the man beside him to his three colleagues who were plying the tools of their supposed trade with the same dogged determination Mugal had just advocated for students. "How did you know we were Voorstoders?" he asked in a silken voice.

"You said 'Lord knows,'" the man replied. "Voorstoders say that. I do a bit of reading in the Archives, bit of a hobby with me. Like to read about those old religions. That Lord-this, Lord-that kind of talk belongs to the old tribal religions, doesn't it?" Old and outworn, said his voice. Old and outworn and suspect.

Mugal smiled, said something inconsequential, and then went away from the man. He hadn't hidden the fact they were Voorstoders as they moved about on Hobbs Land, but he hadn't advertised it either. It came as a shock to learn that he had given them away with two casual words.

"I heard him," whispered Epheron, when Mugal rejoined the others.

"So did I," whined Ilion. "I thought we didn't want people to know we were from Voorstod."

"We're not hiding it," snarled Mugal. "For, if we hid it, and somebody learned we'd hid it, they'd wonder at us. We've just made nothing of it, that's all."

"This is all too difficult," said Ilion. "This Maire Girat is making things too difficult. Maybe some other woman would have been easier."

Mugal glared at him, annoyance mixed with amazement. "Some other woman? Have you been to school?"

"I've been," the youth snorted. "And what is that to you?"

"Were you told in school of Maire Manone."

"I was. Some singer or other. She was before my time. I never heard her. Except from the Archives."

"Some singer or other! The Voice of Voorstod? Who wrote *Voorstod Ballads*? And *The Songs of the North*?"

"She also wrote 'The Last Winged Thing'," said Ilion in a snippy voice. "Which made women and children leak away from Voorstod like water from a cracked jar. Are you saying she's some connection to Aunty Maire?"

"She is your Aunty Maire, lad. And, difficult or not, we'll keep looking until we find her."

SIX

• *Atop the escarpment,* the surface of Hobbs Land was as softly undulating as the plains below, though wooded rather than bare. It had been a considerable time since the last great cataclysm, and that had come in response to the impact of an enormous rocky mass—perhaps belt flotsam? perhaps a comet lost in cold space for millions of years? perhaps even a stranger, plunging out of nowhere?—suddenly showing up and throwing itself down in a gravitic tantrum of self-destruction. Then had been much tumult and wreckage. Then were lakes overthrown and a large sea drained away into the southern ocean and the warm light of the sun hidden for several revolutions behind a cloud of ash. When the skies had cleared at last, however, there had been a new inhabitant upon the coalesced world: a threadlike growth that spread from the point of impact outward until it lay everywhere within the soil and over the stones and among the plants and among the clumsy, prototypical animals. It had come with the outsider. Where the outsider came from, or how it came to be carrying its strange burden, there had been no one then to wonder, and there was no one now who knew enough to ask.

After the great catastrophe, the clumsy animals had evolved with astonishing rapidity. They had acquired tool-manipulating tentacles, and then speech, and then a sense of identity and purpose. After many generations, they called themselves the Owlbrit people, Owlbri being what they called their world. They walked on detachable legs. They spoke by rubbing two or more serrated tentacles together. They never got very far, if travel or expansion was the measure of getting, for their world was the only one they knew. They never did very much, if creativity is the measure of doing. Their racial characteristic was a slight bewilderment which increased with the centuries. They had no imagination and no ambition. If the thread-like growth was frustrated by this quality among the Owlbrit people, there was no indication of it. From time to time the net would create spores and then die, reconstituting itself as though to go at the task in a slightly different way. It made no difference. The Owlbrit built slowly and painstakingly and uniformly, pockmarking the world with their temples and their villages, the last of them not very different from the first, and at last they died too, still slightly bewildered, though pleased that some other creature had come to take up the burden of . . . of whatever the burden had been.

Some essential quality of renewable force or desire had been missing in the Owlbrit people. They had used up what they had, and then there was no more. Strangely enough, they had perceived this deficiency themselves, naming the missing quality "rhsthy." An Alsense machine would have translated this as "poetry." The Owlbrit had lacked poetry.

None of the researchers quite realized this, though some academics had made a footnote or two concerning the possibility of racial ennui. The lethargy of the Owlbrit was one of those mysteries which remain forever unanswered because no one quite formulates the proper question.

No one had wondered very much about the Departed ruins, either, though many of them survived. Entirely too many, Shan and Bombi had decided, though Volsa still exhibited interest in what each day might disclose.

"Tomorrow will disclose another village or six," Bombi told her in a bored voice, as he wiped dust from his eyes. The Baidee turbans had given way to caps; their white tunics had been replaced by rough coveralls of dark and heavy fabric. The High Baidee Damzels could have been anyone, anywhere, so long as the where was dusty and ancient and smelled of earth.

Bombi went on, "I cannot understand your *enthusiasm,* Volsa. We have seen almost four hundred villages by now, usually at the rate of two or three a day. Each has the ruins of little scoopy houses. Each has the ruins of *several* scoopy temples. The temples were built in series, we've established that. An old one fell to pieces before they built a new one, or concurrent with their building a new one. The villages all seem to have the same number of temples, as though *every* village decided to build at the same intervals. Six temples in every village. We don't know *why,* of course, though the Archives suggest many historic parallels which would lend credence to a variety of *contradictory* hypotheses."

He wiped his forehead and sighed dramatically, waiting for comment, which was not forthcoming. He sighed again, and went on. "All the house are *alike.* All the temples are more or less alike, except for the grillwork, which varies over time sufficiently that we might work up a dating scheme based on pattern, if there were any *conceivable* reason to do so. The very plain ones were first. Followed by leaves, followed by various inelegant conceits and useless *frills.*" He sighed once more, saying, "By the *prophetess,* but I'm thirsty." The robot handi-serve beside him gurgled and offered a sip tube.

When he had drunk, he went on with his diatribe. "We have, however, made a noteworthy discovery. We *know* why the Old Ones died—of *boredom.* They had no talent for innovation. One might almost think they had pushed themselves too far in achieving this little and died of *exhaustion.*"

He intended to be brittle and sophisticated and amusing, and thereby succeeded in speaking the absolute truth, though neither he nor his indifferent listeners recognized that fact.

"How many villages do we have left to do?" asked Shan in a weary tone.

"If we do them personally, entirely too many. However, if we don't find something a *wee* bit different soon, I'd suggest we have the rest of the survey done by machine. We could turn the whole job over to something along the lines of a Selter Model 15J environment sampler. We can feed in a planetary survey, and it will do very nice diagrams, and because it won't get *impatient,* as I most *certainly* am becoming, it will maintain better sampling technique than I do!" Bombi laughed shortly and accepted a lengthy drink from the robot.

"We could always program it to call us if it found anything different from what we've already surveyed," Volsa said doubtfully.

Bombi agreed. "Which would give us time to get down to the settlements, which we haven't even seen yet. I must say that my whole being longs for enormous quantities of hot *water!*" The flier they were using had a sonic cleanser, but the quality of the experience was in no sense comparable to the tumbling torrent Bombi envisioned.

Shan exploded, "Hot water! Bombi, this has been a very easy trip. You don't know what a hard trip is. You . . ."

"Do not want to hear about the *Porsa,*" Bombi told his brother sternly. "Volsa and I have heard about the Porsa, and do not want to hear about them *ever* again."

"I was just going to make the point that . . ."

"Don't," said Bombi. "What do you think, Volsa? Shan? I don't want to *shirk* the job, but so far this has been a waste of man-days. We've done nothing a robot couldn't have done as well. Our contract with Native Matters Advisory says we can use whatever method seems advisable."

"Two days," said Volsa at last, looking dreamily at the verdure around her. Green wasn't the usual thing on Thyker. Or on Phansure. She found green rather intriguing. "Give it two more days. Then, if there's nothing distinctive, give it to the robots."

• • •

• *Gotoit's mama cat,* Lucky, had five half-grown kittens hunting in the tall grass at the side of the easternmost grainfield. It was the job of all the settlement cats to minimize the ferf population along the edge of the fields. From the various animals man had used as workmates in pre-Dispersion times and taken with him from planet to planet in the long reach outward, cats had been chosen to accompany these settlers because they did not form destructive packs, did not require constant attention, and could be depended upon to keep the vermin population in check. Lucky and her kits were a demonstration in point. There were several dozen dead ferfs laid out in a row along the footpath, and the nightwatch was only half over.

None of the settlement cats ate ferfs. Something about them disagreed with cat stomachs, but this in no way lessened cat fondness for the chase. Only at dawn, when the count had been increased to over seventy, did the cat and kittens pause in their labors to engage in the lengthy face- and leg-washing all of them felt necessary. They had finished faces and front legs and were starting on the hind legs when Saturday and Gotoit arrived with a sack.

Gotoit admired the line of bodies, conveyed her admiration with strokes and chirrups to Lucky and the kittens, and only then helped Saturday bag the night's catch and walk with it around the eastern edge of the settlement to the temple.

"What does Birribat Shum need all these for," Gotoit wanted to know. "Usually he only wants one or two at a time."

"Birribat Shum is pushing the mycelium all the way to Settlement Three," said Saturday with a slight air of self-importance. "You know, to join the one that's growing there. He says it works better when all the parts are linked up. Ferfs have something in them that he needs. Something different from human waste. We could probably find out what it is and supply it directly if we had to. On the other hand, humans have something in them that was missing before. Once the Gods used up all they brought with them, they couldn't go on any longer. That's why the Departed died."

"The God didn't die for a long time after humans got here, not the last one."

"It took a while. It had to get to know us before it could make the right kinds of spores for the next one."

Gotoit shook her head and jiggled the sack. "How do you know all that stuff?"

Saturday looked uncertain. How did she know? "I just do," she said at last. "I'm the One Who, so I guess that's why."

"Well, it's still a lot of ferfs."

"A lot of work for the cats."

"It doesn't matter. Lucky doesn't mind so long as she doesn't have to carry each one over here individually."

"She told you that, did she," Saturday laughed.

Gotoit was not annoyed at the question, but neither did she disregard it. "Of course she told me I'd have to carry them over. Didn't Birribat tell you he needed them? Didn't I tell Lucky? Of course Lucky told me."

• *By noon of* the last day they had determined to spend upon their survey, Shan and Bombi and Volsa had reconciled themselves to turning the whole matter over to the machines. By dusk of that same day, they had changed their minds.

The land at the top of the escarpment was relatively flat, though it had been cut by river valleys over the millenia, and the resultant cuts had been worn into gentle slopes by wind and rain and the burrowing of creatures small and large. This terrain was forested with the distinctive escarpment trees, slender trunks which rose twenty feet or so into the air and then exploded into a spherical puff of foliage, from the top of which another trunk emerged, and another puff, and another trunk yet, and so on, to a height of eight or nine puffs at about two hundred feet. From a distance the trees resembled fuzzy green beads strung on thick vertical needles. Because of their resemblance to the ancient art of topiary, the trees were called Topes, as a class, though there were at least twenty different species easily distinguishable by the layman.

The villages of the Departed had been set in clearings, which, remarkably, remained mostly clear of trees even after all the time that had passed since they were built. The temples of the Departed, however, were set among the trees. The new thing, which the Damzels found quite by accident, was in what they assumed to be a meteor crater, a raised lip of stone which made a ragged circle around the enclosed flattened space.

Volsa, bored with villages and temples, had walked into the woods to admire the undulant surface above, where the foliage spheres interlocked to create a solid ceiling of feathery puffs. The land rose before her, culminating in a low rocky wall, which she climbed, bemused, thinking how different air smelled when there were many things growing in it. Beyond the wall, the area was only lightly wooded, the trunks so sparsely scattered that from where she was standing atop the stones she could see the entire circle which enclosed the radiating mounds at the center of the space.

She walked their length, their circumference. The individual mounds were perhaps a hundred feet long, radiating from a common center. There were eleven. Her recording instrument, which had a detachable probe point, told her the mounds were not covering anything on the preset list of recognizable substances—though this bit of information seemed doubtful, with digital figures quivering and needles darting restlessly across the faces of dials.

"Bombi," she said urgently into her communicator. "Shan. Come here. I've found something."

When they came over the wall a few moment's later, she was standing in the fifty-foot circle at the center of the radiating mounds, trying to make sense of the readings she was getting.

Bombi stared. "Artifact?" he asked at last.

"I don't think so," she said. "Artifact would be stone, or metal, wouldn't it? The same kinds of materials they built their houses and temples out of? We've set these machines to recognize all those substances, in all their modest variations."

"Maybe your probe simply isn't deep enough. There's a longer one in the flier."

"Well, get it. We'll try."

As they did, without success. Whatever the things were, buried there under the soil, they were not what the Damzels had expected to find. Nor did they have any idea whether these starburst mounds had anything at all to do with Ancient Monuments.

· *Samasnier Girat left* a note on China's door saying he was thinking of her. China knew what he meant. He wanted to try again.

China surprised herself by considering it. Certainly she had sworn never to be with Sam in anything but an official capacity again. They got along all right as workmates. Certainly she had meant it, at the time. After all, he had made her miserable with his picky-picking at her all the time. Asking her strange questions. Demanding answers, when she didn't even know what he was talking about. Saying things like "Well, think about it," when she had no idea what "it" was.

On the other hand, Sam had seemed more relaxed lately. Things had been going extraordinarily well. Even those small annoyances that used to plague him, as well as everyone else in the settlement—parts lost, equipment broken, necessary supplies not arriving on time—even those annoyances seemed to have taken temporary leave. Therefore, it was possible that Sam wouldn't be so picky, possible they might just enjoy being together. Besides, she was curious. She wanted to know what this thing was he was playing at, and maybe . . . just maybe he would tell her.

"Come for dinner," she said, next time she saw him, not staying to watch his face light up.

Red meat was raised over in Settlement Nine, almost entirely for export. The settlers' allotment of it was miniscule. All the settlements had plentiful supplies of poultry-birds, however, for both meat and eggs, so China planned her dinner around fowl. Each settlement had plentiful grain supplies and vegetables, including the so-called fragile vegetables, grown in greenhouses. Fruits tended to be seasonal, but were dried and preserved for settler use. The people in the settlements where wine and cheese were made hadn't seen fit to share their expertise yet, so their products stayed in short supply, but China had credits squirreled away for a special occasion.

She asked Africa if Jeopardy and Peace could come to Africa's sisterhouse for supper.

"You and Sam playing winkies again?" asked Africa with a leer. "Or is it someone else?"

China shrugged. "No one else." She didn't know. Not really.

"I thought it wouldn't be long," Africa murmured. "A changed man, our Sam. All full of human kindness."

"Africa . . ." China murmured. "Don't tease."

"Well, why not? The two of you are a scandal and an amusement to the rest of us. Be nice if you could get along instead of you walking on eggs here in settlement, trying to avoid him, and Sam out there fighting monsters on the hills for his fair lady . . ."

"That's not what he's doing!"

"Well, what is he doing?"

"I don't know, Africa. Except it doesn't have anything to do with me. It's something inside Sam. He wants to be somebody else. Somewhere else."

"Topman isn't enough, huh?"

"It doesn't have anything to do with enough. It's . . . there's something inside him, like a hole. A vacancy. A question. He keeps trying to fill it up. All that playacting, that's just part of it." She had surprised herself considerably by saying this. She considered it to be true, but if anyone had simply asked her to explain Sam, she would have said she couldn't explain him at all. Maybe as she got older, her understanding was increasing.

"Fighting ghost-beasts with his bare hands? That's part of it?"

China shook her head. No one had ever learned exactly what it was that Sam had fought, but ghosts didn't have bones. Even though the bones told no tales. For a while China had worried about that, worried quite a lot, afraid some visitor or intelligent being would come up missing, but except for that Soames man from Settlement Three, no one had, and the bones weren't human. Quite. China thought CM should have done a quick survey, looking for an Out-System ship maybe, but she hadn't suggested it. The skull was at CM, and everybody had looked at it. It had long teeth and big bony ridges over the eyes, and no one knew what it was. If they hadn't thought it might be something from Outside, why should she?

Africa shook her head and laughed. "Send Peace and Jeopardy over. They can spend the night with their cousins."

China seasoned her bird with Hobbs Land spices and fried it in grain oil. She made a vegetable-noodle dish that had been invented locally and was called a hobbspudding. There was fresh bread and fruit, plus the wine and cheese. They ate at the small table near the window which looked west, away from the fields, toward the wooded land.

Sam ate and smiled and smiled and ate, without picking at her and, when he had finished everything but the bones, suggested they take the last of their wine into the bedroom.

She started to say no, but then said yes instead, without really meaning to.

They lay on the wide bed, her head on his shoulder.

"We need legends here," he said.

Oh, hang him by his heels, she thought, her entire body stiffening. Here he goes again.

"Legends of lovers," he said. "Who are the great lovers, China Wilm?" He sounded merely interested, not picky.

This was a new question. "Great lovers?" she asked, relaxing a little.

"I asked that question of the Archives, and they gave me names. Names as empty and dry as dust. They meant nothing to me. Who was Abelard? Who was Romeo? Who was Gercord Thrust or Standfast Murgus and the Lady Vees? I did not know."

"Nor I," she murmured into his neck, feeling his arm tighten around her, his hand slide downward on her skin.

"Samasnier Girat and China Wilm," he whispered to her. "Why shouldn't they be legendary?"

"A legend in our time?" she giggled.

"For all time," he whispered, kissing her before going on to other things. "For all time."

For all time, she thought, wondering why the words echoed so fatefully. For all time. "Do that again," she commanded. "Oh, do that again."

He did it again, and then something else, and then time went away entirely. There was thunder, which they did not hear, and then a downpour of rain, lashing against the window with whispering whips.

A long time later they heard the rain and wondered at it.

"Early," said Sam in a puzzled voice. "Early this year."

Thus far he had not picky-picked at her once.

She was not content to leave it alone. She had to test it.

"What did you mean about legendary lovers?" she asked.

"I have decided legends are like spiders," he said, unaccountably.

"Yes," she urged, doubtful of the direction he was taking.

"Though the closest thing we have to spiders here upon Hobbs Land has ten detachable legs, we all know about spiders." He thought for a time. "Actually, legends are more like spider webs. You see, the spider attaches a bit of web and then swings out into space and attaches the other end somewhere else. And then does it again, and again. And finally, when all the spokes are fastened, it goes around and around, knitting them all together, until the pattern is made. You understand."

She did, of course, though she had no idea what he meant. Spiders were part of the human heritage. Even though there were none here, children learned of them in school as they learned of tigers and elephants and bears, almost mythical creatures of Manhome.

Sam went on. "The pattern links all the points it's connected to. So we men go back in history and come up with a great hero, and we attach our memory there. Or maybe we just go back in time and come up with a fa . . . an uncle, and we attach our memory there. Then we swing forward and attach the other end of that idea to someone or something else. That's what legends are for, to give us anchoring places in time. Else we live such little lives, China Wilm, like a bit of fluff adrift upon a great wind. We need anchors. If we have them, here and there we go in our minds, knowing this story and that, putting our web to this and that, spinning and spinning. Until, when we are done, we are all bound together in the same pattern. Without them, we are strangers to one another. With them, we know one another. We are spiders of the same ilk." He laughed. "Silk. Spiders of the same silk."

"But you said we had no legends on Hobbs Land."

"We don't. We have no common ground to tie us together. So, when I want to say to you, China Wilm, that I love you as the greatest lovers ever loved, I have no names to put to them. What are Heloise and Hero to us? I read their stories, and it means nothing to me. Who are Gercord Thrust and his fair Madain? Do the words make any picture in your mind?"

She shook her head, beginning to comprehend what he was saying. "So when my son Jeopardy seeks to tell Saturday Wilm how he feels, kissing her, he has no words."

"Ah," he said, something wicked and sharp-toothed rearing inside him at hearing her say, "my son." Abruptly, all his easy way with her was aground upon that particular stone in his craw. "Perhaps he will say, 'Saturday, I love you as my mother loves my father.'"

She flushed, not speaking, balking at the word he insisted upon using, finally agreeing, "Perhaps he will."

"And do you?"

She became very quiet. Now his voice was as it used to be, harshly demanding. Now it was like those other times, when he had wanted something from her and she hadn't known what. "Would you be here, Sam, if I didn't love you?"

"How would I know? I don't know who's been here since I was here last." He gestured at the room, her room, into which she could invite anyone she chose.

She could have told him, no one. Perhaps she should have told him, no one, letting him lapse again into that peacefulness he had shown earlier, but it wasn't something he should have asked. It wasn't the way things were done among the Wilms. If she said, no one, then he would say no one until now, how about tomorrow? And if she said, no one tomorrow, he would say, what about next year? And before she knew it, she would be eaten up for all time, pledging herself where no one should have to pledge herself. "Time spins, people change," so ran one saying in an old language. *"Vota errod, Erot vode."* Or that Gharm poet Maire was always quoting. "A vow of forever stands like grass/against the scythes of change." People did change. Even she might.

"You are here now, Sam," she said, knowing it would not satisfy him. Knowing nothing would satisfy him.

"You will not say," he muttered, getting out of the bed and standing at the window to see the rain. "Well, I have no better Hobbs Land words to use than these: I love you, China Wilm, as a creely loves its legs." And he burst into harsh laughter. "The words do not satisfy me, China Wilm. I need others. Perhaps, someday, I will find them."

She did not laugh with him. He was, perhaps, not the same man she had known before, but he was not a new man either. Something dwelt in Samasnier Girat that dwelt in no one else left on Hobbs Land. Wandering around at night was not enough. Fighting monsters was not enough. Exploring the miraculous new lakes and forests—even the brand new ones over near Settlement Three that no one had ever seen before—was not enough. He wanted something she could not give him, something no one could give him, and for a moment she wondered why he was still here, why he had not gone away with the other malcontents, wishing he would go.

So, for a time, she had loved him as she longed to do, but now the gentle time was spoiled, leaving her hurting and close to tears. She resolved once again to stay away from Sam Girat.

• • •

• *Shan, Bombi, and* Volsa arrived in their flier at
Settlement One and were met at the flier park by Sam in a
surface vehicle.

"You didn't need to do this," said Volsa, admiring
Sam from beneath her lashes and thinking that, had she
not been High Baidee, she would have set herself at this
man. "We could have walked over to the guest quarters."

"Topman, I could *not* have walked," said Bombi dramatically, falling about in not entirely pretended exhaustion. "I could have walked no farther than the nearest
bathhouse. I am *filthy.* I want nothing but water, hot water and peace."

"What's this I hear about your discovery?" asked
Sam, with genuine curiosity. "Some kind of strange monument?" Monuments, any monuments, interested Sam
greatly.

"Some kind of strange something," admitted Bombi,
"which we have *no* idea what is, except that, probably, it
has been there for a *very* long time. Animal, vegetable,
mineral, real or mythical, we cannot say. Something
which occurs naturally or something which was built. By
the Departed or by some former race. Or, by visitors,
there's always *that* possibility."

"Remarkable," said Sam, his mind spinning with a
thousand questions. "Remarkable that it was never seen
on survey maps."

Volsa shook her head at him. "The area is wooded.
The mounds might have shown up if there had been no
trees. They would have shown up on instruments if they
were of very dense material, but they don't seem to be any
more dense than the surrounding soil and rock. We just
don't know. We didn't bring the proper equipment to do
excavation. As a matter of fact, we're not trained xeno-
archaeologists, and we'll undoubtedly be criticized for
even putting a probe into the soil. Of course, when the
Ancient Monuments Panel learns of the discovery, who is
to say what may take place? We'll probably be innundated
by experts."

"Interesting," Sam murmured, thinking that the
things they had found might have appeared recently, as
certain other geographical features had, but not wanting

to say so. Evidently these visitors had not noticed the new features, and Sam was no more eager than anyone to have teams from Thyker or Phansure or Ahabar investigating. He brought the vehicle to a halt beside the Supply and Admin building. "Guest quarters upstairs."

"Hot water," moaned Bombi.

"Hot water," Sam agreed. "By the way, I've had some of our better cooks select and prepare food for you, in accordance with the information received by CM from your Religious Center. If anything seems improper or even doubtful, please let me know. I think we depended pretty heavily on poultry, fruits, grains, and vegetables."

They left him to go to the upper floor and make themselves at home. Shan fell onto a bed and was asleep within moments. Bombi got himself under the water shower and began singing Thykerian mind-clearing mantras, loudly and tunefully. Bombi had an excellent voice and had sung during the recurrent opera revivals in Serena. Shan, who had an even better voice, had never evinced any interest in music.

Volsa used the sonic cleanser, which she preferred to getting wet, and then sat by the window, nibbling at the nicely prepared oddments she had found waiting on a tray in the kitchen and thinking of Sam Girat. It was all very well to be restrictive in one's sexual pleasures, but on extended trips into places where there were no Baidee, one might desire to have other companions than one's own brothers. It didn't seem to bother Bombi much. Bombi had a tendency to take it or leave it, in almost any environment, and Shan had a strong touch of the ascetic in his makeup. For herself, however, Volsa preferred reasonably frequent access to acceptable companions. She decided to call Spiggy Fettle and ask him if he would join them for a few days when they returned to the escarpment. No point in making talk here in the settlement.

Here in the settlement. She watched it from the window, in all its dusty frontier guise: low, flat-roofed, sponge-panel buildings with wide porches; mostly unsurfaced roads; greenhouses stretching their glittering length toward the west; fields, which could be seen over the rooftops, green and orange and yellow and purple and dun, in wide rows and narrow, and no rows at all, reaching away on all sides, almost to the western horizon, where the suns flattened.

There were long, evening shadows across the streets. People went by purposefully, without hurrying. Children raced down the street and into a narrow alleyway and out again, shrieking, as children have always done. There were many cats. Volsa had expected that. Most farm settlements used cats, sometimes thousands of them, to keep the vermin in check. The local breed was sizeable, with large round heads, big eyes set well apart, and short hair. Some were plain-colored and some striped, and all had long, sinuous tails. Every now and then one of them looked up at her, standing quite still, tail carried low, one foot raised, eyes bright with a perspicacious, interested stare, as though to say, "Aha. Someone new."

Bombi came out of the shower much refreshed and very wet, his long hair hanging in dark strings almost to his knees. "No fas-dry in there," he complained. "Only towels."

"Sit here in the sun," she suggested. "It will dry quicker." She stood behind him and plied the towels, several of them, until the long strands were only moist. Then she combed and braided his hair for him, as he often braided hers, the long, complicated braids that would end up wound tight under his turban. Volsa had often wished the prophetess had said *minds* instead of *heads.* How wonderful if she had said, "Don't let anyone fool with your minds." This business of never cutting one's hair was a bore.

Music came to them, at first faintly and then more loudly.

"Are you dry enough to get dressed?" she asked.

He nodded, sighing as he heaved himself out of the chair. "You want to go see who's singing?"

"It sounds interesting." She leaned out of the window, trying to ascertain where the sounds were coming from. "Besides, we want to look at the temple, don't we?"

"I have seen enough ruined temples to last me forever," Bombi said.

"Shouldn't we wake Shan?"

"Leave him." Ever since they had found the mounds, Shan had become a pain, twitchy and jumping at shadows. Bombi frowned. "He needs his sleep."

They went out into the air, found the ruined temples, and gave them a cursory once over, enough to know they were exactly like every other ruined temple upon the heights.

"What's the music?" Volsa asked a passerby, a stout woman in a bright coverall.

"The choir?" she asked, surprised. "Oh, I've gotten so used to it, I don't even hear it anymore. The children started a choir, many grown folk have joined, and Maire Girat is its leader. They practice out near the temple. Just follow the road across the stream, that way." She pointed and smiled, then scurried away as they went in the direction she had indicated.

"Happy place," commented Bombi, two lines appearing briefly between his brows. "Remarkably."

"Everyone seems well-occupied," agreed Volsa. "Busy." The two of them walked in the direction indicated, toward the sound of the voices. "We should have brought Shan with us," she fretted. "Except he's been so strange lately. Have you any idea what's wrong with him?"

"Only the Overmind knows," Bombi replied shortly.

"Do you think it has something to do with that time, you know, the Porsa?"

Bombi frowned again. He had resolutely not been thinking about that. He had been very self-consciously not-remembering. Now he did remember, and it made him cross. When Shan had first returned from Ninfadel, he had driven them crazy. He had spent most of every day bathing, over and over, claiming the smell of the Porsa had permeated his flesh. Night after night he had scrambled from his bed, screaming, bringing his siblings running to shake, wake him, talk him into reality again. After ten times, a dozen, it had been too much for Volsa and Bombi. The doctors had been summoned, to give Shan things he could take to make him sleep, to teach him techniques for ridding himself of memory. The doctors couldn't do it for him, since that would be fooling with his head. He had to learn to do it himself.

As he had done, Bombi reminded himself. As Shan had done. Shan had concentrated, had studied, had learned to control it. Give him full credit for that. He had been very strong. Now Bombi gave homage to that strength by saying, "Volsa, he was over that *years* ago. He's all right. He's just tired." And he repeated the words silently to himself, reassuring himself. Shan was just tired.

"So we let him sleep," said Volsa, willing to be convinced. It was what she wanted to believe. He was just tired.

They crossed the stream and noticed the ribbon-willows, which were quite different from the Topes of the heights. They saw the rebuilt temple without, at first, realizing what they were seeing. The thatched roof completely changed the shape of the thing. The brightly painted walls made it seem almost spritely, almost joyous. They both realized at the same moment.

"By the Overmind," whispered Bombi. "A new one."

"It startled me for a moment, too, though I don't know why," Volsa commented. "We knew the children of the settlement had rebuilt a temple. That's what Zilia Makepeace told the Native Matters Advisory, after all. It's what set her off in the first place."

They thought for a moment of going in, but the choir drew their attention away from the structure, and they moved toward the singing. Childish trebles were soaring along with the women's higher voices, deep bass notes anchoring their flight, the lighter baritones and tenors and contraltos filling the pattern with harmony. Highest and brightest of the voices was that of a child of about thirteen or fourteen lifeyears, standing at the front of the group, her voice tumbling through the harmony like that of an ecstatic bird.

"Let's sit here on the grass and listen," suggested Volsa. "They're really quite good."

"Not what I'd call up to professional standards, but yes, quite good," agreed Bombi. They sat down on the grass, among a dozen settlers similarly engaged, falling under the spell of the music, letting the time pass gently.

Back in the settlement, in his room in the guest quarters, Shan Damzel dreamed he was once again on Ninfadel.

The dream started as his dreams had always started, with him just emerging from the Door to see the inside of the high-walled compound where several small buildings squatted on bare gravel amid stacks of supplies. Theoretically, the wall wasn't necessary, not here on the highlands of Ninfadel. Nonetheless, a wall had seemed prudent to the bureau in Ahabar responsible for such things. In the dream, Shan already knew this.

A pile of food crates lay on the sand beside him. All food came from Ahabar. Food could have been grown on the highlands of Ninfadel, but the soil required much labor to produce anything worth eating, and no one stayed long enough on Ninfadel to make the effort worthwhile. Shan knew this, too.

In the dream a uniformed officer came across the sand toward him, holding out his hand, smiling an official smile. The handful of Ahabarian guards were changed every forty days. While on Ninfadel, they seldom went outside the walls. The small Native Matters contingent stayed longer, but even they went outside only rarely. Sometimes they told Shan this, sometimes he remembered it.

In the dream, it was the Native Matters people who explained various things to him, putting their faces close to his, so that he saw their gums, their teeth, their vibrating tongues, repeating things he already knew, a litany he knew by heart.

"We'll tell you how to survive," the Native Matters person said. "Do you understand? If you want to survive, you'll listen.

"First, you never step off the highlands without your faceplate down. Not one step. You don't lift your faceplate anywhere below the altitude line. We had one guy, went down below the line and built himself an observation post up in a tree, slept up there without his faceplate. One of the Porsa slimed up somehow, got him in the night. So you never, we repeat *never*, go below the line without your faceplate down.

"Second, never go beneath the line without one full day's air in your emergency tank. Anytime you have less than that, you get here as fast as you can and get it refilled. One of 'em grabs you and you use up all but half a day's air, don't think you can get by. Next one might swallow you for a whole day. It's been known to happen. Some of them lay in wait at the line, so don't tell yourself you're stepping over just for a minute.

"Third, try not to go more than a quarter-tank's distance away from the line, or you can't be sure you'll get back to refill your tank. There's a counter on the tank, push it when you step over the line.

"Fourth, if any mucous gets on your skin, wash it off while it's still gooey. If it dries on you, it makes sores that don't heal. Don't take off your faceplate while you're washing, either, if you do it down there. They like to grab you down at the river. The best thing to do is wash in the troughs we've piped water to, on the highlands. There are tall beacons by every trough. They're easy to find.

"Fifth, don't try to talk to them. I don't care what kind of Alsense machine you've got, keep it on translate and record, not on speak. They go crazy if you try to talk to them. They just love it. We've had some of them swarm over the line just because some student was trying to communicate with them. It kills them, but they don't die right away. They live long enough to do a lot of damage.

"Sixth, you'll actually see more and hear more if you stay away from them than if you go close. If you go close, you'll spend most of your time swallowed, and from inside you can't see or hear anything much. The way to stay away from them is to stay above the line. That way nobody gets hurt. I know you won't pay any attention, but it's true. You'll see just as much from up here as you will if you get closer. Use spy-eyes, if you like. They'll get slimed fairly fast, but you can bring them back and clean them off.

"Seventh, use the nose filters whenever you see or hear them. I know you don't think a stink can kill you, but damn, it can come close. . . ."

What they had said. What they said to every student who came to Ninfadel. Shan had heard it; now he dreamed it, every word. Perhaps he only remembered it, but in the dream it seemed that he heard it for the first time, felt, for the first time, his own scepticism. Shan was High Baidee. He believed what he himself knew to be true. He did not necessarily believe these Native Matters people from effete Phansure, these Ahabarian guards.

They gave him the breathing hood, a tight, flexible garment with a hard visor-hinged faceplate. The plate was linked to a heavy tank containing two day's worth of ultrapack-air. A tube inside the faceplate could give him water. Another could feed him nutri-paste. The whole assemblage was heavy to carry, uncomfortable to wear.

"How long can I wear this thing?" he'd asked.

"Some people wear it all their lives," the officer had said, making a joke. It wasn't a joke, of course. Shan had seen the recordings of the assemblages lying in the sun among scattered human bones: required viewing for any graduate student who had the arrogance to plan research among the Porsa.

Or the courage, he told himself in the dream, as he had told himself in reality. Dedication, determination, courage. That's all one needed. He went out of the outpost, into the security lock. The inner door closed and locked. The outer door opened. He walked along the high, rocky ground, keeping himself just inside the clearly marked glowing *line*, above which the Porsa died, looking down into sparse growth on the lower slopes of the hills and along the river. The smells were of spice and resin. Below him, by the stream, he saw a group of Porsa and heard them shouting at one another. Unthinkingly, he stepped over the line and went down onto the moist, sucking soil of the hill, turning on his Alsense machine so he could hear what they were saying.

"Piss, shit, snot, pus," said one to another.

"Shit, slime, rot, you," replied the second.

"Fartedy-fart-fart," screamed a third. "Filth. You. Filth. You. Bury in feces."

They fell on one another, melting together, seeming to coalesce, then separating once more. As they did so, they caught sight of him and began sliming up the hill toward him, shouting greetings, great gray blobs of mucous covered with running sores. The stink that preceded them came in a palpable wave. Gagging, Shan thrust in the nose filters he had been holding and then remembered, at the last possible minute, to pull down the faceplate. Shrieking happily, they increased their speed.

"Coming to you, filth. Coming to you."

"Wait, filth. Wait!"

Shan dreamed that he ran, but they caught him. He dreamed that they swallowed him, one after the other, making gulping, liquid sounds.

Shan began to scream and went on screaming.

"Damzel!" someone shouted.

"Let me out!" he screamed.

"You're out," Sam yelled at him, shaking him. "Damzel, wake up. I heard you from my office downstairs. You're on Hobbs Land. You're all right!"

Groggily, Shan thrust himself toward the top of his bed, sat up, tried not to breathe.

"Breathe," Sam commanded, as the man before him turned blue. "There's nothing here to hurt you."

Shan tried a tentative sniff. Nothing. Only air. "Sorry," he said. "I thought I'd learned not to do that anymore."

"You're probably overtired," said Sam, carefully not asking the questions he wanted to, such as, "What were you dreaming about." Instead he asked, "Are you all right now?"

"Fine," said Shan. "Where are Bombi and Volsa?"

"Saw them walking down the street a while ago. You're sure you're all right."

"Fine," said Shan again, calling out as Sam went out the door, "and thank you."

Inside he was trembling, keeping himself from total panic only with an effort. This wouldn't have happened, he told himself, on Thyker. It wouldn't have happened. It had to be something here, something on Hobbs Land. Something . . . maybe those growths. Maybe . . . maybe something else, but definitely something. He lunged from the bed and started to pull his clothes on. It was this place. This place was causing it!

He went out into the street, hearing the music in a

kind of panic, walking swiftly toward it, trying not to run, keeping himself from running only with great difficulty. As he approached the sound, he began to make out the words they were singing.

"Rise up, oh ye stones," cried the tenors. "Rise up, ye great stones. Stand, oh, stand into the light."

"Rise up," boomed the basses. "Stand, oh, stand into the light."

"Rise up," trilled the girl's voice. "Stand into the light."

And there were Bombi and Volsa, sitting on the grass, listening, nodding in time to the music. "Not nice of you," Shan snarled from just behind them. "Not nice of either of you."

Bombi looked up to see him standing there, grinning a death's-head grin.

"What were you two doing, sneaking off without me?" Shan asked. His voice was tight, near to screaming.

Bombi stared at him, not replying.

"I thought you were asleep," said Volsa. "We're just sightseeing."

"Let's get out of here," said Shan, seizing their arms and half-dragging them back the way they had come. "Out, quickly."

"Shan, what's the matter with you?" cried Volsa, tugging herself away from him.

"The noise," he said. "The noise."

"It's only music, and lovely music," she cried.

"In my head," he muttered. "Something trying to get into my head. Swallow me."

"Beauty," she snapped. "Beauty trying to get into your head. It's all right. We're allowed to appreciate beauty."

He shook his head at her, wildly. "More than that," he hissed at her. "More than that. Get out of here."

Bewildered, they followed him back to the guest quarters, where he shut the window against the sound of the distant choir.

"Don't you hear it?" he cried at them. "The thing trying to get in?"

"Shan, go lie down," his brother instructed. "You're

overtired. I hear nothing but music, lovely music, very nice voices, untrained but, in the mass, having a *nice* effect. I do not detect any threat against my religious sensibilities."

"I'm not overtired," Shan shouted. "Not!"

Volsa merely looked at him, thinking he had not acted like this since just after he had returned from Ninfadel. He met her eyes, flushed, and went into his own room, shutting the door behind him. He was quite sure he wasn't mad. Though, at one time, among the Porsa and when he first got home, then he had thought he might be mad. This time he was quite sure he wasn't. Quite, quite sure.

He sat down at his portable stage and began, very carefully, to compose a message to the Circle of Scrutators of the High Baidee. When he had done, he composed a quick, superficially innocent reminder to Howdabeen Churry. In essence, both of them said that Shan Damzel felt Zilia Makepeace had probably been right. Something dreadful was going on.

• *Maire Girat received* word that her nephew, one Ilion Girat, son of Phaed's youngest brother, was on Hobbs Land and desired to see her. The last thing Maire wanted to do was see anyone from Voorstod, but on the other hand the boy could have something to say—about Phaed, perhaps. That he was sick, which she felt unlikely, or dead, which was always possible, given Phaed's inclinations. If he were sick, or dead, she wanted to know. Silly, perhaps. Unreasonable, yes. But she wanted to know. However, there was this other possibility . . .

Maire went over to the brotherhouse and found Sam doing nothing much, which was a wonder in itself.

"I've a message your dad's nephew is here on Hobbs Land," she said.

"My *dad's* nephew? *My* father . . ."

"Phaed Girat's younger brother's son."

Sam went giddy. This would be it, a signal, an invitation. This would be the thing he had been waiting for. "So? Does he ask to meet us?"

"Me, he does. And I don't want to."

She looked so pitiful, he forgot to be angry with her, though he usually was when she got into all that nonsense about Voorstod. "Tell me," he said.

"I'm afraid he's here to bring me back to Phaed."

Sam could not keep from saying in an exasperated voice, "Mam, that's silly. He couldn't bring you back to Phaed if he tried. And to think Phaed would send anyone, after all these years, it's ridiculous. He might send for me, maybe, not for you."

She ignored what he said, her fear overcoming her perception, not really hearing the words. "For me, maybe . . ."

"I know it sounds ridiculous," she said, wiping her eyes, "but I'm still married to him."

Sam did not want to speak of marriage. The idea of it shone in his mind. Lifelong commitment. He didn't care what China called it, that's what he wanted, and he dared not talk of it for fear those who scorned the idea would sully it for him.

"You didn't get unmarried when you left Voorstod?" he asked.

"There's no getting unmarried in Voorstod, Sammy. I'd made my vows to Phaed. I'd made them before a priest, as they do in Voorstod, and there's no undoing of it. The men can undo it, but the women never. For women, vows made before the priest are sacred."

"Not so sacred you didn't just walk off and leave him, though," said Sam, a hint of his buried anger coming through.

Maire gave him a shocked look. "Well of course, I didn't *just walk off and leave him.* After Maechy died, I went to your dad and I told him I could not go on living there in Voorstod, and I begged him to come with me here to Hobbs Land. 'You've riled your belly over the Gharm long enough,' I told him. 'Forget them and come with me. There's no Abolitionists on Hobbs Land for you to pain your guts over, and there's no slaves to get in a passion about, and no marriage there either, so you would be rid of that burden as well.' He disliked marriage, Sammy. That's nothing rare among the men of Voorstod. They do it, because it's the only way they can get virgin brides and sure sons, but it's only what they call a temporary device. They don't believe in it for men. In their Paradise, there will be no wives."

Sam ignored most of this. "So, what are you afraid of? That some priest will be with your nephew, to drag you back to Ahabar?"

She shook her head. "It's so strange, his being here. It smells of conspiracy."

"Conspiracy!" he laughed. "Mam, you're being as paranoid as Zilia Makepeace! The boy is here, he wants to see you because you were famous. Conspiracy!"

She stood up straight, glaring at him, "Sam, I say to you what my grandma once said to my mother in my hearing when I was yet a child. I've remembered her words all my life. She said, 'Conspiracy is dark and dirty, and vengeance is heavy as rock, and being a slaver presses a man down until he can see nothing but black dirt around him, like the walls of a grave. Men become accustomed to that darkness when they are in the habit of death. It pains such men to come into the light.' Now, Sammy, this nephew of your dad's is one of them, and it would pain him to come into the light, as it would pain Phaed himself. Dream your dreams of a kingly father all you like, Sam—oh, don't think I can't tell what you're thinking, you, my own flesh—but believe me, these men sit in the dark still, conspiring with their fellows, deep in that black pit with the stones of hate above them, and there is something dreadful portending. I know it as I know my own name." She broke off, half-choking, leaving Sam amazed and hurt.

He recovered himself and made excuses for her. So she was getting old. She was remembering troubled times, and it hit her hard. He should make allowances, but he didn't need to believe everything she said. "Well, if you're afraid, or for whatever reason, I'll go with you to keep you safe." Her fear made no sense to Sam at all. Still, this might well be the happening he had waited for, the stone under which he'd find his way back to Voorstod, and if she was involved, he would accept that she was afraid and get on with it.

Maire and Sam went up to CM for the meeting, and both of them were surprised to find two persons awaiting them when they arrived.

"Mugal Pye, at your service, Madam," the older one said, eyes crinkled in his best attempt at a pleasant smile. "Young Ilion here is part of our Archives party, and he did want to say hello to his famous aunt."

"You're Domal's son," Maire said to the younger man, ignoring the fatuous comments of the older one. She knew men like Mugal Pye all too well. Phaed was one of the kind, and he too had smiled and smiled and said soft words.

"Yes, I'm Domal's son," the youngster said, staring at her curiously. "Are you really Maire Manone?"

"They called me that, yes."

"The Sweet Singer of Scaery?"

"They called me that too, long ago."

"Mugal Pye," the older man said again, holding out his hand to Sam. "You'd be Sam Girat."

"That's right," said Sam, wondering why he felt squeamish touching this man's hand. Squeamish he felt, and he could not say why.

"Do you sing here, in this place?" Ilion asked Maire, looking around himself, as though wondering if anyone could sing in this place. "It seems very bare and open."

She laughed without humor. "Compared to Scaery? Where the mists make walls and a roof for any homeless man? Where a man may have a dry bed only if he puts his blankets beside the fire?"

"It is damp in the north counties," he agreed.

"Did you have some special reason for wanting to see me, boy?"

He shook his head. "I just wanted to hear about your life here, Maire Manone. People ask about you, you know. I thought I might carry word of you back."

"Tell them Mary Manone is no more, that Mary Girat cares for the babies of Settlement One on Hobbs Land, and that she is satisfied. Tell them that, boy." It seemed innocent enough, and she could not explain why she felt so cold.

Maire and Sam stayed only a little while longer, exchanging compliments and sending messages. Sam took Mugal Pye aside, despite the revulsion he felt for the man, and asked him to convey his best wishes to his dad. "Ask him to write to me," he said. "I think of him often."

Mugal Pye only smiled, without promising, for he had no intention that Phaed Girat be told about this, as yet. He asked Sam and Maire only a few more meaningless questions, to cover up the fact Maire had already told him everything he needed to know.

· *The message written* by Shan Damzel upon Hobbs Land was received on Thyker by Holorabdabag Reticingh, Chief of the Circle of Scrutators of the Divine Overmind, who judged it went overfar into the subject of inscrutable "feelings."

Shan said in his message he felt something was wrong. Shan felt something was happening. Shan didn't know what. Shan couldn't prove anything, but Shan was decidedly nervous. He thought whatever-it-was Zilia Makepeace had felt, he too felt. It was inimical. It was threatening. It should be stopped.

Reticingh was at first concerned about Shan Damzel's health and welfare. "He may be ill," he confided to his plump and sad-eyed assistant, one known as Merthal. "I thought he looked fine-drawn before they left. Sometimes I wonder if he ever recovered from his stint among the Porsa, may they rot."

"Rotting would probably delight them," suggested Merthal, who was not above an occasional jibe. "When Shan came back, he looked half-rotted himself."

The two of them stood upon a small balcony which jutted from the living room of the Chief's apartment, high above a training ground where some of the young Baidee doing their three-years obligatory service were being drilled and redrilled in the close order march and countermarch so useful in parades and processions of all kinds. If anyone ever tried to fool with the heads of the Baidee, the Baidee were ready to defend themselves. Between the brigades and the army, every ablebodied Baidee between the

age of puberty and senility was trained for service, and
that service was extremely up-to-date, relying heavily
upon biological weapons of varying, constantly updated
kinds. A well-equipped and trained research branch kept
everything on the edge of knowledge, insofar as both of-
fensive and defensive material and tactics were concerned.

It was almost a pity that such an effective machine had
so little work to do. The Baidee army had been fully committed only once in the years since the prophetess. The
beings who had come from Outside and who had attempted to enforce their own opinions upon the Baidee
had been fairly well thrashed before they had all "caught
cold and died." At one time, the Scrutators had smiled
when they recalled the story of the invasion, though after
the Blight came and went, they stopped enjoying the
story.

Reticingh regarded the wheeling ranks upon the drill
ground with approval as he said, "I've known the Damzel
clan since well before Shan and Bombi and Volsa were
born," he mused. "The family is rocklike in their objectiv-
ity. Though he is very young, I wouldn't have said Shan
was capable of mental disturbance. Unless he was ill, of
course." He meant physically ill. There was no mental
illness recognized by the High Baidee.

"He says in the message that he's well," offered
Merthal.

"He might only think he's well. I mean, one of the
symptoms of being not well is to think one is well when
one is not." Bodily ills could be treated. Sometimes
mental "troubles" disappeared when bodily ills were
cured.

"Short of bringing him back to Thyker and having
him gone over by the temple physicians, what would you
suggest?"

Reticingh sighed. Madmen were a constant challenge
to the Baidee. Nothing could be done for them unless they
had treatable bodily illnesses. There were many homes for
the "uncontrolled" scattered around Thyker. Some of the
inmates had to be tied up. Some of them had to be re-
strained to keep them from harming others, though they

were allowed to harm themselves if they wished. Some of them expressed themselves, sometimes, much as Shan Damzel was doing.

Reticingh thought it over, slowly, as the High Baidee were taught to do, considering the consequences of each action, the probable outcome of every case. At last, with some satisfaction, he said, "I would suggest, Merthal, that we send one of our temple physicians to Hobbs Land to make quite sure our beloved son is truly well. Young Dr. Feriganeh, I think. He would enjoy it. And you, of course."

"Me!"

"So that I may have your much valued opinion when you return. Besides, Shan's mother would eat me alive clad only in my zettle if anything happened to him."

· *Horgy Endure kept* the peace among his womenfolk by letting each of them know precisely what she could expect in the way of his time and undivided attentions. The fifth, seventh, and ninth nights of each ten-day work schedule were spent with his trainees, one at a time. Ruellin, the blonde, was scheduled for the fifth night, and she arrived at Horgy's apartments at the appointed time, shortly before the usual supper period. It was Horgy's custom to drink a little wine, eat a little food, and then engage in sexual sports for several periods of the nightwatch. Horgy was very good at sexual sports, and Ruellin considered herself fortunate to have obtained the trainee position, particularly inasmuch as she was learning something about agricultural production management as well.

On this particular fifth night, Horgy refused a second glass of wine, which was unusual. He also seemed lethargic with respect to his food.

"Not hungry, I guess," he said apologetically.

"I could go on home," she whispered, hoping he would not agree. "If you're not feeling well."

"No, no," he smiled at her, the white-toothed smile which warmed her all the way through. "Let's just sit a while on the terrace. I simply need to relax a bit."

Horgy's apartments were on an upper floor of the administrative residence. Only Dern Blass had quarters that were higher up. From the small terrace they could look over the ramified roadways and parklands of CM, out through the surrounding woodlands and plains to the place where the escarpment made a winding line upon the northern horizon.

"I understand they're finding interesting things up there," said Ruellin, making conversation as she gestured at the distant escarpment. "The people from Thyker."

"Interesting things happening everywhere," he murmured.

"Really?" She lifted a flirtatious eyebrow. "Are there interesting things happening here?"

"In the settlements," he said, not noticing her expression. "Lakes. Canyons. Water falls that didn't used to be there. Did you know six of the settlements have Gods now?"

"Gods?"

He put a hand to his arm, as though it ached. "Look it up in the Archives. There was one God when the settlers arrived. Where Settlement One is now. It died. You were there when we discussed it at management meeting." He sounded slightly pained or impatient, and she was quick to reassess his mood.

"Of course, I remember. And six of the settlements have Gods now? Where did they get them?"

"Found them. Funny thing. First the children get into this mood to build a temple. I wouldn't have believed it. Zilia didn't believe it. She asked me to go out to Settlement Five with her when she heard about it. There they were, gangs of kids, laying stone, singing. Funny kind of singing, zum zum zum, bittle bittle, as though they'd rehearsed it. So, they get a temple finished, and pretty soon, they find a God to put in it."

"Very . . . neat," she offered, not knowing what else to say.

"They've all got temples, now. All eleven settlements. I'm sure they'll all have Gods before long. Strange."

"Strange," she agreed, wishing he would quit talking about the Gods.

"They call each God by the name of some settler that's died recently. Kind of a memorial, I guess." He grunted and put his right hand under his arm. "I shouldn't have eaten anything. Now I've got a pain."

"Shall I call a tech?"

"No, no," he waved impatiently. "I've just been tired these last few days. I'm supposed to have a med-check, but I keep putting it off."

"Perhaps I'd better run along."

He turned the full splendor of his smile on her. "Sweetheart, no. If there's any remedy for tiredness on this whole world, it's right here next to me." He reached out for her, and she lost herself in their usual and delightful preliminaries.

Later he went into his bedroom while she visited the bathroom. When she came to him, he was sprawled out on the coverlet, face up, the lights dimmed. She was on the bed with him, snuggled against him, before she realized he was no longer breathing.

· *If Horgy had* thought the rapid proliferation of Gods upon Hobbs Land strange, Zilia Makepeace considered it ominous. She wanted very much to talk to the survey team from Thyker, but they were all up on the escarpment, looking at odd formations no one had noticed until recently. From what Zilia was told, once Shan and Bombi and Volsa had started looking for them on the aerial surveys, they found others, a similar formation here, a slightly different one there, some protruding high out of the soil, others barely rounding the surface. Though it was not part of their project, the Damzels had decided to uncover at least one of them, just to see what they were, and the three-man team had been augmented by machine operators, techs, a doctor from Thyker, and even a funny fat Baidee named Merthal who was scrupulously polite but stubbornly insistent upon being supplied immediately with whatever-it-was the Damzels thought they needed. Since the project was being conducted under the aegis of the Native Matters Advisory, as Native Matters person upon the planet, Zilia had to see to all of it without being part of any of it, and her paranoia had given way to sheer annoyance and frustrated curiosity.

She had even sought Spiggy's company, only to find that he, of all people, had been invited by Volsa Damzel to spend some time up on the escarpment. According to Tandle Wobster, who knew everything, Spiggy was enough of a Baidee to be acceptable as a sex partner even if he did eat eggs and didn't own a kamrac. Since she had little enough else to speculate about, Zilia speculated as to how Tandle had learned this interesting fact and ended with the suspicion that Tandle had probably illicitly tapped all their private stages.

Ruminations and suspicions were disrupted by the unexpected death of Horgy Endure, who, as anyone might have predicted, died in bed with one of his trainees. Zilia could not remember which one she had been until she saw the blonde girl at the memorial service, supported by female associates and obviously still in shock. Horgy had had a large circle of acquaintances, a few of them men, many of whom came to CM for the service. Zilia dressed herself soberly and sat toward the back of the hall, hoping the eulogies would not take long. A young person took the seat beside her, and other young persons filled the surrounding area.

"I'm Saturday Wilm," said Zilia's neighbor, offering her hand. "This is my cousin, Jeopardy. We met out at Settlement One when you came there for the visit. All these others are members of the visitation committee that Horgy Endure sponsored." Saturday sighed, and a tear slid gently down her face to drip, unnoticed, from her jaw. "He was very nice to us."

"He was very nice to many people," said Zilia, drily. She herself was almost the only woman in Central Management Horgy had not been intimately nice to. Herself and, possibly, Tandle, though Zilia would not have bet her life even on that. What had Horgy been up to with this child? "So you've come for the service."

"For the vigil, actually," said Jep. "Our group does that, you know. We keep vigil the night someone is buried. It's a sort of symbol of thoughtful remembrance. A kindness."

It was the first Zilia had heard of it. She had not looked at Horgy's report on innovations, and though Dern Blass had been interested in the proliferation of Hobbs Land Gods, no one had mentioned vigils at recent meetings. "At the grave?" she asked, amazed. Graveside services were unknown. Only the family or those appointed for the duty took bodies to a grave or to whatever other form of disposal was used. This, a Baidee custom which had become accepted Systemwide, was almost never contravened. The Baidee considered the body simply as something to be disposed of, a leftover, not something to focus community attention upon. It was customary for families to dispose of bodies, quickly though respectfully, even before memorials were conducted.

"At the grave, yes. So far, the weather's been very good, so we just bring blankets and sort of sing until the suns come up." Saturday's eyes were as limpid and clear as the mountain streams which fell from the escarpment. "Just a remembrance."

Zilia was not to be taken in by childlike eyes. This was another behavior she did not understand. "I'd like to join you," she said. "Would you mind an observer?"

There was a hesitation so brief that it went unnoticed. "Why, of course," said Jep. "We'd be glad to have you. We'll be getting together at the burying ground around nightwatch two or three."

Zilia walked out to the burying ground at nightwatch two and a half, splitting the difference. The place lay in an elevated basin, separated from the CM complex by a raised ridge of stone and shrubs and curly native trees. As she approached the ridge, Zilia heard singing, and once she had climbed it, she saw the lights of several lanterns and the shifting shadows thrown by a small fire.

The children were gathered around an area of disturbed soil which Zilia assumed was the grave. Saturday welcomed her and offered a blanket, since Zilia had not brought one of her own. The singing resumed, a multiversed chant called "Singing up the Gods," which told the story of a scene-by-scene, virtually rock-by-rock, ascent to the escarpment. This was followed by storytelling in which Horgy Endure was given the leading, though fictional, part as he explored strange and wonderful places such as the Isles of Flowers. Then there was a quiet perambulation around the grave and then a repetition of the same sequence, with minor variations. The children seemed to know a great many songs which had no real words but very complicated rhythms, songs which had no end but merely went on until everyone was tired. Sometimes they wore masks while singing or perambulating, blank masks with round holes for eyes and mouths, so they all looked alike.

"Why?" Zilia asked, troubled by this facelessness.

"Because we are not here as individuals," said Saturday. "Who we are isn't important. It's the intent that matters."

"Why do you say who you are isn't important?"

Saturday frowned, tried to speak, frowned again. "Because . . . because there's no . . . no reward," she said at last. "We don't get a gold star or anything."

"Our name doesn't get put on a plaque," said Jep. "Who did it isn't important. Only the fact it was done."

Zilia did not understand this. Nothing was *being* done, that she could see. Whether something was done or not seemed utterly irrelevant, and she could not believe it was important. "What do you think you are doing?" she asked.

"A kindness," said Saturday. "A kindness of eight."

It was true there were only eight of them. Jep, and Saturday, and six from other settlements, not as many as Zilia had assumed there would be.

"Where's your friend Willum R.?" Zilia asked Jep.

"He wasn't feeling well," he responded. "Gotoit and some of the others stayed with him.

Nightwatch ten passed, and eleven. Somewhere in the night was the sound of someone or something digging. "Pocket squirrels," said Jep calmly, in response to Zilia's questioning glance. "The big kind. I saw one before dark that was as long as my forearm."

"I didn't know they got that large," said Zilia, wonderingly. "Really? Or are you exaggerating?"

"I have seen some very large pocket squirrels," Jep said stoutly. "And at night they look even bigger."

The others agreed with him, telling stories of pocket-squirrel oddities from the settlements.

Along about nightwatch thirteen, Zilia fell asleep. When she woke, it was almost dawn, and the children were yawning as they put out the fire and extinguished their lanterns. One more parade around the site, and then they straggled back toward the management complex, Zilia as weary as any, though she had slept four or five periods. She waved them goodbye at the door of her apartment building, washed off the dust of the night, and fell into bed.

Meantime, the weary children trudged back the way they had come, into a small gully, which ran behind the burying ground, where Willum R., Gotoit, and a dozen other shivering children waited for them around a blanket wrapped form.

"You were far enough from the real grave that we could get him up," said Willum R. tiredly, "but we couldn't carry him over where we picked for the temple without that woman maybe seeing us."

"It's short nights now," murmured Saturday. "Nobody'll be awake at Central for a while yet. The grave's all dug, so we've got time if we go quickly."

The body of Horgy Endure, carried on a blanket folded around two poles, was hustled over a stretch of rolling ground to a small eminence overlooking the management complex and was there shallowly interred together with a scrap of the sticky, whitish God-stuff, which Saturday Wilm had brought in a filmbag in her knapsack.

"It's about time," moaned Gotoit, rubbing her aching arms.

"I'll say," agreed Jep. "I'm tired. This is the last one."

"No more vigils," said Saturday. "I'll sort of miss the singing."

"No reason for vigils," Jep shook his head. "Not anymore."

"I've got four left," said Saturday, peering into her knapsack. "I cut fifteen when we raised Birribat. We used

ten in the settlements and one here, so I've got four left.
Why did I do that?"

"Don't throw them away," said Jep. "If you've got
them, you've probably got them for a reason. Keep them
safe."

"I wonder how long they're good for?"

Jep only shrugged. He hadn't any idea.

"Who'll build the temple at CM?" he wanted to know.
"They hardly have any kids here at all."

They had no answer to the question, and even the
most impudent among them could not have foreseen the
day when Dern Blass and Zilia Makepeace and Spiggy
and Jamice and the rest of the administrative staff would
scribe the inner and outer circles of a temple and begin
laying stones near the grave which had just been filled.
Nor did they foresee the day when those same folk would
see to the raising of the God, Horgy Endure.

They went back to their temporary quarters at CM in
a straggling procession, yawning and dragging their feet.
Jep and Saturday lingered behind the others, hand-in-
hand.

"Now we can just live," said Jep, rather wearily.
"Now we can just live, Sats." He put his arms around her,
and they leaned together, two tired children, Ones Who
had done everything the God required and were now entitled to rest.

"Now we can just live," she agreed, kissing him on the
cheek, a small kiss, just to say everything was still there,
intact, between them.

"Come on," cried Gotoit, beckoning. "We need to get
home."

Jep stopped abruptly, shivering.

"What's the matter?" Saturday asked.

"When she said that, I got all cold," he complained.

"When she said what?"

"About going home. Like maybe something's wrong
there."

"Nothing's wrong there, Jep. You're tired, that's all.
So am I. You're tired, and when we get home we have to
go to school, and there's sports practice, and your body
isn't interested in doing anything but sleeping. Neither is

mine. The idea of music practice makes my throat hurt like crazy."

"I guess that's it," he said, returning her kiss and smoothing her wild hair away from her face. They smiled comfortingly at one another and set out after Gotoit and Willum R.

Voorstod

ONE

• *Jeopardy Wilm woke* into a strange world and a strange time, with a headache that roared and howled between his ears. His body was on a bed, arms and legs flung out in all directions. His mind was somewhere else, looking for him. The air smelled wet and moldy. There were voices in his head that he did not know, voices and a horrid wrenching he thought he might have felt once before, long ago, and hated then and now. Both the voices and the wrenching had happened elsewhere, in the darkness before he woke, and he remembered them as he sometimes remembered parts of an unpleasant dream from which he had wakened too quickly.

A moan came from his throat of itself, unintended, making the pain in his head thunder and throb. Nearby a chair scraped on a wooden floor, the noise sending jagged lightning through his skull. It was not a usual sound, not the sound a chair would make in the settlement. Sponge panels made a soft, cushiony sound. This sound shrieked, but he knew what it meant. Someone, someone getting up to see to him.

The face that came to hang over him was not a face he knew. It had an aura of red light around it, a disturbing tendency to swim toward him and then away.

"Wakin' up, are you?" the mouth above him asked, a gaping maw of teeth, ogrelike, with a great oar of a tongue waggling in it. Jep squeezed his eyes shut, then opened them again, and again. The aura faded; mouth and face dwindled to a proper size; and he was able to understand the voice. It wasn't a Hobbs Land voice. He knew the words—System language—but the pronunciation was odd, full of sliding tones which had nothing to do with the sense of the words.

The face turned away, the mouth still uttering. "He's comin' back, Preu. I guess you didn't kill him with the stuff after all."

"I'll see for myself, Epheron." Another face ballooned over him, one with white hair fringing the edges of a dark cap, a face that wavered in his sight, back and forth, back and forth. Jep shut his eyes again, sure he was lost in nightmare.

"Boy," said a harsher voice. "Listen to me. You'll get your sense back quicker if you know where you are and who you're among. I'm Preu Flandry, and this is Voorstod."

Nothing. It meant nothing. "Who's Voorstod," the boy mumbled through dry lips. "Voorstod? Who is that?"

"You're in Voorstod on the planet Ahabar," Flandry said angrily.

"Ahabar," mumbled the boy. He knew the meaning of the word. Ahabar was a planet. One of the inner-System planets. Large. Ruled by a monarchy. Queen somebody. "I'm on Ahabar. Queen somebody."

The man struck him, not hard. "We don't talk of Queens here. Though we may share the planet, this isn't Ahabar, this is Voorstod."

Which left him where he had been before: nowhere. If Voorstod was not a person, what was it?

"He's never heard of Voorstod?" someone said incredulously. "Maire Girat's grandson?"

"Not anybody's grandson," mumbled Jep, coming to

himself a little. "China's mom died. I don't have a grandma."

There was angry murmuring punctuated by snarls, like dogs fighting over a not-very-interesting bone, more out of habit than appetite.

Another man came to the bed, a squinty-eyed man. "Who's Sam Girat?" the man asked.

"Sam Girat?" asked Jep, trying to pull himself up a little. "He's Topman of Settlement One."

"He's your father," snarled a voice from somewhere else, not one of the voices he had heard before.

"You don't need to talk like that," said Jep. "He's nothing to do with me. That's improper, saying my mother's friends have anything to do with me." He succeeded in getting more or less upright and stared around the room. Against the far wall was a stone hollow with a fire in it and a small door next to it. The floor was wood, not polished, as Jep was accustomed to seeing wood, but dry and splintery. The ceiling was crossed with round wood beams, then crossed the other way with flat boards laid side by side. The walls were splotchy and stained, dun and rust colored, as though water had leaked through everywhere, in some places more copiously than others, making islands and peninsulas of stain upon the dank surfaces. A curtained window occupied the center of the wall opposite the fire; plank doors, bound heavily with metal straps and hinges, opened at the middle of the other walls. From where he lay, Jep could see that the door to his right was spiked shut with huge nails, driven deep.

Two of the three chairs by the fire were occupied. The man beside the bed went back to the third chair, slumping into it gracelessly. "Kid doesn't have a grandma! Hah."

"Question is, Pye, does the grandma have a kid?"

The white-fringed man leaned forward to warm his hands at the fire. For the first time, Jep realized how cold and damp the room was, how bitterly cold he himself was. He shivered. The blanket across his body was sodden with moisture, like a fungus after rain. He shivered again and tried to distract himself by identifying the men. The white-haired one was Preu. The younger one with the huge mouth who had spoken first was Epheron. The

squinty-eyed man who had just left him was Pye, and Jep
had seen him before.

"What's your whole name?" asked Jep, pointing.

"My name is Mugal Pye," the man said, turning his
daggerlike eyes upon the boy. "We've met before."

All three of them wore large caps, which had the effect
of making their heads look larger and their faces smaller.
Jep remembered noticing that before. He had been walking out to the temple alone, very early. There was something he had to do for Birribat Shum. And there had been
a stranger on the road, a man wearing a cap, a man who
had said his name was . . . was Mugal Pye.

"What did you do to me?" Jep asked. He could remember nothing after the man told him his name. "Why
am I here?"

The man named Preu told him. "You're here for our
purposes. If you behave yourself, when our purposes are
accomplished, we'll send you home to Hobbs Land."

"What purposes?"

"We're holding you hostage, boy. To bring your
grandma home to her people. If she won't come, you'll be
some damaged, but that's up to her."

"I told you, I didn't have a grandmother. China's
mother is dead."

"I'm talking about Sam Girat's mother, boy."

"But she's not my grandmother! Why would she do
anything for me?" Jep thought with sudden panic that if
his welfare depended upon Maire Girat, he was doomed.
He scarcely knew the woman, only as one does in settlement, by name and face. Saturday knew her because she
taught Saturday music, but Jep knew almost nothing
about her!

"Brat," sneered Epheron. "Ungrateful whelp."

"Nah, nah," breathed Mugal Pye. "He's right, Floom.
When we were there, I heard it for myself. It's only the
mother's line they think of. They don't say 'Dad' and they
don't say 'Granddad.' They do say 'Uncle,' though. The
boy there has three uncles, and no father. And it may be
Maire Girat thinks the same way. She's been there a long
time. If so, we've gone awry, someway. It was her daughter's children we should have brought. Sal's children. We

thought to save ourselves some trouble and may not have done that at all."

"Phaed told me she always felt so soft about the Gharm," sneered Preu Flandry. "Maybe she'll feel soft for this one, too. Whether she counts him family or not."

Jep shivered again, and gagged. Sour bile moved at the back of his throat.

"Better feed him something," said Mugal Pye, with a sneer. "Before he fades away on us."

"Better give me something dry to wear," said Jep, shivering. "Before I catch something and die. I'll be no good to you dead."

"Ah, well," said Preu. "This is boring to be sure. He knows nothing of interest to us, so let the boy have the good of the fire. Send the Gharm to feed him. I'll be getting back to Cloud. We don't want anyone thinkin' I've been away too long. Besides, it's time someone talked to Phaed Girat. Which I'll do soon. Tomorrow. Or next week. Or after that, sometime."

He went out, and the others followed. When it was apparent they were not coming back, Jep got up and approached the chairs. One of them was a tall stuffed thing, much torn and stained upon the seat and back, but warm from the firelight. He curled up in it, trying to soak up all the heat there was. When the fire had somewhat restored him, he fetched the blankets from the bed and hung them across the other chair backs to let the hot light dance upon them. By the time a noise alerted him that someone was coming in, a cloud of steam was rising around the hearth.

Those who came were little people. Though Jep had much of his growing still to do, the tiny man came only to Jep's shoulder, and the little woman only to his chest. The man carried a metal pot with a long-handled spoon protruding from it; the woman carried a bowl, a cup, and a bottle, which glugged solemnly as she set it down. Despite their diminutive size, Jep did not for a moment think of them as children. Something in their faces said they were grown, adult, mature, even dignified. They were very dark and ruddy in color, darker than even the darkest skinned persons of Jep's acquaintance, the color of stained wood, very deep brown, with red lights in their skin and fur. Their heads were covered with fur the same color as their skin, fur that ran down the backs of their necks onto their shoulders. Their eyes were the same ruddy color as their skin, but their teeth were very white. They wore wrinkled trousers and loose shirts of a coarse, colorless fabric. Their feet were furry and bare.

"Something to eat," said the woman, placing the bowl upon the table. She removed the cup, poured into it from the bottle, and held out the drink. "Good. Warm."

"I was about frozen," admitted Jep. "Who are you people?"

The two exchanged glances, almost of surprise. "We are Gharm," the man said.

Jep thought about it. "I think I've heard about you. There's some big controversy about you, isn't there? Maire Girat told Saturday Wilm about you. Saturday said you were enslaved by the people of Voorstod. Is that right?"

They exchanged glances again and moved away from him, almost as though afraid.

"I won't hurt you," Jep cried. "I wouldn't do that. Stay a little while. Tell me where I am . . ."

They wouldn't stay. The food and drink was set upon the hearth and they fled.

Jep looked after them, tears gathering. He shook his head impatiently and laid his hand upon the kettle, finding it warm. He lifted the kettle to the table, filled the bowl and began to eat. The taste was not unfamiliar. Meaty. Grainy. What China would have called an eternal stew.

"Our remote ancestors ate such things when they first discovered fire," she had said to Jep more than once as she threw things together to make their supper. "And first discovered pots, of course. Then they put tough meat and hard grain and harsh herbs together and let them cook until they could chew them and until the whole tasted better than the parts. If they were lucky, their cooks added bulbs and salts to make it tastier yet." China always added good things. Almost always. Sometimes she said, "If they were not so fortunate, they ate it anyhow."

He ate it anyhow, not allowing himself to be fussy, knowing he would have to keep strength and warmth and wits about him. When he had finished, he stayed beside the fire, soaking in the warmth.

Heavy footsteps approached, too heavy for the Gharm. It was Mugal Pye, returned. "Can you write?" he asked from the door.

"Of course I can write," Jep said. "I'm not an infant."

"On paper, with a brush, as well as on a stage?"

"I can," Jep said.

"Then write." The man put down sheets of paper, soft-edged, handmade. There was a woman in Settlement Two who made paper like that. She sold it to people who wished to make fancy, hand-lettered documents and memorials. "Write to Maire Girat. Tell her you are here, in Voorstod. Tell her no harm will come to you if she comes back to her home."

"Her home is in Hobbs Land," said Jep. "In Settlement One."

"Write," said the man, his lips quirking angrily at one side. "She will know what home is meant. Tell her also that she must not inform the Queen or the Authority, or you will surely die." He set a pot of ink upon the table and held out a brush.

Jep took the brush he was offered and dipped it into the inkpot. Writing, as distinguished from entering information in words and symbols, was one of the decorative skills. Everyone was taught the decorative skills, though Jep was not very good at any of them. Saturday was far better at them than Jep was. The thought of her caught him unaware, beneath the ribs like a knife, and he gasped.

"What's wrong?" demanded the gimlet-eyed man.

"I'm all alone," Jep whispered. "My people are all far away."

"Oh now, that's true," mocked Mugal Pye. "Tell that to Maire Girat. Tell her you're lonely, and cold. Tell her you're hungry. Tell her you will never be returned to Hobbs Land unless she comes to Voorstod once more. Comes, and sings."

"She does not sing," said Jep. "I know all the singers, and she is not one of them."

"Does not sing?" said Pye, incredulously.

"She's an old woman," said Jep, laboriously writing the name of Maire Girat at the top of the page. "She's an old woman, and she does not sing."

He wrote as he had been directed. It was a difficult exercise, not something he did every day. The words were not simple ones to do with crops or animals, and the sense of the demands being made evaded him. Why Maire Girat should do something because he, Jep Wilm, was captive, he could not say. He could have used simplex form to make it easy—simplex was a phonic system with no room in it for interpretation, like taking dictation. He chose, instead, to use Phansure High Text, to show it was a serious matter. Between the lines, as he lettered the words of the message Mugal Pye intended, he added a superscription for Saturday, which told her, by allusion, that he loved her and needed her help. He could have directed his personal words to China or to Aunt Africa, but Saturday was a One Who, as he himself was.

"What's this?" demanded Mugal Pye angrily, who understood enough High Text to read the message. "I didn't tell you to write to your sweetheart."

"I must," Jep said. "She'd worry otherwise."

"Damned brat," said Mugal. "You've put it between the lines. I can't even cut it off."

"Leave it," cried Jep desperately. "It won't interfere with what you want!"

Mugal fumed for a moment, but decided after a time that the boy was right. Actually, the second message made the first one more poignant. While the first one had been dictated, the second one had come from the heart. They'd know the boy had written it himself, just from the pain in the words.

When the ink had been dried before the fire, Mugal Pye set bottle and brush upon the mantle and went away. Jep put his head down on his arms and wept. Gharm slipped through the door next to the fireplace like shadows, he and she again. He felt a soft hand on his arm, looked down into a pitying face.

"What are your names?" whispered Jep.

"Nils," said the man.

"Pirva," said the woman, holding out her hands. "Have you finished?"

He nodded, lifting the still-warm kettle into her arms. "Please don't be afraid of me," he begged. "I need someone to . . ."

"We know," she said. "We were listening."

"Are you slaves?" he asked.

The woman nodded, reaching up to pull her shirt away from her neck to show Jep the numbers branded there, along the top of her shoulder, the bare scars of the brand showing against the soft fur of her shoulder. Below the shoulder, the fur stopped, and Jep could see the skin of her chest. She had no breasts there, at least none that showed. Instead, her skin folded down her body, a long, vertical line. The Gharm were made differently from men. They were different about the ears, too, which were furry and flat. He flushed and looked away, noticing as he did so that she also wore a metal collar, with a ring in it, much like the ones used to tether livestock.

"Slaves." He could scarcely believe it. He had no clear idea what it meant, except that they were not free, as he was, had been . . . might never be again. If slave meant captive, he, too, was a slave. "Why?"

Again that quick exchange of looks. "We're not supposed to talk of it."

"I won't tell," he promised. "I won't tell you told me."

"Because the men captured us and put us in cages and brought us with them when they came here," said Nils. "They were bigger and stronger than we. We could not prevent it."

"I thought there was a contract," said Jep. He had heard some such.

"Later, they said we had signed a contract to serve them a thousand years. We signed nothing. We would rather have died there, in our own land." She looked into the fire, seeing things there Jep could not see.

"Why do they want Maire Girat to come back?" he asked. "Why do they care?"

They shook their heads at him and were gone. He heard the locks chunking as they fastened him in.

At the window he pulled the curtain aside to see only darkness and the gleam of the fire on the bars that were set to keep him confined. He let the curtain fall and went back to the fire, so weary he could hardly move. There were chunks of fuel piled beside the chimney. He placed some of the fibrous stuff atop the embers, then spread the blankets before the fire and curled into their dry warmth. Light flickered on his face. The smell of smoke was comforting, like an ancient blessing. He shut his eyes in order to smell it better and thought of Saturday. The last time he had seen her, he had told her they could simply live from then on. It seemed he had been wrong. He had known something was wrong at home. Something had told him that. But nothing had told him not to go there.

He opened his eyes and stared at the rough wood above him. The God knew. The God knew all about it. But it hadn't told him not to go home. After a time his eyes closed and he fell into sleep.

The following day he was given boots and a coat and told he would be working for the farmer who had the place and who could not feed him unless he worked. They locked a collar upon him, not a rough metal one like the Gharm collar, but a sleek, complicated piece of machinery with faceted dials and lights in it, like a piece of jewelry. They told him if he wandered more than half a mile from the farm house, the thing would blow his head off. They set him to digging ditches, and it was harder work than he had ever done.

All the day the mists enclosed him, making a wall at either side, a ceiling above. Sounds that filtered through the mists were dimmed and spread, like water coming through a weir. Each night he scratched a mark on the wall beside the fireplace before he lay down. He had no trouble sleeping. He told himself in time help would come. It was only by keeping this idea before himself, looking at it every moment, telling it over like a holy name, that he kept himself calm. Saturday, he said to himself, will come, will send someone. She could find him if he were at the bottom of a sea.

"We are the Ones Who, after all," he muttered to himself. "The God Birribat Shum knew what was to happen and did not prevent it. The God Birribat Shum will not let either of us die until it is time."

• *On the occasion* of the quincentennial of the monarchy of Ahabar, the Gharm harpist, Stenta Thilion, was to be featured with the Orchestra of Ahabar at the Royal Opera House in Fenice, the planetary capital. This was an event long-awaited. Traditionally, the music of Ahabar had made little use of the harp, or indeed, of any stringed instruments, being rather given over to brasses and percussion instruments of a hundred tinkling or booming kinds. Ahabar loved a good march. Hiking groups were traditionally led by drum and bugle corps. Machinery was the more valued if it made a good rhythmic whumpety-whump the workmen could tap-feet in time with. At least so much was true in the outlands, though the cities were becoming more sophisticated. String quintets from effete Phansure had been all the rage in social circles for some little time, and it was through one such prestigious group that a Phansure composer had been obtained and commissioned by Queen Wilhulmia herself to compose a work for Gharm-harp and orchestra that would encourage the patriotism of Ahabar while displaying the virtuosity of Stenta Thilion.

"Display, but not overtry," the Queen had murmured in the ear of the composer, who had been invited to dinner. "She's not a young person any longer. Perhaps you'd better get to know her work."

"Ma'am," said the composer, who felt himself greatly honored by the commission, "even on Phansure we know Stenta Thilion. I've known her work all my life."

And so he had. Stenta Thilion was a rare genius, one of those who were recognized early and who throughout their lives receive adulation with modesty and good humor. The First Symphony for Gharm-harp and Orchestra, when finished, met with both the conductor's approval and that of Stenta Thilion herself. Rehearsals took place in an atmosphere of welling enthusiasm, and everyone who heard the work used words like *enchanting* and *marvelous* and *a new age in Ahabarian music.* It said much for the political savvy of the composer that he had used several familiar patriotic themes in the work—including a few motifs associated with the royal family—and much for the skill and good nature of the harpist that she played them with appropriate verve and ferocity.

Now there were only a few days left before the concert, which the Queen would attend with her sons, Crown Prince Ismer and Prince Rals, Duke Levenar. As for Stenta, the harpist rested at home with her two daughters, all of them quite excited about the impending event.

"Coribee, Gem, sit," said Sarlia, the eldest daughter, a grandmother in her own right, to her mother. "Sit, Mama-gem. Take tea."

"Don't fuss at me," murmured Stenta, smiling. "Don't fuss."

"Who fusses? Do I fuss? Does Liva fuss? We are fussless, no, Liva?"

"Fussless," agreed her sister. "Totally, Sarlia."

Stenta subsided onto the couch beside them, giggling. "You, fussless? Aha. Then would a new sun rise."

"In a few days does a new sun rise," said her daughter, bowing. "At the concert does the sun shine on Stenta Thilion, great artist."

"Coribee," blushed her mother, turning a dark, brick color. "Oh, coribee." So she disclaimed her own talent and laid it upon the Gods of the Gharm, saying, "as the Tchenka will it."

"No coribee about it. The Tchenka had, perhaps, a part in it. Mostly you did it yourself. Sadly, the Tchenka are mostly likely far away, on the old land. The Old Ones do not say they have followed to this one." Sarlia shook her head in sorrow.

"Perhaps by now," Stenta breathed through the steam of her teacup. "Perhaps by now." There was great longing in her voice, a longing she did not need to explain to her daughters. The Tchenka were the spirits of the ancestors of Gharm, the spirits of the creatures of the planet Gharm, the kindly ones, the guardians. Since the planet Gharm had been first killed and then abandoned long ago, the Gharm did not know what had happened to the

Tchenka. Since coming here, the Gharm had had no spiritual protection, and little kindness.

"I rejoice in my deliverance," whispered Stenta. It was ungrateful to think of little kindness when all in Ahabar had been so kind.

"We pray solace for our kindred in bondage," whispered her daughters in response. "Coribee."

Though it was hard to enjoy one's own deliverance when so many remained behind. It was Stenta's grandmother and grandfather who had made the escape from Voorstod. Stenta herself was the second generation of Thilions born in freedom. Her great-grandchildren, Sarlia's and Liva's grandchildren, were the fifth. Even after all these generations, the plight of the Gharm remaining in Voorstod was a constant pain, not only in an emotional sense, but also in a physical one. What one Gharm felt, all Gharm somewhat perceived, a sensation attenuated by distance but still identifiable. If a Gharm died painfully in Voorstod, all free-Gharm knew of it in their bellies, and wept for it, not only for the pain but for the loss. Since many Gharm died in Voorstod, their deaths weighed upon the free-Gharm in an endless melancholy. The Gharm at home in Ahabar were in many respects no freer than their kindred in Voorstod, though here in Fenice there were thousands of miles and many years separating the Gharm population from the deadly peninsula.

Stenta sat upon a cushioned chair and held out her cup to be refilled by her eldest child. A disinterested observer would have seen no apparent difference in their ages. The slight, lithe forms were of a kind. The tight caps of dark fur were identical. The eyes and button noses and unlined skins appeared no different in the daughters than in the mother. Even the sinuous movements of arms, the mannered extensions of the four-fingered, two-thumbed hands, the ritual courtesies of full and half-obeisance, were the same in both generations, save that Stenta did not bow quite so deeply nor kneel so swiftly. As the eldest, the Gem (for the Gharm saw their old people as jewels to be treasured), she was entitled to deference, no matter that the outsider would scarcely notice how much was given her. Among themselves, they were aware, and what

others thought or perceived about so private a matter was
of no concern.

Now Liva, seeing the strain settle upon her mother's
face at the mention of kindred in bondage, cast a quick
glance at Sarlia and begged, "Tell us of the Tchenka,
Mama-gem."

"You have heard," the older woman breathed into the
steam of her teacup. "Ten thousand times."

"Were it ten thousand times ten thousand, it were not
enough," said Liva, ritually. "No retelling is too much."

"So much is true," Stenta agreed. The stories of the
Tchenka were the heritage of the Gharm, to be passed on
intact and unchanged to all future generations. Even
though the Tchenka themselves might have been left behind—and no one was sure whether they had stayed or
died or followed—still their history should be told. They
were the spirits of the Gharm, no matter how long ago or
faraway. It behooved every Gharm to hear; and hearing,
tell; and telling, teach.

Stenta began, singing in the breathy chant that was the
best she could manage these days, "Long ago was Billa-
needful . . ."

• *Long ago was* Billa-needful, waking out of darkness and emptiness, aware only of a something-hunger.
What am I? Billa asked itself. Why do I wake thus?
Where do I find myself? When is this time, beforeness or
afterness? Who is in this place with me?

Long did Billa meditate upon these questions, until at
last Billa decided to test first whether any other being was
present. So Billa sang one note, sending it into the darkness and emptiness until all the void was filled with the
note. And the note went away into silence, leaving no
echo and no answer.

There is no answer, so then, I am alone, said Billa-
needful. And since there comes no echo, I am in empty;
and since there comes no echo, I am before anything has
occurred; and since I am before, I wake to create; and
since I am in empty, I am All-There-Is-Now.

And long Billa meditated upon these answers, until at last Billa decided to create others which would echo.

I shall make others, said Billa. I shall make some to sing with me. So, Billa-needful sang into the nothing one song, and it was named He-Is-Accomplished. And Billa-needful sang another song, and it was named She-Goes-On-Creating. And He-Is-Accomplished was a male and She-Goes-Creating was a female, and the two of them went out into the nothing where they sang with Billa-needful until all of nothingness was full of song.

And He-Is-Accomplished heard the song and was content, but She-Goes-On-Creating took the song and rounded it and made many worlds of it, large and small, and set the smooth songs spinning around the fiery songs and the cold songs spinning around the smooth songs, and all music gathered up to leave no sound between so that the songs spun in silence. And when Billa-needful saw what she had done, Billa-needful was pleased, saying, "Now may happenings occur and one thing cause another and time come into creation and the reason for my being be fulfilled."

But He-Is-Accomplished was uncomfortable, for there was much doing and confusion among the circling worlds, so that He-Is-Accomplished suffered greatly from itchiness.

"There is peace in silence between the worlds," he said, moving away from the worlds, "and that is where I will dwell."

So Billa-needful encircled all, watching what occurred, while He-Is-Accomplished dwelt in silence and She-Goes-On-Creating dwelt in song, and so all was inhabited. So say all Gharm, so be it, *coribee.*

· *The annunciator at* the door brought all three of them to their feet. "Someone comes!" cried the mechanical voice, like metal foil, blowing in the wind.

Liva motioned the other two to sit. "I will see to it," she said.

"Careful," her mother said, out of habit. "Do not open unless you're sure." There was no such thing as safety, not even here in Fenice. Not when the men of Voorstod were determined upon killing every Gharm they could. How many of the innocent had died for no reason at all save the vicious pride of the Voorstoders? So now, Stenta repeated, "Careful."

"So, Mama-gem," Liva agreed. She peered at the door screen, noting the royal livery on the man carrying the package, the label and shape of the box he bore. "Your gown for the concert, Mama-gem! From the Queen's own dressmaker."

Liva opened the door, presented a finger for the messenger's snipper to painlessly drag away a cell or two, and accepted the box. The royal page stepped inside and opened it for her, thus showing there was no danger in it. In these days of the Voorstod terror, so much was courtesy on Queen Wilhulmia's instructions.

Liva carried the box in one hand, the frock over both arms as she returned to the inner room like a moving sheaf of diamonds, glitteringly resplendent, a preserved rainbow of light.

"Oooh," breathed Stenta, who had been fitted only into the basic garment, before the Phansurian bead-artists had been at it. "Oooh."

Upon the high-necked breast of the dress was worked the heads and bodies of two saber birds, facing one another. Their head and wing plumes arched away onto the shoulders and down onto the drooping, bannerlike sleeves of the dress. Tail plumes filled all the space to the hem, every plume with a gemmed eye. On the back of the dress, butterflies flew from the hem toward the neck, around a space of Phansuri silk at the hip and thigh, where Stenta would sit, filling all the rest with glittering beauty. The saber bird was the clan Tchenka of Stenta's mother. The butterfly was the clan Tchenka of Stenta's father. Stenta had been born out of the Butterfly people into the Saber-bird people, though there were neither butterflies nor saber birds where any of them had lived for generations. On the neckband of the gown was a tiny frog, worked in emerald beads. The frog was Stenta's personal Tchenka. The dress was of scarlet and yellow and every shade between these two: wine and gold, pink and melon, orange and ochre.

The style was an adaptation of that traditional to the Gharm for festive occasions, though there had not been within living memory such a gorgeous or extravagant application of tradition. Sarlia stroked the beads, marveling at their chilly, heavy surface, like flowing metal.

"Mama-gem," said Sarlia, "the sleeves are so heavy. Surely you will not be able to play, wearing this."

Stenta came forward to peer closely at the garment. In a moment she found the seams she sought, opened them, and removed the sleeves. Beneath were other sleeves, close, light ones of Phansuri silk, red as new blood.

"I come on the stage all glorious," announced Stenta with a straight face, walking with decorous steps around the room. "I glitter and shine and bow to the conductor, and he to me. I bow to the audience, holding out my arms so the sleeves hang down like flags. I wave my hands, so, showing yet once more how graceful we Gharm are. I go to the harp. I seat myself, being careful that under me is this place on the dress where there are no butterflies to make uncomfortable places on my bottom. I hold out my arms, straight, letting the sleeves glitter. A woman comes from the wings and leans above me, unfastens my sleeves, and takes them away. The undersleeves are red, very highly visible, so everyone will see how my arms move. So, now I may play. So we have rehearsed it, to make a show. The conductor says I am so small, I must shine like fire for them all to see me."

"Beautiful," said Liva. "I'll hang it up, Mama-gem."

"No," her mother instructed. "The beads are too heavy. You must lay it flat, in the spare bedroom. The Queen's dressmaker told me. Even so, it will stretch a little during the concert. It was made to wear only this one time."

"And the bracelets?"

"What bracelets?"

"The ones in the box with the dress," said Sarlia, drawing them out. They glittered with the same colors as the gown, though their faceted surfaces were set with gems rather than beaded.

"Ah, ah, how kind of the Queen," said Stenta. "She does too much."

"I'll put them with the dress," said Liva. "Then Mama can tell more of the Tchenka."

She went off to the guest room, returning a few moments later to refill their teacups and demand that the story of He-Is-Accomplished and She-Goes-On-Creating be continued.

· *She-Goes-On-Creating* wandered a time upon the worlds and among the stars, singing as they sang, but the surfaces of the worlds were dull and uninteresting, like beads, while the surfaces of the stars were furious and uncomfortable. "I will sing life," said She-Goes-On-Creating, as she stood upon a world, "I will sing life to make things more comfortable." And she put out her hand and sang water into being, and then grass into being, and when they were created, she put them on many of the worlds while she sang forest into being.

After that she sang Water-Dragon into being, and after Water-Dragon, she sang Desert-Dragon, and after Desert-Dragon, Forest-Dragon, and then all other dragons of every kind, and sent them to the various worlds where they were to live . . .

· *"You don't want* me to say the entire catalog, surely," said Stenta. "You have known the list of the Tchenka since you were eight!"

"So we have," Liva agreed. "Dragons first, then fish that eats grass in all its kinds, fish that eats on the bottom in all its kinds, fish that eats other fish the same; then bird that eats grass, bird that eats in the field, bird that eats other birds; so on and so on, creatures of every kind. All the Tchenka, lost forever."

"Well, it may be they are not lost, though such is the story," sighed Stenta. "And finally, She-Goes-On-Creating meets together with all the Tchenka at the foot of the eternal mountain to decide what should be done to keep everything in balance. But the Tchenka of humans would not agree to keep humans in balance, so the other Tchenka killed them, and man has had no Tchenka since."

"Which is why he kills everything," said Liva, "for he is not cousin to the creatures of the worlds as the Gharm are."

"It is why those of Voorstod are so evil," said Sarlia, "for they have no indwelling spirit whatsoever."

"Tss," whispered her mother. "Do not offend the Tchenka by mentioning Voorstoders. I will play you quiet, as She-Goes-On-Creating sang the quiet into which He Is-Accomplished went."

She went to the harp, which stood beside the window, a great concert harp, the largest any Gharm could play, very narrow, to hold all the strings, with the strings set very close, as they could be for the slender Gharm fingers. "I will play the song She-Goes-On-Creating sang to create the saber bird," said Stenta, laying her hands upon the strings.

She played and the-women-her-daughters were silent. Outside in the street, people stopped what they were doing and simply stood, heads turned toward the sound. Wherever the music was, the birds came into being, head and wing and leg, brilliant body and brilliant tail. They moved. One could see them moving in the music. One could tell what they looked like. They danced with their beaks pointing upward. They danced on their toes. They leapt and turned, wings spread wide. It didn't matter, not too much, that they were not on Ahabar, or in Voorstod, that they had died on Gharm with all the trees and forests and swamps and streams which had been Gharm, for they survived still in the music. When the music was over, for a long time, it was as though the birds were in the room, as though their souls were there, listening, brought back from whatever place they had been.

"Go home now," said Stenta to her daughters, her face calm and radiant as dawn, as though she had been speaking to angels. "Go help your daughters feed the children. I will rest, for soon I will play for the Queen."

* * *

· *On the escarpment* of Hobbs Land, Shan Damzel dreamed of Ninfadel.

"Don't forget to wear your faceplate," said the officer at the outpost. "Don't forget to wash off the mucous before it dries."

Shan went away from the outpost. It receded behind him as things in dreams recede, becoming unreachable, unattainable. He was remote now, all alone, standing on the hill overlooking the river. Raucous sounds came to him, and he looked down to see Porsa by the river, and then they were coming at him faster than he could have imagined possible.

He tried to run, but his feet wouldn't move . . .

He only had time to get his faceplate down before . . .

Something inexorable swallowed him up.

· *Jep learned to* dig ditches, at first painfully, and then much less so. At first digging by hand seemed a daft, silly thing to do, when there were machines that could do it easier and better, but here in Voorstod there were many daft, silly things going on. So he worked hard, hoping to finish the task, only to find there were more ditches to be dug, and still more. After the third or fourth agonizing day of it, he realized the labor was set specifically to tire him out, possibly so he would sleep, certainly so he would not have the energy to be rebellious, so he would have no time or strength to think about escape. The farmer didn't need these ditches, or, if he did, he didn't need them done quickly or finished soon. With this realization came sense and a kind of fatalistic serenity. From that moment on he worked easily, gently, as though, he told himself, he were uncovering a God, neatly setting the turves aside in parallel lines and piling the dark soil inside them, making of the task a work of art.

Work was not easy, as it would have been at home. He could not see into calming distance. The whole world was confined by mist, into the compass of his own emotions. There were feelings all around him, anger and hatred and menace. Each time one of the men came near him, he could feel roiling dissatisfaction, barely withheld belligerence. The animosity was not toward him, especially. It was not even toward the Gharm, especially. It simply was, a condition of their being, born in them as gills on a fish, suiting them to breathe only angry and hostile air.

The bellicose atmosphere frightened Jep. He could feel a reflection of it in himself, as well, rising up from a hot well in his belly, something responsively molten there, something heretofor unsuspected. He kept it carefully controlled, remembering the time after Bondru Dharm had died. Then, too, there had been anger, though the children had felt it less than the adults. Of course, the children had been working on the temple. There were no temples here.

Though . . . why shouldn't there be?

That night, when the Gharm, Nils, brought his food, he begged the little man to sit with him a while before the fire.

"I'm lonely," he said, sounding as pathetic as possible. It wasn't difficult. He was lonely, with a deep, aching sense of loss for all familiar and comforting things.

"If the men come . . ." the little man temporized.

"They don't come. Not anymore. Sometimes in the day, but not at night."

"It's true," Nils agreed. "They are living in a house down in Sarby, not far from here. It's warmer there, in the valley."

"All of them?"

"Mugal Pye and Epheron Floom, those two."

"Not Preu Flandry?"

"No, He's gone back, so they say, to Cloud."

"What do those others do there in Sarby? They're not keeping watch on me. This," and he indicated the collar he wore, with its faceted, gemlike inserts, "this keeps me close. So, why do they stay?"

"Making things," the Gharm said. "The Gharm there often see them making things, and they tell us. Jewelry, like. And little boxes. Things."

"Devil things, no doubt," brooded Jep. He had no illusions about the Voorstoders. He had not yet detected any goodness or kindness in any of them. It was almost as though they were a separate race, and Jep spent much time during the lonely days thinking how this might be. Speciation through isolation, possibly. He had learned about that in school. Men had developed a few species since the Dispersion. How long had the Voorstoders dwelt apart from other men, on that planet with the Gharm? How long to turn into devilish creatures, who made devilish things.

"Devil things, no doubt," assented Nils.

The door opened a crack and Pirva slid through, eyes wide. "You didn't come back," she told her mate.

"I know." He soothed her, inviting her to join him at the fireside. "The boy is lonesome."

"Poor boy," she said softly. "Taken from his mama-gem."

"It is not my mother I miss so much," he told her. "I was old enough to leave my mother's house and go into the brotherhouse. It is that I am a One Who."

"One Who what?" she wanted to know.

"One Who serves the God," was his answer. "One Who serves the God Birribat Shum. And there is another One Who, closer to me than a sister. So it is the God I miss, and Saturday Wilm."

"Is that a name?" they asked. "Saturday Wilm."

He nodded, choking down a hot, bitter hard-edged chunk that had come into his throat. "That is her name," he told them. "And she will come for me, somehow. We need each other."

"But that is not the person they expect," Nils said in a puzzled voice. "It is Maire Manone they expect to come, not Saturday Wilm."

"I do not know what Maire Manone will do," he said. "But Saturday Wilm will come. And she will bring . . ." His voice trailed away, for he had just thought of it. She would bring. Of course she would bring. "She will bring with her what we all need."

The little woman laughed, a short chortling sound, without amusement in it. She drew down her collar and ran her fingers over the numbers burned into her shoulder. "What we all need? What other thing than freedom?"

She gave her mate or lover or husband or whatever he

was a significant look. Nils rose. The two of them took up the dishes and cup and kettle, ready to leave and go back wherever they went at night.

"Perhaps she brings freedom," Jep whispered. "If that was so, would your people help to put an end to all this? All this slavery?"

Both the Gharm stopped where they were, like statues.

"We cannot," Nils said. "It has been decided. If all of us try to go, if we rebel, if we rise up, then the Voorstoders will slaughter us all."

"Tell me," begged Jep. "Tell me about it."

Half-unwillingly, they sat down by the fire once more, not relinquishing their hold upon the kettle and the dirty dishes, ready to rise and flee at the first hint of sound.

"Tell me," begged Jep again. "Make me understand!"

Nils reluctantly put down the kettle, took up a stick from beside the fire and scratched some ashes onto the hearth, spreading them into a thin film with the side of the stick. In the ashes he drew a shape, a fat vertical with an even fatter leftward turn at its upper end, the whole like a leg with a swollen foot at the top, a leg very thin at the knee where it joined something long and flat.

"Voorstod," whispered Nils, indicating the whole outline. He ran a finger from the toes to the knee, dividing the fatness into two, a wide calf-of-the-leg and bottom-of-the-foot, a narrow top-of-the-foot and shin. "The line of the mountains," he explained, "running all down Voorstod, like a backbone." He indicated the wider part. "The Sea Counties." The narrower part. "The Highland Counties." He poked a finger onto the foot, just above where the toes might have been. "Sarby County, where we are." Other finger marks went toward the heel. "Panchy County, Odil County." He came to the heel. "Bight County, with the town of Scaery, where Maire Manone once lived." He proceeded down the leg. "Cloud County, Leward County, and the town of Selmouth. Then the three apostate counties, so the evil men call them, Wander, Skelp—Skelp, thin as a child's neck—then Green Hurrah spreading out, right and left, along the shore. Be-

low that is broad Jeramish, a province of Ahabar, with the
army all along the border."

Jep stared at the picture, memorizing what the little
man had said. "What are the Highland Counties?"

Nils stabbed a finger at the lower edge of the foot.
"County Kate is just south of where we are. East of that is
County Furbish. Then, running toward the south is North
Highlands County and South Highlands County, long,
narrow counties squeezed between the sea and the peaks.
No big towns, only villages up there. No ports. On the
west, the mountains come up from the sea like a wall,
with no big rivers, only streams plunging down in white
torrents."

Pirva leaned forward to point to the thin neck of the
peninsula, where it joined the mainland. "County Skelp,"
she said, tapping it meaningfully. "Narrow Skelp. If we
escape by land, it must be through County Skelp. We can
do it, hiding like beasts in the grass, crawling among the
stones, one or two at a time. Not more."

"The people in Skelp are sympathetic?" Jep asked.

"Oh, some of them are, yes. They try. But the slavers
are everywhere, sneaking and skulking. And if they know
one of the people of Skelp has helped us, then that person
loses his eyes, or his hands, or his manhood, or her
breasts, or their children are killed, or perhaps all of
these."

Jep peered at the map. "How about getting out by
sea?"

"There are only the few ports. Old Port in Odil.
Scacry. Cloud. Selmouth. Watched, all of them, like a
mousehole in a house full of cats."

"And in between?"

"In between, rocks and bad tides and places a tiny
boat may come in to pick up one or two, but no more than
that."

Jep sighed. "So you go by ones and twos."

"We do. We choose by lottery. Some of the people of
each Tchenka, each clan, must go out, some of each people must escape, so the race may live. Children. Men and
women of reproductive age. No old ones. Only a few at a
time. We say 'One child for life, one child for death. Two

for the future, two for the sacrifice.' When our babies are born, we weep, for perhaps the child is to be a sacrifice, a sop to the beasts, to be whipped to death to calm the evil men. Not enough of us go to set the Voorstoders into a frenzy, but enough that our people will live, that all the Tchenka will live."

"What are Tchenka?" Jep asked.

They told him as though they were teaching one of their own children, and by the time they were finished with the long catalog of Tchenka, which included every natural and supernatural beast and being upon Gharm, the fire had burned to ashes and Jep was yawning uncontrollably.

"We will talk again," he said. He needed time to understand all they had told him.

Meantime he went on digging ditches. Since there was no purpose to it save the purpose of keeping him busy, he decided to ask Mugal Pye if he could do something a bit more interesting. Mugal came by every now and then to check on the status of the prisoner, to jibe at him as though Jep had offended the Voorstoders in some way. It took some time, but Jep finally figured out that he had offended the Voorstoders by being innocently involved. Their world view did not allow for innocence. Those who were not for Voorstod were against Voorstod by definition, and that included Jep as it would include a baby still in the womb. Mugal kept him abreast of developments and seemed to take an almost sexual pleasure in threatening the boy with mutilation.

Ilion Girat, it seemed, had stayed behind upon Hobbs Land of necessity, since Jep had come out disguised as Ilion. Now Ilion was under house arrest on Hobbs Land, but he could observe what was happening there. He sent word that he knew Maire had received the initial message since Ilion had arranged its delivery himself. He had received no response as yet. Mugal was quick to advise Jep of this, as though Jep's terror here on Ahabar might somehow stimulate action on Hobbs Land. Maire was to give Ilion an answer in a little time, Mugal said. Jep choked down his fear and waited for the little time to pass.

Meantime, however, he sought to do something sensible. "I told the Gharm I'd teach them how to build a house that will stay drier," Jep said to Mugal Pye. "It's a kind we build sometimes on Hobbs Land. It would be more useful than these ditches you've got me digging."

"I don't care what you do, laddy," sneered Mugal Pye. "So long as you keep busy. That collar you've got around your neck guarantees you won't run off. But the Gharm have work to do, and I don't know how the farmer will take to your distractin' them."

"I won't take them from their work," said Jep. "I'll do a lot of it myself."

That night, he spoke again with Nils and Pirva.

"I will build a home for the God," he said. "For my Tchenka, and for yours. When Saturday Wilm comes for me, the house must be built, for she will bring magic with her."

"Magic?" questioned Nils, doubtfully. It was not a concept the Gharm found familiar.

"Holiness?" suggested Jep. "The stuff of She-Goes-On-Creating."

This was totally acceptable.

"I need your help," he told them. "We will pretend it is a house for the Gharm. It must be as close to Sarby as we can go."

They conferred, went away to talk to others, came back again. If one went only a few hundred yards north of the farmhouse, one came to a place that would, if all the land between were not so thickly forested, overlook the town of Sarby.

"The trees will not matter," Jep told them. "So long as the soil runs down to the town. So long as there is not rock between." He was not sure even rock would matter in the long run, but it seemed likely rock would delay things. Jep did not want anything that would add time. Time seemed to him to be a very important factor in whatever would happen to him.

There was no rock between the site and Sarby. The soil ran from the prominence down to Sarby and thence along the steeply curling river all the way to the sea.

Nils and Pirva were with him, as were half a dozen

other Gharm, early the following morning when he stuck
a staff into the most level patch they could find, tied a
rope to it, and scribed the two circles upon which the
temple would be built. He made them small. There would
not be enough help, he felt, to build it large, but that
didn't matter. Small was more appropriate for the Gharm.

He dug the foundations himself. He had watched several other temples being built besides the one he had
worked on in his own settlement, so he knew how to set
about it. The stones of Voorstod were a different color
from the stones of Hobbs Land, but since they were ledge
stones which broke into flat slabs and cracked across into
straight pieces, they were easy to lay Jep saw no reason to
scoop out the floor. A flat floor would be more suitable for
the Gharm, as it was for humankind. He merely flattened
the soil and rammed it hard before putting down a single
layer of large, flat stones as a base for mosaics. He had
seen no small, smooth, colored stones in the streams of
the kind ubiquitous in Hobbs Land. He did not know
what could be found for the mosaics, but that matter
would wait until later.

The Gharm came to help, sometimes one or two,
sometimes a dozen from the town, often at night, after
their work was done and the Voorstoders down in Sarby
had drunk themselves into sodden slumber. Actually, they
came to hear what Jep had to say, which was that he, Jep,
was the One Who had come to tell them that the Gods—
that is, the Tchenka—would soon come here to Voorstod,
and that this was to be their first house.

"You are to lay their pictures on the floor," he said.
"In my home, we laid our own Tchenka, in rock and clay.
I do not know your Tchenka, so you must do it."

This amazed the Gharm. However, a member of the
Grass-serpent clan found some green stone on the hill,
bashed it into small pieces and laid a fringed green snake
with a red eye, the whole set in a bed of clay which dried
hard only after they built a fire on top of it and then
polished the hardened result with fine sand. Grass snake
was followed by a birdlike creature with great round eyes,
laid in pebbles of brown and tan and white, and then by a
dozen kinds of air, water, and land dwellers, some recog-

nizable to Jep's eyes and more not. Some of the mosaic was laid in broken tile and some was laid in broken glass and some was put together out of odds and ends of equipment, whole or in pieces. Still, each morning when he looked at the floor, something new had been laid into the clay during the night, burned hard, and polished. Each night when he fell into bed, something new had been done to the temple. The work moved with astonishing rapidity. The walls and arches seemed to leap into being, smaller and more delicate ones than those he had known in the settlements. In forty or fifty days, designs covered the entire floor, swirling and knotting, giving a different feeling than those in the temples on Hobbs Land. Less peaceful, they were. More pleading. The roof was different, as well. The Gharm had made the roof as they made their huts, out of reed bundles hung upon stringers, rejecting a clay layer for, as they told Jep, it would never dry.

There were no grills for the ringwall. Jep explained how grills were used in his own land, and the Gharm responded with panels of marvelously woven and ornamented cane.

"When will the Tchenka come," they asked him when all had been done that they could do.

"When the other One Who comes for me," he said. "It is she who brings the substance of creation."

"Jep is He-Is-Accomplished," they nodded to one another when he said this. "She who comes is She-Goes-On-Creating. Perhaps he tells us the truth."

They considered this solemnly, without rejoicing. There was no great joy among the Gharm. When Jep urged them, they sang their whispery songs very quietly, so the Voorstoders would not hear: the endless catalog of their Tchenka, songs which had been taught to every Gharm child—though softly, softly, lest the Voorstoders grow angry and defile the songs with blood. In addition to the catalog, there were individual songs, which told of the lives of the Tchenka after they had been created. Outside these theological matters, the Gharm spoke little and complained not at all. When they did speak, most of their talk was of the lottery, which chose those to escape next, those to go out into the world through Skelp and Wander and Green Hurrah into Ahabar, where their kinsmen waited with clothing and food and friends and schooling for some of every clan, some of every blood line, so the people might not die.

When the temple was finished, it turned out to be suitable for living, also, a place in which a number of Gharm might dwell, better ventilated and drier than their huts.

"Will it be sacrilege?" they asked Jep. "Is it evil to dwell in the God's house."

"It's a good thing," Jep advised them. "To keep the God's house warm and dry until the God itself arrives. Then you should build houses of your own. Thereafter he watched, bemused, while they built little houses for themselves which were surprisingly similar to those built upon Hobbs Land by the Departed.

When the temple was finished, he lay upon his bed wondering what he would do with himself now. There were over a hundred scratches on the plaster beside the fireplace. If something didn't happen soon, so he had been told, they would start sending pieces of him to Ilion Girat for delivery to Maire Manone.

When, not many days later, the door burst open in the night, he thought the time had come. He had tried to summon bravery against this hour, with little success. He could face death, he thought, more easily than being cut up in pieces while he lived. Still he took a deep breath, pulled himself up and confronted Mugal Pye over the lantern with a level gaze.

"Good news for you, boy," the man said, with a bubbly laugh which said he had been drinking deeply, perhaps in celebration. "Maire Manone has sent word. After dillydallyin' for half a season, to save your worthless skin she's given us a time not long hence. The Sweet Singer's coming home."

· *The departure of* Maire Girat for Voorstod was only the last in what had been perceived as that long chain of apprehensions, terrors, and decisions that had begun with the disappearance of Jep Wilm.

No one even realized the boy was gone until a day had

gone by. The boy wasn't around on one off-day, but no one worried about that. Young people often went missing for whole days, occasionally whole days and nights. Aside from the thing that had attacked Sam, there were no predators on Hobbs Land, and that thing seemed to have been one of a kind. Sometimes Sam himself wondered why he was not more concerned with the danger implied by the existence of such a creature, but he wasn't. Theseus told him there weren't any others, and he more or less let his people know that.

If settlers stayed in the utilization zones, there were few dangers. If people obeyed the rules on leaving the utilization zones—that is, if they told their families where they were going—danger was minimized. Young people fell off rocks, sometimes, or out of trees. An occasional broken bone was about the worst of it. It had been most of a generation since a child had died from accident.

So no one worried when, on the particular off-day, Jeopardy Wilm was not to be found. When he did not show up by night, Saturday Wilm and China Wilm went to Sam and told him the boy was missing. Then the settlement began looking for him, asking questions, finding who had seen him when.

"Going down the road to the temple," said the people in the clanhome north of the Wilm clanhome. "Very early yesterday morning. First or second daywatch."

So the road was searched, and the temple itself, and the land around. When the sun came up, search parties moved out into the surrounding lands and up toward the New Forest and Cloudbridge, a favorite place for young people to wander.

Meantime, Saturday sat for hours cross-legged in the central enclosure of the temple. Birribat Shum did not say Jep was dead. If Jep had been alive or dead anywhere near, anywhere in the area of any of the settlements or CM or even the surrounding countryside, Birribat Shum would have known and Saturday Wilm would have known. Therefore, Jep was not in any of the settlements or in CM or in the surrounding areas all the way to the foot of the escarpment.

She explained this, as best she could, to a somewhat skeptical Samasnier Girat.

"The God told you this?"

"Not exactly," she confessed.

"What, then?"

"He sort of let me know," she said, trying for accuracy. "It's kind of like asking a question in your head, and then seeing how you feel about the answer. Some answers feel better than others, that's all. Some answers feel right."

This closely resembled the way Sam's mind worked on many occasions. He would have called it intuition, but he accepted that the God might amplify the effect, and he sat down with a map, wondering where else he could look. It seemed ridiculous to look on the escarpment itself, but that was about the only place left within reasonable distance.

On the third day they learned they need search no farther. Maire came to Sam, pale and distraught, bearing a written message which had been delivered to her, so she said, from the young man they had both met, Ilion Girat.

"Jeopardy Wilm wrote it," she said to her son. "Your boy." She held out the paper.

Sam, taken aback by this breech of convention, said, "I've never heard you say that, Mam. You've told me often enough we don't think about fathers on Hobbs Land!"

"Well, I know we don't, Sammy. But someone thinks that, or he'd not have taken the lad. And someone has taken the lad, and holds him hostage against my return to Voorstod." She waved the paper in his face until he took it. "I told you, Sammy. You thought I was a silly old woman. You were angry with me, I could see it. And all the time I was right."

Sam felt strangely wrenched and tugged about. He had been so sure she was being stupid and paranoid, and now here was this letter, this indisputable thing in his hands. He had been so sure she was . . . well, mistaken about Phaed. On the other hand, the message from Jep said *nothing* about Phaed. The ones who had taken him had been the ones here on Hobbs Land, Mugal Pye and this youth, Ilion. There may have been others involved, but not Phaed. Phaed might not even know about it. Phaed would not have threatened to kill the boy! His own grandson!

"This Mugal Pye, is he really capable of killing anyone, Mam? Do you know for sure?"

She screamed at him, anger at his wilful obstinacy overwhelming the gentlencss she'd always tried to use toward him. "You're trying to make excuses for them, Sammy. Well, don't do like I did and lie to yourself! Are they capable of killing anyone, you ask? Wasn't your little brother anyone then? Aren't they *anyone* who die among the Abolitionists? When the bombs go off, aren't they men and women and children bleeding on the ground with their arms and legs blown off? Aren't the Gharm *anyone*? Whipped to death and starved to death and hounded to death, aren't they *anyone*?"

Sam shook his head at her, wishing he had not asked her, for she could not be rational about it. Still, even accepting that a good part of what she said might be true, it still didn't mean Phaed was involved.

She murmured, "Not that I could prove which ones they killed with their own hands. I could only say for sure they planned killing, hour on hour, night on night . . ."

She could not prove it. Sam heard that, forgetting what else he had heard. His own dad was probably not part of any of this. Bad things happened in Voorstod, he no longer doubted, but his own dad was not part of it. Perhaps he was even being used by these conspirators.

Maire went alone to the Wilm clanhome, refusing Sam's company but taking the letter with her.

"So what do we do now?" cried China. "What will you do, Maire? Dare you return?"

"Dare I? No. I don't dare. I'm terrified. But of course I'll return," Maire's eyes were sunk deep, and her face was drawn. "To save the boy, of course. And not because he's Sam's . . . you know. Simply because he is. The thing is, my going back may not save him. I know those men. We can't trust their word. I'll have to think of a scheme to get him out safely."

"What will they do to *you,* when they get you back?" Africa wanted to know.

"Only their vengeful prophet knows for sure. Awateh, they call him, the prophet of the Almighty, head of the whole butcher shop. He'll have the last word on what happens to me. Still, I don't think they'd kill me right away. They must have some reason for wanting me back besides merely killing me. They could have done that here."

She went back to Sam, trembling from fear, and Sam comforted her, telling her he wouldn't let her go alone. He would have gone with her even had she gone blithely, with a song on her lips. This was what Theseus had promised him. He knew it. "I'm going with you, Mam. I will not let you go there alone. Depend upon it."

She wept on his shoulder, while he looked over her head at the wall. It was time for him to meet his father. The man his father. Phaed Girat. He told himself he wanted to know the truth, even while he assumed he already knew the truth. Dad was much maligned, not that Maire hadn't had some right on her side, but she'd no cause to think all the evil of Voorstod dwelt in Dad's skin and hung on his bones. No doubt Mugal Pye was a villain, but no doubt Sam and Phaed, once they were together, could put it right. Thereafter, Maire said things to him, and he to her, neither of them understanding the other, her thinking he was going along to protect her, and him thinking there was nothing, really, to protect her from.

Maire wanted delay. The longer she could delay, the better, so she told herself. She had no intention of going directly to Voorstod. Her only reason for going at all was to guarantee the boy's safety, so she was determined not to put herself at risk until Jep Wilm was free. Though Mugal Pye had promised no harm would come to the boy, Maire trusted him no more than she trusted the wind not to blow on any given day.

Between herself and Sam, they kept Ilion hanging and hanging for days at a time, while messages went back and forth between Ilion and Mugal Pye and, secretly, between CM and Ahabar. Even though Maire agreed to go almost

at once, she told Ilion she would not go alone, and Sam
needed some time to take care of matters at Settlement
One before he could depart. To Ilion, the whole matter
seemed pointless, so he didn't question this excuse. Luckily for Jep, the conspirators had allowed for a considerable
period of time for the old woman to make up her mind.
They had thought they might have to send a few slices of
the boy, quite frankly, before she'd be jostled into action,
and her early acquiescence had startled them agreeably.
They didn't see that having Sam with her made any difference. He would make another hostage, if they needed one.
Within limits, they were willing to be patient.

It was only days before they were to leave when Saturday Wilm came to Maire with a pronouncement.

"I have to go with you," said Saturday.

"Never, child. I'll not endanger another of you."

"It has nothing to do with danger, Maire Girat. It has
nothing to do with what I want, or Jep wants, even. It has
to do with the God. It is the God tells me to go, where Jep
is. There's something there I have to do. Wherever Jep is,
I have to go there. You must stay outside of Voorstod
until we return, both of us, but before Jep leaves there, I
must go to him."

Maire shook her head. She would not consider it.

Saturday gritted her teeth. "Maire, everything you
told me about Voorstod, all the killings, all the maimings
and the slavery, do you want it to go on? Do you want the
Gharm to go free? Maire, do you want the killing to stop?
Maire, are wee babies to be safe in Voorstod? Maire, are
the bombs to stop going off in Green Hurrah and killing
the children?"

The older woman looked at the girl, shaken.

"How do you know these things?"

"Some of them you told me! I guess the God told me
some things. What any person in Hobbs Land knows, the
God knows. What you know, the God knows, Maire. Everything we know becomes all one thing, the thing the
God knows, and what the God knows, so do the Ones
Who, or maybe even just anybody if it is needful. If you
want the killing to stop, Maire, then you have to take me
with you."

Surprisingly, when Maire asked Africa Wilm if she would allow Saturday to go, Africa had already decided it was the only proper thing to do.

Bleakly, she said, "Saturday and Jep are lovers, or soon to be. They are the Ones Who." Tears ran down her cheeks. "I wonder if either can live without the other. Let my daughter go with you." She was not willing to say this, but she said it, and the tears ran until she thought she had no more.

Later that night she went to China's house and cried over hot tea in the kitchen. "I don't know why I'm saying it," she said. "I say it, and I know it's right, but still I cry."

"Perhaps because you know, somehow, it will be best for them both," whispered China, wiping her own face. "But at the same time, it is terribly dangerous for them."

"Terribly dangerous. And Sam, going with them, makes it no less so. He's crazy, China!"

"No," said China soberly. "He's not."

"He acts crazy!"

"Africa, if Sam were crazy, he wouldn't be here anymore. All the really crazy people have gone, or killed themselves. But Sam is still here."

Africa thought about this, shaking the tears from her eyes. It was true. Sam seemed solidly set in Settlement One. However. "You're right about all the other crazy ones having left," she whispered. "But maybe this is Sam's way of leaving."

China felt something lurch within her. She couldn't live with him, but, oh, the thought of his going away. And yet, his going might bring Jep back. Could she trade one for the other? She gulped, swallowed the pain, tried to get it to go down from the place it was lodged, just behind her breastbone. "Trust," she whispered. "It comes down to that. Do we trust it?"

"It?"

"You know what I mean."

"Say it, China! Say it. Do I trust the God?"

"Well, do you?"

"Trust . . . what? What is it? It grew under the ground. We all know that. We don't talk about it. We pretend not to notice it. Half the time we act as though it weren't there at all. Sometimes we'll go to the temple, to help clean it or something. Most times, we don't. It doesn't ask for worship, you know. It doesn't need worship. It doesn't ask for hymns or praise or sacrifice, except for a few ferfs, and that's more in the nature of food. When we sing, we're singing about something else. We're singing about ourselves, not the God. Most of the time . . . we just take it for granted. It's there."

"You want it there, don't you?"

"Of course I . . . Yes. Yes, I want it there. But it should have come out of a fiery cloud. It should have descended from heaven. It should have . . . It should have come through a fiery gate, like that prophetess of the Baidee! But it just grew in the dirt like a turnip, China. How can we feel this way about something so common. Something that just grew in the dirt?"

"Because it *works*. It doesn't threaten us. It doesn't damn us to hell as the Voorstoders do. It doesn't require rituals as the Phansuri say their gods do. It just works."

"Yes," Africa whispered, eyes shut, squeezing tears. "Yes, I know. It works. And that's why Saturday has to go. Even though she may never come back."

· *At CM, Zilia* Makepeace and Dern Blass had become the Ones Who attended to the temple of Horgy Endure. Tandle Wobster helped out on occasion, as did Jamice, but Spiggy Fettle was still up on the escarpment, with the team from Thyker, unaware of the elevation of the God given the name of his former associate. Though information was consistently transmitted from escarpment to CM and back again, the new temple and the new God were simply taken for granted, and no one saw fit to mention them in the transmissions. Of course, no one on the escarpment had asked either.

Meantime the God Horgy sat upon its pedestal in the temple, a man-sized chunk of something or other which broadcast an almost palpable charm. Young women, particularly, enjoyed visiting the temple of Horgy Endure. Many men, on the other hand, found the temple at Settlement Two very much to their liking, while older women enjoyed the temple at Settlement Three where the God Elitsia was enthroned, or perhaps, said some, *en-plinthed* would be a better word. Not that there was any evidence of religious frenzy or even of extreme devotion. If one happened to be in the vicinity of a favorite temple, one dropped in sometimes, because it felt good to do so. There was considerably more intersettlement travel than there used to be, as people became aware that answers to certain problems might exist here, or there, at some distance. Otherwise, the usual work went on, productively and without interruption. People enjoyed life. There was an upsurge in arts and crafts and inventions, as well as what amounted to a renaissance in vocal and instrumental music.

On the escarpment, the Thykerites, augmented by the additional personnel, finished their personal survey of each and every ruin, took samples of several of the buried things, all of which turned out to be more or less of the same material, and decided to return home. Dr. Feriganeh had decided that Shan was physically healthy, though considerably fatigued. Shan was having bad dreams again, though he had been without them for several years. Neither the doctor nor Merthal had been able to find anything threatening on Hobbs Land. Shan was encouraged to take it easy.

"Your feelings and ideas are your own," the doctor reminded him. "So say the High Baidee. I may not interfere. I may not explain that you are wrong or attempt to convince you of error. I may not fool with your head. I may, however, recommend more sleep, more regular meals, and an easier schedule. The mind cannot exist without the body. The body must be healthy to carry the mind."

So much was doctrine, and to so much Shan acquiesced. He had not for a moment lost the notion that something on Hobbs Land was badly awry, but by following the physician's orders he was able to get himself into a state where he stopped having nightmares and didn't feel personally threatened. He told himself only the singing had made him feel threatened, and there was no singing upon the escarpment. When Shan mentioned this, Merthal went down to Settlement One to hear the choir for himself and enjoyed it thoroughly. He, like Bombi and Volsa, found it esthetically pleasing and not at all intrusive. He told Shan this, received a shrug in reply, and let it rest there. Once they were back on Thyker, he told himself, his young associate would recover a proper balance. He had simply been overstressed. Meantime Merthal went about humming to himself, "Rise up, rise up oh ye stones."

The buried things had turned out to be a kind of hard, woody fungus, something similar to a polypore. While their size was extreme, it was not unheard of. The Archives said there were similar things of even larger size on other worlds. Something similar had been found on several of the Belt worlds, and considering the constant bombardment from comets and other trash, a common source was probable. Perhaps there had been a world where these things grew, and it had been broken up, somewhere out there, and the pieces had been drawn into the System, several of them dropping on Belt worlds. This would explain their presence. The group was satisfied with this theory. With a singular lack of imagination, they did not look for other things that might have come from the same source. They took samples for the botanists on Thyker, finished up their documents, and returned to CM, where Spiggy, no less than Bombi, decided that hot water was the first priority.

Spiggy hadn't actively disliked his liaison with Volsa, though it had lacked certain aspects of mutuality, which would have allowed it to be enjoyable. He had felt summoned. He had felt patronized. His reward for service had had the same emotional weight as a pat on the head. "Here, little boy, take this coin and buy candy, the lady is busy now." Well, he had no one to blame but himself. There was no requirement in his contract that he provide sexual services for visiting VIPs. To do so had been his own decision, based at least partly on what Spiggy himself identified as prurience of the first degree.

When Spiggy returned to CM, and after a lengthy

bath, he tried to tell a strangely relaxed and comfortable Jamice how he felt.

"I've always wondered about the High Baidee," he said. "I rejected the teachings as a child, but the curiosity remained. Kind of a nasty voyeurism, I suppose. I wanted to know what they were really like, up close."

"Well," Jamice asked, who was being unaccountably accommodating, "what are they really like, up close."

"Intense," he said. "Self-involved. Not Bombi, who has some sense of fun, even a little self-ridicule. But the other two . . . Well. They burn with a hot, clear flame, put it that way. Especially Shan. He has these nightmares and wakes up screaming, and then he goes around at white heat all day, making up for it. He's a fearful and yet daring youngster, possessed by something very strange indeed. Capable of destruction, of self or others, I have no doubt."

"Best they go home soon, then," said Jamice. "When do they?"

"Immediately," Spiggy said. "Tomorrow, I think. As soon as they can clean up and have a little rest."

"Good," said Jamice, who had said nothing at all to Spiggy about the CM temple or the God Horgy Endure. Thus far, Spiggy had not asked about Horgy Endure. Perhaps he would not. The two had never been close friends. Better, perhaps, he did not ask, not until the Baidee had left. Perhaps the Baidee would all go to bed early, and no one would say anything, and then they would go. Best that they simply go. She did not question why she thought so. It was simply a feeling, but then, recently she had grown to trust her feelings. All of them at CM had learned to trust their feelings.

Spiggy, however, found himself restless and unable to sleep. Perhaps he was too keyed up. Certainly he was on a high, jittery, strung-up, unable to relax. Perhaps he needed a walk. Though it was dark and late and quite cool, he put on warm clothing and went out into the night, finding just enough light to walk by without tripping over things. He went southeast, onto the rolling, low hills which surrounded CM on all sides except where the river valleys came in from the west and departed to the south.

He came upon the temple without seeing it, almost bumping into it before the mass of it obtruded on his senses. Then it was as though someone spoke to him, and he found the door without trying, found the grill to the inner chamber without trying, found the central area where the God stood upon its plinth, and was found by the God in turn.

When he came to himself at first light, he was slumped on the mosaic floor just outside the inner chamber. When he rose, it was with the sensation of something tearing, as though he had been connected to the floor by a pelt of hair-fine filaments. The ripping sensation was not painful. He was not even certain it had been physical. It might well have been totally subjective, a symbolic expression of his being connected to this world. What was remarkable was how well he felt, not at all stiff after what should have been an uncomfortable night.

He went out, into the air. From the height, to the south, he could see a string of lakes dotted with tiny islands where he did not remember any lakes being before. That the islands were real was impressed upon him by the scent which came from them on the wind, sweetness and spice, and he could see the colors of the enormous flowers from where he stood. On several of the islands stood the pillared shapes of small circular buildings with sweetly rounded domes, like women's breasts.

A nice place, he thought, to take a shallow boat and skim along, smelling the flowers, seeing the no doubt charming small birds and animals that lived among them, perhaps a nice place to stop and picnic, a nice place to make love in one of those little buildings.

He wondered if Dern knew about the lake, and then realized that of course Dern did. Everyone did. But they weren't telling. No news of this lake had been sent out into System, anymore than there had been news of the canyon west of Settlement One, or the New Forest, or any of the other recent wonders. These were Hobbs Land things. No one wanted curious outlanders flooding in, asking questions, threatening the . . . the what? The whatever it was.

So, before he went on with his work, worthwhile work, which he was anticipating with pleasure, before he saw his friends at CM again, it would be appropriate to see the Thykerites off Hobbs Land, to get them on their way, before they had a chance to do any further explorations.

Spiggy felt the High Baidee should go as soon as possible, for they would not understand the way, the convenience, the kindness which was manifesting itself on Hobbs Land.

TWO

· *"We're going tomorrow,"* said Sam to Theseus in the night hours, as they stood in the Temple of Poseidon, upon a shining hill, watching phantom horses grazing in the meadows. "The thing is, I want to talk to him. To Phaed. To my father."

"What do you want to say?" asked the hero.

"I don't know. I mean, I figure it out, but then it doesn't seem to be the right thing."

Theseus tossed his sword in the air, spinning, and caught it by the hilt. "I'll pretend to be him, and you can practice. How would that be?"

Sam was doubtful. "You don't look like him at all."

"Oh, I can be him," said Theseus, sitting down on the hillside and compressing himself, becoming squattier and bulkier. A moment later he looked up at Sam, slantwise, with Phaed's remembered face, exactly, even to the big cap hiding most of his hair. "Well, hello, boy! And where'd you drop in from?"

Sam was silent, shocked. It was the voice he remembered, too, and the very words.

"Hello, Dad," said Sam after a moment. "I've come all the way from Hobbs Land to see you."

"That's a long way to come. I always hoped you would, though, no matter how far it is."

"Well, if you missed me, you could have come to me, Dad."

"Not really, boy. I mean, when your mam went away, it was because she wanted to be rid of me, wasn't it? So what kind of man would I have been to go invading her privacy, showing up in her town?"

"You were thinking of her?"

"Well, of course, boy. She's my wife. Mother of my children. I always think of her."

"So you love her still, do you?"

"We're man and wife, Sammy. We made vows . . ." The man looked off into the distance, sadness in his eyes.

"Dad."

"Yes, Sammy."

"I need you to explain something. About when Maechy died."

"Oh, sad, sad, that was."

"Mam said you didn't grieve. She said you just cursed the man for not shooting straight."

The huddled figure shook with sobs. "Oh, I grieved, Sammy. By the Almighty, I grieved. I cursed at the fool who killed him, and I grieved. He was my son, too. Not my eldest, not you, Sam, only a tiny boy, but he was my son, too. The pain was so deep I couldn't weep, boy. I thought I'd die with the sorrow of it. All I could do was curse or I'd have died . . ."

"Then they weren't your men who killed him?"

"My men? What men is that, Sammy? I have no men who would do such a thing. Your poor mam always thought I was involved in things like that, but I was only a farmer, only a man seeing to flocks and fields, as you do, lad. We farmer kings are the true heroes, don't you think? It makes me proud to see you, following in my footsteps so to speak."

Sam turned away, tears in his eyes. It would be something like that. When he really came to it, it would be like that.

"Did you say what you wanted to say?" asked Theseus, back in his own form, tossing up his sword again,
spinning, up and up until it almost touched the heavy
beams above.

Sam nodded. Yes. Something like that.

Later that night, Sam walked back to the village, his
face reflecting only calm, his belt and helmet no longer
causing the apprehension they once had. Lots of people
wandered about at night, now, going out to Bubble Lake
for a swim or into the newly discovered marsh district to
hunt phoenix feathers, or down to the Grove of Fabulous
Beasts with the children. Night-wandering was no longer
odd.

He found Maire waiting for him at the brotherhouse,
wanting to go over her plan once more, to see if she had
forgotten anything.

"Tomorrow we go to Ahabar," she said. "The Door
takes us to Fenice, the capital city. We will go from there
to Jeramish, the area bordering Green Hurrah, where
Commander Karth has offered us hospitality and protection. He will keep us safe from being seized up and made
off with. At least, so he says in the messages he has sent
me."

Sam had heard this a dozen times, but he had never
wondered until now how it was she knew this commander. He asked her now. "How did you come to know
a commander in Ahabar?"

"I met him once, long ago . . ." Her voice trailed
away in memory. She had known him only briefly, she a
young mother with two dirty children clinging to her
skirts, a road-wearied trio who had walked out of Green
Hurrah straight into the hands of an Ahabarian patrol.
Karth had been the officer in charge. She remembered
him as generous and attractive. In the intervening years
she had often thought of him, regretting the vows that had
prevented her responding to his unspoken invitation. She
had not hesitated to send him a reminder of their former
meeting, begging his help. He remembered her, so he said,
and, usefully, he was in command of the garrison now.

She went on, explaining her plan to Sam. "My plan
was to wait there, well-guarded in Jeramish, until Jep was

brought out safe. But when Saturday involved herself, it meant we would have to do it differently. She claims she must go into Voorstod, to whatever place Jep's being held, then they will come out together."

"Which is no doubt the best reason of all for my going along," said Sam, realizing he had found a suitable role for himself. "A girl that age obviously should not have to travel alone." Not among men like Mugal Pye—whom he had liked no more than Maire had. "Now, suppose we get Jep out safely. What happens then? Do they want you to return to Voorstod and sing? Do you think they want you for some symbolic purpose? The old Maire Manone, Sweet Singer, all that." He smiled at her, trying to cheer her.

"Certainly they want me for some purpose of their own," she agreed. "They sought me, particularly. They took Jep because he is my grandson, to their way of reckoning, so it is clear they want me." She turned away, not wanting her son to see the fear in her face. In a country in which children were taught to inflict pain for fun, it would be foolish for any woman to consider herself immune from receiving similar attentions. She didn't know what they wanted with her, but she was sure there was pain in it somewhere. Still, she could not live with herself if Jep came to harm through her. "I'm frightened," she said, wanting him to hold her. If no man had ever held her gently, surely her son could do that, now that she was old.

But Sam had never held her. He did not even think of holding her now. "But you have no idea what they want, Mam," he said, trying to get her to look at it in a less dangerous light. "It could be something fairly innocent."

"Oh, I've tried to convince myself of that," she said. "I've had plenty of practice." She was thinking how much practice she had had. We do it all the time, we women, she said to herself. We marry, and it turns out to be hell. So we hope they will stop drinking, but they don't. We hope they will stop beating us and the children, but they don't. We hope they will stop killing, but they see no reason to stop. Why should they, when they can sit in the tavern and tell one another how fine they are, how powerful and clever they are, how they'll take nothing from nobody. No man's a match for them. No woman's enough. And nothing matters so long as they're faithful to the Cause. Still, we women keep hoping, we keep telling ourselves *maybe things are fairly innocent.*

Sam's voice interrupted her thoughts. "Perhaps they want you there because too many women have left." It was an insight, which had just come to him. "That's possible. They want you there to tell them to come home."

"Oh, perhaps." She nodded, thinking about this. It made as much sense as anything else. "Perhaps so, Sammy. Perhaps there are not enough women left to breed men for the Cause's purposes. I suppose Mugal Pye and his cronies might believe I could undo what once I did when I sang them away. Well, they can only have of me what I have to give, Sammy. As for what good you'll do, being there, I can't say."

Sam couldn't say either, but he burned to go, nonetheless.

· *At first daywatch* of the following morning, Saturday met Gotoit and Willum R. Quillow at the temple.

"You know what's to do," she told them. "The front of the temple's still to be painted."

"I know," said Gotoit. "Don't worry, Sats. Willum and me will take care of it."

"Be alert if it needs ferfs," Saturday said, wracking her brain for any other instructions she might remember when it was too late. "Lucky'll know."

"They've begun talking, you know," said Willum R. "The cats."

"Talking!"

"Well, a kind of talking. Not human talk. They haven't the right physical structure for that. But they've been talking a kind of cat talk. If you listen and watch, you can understand a lot of it."

Saturday thought Willum R. might have gone a little odd, but when she encountered Lucky and two of her kittens outside the temple, Lucky addressed Saturday in a long, complicated yowl, which Saturday found she understood perfectly well as an instruction to walk softly and smell very carefully before getting herself into anything. Saturday replied in human talk that she would do so, and Lucky nodded as though she fully comprehended what Saturday had said. She sat down and licked a front paw with every evidence of satisfaction.

"Have you got the you-know?" asked Gotoit in a half whisper.

Saturday nodded. She had the packets sewn into her chemise where they would lie next to her skin.

"That's good then," said Gotoit, hugging her. "It'll be all right."

Saturday, who was not at all sure it would be all right, returned the hug and tried very hard not to cry.

• *At the third* daywatch, Africa Wilm, with Saturday beside her, picked up Sam and Maire at the Girat clanhome and set off for CM in one of the settlement fliers. It was a virtually silent trip. Africa had tried talking to Saturday, without success. It wasn't that Saturday wouldn't talk, it was that she, Africa, couldn't.

"It will be all right," said Saturday, reaching to stroke her mother's face. This was merely reassurance, with only hopeful supposition behind it, and they both knew it.

There was a time, Africa told herself, when she would have resented what was happening now, resented being *informed* that something needed doing. Now, however, she examined herself for any feelings of coercion and found none. No demand. Simply information. The thing was necessary. The difference now was that she was unable to reject the information or rationalize it away. If one was *informed,* one knew it was true, and there was no point playing with the idea or talking about it. It simply was, that's all.

"Take care of China," Sam begged her, when they arrived at the departure area. "Please, Africa."

Africa merely nodded, saying yes, she would look out for China. Undoubtedly Sam, too, was being *informed* that something needed to be done, as Saturday herself had no doubt been *informed.* Africa hugged her daughter, muttering words of warning and caution which, in the sense of them, were remarkably similar to those the cat Lucky had uttered. Walk softly. Be careful.

Africa didn't stay to watch them go through the Door. She let them out and drove away, tears flowing down her face. She was not being silly, she told herself. She was just . . . just missing her daughter, that was all. Inside her, calm and peace were urged upon her, but she fought against being consoled. It was proper to feel this way. Proper to be lonely. Proper and human to grieve.

The consolation withdrew as though considering the matter. Perhaps, it agreed, it was more proper to grieve. Consolation was proper, but grieving, too, had its time and place.

Inside the reception area, Sam, Maire, and Saturday encountered the team of Baidee who had been up upon the escarpment doing the ancient monuments survey, ten of them, counting the techs. Sam greeted Volsa, Shan, and Bombi by name and was introduced to some of the other persons in the party—Dr. Feriganeh and a busy little man named Merthal. The several technicians were busy with their boxes and bundles of esoteric equipment, muttering among themselves.

"Did you find anything exciting?" Sam asked Volsa, relying upon their brief acquaintance in the settlement to excuse his obvious curiosity.

"A rare fungus of some kind," said Volsa, warming to Sam as she had in the settlement. She turned to smile at Saturday. She had seen the girl before, singing with the choir. "A fungus that grows into long, radially arranged bodies beneath the soil. So far as our botanists can tell, the growths may have been there for centuries. They're dormant. There have been many meteor strikes on the escarpment. We believe it probable the growths are not native to this world, and the planet lacks something they need for development."

"Almost a unique find," said the doctor with enthusiasm. "There are similar growths on two other Belt worlds, similarly dormant. My colleagues will be envious that I have had this opportunity."

"That's marvelous," said Saturday. "All the time we

settlers have been here, and you come along and find something completely new!"

Her remark drew Shan's attention. He turned calculating eyes upon her, recognized that he had seen her before, and said, "I went out for a walk early this morning and saw that while we have been working on the escarpment, the people of CM have built a temple like the one rebuilt in Settlement One. At least, I suppose it is similar. I did not look at it closely. Why was that done, do you suppose?"

Sam responded before Saturday could. "I think it's because we're a little starved for history upon Hobbs Land. We have no monuments, no memorials. We've adopted this indigenous architectural form as a kind of symbol. Not unlike, perhaps, the ritual dress which your group wears. You bond yourselves together by similar dress. So we bond our various communities together by building in this ancient form. It is Hobbs Landian, like us."

"You think it will be a persistent symbol then?" Shan asked. "Or a mere fashion?" It was his youth more than his tone that made the question seem arrogant.

"Only time will tell." Sam shrugged. "When we build a future of our own, perhaps we'll abandon this relic of the Owlbrit people. Personally, I hope we'll keep the little temples. We can begin our history with a continuation of the former one."

"I would have liked something prettier," said Maire, moved by some impulse she could not identify to argue with Sam. "I wish they had built towers instead of these flattish things."

"You disagree with your . . . is it your son?" asked Shan.

"Oh, fairly regularly," she laughed. "We are not in agreement about a number of things."

"Tell me," Shan asked Sam, almost as though he had not been listening. "Do you have a choir at Central Management?"

Sam was caught by surprise. "Not that I know of," he answered.

Saturday and Maire, who had both helped organize

the choir at CM, kept their mouths shut. Shan had no
chance to ask other questions, for Spiggy and Dern Blass
came bustling in, bonhomous and full of farewells.

"Came to thank you," Dern said to the Damzels with
a nod to the others of their party, shaking Bombi's hands
between his own, oozing conviviality. "We've wanted the
survey done for a decade or so now. Good to have it. Will
you be making any recommendations?" He looked hard at
all three of them. "Any recommendations for preservation
or reconstruction?"

Bombi shook his head, responding to the warmth expressed. "We think not at this point," he said. "There are
thousands of village houses, over a thousand temple clusters. Any scholarly work that is done will probably be
done from the survey itself."

"You will recall that there had been some accusations
concerning the Departed," Dern insisted. "Did you find
any evidence of malfeasance, misfeasance, naughty do-
ings?"

"As to the matter you raised originally with the Advisory?" asked Volsa. "We found no evidence that there has
been anything done which would be of concern to the
Advisory. I believe Zilia Makepeace was misled . . ."

"Though perhaps not totally in error," interrupted
Shan, who was standing close beside his sister.

Dern Blass's eyebrows went up into his hair and
stayed there while he regarded the two young Baidee with
astonishment. "You disagree? Perhaps and perhaps not?"

Shan said, "There is no evidence that any settler has
ever committed an untoward act toward any of the Departed. There is no evidence that any remnant of the Departed still exist, and we have covered the escarpment
thoroughly. However, I agree with the Makepeace woman
that some influence of the Departed remains upon Hobbs
Land. I can identify it no more clearly than she did.
Nonetheless . . ." His words trailed away as he gave
Spiggy a long, weighing look.

Spiggy, correctly interpreting Shan's stare, returned it
with calm indifference. Shan had never approved of Volsa's liaison with Spiggy. He had obviously considered
Spiggy to be a self-indulgent backslider who was, when all

was said and done, little better than a Low Baidee. Relationships between them, up on the escarpment, had been strained at best, which did not matter now. Spiggy had come to the departure area this morning for only one reason, to be sure that all of the Baidee went away.

A soft horn sounded, signifying that a scheduled departure was imminent. The board above the gate flashed: *Chowdari upon Thyker.* No one moved. Anticipation of that wrenching, turned-inside-out feeling made it usual for passengers to linger at the gate, shifting from foot to foot, dallying.

Chowdari upon Thyker, flashed the sign above the gate repeatedly, then *Final call.*

Dern bowed, spreading his arms wide, smiling, as though to say, "Well, we can not postpone this occasion further, or you will miss your destination. Farewell."

The Damzels bowed in return. Bombi pushed the gate open, and the group straggled across the gravel toward the curtain of fire at the center of the walled circle. Once they had gone through, there would be a brief wait while the next desired destination was programmed, checked, and confirmed.

"So Shan thinks there's an influence of the Departed," mused Dern. "Who would have thought it?"

No one in the area made any comment at all. No comment was necessary. All of them were from Hobbs Land. All of them knew, just as Dern did, that despite all the casual indirection the settlers had managed, Shan Damzel had still come up with a fairly accurate assessment of the situation. There was, indeed, an influence of the Departed upon Hobbs Land. Or an influence of the influence which had been upon the Departed. So to speak.

"And now, you people," said Spiggy, suddenly very interested in what was going on. "What is this business, Maire Girat? I've looked you up in the Archives, you know. You were a kind of talisman for Voorstod at one time." He took her by the arms and smiled at her, urging her to tell him everything.

"At one time I was," she admitted, responding to his warmth. "At one time I let myself not think about what Voorstod really was. I saw the loveliness of the mists and the aching beauty of the sea and the highlands, and ignored other things . . ."

Sam moved away to speak to Dern, and Maire followed him with her eyes. "I dreamed of lovers and sang about them. I saw children laughing and sang of them. I didn't see the Gharm. No one in Voorstod looks at the Gharm, so why should I have done."

"I've been told of the Voorstod Doctrine of Freedom," said Spiggy, holding her eyes with his own. "Almighty God gave the Gharm to Voorstod, so says doctrine, for freedom's sake." He shook himself, as though to shake off some vile residue. "But what of the Gharm themselves?"

"The doctrine of Voorstod says they are nothing. Less than nothing. Consumables. To be bred and used up."

"It seems to me," said Spiggy softly, "that when a race of man becomes so anthropocentric it regards other living beings as lesser consumables, it could get to be a habit. It might become easy to include other living creatures with the Gharm. Animals. Children. Women. Entire planets. Perhaps they, too, become consumables, to be used up and thrown away."

Maire nodded at him. "So they will not teach the girl child anything important, but they will call her stupid when she is grown. So they will force a Gharm to live where there is no water and call him dirty. So they will demand their children seek their permission for any act but then turn upon them as lazy and unenterprising. Such are the imprecations of Voorstod. Such are the words that lie upon Voorstod souls to hide the guilt inside." She stood rigid, turning her back. "Ire, Iron, and Voorstod: the words I left behind." Tears were running down her cheeks.

"And you will go back? To that?" asked Spiggy. He was the only one who would have asked. Despite his discovery of the God Horgy Endure, he was not yet accustomed to knowing things as others in Hobbs Land were coming to know them.

The horn sounded again. The lights flashed above the gate, spelling out *"Fenice upon Ahabar."*

Maire wiped her eyes and stepped resolutely toward the gate, without hesitation. Sam's face showed only interest and expectation. Saturday took a deep breath. The coming time would be hard. Things would not be clear and trustworthy. She would have to depend upon herself, her own memory of the way things should be. She would have to be strong, and careful. "I will," she promised, promised herself, perhaps, or something larger than herself. "I will."

Spiggy opened the gate. Outside, across the area of sandy ground, partly fused with the powers that ran into and out of the Door, stood the Door itself, glimmering in pale fire. At the other side of it was Fenice, and the road to Jeramish.

"Go with our blessings," murmured Dern, patting Maire upon the arm.

Saturday and Maire bowed him farewell and went. Sam had already gone.

· *Shanrandinore Damzel, despite* the fact that his siblings saw things quite otherwise, insisted upon making a minority report to the Circle of Scrutators.

"Do you really think it necessary?" Holorabdabag Reticingh asked. "You won't do your career any good by poking spears into grinding devices."

"Spears into what, Uncle Holo?"

Reticingh shook his head. "An old saying. I'm not sure what it means, literally, though the sense is that one ought not to waste energy on imaginary enemies."

Shan bridled. "Who claims that I merely imagine?"

Reticingh flushed. Such a claim would be blasphemous, and Shan knew it. No Baidee would accuse another of merely imagining, or of being insane, or of not understanding. "Each mind sees reality in its own way," said the catechism.

"No one makes any such claim," said Reticingh. "Calm down, Shan. It's just that no one sees any reason for concern but you. Dr. Feriganeh doesn't. Merthal doesn't. Bombi and Volsa don't. We can't tell you you're wrong, any more than we can tell you they're right. We can say that the weight of opinion . . ."

"I believe I am more sensitive than any of them,"

Shan interrupted. "I believe I was sensitized by my time among the Porsa. I believe Zilia Makepeace sensed the same thing I did."

"Now she says not, you know."

"What do you mean?"

"She's revised her report to the Advisory. I got a message from Chairman Rasiel Plum, saying the Makepeace woman had thought it over and decided she was imagining it all. She ascribes it to experiences she had as a child in the Celphian Rings. She was badly treated, and it made her suspicious of everyone."

Shan scowled hideously. "If she says that, then I believe the danger to be even greater than I had thought previously."

Reticingh threw up his hands. "What danger, Shan?"

"Something is controlling the minds of those upon Hobbs Land. All of them. Without exception. Including Zilia Makepeace."

Reticingh sat down carefully, slowly formulating what he would do and say next. There was a convention for times like these. Not, thank the Overmind, one he had often had to use.

"Very well, Shan, let us examine the evidence in the conventional manner."

Shan settled himself into a chair opposite and relaxed. If Reticingh was content to examine the evidence, so was he.

"One sign of mental interference of the type you suspect would be total agreement on everything by the people on Hobbs Land. Absolute single-mindedness. Was this the case?"

Shan was about to give a qualified yes when he remembered the last conversation he had had with people from the settlement. He recalled Sam Girat's mother, who had said she and her son disagreed about many things. "No," he said honestly, flushing. "As a matter of fact, when we were leaving, the mother of one of the Topmen told us she and her son were often in disagreement. I think the people do disagree, quite a lot." He thought a moment more, still being honest with himself, as Baidee were expected to be. "I heard children fighting among themselves when we visited Settlement One. And people arguing. Though there was what I regard as an unlikely degree of cooperation, I cannot honestly say there was total agreement."

"Was it considered inappropriate or unacceptable to argue or disagree?"

Shan shook his head, a little angrily. He was as familiar with these questions as Reticingh was, and he knew where they were heading.

Reticingh thought a moment. "Another sign of mental interference might be ardent fanaticism of some kind. Extreme dedication to some system of thought or to some deity. Mind-numbing ritual, for example. Lengthy periods of rote prayer. Did you notice anything of the kind?"

"They built these temple structures," said Shan. "They built them in all of the settlements, I think."

"What reason did they give for doing so?"

Shan recalled Sam Girat's reasoning and quoted it fully.

"Do you find this unbelievable?" asked Reticingh. "On Phansure, virtually every village has a monument to those who died in the great Phansurian brother-war during colonial times. Here on Thyker, we have cenotaphs for those killed by the Blight. Do the settlement people spend inordinate time with this temple construction? Do they spend a lot of time *in* the temples?"

Shan shook his head again. "Not that I could see."

"Are there great crowds of worshippers being harangued? People spending hours in prayer? Anything like that?"

"Not that I could see. But they sing, Uncle Holo."

Reticingh paused again. "Though vocal music is not an overwhelming interest here on Thyker, at least not among most Baidee, you have to admit that a great many people sing. Your brother sings! We cannot ascribe mind-control to all who sing. On Phansure and Ahabar, they have large orchestras and pay much attention to music, and even though the conductors seem to have absolute control over the musicians during a performance, we don't consider that the musicians have had their heads fooled with." He paused to let that sink in. "They choose to take part in an orchestra, and that implies submitting to the director." He let Shan chew on that for a moment before continuing.

"A third sign of mental enslavement would be a continued attempt on the part of the controlled ones to convert others. Did anyone attempt to convert you to any point of view?"

Shan laughed shortly, without amusement. "No, Uncle. No and no. We're not going to find what concerns me through applying the conventional questions! No, and no, and no. They did nothing, said nothing, indicated nothing. They look normal, act normal, except that they're far more contented than people should be . . ."

"Contented?" Reticingh interrupted. "What do you mean by that?"

"They give the impression of being . . . satisfied. No. Not satisfied. Pleased with life."

"Well, from what you tell me, it's a healthful life, without much stress. And, unlike most populations, the people on Hobbs Land are self-selected to be those who want to live that kind of life. I suppose by now most anyone who wasn't well-suited to it has given up and departed." He stared at Shan innocently. "They are allowed to depart if they wish?"

"They are," said Shan unrepentantly. "Still, I believe something . . ."

"You believe something bad, evil, threatening is happening. You don't know why, you don't know how, you don't know what, but something's wrong, is that it?"

"I want to tell the Scrutators how I feel. Just for the record."

Reticingh threw up his hands again. "You have that right, Shanrandinore Damzel. If you had not the right on your own account, I would obtain it for you, as the dear son of my old friends. Still, think about it carefully. You have told me nothing convincing. Others may question your judgement."

"For the record," said Shan stubbornly. "I insist."

"Very well then," agreed Reticingh. "For the record. I will make the arrangements for a hearing and inform you when I have done so."

Dismissed, Shan Damzel went out through the hall and onto the high walkway along the parapet, which led to the top of the grand staircase. He had come up that staircase, slow flight by slow flight, eschewing the gravitics which would have lifted him without effort. Climbing to the ramparts of the Chowdari Temple of the Overmind had the weight and force of ritual, a significance beyond the mere physical effort. It was a symbol of trial, of overcoming inimical forces. The grand staircase wound around the temple, a long flight beginning at the southeast corner of the temple and climbing to the northeast corner, then turning across to the northwest, to the southwest, then up to a point directly above the starting point, where he stood now. From his present vantage point he could look down into the drill grounds where thousands of young Baidee, tunicked and turbaned, identical as grains of sand, engaged in weapons practice.

Odd. It hadn't occurred to Shan before, and would not have now except for Reticingh's comment about the orchestra, but was not the subordination of one's own judgement in accepting military orders "fooling with one's head"? When Shan had been among them, the troops had been harangued for hours at a time by their officers. They had been converted to a proper frame of mind to make them move and march and maneuver as proper soldiers. They had come to an absolute uniformity of opinion upon some matters, many matters.

Shan turned away from the parapet and wiped his forehead. It wasn't the same thing. One could choose not to take part in military service. The alternatives were unpleasant, but one could choose.

He turned back, focusing his attention on the wheeling thousands. Some of these very men might be under Chur-ry's command in the brigades. Some, perhaps, were members of The Arm of the Prophetess, about which Shan had heard whispers. If there was no response from the Circle of Scrutators, and it seemed unlikely there would be none, then there was one body of dedicated Baidee who would see the threat to their traditional freedoms. One group who would realize such a threat could not go unopposed, to spread, perhaps to spread widely.

He wiped his forehead and swallowed bile at the back of his throat. There would be one group he could count on. And at least one dedicated Baidee to lead them.

· *On the moon* Enforcement, Overmajor Altabon Faros tried to think of anything in the universe except his wife, Silene. Often he woke in the night to the sound of her screaming words at him, only to realize words could not come from her lips again. Unless . . . unless he could get her away from Voorstod. Elsewhere, she might have a new tongue cloned. Elsewhere she might be well again, herself again. Otherwise, there were certain secret sweet names she had called him which were forever silent. There were certain sweet plans they had made which were forever dead. If she herself were dead, he would have grieved and forgotten, but she lived and might go on living if he could quit thinking about her enough to go on doing what he was supposed to be doing. Only by doing it successfully could he save her life. So Faros spent evenings and early mornings concentrating on what he knew about what he had to do. Everything he knew about Enforcement. Everything he knew about Authority.

He knew the moon Authority was a small one because nothing larger had originally been needed. There had been room for twenty-one Phansuris and Ahabarians and Thykerites and Moon and Belt people together with their secretaries and aides and servants. Over the centuries, however, Authority had become corpulent, adding an advisory here, creating a panel there, appointing a temporary study commission that survived over the centuries to create other (temporary) commissions of its own. Now Authority filled every cubic inch of the moon's hollowed-out interior and domed surface, and its constant complaint was that there was no room for all its people. Authority had become an entity larger than its purpose and too unwieldy for its duties. It was swollen, gross, quivering with indulgent fat.

And the people were the same. Faros had met them. He knew they were effete and decadent and mostly old, living in environments of unquestioned, though artificial beauty. Though they went away, from time to time, they always returned, to be soothed by privilege and to divert themselves with endless machinations.

Despite the numbers packed into Authority, the moon itself was no larger than it had ever been, no larger and no better defended, which was to say, not defended at all. No one on Authority had ever considered defending the moon, certainly not against Enforcement. Those on Authority did not often think of Enforcement and had never used it. Even when Thyker had been invaded and the twenty-one Members had considered mobilization, Thyker had dealt with the matter itself before one vote could be taken, before one soldier could be awakened and programmed and sent out to wreak destruction.

Authority was incapable of imagining its own demise, a demise that was already hovering over it, implacable fate held in the trembling hands of Altabon Faros and the hard, unfeeling ones of Halibar Ornil.

Ornil. Stocky and thick-skinned Ornil, whose forehead was low and whose eyes were narrow. Who walked with a lurching stride, like a wrestler, and whose hands hung away from his body, as though they were not quite part of him. Whose uniform was always slightly untidy, even moments after he put it on, and whose connection with the aristocratic Overmajor Faros had never been understood. Only Faros knew that Ornil was there to keep watch on him, and he to keep watch on Ornil. The prophets trusted no one. Trust had no part in the Cause.

Occasionally, when it would seem natural for them to do so, the two Voorstoders spent some time together. They did not drink stimulants or take any recreational drug. They did not patronize the brothel maintained at Authority's expense—Faros from lack of appetite, Ornil from prudence. But they might take a meal together while Ornil muttered his assessment of what he assumed was closest to them both. The successful culmination of their mission.

"Thyker first," Ornil had postulated on the most recent occasion. "We'll send the Enforcement army against Thyker first."

Faros knew it would not be Thyker first. To say so

would make him suspect, however, as though he questioned the will of the Awateh, to which he was not privy. So, he said, as he always did, "That's up to the Awateh," being careful to give nothing away, stroking his long, tapering fingers as though they ached and wishing Ornil could talk about something else.

Ornil ruminated, chewing over his ideas as he did his food, messily, noisily. After a time, he said, "Except Thyker does have all those biological weapons. If not Thyker, I'll bet we go against Phansure first."

Faros sipped at the lukewarm drink before him. "If the Cause conquers Phansure, then it can force the Phansuris to build as many more soldiers as it might need for any purpose. So it would seem Phansure could be an early target."

"Not first?" Ornil glared at him from beneath his brows. "Why not first?"

"Perhaps the Awateh has considered Authority as the first target." The only one that made any sense. Which was not to say the Awateh would necessarily do it. Much of what the Awateh did had no sense to it. Only cruelty and pain.

"Authority?" Ornil thought about this, laboriously, as he thought about most things. Then he smiled. "Of course. Authority."

Faros sighed and tried not to think of Silene. "Whatever they do, it will be very soon now. The new man arrives shortly."

Ornil's eyes gleamed. He had no wife in Voorstod. He had no children. He had no family for the prophet to chop up like meat for the pot. Ornil was a dedicated man.

While Ornil gloated, Faros went back to writing scenarios in his head. If the army was dispatched against Phansure and Authority, and if the prophets followed the army, would it be possible for him, Faros, to get to Voorstod and rescue his family while the Faithful were otherwise engaged? While Ornil muttered and chuckled and muttered, Faros plotted how he might get his wife and children to safety.

• • •

· *Maire, Sam, and* Saturday arrived in Fenice to find themselves in the midst of a festival. The quincentennial, they were told. The city fluttered with banners; there were musicians on every corner, a parade down every street.

"You'll stay for the concert this evening," said the young officer who had met them, one who had stared curiously at Maire Girat as he wondered what it was about this woman that had made his commander seem so nostalgic and faraway. "Commander Karth insists that you be his guests for dinner and the concert. He says he'll escort you on to Jeramish tomorrow."

"If Commander Karth wishes us to stay," said Maire. "Another day will make no difference. What is the concert to be?"

"A new work commissioned by the Queen. Stenta Thilion is to play for us on the harp."

"A Gharm harpist playing for the Queen?" queried Maire, with a wry twist to her lips. "Have things progressed so far?"

"She is much admired," said the officer, defensively. "By all men of goodwill."

"And by us," said Maire, defusing him with a smile and a shake of her head. "I have no sympathy for Voorstod views, lad. It's why I came away, long since. And I would not be here now, hating the idea of returning, if I had a choice."

Saturday was regarding her clothes with dismay. "But we have nothing to wear to a fancy concert, Maire. We have only our farm clothes."

The young officer smiled. Girls were all alike, no matter where they came from. His own wife had said the same, and when he had laughed at her, she had told him uniforms made it easy for men.

"If you'll accept the Commander's hospitality, Ma'am," he said to Maire, nodding to show that the other two were included. "His daughter would be pleased to provide something suitable."

· · ·

• *Without warning, on* the very morning of the day Maire arrived in Ahabar, Epheron and Preu seized Jep up and carried him off on a trip to Cloud. They took him, so they said, because "The Faithful wanted to get a look at him." They left the collar on him, taking the box that controlled it along to prevent his running off or causing trouble. He was given a coat to hide the collar and a cap to hide his head, very much like the caps the Voorstoders wore to keep their long hair clean and out of the way. The men of the Cause affected ringlets flowing down their backs into which coup markers could be pinned during special ceremonials of the Cause, so Preu Flandry had once remarked to Jep after he had sneered at Jep's close-cropped curls.

"Coup markers?" Jep had asked Pirva. "The Cause?"

Pirva had not looked up from what she was doing. "The Cause is their society, their religion, their brotherhood," she had said, the words dripping like acid from her mouth. "It's a killers' club. A man gets a coup counter for each Abolitionist or Gharm man, woman, or child he has killed out there in Ahabar or the Three Counties. There are special counters for bombs set off in the three counties, no matter who is killed or mutilated."

"They do not set off their bombs in Ahabar?" Jep asked.

"So far they have not risked bringing the Ahabarian army into Voorstod. With every year that passes, though, while the Authority sleeps and Ahabar withholds its power, the Cause pushes itself closer to the brink. Some of the members have hair to their knees, with coup markers set every inch, but they are not content. So long as another man has as many, their sense of competition will not let them rest. They will carry their murders into Ahabar sooner or later."

"Mugal Pye has this long hair?"

"Him, down to his knees. And Preu Flandry. And Epheron Floom, though his is only a wig to make up for all the time he spent out there in short-haired Ahabar, spying."

Remembering what Pirva had told him, Jep was content to wear the cap. He did not want to be thought one of them, but no doubt it was safer than to parade his distinction. For all he knew, some Voorstoder might decide to kill him as an outsider or Gharm sympathizer and ask for a special coup marker to memorialize the event.

The trip to Cloud was by flier, at first moving along the coast, where there were no roads for surface vehicles and where the heaving seas would have made water travel unpleasant at best. Voorstod had made no investment in short-distance Doors, no more than Hobbs Land had. Few planetary populations did, except where there were great cities separated by considerable travel time, as upon Phansure, where the volume of travel between cities was large and constant. Fixed-destination, constant-flow Doors were too expensive to obtain and operate to be economically feasible otherwise.

The trip was improved, so far as Jep was concerned, when a wind came up to clear the mists and disclose the rock-pimpled surface of the heaving seas, the stone-fanged coastline, and the clustered clutterings of towns and hamlets. They flew over Old Port in Odil County, with its timbered houses staggering down the steep hills toward the bay; they viewed the pastures of Bight County, puffed like piled green pillows between the mountains and the sea, then turned inland to fly along the base of the mountains.

Preu pointed out the town of Scaery, away to their left, its markets and stone streets netted among golden hills. On the right gaped the black maws of mines, horizontal holes in the sides of mountains, with long dun dunes of tailings trailing down the mountainsides and pools along the streams stained green and blue and red by leached minerals. Neither the tailings nor the edges of the pools showed any signs of life. Both were too poisonous for any seed to sprout. From the mines, tiny cog railways climbed down over the cliffs to dump their contents in other dunes beside the roads at the bottom.

"What are they digging for?" Jep asked, as they passed the hundredth such mine.

"Voorstod makes its living out of rare ores and gems," said Preu Flandry, pointing out this and that, as though Jep were a tourist.

Though Preu did not mention it, the workers in the mines were Gharm. The supervisors were Voorstoders, with whips. The flier was close enough to the cliffs that Jep could see that for himself.

In midafternoon they came to the fields of Cloud, soil black as tar and rich as a glutton's dinner, said Epheron, with the town of Cloudport standing on a level plain above the sandy beach—"the only sand beach in Voorstod," he said. The castle and the cathedral towered above the town on a stony arm thrust out from the mountain chain. It had become a day all blue and gold and white, with the sun taking the curse from the wind's chill and no mists remaining at all. As they swung above Cloud and Jep looked down at the people busy in the marketplace, at the children playing in the schoolyard, he thought how little it looked like the Voorstod he had learned to know. It did not look like a land steeped in violence and such hatred that there was no part of it unstained by blood.

The flier side-slipped up the hill and over the castle wall, coming to rest in the courtyard. The first things Jep saw when he climbed out of the vehicle were the hooks set high onto the wall, some of them burdened with dried bundles from which bones protruded, others of which held bodies still twitching or moaning. The second thing he saw was the blackened and twisted loop of a Door framed against looming walls of lichened stone. Above those walls and behind them, the towers of the citadel stabbed jeering fingers into the sun's eye.

"What's that?" Jep asked, pointing out the Door in an effort to distract himself from the walls and their hideous burdens.

"The Door we came in by," said Mugal Pye. "We leave it here as a reminder." He did not say a reminder of what, and Jep did not ask. The Door looked burned past any use.

"Are we going into town?"

"Not likely, boy. There's spies in town. The meeting is here, in the citadel, where we hold our secrets to ourselves and where the prophets will look you over without let or hindrance." The words had a snigger in them, and Jep shivered, wondering if he knew anything they might want to know which he would feel guilty telling them. They would not hesitate to encourage him, he knew. He wondered if he would survive the encouragement.

A figure approached them, a tall man in a long robe with a headdress covering his hair. His eyes were deep set and burning, his mouth was a slit. He carried a staff, thrusting it down onto the stones with each step, like the slow beat of a drum.

"Holy One," murmured Epheron Floom, falling to his knees and bending forward until his forehead rested on the floor. Preu Flandry was a little slower getting down, but he bowed as deeply.

"We have a message," snarled the prophet. "Get up."

"What message, Beloved of God?" whispered Preu.

"The woman remains in Jeramish until the boy is brought out, unharmed. Then she will come in. So she vows."

"Then she will come. Maire Manone will likely keep any promise she makes," said Pye.

"All women are creatures of Satan," snarled the prophet. "An apostate woman is the devil's toy." Actually, since he had talked with Faros, the whole matter of Maire Manone seemed less urgent. Probably even unnecessary. He had thought Faros and Ornil might need to be replaced, a project which could take generations. But this was not the case. The delay had been only brief. The end was approaching soon. The end was coming, in his lifetime.

A younger prophet approached, bowing deeply to the one who confronted them. "Awateh, we've already agreed to send the boy back. He is of no use to us, but the woman may be."

"Satan!" cried the first, thumping down his staff so that the stone quivered beneath it. "He is one of Satan's spawn, and we are commanded to extirpate them all. Our war is a holy war." Even as he thumped and howled, he considered the matter of the blockade. Perhaps it would be better to allow them to placate him.

"Awateh," said the other, shaking his head gently at Preu and Epheron. As the younger prophet led the elder one away, the Faithful sank into another obeisance, pulling Jep down with them.

Mugal Pye approached them as they rose, his eyes on the prophet's retreating back. "He's in a fury," Mugal whispered. "He's been like that ever since he received the message from Maire Manone. Women do not tell prophets what to do, particularly apostate women. This may upset our plans a trifle."

They took Jep through an echoing stone hallway into a smaller place hung with banners and set with high seats in rows. On the back of each seat was carved a different device, and many were filled by men wearing the same devices painted or beaded upon the leather tabards they wore. Their heads were bare; their hair hung loose to their buttocks or knees with ornaments of feathers or beads or bone studding every inch of the lengthy strands.

The seats upon the dais at one end of the hall were fully occupied by prophets. The highest chair was that of the deep-eyed, slit-lipped man, who sat silently fuming while others leaned at his shoulder, murmuring. Mugal thrust Jep out of sight, onto a low bench behind a pillar. By leaning forward, Jep could peer between men's bodies and see without being seen.

One of the younger prophets rose from his high seat and called silence.

"We are assembled tonight to witness the celebration in Fenice," he said.

"Death to all unbelievers," cried a lone voice, the words immediately taken up by others in a monotonous chant. "Death to Satan's spawn," cried the cheerleader, and everyone intoned that for a while.

The prophet silenced the room with an upraised hand.

"While we wait for that event to begin, we thought it expedient to examine this spawn from Hobbs Land, brought here as hostage to stimulate the return of the apostate woman."

Spontaneous cheers, catcalls, and suggestions which Jep tried not to hear.

"However," said the prophet, "the woman will not come out of Jeramish until the boy reaches her there, without injury, so we will not question him . . ."

Beside the speaker the slit-lipped prophet glared at him and thumped his staff, putting on a show of fury.

"The hell with what the woman wants," screamed a voice from one side. "Give us the lad and give her what's left." A chorus of agreement rose and fell.

Two prophets knelt beside the Awateh, holding up their hands, begging him. The speaker held up one hand and waited for silence.

"If he had anything to tell us worth hearing, we could do that," the young prophet said, almost consolingly. "However, he knows nothing of interest. He scarcely knows Maire Manone. He knows nothing at all of Ahabar, and what he does know of Hobbs Land is of no interest to us."

A murmur of questions ran around the high room. "What does he mean, scarcely knows his grandma? Isn't this the grandson? What does he mean?"

Other voices making explanations. Jep put his head in his hands and wiped chill moisture away from his brow and cheeks.

"We can at least *ask* him questions," the violent voice screamed.

The prophet shrugged and sat down. Immediately there was a babble. The prophet let it go on, then stood and raised his arm once more. "He can no more hear you than he could hear one bird in a poultry yard. One at a time."

"How come you don't know your own grandma, boy?" the violent voice howled at him.

Jep was pulled to his feet and pushed out where they could see him. He kept his head down as he answered, willingly enough, that in Hobbs Land she was not his grandma. The angry mutters made him wish he had had some other answer to give them.

"You've heard her sing, though, haven't you?" Another voice.

He could not lie and say he had. He had already made a point of the truth, before he knew what it meant. "I haven't heard her sing, no," he said honestly, by way of explanation adding only, "but then, I'm not very musical."

Either Phaed and his cronies had disbelieved Jep or they thought it wisest to let sleeping beasts lie, for they did not contradict him or amplify his answer in any way.

"Many Voorstod women there in Hobbs Land?" someone asked.

"I don't know," said Jep honestly. "I guess kids aren't very interested in where people came from. I think I've heard my mother say that most of the people in my settlement came from Phansure."

"Not worth making it a target then," said someone, sotto voce. Jep heard it, was glad of it, pretended he had not heard.

"Hear you're quite a Gharm lover," sneered the original questioner, provokingly. "A real Gharm sucker." The taunt was obviously designed to create fury.

An angry mutter swept through the hall.

"The men who took me put me with two Gharm," Jep said in as calm a voice as he could muster. "They feed me. I talk to them when I must, and nobody told me not to. I try to keep busy."

Laughter, one angry voice, others, drunken or amused, the slit-lipped prophet declaiming to his neighbors, the quieter prophet standing before them once more.

"What's your own preference?" the prophet asked him, as though actually curious. "Whose company would you keep?"

"How would I know," said Jep. "Preference for what? My preference would probably be to be home with people my own age, since that's what I'm used to. I miss my school."

The prophet seemed to find this interesting. "And what do they teach you there? About Voorstod?"

Jep shook his head. "They've not mentioned Voorstod to me. I don't know whether they will later or not. Mostly we learn about agricultural methods. Like how much fertilizer to put on different kinds of crops."

Despite the efforts of the provocateur, the group was losing interest. Blood might have excited them, but this ignorance of their very existence was merely dull. Jep could feel them cooling, turning away. Only the slit-lipped prophet still glared, balefully. That prophet, left to his

own will, would have him killed simply because he was
not of Voorstod. That prophet would have him hung upon
the walls to die. So much was clear. Cooler heads had
prevailed, for the moment. Jep had given them nothing to
get angry at. Some of the prophets and others left their
seats and went into a neighboring room where food and
drink were laid out upon long tables.

"You can go eat if you like," Mugal told Jep as he
stared at the platform where the prophet had sat.

Jep decided Mugal Pye was a fool. The slit-lipped
prophet was being served food by his colleagues, and the
last thing Jep wanted to do was go where the fanatic
would see him. "I'm not hungry," he said, adding,
"Who's the man who wanted me killed?"

"The Beloved of God, Teacher of the Just."

"Does he have a name?"

"The prophet, Awateh."

"How come you have both prophets and priests?"

"We have prophets for men, priests for women, pastors for Gharm and animals," said Preu. "The prophets
are of the Cause. The Cause is for men."

"Are they the same religion?"

Epheron gave him an intense, weighing look. "No,
boy, and yes. Long ago they were of the same lineage, but
not of the same strength. Our God is the same, but the
Holy Books are different. One book for the priests, a
similar book for the pastors. A different book for the
prophet."

Jep raised his eyes to the room where the food was
spread. The prophet Awateh was standing there, staring
at him. Jep ducked his head and breathed deeply.

"Relax, boy," said Preu Flandry. "He wanted to eat
you, but he didn't. Enjoy yourself. This is a celebration!
Later we'll be watching how they do it in Ahabar."

There was laughter among those seated nearby who
overheard this comment. Jep tried not to hear it. He sat
sweating as workmen came into the hall carrying the parts
of a large, portable information stage. They assembled it
at the center of the room, then turned it on to disclose a
huge concert hall beginning to fill with brightly dressed
people. Others were arriving, moving up and down aisles,

finding their seats. Jep tried not to watch, afraid of what he might see.

There was a stir at the entrance, and a tall, bulky man came in with a few others. He had an angry face, which grew even grimmer as he saw Mugal Pye and came toward him with a heavy stride.

"What's this they've been telling me?" he demanded. "What fool's business is this?" His eyes went over Mugal Pye's shoulder to the stage. His face grew very red, and he cried out in an enraged voice, "That's Maire!"

Jep's eyes were drawn to the stage. He saw her at once, Maire Girat. Beside her was Sam Girat, and . . . yes, Saturday, Saturday dressed in beautiful scarlet, all three of them in colorful, festive clothing, all of them taking seats next to a stout, uniformed man with many medals on the honors sash he wore across one shoulder.

"What in all the demons of hell is she doing there?" screamed the man. "Why wasn't I consulted about this? What have you sucking idiots been doing with your brains!"

"Now, Phaed," said Mugal Pye.

"Don't 'now Phaed' me," he cried. "Is this your doing, Pye?"

One of the younger prophets had drawn near, and he laid an admonitory hand on Phaed's shoulder. "*Our* doing, Phaed Girat."

"You've brought her to Ahabar?" Phaed breathed, incredulous. "Why in hell?"

The prophet became threatening. "Enough reason to say the Awateh desired it."

"Why!" Phaed demanded. "Desired it why?"

"She is to become the symbol of return for the women of Voorstod," the prophet said stiffly. "If the Sweet Singer returns, so may others."

Phaed turned away. Jep saw his lips. They did not say the word aloud, but they shaped it several times. "Fool, fool, fool."

"We didn't want to tell you until it was time," whispered Epheron to Phaed. "We didn't want you bothered."

"Idiot," hissed Phaed. "Slob-lipped, turd-sucking idiot!"

Epheron's face became dead pale, but he turned away with an apprehensive glance at the prophet.

On the stage, the bemedaled officer leaned across Saturday to speak to Maire.

"Karth," Preu Flandry hissed in a carrying whisper. "Commander Karth."

"What's he doing with her?" the prophet asked. "And what's the woman doing there? She wasn't supposed to be there! When this was planned, she was expected to come here, to Voorstod!"

The men looked at one another, shrugging.

"Who's that with her, boy?" demanded Mugal Pye of Jep.

"Topman Sam Girat," said Jep. "Maire Girat's son. And the girl is my cousin, Saturday Wilm."

"Who's the other girl?"

"I don't know." There was another girl, talking to Saturday.

"Why are Sam Girat and your cousin there? Why?"

"Probably to keep Maire company," said Jep. "She probably didn't want to come alone." His heart told him she hadn't wanted to come back at all, that his capture had brought her.

"Maire's gotten fatter," mused Phaed, staring at the stage. She was stouter than he remembered her, but she was still, he thought, a fine woman. Her skin was smooth, her eyes clear, her hair a wealth and a treasure. The bright garments were flattering to her. Something old and mostly forgotten stirred deep inside him. "She's gotten fatter," he whispered again, almost fondly.

"She's older," said Mugal Pye, angrily.

"She doesn't look quite like herself, I mean," said Phaed softly. "My son's a fine man, isn't he. But she doesn't look like the Sweet Singer I remember."

"The Singer was a young woman. It's been thirty years," said Epheron. "What did you expect?"

"What did *you* expect?" snarled Phaed. "You're the fools who brought her here."

"We expect she'll do what we need done. We've got it all planned," said Preu. "Doesn't matter what she looks like. Or sounds like. It's her being here in Voorstod that's important."

"She's not here yet. You still think she'll come?"

"She's on her way here," said Epheron. "What do you mean, Phaed! We'll send out the boy, she'll come in. Even the prophet thinks so."

"The boy?"

Epheron pointed at Jep. "This is your grandson, Phaed Girat. It's how we got the woman here."

Phaed scarcely glanced at Jep as he sneered at Epheron, shaking his head.

"What's the trouble?" Preu asked.

Phaed pointed at the stage, where the concert hall was almost completely filled. "None of you expected her to be there, did you? In that particular company? You expected her to be here, where she would see nothing, hear nothing you didn't control. But where is she now? This minute, where is she? She's in that concert hall, across from Queen Willy, beside the Commander of the army, where the Gharm's going to *play the harp*. I ask again, you think Maire'll come to Voorstod? After what's been planned?" Phaed was snarling like an animal. He turned back to the stage and stared at it ravenously.

Jep kept his head down, his body quiet, attracting no attention. This man was, by the tenets of Voorstod, his granddaddy. This man had been Maire Girat's husband, and he had obviously not forgotten her. As for the rest, Jep had no idea what was going on, except that something had slipped up, somewhere along the line. Some plan had gone awry. They had not planned on Maire Manone being at this celebratory concert. Something was going to happen at the concert that Maire Manone was not supposed to see.

THREE

• *Maire and Saturday* were well-dressed at the concert because they had been escorted to a shop by the Commander's daughter, Eline, where they had selected clothing with Eline's help and at Ahabar's expense.

"It's the Queen's wish," Eline had said. "She knows why you're here. She knows what those vile men in Voorstod have done. She wants you to have a pleasant evening before you have to go there and struggle with those . . . those . . ." She shut her mouth grimly, and nodded her thanks to the young woman who was running a heatseamer along the garments they had chosen, taking them in to fit. "She thought you'd have more fun if you had some Ahabarian clothes. We've become very dress conscious here in Fenice. It's an affectation we've adopted from Phansure, this concentration on style and fashion. Unimportant in itself, but we enjoy it, the men as well as the women."

"It is kind of the Queen," Maire had said, ignoring nine-tenths of the girl's chatter. She supposed it was kind of the Queen. Queens could be kind, like anyone else, or

think they were. Maire had no wish at all to attend a
concert, to appear in public, to see or be seen. Mostly she
felt inclined to slink or skulk, to be hidden in some dark
corner from which she could spy out whatever trouble
was coming, for she felt trouble, as she could sometimes
feel a thunderstorm gathering. The air prickled, and her
eyes itched.

Saturday, who had said nothing during the shopping
expedition, who had tried not even to hear the conversation, laid her cheek against the warm red gown she had
chosen and wished more than anything that Jep could see
her wearing this dress.

She was dragged out of her reverie by Eline's hand on
her shoulder.

"You're sure now?" Eline asked her, pointing at another dress, a blue one, with a low-cut neck.

"I'm sure," said Saturday. Her chemise would show at
the neck of the low-cut gown, and she dared not lay the
chemise aside until she no longer needed it. Besides, she
hadn't enough breasts yet to go wearing nakedy things.
And the red dress was prettier. It was softer and moved
like leaves in the wind.

Maire noticed Saturday's eyes, dreaming and eager.
Interesting, she thought, what pretty gowns could do to
raise one's spirits. Would women face death and danger
with more aplomb if they could wear beautiful gowns?
Perhaps she and Saturday had better wear these dresses
when they went to Voorstod, to encourage themselves.
But, no. No. The prophets would surely condemn any
woman who looked pretty. Women were sinks of sin. They
weren't supposed to look pretty.

They went back through carnival-crowded streets to
their hotel, where the Commander, his daughter, and the
young subaltern met them for an evening meal. By the
time they finished eating, the streets had cleared a little,
and they walked among a cluster of guards the short distance to the concert hall. Their place was at the side of the
orchestra, at the same level, in comfortable chairs, two
rows of three each, separated from the performance platform and the rest of the audience by a low, gilded railing.
At their left was another, similar enclosure.

"The Queen will sit there," the Commander said, pointing to a larger enclosure directly opposite the place they sat. The great lacquered and inlaid Gharm-harp stood between where they were and where the Queen would be, with the chairs of the orchestra arranged in a crescent to the right of it.

Saturday peered at the platform, a little giddy from the unaccustomed wine she had drunk at dinner. It seemed abandoned rather than expectant. The chairs were empty, the music stages turned off so that their lightless frameworks stood like angular skeletons. It was like a battlefield on which an army had fought and been vanquished, leaving only bones. Not a pleasant mental picture. She turned resolutely toward the audience. There, among people, was movement and life. She kept her attention on the movement, on the chatter, on the laughter.

Beside her, Maire watched her with a slightly troubled frown. "Are you all right?" she asked.

"Things keep pushing in," whispered Saturday. "But I'm keeping them out."

Maire squeezed her hand. Oh, yes. Things did indeed keep pushing in.

"We are being greatly honored," said Eline. "These seats are always reserved for the Queen's guests. I've never been so close to the stage. Usually I sit up there with my friends," and she gestured toward the heavens. "Way up, where the students sit."

High above them faces seemed to cluster against the ceiling like fruits on a tree, pale blobs, mouths opening and shutting among the rustle and flutter of paper programs.

"For this special occasion, the Queen ordered programs printed upon fine paper," said the Commander, passing to each of them a folder with a golden cord and tassels and the great seal of Ahabar on the front. "They are to serve as souvenirs of the occasion."

Sam was between the Commander and the subaltern in the back row, behind the women. Since afternoon, when the subaltern had taken him shopping, he had been delighting in the joyous hubbub of Ahabar. People everywhere. Vehicles everywhere. Laughter and music and

bright colors. Then at dinner he had drunk a great deal of
wine, not feeling Maire's anxious eyes upon him. He felt
he had been in this place before, or read of it, or read of
something similar. Though it was wonderful and exotic, it
felt familiar to him, as though he had been born for such a
place, such bustle and hurry and sense of accomplish-
ment. This is where he should be. Maire should not have
gone to Hobbs Land. She should have stayed here, in
Ahabar, where festival reigned. Surely nothing the Voorstoders did was sufficiently dreadful to have driven her
away from this! One had to understand their reasons, that
was all. One had to know and sympathize with their history. So he told himself solemnly, the wine boiling away at
his mind.

They sat back and watched the place fill, as brightly
garbed men and women trickled down the aisles and took
their seats. At every door there were uniformed men
watching. Sam leaned toward the Commander to point
them out and ask why they were there.

The Commander shrugged. "There are certain faces
we look for. Voorstod faces. I told the Queen that everyone coming into the hall tonight should be searched. She
refused to allow it. She told me this is a celebration." He
shrugged again, smiling at Maire, at Sam, at the girl, Saturday. "What can one do?"

Sam frowned. Surely they would not need to consider
such things tonight.

The orchestra began to arrive, men and women in
close, anonymous garments, each section dressed in its
own color, blue for strings, green for woodwinds, orange
for brasses, yellow for augmenters, red for percussion,
wine for sonics. They settled slowly, squeaking, tootling,
booming, making the seats shudder, creating the sounds
all orchestras have made since time immemorial.

Eline drew their attention to the gilded enclosure next
to their own, where a numerous party of Gharm fluttered
and arranged itself. Eline bowed to them, they bowed in
return. "Stenta Thilion's family," whispered Eline. "Her
daughters, her grandchildren, her great-grandchildren."

The conductor arrived, his tall, black form looming on
its pedestal like a shadow before a rainbow. People ap-

plauded. The conductor bowed as the orchestra settled itself. A door at the back of the Queen's section opened, and Queen Wilhulmia was suddenly before them, standing between her two sons, her hands raised, smiling broadly. The audience cheered as it stood, the orchestra played the royal anthem, everyone sang. Then everyone sat down again, rustling, the lights dimmed, and Stenta Thilion came onto the stage.

How tiny she was. Like a child, and yet with nothing childish in her manner. Her walk was dignified, her face calm. Her dress glittered, throwing light into every corner of the hall. Her sleeves were deep banners that folded on the floor when she bowed to the Queen, then unfolded into glorious flags when she held out her arms and looked up, up at the highest seats, against the ceiling, where there were Gharm gathered by the hundreds, cheering.

They cheered, the audience cheered, applauded, Stenta Thilion bowed again, the deep sleeves falling in graceful folds upon the floor.

Silence then. She sat at the harp and held out her arms to either side, a beautifully theatrical gesture. A dark-clad attendant came in and unfastened the sleeves, folded them slowly, carried them away. Now people could see Stenta's slender arms clad in scarlet silk, her gemmed bracelets, the narrow, long-fingered hands. She smiled at the conductor and nodded her head.

And began magic.

There was not a sound in the hall except the sound of music. There was not a cough, not a whisper, not the sound of a shoe scuffing against the floor. The audience sat as though enchanted.

The opening movement began, light as wind. Stenta's hands and arms moved delicately, swiftly. The wind stopped and something slower, more somber began. Stenta's foot went down, and augmented bass notes marched into the hall, an army, an army with the wind following, blowing it along.

A murmur went through the audience, a sigh of appreciation. Those who knew harp music knew what she had just done was impossible. Those who did not know harp music knew what she had done was beautiful. The Queen was leaning forward, her elbow on the railing, her hand supporting her head, unconscious of the royal dignity, her face soft.

The bass notes again, a horn announced a new theme.

I know that, Saturday thought. That's a song Maire taught me. It was a battle hymn, martial and rousing.

The theme built toward a climax. The drums began. The horns in chorus, carefully, not for one moment drowning out the harp. A red-clad man picked up the great brass cymbals and held them above his head. Light danced across them, shivering.

The music built, and built, the cymbals shivered, and at last the climax came as they struck together with a great, brazen sound . . .

People rising, screaming, crying out at what they saw upon the stage. Maire breathed a word and was over the railing, running toward the tiny woman, the tiny woman who held out her arms and watched the blood fountaining from her wrists, the tiny woman who suddenly had no hands.

The Commander followed Maire. The Queen had been pulled out of her seat and drawn back through the door by watchful guards. The hall was on its feet, beginning to scream, beginning to flee. Maire turned toward Saturday and shouted for her to come, and Saturday was running, listening, the conductor was there, nodding, shouting to his musicians, and then Saturday was at the center of the stage, singing, singing, while behind her Maire and the Commander fought to save the life of Stenta Thilion.

The orchestra played the battle hymn, one Saturday knew, for Maire had taught it to her. Saturday's voice soared above the confusion like a trumpet calling men to battle. The noise in the hall stopped. Men stood and began to sing. This was a song they knew, one they had marched to, one they had known since they were children. Women sang. High along the walls, the Gharm sang. The huge hall howled with sound, as every voice joined until there was only one huge unison chorus of outrage and fury and determination over the body lying so quietly and the two working over it and the Gharm gathered weeping around them.

• • •

· *In the castle* of the Cause, above Cloudport, there was laughter when the cymbal crashed. Men had been waiting for that crash, tossing their heads to make their coup markers flutter, nudging one another as the time drew near. When it came, they pointed out the handless woman, the fountains of blood, roaring with laughter. When the audience screamed, started to run, the laughter grew in volume.

Then something happened they had not expected. Maire Manone was on the platform beside the fallen Gharm woman, binding up Stenta Thilion's handless arms. The Commander was beside her. And there was a girl on the stage, turning to face them, as though she saw them, and she was singing the Ahabar battle hymn, with the horns and drums of the orchestra taking up the music behind her. And suddenly, as every voice in the great hall came alive with that same hymn, rising in a torrent of song, the laughter in the castle of the Cause fell away to a titter and then to silence. It was as though every eye in the hall saw through the stage to those there in Voorstod, to those conspirators, to those who had done this thing, and pledged them everlasting hatred and death.

Jep, his face wet with nausea and horror, crouched at the foot of the pillar and heard Saturday singing. Even while he retched, he could not keep his eyes away from the prophet, that one who had wanted to torture him earlier, that one with the deep-set eyes and the slit-lipped mouth. For a moment, only a moment, Jep saw terror slip across the aged man's face. Other faces were equally fearful, the kind of fear, Jep told himself, of a child in a tantrum who destroys something irreplaceable and suddenly realizes he has gone too far. In the past he has been indulged or perhaps only overlooked. But what he has done now cannot be overlooked. What he has done cannot be explained away. What he has done has damned him, utterly, and so what Voorstod had done this night had damned them all, and even the prophet Awatch knew it.

• • •

• *Saturday, Maire, and* Sam sat against the wall in the Queen's small audience room. They had been brought there for safekeeping, so the Commander said, inasmuch as the world had seen them, and heard them, not only here in Ahabar but in Voorstod as well. Some madman or madmen might try to hurt them for saving the harpist, for singing, or just for having been there, so they had been brought here, where it was safe. Stenta Thilion was elsewhere, among the doctors.

Sam was in a state of shock. Despite what Maire had said, he had disbelieved her. Even when he had believed her, he had told himself it wasn't as bad as she said. People got hurt during these kinds of disputes, but surely, he had said to himself, no one would purposefully hurt a child or a woman or someone obviously noncombatant and innocent. Those hurt were usually soldiers, or the equivalent, he had told himself. Innocent bystanders sometimes got killed, but never on purpose.

Now he knew that they did get killed, purposely, for no military or strategic reason, purely for terror and hatred. Still he kept telling himself his own dad would not be part of this.

But the word Maire had breathed as she went over the railing had been *Phaed*. She had said it as though she recognized his presence. Had she, indeed, recognized Phaed in this bloody work?

Maybe she'd only assumed, Sam told himself. Maybe she hated Phaed so much for other things he had done that she assigned all manner of evil to him as a matter of course. That had to be it. Poor Maire, to be so full of hate for her husband. He pitied her. He told himself he pitied her.

At the other end of the room, the Queen was talking to several of her counselors. "You will want to send certain representations to Authority," old Lord Multron was saying.

"No," the Queen responded, her voice strident as brass as she turned away from the old man toward the Commander. "There will be no more representations to Authority. I require complete mobilization of the army by morning. They are to occupy Green Hurrah and cut off all access from Skelp. They are to cut off routes from the peninsula. They are to put guards on every inch of coastline. Our seagoing forces are to blockade Voorstod from the water. Not one rat from Voorstod is to be able to crawl out of that rat hole."

"Your Sublimity," faltered Saturday, rising from her chair. "I must still go in."

The Queen looked at her blindly, not seeing her.

"She must still go in," said Maire, expressionlessly. "One of ours is still held hostage there."

Maire's dress was clotted with blood. She had torn strips from that dress and had bound the arms of the harpist, had saved her life, though no one knew how long Stenta would live. The musician was old and frail. All her strength had been in her music, in her fingers, and now there could be no music. When they had left her to come here, the medical people had been gathered around, thick as flies, while Stenta's family had knelt outside their circle crying as for one already dead, "Mama-gem, oh, Mama-gem."

"There are Gharm there in Voorstod," said Maire sharply, getting the Queen's attention. "Thousands of Gharm. You don't want them hurt. That would be a bad memorial for Stenta Thilion. Saturday must go in. Later I must."

Queen Wilhulmia tried to focus. "What are you saying? That you have some way to save the Gharm in Voorstod?"

"Perhaps," said Saturday.

"Perhaps," agreed Maire. "You must let Saturday and Sam go in. No matter what else you do."

"Is it your plan to invade Voorstod, Mother?" asked Prince Ismer. His fine features were drawn into an expression of pain and resolution. His younger brother, Prince Rals, stood at his side, blank-faced, unable to comprehend what was happening. At one moment he had been drowsily listening to some quite pleasant music, and the next moment he was being dragged off by guards. He still wasn't sure what had happened to the harpist.

"Ismer, I don't know if we will invade. All I know at

this moment is that no man of Voorstod is to come out of that place. Should I prevent these people going in?"

Ismer regarded the three. "Why should you go into Voorstod now?" he asked Saturday.

"One reason is that my cousin is there," said Saturday. "They'll kill him unless someone gives them a reason not to."

Maire stared at Sam, as she said, "If they think it is only a blockade, they will hope that eventually the blockade may be lifted. While they have hope, they may continue with their prior plans, with what they wanted before all this happened. They may still want Maire Manone. Or they may simply wish to appear reasonable, for a change. They may still be willing to trade a life for a life. Or trade many lives for the lifting of the blockade. It gives you something to bargain with, for the Gharm."

And gives me time for myself, thought Sam. Time to meet Phaed and set this matter straight between us.

"Very well. Let us *say* it is only a blockade," said the Queen. "For now. Maire Manone is right. Let them have hope. Let us conspire to get every life that we can out of there and safe before we take hope away, as I will do. What right have they to hope."

"Sam and I . . . we will go in," said Saturday, looking closely at Sam to be sure he was in agreement. "Maire must stay with the soldiers until we return."

"Once they have you, girl, they may not want me," said Maire. "Remember, if they saw what happened, they heard you sing. They might rather have a girl who can sing than an old woman who can't."

"When the time comes," said Saturday, fueling her determination on outrage, "that's when I'll worry about that, Maire."

· *Men had fled* from the citadel of the Cause. They had removed their coup markers, coiled up their hair on top of their heads, put on their caps, and gone out into the night like skulking beasts, quietly. Their lofty moment had turned to dust and irritation. They were greatly angered at that.

"What do we do with him?" Preu asked Epheron, indicating Jep.

It was not Epheron who answered. Mugal Pye answered. "Take him back to Sarby."

"Why don't we get rid of him now?"

"Because he's a trade! Something to give for something! Kill him now, and we've nothing to give for nothing. Take him back to Sarby. He's no trouble there. Let's see what's going to happen."

"Oh, we've an idea as to what'll happen," said Preu, with a sneer. "Those bracelets of yours worked a pure joy, didn't they, Pye. I've never seen better."

"You got them into the box!"

"Only after Phaed found out where the Gharm was. The Gharm thought they came from the Queen. Couldn't have been better. Timing, setting, everything. Very dramatic." His voice was bitter.

"Bastard!" snarled Mugal Pye. "It was not only Phaed and me. We all decided when it was to be, how it was to be."

"Neither you nor Phaed mentioned the Gharm was a pet of the whole damned Ahabarian world!"

Phaed snarled. "You *knew* that. That's why you sent Pye to me in the first place. It was that riled your guts, Preu Flandry. It was that fact riled all of us. If she'd not been a pet, who'd have cared what we did to her!"

Epheron thrust a shoulder between them. "Whatever's done's done. Now we have to figure what'll happen next. What do you think the Queen will do."

Preu Flandry pursed his lips and spat, glaring at Phaed from the corners of his eyes. "Oh, she'll have the army marching back and forth, I should say. She'll make some threats maybe, askin' Voorstod to turn over those who did the deed, which is us, and which the neither the Faithful nor the prophets will allow. She'll complain to Authority, no doubt."

"Invasion?"

He thought about it. "Either she'll move in the next few hours, out of temper, or she'll cool and won't move at all."

"So, then, we go to ground and keep quiet for a time.

Let things sort themselves out." Epheron kicked at Jep, where he crouched against the pillar. "Take him back to Sarby. Maybe he'll be good for something there."

· *By dawn of* the following day, Commander Karth was at the southern border of Green Hurrah with armies stretching in long east and west wings, curving northward to the sea. The lines would cut off Voorstod from the rest of the land. The order was search and seize. Persons who could not be identified as known and trusted residents of Green Hurrah were to be rounded up and placed in confinement camps at the rear of the lines. The line was to push into Green Hurrah all along its length, filtering out the suspect, leaving only safe persons behind it. Meantime, behind them in Ahabar, agents of the Queen were rounding up all known Voorstoders who were in Ahabar "on business" or "visiting friends." They would join their countrymen in the camps.

The line would move forward until it arrived at the coast and the border of Skelp, the thin neck of land going on northward. At that point, the coasts would be occupied, the seas would be watched, and the only land access to the continent of Ahabar would be closed.

From that point, whenever they got there, Saturday and Sam would go on into Voorstod alone. The Commander had sent word for someone from the Skelp Council to come forward and guarantee them safe passage as far as possible.

Until then, they stayed in the vehicle fitted up as the Commander's field quarters, and did whatever they could think of to relieve their apprehension. Sam stared at the wall and asked himself the same questions he had been asking since he had been about ten or eleven, who he was and whether Phaed missed him, and what there was in Voorstod that he had lost. Maire slept, the sleep of someone who thought she might never sleep again. Saturday sat in a wide window of the vehicle as it moved slowly forward, trying to see in the surrounding countryside those beauties Maire had so often spoken of, and seeing only handless arms, fountaining blood. Until that moment, she had not truly perceived what kind of place she was going to.

Prince Rals had been sent along as their escort. He was only a few years older than Saturday herself.

"I don't understand why you're so determined to go into Voorstod," he said to her. "I'm afraid Mother doesn't get the point, either. I mean, if you want your cousin, we'll just tell the damned Voorstoders to bring him out before the lady goes in. You don't have to go in there."

Saturday, in the grip of sudden inspiration, said, "It's a religious matter."

"Oh," said the Prince, suddenly cut off from his argument.

"My cousin has been . . . defiled," said Saturday. "He must be . . . cleansed before he can come out again. You understand?"

The Prince shrugged. What was to understand? Religion *was*, so much was certain, and one didn't argue about it or with it. Though, for the life of him, he could not recall, despite his comprehensive education as a future diplomat, that people from Hobbs Land had any such beliefs.

"Aren't you kind of young to be doing religious work?" he wanted to know.

"The person doing the cleansing has to be about the same age as the person being cleansed," said Saturday, beginning to develop the fable. She thought this over. "Except babies, of course. With them, it takes someone older."

"It's a kind of . . . ritual, is it?"

"Kind of," she said.

"With sacrifices?"

"Not really," she murmured. "Anybody who's died recently will do."

Despite Saturday's friendly smile and inarguable beauty, Prince Rals decided to go forward and help the driver.

Saturday, meantime, was wondering if there was likely to be someone recently dead where she and Sam would be going. Actually killing someone would not be a good idea.

Actually killing someone would not be what the God
wanted at all.

Then she remembered Stenta Thilion and realized
there would always be recent dead, anywhere in Voorstod.

· *When the Religion* Advisory had been set up
in the early years of Authority, it had seemed wisest to
have it a representational group made up of adherents of
the various religions in System, their numbers roughly
proportional to the numbers of their worshippers, com-
municants, parishioners, or whatever they might be
called. Shortly thereafter, Authority had added a number
of generalists, who had done research in such fields as
religious history, xenotheology, deconstruction of scriptures, the anatomy and chemistry of revelation, and the
social and economic consequences of prophecy. While the
resulting mix suited no one very well, it at least prevented
domination by any one system of thought, a sufficient advantage to guarantee the group's survival, on virtually its
original basis, for well over a millennium.

At the current time, there were half a dozen High and
one Low Baidee on the Advisory, and twice that many
persons representing various of the casual Phansuri sects,
none of which (or whom) took themselves very seriously.
Indigenous religions were represented by xenotheologians
who had studied in the field among the Glothee and the
Hosmer, and at a respectful distance from the Porsa, who
could not, in any case, be said to have any religion beyond
what a few researchers had called, not indefensibly, Holy
Shit. The state religion of Ahabar was well represented in
the person of a Bishop Absolute and three Importunaries.
When the Voorstoders had settled upon Ahabar, one
Voorstod prophet and one Voorstod priest had been
added to the Advisory, and neither they nor their successors had, for one moment since, ceased demanding that
numerous others of their ilk be brought in as well.
"Truth," they said, "could not be represented numeri-
cally."

Each representative had administrative assistants, and
the administrative assistants had aides and senior and ju-

nior researchers, readers, chaplains, haruspices, oracles, and the like. Over time, a very nice system had developed by which persons actually interested in religion as religion (rather than religion as a system of social control, religion as politics, religion as warfare, or religion as spectacle) met over luncheon from time to time to read their scholarly research to one another, while clerks and aides got on with the endless and self-generating paperwork, for so it was still called, despite the fact there was little or no paper involved.

Matters requiring, or pretending to require, decision were referred to the Official Advisory, or OA, which was simply shorthand for those originally selected persons, or their successors, who had been actually charged with advising the Authority. The Religion Advisory, en toto, including the panels and all the subordinates, consisted of several thousand individuals. The Religion Advisory, OA, consisted of about thirty, give or take a few who might be back on planets of origin receiving instruction or have died and not yet been replaced.

No one remembered, offhand, when the OA had last met, though virtually everyone knew that the reason for the meeting had been a discussion of the Voorstod problem. The site of that meeting had been the Great Library of the Advisory, where, it was presumed, any future meetings would also occur. On ordinary occasions, the library was empty or scantily occupied by research fellows or, very rarely, visited by scholars.

Which explained the dogged and martyred attitude of the messenger who did, at last, find Member of Authority, Member of the Advisory, and Notable Scholar, Notadamdirabong Cringh, at one of the long, silent tables in said library. Cringh was deeply involved with a dusty, huge, and very old real book, over which the information stage scanner was laboring with difficulty, and he did not at first see the messenger standing before him with flushed cheeks and an air of frayed annoyance.

"Aaah, yes," he said at last, when the messenger's active fidgeting drew the attention of his aide, who nudged him. "Aaah, yes."

"Message, Notable Scholar. For the Scholar's eyes

only." The messenger held out his skin snip, and Cringh allowed a few dermal cells to be dragged from a finger in return for a square, metallic object, which he recognized, after regarding it thoughtfully for a few moments, as an envelope. It probably contained real paper with words on it. He could not recall having seen an envelope actually in use before, though he had, of course, seen them in museums and read of their being used.

How very interesting, he told himself, squinching his eyelids into a net of tiny wrinkles, pursing his lips into another such net. Notadamdirabong Cringh was an old, extremely wrinkled man. He liked to think his interior was younger than his exterior by a number of decades, despite the illogicality of that wish. He rubbed his hand across his totally bald and equally wrinkled head and asked himself why anyone would go to the trouble of sending a written message in a tamper proof envelope, when one might equally well place a personal message into the Archives directed to Scholar Cringh's identity and personal attention.

How intriguing! He could think of several possible answers.

Perhaps because it was known that other persons might see, either by intention or accident, messages placed in the Archives for private viewing only. It wasn't supposed to be possible, but it was possible, everyone knew that. Some people were unbelievably nosy and would actually go out of their way to see messages directed to other people!

Perhaps because the person sending the message did not have access to Scholar Cringh's identity number. Though that seemed unlikely. The identity number was right there in the roster for all System to see.

Perhaps because the person sending the message was a decorative hobbyist, a what-you-call-it, calligrapher, someone who enjoyed making words on paper.

Perhaps because the delivery of an actual message carried more psychic weight than the delivery of a mere Archives message.

Perhaps because the writing of the message had some

spiritual significance of which Cringh had been heretofore unaware.

Perhaps . . .

"Aren't you going to open it?" Cringh's favorite aide asked, from behind his left shoulder.

"You spoil all the fun," grunted Cringh. "I was going to figure it out, first."

"It might be urgent," the aide said, purring. Her name was Lurilile. She was willowlike in her grace and ferret-like in her abilities. She had a face like a corrupted angel. She was from Ahabar, though no one knew that but herself and those who had sent her. Queen Wilhulmia knew her, of course, and was deeply concerned about her presence upon Authority.

"Urgent, maybe . . . ," Lurilile suggested again. ". . . what's inside?"

Cringh nodded, slowly. The one thing he hadn't thought of was that it might be urgent.

He touched the envelope, which recognized his cellular structure as being compatible with the delivery instructions, and opened along a seam, emitting a tiny hiss of damp air and a small unpleasant smell.

"Ninfadel?" shuddered Lurilile, in the tone of one detecting a fart.

Cringh shook his head as he examined the contents. "Chowdari," he said. "From Reticingh, who was in his bath at the time. Or so he says. Though why he should think I care where he was at the time rather escapes me."

"So?"

"So, there's a copy of a report in here that somebody named Shanrandinore Damzel gave to the Circle of Scrutators, plus a set of questions Reticingh came up with. Reticingh wants to know what I think of them. We. What we think of them. Unofficially."

"We, the six High Baidee members of the Religion Advisory? Or we, the three Baidee members of the Theology Panel? Or we, the whole panel?"

"We, the whole OA. However, Reticingh stresses that it is an unofficial request."

"How can anyone ask something of the Official Advisory unofficially?"

"One wants to say it would make no difference. Nothing ever happens when they're asked officially, anyhow."

"Shit," sneered Lurilile, puckering her lips and making kisses at him. "Everyone knows that."

"Might be kind of fun to find out if the OA can think."

"Might be kind of fun to find out if the OA is alive."

"That, too."

"Though, if taking bribes is evidence of life, we know parts of it are burgeoning."

Cringh smiled sweetly. His colleagues from Phansure were not serious enough about religion to feel guilty about buying and selling it. On the other hand, his colleague the Bishop Absolute from Ahabar certainly was. As were some of the xeno-theo-whats-its. Lurilile had been trying for almost a year to find out who, and Notadamdirabong wasn't going to tell her. He liked having her around too much to give her what she wanted.

"Be interesting to find out," he said again, pulling himself out of the chair he'd been sitting in for several hours.

"Not going to read it here?"

"In my suite, I think. Besides, it's nearly dinner time."

"Wouldn't want to miss that," purred Lurilile, with a delicate elbow punch into the Notable Scholar's well-padded ribs. "No sir. Can't miss dinner."

Cringh smiled sweetly once more. Actually, he had already leafed through the document enough to have seen the page upon which someone had set down a series of brief, though elegantly lettered, questions.

1. How does one define God?
2. How does one know if a God is real?
3. Does a God have to create a race of intelligent creatures in order for that race to consider Him/Her a God?
4. Can a God adopt a people who already exist?
5. If a people become holy because of the influence of something, is that something likely a God?
6. If the answer to the foregoing is "no," then what should we call it?

And finally, the questions Cringh immediately recognized as at the crux of the matter, from the view point of the Baidee:

7. Could the Overmind have created or allowed the creation of some smaller, lesser Gods or pseudo-Gods for any reason at all?
8. If the Overmind could not have done so, then shouldn't we immediately dispose of any smaller things of that description we might happen to discover?

"Unofficially, of course," said Cringh to himself, leaning rather more heavily than was absolutely necessary upon Lurilile. Sometimes he called her Abishag. He had forgotten exactly where he'd encountered that name during his studies, in some ancient volume or other. He connected it to Voorstod, somehow, which meant he had probably read it while researching Voorstoder beliefs, which meant Abishag must have been an ancient tribal beauty mentioned in the tribal scriptures. A young woman obtained to warm the bed of an old, cold chieftain, as he recalled. A chieftain not too distantly related to the ancient chieftains of the Voorstoders. Equally old and cold, no doubt.

"What are you thinking?" Lurilile wanted to know.

"I'm thinking things could get very lively around here quite shortly," he said. "For a change."

"Oh, goody," she replied.

· *At Settlement Three* on Hobbs Land there had been deaths. A couple of the more violent and contentious of the inhabitants, one of them a Soames brother, had decided to leave Hobbs Land, a decision with which the settlement had been in complete agreement and sympathy. However, before the two could get themselves gone, they had happened upon an excuse for a fight, and the fight had ended with both dead. All in all, thought most of the people of Settlement Three, good riddance.

However, there were two bodies to dispose of. For

some reason, it did not seem to anyone that the proper place to put the two bodies was in the Settlement Three graveyard.

"We think they ought to go up on the escarpment," said Topman Harribon Kruss to Dern Blass, with no effort at all toward explaining himself or thinking up a logical reason for the course he was suggesting.

"On the escarpment," repeated Dern, casting a look at Spiggy and Jamice, who happened to be with him.

"It's very nice up there," said Spiggy, apropos of nothing. "I agree, it would be nice to have a memorial park up there. Burial space near the settlements could be put to better use."

"Memorial park," repeated Dern, remembering not to try and make sense out of it.

"For everybody," agreed Jamice, nodding her head. "One nice cemetery up there for all the settlements. Among the topes. It's only a daywatch away, by flier."

"Right," said Topman Kruss, as he left to go make arrangements. "I knew it would be all right."

Out of curiosity, Dern attended the interment. The two bodies were laid to rest in shallow graves in the wedge-shaped space between two of the long, strange mounds Volsa had discovered. Several cats, who had come along in the flier, scattered into the surrounding forest and emerged with dead ferfs in their jaws, which they dropped into the graves as they were being filled.

"Those two people never did get along, did they?" Dern asked the Topman, indicating the two graves. "Seems to me I saw reports about their orneriness all the time."

"They always fought. Each other or somebody else," said Harribon. "Lately, you know, people who don't get along sort of get up and leave. Have you noticed that? I've had four leave from Three, including these two; five or six left Four; and so on. These two were going to emigrate, but they got overtaken by bellicosity before they had a chance."

"I have noticed a number of departures lately," Dern agreed.

"Not in Settlement One," said Harribon. "All their

departures took place years and years ago, shortly after the settlement was started. Funny thing. That's one of the things I was most interested in about Settlement One. I thought their low hostility–high productivity record might be explained by the mix of people they had. Dracun and I were going to find out about that, but then things happened and it slipped my mind for a while. Then later on I remembered it and looked it up. The rest of us settlements had people coming and going, some of them not fitting in, a constant flux. Settlement One lost a few people during the early years, and then they didn't lose any more. It made me curious, so I checked out a few of the families who left. Osmer was one. He came in about year twelve, stayed a few years, then left. Couple of years after he left here, he was executed for killing a dozen Glottles. His family moved on somewhere else after that."

"Almost like he was sorted out to start with," suggested Dern.

"Almost like that, yes," said Harribon. "Well, the rest of us have been getting sorted out lately." He pointed at the graves. "People like these guys somehow just can't stop fighting. Mad at the universe, they are. Born that way, I guess."

"So it doesn't work for everybody," mused Dern.

"It?"

"Don't go dumb on me, Kruss. You know what I mean. In Settlement Three, the God Elitia doesn't work for everyone."

Harribon gave him a long, level look. "In Central Management, the God Horgy doesn't work for everybody. Ninety-nine percent of everybody, but not all."

"Be interesting to see what happens in Voorstod, won't it," said Dern. "You heard about that?"

Harribon nodded. "Sal Girat told me. I've been going over to keep company with Sal quite a bit lately. She says her mother went to Voorstod. Also Sam. Plus the little Wilm girl. Only reason I could figure for the little Wilm girl to go was . . . well. Is that what they went for?"

Dern shrugged elaborately. "All I know is what I feel in my bones, Topman." He turned back to the burials to see a large orange cat drop a final ferf into the grave before the last few spadefuls of earth covered it. Spiggy was watching the cat curiously.

"There," yowled the cat. "That does it."

Spiggy said something yowllike in response, which Dern interpreted as, "Thanks for your help."

"So we'll all bury our people up here from now on," said Dern.

"You feel that in your bones, do you?"

"You brought it up, Topman."

Harribon Kruss rubbed his neck and smiled, wryly. Yes, he had brought it up. And from now on, they'd all bring their people up. Because it seemed like a good idea. Because it was a way, a convenience, a kindness.

· *It took two* days for the search-and-seize line of troops to cross Green Hurrah. Many of the people of Green Hurrah were known to men of Karth's command. The army had been stationed in Jeramish for years, and they had made repeated forays into Green Hurrah, encountering the people who lived there on almost a daily basis. Persons who could not be identified or vouched for by trusted inhabitants were sent to the rear, under escort. Three camps had been set up at the border of Green Hurrah, and two of them were already swollen with internees from Ahabar. By nightfall of the second day, the line of men had reached the coast on either side of the thin neck of Skelp, and barriers were being constructed across that neck and all along the shore.

Across the main roads leading into Skelp, barricades had been set up—deep ditches, fences, overlapping suppressor fields to bring fliers down. Other suppressor fields covered the coastlines to either side, and beyond the fields were automatic weapons to bring down anything coming from the sea.

"What if people from Voorstod tried to go straight out, north?" asked Sam, curiously, pointing at the top of the chart. Across the room, Saturday and Maire sat at the table, remnants of a midafternoon meal scattered before them. Maire was slumped deeply into her chair in an attitude of dejection.

The Commander reached for another chart, showed Sam a line of coast north of Voorstod. "Icecap," he said. "Beyond that, open ocean. Beyond that, the province of Caerthop and more guns. East and west, gunships with suppressors. They'd have to go straight out, off Ahabar, to escape this blockade."

"Can they?"

"Not that we know of. No Doors. No intrasystem fliers."

"No army?"

"No. They've always advocated terrorist tactics, not battle. Their biggest group is their Faithful, the brethren of the Cause led by that group of fanatics they call the prophets. If you ever want to meet a wildman, meet a prophet. But, in addition to the Cause, there are probably a hundred splinter groups, all of them devoted to terrorism of one kind or another, some of them with only half a dozen members. One nice thing about them, they've never been able to work together. No man of Voorstod takes orders from any other man of Voorstod. Has to do with their Doctrine of Freedom."

"Uhm," said Sam, who had never listened when Maire had explained the doctrine. "How many do you think there are in there who would fight you?"

"Fifty thousand Faithful, anywhere from twelve to eighty lifeyears old. Whipped up by their prophets, they'd run naked into the guns; I've seen them do it. Other groups? A few hundred each, maybe a thousand in the largest of them."

"And how many in your army?"

Karth snorted. "Three million, if we call up the reserves. I've a million men involved in this blockade."

"Then there's no question you can go in and crush any opposition."

"No question."

"But many will die if you do."

"Before we got there, they'd kill all the Gharm they could get to, I imagine. Plus many of the women and children. These men are the kind who would kill their slaves and families rather than let us free them."

"No matter what the women want?" The question was

surprised out of Sam. It was not one he wanted an answer to.

"Women have no rights in Voorstod except under System law. It always surprised me that they let their women leave. I always expected to hear they'd locked them up."

"Too much trouble," said Maire, roused from her dejection. "More trouble than we were worth, so they said."

"But no longer?" Karth asked her.

"You've got to understand they're a puritan people, Commander. Sex is a very powerful taboo among Voorstoders. They delay it and forestall it when they can. The prophets of the Cause tell them sex is power, and being celibate stores up their power. The priests tell them married sex is all right, but only that. Both priests and prophets tell them not to look at women, not to think of women, that women are evil snares of the devil. And all women past puberty wear robes that cover all of them but their eyes. So they wouldn't have been inclined to hang on to us, not until now." She sat up, rubbing her head.

"We were commodities, not valuable ones, but there comes a point at which there probably aren't enough boy babies being born to make up for the Faithful who die," she said. "Sam suggested that, and the more I think of it, that has to be it. That's why they wanted me back, so I could keep others from leaving with my songs. But I fiddled around, making plans, trying to be sure we could get Jep out safely, and I may have fouled up the whole thing. I was supposed to be here long ago. I wasn't supposed to arrive at the same time as that concert. I wasn't supposed to be sitting there, watching. They thought to have me safe in Voorstod long before that happened. If they thought at all."

"They didn't foresee what Queen Wilhulmia would do either," said Saturday, shivering. She knew that what had started out as a dangerous exercise was now doubly so. The men in Voorstod would be anxious, fidgety, liable to strike out at anyone and everyone. She could feel their animosity like a palpable thing, like a wind blowing from the north. When she shut her eyes, she saw arms, pointed upward, handless, blood fountaining from the wrists. They were her own arms. She saw a throat cut. Her own throat. She fought down terror and asked, "When is the guide coming?"

"Yes," said Sam. "When is the guide coming?"

"She's here," said Karth. "Been here for a while. I told her you'd finish your food before you started out with her."

"Where does she take us?"

"Right through Skelp into Wander. The Squire of Wander will give you food and a bed tonight, then he'll send you on to Selmouth, in County Leward. That's as far as we've been able to plan. After that, you'll have to deal with the Faithful, for they're the ones who have the boy."

The Commander crossed the room and knelt before Saturday, taking her cold hands into his own. "I can't talk you out of this? It seems a dangerous and useless endeavor, Saturday Wilm. You could stay here in Ahabar, become a concert singer, have young men—maybe even old men—sending you flowers."

She assayed a smile, managed to arrange a fairly good one, a little tremulous. "No sir, you can't talk me out of this."

"It's a religious matter," said Prince Rals from across the room. "So she says."

The Commander looked at Maire, as though for verification of this. Maire merely smiled, a wry smile. Well, it was religious, in a way.

"Is it?" the Commander demanded of her.

"It is," she nodded. "Yes. If you must have a category for it, Commander, you may file it under religious matters."

The Commander shrugged; very well, his shoulders seemed to say. Oh, very well. He went to the door and beckoned. A woman came into the light, a person of middle-life, her hair turning gray at the temples, her face lined. "This is your guide," he said to them.

"I'm your guide," she agreed. "I don't tell you my name. You call me Missus. There's a vehicle outside."

Sam knelt before his mother and reached up to kiss her, his lips gently touching the edge of her own. He hugged her.

"Oh, Sammy. Why are you here?" she asked him. "I wish I knew."

"Here to keep Saturday company," he said. "Why else." For the moment, keeping Saturday company was the only reason he let himself admit to out loud. Later he would consider others. Such as acting the true hero and bringing an end to these senseless misunderstandings between people. Last night, deep in the dark, Sam had lain awake questioning himself, doubting himself, telling himself he was stubborn and intransigent.

"Maybe you're supposed to be," a voice in his mind had said. Theseus, maybe. "Maybe you're supposed to be. Maybe there's a reason."

Heroes, he thought, had to be stubborn perhaps, had to be intransigent, had to cleave to their ideas no matter how many people tried to sway them, even if those people were their mothers or sisters or friends.

The two of them, man and girl, went out into the night with their small packs of clothing and food. No weapons. Carrying a weapon in Voorstod, so said Karth, would get them killed faster than anything. Besides, neither of them knew anything about using weapons. They were farmers. Act like farmers. Sam, ready to object to that, had swallowed his words and pretended to accept them.

They climbed through the barricade, watched stoically by a hundred troopers. Missus put them in the back of the much-used vehicle with their packs, then drove them out of the occupied area and onto the wide road leading north. Theirs was the only vehicle on the road.

"Do the people of Voorstod know they're cut off from Ahabar?" Sam asked.

"We have eyes and ears," said the woman. "There'll be men going out tonight, seeing can they get through. By tomorrow, everyone will know how tight the blockade is, or whether the Queen is only playing with us."

"Do the people of Voorstod know why?"

"Something the Cause did. They're not saying what it was."

In a bleak, emotionless voice, Saturday told her what the Cause had done.

"Seems a small thing to cause so much ruckus," the

woman said. "One Gharm. Here there's hundreds every year. Whipped. Hands cut off. Feet cut off. Blinded."

Sam turned his head away. Surely, he thought, surely she didn't believe that. One, as a terrorist ploy, but not hundreds.

"You don't sound as though you care," said Saturday, sickened.

"If I cared about every Gharm that got mutilated, I'd do nothing but care," the woman responded. "I save my caring for what I can help."

"Your children?"

"What I can help," the woman said, shutting off the conversation.

Skelp was a hilly region where the road ran up through rocky defiles and out onto steep uplands before plunging down again, almost to the sea. From the uplands they could see the coast, off to their right, the sea reddened by sunset.

"Not many people in Skelp," ventured Sam.

"More than you'd think," the woman said. "There's villages west of us, where there's good pasture in the mountains. Mostly herdsmen here in Skelp. And fishermen, down along the shore."

"Lots of hiding places," said Saturday. "For those who escape."

"Lots of hiding places," the woman agreed. "For those who know the country."

"You know the country," said Sam.

"Yes," she responded. "Yes, I do."

They drove on as darkness came. Gradually the land flattened. They passed an occasional vehicle headed in the opposite direction. Night came, velvety dark, but clear enough that they could see the stars.

"I thought Voorstod was all misty," said Saturday.

"Farther north it is," said the woman. "Look there. You can see the lights of Wander Keep, off there to your left."

They were coming down a long slope and could see the scatter of lights burning in the shadow below them.

"The Squire," said the woman. "Still alive, though the Cause has taken one foot and a hand and one eye."

"What has the Cause against the Squire?" Saturday asked.

"He turned his Gharm free. He told a prophet he was a raging fanatic destined for Hell. He told the Cause to quit trapping itself up as a religion, because no God could endorse such evil. So the prophets cried anathema on him and put a price on his head. They do that a lot, the prophets, whenever someone does something they don't like. Then the church excommunicated him. Prophets and priests always go hand in hand on matters important to the prophets. The Squire doesn't care. He has services in his house every day. There's apostate priests live with him, so it's said."

"Where's the Cause strongest?" asked Saturday.

"Strongest? In Cloud, I should say, where the big citadel is. And in Selmouth, in County Leward. And in Scaery, in County Bight. And in Sarby. There's not enough people in the mountain counties, and there's nobody much in Panchy or Odil but farmers."

"Cloud's capital is Cloudport, right?"

"Mostly we just say Cloud. You planning to go there?"

Saturday shook her head, realized she could not be seen in the darkness and said, "No. We're not planning anything. Just to find my cousin and take him out of here."

The woman snorted and said nothing more. The lights grew closer, larger. After a time they could see that the lights were the windows of a fortress, high upon a sheer-sided hill. "Wander Keep," said the woman. "I'll let you out at the bottom of the hill. There's a gate there."

"Thank you for your trouble," said Sam.

"No trouble," said she. "You've never seen me, nor I you. We haven't met, so there was no trouble."

She paused only a moment, for them to unload their packs, then the vehicle sped off into the darkness. Behind them, a voice said, "Put down whatever you're holding and put your hands out away from your bodies."

Sam sighed. Thus far, there had been nothing heroic for him to do, and this did not seem to be the time to try. He dropped his pack next to Saturday's and held out his arms. Metal clanged. Someone came up behind him and beeped at him with a device. When they were allowed to turn around, the device was run over the packs.

"Come in," they were invited. "Come through the gate."

They went into deeper darkness. Metal clanged once more. Then there were dim lights, a dusty path, and long flights of stairs carved from the rock.

"No gravitics, sorry," said their escort. He was a short, heavy man with a hood over his head, showing only his eyes.

"I suppose we've never seen you, right?" asked Saturday, trying to make a joke of it.

"Right," he said, surprised.

"Why is that?" Sam asked.

"Because if the Cause wants to know, you don't know. You're going north where the Cause is, and they want to know all sorts of things."

"Won't they know we stopped here?"

"They will. But they won't know who let you in. Or who fed you. Or whether the Squire even knew about it. Probably he didn't know a thing about it."

They went up three more flights, into a stone room with two cots, a table, an open fire, and a door half open to disclose rather primitive sanitary arrangements. "Food," said their guide, pointing to covered dishes on the table. "Fire, plenty of fuel to keep it going. Eat, sleep, tomorrow early somebody'll be here to take you to Selmouth. There's Voorstod money there, too. Enough to get you wherever you're going."

Saturday had already thrown herself down on one of the cots. "Thank you," she said. "For your hospitality."

"Nothing," the hooded man said, retreating through the door.

Sam and Saturday heard the door clang, heard it lock. Sam went to the window, which had been cut deeply into the rock. Below the barred opening the sheer face of stone plunged downward into darkness.

"Are you going to eat?" Sam asked.

"Later," the girl murmured. "I'm not hungry now." Actually, she was sick from the tension and the long ride, from not knowing what was to happen next. It was easier to say she wasn't hungry.

Sam was hungry. He ate cold roasted meat with an unfamiliar taste, raw vegetables and fruit, half a loaf of chewy bread smeared with soft cheese. He pocketed the money after looking it over carefully, both strips and coins. The room was utterly silent except for the crackle of the fire.

"What am I doing here?" he asked himself aloud. "Why did I come along?" He thought Theseus might answer him.

Saturday sighed in her sleep.

"You came to protect Saturday Wilm," he told himself. "Because she must get to Jep. For some reason."

He knew that reason, of course. They all did. If he had not known before, what happened at the concert would have made it clear. He had no objection to doing that. It couldn't hurt anything, couldn't hurt Phaed, for example, to have the God in Voorstod. It might help. Might do good.

"You know," he said conversationally, "it would be interesting to know if you're interested in all life, or just intelligent life, or maybe just certain races."

The fire made no response. Night air came cool through the window cut in the rock.

"Cats," he said. "That would indicate all life, wouldn't it? Cats and humans and now, probably, Gharm. Of course, nobody can deny that cats are intelligent, so maybe it's only intelligent life."

Saturday sighed, half in sleep, half-awake.

"On the other hand, the crops have done very well. Better in Settlement One than anywhere else, for years and years. So maybe it's all life. Flora as well as fauna.

"I guess the only way one could tell would be to compare two complete planets, one with you and one without . . ."

"It doesn't do any good talking to it, Topman," murmured Saturday. "It can't hear you. It isn't here."

"Yet," said Sam. "Though it feels like it's here."

"Just what we're carrying around inside us. Not enough to do anything much when it's separated like this.

Enough to keep us from panicking, maybe, but that's all. Not even enough of itself to reproduce if we got killed and buried."

Sam thought about that. "Too bad."

"Mom said to remind you. Just in case you get any . . . heroic ideas."

Saturday might not have thought of that, but Africa had. Africa had worried aloud about Sam endangering them both by doing something . . . crazy.

Saturday sighed, still half-asleep. "We'll be more use to it alive, Topman. Let's try to stay alive."

· *On the hill* above Sarby, Jep sat in the temple with half a dozen Gharm, including several he had not seen before. He still wore the collar, though he hadn't seen any of the conspirators for two days.

"Is she coming?" they asked. "She-Goes-On-Creating?"

"She's coming," said Jep. "I don't know how long it will take her, but she's coming."

· *"You know,"* said Rasiel Plum, Chairman of the Native Matters Advisory, as he ran his finger down the list of questions he had been given by Notadamdirabong Cringh, "this is very interesting. Why are you showing it to me?"

Cringh ducked his head into his shoulder and considered the matter. "Well, we two are old colleagues, Rasiel. Two of the twenty-one Actual Members of Authority, so I would naturally turn to you for help."

"I know, Notty, but that's not the reason."

Notadam sighed. "The head of the Circle of Scrutators of the High Baidee wants the questions considered, unofficially, by the Religion Advisory. But, as my aide put it—succinctly, I thought—how can you ask an unofficial question of a very official body? Without causing, that is, a stink?

"Let us suppose I asked the questions. Everyone would assume immediately that the High Baidee is out to destroy someone's religion, someone else's religion, that is. There are those rumors, you know, the old ones about the Blight. We High Baidee are accused—wrongly, need I say, but accusations of that kind color other peoples' attitudes. So if *I* ask these questions, particularly if I include the last few questions, rumor will brew like tea, with everyone smelling it. And once that rumor gets started, people will get anxious, memoranda will begin flying here and there, chaos will result. That isn't what the head of the Circle of Scrutators had in mind, I'm sure, but it's inevitable if I'm known to be involved."

Rasiel nodded, agreeing. That was what would happen.

"However, if the questions come from *you,* Rasiel, they could be considered unofficial. The Native Matters Advisory might simply need to know about something religious because some native peoples have questions. Perhaps the Hosmer are becoming interested in theology. Or something. Coming from you, it's no threat, if you take my meaning."

"Is the High Baidee out to destroy someone else's religion?" asked Rasiel, unamused by the idea.

"I shouldn't think so."

"Not a nice idea at all, Notadam. Not one I would approve of in either an official or unofficial capacity."

"If any Baidee ever did such a thing, Rasiel, it wouldn't be old farts like me. It would be some young firebrands with more energy than sense, and they would do it because they would regard the religion in question as a kind of disease."

"Catching, is it?"

"Seemingly so. Or, perhaps I should say, suspected to be so."

"That could be ugly. People turn all fanatic, do they? Rant and rave against the unholy? Claim to have the only source of truth? Execute people for heresy? Burn people at the stake? Shovel them wholesale into ovens?" Rasiel was a student of human history, including its more barbaric periods.

Cringh took some time before he answered, and when he did, it was with a musing tone that made Rasiel look at him sharply. "No, as a matter of fact, people seem to turn cooperative and kind and virtually incapable of hurting others."

There was a long silence.

"Young firebrands, you say?" asked Rasiel Plum, wonderingly.

"Every religion has its zealots," said Cringh.

"It was some such young berserkers who wiped out the invasion force that hit Thyker, when was it?"

"A long time ago."

"Any current special bunch of firecrackers?"

"A fellow named Howdabeen Churry has a group that calls itself The Arm of the Prophetess."

"Why do they call themselves that?"

"Why do the Voorstod terrorists call themselves the Faithful?"

Another long silence.

"Well," said Rasiel Plum. "I suppose I could ask the questions. Some of them. Unofficially." He looked at the list in front of him. "Let's start with questions one, two, four, and five."

• *Sam and Saturday* were picked up by another vehicle on the morning following their stay with whomever it had been at Wander Keep. This time the driver was a laconic man of about seventy, gray-haired and knob-jawed, who sang tunelessly to himself during the entire trip to Selmouth, seemingly deaf to anything they said.

When he let them out in a cobbled street in front of a tavern, he pointed to the tavern and said, "In there. Tell the provider you're looking for passage north."

"How far north?" asked Sam.

"The word is, you'll learn that in Cloud," said the driver, spitting at Sam's feet.

"Is there a church here?" asked Saturday.

The driver stared at her. "Use your eyes, girl," he said at last. "Or your ears. Towers and bells, that's churches."

"A church?" asked Sam as they turned away.

"Funerals," said Saturday. "Maire told me this religion has funerals."

Sam nodded thoughtfully. Maire had indeed talked of the religion of Voorstod, or rather the religions, for the priests had one and the prophets another, though they often seemed to be the two sides of one coin. It was the prophets who did war and murder. It was the priests who did weddings and funerals.

"If you're looking for funerals, then we need to stay a while in Selmouth," he said, giving the tavern a look over so he was sure he could find it again. It was called the Horn and the Dagger, and the sign showed the one curled around the other.

"Only as long as it takes," she replied. "The woman who took us to Wander said the Cause was strong here. And in Cloudport, and in Scaery, and in Sarby."

"Four places?"

She nodded, looking over the roofs which surrounded them. There were towers, many towers. "Let's walk," she said.

At the third church they saw a group assembled for a wedding. Sam and Saturday watched curiously as the white-robed bride and her strangely garbed husband left the church under a shower of flung grain. Nothing could be seen of the bride but her eyes, and it was impossible to tell if she was happy about her marriage. At the fourth church there was an old man digging a deep grave. The funeral would be the following day, he said, when they asked him.

"Too deep," Saturday murmured as they walked away. "We need something shallow."

At the eighth church they passed, a crypt was open and a group of mourners was leaving together with the black-clad priest. Through the open door of the stone tomb, they could see the coffin upon a bench above a dirt floor. The iron grill that would close across the door stood open, with a huge key hanging from it. Saturday directed Sam's attention to the key, then engaged a stout, veiled, much-interested bystander in conversation.

"Who died?" she asked.

"Herk Madun's young wife," said the woman. "In childbed. The midwife could not save her."

"Have they no medical people in Selmouth?" Saturday asked.

"Where are you from, girl, to ask such a question?" The woman's voice was sternly disapproving.

"From elsewhere," she said. "No offense. I'm only curious."

"Well, our priest teaches a woman pays for her sin by bearing children. The risk of dyin' is what balances the books. No medical person would interfere between a woman and God, not here in Selmouth."

"Her sin? You mean sex?"

The woman flushed and whispered, "Well, of course I mean that. What else is so sinful?"

"What balances the books for the man?"

"Losing his wife, stupid girl. Now he must go to the trouble of finding another, no easy thing, these days."

Saturday thanked the woman for the information. She and Sam walked back the way they had come.

"Can you pick the lock?" Saturday wanted to know.

"With my teeth, if you like," he smiled.

"We'll need to borrow a spade," she said. "Perhaps there is one at the tavern."

However, they found the tavern owner ready and eager to move them forward, out of Selmouth.

"We are too weary to go farther today," said Sam. "In the morning, early, we can leave then."

"But I've got a man to take you now!" The man rubbed his greasy hair and seemed about to cry.

Sam shook his head. "The child is tired. Look at her. She's worn out. No more travel today."

The provider grumbled, muttered, glared, and threatened, but Sam was impervious to it all. Before they ever left Hobbs Land, Sam had decided that Saturday was the symbolic equivalent of sword and sandals. She had emerged at the proper time to give him a reason for leaving Hobbs Land and seeking his father. Accompanying her had been "meant." Therefore, playing out his mystical role included helping her do whatever she thought best. Such roles were frequent in legends. Once that was out of the way, his real quest could begin.

The provider agreed finally that Sam and Saturday

might have a room upstairs to rest in until the morning. The room was dirty, but it looked down into a littered yard at the back where they could see odds and ends of tools lying about among the trash. When darkness came, Saturday took a light-wand from her pack and they slipped down the back stairs and out into the yard. There, after Sam had rummaged around to find a rusty spade and some stiff wire, they trotted off down the alleys, stopping now and again to be sure they were headed in the right direction.

The lights in the street threw long shadows across the empty churchyard. To one side of it the silent crypt loomed, mysterious and awesome in the dim light, the iron grating across its door locking away the world of the dead. Saturday had spent too many nights on vigils to be impressed. It was only a tomb, only a door. Sam used the wire to open the lock while Saturday kept watch. It took him no time at all. With the door half-shut behind them, Sam put the dull spade to the hard-packed ground and, cursing under his breath, began to lay the moist, heavy clods aside. Even inside the tomb, the earth was damp, as it seemed to be everywhere in Voorstod.

"Hsst," said Saturday, laying a hand on his shoulder, and turning off the light.

He stopped digging and held his breath. Outside, along the street, someone was walking toward them. Two figures stopped at the churchyard wall, silhouetted against the glow of the town. They were not dressed as ordinary people. The outline of their heads and shoulders was massive, inhuman.

Said one, "Madun's woman and child were buried here today. He was up at the citadel, demanding a new wife."

"There's no woman to allot him," the other replied.

"Then he'll do without. He should have picked one better suited to childbearing. He was told that."

"He wanted this one."

"Well, he had her."

After a time, they walked on. Sam went back to digging the shallow hole they needed. When he had it deep enough, they used the spade to lever up the coffin lid, which had been nailed shut. The woman had not been dead long. There was little smell of corruption. Saturday lifted the shroud from her face and looked at her, a child, no older than Saturday herself. The stillborn baby lay on her breast, alabaster white, a tiny hand curled against the young mother's throat.

"What are you thinking?" asked Sam, curiously, nervously. He had buried a body only once before, after Bondru Dharm died, and then he had been moving in a paroxysm of grief.

"I was thinking the Baidee are right in some ways," she said. "They say only our minds are us. I think what's so terrible about death is that we leave this behind. If when we died, we just vanished, like a spark of light, it would be better. Then we would realize better what we are. Instead, we worry about bodies. We think about bodies. I see this woman lying so still with this baby and it makes me want to cry."

She turned toward Sam, her eyes luminous with tears. "She's only a girl, Topman. No older than me. She and the baby should have gone out, like festival rockets, sparkling, leaving nothing behind."

Sam was shaken by her intensity, but he said, "Then you would have nothing to bury for the God."

"That's so," she sighed. "I should be grateful. Well, help me lift her down."

They laid the still form at the bottom of the shallow grave. Saturday unbuttoned her own shirt and cut a seam at the bottom of her chemise, ripping the silk away from the filmbag inside, then ripping the filmbag itself. The fibrous stuff inside was moist and smelled of earth. Saturday knelt and put it between the woman and her child.

"You see, you were needed," Saturday whispered to Sam as she rose. "I could not have dug the grave alone."

"Sam, the grave-digger," he said, somberly. "It scarcely sounds legendary. I have higher hopes for this trip than merely digging graves, Saturday Wilm."

His tone frightened her a little, it was so full of determination. She said nothing more while they filled in the hole, breaking up the clods so they would lie smooth, putting the extra soil in the box and restoring the lid so that it looked as it had before.

"Do you often have thoughts like that?" he asked her. "About leaving bodies or vanishing like sparks?"

She thought for a moment, then nodded. "They aren't my thoughts, I don't think. I get them from other people. I think Ones Who do that. I say something and it comes out . . . it comes out as though Africa had said it, sometimes. Or China. Or someone else, Maire even."

Sam nodded, accepting this. "Where will they build the temple?" he asked. "There's city all around us."

"Here," said Saturday, indicating the churchyard. "Perhaps they will pull down the church to make room. They won't need a church then. Perhaps they will build it on top of the graves."

Sam hid the spade in an alley, some distance from the church. From that point, they proceeded openly, two people out for a walk. There were others out walking. They stopped at an eating house for supper, using the money they had been given in Wander. Saturday watched the few women in the place, feeding themselves under their veils, putting drinking glasses up under their veils. So much wasted motion. So much wasted effort. She thought she might be the oldest unveiled person in the room, though there were other girls who looked little younger than she.

When they came out, there was a veiled woman singing on the street corner, with passers-by casting her frightened looks.

The last winged thing came in from the sea.

It blew into Scaery on wings like foam,

footless as angels are said to be . . .

Sam and Saturday walked past. When they were almost at the corner, Saturday said, "Wait."

"Wait?"

"Listen. That's Maire's song she's singing."

"Did you call," it asked, in a voice so low

it was lost in the dusk like a blowing leaf.

"Did you call?" it begged, "out of loss or woe,

did you bring me here where no winged things go,

did you call out of sorrow or grief?"

"Mam's song? Oh, you mean that one she talks of. The last song—what was it called?"
" 'The Last Winged Thing,' Sam. Listen."

"As you called for Peace, who came and died,

As you called for Joy, who drowned in the sea,

As you called for Love, who stayed and tried,

though Voorstod's no place for love to be,

There were people coming, uniformed people, from down the street. The woman saw them, but she didn't stop singing. Her voice rose passionately.

". . . and now that Hope's gone, it's our time to go.

Kiss me, my child. Farewell my child.

Follow me, child, and we'll go."

The men were around her then, holding her fast, taking her away. Through the head-to-toe covering, they could hear her panting breath as they dragged her away, still singing. *"We'll go. We'll go. We'll go."*
"I had no idea they'd still be singing Mam's songs," said Sam. "She's been gone for so many years."
Saturday stared at him, hating him a little. Why hadn't he said something about the woman! "Why did

they take the woman away?" she cried. "Is that song forbidden? It wasn't forbidden when Maire sang it."

Sam shook his head. He didn't know. He hadn't really listened to the words. He hadn't really seen what was going on. He had been thinking of something else.

Saturday subsided, wondering what he was thinking of.

When they returned to the tavern, they went up the back stairs and into their dirty room once more. Saturday took the coverlet into the hall and shook the dust from it. They lay down upon it, side by side, and fell asleep, not to waken until the landlord shook them roughly in the morning.

"You have to go," he hissed at them. "You're expected, in Cloud."

They looked down from an upper window to see the driver, a young man with a large cap. Remembering what Maire had told them about such caps, they assumed he was one of the Faithful.

Sam tied a kerchief around Saturday's head, hiding her hair. He smeared black from the fire upon her teeth. "We know as little as possible," Sam whispered to her. "We were in the concert hall. We saw what happened. It has nothing to do with what we are here for."

Saturday nodded soberly. When she came out of the tavern, the man with the cap began to finger his crotch, as though it were some instrument he intended to play upon. Rape was not out of the question. Maire had warned her. So had Africa. Saturday gawked and breathed at him through stained teeth, watching his interest dwindle. His vehicle was used to transport livestock. The back of it was full of heaving movement and an evil smell.

"You have a choice," the driver sneered. "Back there with the beasts or up front, with me."

"We'll ride with you," said Sam, getting himself into the middle of the seat with Saturday on the outside. "She needs the fresh air, you know how girls get."

"What's she here for, anyhow?" demanded the driver angrily. "We didn't ask for her. Didn't ask for you!"

"I just go along," said Sam. "She has to see the boy,

and then she and the boy have to come back to where the woman is, that's all I know."

"The woman's your mother, isn't she?"

Sam gave no evidence of surprise. "Maybe you've got a different kind of mother from mine. Mine doesn't tell me anything."

The driver snorted. They moved onto the road, heavy with traffic. Now there were towns and villages all along the route, with fields and pastures behind, toward the mountains. Along the shore were fishing villages, boats and ships rocking offshore at their mooring lines.

"No bays," said Sam. "I'll bet you lose a lot of ships when the weather's bad."

"Boats go to Cloud when the weather's bad. To Cloud or Selmouth or Scaery. Where they'd might as well take them now, for all the good they'll do us here."

"Something wrong?"

"The Queen's ships are out there on the water, and they've sent our boats back. A few days of that, and people will go hungry."

Sam hushed himself and sat silent as the road rolled away beneath them. By midmorning, the mists had gathered, and they could see no farther ahead than the nose of the vehicle. It was midafternoon when the driver pointed ahead and muttered, "Cloudport, there."

They could see nothing, then something, then a darkness against the ever-present mists. A vagrant wind blew some of the veils between them and the city away. They saw it almost clearly before the fogs closed in again, a gray city piled at the side of the sea with the citadel crouched on a rocky crag above.

FOUR

· *Sam and Saturday* were met at the gate of the
citadel by two robed men wearing elaborate headdresses,
which exposed only their ears and the fronts of their faces.
These fleshy parts seemed extraneous, like sections of a
mask, and the whole effect was monolithic, as though
these were not articulated creatures who moved themselves but solid lumps moved by some outside force, as
chessmen were moved during play. Saturday recognized
the shape of the ponderous figures, the same as the two
passersby at the graveyard in Selmouth. She caught herself staring, flushed, and dropped her eyes, but not before
they had noticed her doing it.

"Modest women do not stare into the faces of men,"
said one with a snarl. He had a face like a vice, narrow
and unyielding about the jaws. "An immodest woman is a
pawn of the devil."

"Has the woman no veil?" demanded the other, a petulant creature with pursed rosy lips, thick and moist as a
mollusk.

"Young as she is, we did not know a veil was required," Sam returned craftily. "She has a kerchief she can use. What is supposed to be covered?"

"Her face. All but the eyes."

Saturday started to object, then drew a deep breath and forced herself to be silent. Maire had said little enough about this. She had talked of priests, of churchy things, of her own life, of children and gardens and the countryside. She had talked much about the Gharm. But she had said very little about prophets or the Cause. With Sam here, it would be better simply to go along, to say nothing, to let Sam handle it, man to man, as it were. She stood quietly as he tied her kerchief across her face, under her eyes, covering her nose and mouth. She had a shawl with her, which she drew over her head, giving thanks that her clothes were straight and bulky, hiding anything female about her shape. Then she tried to stop thinking of anything, for Sam was being led inside, and she wanted to stay as close to him as possible.

They were brought before a dais with high-backed chairs upon it, the middle and highest one occupied by another of the robed prophets, an aged man with blazing deep-set eyes and a mouth drawn down and bracketed by heavy lines. The seat he occupied was far too large for him, but his fury filled it. The chair pulsed, as though a star burned itself out there. Saturday saw it, then did not see it, a moment's vision which came and went. She looked at her feet, not wanting her eyes to meet the rage facing her, feeling it would be dangerous to try. Sam gripped her shoulder, squeezing it, saying by that gesture, calm. Be calm. Through the contact she could feel his own flesh quiver. He was no calmer than she.

"Why do you bring this whore of Satan to Voorstod?" the prophet cried. His voice was quavery with age, shaped by years of hostility into a wavy edged dagger of sound.

Sam thought it over. The words the prophet had used were a riddle. The riddle itself was the only clue he had to its answer. What would the answer to this riddle be, in a legend? She was not a whore, obviously. Legends did not concern themselves with whores. So she had to be something else. A princess. A priestess. A virgin, sacrifice to a dragon. The old man was dragonlike enough.

"This is my kinswoman, a virgin girl, pledged to a young man you have taken hostage. Our way requires that she go to him in his captivity, be where he is, and come with him out of danger if such is to happen."

"Virgin, pfah," the aged prophet hissed. "My sons say she does not even know enough to cover her face before the prophets of Almighty God."

"It's true she does not," agreed Sam, descending from myth to practicality. "We've come from Hobbs Land, where there are no prophets. We're ignorant of your ways."

"Hobbs Land's lack will be remedied in the fullness of time." The words were a promise. "Why have *you* come here?"

"It would be unsuitable for her to travel alone. She is pledged to my son. It is my duty to my son to protect his honor." He was back with legend again, dragging the words up out of the Archives, from the time of horsemen and genies and knights. On Hobbs Land they would have had little meaning. People there did not talk of honor much, or of pledging. Honor was in what a man did; pledging was what a man said he would do.

Silence.

"There are no fathers or sons of men in Hobbs Land," the prophet declared in a weaker voice.

"That is true. However, we are not in Hobbs Land, and your captive is my son."

The prophet gloomed at him, his mouth making tiny chewing motions. Then his eyes widened, lost their focus, stared blindly at the far wall. His mouth opened and closed. "Our Cause is just," the mouth said loudly, as though independent of the rest of the face. "Death to all unbelievers." A tiny froth of spittle appeared at the corner of the mouth. The eyes wandered, wildly.

Sam bowed his head and said nothing.

"Almighty God gave us the Gharm," the prophet cried, lifting his staff with one stiff arm to hold it above his head. "They are ours to do with as we will. Those here, those elsewhere, they are ours. Their blood is ours. Their seed is ours, for God has made of them a separate servant, that the purity of our people be kept uncorrupted!"

Sam said nothing at all, feeling cold sweat rolling down the back of his neck, under his shirt. Under his hand, Saturday quivered. On the platform, two younger prophets moved to the old man and talked quietly to him, soothing him. After a time they seemed to have some success, for the staff was lowered and the old man leaned upon it, panting.

One of the younger prophets turned toward them. "Ahabar has set a fence about us, Sam Girat. Unholy Ahabar at the order of its whore-Queen. What do you know about it?" He glanced at the old man, worried wrinkles between his eyes.

Sam looked up. "Who am I that I should be privy to the deliberations of Ahabar."

"Do not evade. You were with Karth! We saw you!"

"We were with him because it was his wish to honor the Sweet Singer of Scaery," said Sam, his throat dry. He coughed. If they had seen him, then they knew the reason for the blockade. What was this man playing at? "Maire Manone, who is waiting now, at the border of Voorstod."

"Is she now?" asked a silky voice. Not the prophet. A man lounging at one side of the room, a man with hair flowing to his knees. On the dais, the younger prophet stared at the man who had spoken, then turned away to join the urgent colloquy which was going on behind him.

Sam thought he knew who the speaker was, though he wasn't sure. He stiffened his knees and said nothing, waiting for more.

"Do you know who I am?" the man asked.

"I think we met in Hobbs Land," said Sam. "I've forgotten your name."

"Mugal Pye, at your service. A friend of your father's."

"No friend of mine. You're one of those who stole my son."

"Maire Manone will come into Voorstod, will she? When the boy goes back there?" Mugal drawled the words, as though they were not important.

"When Saturday and the boy and I go back to her . . ."

There was consternation upon the dais. A prophet turned suddenly to ask, "What is the girl's name?"

"Saturday Wilm," said Sam.

"The boy's name is Wilm."

"They are cousins."

"And she is pledged to him?"

Sam nodded. Now what?

Muttering upon the dais. Mugal Pye sat down, glaring at Sam. After a time, when the prophets quieted, he said, "So Maire Manone will come into Voorstod."

"She will."

"She'll come sing for us?"

"She said she'll do whatever she can," said Sam. "She misses the oceans and mists of Scaery, the sweet hills of Cloud. She has written some new songs." Maire had said as much. They were Hobbs Land songs, but Maire had written them.

"The Satan-named infidel whore must be killed now," the old prophet cried, thrusting the men around him aside, coming to his feet. "He who stands beside her must be cut down. Their bodies shall hang on the walls of the citadel of the Faithful. The Squire of Wander shall hang beside them. All Gharm who have fled into Ahabar shall hang beside them. Thickly clustered as grapes, hanging upon the vine, so shall hang the enemies of the Almighty. Let it be seen. Let it be known. God will hang them upon the walls. Those from the counties to the south, they will hang upon the walls . . ."

Under Sam's hand, Saturday shook. The old man meant every word he was saying. His malice and hatred pounded at her like a hammer. He wanted them dead. If he had the strength, he would kill them himself. He was all evil, and if his God was real, it was an evil God. The thought came and went, swiftly, and she concentrated on standing where she was.

Other prophets gathered around the old man, and his voice became muffled. "I have set a price upon the life of the Squire of Wander. I have set a price upon the life of the Queen of Ahabar. I have set a price upon the lives of those who speak evil of Almighty God or of His Holy prophets or of His Holy works. The time draws near when the armies of God . . ."

One of the younger prophets turned from the group and came hastily down from the dais toward Mugal Pye. "Go," he said softly, nodding at Saturday and Sam. "Get them out of here. Take them wherever the boy is. Then get them out of Voorstod."

"If the Awateh wants them dead, I've no objection," muttered Pye, with a sneer at Sam, as though Sam had challenged him.

"The Awateh is not quite fully aware of what is going on," the prophet said, turning burning eyes upon Pye. "The Awateh sometimes forgets that we are blockaded. The Awateh is at this moment unaware that there are a million armed men surrounding Voorstod. All of us agree with the Awateh that what will happen eventually will be as God wills, but we believe it might be *prudent* to take this man and this girl where they want to go, Mugal Pye. Just as it might have been *prudent* not to have done what was done a few days ago."

"The Awateh agreed . . ."

"The Awateh was not as well-informed as he should have been. None of us were. We thought the creature was merely another Gharm who deserved death for her faithlessness. We did not know she would become a martyr to move a million men. The Awateh was surprised by that, as were we all. We were not quite ready for this. Now the Awateh suffers from a slight disorientation . . ."

"Well," sneered Pye. "The Gharm isn't dead. She won't play the harp again, but she isn't dead."

"Which may be why *we* are still alive," murmured the prophet. "If she had died, so might we. You have much bad judgment to answer for, Pye. Get them out of here."

Sam looked at his feet, the shock of what he had just heard immobilizing him. Pye was supposedly a friend of his father's, and from the words just spoken it was clear Pye had been among those responsible for what happened to Stenta Thilion.

"Don't lie to yourself, boy," Maire had told him. Had he lied to himself? Would he have been here, if he had not lied to himself? His forehead was wet and he wiped at it.

Mugal Pye led them out. Behind them, the Awateh's voice rose, raging incoherently. They stopped beside the flier in the courtyard while Saturday removed the kerchief from her face and used it to wipe her neck and forehead, soaked with fear's sweat. She was still sick with apprehension. At any moment the prophets might boil from that doorway to bring them back.

"What was the fuss about in there when they learned her name?" Sam asked in a shaky voice, taking his eyes away from the burdened hooks he had just noticed on the citadel walls.

"The prophet said Saturday is one of the names for the Sabbath Day of the Cause. Not in System tongue, of course. In one of the dead languages. I wouldn't know, but prophets study things like that. Great scholars, they are. They know the scriptures from memory."

"When I was a child, Mam spoke of Sundays." Sam focused his gaze upon a discolored Door, standing against the wall. He hadn't known Voorstod had a Door.

"Sunday's the church Sabbath. We have five work days and two Sabbath days, one for the Cause, one for the church, none for the animals, including the Gharm." He sniggered. "Nobody in Voorstod would name a girl after the Sabbath. For a moment, it confused the prophets, then the Awateh decided it was blasphemy, another reason to kill her." He stared at Saturday. "If you'd gone in there with your bare face, he'd have realized you were the one who sang the battle song, there in Fenice, and you'd have had your throat slit, and not his sons nor nobody could have stopped him doing it."

He turned back to Sam. "You don't look much like a Girat. You take more after your mother."

Sam shrugged, hiding anger. "I am as I am."

"You want to go where the boy is?"

"If we can go to Jep, then we and Jep can turn around and go to the border and Maire will come in. If you still want her with all this going on." Though Saturday wanted to stay a brief time in Sarby, since they had accomplished one burial, they could leave at once if need be.

Mugal Pye gave him a level look. "This'll blow over. Queen Willy won't keep it up. We've made sure the Au-

thority will intervene within a day or two and tell her to
back off. Yes, we still plan to use Maire Manone. It's only
right she should come back to Voorstod, back to her people. She can be a symbol, one way or the other. You and
the kids are no use to us, though, come to think of it, the
girl might be." He grinned at Saturday, like an animal,
teeth showing, relishing her obvious fear. "She's a singer,
too."

"I could not sing in Voorstod," said Saturday, getting
the words out with difficulty. "The mists shut my throat."

"Likely, oh likely," sneered Pye. "Well, since the
Awateh's sons don't want us here, let us go find your
boy."

The flier made the long journey to Sarby far easier
than the shorter trips had been. Though the mists ob-
scured much of the landscape, Pye flew low enough that
they could see something of the countryside. Cloudport,
they saw, as they rose, and Scaery, after some time in
flight, while Saturday wondered how she could get to either place, and when. She had been scared into immobility
in the citadel at Cloud. She was terrified still. It would be
impossible to return to Cloud. If she returned, the Awateh
would know, somehow, that she was coming. He would
wait for her. His prophets would hide, waiting, to move
out of the mists like implacable statues, to seize her and
hang her upon the walls. She knew this as certainly as she
knew her name. She could see her body, dangling, like a
doll, her blood smeared on the stones. The old man's colleagues had argued with him, diverted him, but he would
not be diverted long. He was mad, with a lifelong madness
nothing could divert for long, and he hungered for her
life. She shut her eyes and breathed through her mouth,
tasting bile in her throat.

They flew north across County Bight and County
Odil, turning the corner of the mountains to go west along
the foothills. At last Sarbytown lay beneath them, on the
long slope to the sea beside the running river. Pye turned
a little upslope from the town and set the flier down in a
meadow.

The mists had risen to hang just above their heads.
Meadow grass stretched away like carpet upslope to the

line of trees where Jep was standing among a few Gharm. The Gharm turned and vanished into the woods, but Jep did not move away or toward them.

"You'll have to go to him," Pye sneered. "He got one of my collars on him will blow his head off if he comes to you."

They picked up their packs and went slowly, in what they both hoped was a dignified manner. It still seemed important that they not let their fear show. Beasts chased creatures when they ran. It was better not to run. When they reached Jep, Sam took him by the hand and Saturday patted his arm, gently. There were tears in Jep's eyes, but he spoke calmly, as though aware he might be overheard.

"I knew you would come," he said. "I knew a One Who had to come."

On the meadow, Pye stared at them for a time, the habitual sneer coming and going across his mouth. Strangely, he was trying to remember if he had ever seen any woman looking at him the way Saturday was looking at Jep. Soft, these farmers. Phaed's own son, but soft. Phaed's own grandson, soft. It was the Cause that tempered men, that turned them into steel. Phaed had other sons and grandsons, not born in wedlock, true, but better tools than these. In his heart Mugal Pye weighed the Hobbs Landians, rejected them, and planned what counsel concerning them he would give Phaed Girat. Phaed Girat was behaving like a fool, angry at them all for not having told him what was happening. He had to be brought to his senses. If it was true that Maire Girat could not sing, as Jep had said, then she could serve as a symbol of another kind. She could symbolize what would happen, inevitably, to any other woman who left.

Finally he turned to walk down the hill, toward the town. Sam and Saturday watched him go, then followed Jep through the trees to the farm, through the half-wrecked dwelling into the room where Jep lived, where they hovered beside the smoldering fire as Jep added fuel and blew it into a blaze. He sat between them as he told them about his captivity, about Tchenka and Gharm and of his building a temple. When he had done, they went out to see that building for themselves.

Nils was just outside the door.

"Not him," he whispered to Jep, pointing to Sam.

"Why not?" asked Saturday. "He helped me in Selmouth."

"Not him," insisted Nils. "It is said he is the son of Phaed Girat, and the Gharm do not trust his intentions."

"It's all right," said Sam, repressing his annoyance. "I'll wait for you nearby." He had been more distressed than angered by the little man's words, but he still needed to think about them.

Nils and Pirva and a great many Gharm had come to meet She-Goes-On-Creating. They had brought lanterns and cushions into the temple. They bowed when they met Saturday. She bowed in return. When they were all seated cross-legged, Saturday and Jep at the center of the warm puddle of light, Saturday told them she had been sent to them with the stuff they needed to summon their Tchenka to them.

"It is stuff of holiness," Saturday told them. "It is the stuff of creation from which Tchenka come. It is the substance from which your Tchenka will come again, and the way of it is this."

She described burials. She told them about cutting sections of the web around the first Tchenka raised and keeping those sections to use at other burials. She said there must be many burials, here, there, everywhere. She thought the telling unnecessary, no one had told the people of Settlement One in advance what they were to do, but these people were being persecuted and perhaps they needed to know in advance in order to have hope.

"Meantime," she told them, "I have already done the ritual in Selmouth. Here there are three pieces more brought from my own God Birribat Shum, and these three are destined to be used here and in Scaery and in Cloud."

"She-Goes-On-Creating had intended to do this herself," said Jep. "However, there is much evil assembled against her in Voorstod, so she asks that you do this thing for her. You walk invisibly in Voorstod, and the prophets do not see you. Also you work invisibly in Voorstod. No one notices if you dig or build. From Gharm-hand to

Gharm-hand this stuff can be passed. From mouth to mouth the instructions can be given. Burials must be done in Cloud and Scaery, and when the Tchenka in Selmouth and Sarby are raised, someone must be there to take the stuff of creation, for many more must be started."

"How many more?" Nils wanted to know.

"As many as there are places which need Tchenka in them," said Saturday. "Not only here, but in Ahabar, as well. As many as there are Tchenka to come into this world."

"There are many Tchenka," said Pirva, wonderingly. "So very many."

"We should do it every place there are Gharm," suggested Nils.

"Every place there are people," corrected Saturday. "Whether they are Gharm or human."

"But the humans do not care about Tchenka!"

"They will. In time. No doubt there are Tchenka for humans, as well."

Pirva, who knew what the legends said to the contrary was diplomatically silent on that point. "What if there is not enough of the web?"

"Then cut some of the second web, and of the third," said Saturday. "Each time a Tchenka is raised, you may take sections of the web, provided only you do not take too much. You must leave two thirds of it, for the sustenance of the God."

"Meantime," said Nils in a practical voice, "we must do a burial here. Who is dead today in Sarby?"

"In the town," whispered Pirva. "There are always Gharm dead in the square, where the posts for whipping are." And so speculating among themselves, they went off into the night to find which of their people had been killed that day, while Saturday and Jep went to Jep's room to sleep.

They were wakened later when the Gharm returned. Nils shook them awake and asked them to come supervise the burial, the laying of the stuff upon the dead Gharm's breast, the covering over.

"To be sure this first time we do it correctly," whispered Nils.

"His name was Lippet," said Pirva of the dead Gharm. "He was beaten to death. He was of the Water-Dragon clan. Born from the Night-bird people. His personal totem was the sky bug. What Tchenka will rise from this?"

"I do not know which one," said Saturday. "Only that one will. Or perhaps more than one."

When it was done, the Gharm stood staring at the place on the ground, now filled in, invisible, branches dragged across the soil, leaves scattered upon it to hide all evidence anything had been buried there.

"It is hard to believe," whispered Pirva, her voice catching in her throat.

"Does grain grow from the soil from seeds no one sees?" asked Saturday. "Do trees grow in cracks of the rock? There is nothing hard to believe about it. I am She-Goes-On-Creating, and I say to you that the Tchenka will return."

Pirva threw her arms around Saturday's waist and sobbed. Saturday patted her, hugged her, got her quiet again. "The Tchenka will tell you what they need. You, Pirva, and you, Nils. You are the Ones Who will hear what the Tchenka says."

"How long before we will hear?"

Jep looked at Saturday, shrugging, trying to remember, trying to translate his recollections into Voorstod days. How long had it been from the time Bondru Dharm died until Birribat Shum was raised. "As long as I have been here in Sarby," said Jep. "One hundred days, perhaps. A little longer, maybe. The longer it grows, the easier it will become for the Gharm. And the closer the time, the more you will hear the Tchenka speaking. It speaks like a dream, or like one's own voice in one's ears."

"Like a thought that will not go away," Saturday agreed. "Try to get a burial in Cloud as soon as you can." She shivered, remembering the prophet. "There is great need for it there. There's a slaughterer in Cloud, driving the people like sheep."

"Cloud is a great city," said Pirva, turning the packet of white fiber over and over in her hands. "So I am told."

"Cloud will probably need more than one burial,"

agreed Saturday. "Cloud may need many more than one. But we must start with one, as soon as possible. Then when that one is raised, more, and more, until they are everywhere."

· *While Saturday and* Jep were busy with the Gharm, Sam wandered about the edges of the forest, getting himself into endless philosophical tangles. Theseus was not with him on Ahabar, Sam was quite sure, and while he wasn't completely surprised at that, he was disturbed. He had thought that Theseus would be here with him, invisibly, perhaps, but still providing the benefit of his wider experience in travel and adventure. Theseus's not being here cast doubt upon his reality.

Though his absence might mean only that Theseus couldn't or wouldn't use a Door. Or it could mean that Theseus had reality upon Hobbs Land, but not elsewhere. Theseus might be dependent upon Hobbs Land, dependent, perhaps upon the God? In which case it was not Theseus alone who spoke, when he spoke.

Sam stood beside a tall tree and fretted over this. If Theseus was dependent upon the God, then the conversations Sam had had with Theseus had been conversations with the God. With the God pretending to be Theseus, who had, more than once, been pretending to be Phaed Girat. No one else had such conversations, not that Sam knew of. The God did not "pretend" with other people. Neither Jep nor Saturday had ever mentioned such a thing. So why pretend with him, Sam?

The idea of pretense was worrying. Was pretending the same as lying? If one, for example, "pretended" to a child and the child didn't know the difference, was that a lie? Did the God regard Sam as a child, who needed to be "pretended" to? Had the pretense been intended only as a sop, to keep him quiet for a time, until something else could happen?

And here, here on Voorstod, what was real here? Was there pretense here, as well? People pretending to do one thing while actually being something else? And why had Phaed Girat not yet come to see his son? When Theseus had played the part, Phaed had been eager to see him. Though that had not been Phaed, really, but the God pretending to be Theseus, pretending . . .

"Phaed Girat didn't know anything about their trying to get Maire back," said Jep, when he and Saturday returned from the burial and Phaed's name came up in conversation. "He didn't know they'd taken me. When he saw you all at the concert, he was angry. Surprised, and angry."

"He didn't know?" Sam asked, becoming in that instant wholly confirmed in his opinion that Phaed had been much maligned. Then again, more surely, "He didn't know!"

"He didn't know," Jep confirmed. "But he's one of them, Sam. He really is."

Sam did not hear the warning. He sat smiling, vindicated. Jep fingered his collar and wondered if any of them were ever to be free again. Of course, if they lived until the Tchenka rose up, assuming they did rise up, they would probably go free then. If it worked in Voorstod as it worked on Hobbs Land. If the Voorstoders weren't immune. If the three of them lived that long.

Saturday stayed at his side, sharing his fear, worrying over Sam, who was not afraid. "He's crazy," Africa had said. "He may do something crazy." Fear, Jep and Saturday thought, would have been more sensible than this calm acceptance.

Late on the second day, Mugal Pye came to demand that Saturday write to Commander Karth saying that she would be raped and then tortured to death if the blockade were not immediately raised.

Saturday had been working at controlling her fear since she had entered Voorstod. Since the burial here in Sarby, she had felt more sure of her way, almost as though the new thing growing gave strength to the old thing she carried within her. She had resolved that no matter how much she feared, she would not be moved by threats. "No," she said to Mugal Pye, in a voice that shook only a little. "No." Her throat dried, and she could say nothing more.

Sam put his hand upon her shoulder and faced Pye

with burning eyes, finding a new justification for his own presence at this confrontation. "If you send such a letter, the army of Ahabar won't just sit on your borders. They're being patient now because Maire Manone has asked them to, because she doesn't want more bloodshed. You do something nasty or outrageous to this child, and the army won't wait any longer. If you want the army to stay where it is, do what you have agreed to do. Send us out of here, then Maire Manone will return."

"I spoke to the girl!" thundered Pye.

"But I'm speaking to you," shouted Sam, just as loudly.

Saturday had found her strength. "Kill me or not, torture me or not, I will write nothing."

Mugal went away in a fury and did not come back again. There was much hindsight being explored on the matter of Stenta Thilion, and those who had committed the deed were not in good odor among the prophets in Cloud or elsewhere in Voorstod. Mugal had wanted very badly to hurt Saturday just now, as he would have hurt any of his own womenfolk or children who offended him, but he had not dared.

More days passed. On the fourth day, Preu Flandry and two other men showed up with a device to unlock the collar Jep wore. They took it off of Jep, then the two men held Sam while Preu fastened it upon him. The men went away. Sam shouted at Preu, calling him such names as he knew, which were not much to a Voorstoder. Preu was not impressed.

"Yell all you like, Sam Girat."

"This wasn't the agreement!"

"We made no agreement except to trade the boy for Maire. Well, he'll be traded. You've no one to blame but yourself for coming along unasked and unwanted. We could have kept the girl, too, but we decided not." The younger prophets had decided not. The prophets had wanted no excuse for an invasion. "Settle yourself, man, you sound like a fool. Your father wants to see you, and the collar'll keep you where he can find you."

Sam took a deep breath and told the children to go.

"They must let you go as well!" Jep cried.

"Go," said Sam, shaking the boy by the shoulders, adding softly, "Jep, my father wants to see me. You heard Flandry say so. Go. My father won't hurt me. I know that."

They didn't *know.* They only hoped. Still, some hope was better than none. There was no time to say goodbye to Nils or Pirva. Within moments Preu had dragged the two young people into the flier and they were aloft, flying swiftly eastward, then south along the mountains.

Preu said, "The prophets want you out—not the Awateh, but the others, the younger ones. They figure you're dangerous to have around. If you stay, the Awateh will eventually get hold of you and learn you're the girl who sang, and then he'll make an example of you, and no one knows what Ahabar would do if that happened. The prophets tried a few things, sending messages of various sorts to Maire and the Commander. He didn't answer at all, and she sent them all back, saying no and no and no, she'd come in when you came out, and that was all. She could do nothing about the blockade."

"She told you the truth," said Jep. "She did everything she could in keeping it merely a blockade and not an invasion. Why are you keeping Sam?"

"Ah, well, who knows? We did a deed the prophet approved of. Then, when we'd done it, the prophet didn't approve and he insulted Phaed a bit. So Phaed wants some of his own back, and snatching Sam away under the nose of the prophet, that's part of it, no doubt. Then, too, Phaed simply wants Sam. Sam's his son, after all. The prophets aren't to know we've kept him with us, and if you value his life, you'll be quiet about it."

"How can we be quiet? The whole Ahabarian army will see he didn't come back with us."

"True," mused Preu. "All too true, but Phaed says he'll take that chance."

"I'm not sure Maire will come in, with Sam still here."

"We think she will. Phaed says she will. With everyone in such a temper at Phaed, he's turned to brooding on the wrongs life deals to a dedicated man. I suppose it's only right the old man should have something for all his time and effort, since he got no thanks for it."

Saturday sighed. "Why does the prophet want to kill us?"

"The Awateh?"

"Yes. What have we done that he should want to kill us?"

"Nothing," Preu said, shaking his head. "Or nothing much. He still doesn't know you're the girl who sang, there at the concert, so it isn't that. Mostly it's just that you're not one of us. If you're not one of us, you're an unbeliever. Everyone not part of us is part of the devil: you, the people of Ahabar, the people of Phansure, everyone. Our Cause is to destroy the devil, all of it. We're the only true followers of God. We have the truth. It was revealed to us, long ago, on Manhome."

"But the women don't act as you do," said Saturday. "The priests aren't like you."

"The priests are left over from another tribe. They were driven out when we were. Our leaders were Voorstod and the prophets. They made a compromise. They let the priests live, but on the final day, when our Cause is fulfilled, we will kill all the priests. On that day all the women will go into seclusion, like the wives of the prophets, and they will not need priests ever again." Preu sighed. "Do not think ill of the Awateh. He is impatient, that's all. He's dying. He's waited all his life for the final days to come, and he wants to see it happen, before he dies."

Jep could not believe it. "He really wants everyone dead except his own people?"

Preu bridled at his tone. "Don't say 'he' in that manner, boy. He wants no more than all of us." His voice had turned ragged, and he breathed heavily.

"You believe that, too?"

"Of course I believe it. It is my Cause. It was my father's Cause, and his father's before him. Even on Manhome we killed the unbelievers." He stared at Saturday with wide, unfocused eyes, as though saying the words had put him into some beatific state. His voice rose into a chant. "We killed many. Our slaughterers went among the sheep and put the knives to their throats. We shattered them in the air. We slaughtered them upon the sea. We took them hostage and made great countries pay ransom. But evil men came against us in great numbers and drove us into the wilderness. . . ." He was in an ecstasy of recollection.

Saturday listened, trying not to feel. She hated him. She hated what he said, what he stood for. To her, he seemed totally evil, as did all his prophets and his friends. The world he saw was not the world she knew. She wanted to kill him and knew she could not. Her mind and belly burned, as though with fire. Her throat was tight. She hurt, and there was not enough of Birribat Shum left inside her to stop the pain.

"What will you do if Ahabar invades?" Jep asked, after the chanting had stopped and Preu's breathing had become more or less normal.

"Ahabar won't invade," he said calmly. "The prophets say it won't. Almighty God told them so."

The flier set down beside a barricade at the southern border of Skelp. Maire came running toward them as they got out of the flier.

"They kept Sam?" Maire whispered, horrified.

"They said Phaed wanted to get to know him. We left Sam in Sarby. They said you would come in even if they kept Sam."

"Oh those evil men!" Maire gripped Saturday's shoulder. "You were successful?"

"In Selmouth and in Sarby we were successful," said Saturday. "After those two, we turned it over to the Gharm. They know what's to be done. Cloud and Scaery next. Then everywhere. As soon as they can. It will take a while, Maire. We did the best we could."

"So," Maire mused. "Sam and I need only survive against hostility for a time. Perhaps not too long. Perhaps we can last long enough."

"The prophets may kill you, Maire. They want to kill someone!"

"In Voorstod, death waits at every door. If I don't go, they'll surely kill Sammy, and he's my son."

"They'll expect you to sing."

"A doctor here has looked at my throat. He says I have a growth there. Perhaps Phaed will believe it, or their own doctors will confirm it. Perhaps that will take long enough. Also, there is the blockade . . ." Her voice trailed away. "I have convinced the Queen that she must not invade Voorstod, not just yet, but she gets very angry. I have explained what I can to Commander Karth. He will try to reason with her. The army must not go into Voorstod. Not yet." '

"We know," Saturday soothed.

"What news of Stenta Thilion?" asked Jep.

Maire's eyes filled. "She died. Yesterday. She never came to herself again. When it happened, the Queen wanted to wipe out Voorstod in that moment. I pled with the Queen myself, urging her to be patient. For the sake of the Gharm."

She picked up her pack and went out the door. At the door she paused to say, "I told the Queen that Stenta's body should be kept for a time, then brought here to Green Hurrah where a great tomb will be built by the Gharm to receive her. I don't know if she believes me, but it made her feel better."

Across the barricade, Preu Flandry waited.

"Will you take me to my son?" Maire called in her rough, husky voice.

"That's where Phaed is," called Preu. "You can have a family reunion."

Maire took Saturday into a close embrace, then Jep, then crossed the barrier to the flier.

"So you keep your word, Maire Manone," said Preu Flandry.

"So I always have," she said. "Would others in Voorstod had always done the same."

· *At Authority, Rasiel* Plum had put four of Cringh's questions to the Religion Advisory. The Advisory was extremely curious as to what had provoked such interest, and Rasiel had replied—when hard-pressed— that he had become interested in the subject when the Native Matters Advisory discussed the Departed on Hobbs Land. Rasiel made the connection between Thyker and Hobbs Land simply enough. Zilia Makepeace had asked questions about Hobbs Land temples and Gods. A Baidee team had gone to Hobbs Land and subsequently a Baidee had asked questions about Gods. The connection between the two events was clear, and Plum was sure that Cringh's questions did, in fact, refer to Hobbs Land and the Departed.

"But the Owlbrit are all dead," commented various members of the Religion Advisory. "And their Gods are dead."

"True," said Rasiel. "The questions are theoretical. As Chairman of Native Matters Advisory, however, I am very interested in what you think about the questions."

What they thought about them was the subject of violent argument extending far into the late hours, and continuing day after day. The Archives were searched. Historic parallels were invoked. Gods immanent and transcendent were cited. Deified personages of various races were listed. Everyone admitted that there was no exact parallel for the Hobbs Land Gods. Nowhere else had there been Gods who had been present, living, but not of the dominant or any other known race.

Surprisingly to Cringh, it was the religionists of Phansure who were most positive in their assertions that a God might adopt a people and that it was almost certainly the God's doing if that people subsequently became holy. According to the Phansuris, there was no lack of Gods who might do such things. On Phansure there were many, at least one for each village or town: Gods who were undemanding but responsive to prayer, Gods supportive of life and pleasure, Gods who were nice to have about. Every Phansuri home had its shrine to one or more of them. Phansuri Gods were powerful, but occasionally fallible, as humans were, and the more comforting for that. Beyond the many Gods, of course, the Phansuris believed in a single, unified ethical system which ruled the universe, but this was of interest mostly to ethicists and philosophers. Laymen among Phansuris felt day-to-day life was sufficiently demanding that they did not concern themselves with ultimate causes.

An Advisory member from Voorstod, the prophet, shouted that Phansure opinion was nonsense. Phansuris were known to buy and sell their Gods, buy and sell their religion! Holiness, said the prophet, consisted in doing what God wanted as revealed through his prophets. There was no other holiness, so the question about holiness was moot.

Your religion has no room for goodness and joy, said the Phansuris to the Voorstoders. People had to consider goodness and joy.

Goodness be damned, said the Voorstoder, the only goodness that counted was doing God's Holy Will. The only joy would be found in Paradise.

The Voorstoders took joy in killing people, accused the Ahabarian Bishop Absolute with a snort. Did the Voorstoders also consider that holy?

Right, said the Voorstoder, eyes glowing and fists clenched. When that's what God wants, right.

Back off, said the Ahabarian Importunaries, don't breathe on the Bishop.

A real God wouldn't want any such thing, said those from Ahabar whose Lady of Peace was much honored in Fenice.

Could we concentrate on the first question? pleaded the acting Chairman. Can we define God?

God is He Who revealed Himself to our ancestors, declared Voorstod. God is He Who has come with us all the way from Manhome. God is He Who declared the Holy War, who set swords into our hands, who gave us Paradise as a reward for death in battle. God is He Who has always said He is a jealous God. God is He who created Hell for all unbelievers and speaks through the prophets.

The highest God is the ethos of the universe, said a Phansuri scholar. The creative principle.

But can we *define,* begged the Chairman.

The Official Advisory struggled with definition. Each night Notadamdirabong Cringh returned to his suite, to the comforting arms of Lurilile, shaking his head at the interesting futility of it all.

"Not getting anywhere, are they?" commented Lurilile, so interested in what was going on she forgot, for once, her mission upon Authority.

"Not getting far," agreed the Notable Scholar. "I wonder whether this matter will turn out to be significant?"

• *To Sam, spending* the first night of Maire's captivity, the matter was already significant, though he was unaware of the religious argument going on.

"This Awateh," he told Maire, soon after she had joined him, "wanted Saturday and me both killed. You never told me about him, or any of the prophets." Without meaning to, he said it accusingly.

Maire shook her head wearily. She had only been in Voorstod for part of a day, and the place already pained her like a fresh wound, throbbing and hot. "Sam, you never listened when I talked about Voorstod. Besides, when I grew up in Voorstod, I never saw the prophets." She rubbed her forehead. There was an ache there that threatened to become more than mere pain. "It isn't as though the prophets wandered about the town where a woman might run into them. They stayed in the citadels, praying or teaching or reading their scriptures. So it was said."

"Who provided their food?"

"They had Gharm servants. And only their Gharm servants came into the town except very occasionally when they had a religious procession, with prophets taking part. When they did that, the men and boys went out in the street; women and girls were expected to go to the backs of the houses and hide their faces. Very daring women peeked out between the curtains, but every girl or woman knew if a prophet saw you and looked you in the eye, you'd swell up and die."

"Having seen a few, I've no doubt of it," he said, trying to make a joke of it. He had been unable to reconcile the reality of the prophets with his thoughts about his father. The father-king did not fit in well with what he had seen of the prophets, and he struggled with this dichotomy.

"Have you seen Phaed?" she asked.

"No," he replied. "Did you talk to Jep about Phaed, when he and Saturday returned?"

She shook her head, wonderingly.

"Jep says he was at the citadel in Cloud when Phaed learned you were coming back. He knew nothing about it. I'm not sure he even knows you're here."

She turned a dumbfounded face upon her son. "Phaed didn't know?"

"Jep says not."

She became very thoughtful. "Son. Listen to me. Suppose you were right about the reason they brought me here. Suppose it was a silly business of convincing women to stay in Voorstod—or to come back if they had escaped to better places. Then the thing happened in Fenice, which they planned to happen, but now there is this blockade, which they never counted on. And now the Awateh wants you dead, and Saturday, and probably me, too, which means . . . which means what?"

"That their earlier reason for the plot no longer seems so valid. Or that the blockade has driven it from their heads."

"Say the first is true. That their reason doesn't seem so important anymore. That they don't need the women to come back."

"Because?" asked Sam.

"Because . . . because something important, Sam. What could it be? And Phaed knew nothing about it. I don't understand it. I don't understand it at all."

He understood it no more than she did. They offered one another possible solutions, none of which was satisfying. Maire fretted and rubbed her brow and lay quiet with her eyes closed, trying not to think of anything. Sam could not leave the area of the farm, because of the collar. The two of them were trapped, not knowing how long it would take for the trapper to come by and decide whether they were to be turned loose or skinned and eaten.

Sam wanted Phaed to come. When Phaed came, it would all be straightened out. Phaed had no intention of hurting either of them, or letting anyone else hurt them. When his mother wept, full of frustration and fear, he sat beside her and held her hand.

"Let's take it day by day, Mam. Sooner or later somebody is going to have to talk to us."

· *Phaed came up* the hill a few days later to talk with his wife and son. He came ostensibly alone—that is, without his usual comrades—for reasons of his own, not least because he had come to distrust his fellow conspirators. Things had turned sour, with much pointing of fingers and laying of blame, and he wanted no one overhearing what he said and then quoting it to his disadvantage. Also, Mugal Pye had recommended that Phaed leave Sarby without seeing Maire or Sam, and Phaed was angry at the suggestion. Everyone seemed intent upon doing things behind his back, and he told himself he would make his own decisions—but still, he brought three bullyboys along, though he left them outside in the mists.

The two prisoners were seated before the smoky fire, drinking an infusion of familiar fragrant herbs that Maire had found growing at the edge of the woods. In the steam of the kettle she had momentarily forgotten her fears. The sweet smell reminded her of similar times during childhood, before she knew enough to be afraid, for herself or for anyone. So Phaed saw her, first, as a woman not unlike the girl he had known, her eyes clear and her face untroubled.

"Well, Maire Manone," he said, almost fondly.

"Well, Phaed," she responded, as though she had been expecting him at any moment. Inside herself she felt only dismay. She had thought he would have changed, but he had not changed at all. He was older, but unchanged. Like stone, he had only weathered. She stood up to face him.

"Dad," said Sam, standing up cautiously. "I've been hoping you'd come."

"So this is Samasnier," Phaed said, looking him up and down. "He's grown some in thirty-odd years. But then, so have you, my bird. You're fatter."

"Some women get fatter when they get gray," she said, showing no spark at his words. He had once enjoyed teasing her into anger, making her lose both temper and control. He had been able to do it easily. She wondered if he still could. Not by talking about her weight or appearance, certainly. She did not care that much about either.

"I've been getting messages every day," Phaed confided, shutting the door behind him, shuffling across the room to lean on the back of a chair between them. "Messages from this one and that one, tellin' me what ought to be done with you two. The Awateh wants you, Maire. He wanted you before, you understand. So I'm told. As a symbol. They tell me you were to be the centerpiece of some great recruitment of females."

Maire smiled, a sad, reluctant, and fearful smile. "So Sammy thought, Phaed. He guessed that's what it was."

"Well, but now, with this blockade, poor old prophet's forgotten what he wanted you for in the first place. Furious, he is. Like an old bull, running after some little cow, willing to kill her to stop her running off."

"It seems I've nowhere to run to, Phaed."

"Everyone's thinking of letting him have you, just as a sop, to keep him quiet. Poor old man, he's half mad now, thinks he's going to die with none of the Great Work accomplished." He stared at Sam, making it a contest.

Sam stared back, expressionlessly. There was no contest between them. Why did his father want to challenge him? Hadn't he come here of his own free will?

"Great Work?" he asked.

"The final victory of Almighty God," said Phaed, with a grin. "In the book it is revealed that we shall put whole worlds to the sword." Phaed dusted off a chair and sat down. "So say the prophets, and since they say it, so do I."

"You never spoke so directly when I was with you, Phaed," said Maire softly. "I never heard you say out straight you were a killer."

Sam started to protest that Phaed had not said he was a killer, but then did not. It wasn't the time.

"The Book of the Prophets is a men's book," Phaed replied. "We don't go around quoting it to women. I'm not telling it to you now. You merely overhear it as I tell it to my son. Such is allowed. Women may learn by overhearing. They are so contrary, they will not learn what they are told directly. I learned that with you, Maire."

Maire nodded. "It's true, Phaed. I do not much like your prophets. There is too much death in them."

"You don't need to like them," grinned Phaed, with a sidelong grin at Sam, as though to say, we men understand these things. "You have not had the sword revealed to you in all its glory. We are the descendents, followers of blood and the blade, Voorstod and the prophets."

Sam shook his head. He did not believe his father really meant this. "Those were among the legends Maire left behind," said Sam softly, reaching for his mother's hand. "Left behind wisely, it seems, whether she knew them or not. You need not speak to her so."

"She was always a weeper," said Phaed in a sentimental tone. "But then, many women are. It is part of their infirmity. So, Maire, are you ready to sing for us to bring our women home? The Awateh will recollect, eventually, what he wanted you for, but I can keep you safe, at least until then, perhaps longer."

Sam caught his breath. So, so, he would keep her safe. He had known that. His father could not do anything else.

"I cannot sing," she choked. "The doctor says I have a growth in my throat. Your own doctors can look at it to see I tell you the truth. I will do what else I can, according to my word."

Phaed stood up and stared for a long moment, seeing through her to the child he had married once. He remembered things about Maire Manone. He remembered her skin, her eyes, the little cries she made when he took her, there on the floor before the fire, with the Gharm watching from the corners, him heated by their eyes and her red as a flower from embarrassment. He had not thought he'd regretted her going. He had not thought he'd looked forward to her return, either, but obviously he'd fooled himself. He had wanted her back.

"Well then," he said cheerily, without changing expression. "It seems I must keep you safe from the Awateh. How shall I go about that?"

"I wouldn't know, Phaed," she said.

"I suppose you'll do well enough here," he said. "For the time." He did not wait for a reply. He stood and

walked toward the door. "Come with me, Sam," he said.
"Or lose your head."

Sam gaped at him. "You're leaving Mam here alone?"

"Come with me. Leave the woman here while I decide
what's to be done with her. We're goin' down to Sarby.
Come or have your head blown off, it's all one to me." He
belied this by grasping Sam's wrist. Sam threw off his
father's hand. Phaed whistled and three large men came
through the door behind him. Sam fought them, Maire
fought them. Maire was beaten down upon the hearth and
Sam was dragged away. As Phaed went out the door, he
looked back once, chuckled, and shook his head.

"You never learn, do you, Maire," he said, going out
into the eternal fogs. "Women never learn," again, coming
back from the mists. "Women never learn." Like a chant.

"Oh, Holy Mother," whispered Maire, the words
coming from her childhood among the priests, long for
gotten. "What will he do to Sam?"

"Mam!" cried Sam from the mists. He could not even
fight them because they had twisted a kind of net around
him and were carrying him on a pole like some trussed-up
animal. It occurred to him even as he twisted and
wrenched his body that these men had had experience in
taking captives. Most of their captives had no doubt been
Gharm, small men and women, but the procedure worked
as well for him. Overwhelming force, a net to force immo
bility, and then jeering laughter and twisting fingers thrust
through the mesh to cause additional pain and humilia
tion.

Nils and Pirva slipped through the door behind Maire
and helped her get up. She staggered on her feet, unable to
see clearly. "You must come with us," Nils whispered.
"Even if Phaed Girat intends for you to be safe here, there
are other men who know you are here and who would
take you to the prophet for what credit it will gain them.
Men like Mugal Pye and Preu Flandry. Once they know
Phaed Girat has been here and gone, those men may come
to hunt you down, with sniffers. You must go."

"I can never escape being tracked that way," sobbed
Maire.

"With us, you can. Now come. At once." He picked

up her hair brush, a notebook she had left lying by the fire. Pirva folded her nightshirt and thrust it into the pack. There was nothing else in the room that belonged to Maire.

"We should try to help Sam!" Maire cried. "That thing around his neck . . ."

"Sam won't be hurt," said Pirva. "We have spies there, where Phaed Girat lives. He has the thing to take the collar off. Phaed Girat doesn't mean to hurt him. He wants to . . . to convince him."

"Convince him of what, for God's sake?"

"Convince him that Phaed is right," said Pirva. "That the Cause is just. He will not hurt him so long as he can convince him."

They dragged at her, urging her to follow them. Slipping the pack straps over her shoulders, she followed Nils through the inner door, back through a half-wrecked building and out the opposite side, for once thankful for the thick, cottony fogs that wrapped them all.

"The fogs will be thick tonight," said Pirva. "Some of us will come behind and erase your trail. The men have sniffer animals, sniffers they use to find escaped Gharm, but we know how to send them awry. We have the scent of a female at breeding time, and with this we have already made a false trail, leading far away. So we do when we escape."

Within moments they were inside the forest, headed up the slope. They walked, stumbling in the dark, seeming to cover very little ground. Time went by, and they heard movement far behind them, faint shouts and the blat of a horn.

"Too close," said Pirva. "Too close."

"The false trail was laid this afternoon," grunted Nils. "Our wise-gems say there is truth in your songs. They want you to be safe. Come only a little farther to the place the false trail starts, then we may rest."

They went between two stones and then down a declivity, while frantic activity took place behind them.

"The false trail starts between those stones and goes very far up," whispered Nils. "But you will go down. Down is faster. We can get more distance between."

Behind them a sound halfway between a cough and a bay, char-ugh, char-ugh, singly and in chorus.

"Sniffers," whispered Nils. "Good noses. They have also very good hearing. Lie quiet."

They lay in the litter under the trees, leaf smell in their nostrils, trying not to breathe too loudly. Above them on the slope the noises grew louder, more shouts, more snorts, then the confused sounds retreated up the hill. When the sounds dwindled, Nils poked Maire and beckoned. They went straight along the slope, putting maximum distance, whispered Nils, between them and where the hunters would end up. Behind them were little rustlings in the woods.

"Gharm, putting different stinks on your trail," said Nils in an almost normal voice. "Stinks that go off in all directions."

"You're good at this," remarked Maire.

"We have learned it for four hundred years," said Nils. "And we go on living. So our people run away; so our people are saved from sniffing out; so our people achieve freedom."

"Do you know who's hunting me?"

"It isn't Phaed. He went away. So it is probably Mugal Pye. They had an argument, Phaed and Mugal Pye. They snarled and insulted one another. Now each does things to annoy the other, each lies to the other, each plots against the other with the prophets. So our people say."

"Where are we headed?"

"Where we can hide you for a long time," said Nils. "Until we see whether the Tchenka will come to us as you said. If they do, then you are our mama-gem. Saturday and Jep are our mama-gem. You are our own blood, our own clan, our own people."

"And if the Tchenka don't come?"

"It would be cruel," Nils said, sadly. "You would have done a cruel thing."

"The Tchenka will come," said Maire. "They came to us. They will come to you."

"So Saturday said," Nils replied. "But we must see for ourselves. We do not believe human promises."

They stopped beside a stone. Another Gharm stood

there, waiting. "This is Finner," said Nils. "He takes you from here. Pirva and I must not be gone when the farmer returns, when the men come down from the mountain."

"Can I go back later?" she begged. "Maybe help Sam?"

"We will help him as we can," said Nils. "He will not be out of our sight. Think now of yourself."

Maire shrugged. She was not even sure why she was here, except to save Jep. Jep was saved. Perhaps it didn't matter anymore where she was, or what she did.

Finner beckoned and set off along the slope. Maire followed.

The night went by in long traverses, ups and downs, led by this Gharm and that Gharm. So far as Maire could tell from the stars, they were headed south, into the mountains which lay between Sarby and County Kate. The men who were tracking her had been led westward, toward the sea.

"At the end of the trail we have laid for the sniffers, the men will find boats," said the Gharm who was leading her. "One boat will be missing, the others will have their bottoms bashed in. They will think you have gone out toward the blockade."

"They'll think I made it to the blockade ships? They'll stop looking?"

"So we hope."

"And where will I be?" asked Maire, wearily. "Aside from half-dead of walking."

"Nearby here," their guide told them. "In a cave. It is warm and dry. It is in a place where the wind blows the fog away often. We have supplied it with food. There is water. We are not cruel."

It seemed to be important to the Gharm that she believe this. Maire nodded, accepting it. When she came to the cave, she found it to be as represented, a perfectly habitable space. She lowered herself to one of the pads waiting on the floor and pulled the folded blankets over her, so weary she could move no more.

"Very well," she said. "You are not cruel."

"Sleep," said the Gharm. "We will watch over you."

FIVE

• *"I can walk,"* Sam snarled at the men carrying him. "Put me down and let me walk."

"Put my son down," said Phaed, feigning surprise. "Don't you hear him saying he can walk?"

They put him down, though they did not turn him loose. Sam's hands were tied behind him in a particularly painful way, and Phaed held the end of the rope that bound them. The three burly men who had helped Phaed walked off into the mists, though whether they left or merely walked out of sight among the fogs, Sam could not tell.

"Where are we going?" he asked, trying to sound calm and unangered, though his entire nature screamed with outrage.

"To Sarby," said Phaed. "We've rooms there, just off the square. You'll stay with me for a while."

Sam grated, "I'd feel more like your son, Dad, if you took off these ropes and if I knew that Maire was all right. You don't need to tie me, and those men of yours didn't need to hurt her the way they did!"

Phaed answered unhesitatingly, "Well, of course, boy, you're right, they didn't. It was a reaction, that's all. If she'd kept to herself, the men wouldn't have touched her, but Maire was always one to interfere in what was none of her affair. She knows she's in no real danger. I was only jesting with her, there, a little malice from old times. She understood what I meant. Women in Voorstod don't oppose their menfolk, but Maire never could get that through her head. Thick, some women. They just won't learn. . . ."

Sam heard both the words and the tone. The words were reassuring, but there was a devious gloating in the voice. Which didn't mean, at the end, that Phaed was necessarily a villain. Sam thought he understood Phaed's nature, one that always did and said two things at once, never clearly, never being caught by a promise. Phaed had hit Maire, yes, but then men did beat women in Voorstod; Maire had said as much. Sam didn't like it, but it wasn't peculiar to Phaed. It was a cultural thing. Legends were full of such things. One couldn't argue with things that simply were. He swallowed anger.

The meadow was long grasses, wet with mist, and trousers wet to the knees. The bridge across the river was echoing wood and the glimpse of railings through the fog. The street was the sound of boots on stone, until suddenly the wet veils lifted to show the town square, where the gate of the citadel gulped wide, a dark, insatiable maw. It was not as monstrous as the edifice in Cloud, but the slitted windows of its tower were high enough to look down on all the town. Behind those windows a gray light moved to and fro, as though someone searched for something in the drawing darkness.

"The citadel," said Phaed, gesturing, staring upward, almost hungrily.

"I know," Sam replied, following Phaed's fascinated gaze. "I saw the one in Cloud. And the Awateh, the crazy prophet."

Phaed jerked on the rope, pulled him off balance, and struck him hard across the face. "The Awateh is *my* prophet," he hissed. "No unbeliever has the right to insult him."

Sam went to one knee and stayed there, even when Phaed tugged at the rope. The square was centered on a smaller square of posts, four across, four deep, with manacles attached by iron bands at shoulder and ankle level. "Whipping posts?" Sam muttered, disbelieving. He had seen such things, but only in the Archives.

Phaed jerked him to his feet. "For Gharm and backsliders, boy. Gharm are whipped by their masters or the pastors, backsliders by Faithful chosen for the duty."

A school stood beyond the whipping posts. Sam imagined the lessons, arithmetic and reading and information stage exercises, each underlined by the rhythm of the lash.

"I imagine the children play at whippings a great deal," he said, getting a picture of such play, like a shocking vision. He thought the name *Fess,* wondering where he had heard it. Fess. Something Maire had said.

Phaed nodded, yawning ostentatiously. "With animals, or Gharm brats."

"I imagine sometimes play gets out of hand and an animal or Gharm child dies." The picture came again. A bed. A small form. A spatter of black.

"There are always more of them," said Phaed. "Enough of this commentary, now. Our house is just down the street."

He twitched the rope, making Sam groan, drawing him a bit farther down the street, through a heavy door and up a flight of narrow stairs, where Sam pulled himself erect and turned to face the older man.

"I've told you we don't need this rope. I came of my own will, Dad. Let's talk like men."

There were footsteps on the stairs. Phaed's eyes were opaque as he agreed. "Sure, boy, sure. But later. I've things to see to now."

He opened an inner door, dragged Sam through, removed the collar with a device from his pocket, then untied Sam's hands.

"We'll talk later, boy. But for now you'll stay here. Don't try the door, it's too thick for you to break, and there's bars on the windows." He went out, and the sound of the lock clicking shut came muffled through the heavy wood.

Sam could not remember ever feeling so helpless, so impotent. When Phaed looked at him, he looked through him, as though he saw something else beyond, some shadow Sam, some expected presence incongruent with the reality. Sam clutched his arms around himself, assuring himself that he existed in his own flesh and had not faded to shadow. He could not hear anything except his own voices gibbering at him. This is your dad, he kept telling himself. This is the dad he'd come between worlds to meet. This was the dad he had endowed with the stuff of legends. He did not remember a legend in which a father dragged his son off like a victim and imprisoned him.

"Lie," he told himself. He was lying to himself. In the legends, fathers did exactly that, sometimes. Except, in the legends, it was because they did not know who their sons were! Perhaps the father had the word of an oracle and misunderstood it, or the father did not know he had a son. In the legends, things always worked out that the son came unheralded, unrecognized, but was accepted once his identity was revealed.

Could it be that Phaed did not accept him for who he was?

Sam went to the window. Phaed had told him no more than the truth. The window was too small for him to get through and was also tightly barred. It looked down onto the street and a corner of the square, and he could see and hear those who passed by. He wondered if any one of them would respond if he yelled and felt it was unlikely.

Tapping his way around the room he found that the walls were stone. There was only the one door, heavy and solid as a table. If he put his ear to it, he could hear sounds, barely, the clink of glasses and the mutter of voices. Phaed was drinking with someone—plotting, his mind said, and he sternly rebuked himself.

Back at the window he glared at the street where groups of men went by, in threes and fours. One corner of the citadel gate was barely visible, and he could see men passing through. Passersby in the street showed up clearly in the light thrown by Ninfadel. The moon was directly above, making no shadows.

It was senseless. He had come to meet his father, so why was he captive? He had come of his own will, so why was he a prisoner? He was willing to meet, to talk, to learn, even, and he was shut away alone. The thing was crazy. Phaed could not doubt who he was!

And where was Maire? Up the hill, at the farm? Safe before the fire, with the Gharm providing food, as they had done yesterday and the day before? Why hadn't she been brought here with him? Did she realize that he had no choice but to leave her? Did she realize he had been forced away? She could not believe he had simply gone, leaving her to whatever fate Phaed planned. He had not intended to leave her, and he prayed that she knew that. Though why would she know it?

Because, he told himself, she knows I love her and would not leave her.

How would she know that?

Bleakly, he considered whether Maire had evidence of his affection. Had he ever told her he loved her in a way that made her know he meant it? Had he shown her in any way? He remembered throwing words, like a bone to a hungry dog. "Oh, yes, Mam, I love you, too." Bones of love, without much meat; dutiful attention to occasion, but no spontaneous expressions. A bouquet on her natal day. A bottle of wine at First Harvest. And what else?

Nothing else.

He held the bars in his hands and strained at them, finding the pain less uncomfortable than the question. Had he ever convinced Maire that he loved her?

Did he, in fact, love her?

Perhaps he had never really thought she had earned his love. He had not forgiven her for taking him away from Voorstod. She could have left him here. She shouldn't have given him the choice. It would have been easier for her if she had left him here. He had blamed her sometimes that she had not left him with his dad, or stayed with his dad herself. He had blamed her, thinking she had cared more about Maechy than she did about Sam.

He turned from the window, running his hands along the walls, the stone walls. Out in the street there were men walking, walking among the whipping posts. Whipping posts and hooks upon the walls of the citadels, blood and pain and death. Voorstod.

Maire had never told him about the prophets, or the hooks on the walls. Would his own life end there? Did they kill their victims first? Or did they hang them on those huge sharp hooks still living? Did the metal hooks pass through living flesh, flesh that bled and writhed?

Sam found himself weeping without knowing why. He had never feared death, but now, suddenly, he trembled with fear, slumped to the floor, wept passionately, exhaustingly, until he could weep no more. He lay where he had fallen, empty, worn out from apprehension, at last falling into a doze.

A noise in the street brought him awake. The moon was now making long shadows, and the men below were half-hidden, half-disclosed by the mantic light. Mugal Pye, two other men. Their voices came clearly, a sibilant hiss meant not to be heard, but heard nonetheless through some fluke of acoustics in the narrow street. It was a white-haired man, snarling at Mugal Pye.

"What are you doing here, Pye?"

"Came here because Phaed's son's here, Preu Flandry!"

"What do you need with the son, you've got the mother."

"Hell, no, we didn't get her," Mugal snarled.

Flandry's voice, "How could you not? She's an old woman! You had men, you had sniffers with you."

Mugal Pye's voice in belligerent answer: "Because she got down to the west shore, that's why. The woman must run like a rabbit. There were some fishing boats there. Looks like she knocked holes in all of them but one, and took that one."

"Got to the blockade, did she?" Preu asked, wonderingly.

"Who knows. Got there or drowned! Though it could have been a false trail. We've got one more place to look." This was a third voice, from a man standing clearly in the moonlight.

"The Awateh wants her, Epheron Floom," hissed

Preu. "It's why I came! Giving her to Awateh will get us off the hook."

"What the Awateh wants is an example made," agreed Mugal Pye. "So if we can't find her, what?"

"If we don't find Maire, it'll have to be Phaed's boy, then," said Flandry. "He's here, and there's three of us with you, Epheron. We could get him now."

"Not so fast, not so fast," hissed Pye. "Phaed's got men up there with him. We'll wait until he leaves, until his son is alone, tomorrow . . ." Pye's voice trailed away as he went down the street, tugging on Flandry's arm.

There was no light in the room Sam was in. The men could not have known they were overheard. Sam's world gradually came into focus again. Pye and Epheron had been after Maire, but she was safe. Undoubtedly the Gharm had spirited her away. And Jep was safe, and Saturday. The army of Ahabar was on the borders of this place, and time and the Godstuff would work their spell. The forces of righteousness had conspired to help him, though he had not deserved it. He wept again, this time thankfully. He would tell Phaed about the connivance of the two. Even his own life might not be at risk.

Sam stood up and stretched, feeling something inside himself loosen and break. His life was not threatened just yet. Sometimes the only thing a hero could do was exist bravely under difficult circumstances. A hero was a hero, even in captivity. At least he could try for a certain style and dignity, a certain polish and shine. Theseus would approve of that. So he'd concentrate on surviving.

He lay down on one of the dirty beds and slept.

Phaed pulled him off the bed when it was barely light. Sam told him of the conversation he had overheard, and Phaed reacted with a sneer.

"Bastards," he said. "Oh, yes, those bastards. Well, we've planned for that!"

He tied Sam's hands in that painful way again and dragged him out into the street, across the empty square, down an alley, and into an old building that looked as though it had been deserted for years. Sam could probably have escaped; he thought he was almost as heavy as the older man, almost as muscular, but he didn't try. He had already decided he would bear his captivity and see what happened. He did not respond to Phaed's muttered comments, but merely came along, silently, unresisting.

When they had reached the derelict building, however, he asked, "Why are we here?"

"Oh, you're talkin' now, are you? Well, that's a relief. I thought there for a time you'd gone mute."

"No, not mute," said Sam. "It's just hard to talk with you because you're not what I remember."

"I'm sure Maire remembered me well enough."

"She talked of you seldom," said Sam. "I didn't believe what she said."

"What did she say?" Phaed was interested.

"She said you were a killer."

"True," said Phaed.

"That you killed women and children and other innocent people. That you hunted people down and killed them."

"Why wouldn't you believe that? Any good man of the Cause would do the same."

"I didn't believe it because I'm not part of your Cause," Sam said, barely able to get the words out. "No decent man would be part of your Cause, so no decent man would believe it."

Phaed laughed. "Oh, decent, is it? Like those dogs from Ahabar, hm? Like you farmers? Like you servants who take other men's money to do other men's will? Decent!" He hawked and spat, showing what he thought of such decency. "Slave-men. Not even free!"

"Why are we here," asked Sam, again, gesturing with his chin at the surroundings.

"We're here, boy, because the Awateh wants blood. You say my friends didn't find your Mam to give him, not that I'd intended they should."

"You arranged her escape?"

"Say I foresaw it. I may have dropped a word here and there. The Gharm are easy to manipulate with a word, here and there."

"Did she get clean away?"

"She's where I know where she is, boy."

"Why did the prophet want to kill her?"

"The Awateh's getting old and frumious. The blood of unbelievers makes him feel young again. Apostates are even better. Ordinarily, we'd go catch a few backsliders from Wander or Skelp and bring them in for the old man's delectation, but the blockade's been moved through Skelp and Wander and sits now at the border of Leeward County, so there's no apostates we can get at. We could always accuse someone of our own, but with us in our current disfavor, that might come back to roost upon our shoulders. So Flandry and Pye think you'd make a nice morsel for the old man, buy them some goodwill, which is otherwise in short supply, but I'm not of a mind to oblige them."

"Why not?"

"Why not? Well, now, I'm not sure. Could be I'm a bit upset at all the fingers pointed at me over that harpist Gharm. The Awateh and the prophets agreed she should be done, but when it went wrong, they didn't point fingers at each other. No, they pointed at Preu and Mugal Pye, and even at Epheron, who had little enough to do with it, and at *me,* boy! So I'm disinclined to give anythin' of mine to the Awateh. Let him find his fun elsewhere."

Sam was not so eager to die that he wanted to argue. "You plan to stay here?"

"Pye and Flandry've always talked too much, luckily for us. Well, so when they come lookin' for you, they'll find the house empty. Likely they'll think we two have left Sarby. Perhaps they'll think I've taken you to Cloud, so they'll go whippin' back there to protect their own interests. Meantime, I've got some things stowed about this old place, a mattress or two and a few blankets. A pot to cook a bit in. There's a stove that works in that room over there, and there's water runnin' in there, as well."

"What was this place?"

"Used to be a maternity home, with midwives and all."

"Why did they shut it down?"

"There's one in Panchytown, and that's close enough. No need for two of 'em."

Sam looked down the hall, a long hall, with empty rooms on either side. Fewer babies in Sarbytown. "Phaed, has it never occurred to you that your doctrines don't work too well."

Phaed struck him across the face, knocking him down. "Shut you, boy. I may question doctrine and I may question prophets, but you haven't earned that right. You don't question your elders, either. You'll learn."

"So you intend to keep me here. Forever?"

"Until you learn," said Phaed. "However long that takes."

• *In the cave* in the mountains south of Sarby, a day and a night went by. Maire had slept for much of it. Now she sat in the cave opening, feeling lonelier with each moment that passed, more cut off from life, more separated from her own people. She felt a part of herself was missing, and that part growing deeper and wider with every day.

"It's dying," she said to the silent Gharm beside the fire. "Inside me, I can feel it dying."

"What is dying, Maire Manone?"

"The God inside me. It's been there . . . since Sam was a child. First Bondru Dharm, then Birribat Shum. Our own thing, like your Tchenka."

"So She-Goes-On-Creating said."

"Perhaps it cannot live in any one of us alone. It needs the . . . the what, do you suppose?"

"Whatever it is that grows where we put it, beside the temple. Whatever grows in us all."

"Do you suppose I can get it back? A new one? Or when this one dies, will that have been my only chance?"

The Gharm patted her. "Maire, I am your friend. We have each other."

She wept, trying to smile through the tears. "We're so separate. Each of us, always. So separate. I first knew that when I had babies. They'd cry, and I'd try to help, try to figure out what was wrong. But they were separate, as though there was a wall between them and me. Even when they learned to talk, the wall was still there. What they said and what I heard were always different things. Between me and Sammy! A wall, like stone. He would look at me with his eyes blank, listening politely, but not hearing, not caring. And then we came to Hobbs Land. And after a time there, the wall seemed to get thinner. It wasn't that I could read his mind. I still didn't know why Sam does the things he does . . . all those books. All that reading in the Archives, all those old legends. No, it wasn't that I could read his mind, but I was beginning to see something of the mystery in him. Perhaps, if I'd been able to stay there, I would have understood him at last."

"As the Ones Who say," murmured the Gharm. "A way. A convenience. A kindness."

Maire wiped her eyes. She heard a stick crack among the trees. The Gharm stiffened and crouched.

"A kindness you say?" came a voice from the forest, full of rough, gloating joy. "So we've found you, Maire Manone!"

They stepped out of the trees. Mugal Pye and half a dozen other men, all wearing the large caps of the Faithful. The Gharm tried to run, but they caught him and killed him before her eyes, as though they were killing a chicken. Then they turned to her.

"Phaed spoke to us of this place long ago, Sweet Singer. No doubt he forgot he told us of it. When we did not find you at the shore, we thought to try here. Pity. You gave us a good run."

Maire rose. So. So she had come home again to all the legends she had left behind.

"Where will you take me?" she asked, already knowing.

"To the prophet Awateh," Mugal Pye said with a sly grin. "And we will not bother to tell old Phaed we're on the way."

· *Daytimes, Sam was* chained to a post in an upper corner room of the building. The chain was long enough that he could get from his mattress to the toilet. It was long enough that he could sit at a window, looking out.

Nights he sat on the mattress while Phaed taught him doctrine, hitting him with the butt of his whip whenever he did not respond correctly. After a time, he began responding correctly without thinking what he was saying. So animals were trained, he thought, wondering what one of the High Baidee might do under the circumstances. Find a way to commit suicide perhaps. Under ordinary conditions, Sam might have searched for a way to do just that. However, down from the hill above Sarby, something was growing. Sam knew it and hung on. Part of his strength came from conviction that things would change; part came from curiosity. He wanted to see what the God of Hobbs Land would do to Sarbytown.

"Who is the God of Voorstod?" Phaed would ask.

"The One, the Only, the Almighty God, in whose light all other gods are shown to be false idols created by men."

"What is the desire of the One God?"

"That all living things shall acknowledge Him."

"And how is this to be achieved?"

"By teaching those who will learn, and by killing all others."

"I don't understand this doctrine," said Sam.

Phaed raised the butt of his whip, and Sam fended him off. "I didn't say I disagreed with it, I said I didn't understand it. I'm asking you to explain it to me."

"What don't you understand?"

"If God is Almighty, as you say, then why doesn't he inspire all people to acknowledge him. Why be so wasteful about it?"

"What's wasteful about battle?"

"People getting killed, mostly."

"There's too many people anyhow, most places. There's always been too many men. One man can service half a dozen women or more, it's wasteful having more men around than needful, so we have wars, to clear away the excess. The stupider and slower ones die, the survivors breed. That's the way of things."

"But you don't have more women than men. You have it the other way around."

"Because we're cooped up here on Voorstod, boy! If we were free among the stars, it'd be different." Phaed's eyes glazed as they sometimes did, when he talked of being free among the stars. He had a vision of that future, which he did not share with Sam, but sometimes Sam saw him staring at a wall or out a window, his face lax, his mouth loose, his eyes alight, as though he saw Paradise.

"What will you do when you are free among the stars, Dad?"

"Oh, lad. Lad." His eyes blazed. "There'll be no end to what I'll do."

He never said more than that.

Sometimes they went up to the roof at night, Sam in his chains, Phaed with his book of doctrine, and did their lessons under the stars. From the roof, Sam could see the square clearly, the whipping posts and the gate of the citadel. There were always bodies hanging at the posts, mostly Gharm, sometimes human.

"Do they whip women?" he asked Phaed.

"Women are whipped at home," said Phaed. "Where they belong."

"Did you used to whip Mam?" Sam asked.

"Only when she needed it," said Phaed in an offhand voice. "Beatin' a woman for your own pleasure is counterproductive. There's always Gharm you can whip for fun."

"What pleasure does it give you, Dad?"

Phaed smiled, a lubricious smile, his tongue touching the corners of his lips. "I like it," he said. "You learn to like it."

Days and nights went by. One time Phaed went away for ten or twelve days, leaving Sam chained beside a store of food, reminding Sam before he went that if Sam yelled or attracted attention, the Awateh would be glad to hear of it. He left Sam another book of doctrine, *The Doctrine of Freedom,* telling him to learn it. Sam sat at a dirty window, peering down into the street, silent as a ghost, reading to himself. He was a ghost, he told himself, haunting this old building. People had been born here once. Nothing good was born here now.

"What is the place of women in the creation of the One God?"

"Women have no place. They are not followers of God, they are merely processes by which followers may be created. They are to be kept private, kept quiet, kept healthy

until they have borne children, and then they may be disposed of."

"What are the numbers of those who will acknowledge the One God in the last days?"

"If there is one, and that one the only living one, one is enough."

"What is the reward of the Faithful?"

"Paradise."

"Are there women in Paradise?"

"There are virgins in Paradise, for the pleasure of the Faithful, but they are not human women."

"I suppose you want that explained, too." Phaed sneered.

"What are these women in Paradise, Dad?"

"Pure virgins."

"You mean always?"

"Always. Every time a man takes one, she's a virgin. No other man has ever had her or ever will."

"Why would that please a man?"

"She's yours. She's tight, and it hurts her, and she cries out. Those little cries. The virgins have no thoughts. They never talk, they just sing or make those noises. Your Mam used to cry like that, at first."

Sam swallowed and chose to ignore this. "Then the women of Paradise are nothing but dolls, manikins, things for you to rape. Don't you want more than that?"

"What more than that is there, boy?"

"Don't you want to know her thoughts? Don't you want to know what she is?"

"Why would I care?" asked Phaed. "She's a woman. Nothing about her would interest me. The Almighty knows that. Why else would he put pure brainless virgins in Paradise?" He watched Sam then, seeing the expression on his face, and then he laughed, mockingly. "When I married your mam, boy, I thought I'd come close to having one ahead of time!" And he roared with laughter again.

Sam swallowed anger. "But you care for her! I know you do!"

Phaed snapped, angrily. "I do what's convenient, boy.

Perhaps soon now it will be more convenient for me to remember she left me and made me a mockery."

Sam shook his head. "You let her go, Dad. She asked you to come with her. Why pretend now that you cared?"

"Why not pretend whatever I like if it makes my life easier? We learn that, you see, we Faithful. We learn to say to ourselves whatever we need to say to make the task easy. We learn to say, 'For God and Voorstod,' when we blow up some old lady in the toilet or some schoolyard full of children. We wouldn't necessarily do it for ourselves, you see, but we can do it for God and Voorstod. It's the same thing with your mam. It may make it easier for me if I say she betrayed me."

"But it's not true," blurted Sam, unable to keep quiet.

" 'What I say ten times is true.' That's one of our proverbs. We teach the young men to fill their heads with such words. Prayers. Chants. Endless circles of noise. The same sounds repeated over and over until they fill the mind. 'Resolution is the weapon of God; thought is the enemy of resolution; words keep thought out; therefore, learn words,' say the Scriptures. Even on Manhome, our sons learned words, by rote, to keep them from the dangers of thinking. What God wants followers who think and doubt? The Almighty wants Faithful, who obey!"

Time seemed endless. Day succeeded day. Sam counted, and lost count, and counted again. At least ninety days, he thought. Certainly no less than eighty. Sam learned Scripture. Sam learned doctrine. He believed none of it, but he learned it. Between the harsh lessons he made resolutions, what he would do and say when he returned to Hobbs Land. When he returned to Maire and Sal and even China. The things he would be sure to say to the women. The things he would be sure to do for the women. So they would know he cared for them.

He had thought his pronouncement of his commitment was enough. "Marry me, China," he had said, in effect. What he had meant was, "Marry me so I can stop wooing you, stop worrying about you, stop being jealous of you. Marry me so I can put you in a box and punish you if you climb out."

And the same with Maire, and Sal. "Here's your birthday bouquet, Mam, now take this ration of reassurance and don't bother me for a season. Here's a Harvest gift, Sal, now do not pester me for more."

So much easier that way, to put them in boxes and consider that the lids would keep them safe and away from other suitors, other sons, other brothers. Particularly easy when they had no other sons, no other brothers.

Though, a voice whispered, they might find them, somewhere. Blood kinship was not the only tie of the heart.

A night came at last when they went to the roof and there were no bodies in the square, a night when Phaed kept losing his place in the book, getting angry, putting down his whip, then looking for it, and being unable to find it. At last he set the book aside and merely sat, looking out over the city. It had never happened before.

"Can we just talk?" asked Sam.

"Why?" grunted Phaed.

"The thing is," said Sam to his father. "The thing is, Dad, I want to talk to you."

"What do you want to say?" asked Phaed.

"I want to tell you this chaining me up is foolishness. I came here all the way from Hobbs Land, of my own free will, to see you."

"Well, and now you're here. Where you should be. Learning what you should have learned long since."

"Well, you could have come to me, Dad."

"Why would I have done that? What are women or brats to go running after them. A man can get another woman. A man can get other sons. There's no trick to it. You've done it yourself. That brat Jep was yours."

"You can get another son, but it wouldn't be me. You can get another wife, but she wouldn't be Maire. Surely you've remembered Maire, thought of Maire."

Phaed sniggered. "Well, of course, boy. She's my wife. Mother of my children. I always think of her as a sample of what a man should try to avoid."

"Don't you love her still?"

"I've taught you what love is, Sam. Love is the obedience to God. I wanted Maire. That's a different thing.

Men who take the chance of death in the service of the
Cause are entitled to have what they want."

"Dad."

"Yes . . ."

"I need you to explain something. About when
Maechy died."

"He died, that's all."

"Mam said you didn't grieve. She said you just cursed
the man for not shooting straight."

The huddled figure shook with laughter "Oh, I
grieved, Sam. By the Almighty, I grieved. Our one chance
at that bastard from Ahabar, and we missed it. All we
managed to do in was one infant child, and him one of
us . . ." He laughed, his jowls jiggling in the half light.

"We? Then they were your men who killed him?"

"My men? Of course they were my men. They're always my men if they're men of the Cause. Your mam
knew that well enough, that they were my men. . . ."

Sam turned away, too hardened and weary for tears.
Maire had known what Phaed was. When he really came
to it, Maire had always known, and there was nothing left
here of legends. There was no father-king. No hero. Only
what Maire had said was here, stones of hate, heavy,
heavy.

"The prophets are leaving Sarby," Phaed said suddenly. "Going to Cloud, they say. The Awateh needs
them, they say."

Sam swallowed bile. "Did the Awateh send for them?"

Phaed squinted at the sky, his mouth twisted tight. "I
don't know," he said at last. "Nobody knows. I have to go
there, find out."

"Well, if the prophets are going, you can let me loose,"
said Sam. "There'll be no one here to capture me for the
Awateh if the prophets are going."

Phaed had a crafty look. "I'm not sure that's wise."

"What about Mugal Pye, and Preu Flandry? Where
are they?"

"They haven't been back since they went lookin' for
your mam." Phaed chewed his lip and said in a distracted
voice, "If they'd found her, they'd have come back to

gloat, so I think they never found her. They may be hidin'
out."

"So let me go. I'll wait here for you." And he would.
If he could not admire the old man, he could at least
forgive him. He was no worse than the others.

"Somebody might know who you are. I'll leave you
here with plenty of food. Until I come back."

"Before you go, Dad, talk to me."

"I've talked to you until I've turned blue, boy. What
do you want to know now?"

"Aren't there any among the Voorstoders who are different? Any of the men, I mean? Aren't there any who
argue against all this whipping and killing?"

"Now and again."

"Do you ever listen to them?"

"Before we light the fire under 'em, sometimes. A little. For the laugh."

Sam shook his head, and his father patted his shoulder, almost kindly. "Don't you understand yet, boy. Once
you've been given the answers, there's no questions anymore. Once your father speaks and tells you what God
wants, you don't need to worry about it. That's the trouble with all you poor fools on Ahabar and Hobbs Land
and Phansure. All the time thinking, a servant to your
doubts, a slave to your worries. We're free men, we of
Voorstod. Free, don't you see?"

"What do you want sons for?" Sam whispered.

"To be like us, boy. To be just like us."

He went away, leaving Sam to lie on his bed and stare
at the faceless night.

The day Phaed left was the same day the prophets left,
with their wives and children, and it was also the fourth
day there had been no blood shed in Sarby, though no one
had taken overt notice of that fact. It was almost as
though the people of Sarby had agreed not to notice it.
From the roof, Sam had noticed there were no dead at the
whipping posts, though he didn't know whether it was
true elsewhere in the city as well.

On the eighth day, several Gharm slipped up the stairs
in the old building and told Sam they'd been directed by
Nils and Pirva to keep an eye on him, which they'd been

doing. By now they were pretty sure, so they said, that Phaed wouldn't return, so it was time to cut him loose. One of them had brought a cutter for the chain. They turned Sam free, suggesting that, since he had no money to take him to Green Hurrah and it was a long hungry walk, they'd heard there was a job available for a temporary manager at a farm east of town.

"No slaves there?" Sam asked, wonderingly.

"No slaves around Sarby. Not anymore."

"How long?"

They looked at one another, tallying up. "Eight days," they said, wonder on their faces.

There had been no whippings or bloodshed for all those eight days, said the Gharm, though the idea of whipping had occurred to a number of people during that time. They whispered to Sam of one housewife, furious at her cook for wasting food, who had determined to whip the Gharm half to death. The woman sat in her parlor, talking of it to herself, finding the idea satisfying. In fact, the idea was satisfying enough that she did not need the reality. It was even a bit boring, the woman said to herself aloud, so the cook could overhear her. It wasn't a new idea. Not interesting, the woman said, forgetting about it.

The Gharm cook, who had stolen the food for escapees and who had been shaking in her sandals, stopped shaking and gave thanks to her Tchenka.

And there was a gang of bullies who caught a child Gharm in an alley and decided to see how many stripes a Gharm could take before it died. However, they fell to arguing about the possible number, the argument led to ennui. They decided they were hungry and went home to eat, leaving the Gharm considerably frightened but quite alive and uninjured, to tell the other Gharm of his narrow escape.

Shallow under the soil the net had pushed its way down from the hill and under the town, moving with almost visible speed, stretching and turning, making a new track along rock, through soil, netting through gravel, burrowing through root and wall, wider and wider until it had underlain all of Sarby. Upon the hill near the farm, where the little temple had been built, the net was thick and wooly around the hard, wonderful thing it had been growing.

Though all the prophets were gone, the priests had stayed. There was no reason for the priests not to stay. In fact, there was good reason for them to continue in Sarby, for people began coming into the churches, rather vaguely, as though looking for something they had thought might be there. A ninth day went by, a tenth, an eleventh. Two full weeks, with no blood upon the stones, no blood in the soil, no *voorstods,* no whip-deaths.

• *At this same* time, in Selmouth, certain persons living in an area of town surrounding an old church and graveyard got it into their heads to build a small circular temple in the churchyard. The priest in charge of the church had no objection. Even when the stones from the cemetery were taken up and used in the building, he did not complain. Even when one wall of the church was taken down, and its stones used over, he did not think it in the least odd. As it was, the temple was done just in time, for inside a crypt in the churchyard, a crypt which had not been disturbed by the building, the people found an object which they raised and placed at the center of the new temple with a good deal of unquestioning pleasure.

Among those helping raise the object was a busy Gharm with a sharp knife and a number of film bags. No one knew who he was, but everyone agreed he was extremely helpful.

"What is this?" they had asked him, thinking he might know for they did not.

"A Tchenka," he had told them. "This is the Forest-bird Tchenka. It will take care of you. Soon, perhaps, it will walk among us." The Gharm had assigned the Selmouth God this appellative. From what She-Goes-On-Creating had told them, they felt the God would not care.

The Forest-bird Tchenka soon came to an understanding with some Voorstodian cats, and a standing order was placed for the delivery of small scaled varmints. Though there were no ferfs on Ahabar, there were other things which secreted the same substances and could be used for the same purpose.

Shortly thereafter, the Gharm accomplished three more burials at Cloud, in addition to the one that had taken place there some time before. Cloud always had corpses. Of the total of four burials in Cloud, two had been Gharm and two human, one a child. The following night there were three burials at Scaery in addition to Scaery's previous one. In addition to these six rituals, ten Gharm carrying film bags of whitish fiber were sent off into the countryside toward other Voorstod towns and hamlets. Not quite one hundred days had passed since Saturday Wilm had come to Sarby.

· *Commander Karth had* offered hospitality to Jep and Saturday when they returned from Voorstod, an offer which they had promptly accepted.

"I thought you might have to get back to Hobbs Land," the Commander had said.

Saturday had shaken her head. "No, sir. We must stay here and try to keep anyone from invading or doing anything else violent. It would be better if everything was very quiet for a time. If Jep and I are right, you will see changes start, in there."

The Commander passed this on to Crown Prince Ismer, who passed it on to his mother, the Queen, who was still in deep mourning for Stenta Thilion and still greatly desirous of exacting bloody punishment on Voorstod.

"What changes are anticipated?" she wanted to know. "Let me talk to these children."

The children were brought to Fenice and housed in the palace. They had breakfast with the Queen. She didn't want them terrified by the Privy Counselors, though, for the most part, the Counselors were far from terrible. She did ask Ornice, Lord Multron, to come along. He was too grandfatherly, she thought, to frighten anyone.

After what Jep and Saturday had been through with the prophets of Voorstod, the Queen and her counselor caused no trepidation at all.

"You may call me Ma'am," the Queen told the children. "Having children call me Pacific Sublimity always makes me want to laugh."

"Yes, Ma'am," said Saturday. "These are very good eggs."

"They are, aren't they. They are lorsfowl eggs. Do you have lorsfowl on Hobbs Land?"

"We have chickens from Manhome," said Jep, "though I think they've been elaborated somewhat to fit the environment, just as we have. And binnies. I think they were originally from Phansure."

"Thyker," corrected Saturday. "Quarshes were originally from Phansure. I do not like quarsh eggs. Binny eggs are very good, which is a pity, because the Thykerians don't eat them at all, do they?"

"Only the High Baidee reject them," offered Ornice, Lord Multron. "The other people on Thyker eat them."

Jep sighed. "I guess we didn't know there were any other people on Thyker but High Baidee. I saw some High Baidee once. They came to the settlement, but they didn't stay long."

"They were doing an Ancient Monuments survey," Saturday informed the Queen. "They were sent by the Native Matters Advisory."

"Advisories!" snorted the Queen. "Unethical. Unlawful. Bribe-taking advisories. A plague on them."

"The Religion Advisory has presumed to question our blockade of Voorstod," explained Ornice. "They wish us to remove it while they consider whether the assassination of Stenta Thilion can be considered a religious matter."

"Well, of course it can," said Jep, hotly. "I've met the prophet Awateh, and he's very religious, but he's also completely off his head. It seems to me religious toleration stops when they intend to kill you or hurt you with it. Africa, that's my aunt, she always said noninterference was a two-way street."

"See there!" crowed the Queen. "Isn't that exactly what I said, Ornice? Exactly!"

"Furthermore," said Jep, "it seems to me we've got a duty to convert the people away from such a religion as quickly as possible. Before they kill anybody else."

"Ah," said the Queen. "And is that what you've been doing, by any chance."

Jep looked at his feet, flushing.

"Your Sub . . . Ma'am," said Saturday, "would you think it dreadfully impolite of us if we didn't tell you what we've been doing. Shouldn't, I mean. We can tell you what to expect, if that would be all right."

"By all means," said Wilhulmia, intrigued. "What shall we expect."

Saturday cleared her throat. "Some time fairly soon you should expect some of the people in Voorstod to come to the border and say they want to leave. Jep and I are pretty sure about that. If peace comes to Voorstod, there will be some people who just won't be able to stand it."

The Queen looked at her counselor, who returned the look. "People so dedicated to violence that they will not accept any other lifestyle?" she asked.

"*Can* not," said Saturday, definitely. "Right, Jep? *Can* not. It tears something apart inside them."

"One way of saying it might be that certain people are hardwired," said Jep. "In our equipment maintenance classes, we have to learn a lot about agricultural machines. Some of our machines can be programmed to do different things. But some others, harvesting machines mostly, are hardwired for plucking or mowing or whatever. Saturday and I think that some people are hardwired a certain way, and they invent religions to go along with the way they are. Like they're hardwired for bigotry or violence or being ignorant—or maybe ignorance is just a kind of bigotry. People say they don't want to know a complicated truth, you know, because they already believe something simple, something that's easier on their minds. Well, then those people convince others, followers, who maybe aren't hardwired, but who are . . ."

"Impressionable?" offered the Queen.

Jep nodded. "Born followers, maybe. The followers might be able to change their minds, but the leaders, the hardwired ones, they can't."

"And Voorstoders can't?"

"Some Voorstoders can't. Probably most of the prophets can't. That's why they become prophets. Why would you want to be one, otherwise? Why would you want to scream your head off and threaten people with death and torture and Hell and make women cover themselves up unless you were hardwired for being crazy? The point is, if somebody's hardwired and you're not, the only thing he'll let you be is a follower. If an ordinary person tries to talk to a hardwired person and be nice to him, it doesn't do any good. It's like being nice to a fruit-plucking machine. It'll pluck out your eyes if you get in the way, no matter how fast you talk or how nice you are. Punishment doesn't work, and talking to them won't work, and arguing with them won't work, any more than arguing with a plucking machine would work."

The Queen cast another significant glance at her counselor. "So, some of these hardwired people will come to the border and ask to leave."

"Probably," said Saturday, agreeing to another helping of eggs offered by a liveried serving man. "If it happens, you should send them as far away as you can. If you can't send them out of the System, then try to send them where there aren't any people they can hurt. They'll make slaves out of people if they can. It's just wired into them, and by now their religion is all set up to make it even worse. It's never going to come out right unless there's some race of beings somewhere who *like* to be made slaves of. Then I suppose it might come out even."

"I see," said Wilhulmia, after a considerable pause. "And when will these men come out?"

"Not for a while yet," said Jep. "How long is the year on Ahabar?"

"Four hundred and three days."

"Well, probably less than a quarter year from now."

"And then what?"

"Well, after the men leave, you can remove the blockade. That's all."

"And then the Voorstoders will come out and start setting off bombs once more?"

"No. They won't. Everything will be fine. You'll build a tomb to Stenta Thilion, maybe in Green Hurrah, a beautiful big one, in her memory. And maybe the people will build a little temple nearby. And that's all. You might

even start talking to the Voorstod people about their becoming part of Ahabar."

"How do I know this is true?"

"You don't. We don't either, really. But from what we
know about things . . . well, it's what probably will happen. All we can do is wait, and watch. Meantime, you
don't want anybody killed who doesn't have to be, so
don't kill anybody. Just wait, and watch, and pretty soon
it will probably happen the way we said."

"And you won't tell us how, or why?"

"I could, but it would be better not to. No, I'm not
even sure I could. And I know it's not a good idea. Putting things into words is sometimes a bad idea. Other
people take the words and twist them, and the real thing
becomes something else, something it wasn't intended to
be."

Queen Wilhulmia, who had heard words being twisted
during most of her life, understood exactly what they
were saying and did not press them. She sent them back to
Commander Karth with instructions to keep them safe,
watch them closely, and hold everything status quo.

· *On Authority, acrimony* gave way to violence. The Voorstod prophet assaulted one of the Phansuri sect leaders, and was prevented from killing him only
with great difficulty. The Phansuri had merely questioned
the ethical basis of the Voorstod idea of God when the
prophet had begun frothing at the mouth and demanding
that the Phansuri be executed for insults to the Faith.

Rasiel Plum, reminding Notadamdirabong Cringh
that he, Rasiel, was only a cat's-paw in this matter, suggested that the discussions be halted. "They'll begin coming to meetings armed," he warned Cringh. "They'll start
killing one another, mark my words."

Cringh had already come to the same opinion. When
the questions were withdrawn from discussion, however,
he found to his dismay that it was too late. The entire
Advisory had been drawn into the matter, had, as it were,
taken sides. Messages had gone to religious bodies on
Thyker, on Ahabar, on Phansure. Messages had gone to

the Confreres of Theoretical Theology at six universities.
A professor emeritus was to speak on the subject at an
upcoming interplanetary conference on Faith as a Species-
Specific Phenomenon. The matter of "Four Questions Re-
lating to the Departed," as the whole controversy had
been labeled, had already spread far beyond the Advisory
and become a subject of dispute by groups throughout the
System, including by the Circle of Scrutators at the Temple of the Overmind. It had thus come to Howdabeen
Churry's attention, and Howdabeen Churry decided the
time had come for action.

The prophet who had assaulted the Phansuri was sent
home in disgrace, encountered the blockade, and was interred in one of the camps at the rear of the Ahabarian
lines, though not before he had passed on certain messages for the prophets inside Voorstod, which he had
lately received from certain persons on the moon Enforcement. Overmajor Altabon Faros and Submajor Halibar
Ornil had been busy. They had put together the final pho-
neme, and ultimate success was now within the Awatch's
grasp.

When Commander Karth received a message from the
camp director telling the Commander they had a prophet
interned, Jep suggested that the prophet not be allowed to
return to Voorstod.

"The people inside Voorstod don't really know what's
happening," he said. "It's sneaking up on them. The
prophet from Authority might notice the difference or
have some new information which could interfere."

Jep was right in assuming so. He was wrong in assuming that the information had not yet been passed along.
The good news from Enforcement had already been received by the Awatch.

• *In Voorstod, the* underground networks of
fragile fiber spun and spun, widening with every passing
hour. At a farm above Sarby, a God was Dawn Discovered and raised, and the Gharm began plastering the temple there. In Selmouth there were manifestations, and it

was rumored that the Gods of the Gharm, the Tchenka, had visibly returned.

Sam took a job on a farm east of Sarby in order to get the wherewithal to travel south, out of Voorstod, back to the blockade lines. With every person or Gharm who passed, he sent a message as to his whereabouts. Maire, he knew, would be looking for him.

Queen Wilhulmia fretted and tried to be patient, not unaware that there were spies in Ahabar asking questions, for there were usually spies in Ahabar asking questions.

On the moon Enforcement, Altabon Faros cached the recorded phonemes which would make mobilization of the great army possible, prayed to whatever force of mercy there might be in the cosmos, wept yet again for Silene, and went to confer with his colleague.

And on Hobbs Land, shallow under the soil, the network of the Gods—which had long since reached the escarpment and made the laborious, slow climb upward through the pillared stone of the ramparts—reached the fertile soil at the top and sped through its moist depths toward the memorial park of the settlers, the memorial park laid out within the arms of great, radiating, thought-to-be-dormant mounds.

SIX

· *At home on* Thyker, Shan Damzel dreamed of Porsa and screamed.

Volsa came into his room and shook him awake.

"Why are you doing this again?" she asked. "I thought the doctors taught you how not to do this."

"They taught me self-hypnosis," Shan gargled, struggling to come awake. "I've been . . . I've been too worried about this other thing. It's hard to concentrate." He settled himself, almost upright upon his bed, feeling shamed. "I'm supposed to do the exercise each night, before I sleep, particularly when I'm not physically tired, but I keep thinking about this other thing instead."

"This other thing? Being, I suppose, Hobbs Land?"

"Hobbs Land. Yes."

"And the matter of the Four Questions, the Hobbs Land Gods."

He frowned, sulkily. "You've heard about that, have you?"

"Hasn't everyone? What are you afraid of, Shan?"

"I'm afraid . . . I'm afraid of being swallowed. Being

. . . being inside something suffocating that won't let go."

"And you think the Hobbs Land people are inside something that won't let go?"

He nodded, angrily. No matter what anyone said, he did think so.

"They're good, remarkably contented people."

"I don't care. That's not the point."

"What is the point, Shan?"

"If what swallowed them gets off Hobbs Land, it could swallow me too. It could have swallowed me, while I was there!"

She sat beside him for a time. After a while, he fell asleep. There were no more dreams that night.

When he rose in the morning, he went directly to the information stage and demanded, "Find Howdabeen Churry. Tell him I need to see him at once."

· *Sam left the* farm near Sarby after working on it for about a hundred twenty days. He was almost sorry to leave. The farm owner was a kindly man, one who had recently cut off his long hair, so he told Sam, because it seemed to get in his way. His wife and children were also good people, in the way that Hobbs Land people were good, in that they worked efficiently, enjoyed life, and were considerate of one another's feelings.

"I want to go to Cloud," Sam told the farmer. Sam thought his best chance of getting information about Maire would probably be in Cloud, though he had asked questions of the Gharm in Sarby, to no avail. Nils and Pirva were away, probably creating more Tchenka, so he couldn't ask them. "What's the best route to Cloud?"

"I'd stay out of the mountains just now," he replied. "I keep hearing of bad things up there. Men leaving the towns and going up there, rampaging about. Fighting. Killing each other. I'd stick to the roads if I were you. East from here to Panchy, then take the southwest road out of Panchy around the mountains' feet down into Bight. Will you want to stop at Scaery?"

Sam thought about it. "Yes. I'd like to stop at Scaery."

"Well then, you turn east at a place called Bilsville, and that takes you into Scaery. From there, the road runs straight down the coast to Cloudport, and there's public transport between those two towns. Lots happening in Cloud, I hear."

"What do you hear?"

"Oh, lots of fulminations. The prophets are unhappy with things, so I'm told. They're thinking of going back into the mountains, too, and setting up a new county there."

"What's made them unhappy?" Sam asked, wanting to know how the farmer saw things.

"No one knows." The farmer shook his head, a confused, slightly angry expression on his face. "Everybody tells me about it who comes through, but nobody knows why."

As Sam went east into Panchy, he saw only a few men wearing the big caps of the Cause, and they seemed, by and large, to be either drunk or bewildered. Most of them were headed for the hills, and Sam was grateful the farmer had told him to avoid that route. Panchytown was on the coast, out of his way, so he did not go there, but he heard of Panchytown's temples from a traveling merchant who gave him a ride into County Odil. "Funny little round buildings," said the man, shaking his head. "Never seen anything like them."

There was little traffic on the back road along the mountains, but Sam was lucky enough to get rides to take him through Bight County into Scaery. "Watch yourself," said the last driver, as he let Sam out in front of an inn. "Things are in a mess here in Scaery."

"What kind of mess?" Sam asked.

"The Gharmgods," said the man. "They've invaded the town. They're marching every night. With the prophets countermarching. On the edge, the prophets. Very vehement, they are. They could do anything. Just watch yourself, that's all."

Tchenka? What else could it be? Sam took himself into the inn and got a room facing the street. If there were to be parades, he wanted to see them.

They came after midnight, when the lights of the city

were out, down the dark streets in undulant processions. A snake the length of several houses, green as emeralds, with Gharm capering after it, making a happy noise on bells and cymbals and tiny drums. A roof-high bird stalking behind the snake, brooding violet veils of feather sprouting from its wings. And again, Gharm behind, singing.

A gong banged, a trumpet blatted, the snake and bird vanished. Into the street surged a crowd of men with robed prophets leading them. Carrying the symbols of their Cause, whips and banners, they paraded down the street, blowing their trumpets, banging their gongs, screaming in unison, "Ire, Iron, and Voorstod." When they had gone, the green snake came out of an alley and coiled itself before the inn, looking up with glowing turquoise eyes into Sam's face. Bird and snake moved away to be succeeded by other creatures, who were driven away by the prophets, only to return again. All throughout the night, the Gharm danced, and laughed, and sang, and tum-te-tummed on their tiny drums, making a noise like rain in a dry and thirsty land.

"Coribee," they cried when they saw Sam watching. *"Coribee."*

Sam had breakfast in the inn tavern, meal cakes and cheese and lorsfowl eggs, which he had never eaten before.

"D'ja see the parade?" asked the cook, a bulky woman of uncertain age. "D'ja see that big serpent. Wan't he somethin'."

Inspiration struck Sam between one bite of egg and another. "They've come as a sign from the Almighty to the prophets," he said. "That the prophets are to leave this land and go to a new place."

"I din' know that," she said, amazed. "Whafor?"

"Ah, because their work will be accomplished sooner from the new land," said Sam. "So says Almighty God."

"I'll be," said the cook, shaking her head in amazement. For some time she went on with her work, interrupting herself every now and then to say, "I'll be."

"Do you remember Maire Manone?" Sam asked after a time.

"I do," she said. "I'uz on'y a wee brat when she left,

but I 'member those songs of hers. 'Scaery in the Mist.'
'Little Boat.' 'Crows Among the Corn.' We still sing 'em."

"Do you know where she lived, when she was here in
Scaery?"

The cook didn't, but she told him who would know.
Later, as Sam was going out to find that person, he heard
the cook telling a group of workers from nearby buildings
that the Almighty was sending a message to the prophets.

"Where'd you hear that?" someone asked.

"It's the truth," said the cook. "The prophets know it
themselves."

The person who would know where Maire had lived
was a music seller with a shop downtown in Scaery. He
remembered Maire Manone and directed Sam to a farm
on the outskirts of town, in an area now built up, though
the Manone house had been preserved by a local musicians' group, as a memorial. He gave Sam directions for
getting there, suggesting he take the public conveyance,
which went within one street of the place. Sam did so,
listening with interest to the comments of the passengers.
Most of them were intrigued by the phantom animals.
None seemed afraid. Only a few spoke of the prophets'
attempts at exorcism.

The house, when he found it at last, was empty. It had
a plate on the door identifying it as the first home of the
Sweet Singer of Scaery. A neighbor woman came out of
her house and told him if he wanted to see the place there
was a Gharm in back with the key.

Sam went there and found her. She was an old Gharm.
Older than Stenta Thilion had looked.

"May I see the house?" he asked.

Wordlessly she unlocked the door and led him in. In
the tiny hall was a table with a pile of thin songbooks on it
and a sign offering them for sale. On the wall was a picture of Maire as a very young girl, golden and slender,
with huge, wondering eyes. He stared at it for a long time,
trying to imagine her as a child and failing. He went into
the room to his right, the living room, where the wide
floorboards were covered with a thin layer of dust. His
eyes were caught, suddenly, as by a trap of teeth and
chains. He saw all at once the dark spots Maire had spo-

ken of, the dark spatter through the dust, and her words came back to him whole, as though he had told them over to himself every day for years, words he had scarcely heard at the time.

"This is Fess's blood," he breathed, hardly noticing the way the aged Gharm's head came up, tilted, listening. "My mother wept for her every day of her life."

"Who is your mother?" whispered the Gharm.

"Maire Manone," he said. "When she grieved, I thought she was exaggerating. Making it worse than it really was."

"She could not have done that," wept the Gharm. "It was as bad as any words could make it. I am Lilla."

Sam shook his head. "I thought you escaped. Mam told me you escaped."

"We did, but we went no farther than Wander. For many years I have worked there, for kinfolk of the Squire. A few days ago, when things began to boil here in Voorstod, I returned. I am old. Soon I will die. I wanted to see the place my child lived and died. The place she is buried, out back, beneath the tree. I came in trepidation, but I had been here only two days when the Green-snake Tchenka came and blessed Fess's grave."

"It is partly because of Maire that the Tchenka returned," said Sam, begging a boon for Maire, knowing she would have done it for herself. "Please do not hate her any longer."

"I never hated her," said Lilla. "I loved her as my own child. We Gharm nurses often love the children we raise, particularly the girls, for they were not made evil by the prophets."

"Is that what they do? Make evil?"

"We have a saying, we Gharm. *A man who claims to carry the truth, carries an empty sack.*"

"Did you know Phaed Girat?"

"I knew of him. Before we escaped."

"He is my father."

"I think he is a wicked man."

Sam said doggedly, "Are you so sure he is wicked, Lilla? Perhaps, away from here, he might change."

"We Gharm have a saying. *Perhaps, away from the*

pond, the frog would grow feathers. Give Maire my love when you see her again."

He explained when he had last seen Maire, and where, and Lilla promised to inquire among the Gharm. "Perhaps someone has heard something," she said. "We will find her."

"She's probably back with the blockading force by now," said Sam. "But no one seems to know for sure."

"When you see her, tell her I can die content, with the Tchenka come again."

"I will," Sam promised. "When I see her."

By nightfall, when Sam returned to the inn, it was all over the town that God had told the prophets to leave Scaery and even Voorstod. That night, when the great luminous beings walked in the streets, there were no prophets trying to drive them away. All the prophets, so said knowledgeable residents when morning came, had gone to Cloud.

There was public surface transport between Scaery and Cloud. Sam bought some food and drink, paid for a seat, and lounged in comfort as the miles spun by down the coast. It was a Voorstod day, said everyone, with fog thick as a blanket. Still, as they left the outskirts of Scaery, Sam caught the unmistakable outline of a Hobbs Land style temple.

"Many of those around?" he asked his seatmate.

"They're building them right and left," the man said. "Don't know why. Has something to do with the Gharm, I think."

"The slaves," suggested Sam.

"Slave . . . No." The man seemed confused. "That was something else, wasn't it? Not Gharm. The Gharm wouldn't have liked that at all."

The transport was slow, stopping at every crossroad and village, and it was early evening before they came into Cloud. Except for one of the little temples along the road as they came into the town, it was just as Sam remembered it, with the mists blown aside by the evening wind to show the citadel crouched on the cliff above, like something about to spring.

"Must be stuffed full as a feather quilt," said Sam's

fellow traveler, pointing at the castle. "Prophets packing into it for a long time now."

"The Awateh?"

"Him too. At least I haven't heard he's gone anywhere."

There were very few men wearing large caps in Cloud. Sam found an inn and asked the landlord why there were so few.

"Cut their hair, I suppose," said the landlord, uninterested. "Cut mine off, I know. Damn stuff always getting in the way. Can't imagine why I wore my hair that way for so long!"

"What's going on up at the citadel?"

"I heard there was slaughter up there recently. Emptied the dungeons out. I hear they got word today they're supposed to go to another land."

"Where'd that word come from?"

"Scaery, I think. From the prophets in Scaery."

"I thought all the prophets from Scaery were down here."

"I thought so too, but evidently not. There had to be at least one of them left in Scaery to send the word, isn't that right?"

Sam agreed it was probably right. All night the luminous creatures of the Gharm prowled the streets of Cloud to the sound of drums. All night the prophets pursued them with gong and trumpet and symbols and loud unison chants from the Scriptures, the same words Sam had learned in his chains. From the Scripture chosen, Sam gathered the luminous creatures were supposed to be jinni, creatures of the devil.

In midmorning of the following day, the prophets left. The enormous timbered gates of the Citadel were opened by a dozen sweating men. Closed vehicles went into the courtyard and one by one were filled by prophets, or by their wives and children. The Faithful—wearing their long hair loose, with gemmed coup markers pinned to every inch of it—were much in evidence, one or two leaving with each vehicle, some loading crates into still other vehicles, some walking purposefully along the wall toward the flocks that had been penned for some days against the

walls. When the gates were opened, the restless animals
began to move toward the road.

"They are taking the flocks to raise in their new
home," said the bystanders. "Far away."

Sam searched the faces of the herders, looking for
Phaed. Not there. He watched the followers still clustered
at the gate. Not there, either, though all the Faithful
looked much like Phaed. They all looked like Phaed and
Mugal Pye, or like the men he had seen from the window,
there in Sarby. They had a certain massiveness about
them, about even the smallest of them, an immovable
heaviness, as though they had been carved from stone.
Maire had said something about that once. Sam wiped his
face, wet for no reason he could name, and went on
searching their faces.

When only a few vehicles were left, when the flocks
were streaming down the road under a rising cloud of
gray dust, a handful of long-haired followers plunged
back into the citadel. The bystanders heard shouts and,
after a time, the rending of wood and a tumbling of stone:
the sounds of a ruinous search.

"They're looking for jewels," whispered the bystanders. "For gold. For anything that may have been forgotten
and left behind!"

Finally the last of the vehicles pulled away into the
gray cloud raised by the plodding animals, and Sam
joined a dozen other curious bystanders as they wandered
through the gaping gates into the courtyard of the citadel.
He had stood here before, with Saturday Wilm, being bul-
lied by the prophets as he veiled her face with her own
kerchief.

It looked the same, except for the bodies on the walls.
Most of them so fresh that the blood was still wet. Except
for them, the courtyard was empty. Except for the bodies,
and for the men Sam saw just then, coming down the
stairs. Mugal and Preu and Epheron, all three of them,
gloatingly laden with a heavy box they had found somewhere.

Sickened at the sight of them, Sam turned to leave.

The corpse above the door dripped blood on him. He
looked up, aware in that instant that his first reaction was

one of irritation, ashamed of that, looked up almost as
though to say, "Sorry, I know it wasn't your fault," and
saw the long, gray-blonde hair hanging almost to her
knees. Her face was hidden in her shoulder, under a veil
someone had thrown over her. The wind caught it as he
looked up, so that he saw her from below, as he had so
often done as a child.

"Maire!" he screamed. "Mam!" He flung himself at
the sheer wall, trying to climb it.

Some bystander came to him and held him, someone
he did not know. Gharm ran across the stones to him, to
put their hands on him.

"Maire!" he cried again. "Oh, Maire."

His heart seemed choked in his breast. He could not
breathe. His eyes were dry, and they hurt. He turned, full
of rage, to see those three there, before him, still carrying
the box and staring at him with wide eyes and open
mouths. He launched himself at them, so full of blood and
strength that it would have taken a great company of men
to have stopped him, launched himself straight at the
throat of Mugal Pye.

"I have fought monsters before," he screamed, or
words he thought were those words, though all the bystanders heard was one shriek of rage. Mugal Pye's throat
was not thick enough to withstand his onslaught, the man
went down, broken-necked, his head at a cocked angle
and his mouth still pursed as though to ask what was
happening.

Epheron Floom ran, tried to run, was run down, and
his back broken in the instant, all at once.

"No, Sam," cried the old man, Flandry, his back
against the wall, hands before his face. "No, Sam, we
didn't do it. The Awateh's sons had sent her back in the
woods, with the women. The old man had forgotten all
about her. No, Sam, we didn't. It wasn't us!"

"Who?" howled Sam. "Who was it then, Flandry?"

"It was Phaed! The Awateh was furious at him, told
him he was a backslider, so Phaed told the Awateh she
ought to be done before we went. Him, Phaed, your dad!
When Phaed came down from Sarby, he told him."

Sam raised his hand and brought it down and the old

man sank to his knees, still saying, "Not us, oh, it wasn't us, Sam."

Sam turned back to the figure above the gate, the dripping figure with its long hair hanging loose, as he had never seen it.

He said, "I've been to Scaery, Mam. I've seen your house. I've seen the blood spots on the floor. Lilla was there, and she said to tell you her love."

The people, who had been frightened away from him as they might have been from some wild beast, came back to him, shaking their heads at one another, putting out their hands to take hold of him.

"His mother," they whispered to one another. "He didn't know she was here. His mother."

He stood with his hand outstretched, talking to the woman on the wall, needing to tell her what he had never told her.

"You were right, Mam. You took me away for good reason. I did love you, Mam." His voice broke.

"Sam Girat," said a small voice. He looked down to find Nils and Pirva standing beside him. "Sam Girat. Come with us."

"That's my mother," he said, his face empty. "My mother. They called her the Sweet Singer of Scaery."

"We know, Sam. Come with us. Our people will take her down. We have some Godstuff to put on her body, Sam."

"I looked for you," he said to them, unable to explain to himself what they were doing there. "I looked for you."

"We were searching for Maire. They took her from a place we thought was safe. We found her a day too late, Sam. Come with us."

He went with them. Behind him small persons came with a ladder and a hoist to bring Maire Manone's body down from the wall. Hers and the others that hung there. The Gharm took them all down, piling them all in a wagon, except for Maire Manone. Her body they washed and wrapped in fine weaving and laid on the steps of the citadel.

"Long ago," they whispered to one another. "She

helped our people escape. Long ago, she sang of freedom."

During the afternoon, a crew of men levered up several huge stones in the courtyard of the castle and dug a shallow grave in the exposed earth. That night Maire was laid in the grave. Nils and Pirva and Lilla were there with Sam, who seemed possessed of a grief they could not allay.

"I never told her," he said. "All those years, I didn't believe her, don't you see. I thought she robbed me of my dad. All those years, I never told her I loved her, I never really listened to her. . . ."

He looked across her grave to the place the burned and twisted Door had once stood, not seeing it, but not realizing it was gone.

· *Everything happening in* Voorstod was reported to Commander Karth by various of his spies, some of whom had been in Voorstod for generations. The processions of mystical animals, the departure of the prophets, the bodies on the wall, all was reported within hours of the time it happened. Among the matters reported to him was the death of Maire Manone, her death, her burial, the fact that she had been laid to rest with the Godstuff upon her breast. He did not understand this last. He assumed it was some religious thing he had not heard of before. He did not bother to repeat it when he told the children. Thus they wept, deprived of considerable comfort.

"Poor Sam," said Saturday. "He never thought Phaed was that bad, you know. Even when he was with me in Cloud, he didn't really accept that his dad was part of all that."

The Commander left them to their grief for a time, but he needed answers. "What would those strange creatures in the streets be?" he asked them at supper.

When he said he did not know the word *Tchenka*, Jep told him about Tchenka in exhaustive detail. He had had a long time at the farm above Sarby to learn about them.

"And you really think these things are the Gods of the Gharm, manifesting themselves?"

"Would that surprise you?" asked Saturday, who was not at all sure what she thought about Tchenka.

The Commander had to confess that in light of everything else that had been happening, no, it did not particularly surprise him. He sent word of these manifestations to the Queen, wondering whether she, too, would be very little surprised.

Saturday and Jep lay awake long that night, Saturday curled in Jep's arms, wondering what the Tchenka really were.

"Do you suppose," Jep said, "maybe the God gives the Gharm power to dream the Tchenka into being? Because they need them?"

"Like a self-induced hallucination?"

"No, because human people see them too, according to the Commander."

"Like a mass hallucination, then."

Jep shook his head and hugged her tighter. "Is the New Forest on Hobbs Land a hallucination, then?"

"You think the Gods did that too."

"It didn't used to be there, Saturday Wilm. People remembered forests like that, but it didn't used to be there. The thing is, we need forests, we people. Don't we? Just as the Gharm need their Tchenka? We need wonderful places."

"You're right," she snuggled against him more closely. "It didn't used to be there."

· *Sam, escorted by* a small group of Gharm, showed up at the blockade line very early one morning. The prophets had made camp at the southern edge of Leward County, waiting for the flocks to catch up; Sam's group had circled around them on the way to Wander. Just outside the command post, the Gharm left him, crying, "Corribee, Sam-gem. Coribee." He stood with his head down, slack and boneless, not moving until Saturday, Jep, and the Commander came out to meet him.

"The prophets are not far behind me," Sam told them in an exhausted voice.

"I know," said the Commander. "We've got a Door

set up for them." He pointed to it, one of the large Doors used for transport of bulky material. "That's the only Door to Fenice they had in the town of Splendor Magnus. The townsmen aren't happy with our having borrowed it, but it was the nearest, and I had the Queen's warrant. There's been a crew of Doormen here for three days, converting it to the new destination."

"You had to take their only Door?" asked Saturday, casting a worried look at Sam.

"We had to take someone's," said the Commander, putting his arm around Sam's shoulders and leading him into the command module. Though he thought Sam looked very ill, that he needed a med-tech or perhaps had needed one for some time, he did not refer to Sam's appearance. "There aren't any extras lying about. When we want to leave Ahabar, we go to Fenice, where the off-planet travel hub is, but the Queen commanded that no Voorstoders be allowed any farther into Ahabar than absolutely necessary. So, we went to the trouble and expense of modifying a Door. When the people from Voorstod are gone, we'll have to put it back where it was."

"It won't be long," said Sam in a tired voice. "We saw the encampment of the prophets. They will be here by tomorrow."

"Will you stay to see them leave?" the Commander asked.

Sam didn't answer for a moment, then he nodded. "Yes, I need to see what . . . who . . ." His voice trailed away.

"We can't stay any longer than that," said Saturday, giving Sam a troubled look. "I have the feeling we should be getting back." It was more than mere feeling. It was an urgency. Sam turned his weary, grieving face toward her as though to plead for some unspecified boon, but all she could do was press his hand between her own. Whether returning to Hobbs Land would help him or hurt him, she couldn't say. Still, she knew they must go.

"There are green snakes in Voorstod," said Sam, his face quite expressionless. "And forest birds."

"We have heard," said Saturday. "The Tchenka."

"No," he shook his head at them. "Not Tchenka.

Green snakes. Forest birds. Little ones. Real ones. I saw them, along the wayside, in the trees. Snakes. Birds. And other of the ancestor beasts of the Gharm as well."

When they got him inside, he fell into an exhausted sleep.

When morning came, the Commander sat at a table near the Door, among a crowd of Archivists, busy with their recorders. Jep, Saturday, and Sam stayed in the command center, looking out from the darkened interior, where they would not be seen. Nothing was to occur that might upset the prophets. The Commander didn't want them howling for Saturday's blood, or Jep's, or Sam's. The Commander wanted them to go through the Door and away, forever.

"Couldn't you arrest the Awateh for the murder of my mother and execute him," Sam asked, still in his depressed, expressionless voice.

"We could. However, there might be riots, violence, more people hurt. We think this way will be most sensible. Can I trust you to stay calm, Sam?"

"Yes," Sam said. "I want no more innocent blood shed. I'll be calm, Commander, but later . . ."

"What do you mean, later?" Jep whispered, when they had gone inside, but Sam didn't seem to hear him.

The vehicles came at last, throwing up a long bushy tail of dust, stopping at the barrier. Veiled women stood in silent groups. Children, no less silent, gathered nearby. Gharm, light chains attached to their collars, were fastened to the carts, into which bulky bundles were shifted by long-haired men who stared around them with suspicion. One of the Awateh's sons got out of a vehicle and approached the Commander, shifting his weight from side to side, fists clenched. His eyes showed white around the edges, as though he was about to bolt.

"We wish to leave Voorstod," he said. "The father of Queen Wilhulmia offered us land of our own if we would leave Voorstod. Now we wish to go." He did not say the rest of what he was thinking. "Now we wish to go to a place of temporary safety while we complete our plans to destroy you all!" The prophets did not feel they had been routed. Though the manifestations in Voorstod were disconcerting, the prophets had not been driven away by the ancestor-spirits of the Gharm or by the apostasy of thousands of their followers. The prophets themselves were proof against whatever was happening in Voorstod. They had chosen to leave now as part of a coldly calculated and purely temporary retreat. For a time they would play the part of defeated men. So the Awateh had ordered.

Such subterfuge had formed no part of their training, however, and they did it badly. Even the Commander thought so, as he regarded the young prophet with suspicion.

It had been Wilhulmia's great-grandfather, not her father who had promised resettlement land. The land the former king had offered was upon a Belt world which had long since been occupied, but the Commander did not bother with details.

"The offer of resettlement land still stands," he said. "How many of you are there?"

"We are five hundred prophets of the Cause, with our wives and children and an equal number of the Faithful. We have certain requirements," said the prophet, sweat standing out along his clean-shaven upper lip. "We require a habitable environment, with sufficient water for growing crops and for our flocks. We have brought certain Gharm with us to till our fields . . ." Actually, he needed none of these, but he was acting his part.

"You will not be allowed to take any Gharm."

Though the prophet had been prepared for this, the actual words caught in his throat. "But we must have . . . must have . . . servants."

"There is a native race on the resettlement world."

The prophet mopped at his lip. "We have brought our flocks and our possessions, for so we are commanded to do. 'Take up all that is yours,' says our Scripture. 'Your flocks and your people . . .'"

"What is yours, you may take," the Commander interrupted. "Each woman and each child over the age of ten will be asked if they wish to go. No person will be required to accompany you."

The prophet fought down a scream of rage and asked, "When may we go?"

"Now," said the Commander, gesturing at the Door. "Men through first. Then we'll ask each woman if she wants to go, any who say no can stay here. Same with the children over ten."

"That's unfair!" shouted the prophet, barely controlling himself. "You could keep our women, our families."

"Why would we want them?" asked the Commander coldly. "We do not consider your people civilized. We believe you to be barbarians who have chosen the most primitive and bestial elements of human nature and codified them into a cult. If you do not like the terms, you can go back to Cloud."

Sweat started out on the prophet's face. He trembled with fury as he completed his assigned speech. "We prefer not to return. The devil is loose in Cloud. Jinni stalking in the streets. It is no longer an appropriate place for us."

"Then forward," suggested the Commander, almost gently, sensing an end to whatever had been rehearsed. It had been rehearsed. He was sure of it.

The prophet returned to the others of his group. After a pause, they straggled away from their flocks and families and went to the Door and through it. Soldiers gathered around to help the long-haired men herd the animals through.

"There," growled Sam from the door of the building in which he sat with the children. "Oh, there."

The others followed his glare, looked where he was looking, saw only the backs of the Faithful, going toward the Door with the animals before them.

"There," growled Sam again. "And now he's gone. Phaed. Not now. No. But the time will come, Phaed."

Then the men were gone. The women went next, one by one, and the children. Only two of the younger women chose to stay on Ahabar. One of them had no tongue, but she screamed and threw off her veils, falling to her knees at the Commander's feet to clutch at his knees. Her children were with her.

Most of the older women never looked up or removed the veils from their faces. "Do you want to go with your husband." A nod in response, soundless.

After a time the last had gone and the Door was turned off.

Saturday came out of the building to stare at the pale oval of dying fire. "So much hate," she said. "So much pain, removed, as though it had never been. I can't believe it."

"Will that be all of them?" the Commander asked.

Sam shook his head. "I was told there were some of the Faithful back in the hills. I imagine they'll either kill themselves or come out. If you can, you might leave the Door set up for a few days."

"I'm certainly not going to run the risk of having to set it up again," snorted the Commander, signaling the Doormen who had supervised the departure to lock the controls. For the protection of everyone involved, the transfer had been one-way.

"Where are they being settled?" asked Saturday. "Where did the Queen decide to send them?"

The Commander smiled, a thin-lipped smile which, just for an instant, looked very much like the smile of the prophets. "We have sent them to the kind of place they asked for. A habitable place, appropriate for agriculture. It's underpopulated. It even has a native race for them to enslave if they wish."

"To enslave?" Saturday was appalled. "Where?"

The Commander pointed straight up, where the moons of Ahabar were in conjunction.

"We've given them the highlands of Ninfadel," he said.

· **When Howdabeen Churry** reccived Shan's request for an immediate secret meeting, he responded with polite alacrity and considerable curiosity. He had received Shan's previous message; he had learned of the Four Questions. He had planned to act on the basis of those things alone. However, more information would not be amiss. What had his disciple, Shan, found on Hobbs Land that The Arm of the Prophetess should be cognizant of?

They met in Chowdari. Shan, in a tight but determined voice, went into somewhat lengthy autobiographical detail before getting to the point, which was, he said, that he felt personally threatened by the Hobbs Land Gods.

"Volsa goes on and on at me about their being completely beneficent, if they're anything at all, but it seems to me something could appear to be beneficent, for its own purposes, couldn't it?"

"You mean as a kind of lure?" Churry's steely eyes turned silver in concentration. "Bait?"

"Precisely. Presumably the fish thinks the fly is beneficial, too, until he feels the hook. It is my opinion that the Hobbs Landers simply haven't felt the hook yet."

"What makes you think these so-called Gods are inimical?"

"In the first place, I don't think it's 'Gods,' " said Shan. "I'm sure it's all one thing, or was, originally. There was one there when they settled the planet. It died leaving a seed or something from which the new one came. All the settlements have built these little temples, as though waiting for one of their own to sprout. There's even one at Central Management. They may have clones of their own by now, for all I know."

"But you said inimical?" prodded Churry.

"Oh, well, one doesn't know, does one?" he said with tightly controlled sarcasm. "There are three possibilities, I suppose. It could be beneficial. It could be neutral. It could be inimical. What are the chances of one alternative over another? There are more creatures that eat other creatures than there are creatures who don't." He shamed himself by giggling, hysterically.

Churry gave him a look like a lash. "Control yourself, Damzel. You're not making sense. You've said it's some kind of vegetable. Existing only on Hobbs Land."

"That's it, isn't it? So long as it's only Hobbs Land, one might afford to wait and see. But if it got off Hobbs Land . . ."

"You think it will?"

"I believe it has."

Churry leaned back in his chair. "Interesting." He tapped his fingers on his booted leg, a rhythmic tid-a-rum.

"I think it's on Ahabar. I think somebody took seeds from Hobbs Land to Ahabar."

"Why?"

"Why did they do it, or why do I think so?"

"Why do you think so."

Shan wiped his nose. His nose kept running. It had started on Hobbs Land and had gone on ever since. "Because when Stenta Thilion was killed—even I knew who *she* was—everyone knew Voorstod had done it. When the Ahabar army was mobilized and set up the blockade, everyone approved. Voorstod is a boil up the ass of civilization, and everyone was ready for it to be lanced. We expected Ahabar to invade."

"And?"

"And nothing. One account I watched accused Wilhulmia of a failure of will. Another said she could not bring herself to the slaughter of Gharm which would result inside Voorstod."

"And?"

"And nothing, Churry. Half an Ahabarian year, and the blockade is still there, and everything is quiet as a damned grave. That's so unlikely it screams of machinations behind the scenes. You've read about the Voorstoders enough to know what they're like. Do you really think they've stayed quiet for half a year?"

"And your thought is that someone has taken some Hobbs Land God seeds into Voorstod and planted them, eh? Isn't that pure supposition?"

"Not quite pure." Shan giggled, caught himself. "When we left Hobbs Land, there were a group of Hobbs Landers also ready to leave. The group included the Topman of Settlement One—which, incidentally, is where the Departed God was for thirty-some odd years—and his mother and a young girl I'd seen singing at the settlement. The three of them had that determined but depressed look that always reminds me of military training, when you get told off to do something dangerous. You can't refuse. You want to do it well, but you don't want much to die in the attempt, though that's possible. You go off in this mood of depressed determination, carrying yourself on will alone. I recognized that kind of expression on the women's faces."

"So?"

"What I'm saying is, this was not a farmboy and his momma and daughter going off for a visit to the kinfolk. The three of them had some great purpose, at least the women did. So I decided to push a bit and see what they said. I'd noticed one of those temples at their management complex, and I asked about it.

"The Topman spun me a line. He didn't want me to know why they'd built it."

"And," prodded Churry.

"And, when you're going through a Door, there's a destination listing behind a panel on the wall of the waiting room."

"I know."

"Our destination was Chowdari, and the destination under ours was *Fenice upon Ahabar*." Shan fell silent, waiting, wondering if he had said enough, or too much.

"There's something else. I can see it in your face," said Churry.

"I asked Archives to search for the three Hobbs Landers on Ahabar, see if there was any reference to their arriving or to the purpose of their visit. I knew the Topman's name; he'd introduced himself to us when we came to his settlement: Sam Girat. It was a long chance, really, but as it turned out, Archives couldn't have missed them if it had tried. They were at the concert hall when Stenta Thilion died, sitting with the military Commander and his daughter, right across from the Queen. You saw the account! It was replayed for days, until we were all thoroughly sick of it! The Hobbs Land girl was the one who sang the battle hymn. The woman saved Stenta's life, temporarily. After the tragedy, they disappeared. Into Voorstod, I believe."

"To plant their seeds?"

"Possibly. Maybe we'll know soon. Ahabar can't keep the blockade there forever. Presumably something has to happen. I understand Authority has been making rumbling noises, demanding that the blockade be raised."

Churry shook his head and grinned unpleasantly. "Everyone in the System knows the Religion Advisory has been bribed by the Voorstoders. Well, well. What are you really afraid of, Shan Damzel?"

Shan shook for a moment. Whenever he thought about fear, he remembered it. Absolute, bowel-loosening fear, of drowning in glop. Of suffocating inside something that would not let go.

"It could swallow us," he said, his voice shaking. "If it's swallowing the Voorstoders, it could swallow us."

"And if it is beneficent?"

Shan shook his head, eyes wide. "Don't you see, it doesn't *matter*. Beneficent or not. Unlike my fool of a sister, you know that, Churry. You of all people . . ."

Churry smiled again, this time almost fondly. "Yes, I do know that," he said. "The prophetess was quite clear, wasn't she? She didn't differentiate between bad and good. She just told us to let nothing stop us from being ourselves. Whatever we are."

Churry turned for a few moments to the food and drink on the table beside him, which gave him time to think. He offered hospitality to his guest. When this politeness had been complied with, Churry asked, "You're turning this matter over to me, are you?"

Shan sighed in relief. "Yes. I can't get any further with it. Reticingh asked some questions of the Advisory for me, through Native Matters, I think, but the result was inconsequential. I had hoped the Advisory would become frightened and do something, but all they did was argue. Even our High Baidee representatives didn't share my concern. I don't have the authority or the money to do anything more about it on my own."

"Do anything about it. Meaning what, exactly?"

"Meaning killing it," whispered Shan. "Meaning killing it, before it spreads any farther."

• *A small item* on System News mentioned the partial withdrawal of the blockading force around Voorstod. Though the land blockade would be continued indefinitely, Voorstod was no longer to be shut off from the sea. The fisheries could get on with their business.

Howdabeen Churry watched these developments with

a good deal of interest. The question of the Hobbs Land Gods had been generally known for some time, but neither Authority nor the Circle of Scrutators had become exercised enough to do anything official. Now Shan thought the threat was spreading to Ahabar. Obviously, something had to be done, and The Arm of the Prophetess was the only group ready to do it!

"My thinking is," Churry said to his trusted lieutenant, Mordimorandasheen Trust, Mordy, "that if we go to Hobbs Land and simply destroy these so-called Gods— Shan Damzel says there can't be more than a dozen of them—what follows will prove to us whether there's any threat or not."

"Wasn't he more worried about the ones he thinks may be on Ahabar?" asked Mordy Trust.

"Well, yes. But Ahabar has quite a large army, and the only outside Doors are in Fenice, which would mean fighting our way half across a continent or figuring out some time-consuming and surreptitious way of getting to Voorstod. Hobbs Land doesn't even have a militia. Half a dozen security people, and that's about it."

"Better odds, is that it?"

"Well, frankly, I don't anticipate any opposition on Hobbs Land at all. It will be a preemptive, sanitary strike, to wipe out something that may be dangerous. So long as that's all we do, nobody is going to become violent over it."

"So long as that's all we do. We won't carry any weapons, then."

"Don't be silly," laughed Churry, delighted with the prospect of action at last. "We may need to bluff a few farmers into moving off. It's at least partly a training exercise, so we'll go in full battle kit, of course."

• *Sam, Jep, and* Saturday stopped briefly in Fenice to be decorated by the Queen. Maire received posthumous notice of a respectful kind. At Sam's request, it was a private ceremony, though Queen Wilhulmia had longed for something a bit more weighty and regal. Since the Hobbs Landers were mourning Maire Manone, how-

ever, she forced herself to be understanding. When she
placed the Order of Ahabar around Sam Girat's neck and
pressed her cheek against his own, she didn't like the
looks of him. Physically he seemed well enough, but there
was something sadly wrong with him otherwise.

It was announced at the ceremony that Stenta Thilion
was to have a tomb in Green Hurrah. A planetary contest
for the two inscriptions on that tomb would be sponsored
by the palace. One inscription was to memorialize the life
and great talent of Stenta Thilion; the other was to decry
the ugliness of fanaticism. The Queen made this announcement just before she bid Sam and his party farewell.

By this time, though no Ahabarian was aware of it,
the underground net begun with the burials in Selmouth
and Sarby and continued in Cloud and Scaery and dozens
of other Voorstod hamlets, had covered all of Voorstod
but the mountains, had crossed the border into Green
Hurrah where it had spread swiftly through the fertile
area, and was now exploring the deep soil of Jeramish.
Ahead of this line went certain missionary Gharm, quietly
and largely unnoticed, carrying out burials here and burials there. By the time of the winter rains, they felt they
would have raised Tchenka almost halfway to Fenice. Everywhere near Voorstod upon Ahabar, biologists were
noting the sudden emergence of new species that the
Gharm greeted as old friends.

· *Upon the moon* Ninfadel, a flurry and swirl of
arrival: prophets, carts, men, flocks, women and children
last, many of them crying from the pain of the Door.

The guards that met them were sanguine, quiet-faced,
saying Ninfadel, Ninfadel, you are on the moon Ninfadel
—to general disbelief and fury, waved fists and maledic-
tions. The prophets were not armed, but the guards were
both armed and watchful. They took no notice of the
threats.

"We've drilled new wells for you and your animals.
We've erected pens to hold your flocks. There's a bright

yellow luminescent line out there. Stay above it, and you'll be perfectly safe."

To the assembled multitude, the guards and Native Matters persons gave their usual lecture: point one, point two, point three, to the end. They passed out face masks and nose plugs. Inventories of both were virtually depleted when they were through. After the lecture, prophets and the Faithful rose in their wrath and departed, not having listened; the flocks, women, and children followed, not having understood.

Most of the face plates and nose filters were left lying on the ground inside the walls. Guards and Native Matters persons shrugged. Porsa or prophets, the shrugs said. Good riddance to either. Neither group had been ordered to look after Voorstoders who refused to be enlightened about their circumstances.

The Voorstoders received enlightenment almost at once. Their flocks of vlish and dermot moved, for the most part, at the direction of the herdsmen. A few animals, however, dazed by the the Door and attracted by the scent of herbary, broke from the herds and ran down the hill. Herdsmen ran after them. Though the highlands widened south of the outpost, at the outpost itself the hills sloped steeply and the margins for error were small. The animals plunged downward, ever more swiftly, crossing the yellow line. All but one of the herdsmen skidded to a stop. That one had paid no attention to the warnings, and he plunged after the animals, whooping, as though it were a game.

The entire Voorstod population had the best possible view of what occurred thereafter. They heard and smelled it as well.

The prophet glared, belatedly inserting his nose plugs. His sons approached him, instinctively seeking reassurance.

"We can't . . . we can't live here," said the eldest.

"We can live here," said the Awateh loudly, and then more softly, "for a short time." He raised his voice again, shouting instructions. The animals were herded into the pens which had been provided. The wide black tents were set up, those for the men first, then those for the women.

At the point the pens had been built, the highlands were a mile across. The Voorstoders could still smell the Porsa, but not overwhelmingly. They could see the heaving forms, hear the shouts, but not loudly.

Highland brush was gathered, and fires were lit. Food was cooked. The Awateh sat in a tent alone with his sons, all fifteen of them, the youngest not yet twenty.

"On the moon Enforcement there are two of the Faithful," said the Awateh, beginning a litany all of them knew well.

"Praise Almighty God," his sons intoned.

"Halibar Ornil is the servant of God. Altabon Faros is the servant of God. Before we left Voorstod upon Ahabar, we received word from these Faithful that time is fulfilled. The army of Enforcement is being turned to God's service."

A spasm of ecstatic movement went among them. "How soon?" breathed the eldest of the sons.

"Only so long as it takes to teach the army of Enforcement the words of God." The Awateh visualized the army of Enforcement as a kind of angelic host, hovering, awaiting a single command, but he knew intellectually that this was not accurate. According to the latest word received, Ornil and Faros, working alone, had managed to program less than one-hundredth of the army. Once the Commander's unconscious body had served its purpose, it had been disposed of in a manner that suggested accidental death. There was now a new commander, with new-broom attitudes, poking into corners, looking up directives and seeing whether they had been complied with. Ornil and Faros were unsuspected and were proceeding with the Great Work, but they were doing it slowly, daring to do nothing that would seem suspicious. Considering the vast size of the army on Enforcement, the Awateh had decided to move at once. One-hundredth was quite enough for a first step.

"Then we need survive upon these heights only a little time," said the eldest son, optimistically.

The prophet nodded. "Only a little longer."

"Where?" asked the youngest son, greatly daring. He had been accustomed to saying nothing, asking nothing, in a culture where seniority was everything. "Where will the soldiers be sent, Father? Phansure?"

For many of those in the wide black tent, it was the only time they had ever seen the Awateh smile.

"When we struck at the traitorous Gharm in Ahabar, there were three who offended us," said the prophet. "Two offended greatly, because they are of our blood, apostate, deniers of Almighty God and of his prophets. The other one offended us by calling up hatred against us, by singing a devil's anthem into our faces. I learned of her identity too late to take her when she was in our hands.

"One of those three is dead. She was hung like rotten fruit upon the walls of the citadel at Cloud. Our faithful servant, Phaed Girat, saw that she was put there.

"One of the others is her son. The third is a girl of Hobbs Land named, blasphemously, Saturday Wilm."

"You will send the soldiers of Enforcement to Hobbs Land to kill two people?" asked the youngest son, incredulously. He had heard there were only a few thousand people upon Hobbs Land. It made no military sense whatsoever. "To kill two people?"

"To kill *all* the people," said the Awateh. "And their false gods whom they arrayed against us in Voorstod upon Ahabar. Those gods came from Hobbs Land."

There were expressions of wonder and anger.

The Awateh went on. "*First,* some smallest part of the army of Almighty God will go to Hobbs Land while at the same time another small part goes to Authority. And then, when Hobbs Land is no more, when Authority is taken, thereby removing any threat to our continued work, the soldiers will go in their millions to Phansure. After Phansure is taken, they will go everywhere in the universe, in God's name."

"When?" the son asked.

"As soon as there is a diversion," said the Awateh. "Something to focus the attention of the System elsewhere."

"A diversion," the son breathed. "But that could be a long time."

"As Almighty God wills," breathed the Awateh, still smiling. He believed it would be soon, very soon.

• • •

· *China Wilm, who* had wished change upon
Sam before he went to Ahabar, considered him unduly
changed now. At first she hardly knew him. He looked at
her out of haunted eyes, his cheeks sunken from loss of
weight. He seldom remembered to eat. China, despite her
far-advanced pregnancy, took him in. Sometimes a
woman did that with a lover, usually not for long, but it
was certainly acceptable behavior if the man needed care
and couldn't find it among his sisterhouses—which Sam
couldn't, because Sal was grieving so over Maire that she
wasn't competent to look after herself or the babies. Harribon Kruss came over from Settlement Three to look
after Sal. That was sometimes done, too, when there was
no brother to look after things.

China took Sam in and fed him, petted him, and cos-
seted him with delicacies. Within a few days he looked
more like himself physically, though the look in his eyes
had not changed.

"He should be back at the job," said Africa, who had
been holding down Sam's job and her own for far too
long.

"Look at him," whispered China. "Don't push him,
Africa."

"Seems he should start to get over Maire's dying. It's
been a while now."

"It isn't just Maire's dying. It isn't her death he can't
get over. It's that she knew she was in danger of death and
he pooh-poohed it. He had never understood what she
was trying to tell him, but even that isn't what's eating at
him. It's that he never really tried to understand. She told
him things, and he heard them, but he never asked himself
what they meant to her. He only asked what they meant
to him. He had his dad built up as some kind of misunderstood hero. Now he feels guilty, and he won't let go of it.
You know Sam. He always has to wring every drop of
blood out of everything, even when there isn't any blood
to wring."

"Birribat Shum will. . . ."

"I know. I think so, too, if we give him time. There had to be a reason for everything."

"Reason?"

"For the way Sam was, before he left. For the way he is now. Not quite like the rest of us. Maybe a few oddities are needed, from time to time. A few strangenesses. We have to give him time." She did not specify which *him* she meant.

So they gave him time. One day Sam went into the office and Africa asked him to fill out the requisitions. The next day it was the production report. Within ten days he was back at the work, not with any appearance of joy, but doing it in between long spells of sitting gazing out the window at nothing.

Sal recovered gradually. She hadn't seen Maire's body, and no one had told her how Maire had died, just that the prophets had killed her and she was buried in the court-yard at Cloud. One day, Sal was told, there would be a God Maire Manone in Cloud. They could go there, the whole family. The thought seemed to comfort her, though it did not comfort Sam.

Either Sal or China fixed him lunches, to be sure he ate. Sal's children were sent to demand stories. Sal thought this would help Sam, but he sent the children away, refusing to open the books. Harribon Kruss, who spent a lot of time with Sal, took Sam fishing for creelies. Through it all, Sam moved like a ghost, like a spirit, an inhabitant of a world the rest of them could not see. China thought of him as a kind of hollow man, going through the motions. There was nothing inside him.

Not long after the fishing expedition, however, which had taken them up through the New Forest—vastly in-creased in size and awesomeness—and past Cloudbridge —which was enough to make a man catch his breath in wonder—he began to read legends again, starting with the books he himself had made. He kept asking himself what they had meant to the people who wrote them, rather than what they meant to him. It was not long before he noticed what had escaped him before. The legends spoke of victors. The stories told of survivors. Heroes were those who had died valiantly, with immortal words on their tongues, or those still alive when the story was over. Of the myriads slaughtered, of the uncountable maimed and enslaved, of the unnumbered victims, there remained only the poet's voice or no voice at all. They could not speak for themselves.

· *Dern Blass had* been curious about the Voorstod Matter, which is what he had called it to himself, ever since Jep Wilm had been abducted. His curiosity had not been in the least satisfied by Ilion Girat, who seemed to know nothing and who, in any case, had been sent back to Ahabar (and internment) soon after Sam, Maire, and Saturday had left. Dern's curiosity continued unabated after Sam and the children returned, but anyone could see that Sam Girat was in no condition to talk about anything, and humane considerations suggested that Jep and Saturday should be let alone for a time as well.

When Dern considered that enough time had passed for everyone to have settled down and recovered, however, he invited the returnees to join him, Zilia, and Spiggy, and fill them in as to what had happened. The two Phansuri engineers, Theor Close and Betrun Jun, happened to be on one of their periodic visits to Hobbs Land, so Dern asked them to come along. Dern liked both the Phansuris. They spoke his language and understood him better than many on Hobbs Land did, and they, too, were curious about what had happened on Voorstod.

Dern invited some settlement people as well, Sal Girat and Harribon Kruss, China and Africa Wilm. He didn't want what he thought of as an official debriefing; that would be too formal and constrained. He wanted chat. He wanted colorful details. He knew parts of it were painful but he wanted to know about all of it, even the painful parts. The twelve of them would fit nicely into one flier and Dern planned to give the whole thing a pleasant informality by flying up to the new memorial park for a picnic. On his time report he would call it an inspection trip.

Jamice didn't want to go along because she was getting over a stuffy head she had picked up from some visitor—despite all advances in medicine, there were still bugs busy mutating for the sole purpose of giving humans stuffy heads. Dern Blass appointed her acting director for the day and told her to stay in bed. Acting director, as Jamice well knew, meant less than nothing so long as Tandle Wobster was in the office, so Jamice stayed in her darkened quarters and plugged in her sleep inducer while her colleagues assembled at CM, to find that the CM commissary had packed food and drink enough for twice their number. Dern asked Spiggy to pilot, and they had an uneventful and largely silent flight.

Spiggy was the only one in the group who had seen the radiating mounds from ground level, though Dern had flown over them, just to see what people were talking about. They landed nearby, in a cleared plot convenient to the site, and all wandered into the mound area, marveling at the things.

"I don't remember the mounds being this high," said Spiggy. "I recall them coming up to my shoulder, but these are over my head."

"The way I hear it," said Dern, "you were kept very busy up here and can be excused for not having paid that close attention to your surroundings." Dern had no moral qualms about Spiggy's involvement with the Baidee, but neither did he intend to let Spig escape without joshing.

A number of bodies had been buried near the mounds since the first two from Settlement Three. Three of the oldest settlers had died in Settlements Two and Six. There had been an accident at one of the mines, which had killed four. Though the graves were unmarked, it was easy to see where they lay from the slight dimpling of the ground. While Zilia and Africa unpacked the food and drink, the others of the party walked along the mounds examining the cracked and fallen soil around them and exclaiming at their size, excepting Jep and Saturday, who were unaccountably quiet.

"What do you think?" asked Dern, encountering the two youngsters at the end of a mound.

"I think whatever this would grow into would be huge," said Jep.

"Dormant, the Baidee experts said," Dern smiled.

"Dormant for how long?" asked Saturday.

Dern hadn't thought to ask that question of the Baidee scientists. He found himself wondering if the Baidee scientists had asked that question themselves, and he stopped smiling.

"It's only a hundred feet long," he said, gesturing at the mound. "Some trees have roots that long."

"This thing," said Saturday, "is circular and is almost two hundred fifty feet in diameter. The visible part is about twelve feet high. There's a circular mound started up in the middle. It's all one thing, Director Blass."

"Well, yes," he admitted, rubbing his chin doubtfully. "I suppose it is."

They went into the nearby Departed village, just to look around, and found the Theckle brothers from Settlement One, roaming among the ruins.

"What are you doing up here?" asked Sam.

"Picking gravesites for us," said Emun Theckles.

"Having a nap under the trees," said his brother, scratching the back of his neck.

"Are you really picking a place to be buried?" asked Saturday, curiously.

"That's the idea I had," said Emun. "Woke up this morning with the idea very clear that I should come up here and pick a place to be buried. Then when we got here, we were both sleepy, so we had a nap." He brushed clinging, hairlike fibers from the back of his neck. "Now we're hungry."

Dern laughed and asked them to join the party. He had no objection to their hearing what had actually happened in Voorstod. They all sat down, and Dern asked for the tale. Jep began; Saturday continued; it went on for some little time. At the end of the rather rambling narrative, in which Saturday and Jep shared about equally, with Sam saying so little that it almost seemed he had not been involved, Zilia shook her head and said, "Now wait a minute, Jeopardy Wilm. There's something here I don't understand. You're saying that the Gods in Voorstod changed the people there. The Gods here on Hobbs Land have not changed us."

Dern Blass, who was able to appreciate the changes in

Zilia more than any of the rest of them, decided not to comment.

"Well it did, you know," said Africa in a kindly voice. "It's just that it didn't need to change us much. Most of us were already fairly peaceable people, fairly kind, decent to our families and friends. Mostly what it changed was our response to surprise and fear, I think. In my experience, and from what I've read in learning management, most of human nastiness comes out of shock or fear."

"I was afraid," said Saturday. "In Voorstod. I was out of my head with fear sometimes."

"We were separated from Birribat," Jep mused. "And there was something real to be afraid of."

"The Gods don't interfere with real fear," nodded Africa. "Not when there's a reason. You get a malfunctioning harvester after you, the Gods won't stop your running."

"Interesting," said Theor Close, the Phansuri engineer. "A panic suppressant that can distinguish between real and imagined fears?" He felt the whole matter could be explained in terms of chemistry, if the proper Phansuri researchers could only come to Hobbs Land and investigate.

Zilia shook her head. "You're saying the prophets were afraid?"

Saturday nodded. "Were. Are. Of everything."

Sam said, "I've been reading . . ." His voice trailed away.

No one said anything, waiting.

"I've been reading about Manhome. About the retributive religions, the surviving ones. They all came from a pastoral background. In primitive times, everything out here in the dark was a predator. One had to guard against everything that threatened the flock, had to kill it if possible. At night, the flock had to be sequestered, put in the fold and guarded. The shepherd had to stand guard, sleepless, night after night. Many of these societies had a taboo against dogs, so they had no guard dogs. They had to be their own dogs, always alert. The shepherd had to be afraid of everything . . ."

Africa said, "I imagine wives and children were

thought of much as he thought of his vlishes or dermots . . ."

"Sheep," said Sam. "Back at that time it was sheep."

"Sheep, then. The sheep were property, the wives were property, the children were property, and they had to be guarded. Because they were a pastoral people, they didn't have secure caves or houses. They had fragile tents. They didn't have secure lands; they migrated, on foot. They were probably afraid all the time, of everything. They would have been very alert, I suppose. Very nervous."

"Over time, I suppose," said Jep, "only the people survived who were very alert and perpetually frightened and thus very irritable and quick to attack. Perhaps it became a racial characteristic."

"Reinforced by the religion," Sam went on, staring into his plate. "It explains why violence and war went on under the name of religion for so long. Fear and hatred were simply racial characteristics of the people who had that religion—those religions. It's a logical explanation, though I have no idea whether it's true or not."

Zilia said, "The prophets couldn't . . . couldn't change, was that it?"

Jep said, "It has to be genetic. I think the God could pacify any merely environmental influence. Either Sam's right, and these people were the descendents of a race which selected for fear and apprehension, or maybe even now and then there are people born in the human race who are hardwired for hatred. They can induce some others to go along, followers, people who've had bad rearing or traumatic childhoods . . ."

"Like me," said Zilia, without rancor, suddenly seeing the point.

"Well, yes. Like you used to be. As I say, these followers may go along as long as the leader is influencing them, but they can change. The selected ones or the mutant can't. Something inside them won't let them trust anything or anyone. They have to fear. They have to attack."

Emun Theckles, who had been listening to this with close attention, made a sudden, revulsive motion.

"What's the trouble?" his brother asked.

"I was thinking of Enforcement," Emun said. "The soldiers of Enforcement are programmed that way. They trust no one, believe no one. They, too, are hardwired to hate."

Theor Close raised his eyebrows at Betrun Jun. China leaned toward the Phansuris and whispered, "Emun worked on Enforcement for forty years. He was a maintenance engineer for the army."

"If they trust no one," asked Dern, "how can you deal with them?"

"They're programmed to ask questions," said Emun. "When they ask questions, you'd better have the answers they've been programmed to accept, that's all."

"True," murmured Theor Close. "You read a catechism of attitudes and opinions into the Enforcement soldiers, then they will seek that set of attitudes and opinions. Any living thing not manifesting that set, dies."

"Enforcement would kill a poultry-bird because it didn't recite the proper formulae?" Sam barked in unamused laughter.

"Unless it was programmed to ignore poultry-birds," Betrun Jun agreed. "Mostly, the Enforcement machines are programmed to ignore all living creatures except those fitting a certain pattern. Manlike, for example. Or like some alien people."

"Let's quit talking about it," said Zilia. "It's over. The Voorstoders were the only tribal religionists in the System. The Gharmgods are now all over Ahabar. Phansure never did have that kind of religion. And the prophets are safely away from us all, on Ninfadel."

"They have a Door," said Sam in a bleak, uninterested voice.

Everyone looked at him, wondering if he had gone mad.

"What do you mean," asked China at last.

"They had a Door, the one they came through into Voorstod. It was in the courtyard of the citadel. When I went up there and we buried Maire . . . Maire's body, I saw that it was gone. I didn't remember it until just now. They must have taken it with them."

"You didn't tell anyone?" asked Dern Blass, unbelieving.

"I didn't remember it until just now."

Again Emun made the revulsive gesture. "Bad," he said. "People like that shouldn't have Doors of their own."

Spiggy said, "So they could . . . go through it from Ninfadel and come out . . . where?"

"I don't know where," said Emun. "Maybe anywhere."

Theor Close raised his eyebrows into his hair. "What did this Door look like?"

Sam described it. Jep and Saturday added a few words.

"You have reason to be concerned," the engineer said, casting his colleague a doubtful and worried look. "Doors of that type have not been made for civilian use for millennia. They operate one way only. They need no *other end* in order to function. They may be set, approximately, for any destination."

"Where would the prophets go?" asked Africa Wilm "To Thyker, perhaps. To the Baidee."

"The Baidee are free thinkers," remarked Dern "They would not put up with the prophets' claim to know the only holy truth. It's unlikely the prophets would go to Thyker, but we don't know where else they might go Perhaps just Out, away. Let us hope so. Whatever they intend to do, we must tell the people on Ahabar, immediately."

· *Howdabeen Churry counted* on youthful zealotry and a few ancient weapons to carry out his plan regarding Hobbs Land. A year before, one of his minions had been digging into old military records and had found mention of certain devices that had been ordered from Phansuri armorers and stored in the desert at the time of the Great Invasion. The minion had found no record indicating they had been disturbed since. When The Arm of the Prophetess had made a foray into the desert and uncovered one of the repositories, it had found the arma ment as described, much of it still in its original shipping cases.

Among other interesting devices was a thing called a Paired Combat Door, one of which was always keyed to the other, while the other could be keyed onto any existing Door within System range. The two interconnected Doors could be assembled quickly and taken apart as quickly. They would allow an invasion force to set up one Door at their home base, invade through an existing planetary Door, blow up that Door, and set about hostilities while carrying an escape route with them.

Even when quite new, the Combat Door had come without a guarantee. Nothing that complex, designed to be set up that quickly, could be guaranteed—so the disclaimer attached to the device stated, estimating a fifteen percent chance of failure during any sustained period of use. Churry chose not to mention this to his troops. He merely punched up the manuals for assembly and disassembly, uttered a perfunctory prayer to the Overmind, in whose service he was engaged, and suggested daily drills until proficiency was attained.

In a remote desert region of Thyker, both Doors were tested by being assembled and interlocked, and successfully transmitting men and materiel from point A to point B and back again. Everyone arrived intact at both places. Howdabeen Churry permitted himself a small sigh of relief. Losses at such an early stage of the exercise would have been difficult to explain away.

When the troops disbanded, with instructions to arrive early in the morning for the actual invasion, Churry sat with Mordy Trust over glasses of oasis wine and the charts of Hobbs Land which Shan Damzel had given to Churry in Chowdari.

"We go into the Central Management area," said Mordy Trust, reviewing the plan for one last time. "We blow the Doors behind us as we come in, to prevent Hobbs Land from sending any messages out. The flier park is nearby. We take twelve fliers from the park. One team goes to each settlement and destroys any God they find there, the twelfth team stays in CM and destroys the God there, if they've got one, then everybody goes to this

point here," and she pointed out a place north of CM,
halfway between Settlements Ten and Five, which had
been computed to be the minimum aggregate distance
from all settlements. "There the twelfth team will have set
up the return Door. Everybody returns through that Door
except the pilots, who take the fliers out on the plain
about here," she pointed, "leave them there, and return to
the Combat Door together in one flier. We de-bond that
one flier with the de-bond rifle we found in the old armory, then we return to Thyker through the Door, which
we have concealed as well as we can. We will have destroyed only the Gods plus one flier, and we will have left
nothing behind us except one Door, which they probably
won't find and which they can't use for anything if they
do find, because it's permanently keyed to the one here."

Churry nodded his agreement. "After returning here,"
Churry concluded, "we disassemble this Door, leaving
Hobbs Land without communication for the near future
but otherwise essentially unharmed. Our Door, the one
we leave there will be well hidden, and later we can sneak
back and see what's happening."

Mordy nodded. "They'll be effectively cut off. It'll take
a long time before anyone finds out what happened. By
the time it is generally known what did happen, we will
have put phase two into action, our propaganda campaign
concerning the danger posed by the Hobbs Land Gods.
By the time people realize we have killed something that
could have taken them over, they will be very glad we did
and ready to assist us in doing the same on Ahabar."

Every member of the Arm was sure of this. Churry
himself was sure of it. Churry had computed the time it
would take to get another Door built on Phansure and
shipped to Hobbs Land. He felt the farm world would be
effectively cut off for at least half a lifeyear, plenty of time
to confirm the danger posed by the Gods. Everyone would
be glad, when they finally found out.

"We can go there anytime we want to," he mentioned
to Mordy Trust. "To collect evidence."

"Provided they don't find our Door." She considered
this the weak point in the plan.

"It's in a broken area where no one ever goes, according to Shan Damzel. They're unlikely to find it."

"When we do the raid, they'll see us flying toward it, or away from it."

"That's why we're using their own fliers. They won't know who's inside them. They're used to seeing their own fliers going back and forth. No one will pay any attention."

"And then?" she had asked.

"Well, Mordy, we see what happens. The purpose of leaving a Door hidden there is so we can see what's happening. If these people have been swallowed up and changed, that offers a threat to the rest of us. Shan Damzel is sure they have been and it does, and so am I." Churry had said this often during training. Though he did not realize it, he had portrayed the Hobbs Landians as monsters, possessed by terrible things. He hadn't meant that, but it is what his followers had heard, more or less.

"It won't be necessary to kill anybody," Mordy said flatly, reaffirming what she'd been told.

"Of course not, Mordy. They're farmers on Hobbs Land. They won't put up any fight. They see a fully armed Baidee coming through a Door, they'll turn tail and run."

He had often said this also during training. He had visualized the scene frequently, himself at the head of an intrepid band making the strike, finding out what needed to be known with no nonsense about it. There had been many such raids, many such decisive actions in the history of the Baidee. Since he did not know what was in his followers' minds, he did not see the fundamental dichotomy in his vision. Farmers would run, but farmers would be harmless. Monsters wouldn't be harmless, and monsters probably wouldn't run.

Churry had visions of medals and glory, after the fact. System would approve and admire, after the fact. So he assured himself, right up to the moment his hundred and twenty fully armed and equipped Baidee troops stamped their booted feet upon the sands of Thyker, readying themselves to go through the Combat Door into Hobbs Land.

· · ·

· *Tandle Wobster was* the first to see the Baidee
invaders. She was also the first to die. She happened to be
in the vicinity of the Doors, on her way back from the flier
park, when the first Baidee came through. Seeing the
weapons, she panicked and ran for the Security building.
The young trooper shot her in the back to keep her, he
said later, from setting off the alarm. Actually, she didn't
think of anything when he shot her except that this was
one of the possessed, possibly a monster. He'd been taught
to shoot at anything moving, and he did.

Hearing the weapon, the security people, all three of
them on duty, came out to see what had happened, and
the same trooper, seeing weapons in their hands, fired
again. More monsters, he told himself, without realizing
it. One of the security people got off a lucky shot with a
stunner and paralyzed the trooper's right arm. All three
of the security people were dead before they hit the
ground.

Churry came through in the next bunch, took one
look at the bodies, made a thin-lipped grimace, sent the
offending trooper back through the Door, and ran for the
flier park. Others at CM, alerted by the firing, had peeked
out, had seen what was happening, and the more foolhardy among them had found weapons of sorts—power
tools or something they could use as clubs—and tried to
defend CM. Two troopers dropped, shot through the
heads by fasteners fired from the guns used to put sponge
panels together. One of the Hobbs Land tool wielders was
killed, the other escaped.

Meantime, a clerk in the personnel department got to
the main network stage outside Dern's office and sprayed
a warning to all the settlements that CM was being invaded. The clerk did not know enough to key the audible
warning, which meant that the warning light blinked
unobserved in most of the settlement administrative offices. It was lunchtime, and no one was there. In Settlements One and Ten, however, people were present, the
audible alarms were set off, and both defensive and offen-
sive tactics were hastily planned.

The invading force was unopposed as it took twelve fliers, disabling but not destroying all others in the park. Eleven of them set off for the settlements. The twelfth, which contained the linking Door and was commanded by Mordy Trust, lifted only briefly, then set down again outside the temple of Horgy Endure. The God Horgy was dragged out of the temple by grunting Baidee. Churry had decided not to destroy the temples. He didn't want to appear wantonly destructive, and the temples themselves weren't implicated in the possible swallowing Shan was afraid of. Once outside, the God was laid on an incinerant pad, another was thrown over the top, and the assemblage was ignited.

Five people came running out of the management area, brandishing one thing or another and screaming at the Baidee to leave the God alone. Mordy Trust started to tell the troopers to ignore them and get into the flier, but she was too late. None of the intensive drills in which the Baidee had engaged had focused on withholding reaction or minimizing damage. Every drill had had as its purpose shortening reaction time to any observable threat. The troopers saw threat and reacted with deadly force. The five Hobbs Landers went down in a flurry of broken bone and spattered blood before Mordy could get her mouth open. Several of the missiles used, which were lethal at great distances, went on down into the management area and killed other persons who were merely standing there, watching. One of the missiles hit a fuel store in a repair building and set it on fire. The fumes of the fuel were lethal. One hundred CM staff members died from inhalation of poison before the confused, grieved fire-squad got the flames out.

Mordy didn't stay to see the God burn. She had decided that things were already out of hand. Praying that the damage in Central Management had been the only damage done, she got her troopers into the flier and set off for the meeting point. Her group had yet to find an appropriate hiding place and set up the linking Door.

Meantime, in settlement after settlement, the Baidee troops encountered what they interpreted as resistance or threat by monsters, with the same unthinking responses they had shown at CM. Some settlers moved to defend their temples and were killed. A few troopers were killed by hidden defenders. Despite the carnage, each of the Gods was pulled from its temple and burned. In one settlement, the God was defended by children, though the troopers did not realize until they had killed them that they were children, some of them not more than eleven lifeyears old. The God in that settlement had been less solid than in the others, more crumbly. When they threw it down upon the mat, it broke into fragments, dirtying their uniforms with the fine, black dust.

Sweating and sick, one of the troopers said to Churry that they ought to kill everyone. "They've seen us," he said. "They've seen us, and we've killed the kids, and we have to kill them, too, so they don't . . ." The trooper had begun to doubt that the victims were monsters. They acted like people. They acted like kids. And killing people, kids, wasn't going to set well with those in Authority.

Churry slapped him, hard, and told him to get into the flier. All the way to the meeting point, he kept wondering if that had been the right response. Maybe the man had been right. They had sufficient weaponry with them to wipe out the settlements. Maybe . . .

Common sense prevailed. What had happened was unfortunate, he told himself, but explainable as the kind of mistakes untried men make in their first combat situation. If the Baidee wiped out Hobbs Land, however, no explanation would be acceptable. Besides, they couldn't guarantee to wipe out everyone unless they stayed here for days, and it would mean killing the children and babies as well, and by that time they'd be outlawed in the System.

While carnage and destruction went on among the settlements, Dern Blass's group on the escarpment finished its lunch, got into the flier, and returned in leisurely fashion toward CM, following the line of the river which would take them past Settlements Seven and Five and then south.

"Smoke," said Sam, suddenly alert.

"Right," said Spiggy, who was piloting. "At Seven."

"At Five," said Dern, pointing ahead of them, then off to the left. "And Six."

Spiggy dropped to a lower altitude and took refuge behind a convenient hill.

"Voorstoders?" asked Sam. "It couldn't be!" Who else would invade Hobbs Land? The prophet had threatened to do just that!

"I don't know who," said Africa. "Take us up a little, Spig."

From the slightly higher altitude they saw the telltale sparkle of a Door, off to their right, in an area heavily cut with canyons. A dozen fliers rose suddenly from the site and sped south.

"Those are *our* fliers," cried Dern, outraged.

Spiggy held the flier low. "They haven't seen us," he said. "Perhaps better they don't."

"Who in hell," muttered Sam.

"Baidee," said Saturday, suddenly sure of it.

"Baidee!" blurted Harribon.

"Not the girl," she said. "Not the fat one. The other one. The one who talked to me when we left for Ahabar. The one who wanted to know why there was a temple at CM. The one who wanted to know if CM had a choir."

"Shan Damzel?" asked Spiggy. Then, suddenly, "Shan Damzel!" Yes. Shan Damzel might, could . . .

"What are they doing here?" cried Harribon Kruss.

"They came to kill the Gods," said Saturday. She howled angrily. "He's afraid of the Gods, so he sent these people to kill them. They think they have."

"Get us into CM," Dern directed Spiggy. "Quick as you can."

"Quick as I can without letting those bastards see us," amended Spiggy. "Twelve fliers, Dern. And there's smoke, everywhere. That's not just Shan Damzel and his sister. That's a bunch; they're armed, and we aren't!"

They hovered just below the ridge, waiting for twelve fliers that did not return, not seeing the one that did, though they saw the cloud of dust when it was de-bonded. Only when there was no further activity did Spiggy speed the flier south and set it down outside the CM offices. Dern ran toward his office, shouting something about communications. Spiggy summoned two engineers from the nearest repair shop and went to examine the Doors.

All gone, blown, destroyed. On his way back from the tumbled wreckage, Spiggy discovered Tandle's body, crumpled like a doll.

He stood up to confront Dern Blass, his eyes blazing, who cried, "Messages from the settlements coming in upstairs, Spig. Get up there and start putting information together. Anybody know where Jamice is? Find her, get her to help you. Ah, God, poor Tandle. Shit, Spiggy. Get Sam and Africa Wilm to help you, too. Find out what's happened."

What had happened was that all the Gods had been burned. What had happened was approximately three hundred Hobbs Landians dead, a twelfth of their total strength, another two or three hundred wounded, some seriously. Among the wounded were Friday and little Wednesday, two of Africa's children. Among the dead were Willum R. Quillow, almost-twelve-year-old Thash Tillan, and the even younger Miffle twins, who had died attempting to defend Birribat Shum. Wounded and dead were brought to CM, where a hospital was set up, and a temporary morgue, in the largest gymnasium. Hastily mobilized clerks were set to securing identification and filling out forms. Medically trained people from the settlements poured into CM to care for the wounded.

"As soon as people have been identified for sure," Dern directed, "take the bodies up on the escarpment and bury them. Call the settlements and ask for volunteers."

"Let's not forget there's a Door out there in the canyons," said Sam. "We saw it!"

"We weren't supposed to see it," said Africa, wiping her face. Her children would survive. Other children hadn't. She could not stop crying over them, but duty would not wait while she grieved. "I'll take a crew and find the damned Door." She didn't wait for approval. A moment later they could hear her voice raised, demanding volunteers.

"What's the Door out there for?" asked China, who had spent the last hours carrying bodies, alive and dead.

"So they can come back," said Sam with absolute certainty. "We weren't supposed to know it was there. They set it up so we can't get out, but they can come back."

"Well," said China, "I imagine Africa will see about that."

"Who do we tell?" asked Spiggy of Dern. "How do we tell? We used the Doors for all communication."

"We have a radio data link from our Archives to Transystem headquarters on Phansure," said Dern. "Nobody uses it for anything. It's too slow. Takes too much redundancy to get anything through accurately. I've never used it, but old Mysore Hobbs the first insisted on it. He said the Doors might break down. He always had this thing about Doors. He didn't trust them. I thought we'd never need it, not in a million years." His own face was as wet as Africa's, as China's "The instruction manual's on my desk," he mumbled, mopping at himself. "Oh, God, I already miss Tandle. She'd have had it all set up."

"Let me do it," said China, beckoning to Harribon Kruss. "Harribon and I are good at that kind of thing." They went uplevel to dig out the manual and set up the emergency linkage.

Since the death of Bondru Dharm, Jep had not felt so grieved. None of them had. They worked, and cried, and worked. Whenever they thought the worst was over, they heard that someone else they knew had died. They cursed, and worked. Missiles had gone all the way through rows of sponge panel buildings, breaking water lines, setting fires. Essential machinery had to be checked for damage. Children had to be comforted. Wounded had to be cared for. Burial parties had to be manned. Pain and weeping. Blood and sorrow. And eventually night came, and people fell onto whatever flat surface was available and slept.

A day later there was more of the same, but it came in more orderly chunks. Everyone knew who had died and pretty much who was dying. Everyone knew who lived and would probably go on living. People, including Mysore Hobbs on Phansure, knew who had done it. There was no question whatsoever. One of the Baidee troopers had been found in Settlement One, still unconscious from a blow on the head administered with a large rock by Gotoit Quillow while the trooper was attacking Willum R. The trooper was now chained to a wall in the basement of CM, his uniform, weapons, and equipment set aside as exhibit A, his head shaved in order, they all agreed, that his head wound could be treated. Actually, when Sam had seen the length of the hair which had been hidden under the turban, he had had a violent reaction and had assaulted the unconscious man with his belt knife, sawing everything off but uneven stubble.

"It's the same damned kind of thing," he kept muttering, remembering the men of Voorstod. "It's the same damned kind of thing."

"I don't feel any different," murmured Zilia. "They burned all the Gods, but I don't feel any different."

Jep patted her on the arm. "Never mind, Zilia. All they did was cut off the Gods' tongues. They'll grow new tongues. We'll bury a few of our companions at the temples, and the Gods will grow new tongues. The Gods are still there." He gestured outward, circling his hands, lifting them to describe circle after rising circle, until his pointing fingers reached the level of the distant escarpment. "I imagine it's reached all the way to the top by now."

Zilia tried to read his face. "What was in the temples wasn't the God?"

Jep shook his head. "What's in temples was never the God. What's in the temples were just mouths, to talk to us. Birribat Shum isn't dead. Horgy Endure isn't dead. The damned Baidee have killed some of us, but they had no idea where to find the Gods."

He spoke with complete authority. He would not have needed to speak at all. Once they thought of it, each of them realized that nothing had truly been destroyed. Even those who had died were part of what grew on Hobbs Land. A way. A convenience. A kindness.

They went on doing what had to be done, comforting one another as best they could. None of them recalled what Sam had told them upon the escarpment. In their grief and immediate pain, none of them remembered that the prophets had taken a Door with them to Ninfadel.

· *Twelve of the* troopers of The Arm of the Prophetess were dead, though their bodies had been carried

back to Thyker. One trooper had been inadvertently left
behind on Hobbs Land, and Churry hoped he too was
dead so he couldn't talk. Churry was angrier than he
could ever remember being. Though he didn't quite realize it yet, he was angry at himself. He had always delighted in the fact that he had never found it necessary to
raise his voice. He had always told himself his zealotry
was a different kind than that of other folk. He did not
rant. He thought of himself as quiet and quite deadly. He
told himself he would not hesitate to use force, when necessary, but would never stoop to it when it was not. His
self-assessment had never been tested, but he had believed
it implicitly, believed it as an article of faith, as he believed
in the Overmind.

Now he writhed in a fury of self-hatred. He had never
anticipated a time when he would accuse himself of having been a fool. Who would have thought it necessary to
train soldiers not to kill? There was nothing about that in
the manuals. Who would have thought it necessary to
carry weapons which didn't kill? There were no such
things in the armory.

As for Mordy Trust, she was shocked into virtual immobility. She sat with her face blank, not speaking, while
the others gathered around her, murmuring incoherently.

"So far as we are concerned," Churry snarled at his
remaining one hundred seven men and women, coming
very close to raising his voice, "the twelve men who died
today died right here on Thyker during an unfortunate
training exercise. They went out and didn't come back."

The troops, who had never given any thought to killing unarmed children and elderly women, and who certainly hadn't given much thought to dying themselves,
were now finding themselves unable to think of anything
else.

"How about Nonginansaree?" whined Nonginansaree's brother. "He didn't get back."

"Let things cool down, we'll go back and find him,"
said Churry. "But let things cool down. You get out of
those kits. Put them in a pile out behind the barracks." He
ticked off the three worst foul-ups he had personally observed and told them, "You three dig a pit. Put the bodies

and the combat kits in the pit, cover it up, pack it down, smooth it out, and park a truck on top of it. The rest of you, get your ordinary clothing on, and get back to daily life. When you hear about the training fatalities, be properly surprised."

"Shouldn't we . . ." said someone tentatively. "Shouldn't we . . . reparations. Those kids . . ."

"What kids?" demanded Churry. "I know nothing about any kids."

This came frighteningly close to fooling with their heads. They all knew there had been kids, and women, and men, mostly unarmed, hundreds of them. Baidee did not lie, not usually. Certainly they did not assert conditions contrary to those which could be observed. They had observed people, not monsters, being killed.

Churry saw the doubt on their faces. "We don't *officially* know about any kids," said Churry, more gently. "What happened was unfortunate, but none of us planned it. All we can do now is remember why we went there in the first place, which is still important to us, and give things a few days to settle down."

Still murmuring incoherently, the others obeyed him, though they did so with backward glances and a few peculiar looks, which Churry did not relish. When all had gone, Mordy remarked in a dead calm voice, "All we can do now, Churry, is see that all future training includes learning when not to shoot."

Churry, who had over and over again visualized the raid into Hobbs Land as a militant but orderly progress of his people, while the farmers ran shrieking in the opposite direction, was by now fairly sure all two or three hundred of the Hobbs Land corpses would eventually be laid on his shoulders. He had been responsible for training the Arm. He had been responsible for commanding the exercise. Now he nodded somberly at Mordy's comment, thinking that now was a less than perfect time for her to have given him such excellent counsel, thinking that though she might not realize it, there would be no future training at all for either of them to be involved in.

· · ·

• *Shallow under the* soil, behind the barracks of The Arm of the Prophetess, in the desert outside Chowdari, lay the bodies of twelve troopers and the combat uniforms of one hundred nineteen, including those covered with the fine black dust Birribat Shum had shed when he broke into pieces outside his temple in Settlement One. If there had been water, conditions would have been quite perfect for the growth of the God. Thyker, however, was a hot desert world. On this particular spot, rain had last fallen fifteen years before and might not fall for fifteen or twenty more. Under the soil the bodies desiccated slowly, mummifying in the heat. Abroad in the land spread rumors of a desert training exercise from which twelve men had not returned. Fliers searched for the missing men, but did not find them.

In Chowdari, Churry contacted Shan Damzel to tell him that finding the answer to his question would have to wait, possibly for a very long while.

"But it's growing," cried Shan. "In Ahabar. I'm sure."

"Use a sleep inducer and forget it," snapped Churry. He was out of sympathy with Shan Damzel. "Let me tell you, Baidee. Now that I've had the experience, it seems to me the people on Hobbs Land behaved almost exactly as I would have if some uniformed troop came plunging through a Door at me. If those people have been swallowed by anything, I can't see that it has hurt them in the least."

Shan gulped and tried to protest, but Churry shushed him with a few brusque words and without offering explanation. Churry was too furious with both Shan and himself to offer explanations or excuses or even information. As a result, Shan had no idea what had happened on Hobbs Land.

• *On Hobbs Land,* shallow under the soil, the net had spread across the escarpment, beneath the ancient villages, beneath the ruined temples, toward and around and then deep, very deep, beneath the strange radial growths which had been dismissed as "dormant" by the team from Thyker.

In the network was Maire Girat, remembering Voorstod of her childhood, every day, every detail, faces and words spoken, rain that had fallen, sun that had shone, rocks foamed with spray at the side of the sea, all there, all in the network, what Maire was and what she knew of others' being. In the network were Jep and Saturday and Sam, everything they had done or been upon Hobbs Land, everything they had seen or heard while they were upon Ahabar, all saved, tucked away, kept as though in an Archive—every thought, every response, every recollection. What had happened to them in Voorstod, as well. What they had felt. What they had feared.

There, buried deep in the escarpment was Emun Theckles, walking the gloomy halls of Enforcement, looking into the red lenses of violence, taking out his tools, smelling something wrong, sniffing death and destruction. The network sniffed with him, remembering. Everything was there, every soldier he had worked on, every maintenance diagram, every schematic, everything he had learned from his colleagues about their work on other soldiers, all there, deep, buried, waiting.

Buried deep were Flandry and Pye and Floom and what they had planned while they had visited Hobbs Land. Buried deep were Shan Damzel and his horrified dreams of Ninfadel, his hopes concerning Howdabeen Churry, his fear, his rage.

Buried deep was the Baidee soldier who had been left behind when The Arm of the Prophetess fled, everything he knew, everything he thought.

There had been time for each set of information to be added in orderly fashion. There had been time for every eventuality to be accommodated. The recent great sorrowfulness had been part of the pattern. There had been death and grief, but death and grief had stayed within acceptable limits, and no critical damage had been done. Those beloveds no longer living on the surface lived still in the network beneath. The network grieved only for what they might have become. What they had been, the network still possessed.

Each thing had happened in its time. Each inevitability had been set up, quietly and mechanically and withou waste. Paths had been smoothed for some; obstacles had been overcome for others; bait had been set out for the vermin; and traps had been set, to be tripped in the fullness of time.

But there was to be no fullness of time. There was only now. Now, when something unremembered came heaving into the light, like a rotting body emerging in the jaws of a digger, shockingly and without warning. The network had not accounted for that unremembered thing, had not planned for it, had not known of it. None of the Voorstoders had thought of it, while they were on Hobbs Land. Sam Girat had not thought of it, not until now. It was something he had known, but had not known he had known. One of those oddities, one of those unaccountables.

The network was not perfect. Still, it did not engage in recriminations. Such were wasteful. Such were inefficient. When action was wanted, action was all that could happen. All orderly growth was abandoned. Shapes heaved and changed, cells ramified, structures shuddered and expanded like storm clouds, boiling with almost visible motion. Now all order was lost in this burgeoning growth.

The inevitable had been assumed. The immediacy of the inevitable had been underestimated. The network, even while it roiled with frantic life, was no longer sure it could grow fast enough.

SEVEN

· *The Archives link,* on which Mysore Hobbs
had insisted when Hobbs Land had first been settled, announced itself in the middle of the night, and Mysore
Hobbs II became the first person outside the invading
force and Hobbs Land itself to learn what had happened,
who had died, and who else was likely to. Dern Blass's
image was there, on the stage, a little incoherent at times,
but clear enough to be shockingly understood. Though
Dern Blass didn't tell Mysore what had motivated the
Baidee, not precisely, his message did offer intriguing
hints as to what *might* have moved them to do such a
dangerous and provocative thing. There was no question
that it had been Baidee who had made the raid. The best
possible proof of Baidee culpability, as the image showed,
lay in the person of one Nonginansaree Hoven, approximately eighteen lifeyears old, now under detention, nearly
naked, at CM, together with all his weapons and typical
Baidee clothing, including his zettle. Dern Blass had a few
superheated words to say about the words embroidered
thereon.

While Dern Blass grieved over his dead settlers, wantonly killed, Mysore grieved with him. When Dern spoke angrily of the blown Doors, however, Mysore Hobbs realized at once that the attackers had not destroyed them for mere destruction's sake. The only reason to destroy the Doors would have been to keep the foray secret for some little time, that is, unknown by System at large. Because the Archives link was archaic and inefficient, the invading force had not imagined such a thing would exist, and though it was archaic and inefficient, Mysore learned of the outrage within a few watches of the time Dern began the telling. He also learned the name of the captured soldier.

He sent Hobbs Transystem staff members quietly to Thyker, where they were able to establish Hoven's membership in an ultramilitant group of wild-eyed youngsters known as The Arm of the Prophetess, commanded by Howdabeen Churry. An information stage specialist began backtrailing charges for food and drink and transportation, thus uncovering evidence that Churry and Shan Damzel had several times been in the same place at the same time, not long before the raid itself. The same backtrailing was used to locate other possible members of the Arm.

It was only half a day, Phansuri time, after learning of the matter that Mysore Hobbs came through the Door from Phansure to Chowdari on Thyker like a fat stroke of lightning, surrounded by thunderclouds of aides and specialists in System Law, demanding to be seen at once by the Circle of Scrutators, preferably by all of them assembled.

"Not available," he was told by a cowering underling.

"They must answer at once to this outrage," Mysore trumpeted.

"On retreat," he was told by another, more supercilious underling, who had no idea what was going on.

Holorabdabag Reticingh had ordered the underling to forestall interruption. He himself was not sure what had happened, though, since Mysore Hobbs had made no effort to keep the matter quiet on Phansure, System News was already seething with rumors. Reticingh wanted to delay confrontation until he could learn specifically what had happened. It was not the first mistake made by Baidee on that day. It was not to be the last.

"Tell your Scrutators they will regret their incivility," smiled Mysore Hobbs with a dragon's toothy grin. "Whether they were on retreat or not, they should have made time to talk to me. I could have enlightened them as to the murders of over three hundred unarmed and inoffensive civilians upon Hobbs Land, including many children. *Young* children. I could have told them about the destruction of Doors which will require much time and enormous expense to replace. I could have told them that we have a member of the invading force captive. He is a High Baidee, member of a group called The Arm of the Prophetess. Here is his picture, another of his clothing. Here is a medical report on his condition. Since I could not inform your foolish masters of these matters, I leave you with two names to give to them with my compliments. Shan Damzel. Howdabeen Churry!"

And with that, he turned about and went back to the Hobbs Transystem complex on Phansure, from which location he subsequently refused to speak to anyone from Thyker, either during or after his completion of certain arrangements with the other farm worlds.

"Tell them," he told his secretaries when Thyker tried frantically to reach him, "that I am on retreat."

This information was promptly received on Thyker, and the underling carried the message to Reticingh and his fellows.

"You should have talked with him," said Merthal, who had been summoned to lend aid and assistance.

"How could I talk to the man when I don't know what has happened. I can't talk to him until we know exactly what occurred. What has Churry been up to?"

"He can't be located," replied Merthal, who had been trying to find Churry since the first rumors had reached the Circle of Scrutators. "They say he's on desert maneuvers."

"How about Shan Damzel?"

Shan Damzel was summoned and asked to tell the Circle what he'd been up to for the past few days.

"I've been here at the temple," he said sulkily. "Every day for the past five days, as a matter of fact."

"Doing what?" asked Reticingh.

"Meditating. I haven't been sleeping well."

"Reticingh," said Merthal, "I've just thought . . ."

Reticingh made an angry and impatient gesture. "Are you involved in this business?" he snarled at Shan.

"What business?"

"This destruction of the Hobbs Land Gods?"

Thank the Overmind, said Shan silently. At least it's dead on Hobbs Land.

"When did this happen?" he asked, with spurious innocence.

"Yesterday."

"I've been here in the temple, meditating."

"Reticingh," Merthal interrupted again.

"What!" snarled Reticingh.

"Something just occurred to me."

"And what was that?"

"Thyker gets about two-thirds of its total food supplies from Hobbs Transystem."

Shan looked up, dazed, wondering what this had to do with anything.

"Mysore Hobbs *is* Hobbs Transystem," Merthal went on, relentlessly. "And he's very upset."

"He wouldn't," breathed Reticingh. "He wouldn't do that?"

"Do what?" asked Shan, suddenly aware of factors and considerations which had not previously crossed his mind. "Do what?"

"Oh, shit," muttered Reticingh. "Oh, for the love of the Overmind. Oh Hell, Shan. What did the Hobbs Land Gods ever do to you that you had to stir up something like this?"

· *The same question* had occurred to Mysore Hobbs. It wasn't that Mysore Hobbs cared about the Hobbs Land Gods. Mysore Hobbs had no interest in the Gods one way or the other. He was a Phansuri, who could take Gods or leave them alone. However, he was also a conscientious man whose self-image demanded very high standards of conduct, and if Gods meant something to the settlers, then their Gods should not be interfered with. The settlers had been guaranteed that courtesy under the terms of the contract.

The government of either Phansure or Thyker would have considered it acceptable merely to refer the matter to Authority. Mysore Hobbs, however, had no intention of involving Authority. Whenever one invoked Authority, one invoked, by association, that unliving army stored away on the moon Enforcement, just waiting to be called up. Authority and Enforcement were two words for a single idea, like bread and jam or roast grom with kotopek. If a hundred or so Baidee could make such a mess of a simple raid which had been largely unopposed, consider what unthinking destruction such an army might accomplish! Mysore Hobbs shuddered to think of it. No, he did not intend to involve Authority.

Instead, Hobbs sent for his operations manager, who communicated with the other Hobbs agricultural projects. Food scheduled for shipment to Thyker was to be re-routed to Ahabar or Phansure or the supply center for the Celphian Rings. No food was to be shipped to Thyker from any Hobbs Transystem Foods source except from Hobbs Land itself.

• *On Thyker, at* the main receiving station outside Serena, where the day shift of warehousemen and transport workers had been waiting since early morning, a shift supervisor was attempting to explain to a higher-up in Chowdari that no foodstuffs had arrived from any of the Belt worlds, that his complaint to Hobbs Transystem had been greeted with the information that all future shipments were to come from Hobbs Land only, but that the supervisor had been unable to reach Hobbs Land.

"Can't reach Hobbs Land?" asked the higher-up with a sinking feeling.

"Something wrong with their Doors! I sent messages through all three of them. All I get is sparks!"

"I'll have Chowdari try and call you back."

Chowdari was also greeted with sparks and the warning howl that meant system malfunction. A message sent from Chowdari to Fenice upon Ahabar, asking Fenice to attempt to reach Hobbs Land, had similar results.

Maintenance of Doors was an Authority responsibility. The Bureau of Doors, unlike other Authority subdivisions, had a well-earned reputation for actually working. Its people were trained to a fare-thee-well, and they liked to be kept busy. By noon the station outside Serena had been informed by the Bureau that Hobbs Land had no functioning Doors and was therefore unavailable. By midway in the afternoon, the import center at Chowdari was aware that Thyker was under embargo.

"I don't understand!" screamed the Thykerian shipping manager, who really did not understand. "What have we done?"

A Phansuri employee of Hobbs Foods enlightened him.

The shipping manager went personally to the temple and demanded to see whoever was in charge at the Scrutator level. He got, not by chance, Holorabdabag Reticingh.

"They say they're going to what?" demanded Reticingh for the third time. "They really say that?" He was rejecting the idea, hoping against hope it wasn't so. Still, he could not pretend he was surprised. Mysore Hobbs was not a patient man. The Scrutators should have seen him when he arrived on Thyker. It had been a mistake not to do so. Mysore Hobbs intended to hold their feet to the fire.

Reticingh reflected sadly that something of this kind had been almost inevitable ever since Shan Damzel returned from Hobbs Land. Something of this kind had been brewing, in fact, ever since Shan, bursting with pride in his own strength and stability, had chosen to do research among the Porsa. Two guards were sent to fetch Shan, who returned with them in a sullen and unforthcoming mood.

"Three hundred dead," said Reticingh. "In Hobbs Land. Late yesterday, I suppose, our time."

Shan blinked in honest astonishment. Churry had assured him there would be no killing.

"They have one Baidee in custody," said Reticingh.
"The clothing, the armament, the equipment, all Baidee.
They were seen by hundreds of people. Think of it,
Shan. Baidee, from Thyker, made an assault upon the
religion of the people of Hobbs Land and killed hundreds
of innocent, inoffensive people in the process. Several
Baidee, perhaps ten or twelve, were killed by the Hobbs
Landers, defending themselves, but the bodies were re-
moved by the invaders."

"I was here yesterday," protested Shan. "I was meditating. I haven't been sleeping well."

"I know damned well where you were," roared Reticingh. "What I want to know is where were you before
that, and who did you talk to."

Shan shut his mouth stubbornly and looked out the
window, across the drill ground.

"Does this tie into that 'lost platoon' out there on the
desert?" demanded Reticingh.

"I don't know," said Shan, who considered that he
didn't know for sure. "I don't think so."

"Well, Shan Damzel, perhaps you'd like to think about
the following. Less than one-third of the food we need on
Thyker is raised here on the planet. The rest comes from
the Belt worlds. As of this morning, Mysore Hobbs has
shut us down to receiving any food at all, except from
Hobbs Land."

"That ought to be plenty. There aren't that many of
us, and it's a very productive farm world," said Shan in a
slightly surprised voice.

"Except that the Baidee raiders blew the Doors on
Hobbs Land," said Reticingh in an ominously soft voice.
"So there's nothing coming out. The Phansuri our import
manager talked to seems to think there's some other way
for Hobbs Land food to get to Thyker, but he didn't tell
us what it was. He suggested the import man ask around.
The import man came to me, so I'm asking around, Shan.
We very much need to find that alternate way, Shan, or
there are going to be a few million very hungry people
informed that they're hungry because of the Damzel and
Churry clans. I can imagine what your mother will say.
Think that over."

Shan was taken under supervision, which is what the Baidee called putting someone in a small room with no access to the outside. After he had had time to think, Shan admitted he had "suggested" to Howdabeen Churry that the Hobbs Land Gods might be dangerous, but Churry hadn't said anything to him about killing people or blowing Doors. This was true. Churry hadn't confided in Shan. Churry had told himself he was acting swiftly to forestall possible danger. What he had actually been doing, in Reticingh's opinion, was using Shan as an excuse for some excitement.

Howdabeen Churry stayed unavailable for the better part of two days, by which time some depots were already starting to run short of food. Those Baidee who attempted to go through Doors to other places were informed very politely by representatives of the governments of their putative destinations that, inasmuch as there had been extraplanetary hostilities allegedly committed by Baidee, no Baidee travelers from Thyker were being accepted.

· *On Hobbs Land,* all the bodies of those killed by the Baidee were taken up on the rampart and buried, that is, all but the one from each settlement and one from CM chosen for burial near the temples. Everyone who had gone to the escarpment on burial detail had commented on the increasing size of the mounds. They were taller than they had been the last time they were seen, and they were changing in shape. Also, the new mound at the center of the radiating ones was pushing up like the stalks of asparagus grown in the fragile vegetable houses. As though that were not quite surprising enough, other sets of radiating mounds, which were scattered over the escarpment, were also growing; some of them were growing very fast. Dern heard this without surprise. At this point, he felt, nothing could surprise him.

Saturday felt a moment's trepidation when she heard about it, but then relaxed almost immediately. It was all right. It was perfectly all right. She didn't feel she needed to discuss it with anyone, not even Jep. Everyone knew about it, but no one took time to discuss it.

The fires were out, and all the emergencies had been dealt with. Everybody who was going to die had probably died, said the medical people. Dern had made an all-settlements announcement that morning, reminding the people that, even though they were isolated at the moment, they were mostly healthy and would be well fed, with wider menu choices than heretofore, since no items could be earmarked only for export at the moment. Medical supplies on hand would last for an extended period. True, they would have to do without things like new clothing, new shoes, and new amusements from off-planet, at least for a time. A spinning and weaving class would be scheduled at the artisan center ten days hence, as would a course in shoe repair. A new drama group was being organized as well.

According to Mysore Hobbs, half a year, Standard, was the quickest time in which a Door could be built on Phansure and shipped to Hobbs Land—which were not at the best possible points in their orbits for this exercise—though it would probably take longer. Assembly of the new Door would take the Phansuri technicians some time after that, so there would be no off-planet materials for that long. Unless, that is, some other way of ingress could be found, in which case a Door might be brought in disassembled and then assembled by Phansuri technicians, cutting the total time by about two thirds.

Harvested food was to be stored for the time being. Nobody had decided yet what would happen after the warehouses were full. As for perishables, don't bother to store them, said Mysore Hobbs. Raise what you need for yourselves and plow under anything else.

"How do you plow under milk vishes," Africa had asked, annoyed. "You milk them or else." The dairymen went on milking the vishes and herding the dermot, but the Settlement One field people were already turning over about a hundred square miles of hardy salad stuff.

Africa and her volunteers had found the Door the Baidee had left in the twisted canyon land north of CM. Nothing would go through, which meant that the single-destination interlock had been disconnected, so said Theor Close and Betrun Jun, the Phansuri engineers who

were now trapped on Hobbs Land along with everyone
else. They gave the Door a good looking-over, trying to
decide how it could be dismantled or set for some other
destination. Obviously, since it hadn't come in already set
up, it was designed to be dismantled, but, with no procedure manual, neither of the engineers wanted to be the
first to try doing it. They agreed between themselves that
it was a single-destination Door of a very archaic type and
that they lacked the knowledge, the parts, and the mind-
ess intrepidity to try and modify it.

Eventually, at Theor's suggestion, a crew simply
pulled the Door over on its face and built a fence around
it. Anybody trying to come through from off-planet would
end up inside solid rock. Africa and Sam had wanted to
hide near the Door and intercept whomever came in, but
Dern Blass said no. He was unwilling to risk further loss
of life. Besides, Mysore Hobbs had something else in
mind.

Across the System, all eyes and ears were focused
upon Hobbs Land, which was cut off from all aid. The
twenty-one Actual Members of Authority had called
themselves into emergency session. Thyker had been summoned before an Authoritative Commission to Answer
Questions. Enforcement was put on alert status.

From Enforcement, Altabon Faros had sent an urgent
message to Ninfadel.

In his tent, the Awateh smiled on his sons and gave
certain orders. Almighty God had willed the diversion to
occur sooner, rather than later.

Outside the Settlement One temple, where
they had recently buried Willum R., some of the mourners remained for a time beside the grave. Jep sat with
Saturday, Sam with China Wilm, Africa alone against the
temple wall. Gotoit Quillow was around behind the temple with Deal and Sabby and Thurby Tillan, all of them
talking about their dead comrades and crying. Jep
thought it seemed he had done nothing much but cry or
feel like crying since Mugal Pyc had stolen him from Set-

tlement One. He had thought coming home would fix everything, but it hadn't.

Saturday was stretched out on her stomach, head propped on a hand, staring at the grass blades a few inches below her nose. Sam sat under a tree with China, hugely pregnant between his knees, her back against his chest, his arms around her. They weren't talking. None of them had talked much today.

"What's going to happen now?" China whispered to Sam. In the quiet, the whisper carried. They all heard her

"I don't know," Sam said. "We might know better if we knew exactly what the Baidee had been trying to accomplish when they came here."

"I think that's obvious," said Africa. "According to all the witnesses, they were mere youths. They wanted to play at being soldier, and they wanted to see what we would do after our Gods were destroyed."

"I know that," said Sam. "I mean in addition to that."

"I don't think there is any addition to that," Africa went on. "I think that was all of it. They wanted to see what we'd do. They are Baidee. The idea of real Gods frightens them."

Sam mused, remembering the nightmare from which he had wakened Shan. "That Shan Damzel, he was the one. He was a very frightened man."

"Frightened men do stupid things. Now we've found their Door and shut it, so they can't see, they'll be frightened again. They don't know what we're doing."

"What are we doing?" asked China, wiping her eyes

"We're grieving over our friends and relatives who have been killed in a exercise of pointless violence," said Sam, who had thought he had left that behind, in Voorstod.

"When we've done that, probably we'll pretty much do what we always did." Saturday wiped her face and squeezed Jep's hand.

One of the settlement cats came from behind the temple and addressed Saturday at length.

"What did she say?" asked China.

"She says if we aren't going to use the milk, at least let the cats have all they'd like of it, and would we please te the dairy people. She says not to store anything in the empty warehouses at CM until the cats have been through them, because they're alive with ferfs, and she says cats are needed up on the escarpment to hunt ferfs, but they can't stay up there by themselves because there's nothing to eat."

"I'll arrange it," said Sam, getting slowly to his feet. He pulled China up after him, and the two of them walked slowly down to the creek and across, heading toward the settlement.

"Poor Sam," said Africa.

"Why poor Sam?" asked Jep.

"Because he's spent his whole life looking for something, and he's just figured out he was looking for the wrong thing, but he doesn't know what the right one is yet." She looked down at her knotted hands and thought them perfectly symbolic of China right now. Tightly knotted up, full of compassion, full of apprehension, not knowing which way to go. Poor China. Poor Sam.

"If we knew, we could tell him," mused Jep.

"I can't tell him, because I don't know," Saturday said. "I know some things. They come to me solid, like pieces of wood, all carved to fit and nailed down. I just know, and I open my mouth and out it comes, and that's that. No questions. No hesitations."

"That's the God talking," Jep asserted.

"I suppose it is. But when it comes to other things, I haven't the least idea. Maybe those are things the God isn't interested in." Saturday sat up and brushed the grass off her trousers.

"What kinds of things wouldn't a God be interested in?" asked Gotoit Quillow from behind them. The crying session was evidently over, for both the other Quillows and Thurby Tillan were with her and nobody was blubbering. "I should think the God would be interested in everything we're interested in."

Saturday had spent a lot of time while on Ahabar thinking about that matter. "I thought so, too. But then I got to thinking about what the God actually does. I mean, the God is interested in something, it would probably do something about that, wouldn't it? So, if it doesn't interfere with what we do, day to day, it probably doesn't care very much what we do."

Africa looked up from her hands and said, "Perhaps it's simply that, within rather broad limits, it doesn't matter what we do day to day. There are probably thousands of equally effective ways of raising food and getting along together. The God is not interested in minutiae, though it helps us toward efficiency by improving our communications and running off people who are disruptive."

Saturday nodded to her mother. "And it's not just our communications, but cats' too, and probably anything else on Hobbs Land that has any intelligence at all. So the God cares about intelligence."

"What else?" wondered Gotoit.

Africa pondered this question. "It cares about diversity; Saturday's right about the cats. Also, the people who've left tended to be those who thought man was more important than other parts of creation, and themselves more important than other men," Africa mused. "Me-and-my-image devotees. Human fertility worshippers. The kind of people who will happily kill other species to make room for more humans, advocates of the old 'fill up the world and ruin it' philosophy."

"I wonder what would happen if I decided to do something to destroy intelligence or diversity. Would it stop me?" Jep asked.

"It wouldn't have to," said Africa. "You simply wouldn't do it, because you'd have been informed it wasn't a good idea." She stood up and brushed off her trousers. "Still, I get no sense that my autonomy has been destroyed. I believe I still have free will. I don't think the God is directing us, except in a few specifics, and even those seem designed merely to increase our general welfare and freedom of choice."

"So, then, what was Shan Damzel afraid of?" asked Jep.

The people sitting about shrugged. Africa shook her head. Saturday said, "I don't know, Jep. I'm just positive Shan caused all this mess, and I've been trying and trying to figure out what might have made him do it, and I ju can't. He must have been afraid of something else entirely. Something we don't know anything about."

· *Sam and China* went to the settlement office and made arrangements for extra milk for the cats, intensive cat sweeps of the warehouses, and round-trip cat transport to the escarpment, before walking over to China's sisterhouse, where they sat on the porch, unwilling to separate but unable to do anything together that was either constructive or enjoyable. They felt a pained solidarity, a joint grief, which nothing seemed likely to transmute into either recovery or catharsis.

"You're not yourself yet, Sam," said China. While they were in the office together, she had decided to get it out in the open and talk about it. Sam had said almost nothing about Voorstod. Most of what China knew, she had learned from the kids. "Are you still grieving over Maire?"

"I've been . . . grieving over something," he said with a grimace. "It won't come clear for me. I'm not sure yet what it is I'm grieving over."

She sat very still, not understanding him. When he said nothing more, she whispered, "What else could it be, Sam?"

"I don't know." He put out his hands, palms up, looking at them as though they should have held an answer. "I went to Voorstod for a reason, China. Not only my reason, I know what my reason was. But why was I *allowed* to go? It wasn't to protect Saturday or Jep. They would have probably done fine without me. What was my purpose there?"

"Perhaps your reason was all that was necessary, Sam. To see your dad. To find out about him."

He was silent a long time. At last he said, "I have the feeling there are things going on, things I have never seen. Things I have never recognized. As though I'd lived in some other world than this, all my life."

"Like what, Sam?" she asked gently.

"Well, there's the business of Maire. To save Jep, Maire Girat walked into Phaed's hands, knowing she was risking her life. Gotoit Quillow assaulted an armed trooper with a rock to try and save Willum R.'s life. Maire died, Gotoit lived, but they were both doing the same thing. How many million women over the millennia have died, trying to keep their children or themselves or their loved ones from being slaughtered?"

"Many, I suppose. And many men, as well."

"There's little or nothing about them in the legends, China. The legends were my world, and there's nothing about those people. Nothing at all."

China knew that. She made no comment.

"All my life, China, I've been looking for the *single wondrous thing.*" He stood up and moved around, running his hands through his hair. "I put those stories into books, so I could take them down and look at them, feel them, see how the words looked on pages, the way our forefathers saw them, find in each one of them the *single wondrous thing.* In the legends, they always go after the *single wondrous thing.* The Holy Grail. The Enchanted Sword. The Kidnapped Wife. The Ring of Power. The Marvelous Jewel. Eternal Life. Summer's Return. The Throne. The Crown. The Golden Bough. Whatever. Always seeking that special thing. The answer. The ultimate answer.

"That was my reason for going to Voorstod, really. I thought I'd find it there, with Dad. I thought it was one of the things Maire left behind."

"Are you sure there is a single wondrous thing, Sam."

"Why do we want one so badly, if there isn't? Why do we long for quests? Why do we . . ."

She shook her head at him, beginning to feel as she had when he used to pick at her like this, questioning, questioning. "*We* don't, Sam. I don't. Africa doesn't. Sa doesn't. I don't think women do, much. I don't think we have time. Our lives are made up of many things, not just one. Many answers, not just one. It's men that want one answer for everything. They're always making laws, as though they could make one law that would be just in all cases. They can't. They never have. I think men get derailed, sometime during their growing up. Instead of settling for what's honest and real and sort of thoughtful, they go off on these quests. They go strutting and crow ing, waving their weapons and shouting their battle cries. They say they're seeking something higher, but it always seems to end in pain, doesn't it?"

"I don't know . . ."

"I mean, like those laws they make. It's almost always men who make laws, absolute laws, that don't take into account what might be happening in each individual case. They particularly like to make laws regarding women, or children, as though the law could pin us down and make us be something we aren't. Often the laws are unjust and cause great pain. But men are willing to trade justice for the law, because they can make the law but they can only approach justice, carefully and case by case. Like, on Thyker, those High Baidee make a law that says no killing, ignoring the times when killing is the only merciful thing to do, but then they make exceptions for war, because they like war. I know all about it. We women know all about it."

He stared at her for a long moment, realizing the truth of what she said, then slumped to the floor beside her. "I guess that's what I was saying. While all around me people were trying to live case by case, I was still questing, still looking for absolutes. While Maire was dying, I was still looking for the one perfect thing. Why didn't I see? Why didn't I feel the threat? Why did I come trailing along after, sorry when it was too late?"

She put her arms around him. "You were always after me for answers, Samasnier Girat. I swore I'd never love you again, you bothered me so, wanting answers. Now here you are again, wanting answers. Sam, I don't know why! I don't know the answer."

"But I need to," he said quietly. "It was born in me, China Wilm. Born in me and the God has not taken it away. If it were useless or futile or destructive, wouldn't the God have removed it? If the God let me go to Voorstod, didn't the God have a reason? Perhaps I am hardwired for fruitless quests. Perhaps I am driven by guilt to make up for Maire's death. Perhaps the anger in me is too hot to be cooled." He sighed, put his arms around her, held her close.

"Phaed Girat lives. My father. Murderer of my

mother. He who was left behind with the other bloody legends. And it isn't over between us."

"Sam," she cried, feeling his words like a knell.

"Sam," he agreed. "Who has still at least one answer to find."

He kissed her and walked away from her, and she wept to see him go. It was not that she feared losing him so much as she feared he was losing himself. As though there were something within him even the God Birribat Shum could not—or would not—make quiet.

• *On the third* day after the Outrage, Howdabeen Churry was located and brought in to be questioned by the Scrutators concerning the matter of Hobbs Land. Though he had been unequivocally identified by Shan Damzel, Churry did not at first confess to being involved.

When asked where he had been three days before, he said, "We were holding training exercises several days ago. Some of my men disappeared. I've been conducting a search, as a matter of fact." All of this was true, though specious. Howdabeen had indeed been going through the motions of a search.

"Do you know Nonginansaree Hoven?"

"Of course. He's one of my men."

"Presumably not one of the missing men."

"No."

"Hoven is on Hobbs Land."

"Whatever is he doing there?"

When informed that the Hoven trooper was wearing shackles in a cell at the detention facility at CM, Churry shook his head and refused to answer any more questions. There was no religiously acceptable way that Reticingh or any other of the Scrutators could force him to do so. They could not fool with his head no matter how much, as Reticingh said to his sister over a scanty dinner, Churry's head needed fooling with. Of course, Churry did not need to confess in order to be found guilty of grave transgressions against System peace.

Churry's strategy, insofar as it could be called a strategy, had been to let things blow over, just as they would have done if the damned Hobbs Landians hadn't had some method of communication Churry hadn't counted on and still couldn't believe. Let it get to be old news. Let the anger cool. The Baidee who controlled the planetary government did not impose a death penalty for any infraction except head-fooling, but they did sentence malefactors convicted of major crimes to lengthy sequestration. Churry had already resigned himself to years, perhaps to life, in a penal colony somewhere in the southern deserts. However, the longer things dragged on, the less urgent the matter would seem, so he would delay. So he had thought.

It had not even occurred to him that people might go very hungry on Thyker before anything blew over at all.

"Mysore Hobbs says there is another way for food to get from Hobbs Land to Thyker," Reticingh grated. "He intimated that the persons responsible for the raid would know about that."

Once he understood the supply situation, Churry knew when to bow to the inevitable. "Let us say," murmured Churry, "that the raiders might have had a . . . oh, something like a Combat Door with them."

"Which would be what?"

"Which would be . . . ah, a Door that could be set up and taken down quite rapidly, perhaps. A Door that could be moved from place to place easily. A Door perhaps keyed to some other Door on some other place." Churry fell silent, thinking of the dimensions of that Door. It was narrow. Hardly wide enough for two troopers to walk through abreast of one another. Two of the Hobbs Land Doors they had destroyed had been bulk-shipment doors, designed for continuous feed and wide as a house.

As though reading his mind, Reticingh asked, "How large might this Door be?"

Churry looked at his shoes.

Reticingh snarled, "Large enough, for example, to get the parts of another Door through, if they were trans-shipped from Phansure through Thyker? Which would, of course, take some time, because there aren't Doors just lying around on Phansure, ready to be shipped."

Churry swallowed painfully. "Large enough for that, I suppose. If the parts weren't too big."

"I have a feeling that's the *minimum* time Thyker will be on short rations," said Reticingh. "Until at least one new Door gets to Hobbs Land and is installed. I would hesitate to say what the maximum time may be."

•   *The news that* the blockade of Voorstod had been withdrawn paled beside the developments following the Hobbs Land raid by renegade Baidee. Renegade Baidee is what System News called them. Renegade Baidee is what the planetary government of Thyker called them when it announced, even before it was petitioned by Hobbs Transystem Foods on behalf of the settlers, that generous reparations would be paid. The examination of Howdabeen Churry and Mordimorandasheen Trust by the Circle of Scrutators, the subsequent questioning of the Circle of Scrutators by Authority, these events were fully covered by System News and were followed by almost everyone in System. The food shortages on Thyker and the resultant rioting were fully reported along with the announcement that the entire Arm of the Prophetess was to be sent to Hobbs Land as a convict crew to load food through the only available Door to Thyker. Hungry High Baidee were dismayed to learn that early shipments, scanty enough in themselves, would consist almost entirely of mammal meat and processed eggs. Dern Blass had his own methods of retaliation.

The entire Arm had been found out, the name of one leading to the name of another, as such conspiracies do. Baidee were not accustomed to actually telling lies, that is, saying things they knew to be untrue. Most of them had simply swallowed their pride, admitted their guilt, and asked how long it would take to expiate.

Since Shan Damzel, while admitting to having provoked the entire incident and having had guilty knowledge of it, had not done any killing or raiding or taken part in the plans, he was sentenced to the same duty, but to a shorter term. Shan's siblings were swift to declare their own judgment before Shan was taken away.

"People *dead* because of you," said Bombi, sounding more annoyed than grieved. "*Children* dead because of you, shot down in their innocent blood. The whole family is whispering to one another, wondering if you have gone beyond the *bounds.*"

"Churry never said anything about killing anybody," said Shan for the twentieth time. "He was going to go in and kill the things, and then we were going to see what happened."

"Let us suppose the same thing happened here," snarled Bombi. "Suppose the *prophetess* came back to Thyker, and suppose someone from Hobbs Land just happened by and shot her *head* off, what do you think would happen?"

"The prophetess is . . . was a human being."

"So were those *hundreds* of people you killed."

"I didn't kill anybody."

"Just as good as."

Mixed with his dreams of the Porsa, Shan began to have dreams of mutilated bodies, broken faces, shattered children running from him, screaming. He thought he might rather be dead.

Phansure agreed to complete a Door in record time. The parts, including extras to allow for possible transport losses, were to be transshipped via Thyker to Hobbs Land, where Theor Close and Betrun Jun would set it up and put it to work. By that time, people would be notably thinner on Thyker, and the convict crew could look forward to little sympathy upon their return. If they ever returned. Except for Shan Damzel, the Baidee had been sentenced to a very long stay on Hobbs Land, where they were to load the Door by physical labor, using no machines, until everyone on Hobbs Land agreed that reparations were complete.

Jebedo Quillow, uncle to Willum R., said it would be a cold day on Collus before he would consider reparations complete. Dern Blass, still grieving over Tandle, thought the same. They were not alone among those who were determined that The Arm of the Prophetess would wither with age down to its last finger before it left Hobbs Land again.

The prisoners came through the Combat Door just eight days, Thyker, after the raid. What passed for justice on Thyker had always been admirably swift. All but three of them arrived quite safely. One of the three arrived inside out, and the other two did not arrive. This upsetting occurrence led to the disclosures that the Combat Door was not totally reliable and that Howdabeen Churry had known it all along.

Howdabeen Churry wondered then, and later, whether a death sentence would not, in the last analysis, have been more merciful.

· *The same day* the prisoners arrived, Emun Theckles came hesitantly into Sam Girat's office at Settlement One to remind Sam of what he had said about the Door.

"Which Door?" asked Sam, who was thinking joylessly about other things.

"The one the Voorstoders have. You and Dern Blass were going to let somebody know about it, before the Baidee raided us. Then I suppose you forgot. At least, I haven't heard any more about it."

"I forgot," Sam admitted, counting up the days that had passed. Six or seven. Everyone had been very busy.

"Who needs to know?" asked Emun.

Sam rubbed his head wearily. "Actually, Queen Wilhulmia should probably be informed first. Though I suppose Authority should be told, as well."

"I'm going to worry about that until it's done," said Emun in his quavery, slightly fussy manner. "From what you said, up there on the escarpment, those prophets were dead set against you. You and Jep and Saturday. If I were you, I wouldn't like the idea of somebody who hated me having a Door that could set him down on my front porch."

Sam thought this was hyperbole. "Theor Close did say something about that, didn't he."

"That Door's probably one of the real old ones, the kind people used to use to go Out. The kind the army still uses."

Sam stared at the old man, wondering if he'd heard correctly. "The kind the army uses?"

"Enforcement wouldn't be much good if it was limited to going through existing Doors, would it? Sure, the public Doors always have a Door at the other end. Either fixed-destination or varying-destination Doors always use a Door at the other end because that's the safest way, the way least likely to disrupt. That's the way the Baidee Door was, too. But military style Doors, Enforcement Doors, you can tune them. You know the settings for the nearest Doors, if any, to where you want to go, and you can tune the military Door to be so far north or south, or east or west, or up or down of one that's already there. If you know the planetary diameter, that is, and have the right tables for that planet, showing the curvature at the proper longitude.

"Or, if the planetary body is listed, you look up the approximate settings in the Galactic Ephemera and have a computer figure the absolute time and send a three-dimensional beacon array through and see which ones send a signal back. Or you send a soldier scouting array through, and any soldier coming out on a surface sends a back pulse describing where he is and what he can see, and you tune from there. There's five whole aisles of scouts on Enforcement, just waiting to be sent somewhere and then figure out where they are."

"So you meant it! If the Voorstoders have a Door, they could come through anywhere!"

"It wouldn't be what we'd call safe. They'd have to expect some losses. Without a Door at the other end making constant feedback corrections, as things shift, you end up out in space or inside rock or at the bottom of a sea. But, yes, with a good technician they could come through anywhere. I thought that's why you were worried, because you knew that."

Sam allowed that he would have been a good deal more worried if he had realized what it meant. He also asked Emun to excuse him, because he needed to get to EM and see that the proper warnings were sent.

He and Dern spent the afternoon directing warnings to various individuals and offices: Queen Wilhulmia; the

Bureau of Doors at Authority; Authority itself; the planetary governments of Thyker and Phansure; the supervisory bodies of other Belt worlds.

"Ninfadel!" Sam shouted, mostly at himself. "I'm not thinking, Dern. That's the first place we should have informed! Ninfadel!"

The message was accordingly sent. There was no response, but they expected none. Response would be relayed through Ahabar and might not arrive for some time.

Queen Wilhulmia's aides received the warning and passed it on to her and to Commander Karth, who attempted to reach Ninfadel and was unable to do so. He attempted to rouse the guard post by all available means and received no answer. The Door on Ninfadel was not available to Ahabar.

After a day of this, a ship was readied, one which would carry a company of Royal Marines, all of whom had seen duty as guardsmen upon Ninfadel. Ships were so seldom used that preparations took some time. Queen Wilhulmia and those of her advisors who knew what was happening were considerably worried by the time the ship lifted.

The news was received on Thyker and was generally dismissed.

"I can't imagine that a thousand or so Voorstoder and their families, without arms, can do much damage to Thyker," said Reticingh.

"Isn't it Ninfadel where the Porsa are?" asked Merthal. "I wonder if they could come through the Door as well. That's all we need, a plague of Porsa."

Reticingh changed his mind about the damage that might be done and set a planetary watch into effect, along with a message to biological research.

The same thought occurred to people on Phansure. Patrols of sparsely settled areas were increased. Satellite surveillance systems were programmed to report the telltale sparkle of Door usage in non-Door areas.

No one on Hobbs Land, no one on Thyker or Phansure or even Ahabar itself considered another place the Voorstoders might go—or might already have gone—which was where they actually were. Eight Thykerian days after the raid on Hobbs Land, five hundred prophets and an equal number of the Faithful went through their archaic Door into the large reception bay on Enforcement. They had not needed to tune their Door on Ninfadel. They had needed only to set it as instructed by Ornil and Faros and come through en masse at a prearranged time. Ornil and Faros had previously killed the watch officers and disconnected the alarms. Except for a few men locked in their quarters, the moon and the army of Enforcement were entirely in the hands of Voorstod.

"Awateh," murmured Altabon Faros from his knees, his head bowed, thinking of Silene.

"Faithful son," murmured the Awateh in return. He had not liked the wrenching, inside-out feeling of the Door. He did not anticipate the next, similar event. To postpone it, he looked about the cavernous reception bay, large enough to handle the largest Doors ever made, large enough to transmit the largest soldiers ever constructed. The Doors themselves were like the piers of giant bridges. "Can you leave that one open to Ninfadel?" he asked Faros.

It was Halibar Ornil who answered. "We can, Awateh, if there is good reason to do so."

The Awateh had had a vague idea of retreat or escape. He had no intention of mentioning this, certainly not of explaining it. He drew himself up to his full height and glared at Ornil.

"You have my command! Is that good reason?"

Ornil prostrated himself. It was not good reason. Leaving unattended Doors on continuous two-way feed was dangerous. Unquestioning obedience, however, was the measure of the Faithful. "Certainly, Awateh," he murmured.

"Get up," the Awateh prodded him with a toe. "Where does that other Door go?" He indicated the second of the enormous reception bay Doors.

"It is set for Authority, Holy One. The soldiers have been prepared and are waiting to go through. We will send them immediately, when you command it."

One of the prophet's sons spoke up. "How do we get

to Hobbs Land. The Awateh wants to go first to Hobbs Land."

Faros pointed behind them, some distance from the two permanently installed Doors, where another huge Door stood amid scaffolding and braces. "An army Door, Holy One. As soon as you are ready, we will begin tuning it."

"Tuning it?"

"To find Hobbs Land, Holy One."

"One would think it would have been done," snarled a son. "Since the prophet commanded it long since."

"Forgive us," said Faros. "But the Doors on Hobbs Land were destroyed when the Baidee invaded. This is the only one we can use, and if one wishes to make a surprise attack, it cannot be set until the time it is to be used. We regret the inconvenience this causes, but it is the nature of the device . . ."

"No matter," murmured the Awateh, smiling horribly. "While they do that, we can watch the soldiers go to Authority. I want to see them go."

• *Sam Girat woke* in the night, suddenly, as from a prophetic dream. He rose, dressed, and left the brotherhouse to find Theor Close and Betrun Jun just coming from the direction of the guest quarters, where they'd been staying for the last few days. Since the Combat Door was still the only access to Hobbs Land, and since the failure rate of that Door was currently exceeding nineteen percent, the two engineers had wisely decided not to return to Phansure through it. Instead, they had stayed upon Hobbs Land, exploring its wonders and boning up on Door installation. Better use two engineers already on site than transport others through a Door which might spit them into the heart of Collus, or simply abandon them in space, so they said. The Door engineers on Phansure rather reluctantly agreed. Door techs were jealous of their knowledge and their skills, but they took no great pleasure in thoughts of annihilation either. Instead of themselves, they sent information.

As the three men were standing in the street, looking

about themselves curiously, in the manner of those who have heard a summons but are unable to locate the caller, Emun and Mard Theckles also came out into the street.

"Trouble," said Emun, simply. "I can smell it. It used to smell like this on Enforcement, when one of the things went rogue. Can't you smell the hate?"

"Enforcement?" breathed Sam, remembering his breakfast with the old man, long ago. Ages ago. Earlier this year.

Theor Close nodded, quickly agreeing, his mind leaping over possibilities, like a rider going around a series of jumps. "Could be that," he said. "It has that feel to it."

"Where?" Betrun Jun asked Emun. "What direction? Can you tell?"

"That way," said Emun, pointing off to the northwest. "Toward the escarpment, I think."

Sam's mind, so long functioning at about one-tenth of its capabilities, came suddenly and shudderingly alert, startled into full consciousness. He had been swamped in matters unresolved, stuck in darkness, in a swamp of dissatisfaction, tangled in ancient memories, unable to forget the last sight he had had of Mam, the one he had had of his dad, the back of him, going away, scatheless. The two visions resonated against one another, making a subliminal vibration which damped his conscious thought, leaving only a shallow habit-self to deal with the business of daily living. Now his mind shuddered to its roots, quaking, erupting in agonized, panicky awareness.

"You're saying Enforcement. No, more than that! We're really saying Enforcement-Door-prophets. All three. That's it, isn't it. It's that damned Door the prophets had, the one we warned people about. Somehow the prophets have gained access to the army?"

"Unless we believe Authority has set Enforcement upon us without warning and for some unknown reason," said Theor Close. "Assume your unlikely triplet, Sam Girat. Door. Prophets. Enforcement. If it's true, who should be told?"

Sam shuddered. "Everyone! God, Theor. Everyone! Mysore Hobbs, for a start. Authority, at once. Phansure, Thyker, and Ahabar, at once. Mard, can you take care of that. Get to CM, wake up Dern Blass and see that warnings go out at once. Remember, send multiple messages through that damned Door, to allow for some of them being destroyed. Dern Blass may want to use the Archives link as well, though it'll take watches to get the information there. Alert our own people. Get them up and moving. They may need to run."

"And we?" asked Theor Close.

"We have to find whatever it is. See what it is," said Sam, knowing what it was. "We could be wrong." He knew they were not wrong. "So far we're only frightened of shadows. We have to be sure." He was sure, yet prayed he was not. "We'll take the little flier." Inside him a volcano roared, splashing white-hot radiance in all directions, lighting deep crevasses of his mind, sending the dark things there scurrying away, though not before he had seen them and recognized them for what they were. He shuddered and ran for the flier.

Sam piloted. Theor Close and Emun Theckles sat behind him on the double seat. As they flew toward the north, the lights of the other flier sped away toward the east. Betrun Jun and Mard Theckles, going to spread the word.

"How much do you know about the army?" Theor asked Emun. "About the technology?"

"I did maintenance and repairs," said Emun. "I wasn't taught a lot about the theory, but I picked up a good bit. You have to, you know. You have to understand why things work as they do. Especially when they go wrong."

"It's my understanding the army was programmable," Theor went on. "It could be given a set of attitudes and opinions, to agree with the attitudes and opinions of those mobilizing it."

"True," said Emun. "And a set of passwords and command words and phrases. These could be changed from Authority, during an action. The big destroyers have a thing like a Door built into them, a command receiver unit about the size of my head. They can be reprogrammed almost immediately, by anyone with the proper passwords. Smaller soldiers only have a command re-

ceiver like the Archives link between Hobbs Land and
Phansure. It can take a lot of time and many repetitions to
make changes in them, depending how far the action is
from Authority itself. Most battle plans depended on the
big destroyers reprogramming the little ones."

"If our warning reaches Authority . . ." Sam said if,
knowing it would not. No. That wasn't the way things
were to be. Something else. Something dark and hidden
that he couldn't see at all. Fate. Destiny. Dark forces
working against one another, like Titans wrestling far below the surface of this world. What was going on?

The land ahead of them sloped up abruptly, and behind this slope the cliffs of the escarpment loomed black
against the stars.

"If our warning reaches Authority, it can override any
commands the army has been given. If Authority has the
passwords," Emun finished the thought.

"Which it will not have," Theor Close remarked in a
dead quiet voice. "The first thing a takeover force will do
is substitute their own passwords for any currently in effect."

"Well, yes," Emun agreed. "Except there's a Final
Command, which is known to every one of the twenty-one
Members of Authority, and which *can't* be replaced. It's
in a sealed unit on the soldiers, and if you try to fool with
it, the thing destructs. It's the fail-safe device."

"So, so," mused Theor. "In that case, if you are steal-
ing the army, the first thing you do is attack Authority,
hoping you can wipe out all twenty-one of the Members
before anyone can possibly use the Final Command."

"Oh God," said Sam with horrified comprehension.
"Are you saying Enforcement may be loose, and we can't
stop it? *Nobody* can?"

"Like the Blight on Thyker," said Theor in a dull
voice.

They rose to the edge of the escarpment and looked
over it, hills and gentle valleys, tufted forests, all in shades
of darkest gray. Away to their left lay Bubble Lake, a
rising cloud of prismed color. Closer was the New Forest,
looming and shadowed. Canyons and rivers, dunes and
caverns, the marvelous landscapes of Hobbs Land spread

beneath them. To the west was a flicker, a scarlet shimmer in the darkness.

"There," said Theor. "Something came through there."

Sam dropped the flier to the tops of the trees and wove down the valleys toward the sparkle.

Above, to their left, another sparkle, brighter, falling, leaving a trail of fire.

"They're sending through scouts in an array," said Emun. "Still trying for the range. They haven't figured out the surface yet."

"Array?"

"A cube, a lattice of scouts. When they arrive, they pulse back through the still-open Door. They pulse if they destruct, from coming out in rock, or if they fall, from coming out in air, or if they have no weight, from coming out in space. Some of them will end up on or near a surface, and those pulses accumulate into a description of the surface. Then you send in a beacon array to mark the surface, and then the rest of the soldiers. The beacon array moves with the planet surface. It feeds back, keeping the Door open. One way, of course."

"That one we just saw?"

"Became a meteor." Emun pointed upward. "There's another. If we were on the surface, you could feel the shock waves from the ones detonating underground. This is a very broad, rather scattered array. Whoever's doing it has never done it before."

Theor nodded in agreement. "Whoever's doing it knows the theory but not the practice. Wasteful as all Hell, of course, which is why they use cheap scouts to start with. I don't suppose they amount to much except a fire-arm and a back-pulse."

"Do you need to see anything more to know this is happening for sure?" Sam asked in a tight voice, his mind far from this place. This was happening, here, but the reasons were far away, in time, in space. "Have you seen enough to warn the settlements?"

"They've straddled the escarpment," said Emun. "Look below." They looked down to see sparkles in the air and on the ground of the plains. "They've come ou along the edge of the escarpment and some of them are caught there, in crevices of the rock. The first mistake they'll make is to rotate ninety degrees and try to bring their scouts out along the wall. That's the only surface they're sure of."

The three watched in wonder as the sparkles grew thick upon the wall, falling in long streaks, like burning wax from a candle, then stopped. There was a long time of darkness. Then the lights began again, this time all of them on the plain below.

"They've figured it out," said Emun.

"Have you seen enough?" Sam asked again.

"Enough to go warn the settlements," said Theor Close. "We can start evacuation through the Combat Door."

"And lose twenty percent of our people?" Sam cried, suddenly concentrated once more upon the immediacy of the problem. "No! Get them up onto the escarpment, up at the memorial park. Have them take food enough for a long stay. Medical supplies, whatever they think they'll need. Get off the plain." He thought, letting his mind seek the answers, letting the words come. "If the soldiers are coming out down there, the prophets will be behind them." He knew this was true. He could see it. Oh, yes. "Sending an army here is sheer vindictiveness. The old man is getting even with Saturday for singing there in Ahabar. And with me, just for being with her, or for being Maire's son, or because despite everything he feels guilt and must crush it with more violence yet against any who make him uncomfortable! He will come, to see the end of us, and the others will not stay behind. Even if they did not want to be here, he would bring them along."

"It'll take them time to reach the settlements, won't it, Emun?" asked Theor.

"Not as long as you might think."

Sam thought, concentrating every cell upon the problem. "The important thing is to get our people out of the way, get our fliers out of range. The prophets will come through behind the army. We must prepare to attack them from behind and capture some of them."

"I don't understand?" said Theor in a puzzled voice.

"Some of them will know the *passwords*. The ones we'll need to change the programming! If they know them, then our God can find them out. Maybe. Meantime, we're alerting everyone possible; maybe someone can use that Final Command."

"We can get the closer settlements moved first, without baggage, and the further ones moved next."

"Then I'm going to drop off down there, in front of their lines somewhere, and have you fly this thing back."

"Sam!" protested Theor Close. "Why?"

Emun quavered, "You wouldn't have a chance, Sam Girat."

"It's something I need to do," he said, turning the flier in a sharp arc and speeding away toward the southeast. "Something only I can do. There is an unfinished matter here, one which has weighed upon me. It needs to be done with. Whatever happens."

"At least, let us take time to rig you up with a transmitter," Theor Close begged. "We need to know what happens to you, Sam."

Sam shook his head, almost amused. "Haven't you figured it out yet, Theor? You will know whatever I know. If not you, then Saturday, or Jep. The God knows what I know. Ask it."

· *In the reception* bay at Enforcement, the Awateh shifted in impatience. He had soon tired of watching the soldiers marching into the Door. They were small soldiers mostly. There were no large landscapes on Authority in which large soldiers could maneuver. He much preferred the unequivocal horror of the monsters waiting to be sent to Hobbs Land.

"We have a surface, Holy One," said Ornil.

The prophet gestured his permission to proceed. Ornil bowed. Faros bowed. They spoke certain commands, a barrier rolled aside, the soldiers came into the bay and began marching or rolling or hopping through the Door to Hobbs Land. They went past in seemingly endless files. When the last of them had gone through, including one carrying a smaller Door that would allow persons to return, the prophet summoned his followers with a word and strode after the soldiers, his lined faced eager with anticipation. Behind him the others marched or swaggered, their coup markers glimmering in the dimly lighted bay.

Ornil and Faros looked after them. The cavernous space was quiet. The last soldier had gone to Authority. The last of the Faithful had gone to Hobbs Land. The Doors stood open, all of them, and Ornil and Faros stared into the curtains of pale and empty fire.

"Two generations, almost three," muttered Faros, turning his eyes away. Staring into the Doors made his head ache. "How many years? To get us here? To get this thing done? And now what?" He leaned his forehead against the console. His hand rested upon the control of the Hobbs Land Door. So easy to shut it down. If it was shut down, the Door the prophets had with them would be useless. So easy to keep the prophets from coming back. He didn't move his hand. If he moved his hand, Ornil would kill him. He considered whether, for Silene's sake, he should allow himself to be killed.

"The Awateh will punish those who merit punishment," said Ornil as he also turned away from the aching shimmer. "He will return here to send the army to Phansure, and Thyker, and Ahabar. When all have been killed except our people, we will settle where we will." He said it without joy, flatly.

"Do you suppose he'll give us a choice?" Faros closed his eyes, concentrating. If he went back through the Door to Ninfadel, Silene and the children might be there. On the other hand, they could still be in Ahabar. Which place should he go first? And how escape from Ornil?

He decided he would go to Ahabar. He would kill Ornil, and then go to Ahabar. Faros had no sooner made the decision than he smelled something. The smell was terrible, but his first thought was something wrong on the console, and he stared at it for several moments before he looked over his shoulder and saw what was behind him. There were many of them, sliming out of the Door from Ninfadel, pouring into the Door to Authority, a few wandering out of the line and toward the place he stood, moving very fast. By the time he understood what he saw and opened his mouth to shout a warning, it was too late for Ornil, too late for himself. As the Porsa swallowed Faros, his hand on the lever was dragged down, closing the way to Hobbs Land.

· *Notadamdirabong Cringh was* awakened in the middle of Authority's "night" by Lurilile's shaking him.

"Get up," she said. "Damn it, Notadam, get up."

"What . . . ?" he managed, his mind full of a dream in which he had been young again, young enough, at least.

"Notable Scholar, wake up or I'll dump cold water on you," threatened his Abishag. "There's a great badness afoot here on Authority."

"Badness?" he quavered. "What?"

"Machines. Killing machines. Loose in the corridors. Loose in the environments. Wandering about thundering at people. We have to get away."

"Get away?" he said stupidly.

"Abandon ship," she shouted at him. "Yield moon."

He sat up, suddenly clearheaded. "The Doors from the arrival and departure center will be jammed."

"Since that's the way the things came in, it's unlikely they'll be jammed with people."

"There are other Doors, down in Supply," he said, his mind clicking away like a machine.

They were interrupted by the door chime. Lurilile opened it, finding Rasiel Plum leaning upon the door.

"We're under attack," he breathed heavily, holding his chest. "Under attack."

"So the stage said," replied Lurilile. "I was sitting up late, seeing an old drama, something from Manhome times, something like this, an attack at night. I saw the warning. The Notable Scholar was just suggesting . . ."

"Just suggesting we try to get down to Supply," said Cringh, coming to the bedroom door with his robe half-fastened. "The general access Doors will be full of these monsters."

Rasiel sighed, a very old sigh. "I was thinking more in terms of the Final Command, Cringh."

"Which would be what?"

"The words that will shut off the army."

"Is there such a thing?"

"There is. As one of the Actual Members, I know what it is. So do you!"

Cringh furrowed his brow. "Oh. Well, yes. I was told about that, wasn't I? Presumably there are nineteen other people, many of them younger than we, who also know what it is."

"Not here," sighed Rasiel. "I did a quick inventory while I was getting here to you. Half the Actual Members have gone to that gala on Ahabar, the dedication of the tomb of Stenta Thilion. Most of those who didn't go weren't able to go, too old, too tired. There may be three or four younger than we on Authority who know the phrase. You'll recall that the phrase is, '*A key for the last lock.*' I'm reminding you because I may not live to use it, and somebody has to."

"Where do we say it? Where do we transmit the order from? I'm not sure I ever knew."

"From the robing room behind the Authority Chambers, except that when I asked for a view of the robing room, all I saw was metal monsters thundering around. As I recall, there's two or three other places on Authority, including one where you were going, in Supply. Half a day's foot journey from here, in good times."

"I'll get your medicine," said Lurilile to Cringh. "We'll start out at once." She went into his room, burrowed among his things, filling her pockets, murmuring to herself, "*A key for the last lock. A key for the last lock.*"

As they were about to go out into the wide passageway which connected the urban residential suites used by upper-level Authoritarians, heads of advisories, heads of panels, and a few of the Actual Members, they heard a monstrous rumbling from one end of it, an approaching roar.

"Back inside," hissed Lurilile, pulling at Notadamdiabong Cringh's robe. "Back."

As the door slid closed before them, they caught a

glimpse of a treaded and armed monster entering the passageway at the far end and a bolt of lightning seared their vision, melting droplets from the door.

"God," breathed Rasiel Plum.

"Devil," spat Cringh. "Who in hell has set those loose?"

"Thyker?" suggested Rasiel.

"No," Cringh said angrily. "I would have known. They wouldn't have done that without telling me. And there's no reason to. Authority hasn't even suggested retaliation against Thyker for the raid on Hobbs Land."

"There's only one other group it could be," said Lurilile. "The ones who left Voorstod."

"God," breathed Rasiel Plum once more.

"There's the supply chutes," suggested Lurilile, feeling an approaching rumble. The two old men followed her through the services door into the central services area. A hatchway gave access to a system of ducts, complete with ladders.

"In," she said. "In and down."

Gravity was light. Rasiel began the climb, Cringh close behind him, Lurilile remaining behind long enough to pull the hatch tightly closed. The ducts had their own lighting system, their own scurrying little telltales, running up and down tracks let into one wall of the ducts. Twice they scrunched tight to the opposite wall as a supply pod raced past on the tracks.

"If we knew where those supplies were going, we could piggy back," panted Cringh.

"You'd be whipped off at the first corner," Lurilile commented. "We're down two levels. You two stay put. I'm going to reconnoiter." She thrust open a hatch and slithered out, like a lizard.

"Where'd you get her?" Rasiel asked.

"I think she's a spy, assigned to me," Cringh murmured. "Undoubtedly from Ahabar. I've enjoyed giving her all kinds of misinformation mixed up with truths that took me a lifetime to learn. She's been so kind. I didn't want her to get the information and leave me."

"A spy? Why you?"

"As a member of the Religion Advisory, I suppose

was spyable," he replied. "Ahabar was pretty annoyed with the Advisory. Can't say I blamed them."

Lurilile came squirming back. "This level is empty. There's a tube car vestibule down the main hall. I suggest we get to it."

"Why is this level empty," whispered Cringh.

"Because it's a storage level," she replied. "There wouldn't be anyone here in the middle of the night, would there?"

The moon Authority was small enough and enclosed enough that it found it expedient to celebrate nighttime simultaneously throughout. What was "night" for Notadamdirabong Cringh was night for everyone else, as well.

They crept quietly along the wide corridor, past bays heaped with supplies and equipment, past immobile handling machines, past brightly painted ducts bearing enigmatic labels: *Wet cargo, Waste direct, Waste indirect.*

The vestibule was pale green, as all transport facilities were, making them easy to locate. Inside, they found a six-man pod, ready in the tube.

"Supply area directory," whispered Lurilile.

The listing swam onto the stage. *Arrival Stage. Main Sorting Units. Noxious Waste. Temporary Work Crews. Permanent Supply . . .*

"Location of Doors in supply area," she whispered.

The listing shortened itself abruptly. *Arrival Stage. Noxious Waste. Temporary Work Crews.*

"Two-way Doors only," she said again. Arrival stage was for incoming supplies. Noxious waste led to the center of Big Sun, and nowhere else.

There was only one remaining location. *Temporary work crews.*

"Temporary work crews," Lurilile tapped into the destination pad. The top of the pod sealed around them with a hiss.

"Implement," Lurilile tapped.

"Remarkable how efficient she is for an office–home aide, isn't it?" said Rasiel. "If I didn't know better, I'd think she might be an Ahabarian secret service operative."

"Pretend she is," said Lurilile. "It will make you feel better about doing what she tells you to do."

The hissing drone of the transport tube, combined with the featureless walls—which blurred by like blown fabric, shimmering—were hypnotic. Rasiel shut his eyes. "I have a family here, you know. On the other side. In the lake environment."

"If we're lucky, we'll stop the soldiers before extensive damage is done," said Lurilile.

"The Ahabarian secret service does not want Authority dismembered then?"

"The Ahabarian secret service doesn't really care what happens to Authority," she answered. "But neither does it have any desire to see senseless destruction and mayhem among the relatively innocent."

"*Relatively* innocent?" asked Rasiel.

"Almost everyone on Authority knew about the bribes being taken by Theology Panel. No one did anything about it."

"Relatively innocent," agreed Cringh.

"Everyone was content with not rocking the boat," said Lurilile. "Which seems to be Authority's style. Who cares if it goes on existing or not? It doesn't do anything useful. You're all mere artifacts. You should be in a museum!"

The hiss dropped to a lower register, becoming a hum. The pod slowed. They slipped into a vestibule and the lid opened automatically. Lurilile's fingers were poised over the destination pad, ready to send them elsewhere if needed, but the vestibule was empty, soundless.

"Out," she whispered.

They crept into the chill, boxlike space, into the lock, out of the lock into the area used by temporary work crews. A dining area. Dormitories. A recreation area. And at last, a Door.

"I want you two gone," said Lurilile. "I want you two down on a planet somewhere, alerting everyone. I want a dozen agents up here as soon as possible, to help me. Where's the army command module, Rasiel?"

He shrugged. "I was told once. Years ago. Down here somewhere. All I can remember is that it's in the supply area. Do you remember, Notadam? It would be red, wouldn't it?"

"It would be *listed,* wouldn't it?" Lurilile demanded.

Notadamdirabong shook his head uncertainly. "I don't know. Maybe not. To keep bad guys from finding it. In which case, it might not be red, either."

"What in hell am I looking for then!"

Rasiel shrugged, fighting impotent tears. "I don't know. The one in the Authority Chambers robing room is behind a painted panel. I haven't even seen that one in twenty years."

"Shit," she hissed in disbelief. "I've got the key and no damned idea where the lock is or what the damned lock looks like."

"You can try the phrase everywhere. Maybe it's an ear tied into the general information banks."

"I can stand on my head and whistle the Ahabar battle anthem, too. It would probably do just about as much good. Are you two going to go, or do I have to do that by myself, as well?"

Shamefaced, Rasiel Plum agreed to go. Lurilile keyed Phansure as the destination. "Don't forget to tell them the Final Command before they come up here to help me, Rasiel Plum. I may not be around when they arrive."

When he had gone, she keyed Thyker and gave Cringh a hug before pushing him through. He was a nice old man. Pleasant to be with, with no sexual pretensions. She had enjoyed his company. She was glad he wasn't going to die, not just yet, artifact or no.

She had not mentioned it to either of them, but she found it very ominous that there were no crowds jostling their way into this area. Surely she was not the only person still on Authority who knew of the Door in Supply as a way of escape.

Sam stood on a low hill in darkness. Before him were the sparkles that told of arriving soldiers. Now and then the earth shook. Now and then a meteor streaked across his field of vision. These accidents became less and less frequent. Finally, they stopped altogether. Now there was only the recurrent glitter of soldiers or scouts or whatever they were, arriving on the surface, at first singly, then by the dozens.

A thing arrived at the foot of the hill and rolled clankingly around the base of it toward the southeast. It was three times Sam's height, perhaps ten feet across and four times that in length. It had several turrets on it, arms equipped with pinchers and grabbers, grills and eyes, and structures Sam could imagine no use for whatsoever. It was obvious he could not extrapolate from known agricultural machines. The thing that clanked away beneath him was designed to do more than merely kill quickly and cleanly. It was designed to kill, yes, but to do so torturously, slowly, with maximum pain and observable horror.

"Hi," called Sam, without planning to.

The turret at the top of the thing swiveled. Gadgets got a fix on him almost at once.

"Who is the God of Voorstod?" The machine bellowed.

It took Sam a moment to identify the familiar words, familiar and yet so out of context in this place. These were words that belonged to the mists and the stones of Voorstod, not to the wondrous vistas of Hobbs Land.

"The One, the Only, the Almighty God, in whose light all other gods are shown to be false idols created by men," Sam called in a loud voice. They were the words Phaed had trained him to use in response to that particular question. So the machines had been programmed with the words of Scripture. With the documents of doctrine. He should have known that. Perhaps he had known that. Perhaps that was why he was here.

The machine made a weaving motion of jointed arms, a clattering of servo-mechanisms. Then, abruptly, it turned and went the way it had originally started, southeast, away, leaving Sam behind.

"Oh, I learned my lesson well, Phaed," Sam commented to himself as he went down the hill toward the sounds he could hear faintly accumulating before him. Like the accumulating sound of a sea, when the tide turns. Like the sound of a rain storm, growing from a gentle sprinkle to a torrent.

"What is the desire of the One God?" came the challenge from the darkness confronting him.

"That all living things shall acknowledge him," cried Sam.

"And how is this to be achieved?"

Sam shook his head and bellowed, *"By teaching those who will learn, and by killing all others."*

The creature clanked past, its lenses fixed on some unimaginable epiphany. It was not programmed to teach, therefore it would kill.

The soldiers let him alone. They challenged him and let him alone when he responded. After the soldiers, would come the prophets. And their followers. He was going there, where they were. He counted sparkles of light, to his right and to his left. A rank of soldiers some hundreds long, some hundreds deep. Enough to kill every person upon Hobbs Land ten thousand times over. He walked through them, answering their challenges, not breaking stride, his legs moving of themselves.

Strange. One had legs, and a body and a face, and one did not think of that often. One had joints and skin covering the lot, and one did not think of that. Parts were obedient, doing what they were required to do. Sometimes they ached, if badly used, but they were not treacherous. Now, among these great warriors, all human parts seemed ludicrous and inadequate. What could they do but die? What good were arms against these? How fast could legs run in a race against death?

Assume there were no monsters. Assume there was only death, as there had always been death. Inevitable. The end of man as of everything. Which arms could not oppose nor legs outrun nor eyes find a place deep enough to hide oneself in. Then what was the task of man? Of a hero? What was man to do when there was nothing man could do? Why did he walk calmly forward, separated from his own terror only by a thin wall of something strange and flexible and yet quite impervious.

Something which was not death.

"Birribat Shum?"

"Yes."

"Elitia Kruss?"

"Yes."

"Horgy Endure?" he almost laughed.

"Yes. That too."

"The God knows what I know," he said to himself, not needing an answer. The God knew what everyone knew, and what everyone was. And if Sam could find a prophet or a follower and make him stand still long enough, the God would find out what he knew as well.

If there was time.

"What is the place of women in the creation of the One God?" bellowed a monster from a hundred yards away.

"Women have no place," cried Sam. *"They are not followers of God, they are merely processes by which followers may be created."*

As Maire was considered to be. Phaed had told him of the Paradise of the Faithful. Food and drink and virgins. Gardens and virgins. An ecstasy of the senses for the men who had died in the faith, and no mention of the women. *"They are to be kept private, kept quiet, kept healthy until they have borne children, and then they may be disposed of."* His mind finished the quotation.

China Wilm. Saturday Wilm. Maire Manone. All the women. Disposed of.

"What are the numbers of those who will acknowledge the One God in the last days?" trumpeted a huge, rolling monster, aiming its cannon at Sam.

"If there is one of the Faithful, and that one the only living one, one is enough," Sam replied.

Jeopardy Wilm. Willum R. Dern Blass. Spiggy Fettle. All the men who were not of the Faithful, also disposed of.

The nonlegendary. The day-to-day scufflers. The watch-to-watch managers. The growers of food. The builders of houses. Those who lay on their bellies in the grass, watching bugs. Those who listened for birdsong. Those who would not overbreed or overbear. The co-existers. Disposed of. In order that the last man living may be one of the Faithful to utter the name of Death.

But, whispered Sam, if there is one of the Gods, that one is enough for the utterance of a different name.

Sam walked on toward the west. Somewhere ahead of him was Phaed Girat.

• **Settlement One was** already awake and moving when Theor and Emun returned. There were two dozen fliers being stuffed with persons, cats, and almost no baggage.

"Where did the fliers come from," Emun asked China Wilm.

"They showed up," she said. "We're first in line. Then the fliers will evacuate Two and Four, then Three and Ten, then Eleven and CM. Meantime, Five through Nine are putting together food supplies for all of us. They're farther east and will be last out." She was not in a panic. She sounded very matter of fact.

"Where's everyone going?"

"To the escarpment," she replied. "The first few loads have gone already."

Theor Close decided Sam had been right. The God knew what they all knew. He might as well go along with everyone else.

• **The convict laborers** were wakened by Dern Blass, who trumpeted orders, some of them contradictory, and then left Howdabeen Churry to sort it out. It took a few moments before the sleepy off-shift understood what was happening.

"Voorstoders?" Shan Damzel asked, disbelievingly. "How did they get access to the army?"

"Presumably the same way we got access to Hobbs Land," snorted Mordy Trust. "Through subterfuge, lies, and sneakiness. How isn't going to help us right now. What are we to do?"

"Dern says we may be evacuated to the escarpment after everyone else has gone. Which is only fair, I suppose, from their point of view. Blass says we can go to Thyker through the Door if we want, but it's chewing up one shipment in five right now. He suggests we pack some food for ourselves and the others. He also suggests we might ask for some weapons, which might not be a bad idea. According to Blass, the army is west of Settlement One, moving rather rapidly."

"How did he find out?"

"He says the God Horgy Endure told him," said Churry with an expressionless face.

Shan heard this without a quiver. The interesting thing about the Hobbs Land Gods was that they did tell the settlers things and the things were always true. Not commands. Not beliefs. Just things. Like, it's going to rain. Like, there's a fire in the chemical stores. Like, that yellow cat just had five kittens, tell her how pleased you are. Like, somebody is hurt out behind the tread repair shop.

Now: the army of Enforcement is coming. Get out fast.

Shan went to help the men who were loading food, wondering only briefly if he had been swallowed yet.

· *On Authority, Lurilile* went on soft feet down endless metal aisles, listening for sounds she did not hear. Soft whish of air, rumble of liquids in pipes, clutter-clutter sound of fans, wink and beep of monitoring devices, dials quivering, light arrays flickering, all normal, all usual. Why no sounds from above?

She almost passed by the main environmental monitoring station. Inside the half-glassed door, banks of stages showed here, there, everywhere, with telltales beside them reading off temperature and humidity and parts per millions of pollutants. Pollutants off the scale. Temperatures above levels where humans could live. Fiery temperatures. Flames dancing on the screen among charred bones.

"Where?" she breathed.

The great library of the Religion Advisory, said the stage.

"A key for the last lock," she said firmly.

No magic. The flames went on. Wherever the ear she needed to reach was, it was not here.

"Schematic of the supply area," she commanded.

It swam onto the stage before her.

"Command module for Enforcement," she ordered.

A quivering as the memory searched and did not find.

"Command override," she said desperately.

Nothing.

"Find command override and give it this message," she told Archives. "A key for the last lock. Implement."

Again that searching quiver. Oh, Archives wanted to please, wanted to find whatever it was she was searching for, but it could not. No one had told it where the thing was. Or, it knew the thing under another name.

What other name?

"Where is the last lock?" she asked.

Nothing.

"Where does the key go?"

"What key?" asked the stage. "Define key."

Lurilile sat for a moment more, gathering strength. Surely when they ran out of people to kill on the upper levels, they would come down here. Was there anywhere to hide? What were her chances of finding what she sought? Could she in good conscience go home, to Ahabar, to cry on her father's shoulder?

What would Queen Wilhulmia do, in this situation?

After a time, she left the small room and began her search once more.

EIGHT

· *Shallow under the* soil, the radiating mounds had lain, dormant, as the people from Thyker had said, but they were dormant no longer. Urgent information had come to them and shocked them into burgeoning growth. As they pushed upward, the soil had grown shallower still, cracking above them, falling away from the emerging shapes beneath, revealing hard wooden structures which came straight from the ground like walls, echoing beneath curious knuckles like a knocked door.

Eleven radiating walls were all there were at first, eleven spokes from a central hub. When they had shed the soil from their tops, however, a groove formed and deepened along the top of each, splitting each wall into two and then into two again. Forty-four radiating walls, a hundred feet long, moved slowly upward and apart, thickening and lengthening as they grew, thrusting upward at their centers, arching high into gigantic wickets, fifty feet high at the center, rising still higher as the ends flattened and joined into a solid outer wall and into a central ringwall, pierced by smaller arches. Here and there the outer wall puckered, dimpled, and opened to make a man-sized hole into which children raced, shrieking, only to race out again, stunned at the strangeness of the open-topped, torus-shaped enclosures.

Inside, the floor scooped down and covered itself with an ornamental fiber, almost a mosaic of nappy carpet in colors of gray and cream and green and rose. Into the ringwall arches vinelike tendrils twined and knotted to make ornamental grills, hard, almost metallic barriers between the outer ring and the central space where the tower thrust skyward in visible movement, massive-walled, open-topped, the buttresses of the tough, interconnected arches holding it stiffly erect as it grew.

A flange extruded lengthwise on the top of each arch, grew tall and narrow, split in half lengthwise, spread to the sides like great leaves spreading beneath the sun, widened, overlapped, and then grew together to make a laminated roof, a continuous fabric, which wrinkled and ramified on its upper side, thickening itself with veins, roughening until it resembled thatch.

The settlers who had been among the first evacuees watched this process by lantern light, their interest mixed with moderate apprehension. Prudently, they moved a distance away from the emerging temple-shape and those others developing behind it. They asked one another if this resemblance to the stone and thatch temples in the settlements was coincidence or whether one, either one, was a pattern for the other. They cautioned the children, but they, moved by perversity as much as curiosity, ignored prudence and caution to go darting inside, to run shrieking around the central space then plunge out to report on the mosaiclike floors, the woven grills, the whatever-it-was in the middle.

At the bottom of the tower, they said, a mass was forming. A seething shape urgent with power, vibrating with force.

"Is it like in the temples?" they were asked. "Is the thing in the middle a God."

"Maybe," they said. "But a different kind. Like a storm cloud in the wind. All rolling around."

Other fliers came from the settlements, discharged

their human and cat cargoes and ascended once more. From the air above the westernmost settlements, the soldiers of Enforcement could be seen far to the west, the newcomers said apprehensively, exchanging their apprehensions for wonder, and marveling with those who had come earlier when they saw the growths.

Together the settlers built campfires in the narrowing spaces among the great growths, and the chain of these fires threw fitful glares upward onto the curving walls growing into the night. There were others, cried the irrepressible children, rushing in from explorations. Other ones growing beyond the light, growing up to meet the stars. Others beyond the village. And others still beyond that. "Growing like mushrooms," they cried. "Growing like asparagus."

Saturday and Jep Wilm joined hands and went into the nearest of the weird growths, finding their way around the floor to the place the ringwall door would have been in a settlement temple. In this templelike space there was no door. There was a grill, one they could see through, but they could not get their hands through to the convoluted tubes and corrugated shapes that were growing there, could not find the source of the strange, chemical smell that permeated the space. Saturday knelt, craning her neck as she tried to look through the grill upward, to the place the enclosure ended. She could not see the top.

"I think it's open up there. But it's not saying anything," she whispered to Jep.

He shook his head. "Nothing."

"It's not really like being in a temple. It's more like being inside an engine. I feel movement all around. Like something running, very quietly."

"What's it doing, do you think?"

"I don't know. I don't know if it's something for us, or something against those things."

"The things from Enforcement?"

"Yes. Them."

Outside once more, they stood staring at the tower outlined against the stars, faintly orange-flushed along its edges by the light of the circling fires. It might have been a huge smokestack, inclining slightly but unmistakably to ward the south, supported around its circumference by the buttresses of the enclosing arches. It was even more like an enormous cannon, but Saturday and Jep had never seen cannon. With de-bonders available, no one needed cannon. Because of the vast difference in scale, they did not think of the launchers the settlers used to distribute trace minerals.

Fliers came and went. People unloaded hastily packed crates of food and bedding, then settled down in the midst of mystery, only to get up and wander nervously about once more, putting their hands on the wooden walls, knocking as though for admittance. Anyone who liked could have gone inside. Only the children did so, daring each other to enter again and again. After a time, even the children stopped their incursions, driven out by the strange, powerful smell.

A group from Settlement One had gathered beneath the trees halfway between the first-discovered mounds and the Departed village. Sal Girat was there, with Africa and China Wilm, and Theor Close, who had brought the word from Sam. Vastly pregnant, China crouched among her friends and kinfolk, weeping over Sam.

"Gone off like that," she cried. "Sacrificing himself! For what?"

"Nonsense," said Sal. "That's not what he's doing at all. Sacrifice isn't necessary. You know that." The words had come out automatically, without thought, but she stopped with her mouth still open, stricken with a moment of total recall, a visionary episode so vivid it was as though she lived it rather than merely remembering it. She was seeking an Old One, one of the Departed, crouched against the wall in a tiny, circular house. Sal was so close she could smell his earthy, slightly acrid smell. A linguist was crouched beside the Old One and had just asked, "Is sacrifice necessary?"

"Necessary?" scratched the Old One with horny tentacles. "Necessary to what? Is life necessary? No, sacrifice is not necessary. It is a way. A convenience. A kindness."

Sal shut her mouth, which was suddenly dry. "Sam wouldn't do anything foolish," she said. "He isn't a foolish man."

China stared at the firelit towers and asked herself if that were true. Wasn't he? Wasn't he a foolish man? Wanting that one perfect thing, whatever it was. The absolute. The marvelous. Playing about in helmet and sandals. Pretending to be all those ancient warriors. What was he doing now? What was he questing for?

She put her face into her hands and went on weeping, feeling the first stirring of birth, the first uncontrollable surges of her own body taking charge of things. "The baby's coming," she gasped to Africa. "Sam's baby. Right now."

Africa frowned at her choice of words. The baby could not be called Sam's baby, not in any well-managed society, but Africa did not take time to argue. Instead, she moved swiftly and efficiently to attend to matters, sending someone in search of a medical tech while she herself considered what she might use for a tent to make a private space around them.

Sal held China's hand, wondering bleakly if this birth might be a trade-off, a life for a life.

· *On the plains* below, some distance to the west Sam walked toward the line of soldiers, where the prophets were, where his father would be found.

"Phaed," Sam sang, not melodiously, rather a keening hum, a way of keeping his goal in the forefront of his mind. "Phaed," whom he was being allowed to meet once more, in order that all things should be resolved between them. Phaed: wife-murderer, woman-killer, culprit of the Cause, one of the Faithful, faithful indeed, to the most ancient and bloody of all religions. Me-worship. My sex worship. My tribe-worship. My kind-worship. Vowing rage and destruction against all else.

"Phaed." Dream-dad, fable-father, king and hero, lost somewhere in Sam's childhood and never found again. Was it a voice he remembered, from before he was six, whispering voice telling tales before the fire while ochre light gleamed on the eyeballs to show that sly knowingness, that virile intelligence, which meant a more-than-human creature hunched beside the fire, lord-fo king-wolf, great-bear. Prowler in the dark. Inhabiter of dreams. Troll-papa.

Did he come with a mask, father-player, full of false jollity, mirth made manifest, mockery falling from his lips like apples into Sam's lap? Tell me, Dad. Tell me the story of when you murdered Maechy. Tell me about those times you worshipped your god with blood, those times you killed, mutilated, raped, tore.

"Phaed."

Was it a face he remembered? Was there a face there, anywhere? Eyes with a certain look of pride at a son's first words, first steps, a son's finger on the trigger of his first weapon. Was it weapons he remembered? Only in play, the finger pointing, stick pointing, noise of rat-a-tat, immemorial childplay at killing. Maybe it was that sound he thought of, Phaed's sound, in the night, rat-a-tat, killing something.

Was it a smell he longed for? The smell of semen and smoke, the smell of whiskey and sweat, the sour, old-soapless smell of men who spent too much time together in closed rooms, socks and shoes full of that smell, trousers stiff with it, so old it wasn't merely smell anymore but more a miasma, rising ectoplasmic, a living presence, melting on the tongue like a thick syrup of old cheese.

Was it that licked-up smell? Sickening and yet strong, strong as stones.

Was it a touch? Could he even remember a touch? A stroke, a pat, a hug. Blows aplenty, shoves, a closed fist knocking his thin, boy's shoulder, a hard hand aimed in a butt-swat, a knuckle knocking the skull door open, boring into a cheek like an auger, painful as truth.

None of the above. Not smell, sight, sound, taste, touch. What, then? What memory of him pervaded, haunted, kept Sam wondering after all this time?

"Phaed?"

Sam had to know. Sam had to know him again, ask him, perhaps, look at him with these new eyes to see behind the old veils. Only when he had finished with this could he go on, on—to whatever. To a future if there was a future. To an end if there was to be an end.

Before either, Sam had to find him, there, somewhere,

behind the clanking, monstrousness of the soldiers, filing endlessly past.

"What are the acceptable names of God?"

"Almighty, All Knowing, All Wise."

"Who were the peoples of God?"

"Ire and Iron and Voorstod."

The great metal soldier shouted with laughter and spun a knife at the end of a tentacle. "Ha, ha, ha, ha. Ire and Iron and Voorstod. Ha, ha, ha, ha." It leaned forward, poked Sam in the chest with a jointed, jawed extension. "Ire and Iron and Voorstod."

"I know," said Sam, inadequately. He did know. Phaed had told him, chained him up in the old maternity home and told him, for hours at a time. Ire and Iron and Voorstod, the three peoples who had followed Voorstod the prophet away from Manhome. Voorstod with its pastors, Ire with its priests, and Iron with its prophets: the first to rule the slaves, the second to rule the women, the last to rule the men—to rule the men, or to be used by the men, to rule. That had always been the way of men's Gods, old men's Gods. To use the Gods to rule.

"Ire and Iron and Voorstod," cried the soldier, striding the east.

Sam shivered and went on. Far to his left he saw a prophet stalking along, long legs like pistons, face hard as steel, his staff striking the ground, sending up little puffs of dust. He was too far away to see, yet Sam saw him, the prophet stalking, following the soldiers, ready to witness destruction.

"Tell me," Sam said conversationally, "if you had no enemies, how would you live? If you had no predators abroad in the night, no fanged creatures ready to seize your lambs, how would you live? What purpose would your life have?"

"Ire," cried a great soldier, stamping its feet to make the ground shake.

"Iron," cried another.

The battle cry of the prophets. Sam had heard it before, that night in Scaery, when the Green-snake people and the Forest-bird people had paraded through the streets and the prophets had driven them away with trumpets and cries and quotations from the Scriptures. Old rage, never allowed to cool. Old hatred, never allowed to mend. For these were the fires from which they drew their heat. Without them, they were nothing.

Had Phaed quoted Scriptures when Sam was a child? Could he remember Phaed at all? In the kitchen among the food smells? Waking in the morning? Combing his hair? With all that hair, he must have combed it sometimes, perhaps in the warmth of rare, sunny afternoons, in the grassy plot beside the house, where the herbs grew against the wall and the hummers made soft noises in the flowers.

He could remember Maire there, combing her hair, but not Phaed. Where could he remember Phaed?

He could not find the look of the man in memory. The presence, yes, but the man, no. The presence—like Almighty, All Knowing, All Wise Himself, hovering, aware, threatening dreadful punishments—but not the man. The feel of the striking fist, the boring knuckle, but not the man.

There had been a time he had heard Phaed's voice. There had to have been a time. Maire saying something, something about needing. And the man, unseen, saying, "A man doesn't need anybody." Ire, and Iron, and Voortod, and a man doesn't need anybody. Anything.

The speaker not seen. A voice in the night, voices, raised, and the sound of pain. And the man, like God everywhere, but elsewhere in the dark, always elsewhere, in the dark. Old men's religions and old men's legends, always elsewhere, in the dark, so they could not be seen too clearly. So they could not be examined too closely. So they could go on, breeding, fulminating, burning, and rotting in the dark.

He had never thought of Phaed as living in the daytime. He was like the night creatures who came from their burrows at dusk. "Deep," Maire had said. "Deep and black as the tomb, with the stones around and over them."

"I was only six," said Sam to himself, explaining to himself what that meant. What you can see when you are six is only what you can see, hands, mostly. And knees.

Faces are above you if they do not kneel down. Phaed never knelt down.

Where are you, Phaed?

Far to the right the Awateh and two of his sons went by, the Awateh moving like an automaton, short steps, head trembling upon his neck, like a mechanical toy, jerk, jerk. Sam was upon the hill; they were upon the flat. He did not call to them. They did not see him, but walked on into the east.

Why hadn't they seen him?

Because their eyes were fixed on something else?

Sam stood, unmoving, then turned slowly around to look behind him.

Green snake and forest bird, flame fish and shelled beast, hill gant and valley slithe, purple and scarlet and mauve and blue, dancing ahead of the soldiers, ahead of the prophets, leading them on into the east, rising up out of the ground like smoke, forming in the air as from mist, shadow connecting to luminescence connecting to shadow. The Tchenka of the Gharm? The long-ago God of man? Marvel and mystery and joy and voices singing ecstatically between the stars.

"I know," said a voice within Sam's hearing. "I know what Maire knew."

And Maire's voice, singing as he had not heard it since he was a child. Like a prophet bird, a voice of God.

"Your Gods too, Samasnier Girat!"

And they were there, beside him, striding away, leading the prophets away, men in armor and high-crested helmets, waving swords and banners, shouting their battle cries. "Legends," cried Theseus. "All the legends." Battle hymns. Choruses crying war.

Theseus stooped above him, slender and strong, his hairless skin gleaming like bronze, a sword in his hand, sandals on his feet, a marble man, a monument come to life. "I raised up the stone, Sam. Beneath it were the sandals, this sword. I found my heritage. Now, I'm on my way to find my father."

"I," said Sam with a sob. "I, too."

"Then the killing can begin," cried the marble man.

stepping over him and stopping to look under a stone. "Under here," he cried. "Perhaps under here."

"You've already found it," Sam cried. "You needn't go on! You've already found it!"

"Perhaps," cried the marble man, "under the next stone. Or the one after that."

Sam left him behind, still turning over boulders, still peering at the darkness beneath. "Phaed," he said. More than any other legend, more than any tie with the past or the future, this one, this tie of the cells, this claim of the bone, this seeking hunger of the heart. "Phaed."

"What freedom does my faith give me?" bellowed a huge, armored thing on multiple wheels, its torso rearing skyward over a tangle of blades.

"The freedom to hate!" cried Sam. *"The freedom to kill what I hate."*

And what do I hate? he asked himself, knowing the answer, for Saturday Wilm had told him the answer.

I hate what I fear.

What do I fear?

"Phaed!" he called into the thunderous night. "Phaed."

* *On the height,* the lengthening towers had reached the limit of their growth. The curious chemical smell had grown into a stench that drove the people from it, sneezing and choking. China Wilm, laboring in childbirth, identified the smell and the chemical that gave it off as the curious product of certain fungi. "Gyromitra," she murmured, between pains. "False morels. That's the class of fungus upon Mahome. We have related species in the mushroom house. They can only be eaten after we boil away the rocket fuel."

"Rocket fuel?" Africa asked her, mockingly, thinking she was delirious, or joking.

"I'm serious," cried China. "They secrete monomethyl hydrazine. The same stuff used in chemical robes. We boil it away when we process the fungus. This must be a similar species . . ." and she was panting again.

"Where's the smell coming from," Africa asked the children.

"The base of the towers," said Saturday. "Inside the grills, there's this strange twisty growth, all tubes and wrinkled, like brains.

"Get people away from here," cried China. "That stuff is poison."

The smell had already driven people away. They moved restlessly, gathering up their belongings and shifting about, like disturbed bees.

Clouds gathered overhead. It was not the rainy season. Clouds were not unheard of at this time, but they were rare. Still, the light of the stars was covered over, and the dull mutter of thunder began to roll across the highlands.

Young people who had been exploring came to Saturday, and she to her mother. "Over past the village, there are several mound–temples without any towers in the middle. There's no bad smell there, either. The others say they've got tight roofs, and this looks like a longtime rain."

Africa glared at the lowering skies and agreed. The first hard drops of rain were already falling, hitting her face like ice. She and the Wilm brothers, trailed by the other evacuees, carried China through the Departed village, past the little ruined temples, and into a space where several mound complexes had ramified into doughnut-shaped structures with no towers. In these structures, the roofs ended at the central shaft and the central grills were tightly woven with leafy flaps, like shutters to let the air in or out. People moved hesitantly along the arches, found the space warm and welcoming, laid claim to sections of padded floor, then curled on the curving floors like fragile worms in a nutshell, safe, for the moment, from what was happening.

Everyone knew something was happening, though they did not know what. Dern Blass knew. Spiggy, sitting with his back against an arch, listening as the rain pounded on the false-thatch above him. Zilia, rocking a baby who was frightened of the echoes. Jamice, squatting on the pseudo-carpet, turning a Phansuri spirit rod between her fingers, as though in meditation. China, panting behind the screens Africa had rigged. Sal and Harribon sitting side-by-side, holding hands. In each of their minds, as in every other settler, there had opened a vacancy, not so much a hole as a screen, like a white page, waiting for a message to be written upon it. The screen covered the place terror came from. Terror couldn't get through it. The people knew this and were grateful for it. They were attentive to the vacancy. It was there that they would find the final words. Either the Gods would give them words to let them live, or the Gods would help them die. The Gods themselves did not know which. This thing had never been done before. The Gods didn't know whether it would work, whether there was time. Whatever happened, the end would come into their minds upon that waiting blankness.

"I should be doing something," fretted Harribon.

Sal looked at him, and he flushed. It was only habit, his saying that. There was nothing he or anyone else could do. Still, here and there among the circled masses, there were those who said it, men mostly. "I should be doing . . . something . . ."

Thunder came, an enormous shouting of sky and a cracking of split air. Saturday and Jep were at the entrance with a dozen others, seeing what they could see. Several of the great chimneys were within sight, several with lightning striking at their tops, again and again. Burning lines, like glowing fuses, ran down from the tops of the towers. Then there was fire and smoke and a roiling haze and a contained thunder.

"Come see," cried Jep to Theor Close. "They're going off like guns!" Guns he knew. Guns he had seen, in old dramas.

Theor came to see. Certainly something had been, was being propelled up the gigantic barrels and out into the sky. High above the edge of the escarpment, they could see the missiles exploding, making a spreading shadow across the night sky. Lightning appeared green behind the haze, vividly green, like new grass. Saturday ran to tell her mother.

"What's happening," panted China.

"The towers are going off like big guns," Africa told her. "Shooting something up into the sky."

"Using the MMH as a propellant," China muttered. "What set it off?"

"Lightning," said her sister. "Lightning hits the tops of the towers and then runs down the side as though there were a fuse there."

"Probably is," gasped China. "A line of oxygen-rich, punky tissue, perhaps even tissue laced with the propellant fuel."

"What is it firing off? Seeds?"

"Spore cases," China murmured. "Probably." Then she had no time to say anything more, as she and the med-tech struggled to let a seemingly reluctant child come forth into the world which might survive barely long enough to receive it.

· *When the last* of the Central Management people had departed for the heights, they had left the Baidee prisoners behind to comfort themselves with a final word from Dern Blass.

"Consider your sentence interrupted. You can go back to Thyker through your Door, the way you came."

Since every member of Churry's group knew that the Combat Door, which they had disassembled and moved to CM as their first act upon reaching Hobbs Land, was losing about twenty percent of its shipments on a random basis, the Baidee decided to put off escaping through it until the last possible minute. They did draw lots for the order of escape, so there would be no confusion when the time came. Their only alternative action, self-defense, depended upon their being furnished with weapons. They had already sent a dozen pleas to Thyker, one after the other, hoping at least one would get through. Now they repeated the exercise. It would have been wiser, they all knew, to be somewhere else, but if they were somewhere else, they couldn't use the Door.

"What are they like?" asked Shan Damzel from a dry mouth.

"They, who?" responded Churry.

"The soldiers of Enforcement?"

"I don't think anyone knows, except the people who made them and the people who maintain them."

"If you want to know," said Mordy Trust, who was scanning the horizon with a long-distance viewer, "Look here. I think the first one just showed up."

They shared the viewer to look toward the west where a lurching monument clanked along the horizon, a thing the size of the barracks in which they lived, bristling with turrets and eyes and lashing tentacles.

"Did you ask Thyker to send de-bond rifles?" someone asked plaintively. "You did specify de-bonders, didn't you?"

Above them in the sky, something popped. It was a small sound, like a cork withdrawn from some aerial bottle. Haze spread across the sky, covering the stars, which twinkled briefly green.

• *On Authority, Lurilile* crept mouselike through enigmatic spaces. Now and then she would cry out, "A key for the last lock," her voice falling to silence among crates and sacks and against walls of dials. Wherever the last lock was, she had not found it. Perhaps Rasiel Plum had been wrong. Perhaps there was no last lock in Supply. Perhaps it was in Administration, or Environment, or Planetary Liaison.

She went back to the temporary worker's quarters and reassured herself that the Door was there. She set it for Ahabar and left it at the ready, needing only the push of a button to set off. Why had no one come through this Door to help her? Why was she still alone?

She went back to the monitoring screens and checked the upper levels. Among the ruins there were moving blobs. At first she did not identify them. When she realized what they were, she could not at first believe they were there at all, though it was easy to imagine what had happened. Someone had left a Door open. A Door between Nintadel and Authority. Now Porsa had come to Authority. Porsa had come to Authority, and she, Lurilile, had left a Door on Authority open to Ahabar.

She watched in awe as a soldier of Enforcement reduced a Porsa to bubbling stew with a flame gun. When the soldier moved on, the unburned remnants blobbed themselves up and began sliming off in all directions. If they found something to eat, shortly there would be twenty Porsa where one had been before.

Lurilile Ornice, daughter of the Chief Counselor of Ahabar, bent double and retched. Then she went back to the Door to Ahabar and shut it down. The Porsa were intelligent, but they were not familiar with Door operation. They would slime through an open portal, but they were not likely to program one for a destination.

She went to the vestibule, got into the car and set her destination as Noxious Waste. The Door which led out of Noxious Waste had only one destination. She went to that Door, keyed it to continuous feed, and locked it on that setting. Then she found her way back to the Supply area, not by car but through long corridors with many compartments. She opened every gate and locked it open, every hatch and locked it open. Some doors without locks she wedged, to be sure they could not swing shut. Once more in Supply, she found the protein stores and went back to Noxious Waste, strewing protein chunks behind her, leaving a clear trail. Then she left Noxious Waste by car and made her way into the wall-ducts once more. It was futile to search Supply for the lock any longer. Instead, she would work her way to the small robing room behind the Authority Chambers, hiding in the walls until after the Porsa left.

They would leave eventually, she assured herself over a bubbling hysteria which threatened to break forth. They would swallow every living thing they could, and once whatever they had swallowed died, they would digest it. That was the nice thing about Porsa, they never started to digest you while you were still alive. If the Porsa got as far as Supply, they would find a trail leading them to Noxious Waste. In Noxious Waste, they would find an open Door. If they decided to go on exploring through that Door, it would take them into the heart of Big Sun and nowhere else.

Lurilile argued with herself whether she would report her destructive and genocidal actions to Native Matters

Advisory. If there were any Native Matters Advisory members left.

But, of course, there was at least one member left. She herself had saved him. If she survived, she told herself with utmost seriousness, she would have to mention her unforgivable activities to Rasiel Plum.

"Phaed," said Sam. He had reached the end of the line of soldiers, of prophets and Faithful. He had seen them all go past, on the horizon or close by. He had not seen Phaed. He did not think it likely that Phaed had slipped by, far to one side or the other. The God who had brought him to this place would not have allowed it.

"Phaed! Phaed Girat!"

An answering call. "Well, and is that you, Sammy?"

He came up out of the darkness of folded ground, like a man cresting a hill on a pleasant afternoon. "What're you doin' out here, Sammy. The Awateh expects to find you in your settlement, snug in your bed. A most furious prophet, our Awateh. He desires the doin' of you, and that little girl, and all your people." Phaed's eyes were fixed on the backs of the retreating soldiers, the retreating prophets. He moved as they did, forward.

"He'll find me," said Sam, gently. "Or I'll find him. Shall we walk along behind the army, Dad? Shall we see what there is to see?"

"I didn't think you had much love for seein' corpses, Sammy. Not you nor your mam."

"Mam's dead, you know."

"I'd heard something of the sort."

"Hung on the walls of the citadel."

"Well, that's customary."

"She was with the women. The old man had forgotten her. She would have been safe except for you. I hold you responsible for it, Dad."

"Hold what you like, boy, but I don't need to answer to you. A man doesn't need to answer to his sons. That's not the way it's done. It's the other way around." The words were angry, but the tone of voice was calm. As though it didn't matter.

"Did you answer to your dad then?"

"He died."

"Then you didn't answer to anybody? Is that it?"

"To the prophet, you fool. I answered to the prophet. And when he needed proof I was faithful, I gave him what he wanted, that's all. No more than my duty."

"But you think I should answer to you? When you killed my mam? When you left me for the killing?"

"I didn't kill her. I only reminded the old man where she was. As for you, I stopped standing between you and the prophet, that's all."

"You think fathers shouldn't stand between their sons and the legends, then."

"Who said legends?"

"Aren't the prophets the same as legends, Dad? Aren't the prophets the same as Gods? Doesn't a man who speaks for God take the power of God to himself? Doesn't he become legendary, just for that reason? So a God can hurl lightning and a prophet can hurl curses or men can make laws, but if curse or law can kill as surely as lightning does, what's the difference?"

"What are you babbling of, boy!"

The horizon bent and wavered. Across the near distance, the Tchenka danced. Mist came up from the ground and clothed Sam in helmet and swordbelt and sandals. Phaed turned and actually looked at him, then frowned, not sure what he was seeing.

"I'm talking about legends, Dad. I'm talking about fathers passing killing on to their sons. Ages ago, Dad, kings sometimes left their sons in faraway nests, like cuckoo eggs, not even telling the woman who they were. Then they'd hide a secret under a stone and tell the mama when the son was big enough to raise the stone he could learn who his father was. It was like saying, 'Only when his strength rivals my own can he know who I am. I want no weakling. I want none who fears to use the sword. I want no son who is satisfied with kindness. I want only a son obsessed with finding me, who will come again and again to this stone, this stone too heavy for mortal men, to raise it, to look into the darkness beneath it, for only he will care about what I care about. And the fathers were right, of course. Only the sons of legend ever got the stones heaved up. Only they went questing, trying to find meaning in what had none.

"I was like that, Dad." Sam nodded, knowing it was true.

"I left nothing under a stone for you."

"Oh, but you did. You left your own self hidden there deep. Maire herself said so, when I was very small. She couldn't tell me who you were because she didn't know. She didn't understand you. But she said you lived deep in the dark, with stones around and over you. I thought that was a mystery."

"A mystery?"

"I thought so. Of course, there was no more mystery to it than to the life of a mole, which is all dank earth full of worm-ends dug under the great stones. Stones of hate. Stones of rage. A self-buried man, you were, Phaed, that's all. I kept heaving up, looking for who I was by knowing who you were. It's what we've always done, you know. Told ourselves we were our father's sons. Thought we couldn't know who we were unless we knew who you were. Turns out you weren't anybody much, but your having progied me doesn't define me, and I am who I will yet be, Dad."

Phaed growled, deep in his throat, and launched himself at Sam. Sam caught his wrists in his own hands and held him off, without effort. "You don't have three or four bullyboys to net me and tie me now, Phaed. Only you and me. I've raised your stone. I see what's writhing around in the muck there. Come on, Phaed. Let's follow the prophets and see what happens."

Death might happen, or life. Whichever, Sam wanted to see it. He took his father by the arm, feeling the tough muscle there, no flabbiness of age at all, only this stringy muscle over hard bone. "When you've killed us all, Dad, what then?"

Phaed smiled his wolf smile and shook Sam's hand from his arm. "Awateh hasn't said, boy. Ahabar, I shouldn't be surprised. There'd be a certain pleasure in that."

"What will you do?"

"What do you mean, boy, what will I do?"

"There'll be nobody left to kill, Dad."

His hand twitched at his belt, where his whip still hung. "Oh, there'll be disciplining still to do, I imagine. We'll need some to serve us. The Gharm, likely. Plenty of them left on Ahabar, and we'll save a number for ourselves."

"Oh no, Dad. Let me tell you a tale. A legend of my own. The Gharm are all dead, hadn't you heard? A kind of plague came swiftly and killed them all. Right after you went to Ninfadel. They're dead. There are no more Gharm."

Phaed breathed heavily through his nose. "All of 'em?"

"So I heard. Yes." Sam smiled at the sky where the stars showed green through a high veil of mist. A wind had come up and the clouds above were whipping about in it, first one way then another, as in a caldron, the clouds themselves showing green.

"Well, there's others. Maybe we'll keep some Ahabar babes and bring them up to the whip. Maybe we'll . . ."

"No, no, Dad. I hadn't finished my tale! The soldiers have already gone there. They're killing everyone, didn't you know? Everyone on Phansure, and Ahabar, and Thyker. All the moons and little planets, too. Soon there'll be no one left. Except for us few left here on Hobbs Land, and we'll be dead soon. I only came to say goodbye, and because I was interested in knowing what you were going to do now."

"Do now," said Phaed, panting. "Do now?"

"Were the women left on Ninfadel, Dad?"

"The prophet thought that best."

"Ah, well that's a pity. They must have gotten lonesome after the prophet and all you men left, so they went through the Door. There were soldiers there, naturally, and your women didn't know the answers to the questions. I know you told me there was no sense teaching women anything important. Well, so, the soldiers killed them all, the women and children, all the animals. Everyone's dead but those of you here, Dad. You prophets. You Faithful. You men."

Phaed made a munching motion with his jaw, as though chewing at something hard. "All but us."

Sam watched Phaed's face, wondering at what he saw there. This was the end the man had foretold, the end he had longed for, and yet, now that he thought it had come, he did not rejoice!

"But isn't that all right, Dad? It must be all right. You told me so yourself. Kill, and maim, and torture, and howl, and threaten. Utter curses. Make laws. So long as the last one alive is one of the Faithful, that's all that matters. You taught me that yourself!"

Phaed began to run, long strides, his breath heaving up out of his chest. Sam took a pace or two after him, but then slowed down and watched him go. Far ahead was a prophet, and Phaed was trying to catch up to him.

Sam kept on walking, not hurrying. After a time he came within hearing distance of the two.

"My son says so," Phaed was crying in a frantic voice. "Gone. Everything's gone. The soldiers are already killing everything, everywhere. We'll be the only ones left. We and the people here on this place."

"Then the task is complete," sighed the prophet. "The Great Work is accomplished. We may die. Paradise awaits."

"But . . ." cried Phaed. "It wasn't supposed to be so *quick*!"

The prophet had left him. Phaed began running again, passed the prophet and went on toward the east. Sam could hear him panting.

When Sam came up to the prophet, he said curiously, "Is there any need to keep on walking? Now that it's over?"

"True," said the prophet. "Oh, that's true." He sat down on the ground, put his head upon his knees and began to sway gently, as though rocked in someone's arms.

Sam brushed at his own face where a fine dust was settling. The same dust settled on the crouched prophet, who did not move to brush it away. Sam breathed in the dust and sneezed, spewing it out again, before continuing in the direction his father had gone. He passed a great soldier standing motionless at the foot of a hill.

"What is . . . ?" called the soldier. "What is . . . ?"

Sam stood quietly, waiting for the question, but after a time the soldier stopped asking, as though it had forgotten the challenge. Little lights flickered on the soldier's head and at the ends of extensible arms. The lights dimmed, flickered, went out.

Sam brushed dust from his eyebrows, leaned over and shook dust from his face. The stuff was dark and powdery, yet it did not cake. Each infinitesimal particle fell away separately, as though rejecting him. He held out his hand, flat, seeing the dust accumulate from the air, covering his skin. When he turned his hand over, it fell away. Sam was not what it wanted to rest on. Sam was not fertile soil for it.

As he went farther east, he saw more and more of the halted soldiers. The farther east, the more blurred their outlines were. Sam stopped beside one elephantine warrior with a pair of giant treads, and poked a finger between two adjacent plates. The space, which should have been open, was filled with a hard, wooden growth. The same growth, tissue thin, lay across every surface. The soldier was being encased, enclosed.

The core of every soldier of Enforcement was of psuedoflesh, an organic compound. Fungi needed organic compounds in order to grow. Sam found himself wondering if pseudoflesh might not be a good growth medium for the mushroom house . . .

Phaed was just ahead of him, talking to a circle of prophets.

"My son says the soldiers have gone to Ahabar, to Phansure. Already. Already killing everyone. They killed your families too. There aren't any left . . ."

Sam moved gently through the hesitant group and took his father's arm. "You should go tell the Awateh, shouldn't you? Isn't he up there ahead somewhere? Let's go tell him, Dad."

They began walking, arm in arm, Phaed stumbling from time to time. The dust fell endlessly from a green sky.

"Sing me a song, Dad," said Sam. "Sing to me about the Gharm contract."

Behind him the prophets sank to the ground, brushing fruitlessly at their eyes, at the corners of their mouths and nostrils. There was dust everywhere. Sam shook himself like a wet cat, arm by arm, leg by leg, and the dust flew away. Phaed trembled and brushed at himself, but the dust stayed, seemingly rooted into his skin, making him furry all over, as though he were covered in velvet.

"Sing to me about the Gharm contract, Dad?"

"Can't remember," said Phaed, wonderingly.

"Oh, but you sang it to Maire when you were courting. She told me. Maybe you and Mugal Pye sang it when you were making the gadgets that killed Stenta Thilion. Surely you remember the song?"

"No breath to sing." Petulant now. "Can't remember."

"Tell it to me then, Dad. Tell me the story."

"Stories like that aren't for children."

"But I'm grown now, Dad. I'm a man."

"Not a free man. A man who does what other people tell him isn't a free man."

"But you do what the Awateh tells you."

"That's different. He speaks for God."

"Tell me about your God, Dad. What kind of a thing is your God?"

"Demands . . . Obedience . . . From his sons . . . All his sons . . ."

"Does your god care about anything but men, Dad? Does he care about trees and birds and fish in the streams? Does he care about womenfolk? What about planets? Like that one the Gharmfolk had? The one Voorstod destroyed?"

"Demands . . ." said Phaed. It was all he said.

They walked on eastward. All around them the soldiers of Enforcement stood still, like monuments to a war which was not to be fought. Well, Sam had longed for monuments, and here they were. Lines of them, like standing stones. Towers of them. Menhirs. Dolmen. And among their immobile forms the shuffling prophets, still moving toward the east.

"Let's tell them they can stop, Dad."

Sam told them they could stop, and they did stop, falling to the ground in heaps, suddenly looking less man-like than plantlike, strange convoluted shapes, which took their outlines from natural things. Rocks. Brush. Low trees.

And at last, the final ones. Three figures moving as in a dream, slowly, almost floating.

"There's the Awateh, Dad. He has two of his sons with him. I think we ought to tell him about the people all being dead, don't you?"

They came up to the Awateh where he pushed forward like the prow of a boat, breasting the falling dust, tiny step after tiny step. "My son says," said Phaed. "Already killing on Ahabar. On Phansure. On Thyker. Already dead, families, flocks, none left but us."

The prophet's sons dropped, unspeaking. The Awateh leaned forward. Only the white of his eyes showed clean in the enveloping growth, his eyes and his teeth when he opened his lips and said, "Done? All done? All dead?"

"All dead," said Phaed. "All but us."

"Not!" cried the Awateh. "Not! This one, here . . ." he turned the white orbs on Sam and raised one hand as though to strike. It stayed there like a stout branch, sway-ing but unbending. The eyes went. The teeth went. The shape grunted for a time, and then was silent.

Sam turned to his father and saw another stumpy and contorted thing with an eye and a mouth.

"Tricked us," said Phaed Girat, the one clean eyeball gleaming in the starlight. "Didn't you?"

"Not I, Dad," said Sam, weeping. "God did it. He was waiting for you, not I. We were the bait in God's trap Saturday and I, sent to catch all Voorstod, Dad."

The mouth went away. Wood grew over the eye. Sam sat down and cried, clinging to the harsh trunk, hearing for a time the breathing that went on.

"My father died, too," whispered Theseus. "I went to find him, but because of me, he died. Some things . . . some things are better let alone. A man may not face both ways at once. If he looks back, he cannot look for ward . . ." The voice faded into remote distance and was gone.

"Come home, Sam," a voice in his ear. "Come home."

He looked up to see her standing there, leaning forward, offering him her hands. "How did you find me, China Wilm?"

"China couldn't come just now, but she thought you might be lonely," the Tchenka said. "She sent me to tell you she has a new girl child, up on the escarpment. And she thought you might need some company—leaving these legends behind."

He took the Tchenka by the hand, his eyes still filled with tears of grief for a man he had never known, could never have known, had only longed to have, as a man longs for dreams.

"I sought the wondrous thing," he complained, like a sleepy child. "I did."

"Well, Sam, didn't you find it?" asked the Tchenka. "Maire knew what it was. Remember?"

He remembered. Maire had found it before him, long ago, when he was a child. She knew that ancient evils could be left behind. One could choose not to remember. One did not have to dig into the slime pits of old anger and old hate. Forgetting was possible. The Hobbs Land Gods would allow it. Would make it easy. The pits beneath the stone could be left empty forever, if he so chose.

"There are no legends here," said Sam.

"That's it," said the Tchenka. "Come home, Sam."

• *When the Royal* Marines reached Ninfadel, they found that the Porsa had overrun the heights and swallowed all the Voorstod families and flocks, as well as the Ahabarian guards and the Native Matters staff members, before deciding (in what passes among Porsa for decision) to go through the Door the prophets had left open behind them. Not all the Porsa had been involved. Only those who had been selectively and secretly breeding themselves to live at higher and higher altitudes. It took the xenologists some time to figure this out.

All of the high-altitude-tolerant individuals had gone,

via Enforcement, to Authority. After eating everything organic that the soldiers had left edible on Authority, the Porsa had explored the moon and had found a convenient route left open to a Door marked *Noxious Waste*. It was known that Porsa could read. The words "noxious waste" had evidently been most attractive to them. All of them had gone away by that route.

Some persons were left alive upon Authority—those who had shut their doors, who had locked themselves in, who had kept quiet so the soldiers didn't find them before the soldiers were stopped. For the soldiers had stopped, eventually. A woman had stopped them. She had shut herself into the robing room just off the Authority Chambers, where she was found sitting quietly behind a painted panel, reciting a phrase over and over before a red grill. "The key for the last lock," she said, again and again, not ceasing to do so even when the medical techs took her in charge.

Her name was Lurilile. She was the daughter of the Chief Counselor to the Queen of Ahabar, and she had shut the army down. She had done it alone because the two old men she had sent through the Door had emerged unconscious at the other end and had stayed that way for some little time. Partly because of her fortitude—and partly because no one had returned to Enforcement to send them—the soldiers who were to have killed everyone on Ahabar and Phansure and Thyker were still on Enforcement, immobilized for the foreseeable future and perhaps, so hoped Rasiel Plum to his old friend Notadamdirabong Cringh, forever.

· *It came to* be called the Greater Invasion of Hobbs Land. When it ended, the Baidee prisoners took up their labors once more. Most Hobbs Landians ignored them insofar as was possible, though some seemed inclined, in the emotional aftermath of their survival, to regard them more as misled accomplices than as instigators of violence. Within thirty or forty days, a few of the Baidee considered less culpable, or perhaps merely more personable, were recruited to sing in the CM choir, which they agreed to out of boredom as much as for any other reason. The choir, augmented by its Baidee members, sang when the new Horgy Endure was raised.

"Tell me about it," Shan demanded from a Baidee who had sung on the occasion.

"Nothing to tell," the man said. "They dug it up and brushed it off and put it in the temple, and then we sang 'Rise Up, Ye Stones' for awhile, and I came back here."

Shan shook his head in disbelief. Here on Hobbs Land, he was a murderer. No one wanted to be his friend, or even his acquaintance. Churry's men resented him. Except for Churry himself, who saw no point in blaming someone else for his own stupidity, Shan had no one to talk with about what he saw, what it meant, to have a God that grew underground, like a radish.

"What does it mean?" snarled Churry. "It means in primitive times men worshipped trees, or stones, or volcanoes. It means in Phansure men worship idols. It means on Thyker we worship the Overmind, of which no image exists. It means on Hobbs Land, men worship something that grows like a radish! That's what it means!"

That wasn't what it meant, as Shan had already puzzled out for himself, but he did not argue the matter. The work he was doing was so laborious that he was worn out by the time his shift ended. He had no energy left for argument, or for dreams. He didn't care anymore whether he had been swallowed or not.

One evening, when their shift was over, Shan and Howdabeen were visited by Samasnier Girat.

"Tell me about your prophetess," said Sam, to their astonishment and considerable discomfiture. "Tell me all about this Baidee prophetess."

They told him about Morgori Oestrydingh, describing the advent of the old woman and the dragon as they had seen it in the temple a thousand times since childhood, reciting her words from memory. Sam listened, and went away, and came back again, asking them to repeat themselves.

"Your understanding is that the prophetess was seeking this lost race of beings, the Arbai, but she had not yet found them?"

Shan said that was true.

"And she was very old?"

"Very old. Her hair was white and wispy. It flew around her head like smoke."

"One would think she would have taken someone younger with her," said Sam. "To continue the search."

Howdabeen Churry shook his head. He had never thought of that.

"This Door," Sam said. "The one she came through, is it still there on Thyker?"

Oh, yes, they assured him. It was a holy shrine. No one would dream of touching it. However, it didn't work. Or, more accurately, no one knew whether it did or not.

"Have the Phansuris ever looked at it?" Sam asked.

They replied, somewhat embarrassed, that no Baidee would allow a non-Baidee to have access to the holiest shrine of the Overmind. Sam smiled his thanks and went away again. He had a high regard for the genius of Theor Close and Betrun Jun. He believed they could figure out anything they set their minds to.

Subsequently he spoke to Dern Blass and to certain other of the people at CM and the settlers concerning the prisoners. They had been misled, he said. Mistaken and misled, and could that not be true of anyone? After a little thought, everyone agreed with him.

When the new Door reached Hobbs Land and was installed, there was general agreement that the prisoners should be sent home. By that time, Shan had been well and truly swallowed. By that time, Shan was also a member of the CM choir. When he went back to Thyker, he carried with him the substance necessary to bring the God to Thyker—at least to all the fertile parts of it.

Shanrandinore Damzel went home, and Mordimorandasheen Trust, and Howdabeen Churry. They dug up the mummified bodies of the Hobbs Land invaders and buried them again in moister climes, as, for example, in the gardens of the temple at Chowdari. Though Chowdari was set in the midst of the desert, it had fountains drawn from deep aquifers to water the flowers and grass. There was moisture enough that the burgeoning network soon underlay the temple itself and a great part of the training grounds. It was not long after the net reached its outermost limits that revelations came to the Circle of Scrutators in an almost continuous sequence. It was revealed that Baidee might cut their hair, might do without turbans and kamracs and zettles, might eat eggs, might be friends with people of other opinions. Various Baidee began reassessing the words of the prophetess in the light of current understanding. Surprisingly, once stripped of the millennial old accretions added by generations of old men on the Circle of Scrutators, the words of the prophetess seemed quite sensible.

"Which," said Bombi Damzel to his brother, "when you *really* stop to think about it is *quite* understandable."

Shan said nothing at all. He, like some other members of The Arm of the Prophetess, had decided to become a missionary. He would carry the God first to the Celphian Rings, and then . . . then Outsystem. Going Out-System had its risks. Shan believed the risks were outweighed by the eventual outcome. It would be a way, a convenience, a kindness.

Sam gave a picnic bonfire on an off-day when certain invited guests could come from several of the settlements and from CM. So far as anyone knew, Sam was celebrating their deliverance from the army of Enforcement. The guests brought a generous quantity of beer, however, and by the time lunchtime came, everyone was celebrating whatever he or she felt most joyous about at the moment. Children shrieked, and people played musical instruments, and sections of the Settlement One choir sang antiphonally at themselves while the great bonfire Sam had collected fuel for for weeks burned itself down to embers and everyone laughed and sweated and turned red in the heat of it.

Sam had a further purpose of his own, which he had not discussed with anyone. He sat with China Wilm a little distance from the fire, half-reclining against a blanket covered pile of something as he played with the girl child, now almost a half-year old but thus far unnamed.

"So why this celebration now, Sam?" China asked

him, as she watched him dandling the baby on one knee, doing horsy with a girl child far too young to be horsied around.

"Now's a good time," Sam said lazily.

The child chirruped in a voice like a bird.

"She sounds as Saturday did when Saturday was a babe," said China. "She's going to be a singer. Samasnier Girat, would you like it if I named her for your mam? Would you like it if I named the child for Maire?"

Sam stopped dandling and looked at the baby. She stared back at him with eyes which were totally aware.

"She knows she's my child," he said, surprising himself. "And she knows about Maire."

China started to object to this, then stopped. The child did know she was Sam's child, so why object? Children these days knew many things. So did cats. So did the strange trees out on the flatlands, the trees that sighed when the wind blew through them and murmured charming nonsense in prophetic voices.

Several people were raking coals out into the roasting pit. Several others were tossing more fuel into the flames. Sam sat where he was and watched, moving his leg gently with the girl baby astride it.

Across the fire, Saturday Wilm exclaimed, got up, and ran toward a figure which was suddenly standing there.

"Isn't that your mam?" asked China Wilm, almost without surprise.

It was Maire Girat, looking at them from across the fire, her face younger than when they had last seen her. Saturday stood beside her, clinging to her hand. Someone started a song they all knew, and the people joined in, all of them, their voices rising in intricate harmonies. Maire Girat smiled and waved and vanished, leaving Saturday still singing. Jep went to stand beside her, holding out his hands to her and smiling.

"Wasn't that your mam?" asked China again.

"As the Green-snake Tchenka is the Green-snake Tchenka, so that was my mam," agreed Sam.

"But she was buried upon Ahabar!"

"But she lived here and is remembered here. As th

Gharm remember the green snake from the planet from which they came, the one that Voorstod destroyed. I saw the green snake myself, on Ahabar. Not the Tchenka, the real one. It was there, little and jewel bright, slithering through the grass. New born or hatched or however they come. The God missed it, so it made it."

"How does the God do that?"

"I don't know. Perhaps those busy and curious folk from Phansure will find out. Now that we have a safe Door again, many folk will come and go, seeing what the God can do. I would not be totally surprised to see Maire walking down the street of Settlement One, though I do not believe the God will do that."

China thought about that, and decided she agreed. The God would not do that. A visitation, yes, but not reanimation. Such would not be proper except in a case of great need.

"The child has had enough jigging, Sam. Tell her a story."

"You mean tell you a story."

"No, I mean tell us both. She will know what you mean."

Sam thought for a time. The fire was burning down nicely, getting itself a good thick bed of coals, just right for what he had in mind. People were gathering around, roasting diddle-nuts and sausages, wrapping rough-skinned tubers and bundles of creely legs in ribbon-willow leaves and laying them upon the coals of the roasting pit.

"Once on a time," Sam said, "was a man, Samasnier, who told himself there was a secret hidden under a stone."

From the grass at his feet a tiny man sprang up out of nothing, dressed in a tunic, barefooted, looking very heroic and handsome. The child reached for it, but her hands went through it. It was only a vision, a tiny Tchenka, made of jellied smoke.

"Samasnier asked everyone where the secret was, but no one would tell him. Samasmier thought his dad had hidden it, or maybe someone else entirely, but who it was did not matter, for Samasnier was so curious, he had to know what the secret was, no matter who put it there, for heroes always find out the secrets, always."

The little manikin turned about, looking curiously behind pebbles, around blades of grass. The child reached again.

"So, when he was very young he began turning over rocks, looking for the secret thing. And the bigger he got to be, the bigger rocks he turned over, bigger and bigger yet, looking for the secret thing, the single wondrous thing."

The manikin turned a pebble over, then another, making comic faces when he found nothing there. The child crowed with laughter.

" 'Come away, Samasnier,' his friends cried to him 'Come away and play. You're breaking your back over those silly rocks!'

"But Samasnier wouldn't give up looking . . ."

The child tired of the game and reached out to he mother. The manikin vanished. China Wilm took the baby and put her to the breast. Sam pulled China against his chest, his arms around her, and she settled with a sigh of satisfaction.

"Samasnier," he went on with his story as he watched the fire slowly dwindling, "Samasnier could not be tempted into accepting the day or being contented with the night. He could not be tempted into seeing beauty of singing music. When a man wants to be a hero, such things stand in his way. He just went on reading of heroes past and raising the stones and raising the stones . . ."

"Why did Sam do it?" whispered China.

"Oh," said Sam, "he'd started from anger, that his day had been taken from him. And then he read too many books in which anger and vengeance figured greatly. And he'd become convinced of his own importance. He hadn't found a God yet, to tell him he was only part of creation not all of it. He thought every vague question bubbling about in the back of his head deserved an answer. He was spoiled."

Spoiled, perhaps, he said to himself. But a hero, nonetheless. With a destiny still awaiting.

Across the glowing embers of the fire, Jep and Satu

day Wilm were dancing an extravagant minuet at the center of an admiring circle of cats.

"He knew he would be a hero," said Sam. "Somehow."

"The fire's almost out."

"Not quite," said Sam, reaching out one hand to pull the blanket off the pile of things beside him."

"Those are your books, Sam."

"I know," he said, tossing the top ones onto the coals and watching with approval as they burst into flame.

"But they're so beautiful! You can't just . . ."

He tossed another armload. As the baby saw the blue and purple flames that danced along the spines as the glue burned, she cried out and clapped her hands.

"I don't understand what you're doing!" cried China.

"Burning the books, China Wilm. Saying what Maire said: 'Thank God there are no legends here.' "

"But you worked so hard on them. You loved them so!"

"I thought I did. But we need no bloody heroes, China Wilm. No more heavy legends, full of death and pain. No more heroes raising the stones to find marvelous things, and leaving the holes to become graves for those they've killed."

She turned to face him, her brow furrowed, tears in her eyes.

"But Sam, Sam," she cried. "What will you do without your books?"

He put his arms around her, held her close to him beside the fire as he watched the old bloody stories burn. He had not really thought what he would do without them. He had disposed of his sword belt. What would he do without a sword belt? And his helmet? He had flattened the top of his helmet, turned it upside down and planted herbs in it. He had done that yesterday. China would laugh when she saw it. And his books?

"What will you do without your books?" she asked again, worried about him.

It came to him what he would do for a while, until the time came when he would do something else. Perhaps the

God told him, he thought. Or perhaps he thought of it for himself.

"Write new ones, China Wilm," he told her, while the child laughed and the people sang and the fire sizzled in its embers.

"Listen to the God, and write new ones."

ABOUT THE AUTHOR

· *Sheri S. Tepper* was born in 1929 in Denver, Colorado, and has lived in the West most of her life. She worked in the administration of a multi-state non-profit organization until her retirement in 1986. Until recently, she divided her time between writing and—in association with the American Minor Breeds Conservancy—raising various minor and rare breeds of domestic livestock and poultry. She currently lives in New Mexico where she runs a small inn. She is married, has two adult children and one grandchild.

In the few short years Ms. Tepper has been publishing, she has written over a dozen novels which have garnered the respect and admiration of both readers and critics. In addition to *Raising the Stones,* her most recent works include *Grass* (a *New York Times* Notable book and Hugo Award nominee), *The Gate to Women's Country, After Long Silence,* and *The Awakeners* (published in two volumes as *Northshore* and *Southshore*). Doubleday Foundation will publish her new novel, *Beauty* in August, 1991.

Special 16-Page Preview of

BEAUTY

the stunning new novel by
Sheri S. Tepper

During the time Sleeping Beauty is caught in her enchanted castle, the world alters dramatically. The following scene gives a glimpse of these remarkable changes.

Beloved was facing me, weaving a little on her legs, a look of faint astonishment in her eyes. Though she could not have seen me, her right hand was extended as though to hand me something. It was a spindle, precisely as it had been described to me; a spiky thing that looked rather like a spinning top. I put my hands behind my back. The spindle fell even as I moved toward her, and she went down with it, crumpling, knees and hips and then shoulders and arms, falling in a loose pile, like washing. I kicked the spindle thing away and knelt beside her. Her face was quite peaceful, as though she were sleeping, as indeed she was, though a sleep of a strange and terrible depth. Her breast barely moved. Her skin was chill. A pallor had fallen over her skin, so that she seemed to be carved of ivory.

For a moment I could not think at all. My mind was blank. I straightened Beloved out, pulled her skirts down, and folded her hands on her breast, my tears spotting the satin of her bodice. I left the spindle where I had kicked it, not daring to touch it. I hadn't really . . . I had thought the curse wouldn't function if it couldn't find me. . . . I had never considered that . . . Or had I? I didn't know. Had I planned it, or not? The wording of the final curse referred to "Duke Phillip's daughter on her birthday." She was as much his daughter as I was. It was her birthday as much as mine. I had known that!

I fled back through the dining room, seeking help, and was sent sprawling when I tripped over the body of one of the footmen lying beside a tray load of scattered flagons.

In my daze I assumed he had seen what happened to Beloved and had fainted. Even when I reached the hallway and began to find other bodies, I did not immediately realize what had happened. Only when I found Aunt Lavender fallen prone across the virginal did I realize that the malediction had been modified by Aunt Joyeuse not only to send Duke Phillip's daughter to sleep, but to include everyone at Westfaire. I had worried about what people would do with a princess who slept for a hundred years! It seemed they would do nothing at all, for she was not to sleep alone. When she regained consciousness, a hundred years in the future, all her court would still be around her, though it was not Beloved's court, but mine.

I found Doll and Martin asleep in the stables and Dame Blossom asleep at her loom. In the village everyone slept. The shoemaker and the tailor and the potter and the tanner and all. I howled for some little time, as frightened as I have ever been, while I ran about through the barns and stables, the armory, the dormitories of the men-at-arms, the kitchens, the granary, the orchards, through every house in the village by the walls. Everyone was asleep, guests and all. Every living thing. The cattle in the byre were asleep, and the chickens in their pens, and the swine, the piglets laid out like rows of barely breathing bottles at her mother's swollen teats. Wasps slept on the fruit on the sunlit walls. Spiders slept in their webs. The weevil slept at the heart of the rose. Papa's dogs lay indolently in the sun, as unmoving as the painted wooden saints in the chapel.

And in that chapel Father Raymond slept beside Papa —who had arrived home only that morning—both of them on a bench, propped upright by each other's body. Papa's mouth was open, and the faint, infrequent breath hissed across my ear when I leaned down to shake him. I inadvertently dislodged him, so that he fell sidewise, onto the bench, but his sleep did not break, nor did that of Father Raymond when I clung to him, wetting his su plice with my tears. He held a piece of paper in his hand. Evidently something he and Papa had been looking at. It caught my eye because I saw my name on it.

It was addressed to Father Raymond. "Tell Beauty that I love her forever," it said. "Tell her I honor her always. Tell her I would never have done anything to hurt her. Tell her no matter what distance separates us, I will love her still." It was signed by Giles. Father Raymond had not shown it to me. He had shown it to Papa! I hated them both for that, but I could not stand there doing it. I put the letter in my pocket and ran on.

The sleepers even included Sybilla and her mother. I found them in the scribe's office, lying atop Mama's marriage contract in an uncomfortable-looking heap. I left them that way, hoping when they awoke they would have cramps. Of all living things in all the lands of Westfaire, only Grumpkin and I were free to move about, because we were cloaked in magic and invisible to the enchantment. Grumpkin wanted to leave my pocket, but I did not dare let him go.

I cannot remember what I did then for a while. Though a few other guests had been expected, none arrived. It was as though the castle had been set aside from mortal lands. The sun sank slowly, and I with it. For a time I huddled on the stairs, crying, Grumpkin patting my face with his paws and making the small, trilling noise he makes when he seeks catly companionship, his love call. I clung to him and wept. I reread Giles's letter and wept.

Tears changed nothing. Eventually, my eyes dried and I realized I had no choice but to go. There was no way I could stay in this place. No way I could maintain myself. I made myself think carefully about going away, made myself consider calmly the things I would need to take with me, gritting my teeth so hard that later my jaws hurt. I needed money. The keys to Papa's chest were around his neck, and the coin he had available, poor though Sybilla had said he was, was locked in the chest in his room. Also in the chest were two warrants making claims upon usurers in London, and I took them both. Papa or his man of business had evidently tried to delay the final reckoning by deferring payment of current expenses and putting current income into the hands of the Jews to collect interest. Usury was a sin for Christians—but then so was lust, and Papa had not balked at that. I think anything done to excess must be sinful, including pilgrimages, but if so, the poor man was paying for his sins. If he had not neglected Mama, I kept telling myself, none of this would have happened.

The aunts had some jewels, which I did not hesitate to purloin. They would not need them for one hundred years, and I needed them now. There was the Monfort parure of emeralds and diamonds that Papa intended to give Sybilla for a wedding gift. I took that, too, though I suspected the gems might not be the real ones. Surely Papa had sold them, poor as he was. I wondered how much Papa had received for the jewels when he had sold them and what he had spent it on. If, indeed, Grandfather had not sold the emeralds in his own time and put the money into rebuilding Westfaire.

The last thing I did before I left was to drag Beloved in from the garden. I could not carry her up the stairs into my tower room, which seemed most fitting, but then what is fitting at such a time? Where are Sleeping Beauties supposed to lie? Towers come inevitably to mind. Towers or perhaps bowers or enchanted tombs of glass. I could manage none of them. Half fairy or no, I had no power that I was aware of. Perhaps my mama would have managed better. Besides, the tower was burned and there was nothing there except my mysterious thing, sitting untouched upon the window ledge, with charcoal all about it.

As it was, I got Beloved onto the table in the small dining room and covered her with a brocade hanging bringing it neatly up under her chin, placing a cushion under her head, doing what I could to make her long sleep a comfortable one. I wondered if she would turn over in that sleep and found myself giggling hysterically at the thought. "I'm sorry, Beloved," I cried. "Sorry!"

It was pure hypocrisy. Suppose I had known what was going to happen, wouldn't I have done the same thing again? I may even have known what would happen without admitting it to myself. Even then I caught myself thinking, Better Beloved than I. She would be thrilled to be awakened by a prince, and why not? It was a far finer fate than a weaver's daughter could ordinarily expect.

As I stood looking at her I was aware of two things: first, that Westfaire was redolent of that odor I had always associated with the chapel; and second, that there was an aura of glamour that flowed from Beloved's form in a swelling tide. When I went out into the hall, the aura came after me, a shining mist of silent mystery, an emanation of the marvelous. Every stone of the hallway throbbed with it, giving my footsteps back to me like the slow beat of a wondrous drum or some great heart that pulsed below the castle, making the very stones reverberate with its movement. Above me the lacelike fan vault sparkled like gems; through the windows the sunbeams shimmered with a golden, sunset glow. Once outside, I looked up at the towers and caught my breath, for they had never seemed so graceful. Over the garden walls the laburnum dangled golden chains, reflowered on this summer evening as though it were yet spring. In fact, springtime had miraculously returned. In the corners the lilacs hung in royal-purple festoons, and roses filled the air with fragrance deep as smoke.

All around me beauty wove itself, beauty and the strange, somehow familiar smell of the place. Westfaire became an eternal evening in an eternal May, the sun slanting in from the west as though under a cloud, making the orchards and gardens gleam in a green as marvelous as the light in the gems I carried. Slowly the sun moved down, and I feared it would not rise again on Westfaire for a hundred long years.

I took myself away from the castle, across the wide gardens and lawns to the tall inner walls built when the castle was renewed. Outside these walls the moat reached around from the lake on one side to the lake on the other, filled by its waters. The heavy bridge was down. My footfalls thudded on the timbers as I crossed, then fell silent in the dust of the village street. Little shops and houses huddled in quiet, thatch glowing like gold, walls flushed by sun. Beyond the village lay the paddocks and the commons, and past them, the outer walls, all that was left of the first Westfaire, built so long ago that men had forgotten when: low, massive ramparts with squat watchtowers and a fanged portcullis, and beyond that the final bridge and the road leading to the outside world.

I went out, hearing my lonely footsteps, remembering the sounds of carriages and horsemen, listening in the silence for a sound that did not come. Beyond the last bridge, at the limit of the castle lands, I stopped in amazement to confront a waist-high hedge of briar rose that rustled with savage and implacable life, pulsing in the smell of magic as it grew ever taller. Was this part of the curse or part of the amelioration? To either side of me the hedge stretched in a wide circle, enclosing the outer walls, reaching back on either side to the shores of the lake, hiding what had always been my home.

I pushed my way through, crying out as the thorn tore at my arms, thankful for the thick fabric of the cloak I wore. Once outside the limits of the enchantment, I took off the cloak and changed my clothes. It would not do for a woman to walk about on the roads alone, though it was safer in the country than in the cities, where gangs of youths roamed about seeking unprotected women to abuse and ruin. I had already decided to wear my grubby boy clothes, which would attract no one's interest. The tears still running down my face, with my hair twisted up under a grubby cap, and with everything I owned in a sack over my shoulder, I went away from there. At the roadside not far distant stood a pale arm of stone, which emerged from the forest in a tumbled wall topped by a rock shaped like a cat's head. Under that rock was a little cave Grumpkin and I had discovered long ago. We called it the cat-hole. It was a place to secrete treasures, a place for Grumpkin to hide in, a place I had hidden in once or twice myself as a little child, though I had outgrown it long since. Now I stopped and put most of the wealth I carried inside it, stopping the opening with a few head-sized stones well wedged into place with smaller bits of rock. The aunts had often warned against the robbers at large in the world, robbers and ruffians and villains of all sorts. Hiding a part of what I had would save it against later need.

I kept some coin in my sack. Though they might not be real, I kept the emeralds wrapped up in rags: collar, circlet, two brooches, and a bracelet. I kept one warrant on a usurer. The rest of the jewelry and coin and the other warrant, I secreted away. Once this was done, I started on my way again, wishing I had a horse. It had been a weary and frightening day.

As I came from behind the stone I saw a shattered beam of sun on the flower-gathering hill, as though a man in armor had moved and reflected the light. I thought of Giles, my heart leaping up. He had known I needed him and had come home! Grumpkin cried, and I held him in my arms as I ran toward that gleam of light, telling myself it was Giles, it couldn't be Giles, perhaps it was only a light, but perhaps he had a spare horse he might let me ride, or even a horse and saddle I might buy. I had not gone far before Grumpkin snarled, sensing presences I did not. He would not have snarled at Giles.

The men and women I came upon were doing something incomprehensible. They moved among contrivances, among strange apparatuses, boxes that hummed and winked and made noises like the midnight peeps of startled birds. There were five persons, some men, some women, though it was hard to tell which were which. They were clad much alike, and my impression of maleness and femaleness came more from stance and stature than from any other noticeable difference.

I saw them before they saw me. I should have stopped, turned, gone somewhere else, but it is a measure of my distraction and pain that I simply kept walking, mouth open, eyes fixed on them, wondering vaguely who they were and what they were doing on the May-flower hill.

"Did you get time-lapse shots of the hedge?" the oldest of the men cried, his voice urgent.

"Time lapse, hell," answered the tallest, heaviest man, his eye fixed to the end of the convoluted box he held upon his shoulder. "It's fast enough to show without lapse. Look at the damn thing! It's fairly crawling into the sky!"

I turned. The hedge had grown up behind me and was now higher than my head. Tendrils at the top reached upward like hands, clutching at the clouds. I felt a sob pressing upward and choked it down. Now was no time to give way, however much I needed to do so.

"What are you doing?" I cried, stepping from behind the bush.

They turned, mouths open, staring. Almost simultaneously, two who had not spoken before said:

"Oh, shit!"

"That's torn it. Hell!"

Not a polite greeting, considering everything, though not necessarily hostile.

"What in the bloody hell are you doing here?" asked one of the women in an offended voice. "There's not supposed to be anyone here!" Her accent was strange. It took me a moment to figure out what she had said.

I shook my head, almost unable to respond. "Coming home," I mumbled. "From market."

I saw them mouthing the words, having the same difficulty I had had in understanding what they heard. Evidently my tongue was not their native speech.

The oldest man turned to one of others, throwing up his hands. "What do we do about this, Alice?"

"How the hell am I supposed to know, Martin," the one called Alice replied. "If this shows up on the monitors, they'll have our guts for dinner."

"What's your name, boy?" Martin asked. His gray hair was combed back from his face, almost as short as the woman's.

"I am Havoc, the miller's son," I mumbled. It was the name I had used with Martin since I was tiny. There was no time or need to invent another.

"Damn," he said again, thrusting parts of his apparatus into cases. "Jaybee, you got enough footage? Bill, ready? There are only minutes left."

The man addressed as Bill turned his face toward me, grimacing. He was shorter than I, the height of a child, with hair the color of ripe apricots, and he wore the same kind of singlet and trousers as the others. "Ready," he said, staring at me with something like pity in his eyes.

I did not understand the word "footage."

"Janice?"

The other woman looked into the eyes of her contrivance and nodded. "Plenty," she said in a cold voice. Her hair was white as snow, but she was not an old woman. Her eyes, when she looked up at me, were hard and black, like fowls' eyes.

"What are you doing here?" I wanted to know.

The white-haired woman laughed, a quick bark of laughter. "A documentary, boy. We are recording the banishment of magic from England—and from the world. Now, do you know any more than you did before?"

"That isn't true," I said, shaking my head. "No."

"Not yet." She smiled. "But soon."

The one called Jaybee stared at me as he had been since I came from behind the bush. His jaw moved restlessly, like that of a boar pig, and I resolved to stay away from him, for tushes or no, he had that look to him that says all pigs are sows to him. "We need to get rid of this kid," he said, glaring at me. "I'll do it."

"No!" shouted the Alice one. "Killing him would show up on the monitors. Don't! We've only got a minute left."

Jaybee sneered at her and grabbed me by the shoulder. When he jerked me, my hat fell off and my hair tumbled down. He shouted, then laughed and grabbed me up from behind, one great hand clamped on each arm near the shoulder, holding my arms tight as he turned me toward a thing standing behind us, like a great barrel with a door in it. On my shoulder, Grumpkin snarled and scratched at him, but he paid no heed. Both of us were thrust through the door and the others tumbled in after us, all of them shrieking at Jaybee, telling him to put me out, and him fending them off while holding on to me.

Alice staggered to a certain part of the barrel where there were buttons and a flickering of light. She bent over them, muttering. Then we were all twisted inside out. I was. I presume the others were, for Janice cried out and then cursed. Grumpkin screamed. So did I. It felt as though I were being slowly torn apart from inside by rats.

[As was I, Carabosse—the fairy of clocks; for I took hold of the thing she was in and went with her. Or tried. A barrier stretched from the bottom of the world to the top, from side to side. Impenetrable. My powers were absorbed by it, like a sponge. I could not move it. I could not get through. I was being sucked dry, sucked out, killed. I felt Beauty leaving me and could do nothing about it at all. And then she was gone. What she carried was gone with her. All our hopes gone. I was still there, sitting on the hi

and weeping when Israfel found me, I who had not wept since the fountains of the deep were sealed.]

Then everything stopped. Quiet came. The pain went away. The others began to stir and bend and mutter. And the little man, Bill, opened the door into the twenty-first century.

With *Beauty,* Sheri S. Tepper, the author of the Hugo-nominated and *New York Times* Notable Book *Grass,* has written yet another mesmerizing novel. Set on Earth, *Beauty* is a recasting of the Sleeping Beauty tale. But as with all Tepper's works, the novel is more than this, exploring with real depth and perception one of the fundamental truths about what it means to be human. Told in Tepper's magnificent prose with surefire pacing, *Beauty* won't disappoint.

For the summer's best in science fiction and fantasy,
look no further than Bantam Spectra.

SPECTRA'S SUMMER SPECTACULAR

With a dazzling list of science fiction and fantasy stars, Spectra's summer list will take you to worlds both old and new: worlds as close as Earth herself, as far away as a planet where daylight reigns supreme; as familiar as Han Solo's Millennium Falcon and as alien as the sundered worlds of the Death Gate. Travel with these critically acclaimed and award-winning authors for a spectacular summer filled with wonder and adventure!

Coming in May 1991:

**Star Wars, Volume 1:
Heir to the Empire**
by Timothy Zahn

Earth
by David Brin

King of Morning, Queen of Day
by Ian McDonald

Coming in June, 1991:

**The Gap Into Vision:
Forbidden Knowledge**
by Stephen R. Donaldson

Black Trillium
by Marion Zimmer Bradley,
Julian May and Andre Norton

**Chronicles of the King's Tramp
Book 1: Walker of Worlds**
by Tom DeHaven

Coming in July 1991:

**The Death Gate Cycle,
Volume 3: Fire Sea**
by Margaret Weis and
Tracy Hickman

**The Death Gate Cycle,
Volume 2: Elven Star**
by Margaret Weis and
Tracy Hickman

Raising the Stones
by Sheri S. Tepper

Coming in August 1991:

Garden of Rama
by Arthur C. Clarke
and Gentry Lee

Nightfall
by Isaac Asimov
and Robert Silverberg

Available soon wherever Bantam
Spectra Books are sold.

AN278 - 8/91

MM/RAISING THE STONES